The Dark Amulet Collection

The Dark Amulet Collection

The Complete Series

Jennifer Ealey

The Pale-Eyed Mage
The Dark Amulet Book 1

Part 1

Chapter 1

Sheldrake was a mage. His wife, Maud, was a shape-changer. They lived in a large, thatched cottage, grandly named Batian House, surrounded by an idyllic cottage garden, situated less idyllically, on the main road out of Highkington, the capital of Carrador. Behind the cottage lay stables and a working farmyard that opened onto paddocks stretching to distant bushland. All day long and most of the night, carts, carriages, horses and pedestrians passed within fifty yards of Sheldrake and Maud's front door. After a festival, the sounds of wheels, hooves and feet would be compounded by voices raised in song, chatter and argument.

For years, Sheldrake and Maud Batian had considered growing a hedge to deaden the noise, but firstly they were proud of their garden and liked to give passers-by the chance to admire it and secondly, they watched with interest the parade of life that passed along the road. They would often sit out in their front garden and wave to people they knew. Sometimes one or the other of them would lean on the front gate and exchange words with people, friends and strangers alike, as they passed, not letting on for a moment that their interest was as professional as it was friendly.

But not tonight.

On this cold, dark, rainy night, no one was travelling past their front gate and so did not hear the screams that issued from the idyllic cottage. Maud was giving birth.

Tall and spare, Sheldrake generally tried, often unsuccessfully, to appear phlegmatic. Right now, he paced the corridor outside, firmly banished from the bedchamber by his wife and their head groom, Beth, who was assisting with the delivery. Clive, their butler, trod heavily up the stairs, bearing a crystal decanter filled with a particularly fine whisky and one glass on a fine silver tray.

Sheldrake frowned in irritation at the tray. "Clive, you can't expect me to drink alone. I need moral support. Go back and get a glass for yourself."

Clive placed the tray on a small inlaid table, then grinned as he withdrew a second glass from his pocket, with a slight flourish. "One must be prepared for all eventualities, sir."

Sheldrake gave a snort of laughter. "Good man." He ran his hand over his immaculately neat black hair. "This is the most harrowing experience of my life. I had no idea Maud had such a loud voice...or would have to endure such pain."

Just as he was taking a filled glass from the tray, another scream rent the air, making his hand shake so much he nearly dropped it. Clive's big hand came down on his shoulder.

"Easy does it, sir. She'll be all right. My Beth's in there looking after her and she's birthed hundreds."

"But Maud is not a horse."

"That's right, sir. Not at the moment," said Clive in a calm, comfortable voice. He gave a reminiscent smile, "Eh, but she's a fine galloper when she is, though. Isn't she, sir?"

Sheldrake gave a reluctant smile. "Yes she is. But she is her true human form now, just as she must be, to give birth, and I don't know that Beth has as much experience with people."

"Don't you worry, sir. Animals are all much the same. It will be fine," Clive said, just as he would to any child, dog, or horse in distress.

On the other side of the door, Maud lay on a heavily carved four-poster double bed, her long, dark brown hair in a tangled halo across the pillows, her teeth clenched as another wave of pain began its crescendo. As the contraction reached its peak, Maud opened her mouth and howled.

"That's it, pet. One last push. The baby's coming." A thin, dried up woman in her fifties knelt on the floor at the foot of the bed, the head of the baby already in her hands. She wasn't a healer, at least not primarily, but she'd brought hundreds of foals, lambs and calves into the world and she had known for months that this baby would be a boy. "That's it," she said, as the baby gushed forth into the world. "You've done it. Good girl."

For long moments, tense silence filled the room before healthy little lungs bellowed in distress at the sudden change in circumstances. Both women smiled, tears of relief in their eyes. Beth tied and cut the umbilical cord, then gently wiped the child over with a soft damp cloth before wrapping him in a warm blanket and handing him to his waiting mother. Once Beth had tidied away the afterbirth and straightened the bed covers, she opened the door and beckoned Sheldrake to enter.

"Come and meet your new son, sir."

Sheldrake nearly catapulted into the room in his eagerness to see his wife and new child. Clive was close behind him, relieved despite his calming words. Sheldrake sat on the edge of the bed and together, he and Maud looked fondly down at the bright pink, scrunched up face of their first born, marvelling at the little nose and mouth and the perfect tiny fingers.

Then the child opened his eyes.

Sheldrake froze. Maud gasped in horror.

"What is it?" asked Clive urgently.

"His eyes," breathed Maud. "They're white."

Sheldrake frowned and leaned closer. After a close inspection, he shook his head. "No. They are not white. The pupils are black and the irises are a very pale lavender… hmm… but they look white."

"Can he see?" demanded Clive.

Beth intervened. "A new baby's vision is blurry anyway. He can't focus or track yet. So you probably won't be able to tell for a few weeks. He will be trying to focus on you, Maud, but if he turns his head to you, he could be just following your voice or the sound of your movement at the moment." She shrugged. "Most babies have bluey coloured eyes at birth and then often the colour changes. So maybe his will, too."

Even as they watched, the seemingly white eyes darkened to a faint lavender as the light reacted with the melanin in his irises, but they were still unnaturally pale.

Beth shrugged. "A small change often happens the first time the light hits their eyes, but you won't know his final eye colour for months yet."

Maud gave a strained smile. "Never mind. I will love him anyway. He is perfect in every other way."

But Sheldrake knew what she feared. "Don't worry, my love. The merit of a person is not determined by his eye colour. My grandmother's morals would have been just as bad, had she had blue or brown eyes."

"But the power, Sheldrake."

Sheldrake grimaced. "Yes, dear. Madison was powerful, but I do not know that any direct link was made between her eye colour and her particular powers. Besides, we too are powerful. So I think we can assume that our son will inherit at least some degree of magical ability, don't you? It would be stranger if he did not."

"But will he be able to manage it? Will he use it justly?"

"That will be up to us to determine, don't you think?" Sheldrake looked at Beth and Clive, before adding, "All of us."

Chapter 2

During the following two years, Jayhan grew into an unremarkable toddler. Everything about him was normal, except for his eyes. He was a dear pudgy little boy, with a shock of blond hair that would darken to auburn by the time he was five.

Everyone, when they saw his eyes for the first time, drew back in consternation. Most adults tried to cover their reactions, partly out of kindness and partly out of courtesy. But many children, especially those in the village jealous of his privileged position, would stare unashamedly and whisper ostentatiously behind raised hands to their friends.

On the day after his eighth birthday, as Jayhan was trotting down the street holding his father's hand, a jeering voice called out "Spooky!"

Even before Sheldrake could turn around, the children had fled. The mage frowned ferociously around the empty streets but could see no one to berate.

Worse still, his reaction encouraged the jeerers. The voices continued their taunts from the cover of the side streets.

"Spoooooky!"

"Ooh. Ghoul eyes!"

"Crow's eyes. Hey, your mother's a crow."

"He's a ghoul. He's a ghoul!"

"Back from the dead."

Jayhan didn't understand what they were saying but he knew why. When they arrived home, just as his father was thinking Jayhan hadn't noticed, the boy asked, "What's a ghoul? What is back from the dead? I thought when people died, they stayed lying down."

Sheldrake was discomforted by his questions and tried to fob him off. "They do, Jayhan, they do. Just ignore those stupid children. They don't know what they are talking about."

"They hate my eyes, don't they, Dad?"

Sheldrake huffed. "Nothing wrong with your eyes. You can see out of them, can't you? What more do you want?" After a moment, he said dismissively. "Ignorant people annoy me."

Jayhan glanced up at him but could tell he wouldn't get any more out of him. That didn't mean he would let the subject drop though, just that he would have to look for other avenues to find out.

Remembering the comment about crow's eyes, Jayhan took himself out into the garden and set himself up to play with a pair of wooden horses and a tiny carved carriage under a camellia tree where he was hidden behind a large lavender bush.

He watched a pair of blue wrens flit from branch to branch then onto the lawn for a while before flitting back into the bushes and disappearing. A black bird came and went, then two pairs of red-rumped parrots swooped in and pecked their way across the lawn before something startled them and they flew off in a flash of colour. For a while the lawn remained empty and Jayhan became so absorbed in his game that he nearly missed the crow when it landed in the middle of the lawn looking for bugs.

Jayhan studied its eyes. Their irises were bright white.

Jayhan sat back on his heels and thought about it. He had never particularly noticed the colour of crows' eyes before, but now that he had, he thought they were very interesting; different from other birds. Then he pondered the remark that his mother was a crow. He watched the glossy black, intelligent bird working its way across the lawn and decided that would be no bad thing. He knew his mother shape-shifted and could become a crow, if she wanted to, but that her true form was human. On the other hand, he doubted that the boys in the village knew that. More than that, he could tell they had been trying to upset him. He decided he would seek out Beth and talk to her.

He found her in the tack room in the stable, sitting on a stool next to a brazier, polishing a worn bridle that was nearing the end of its days. She looked up and smiled as he entered, no longer even noticing his pale lavender eyes.

"What have you been up to, young one? You have muddy knees again."

Jayhan grinned, knowing she didn't care. "Watching a crow. It has even paler eyes than mine. Bright white they are."

She looked at him a moment then said, "They must be beautiful then."

He put his head on one side and thought about it. "They look very bright because crows are so black. I like bright things." He scuffed the toe of his shoe in the dirt, "But Beth, the boys in the village called me Crow's Eyes and said my mum was a crow. I don't really mind either of those things but I think they were trying to be mean. And they called me spooky and ghoul and said I was back from the dead." He grimaced in memory. "What's a ghoul anyway? And I never died. So how can I be back? And anyway you can't come back from being dead... can you?"

"Jayhan, Jayhan, settle down. Too many questions." She put down the bridle with one hand while she held up the other to forestall his protest. "Give me time. No, you can't come back from the dead." She ticked her answers off on her finger as she talked. "A ghoul is make-believe evil spirit that digs up dead humans and eats them." Beth gave a brief laugh as Jayhan screwed up his face in distaste. "Yes, lucky they're make-believe, isn't it? And being spooky means..."

"I know what spooky is... and creepy," cut in the small boy. "I've often heard people say it when they thought I wasn't listening."

Beth looked stricken. "Oh Jayhan." She held her arms wide in invitation and Jayhan walked straight in and hopped up onto her knee. She hugged him to her and rocked him gently back and forth.

For a minute or two he let his head rest against her shoulder, mostly because Beth needed him to. Then he sat up abruptly and chortled. "I don't care if people get creeped out by my eyes. They're just being silly. Eyes can't hurt you no matter what colour they are." For a moment he looked uncertain. "Can they?"

Beth shook her head. "No young one, they can't." He felt her ribs tighten slightly as though she were about to say something more but she let her breath out and remained silent.

"But...?"

She gave a lop-sided smile. "You know me too well. But... some eye colours are owned by particular people or types of people."

"Oh." He glanced up at her, then looked down. "So am I a particular type of person that gives people the creeps?"

Beth laughed. "No. You are a particular type of person who distracts me from my work." She lifted him off her knee. "Now off you go and entertain yourself for a while."

Jayhan obliged but he had heard a forced note in her laugh and knew that she had dodged talking to him about it. One more line of enquiry closed.

Jayhan gave up asking and no one noticed when he started to avoid looking at people or that his sunny smile had dimmed a little. And when his father invited him to accompany him to the village, Jayhan found excuses not to go.

After the fifth invitation was avoided, Sheldrake scowled at his son. "Your studies can wait. Don't you like to do things with me? Perhaps I should get someone else to tutor you in magic."

Jayhan's eyes widened in horror. "Oh no, dad. I love being with you. It's just...."

"It's just what?"

"I don't really like the village."

"The village has a lovely little shop with lovely little treats."

Jayhan produced a smile. "It has chocolate frogs, doesn't it?"

Sheldrake ruffled his hair. "Yes it does. So let's go."

As they walked through the village, Jayhan kept his eyes cast down until his father reproved him and told him to hold his head up. So when the village kids jeered at him he glared back defiantly, and the intense gaze of his pale eyes cowed them more than any rebuke his father could make.

Chapter 3

During his lessons the next afternoon, as Jayhan dragged his way through a tedious page of arithmetic - his tutor was not a gifted educator - he thought about crows' eyes and the village children's taunts turning to fear. He pondered their reactions, surprised that just looking at them had turned the tables. He was just wondering whether they would have reacted in the same way if his father had not been there, when he was taken to task for having added every pair of numbers when he should have been subtracting.

He was brought abruptly back to the present by Eloquin demanding, "So, are you clear now on what you have to do?"

Guessing and hoping it was what she had said at start of the harangue, Jayhan nodded. "Yes Ma'am," and began the page of arithmetic all over again, this time subtracting. He was up to the fifth question when suddenly the image of a well-dressed middle aged woman swam into his mind; a woman with eyes like his. Where had that come from?

As he struggled his way down the column of subtraction problems, the woman's face stayed in his mind. Perhaps he seen her portrait somewhere? Maybe. But where?

"Jayhan, if you want time to play before dinner, you must finish these questions and get every one of them correct." Eloquin was an attractive, dark-haired young woman who had been forced into the post of tutor as a consequence of her dissolute father gambling away the family fortune. She just wanted her young charge to complete his work in time for her to walk into the village to meet her sister, who was now working as a seamstress, and a rather interesting young man, who apparently worked somewhere in the city. She sighed in exasperation. "*Jayhan*, are you listening to me?"

The boy gave his head a little shake and let the image of the pale-eyed woman drift away as he applied himself to earning some play time.

He woke the next morning to the sound of honeyeaters squabbling in a bush outside his window. The sky was still grey, and colour had not yet crept across the lawn. Flowers and shrubs were shades of grey. Instead of bouncing out of bed in his usual fashion, Jayhan lay back and concentrated on remembering where he had seen that portrait. He let his mind wander the corridors of the house, around the entrance hall, into his parents' bedroom and, when none of these walls yielded the portrait, he changed tack and began to think of cupboards, spare rooms and the attic. He was just ruing his poor memory and from there, letting his thoughts drift to his difficulty in learning spells from his father when, with a jolt, he remembered where he had seen the portrait. It was in his father's workshop, the site of so many disastrous efforts by Jayhan to spellcast.

He had spent so many frustrating hours in Sheldrake's workshop, trying to master even the simplest of spells. Spellcasting did not come easily to Jayhan. He forgot the words or the gestures or some aspect of the spell that could cause problems. Just a week ago, he had levitated himself with a flourish, only to rise sharply upwards and hit his head on a beam. In the shock of the unexpected pain, he had lost control of the spell, sending him crashing to the floor. Sheldrake had not been pleased.

Jayhan waited until he had seen his father leave the house and walk through the front gate towards the village. Then he wandered casually across the back lawn, past the stables checking that Beth was not looking in his direction, and then along the paved path that led to his father's workshop. Even though the workshop contained many valuable artifacts, books and potentially dangerous chemicals, the door was not locked. A magical ward warned Sheldrake if family members, including Beth and Clive, entered his hallowed ground and immobilised non-family members before they could. Happily oblivious to this, Jayhan lifted the latch and pushed open the wooden door. Once inside, he meticulously closed the door behind him. Ignoring the temptations offered him by fascinating potions, vast arrays of tools and the marvellous scaled model of Carrador that dominated one side of the room, he walked to the back, right-hand corner.

There, partly concealed by a workbench, hung a large oil portrait, dulled by dust, cobwebs and neglect. Jayhan climbed up onto his father's stool and from there onto the work bench. Sweeping aside tools, nails, screws and bits of wood shavings, he knelt on the dirty wooden benchtop and studied the painting.

The woman in the portrait was standing in front of the side entrance to the stables Jayhan had so recently passed, holding the reins of a beautiful chestnut gelding. The cottage's front garden, in the full bloom of early summer, was visible in one half of the background. The woman wore a stiffly tailored green riding habit, her black hair swept up under a perky, impractical riding hat. Her straight black eyebrows gave her a stern expression that was lightened by a slight lift at the corner of her mouth. But it was her eyes that held Jayhan's attention. At first glance, they appeared to be stark white but when Jayhan leaned in closer and brushed a cobweb out of the way, he could see that they were actually, like his, a very pale lavender.

But who was she? Had she been teased by children in the village too? Maybe the lady in the portrait wasn't a real person, but a picture of one of these make-believe ghouls that ate dead people.

Na, he thought, *if someone was going to paint something scary like a ghoul, they wouldn't put pretty flowers in the background. Anyway, she doesn't look one bit scary.*

Actually, to other people, she did, but Jayhan had lived with his eye colour all his life and thought it looked perfectly normal.

A thought struck him and he peered down the small gap between the portrait and the workbench, trying to see whether there was a name plate at the bottom of the painting, as there were on the portraits that hung on walls in the house. He spotted a small golden rectangle, which he felt sure was the name tag he was looking for. He leant further down the crack trying to see. Suddenly his left hand slipped on something slimy that had been left on the bench and he plummeted head first into the gap. Then his trousers got caught on a nail sticking out of the benchtop and he was left dangling upside down, unhelpfully facing away from the painting.

It was at this unfortunate moment that the door was flung open and Sheldrake stormed in. He had worked himself up into a lather of outrage, liberally laced with fear for his son's safety.

"What are you doing in my shed?" he roared, fully intending to give his errant son a reprimand he would never forget. Then he saw the legs sticking up from the back of his workbench and stopped short. "What on earth are you doing?"

Jayhan's heart lurched as he heard his father's roar, knowing full well he shouldn't be in the shed on his own. He knew his father could be stern but not deliberately unkind and as Jayhan was a plucky little lad, he said from his upside down position, "Hello Dad. Sorry Dad. I'm a bit stuck. Could you help me please?"

With amusement fast dissipating Sheldrake's anger, he managed to say sternly, "I should leave you hanging there as punishment for coming into my workshop when I have expressly forbidden you to enter on your own."

"Please don't, Dad. I'm starting to feel sick."

Sheldrake shook his head in fond exasperation. "You, young man, are a rapscallion of the first order." He leaned over the bench, grabbed two handfuls of Jayhan's trousers and pulled. This succeeded in detaching the trousers from the nail that had caught them but, from where he was standing, Sheldrake found it was impossible to lift Jayhan high enough to get him clear of the back of the workbench. "Right. I am going to have to lower you down, then you'll have to crawl out from there. Be careful of those boxes. Don't knock anything over on your way out."

Once this operation had been completed, Jayhan stood before his father and dusted himself off.

"And just what were you doing in my shed?"

"Nothing, Dad." When Sheldrake looked sceptical, he shrugged. "I just came to look at that picture." Jayhan pointed. "See? She has eyes like mine... Do you think the village kids teased her too? Did they say she was a ghoul too? I don't reckon she was. She doesn't look like she eats dead people, do you think?"

"Who told you what a ghoul is?"

"I asked Beth."

"Hmph." Sheldrake looked into the cheerfully determined little face, as he realised that his son had sought his own answers when his father had dodged them. "You have an enquiring nature which is an asset in a mage... but no more sneaking into my shed. Understood?"

Jayhan beamed. "Yes sir."

Sheldrake turned to lean his elbows on his workbench to study the portrait and Jayhan copied him, although it meant his elbows were above shoulder height.

"That lady there is my grandmother, your great grandmother. Her name was Madison... and now you mention it, yes, I expect she was teased, though I must say I hadn't thought of that before... Perhaps that was one of the reasons she..." He looked sharply at Jayhan and stopped what he was saying. "Jayhan, we have all been teased by village children. They are envious of our lovely house, our well-cut clothes, our money and our status. Their parents are polite and respectful towards us as a general rule but the children, especially those who live on the streets beyond their parents' control, can be openly resentful and unkind."

"Really? You got teased too. What did they say?"

Sheldrake gave a short laugh. "I was a skinny little kid. They called me String, Slim, Stick, Scrawny, Pole... things like that. I disliked it intensely. I wanted to be big and strong and bulky." He looked down at himself. "But I never got any broader. I'm still as skinny as a rake." He gave a slow smile. "But I am strong now, though I mightn't look it."

Jayhan smiled at him. "Of course you're strong. You're my dad."

At that, Sheldrake actually put an arm around him and gave him a squeeze.

Jayhan thought about all the times people had recoiled from his eyes and knew the children's envy wasn't the only reason. "You know it's not just the kids in the village. Everyone hate my eyes, except maybe you and Beth and Clive. What's so spooky about them? Do dead people have white eyes? Is that what's wrong?"

"Your eyes are pale lavender, not that anyone notices. So were Madison's," replied Sheldrake. "And no, dead people's eyes stay the colour they were in life, Jayhan, just the cornea goes a bit cloudy after a couple of days."

"Hmph. Then why, Dad? I know you know."

Sheldrake heaved a sigh. "Ah Jayhan. Sometimes you are too inquisitive for your own good. I want you to be older before I tell you." Seeing Jayhan's face tighten, he held up a warning hand. "I will give you a compromise. I will tell you this much: People fear you because they feared your great grandmother."

"But that not fair. I'm not her," Jayhan protested hotly.

"Life is not fair, Jayhan."

"Humph." The boy looked down and scuffed his shoe back and forth along the ground, watching it drag a groove in the dirt floor. After a minute, he looked up and, rather to Sheldrake's surprise, smiled. "I guess that's true. It's not fair that we have a better house than the people in the village, is it?"

Having a sense of entitlement, Sheldrake was tempted to take issue but decided not to. "That is what the villagers think and why they take delight in teasing us."

"So why was Great Grandma so scary?"

"I won't tell you that. Instead, I will give you several books which contain information about her. Only you may read them. Do not ask Beth or Clive or your mother to help you. Discuss their contents with me, as you need to."

"But Dad. I'm only just learning to read. I can't read big books."

Sheldrake gave a triumphant, mischievous smile. "Exactly. So now you have a reason to work hard at your reading."

Chapter 4

The pile of books in the corner of Jayhan's room inspired him to study hard for a good fortnight. But at the end of that time, he opened one of the heavy leather bound tomes and found that he could read it no better than he had the day his father gave them to him. Disgruntled, he complained to his tutor, Eloquin, but she merely counselled him to have patience and study harder. Since he had given it his level best for the last fortnight, he knew he couldn't study harder. In fact, he was so peeved she hadn't appreciated his efforts that he decided it wasn't worth the bother. He dragged the pile of books into the back recess of his wardrobe, deciding to banish them from his mind and find other ways to learn about his great grandma.

After stowing the books, Jayhan stomped dispiritedly down the hallway and into the library where the ever-patient Eloquin was waiting to instil him the wonders of reading. With equal patience, he endured her uninspiring rendition of a dreary little story about a boy walking his dog. While Eloquin attempted to emulate a doggy bark, Jayhan heard the sounds of a large cart drawing up outside. Bryson, the carter, had arrived with their week's supplies of vegetables, meats, sacks of grain and kegs of ale.

Jayhan was manfully training his attention on the fascination of the dog wagging its tail, when a loud crash sent him running to the window to see what was happening.

Outside in the driveway, a horse was rearing between the shafts of a cart laden high. The horse's eyes rolled in fear as a large black cat stood stiff-legged in front of it, back arched and hissing her displeasure. The horse's owner was nowhere in sight, presumably inside the house with his first load for the kitchen.

Jayhan saw Beth arrive from the stables at a dead run, kicking her ferocious cat out of the way and lunging to grab hold of the horse's bridle. But the cat was not so easily dismissed. It spat and dug its claws into her boot as she kicked, unbalancing her.

Suddenly Beth was falling beneath slashing hooves. As Jayhan held his breath in horror, a small scrawny figure, dressed in tattered leggings and jerkin, catapulted himself at Beth, thrusting her out of the way just as the horse's hooves descended. The boy rolled lithely onto his feet, leapt up to catch hold of the reins and vaulted onto the back of the plunging horse. Grabbing the horse's mane with one hand, the boy leaned forward, crooning softly to the horse and stroking its neck in long, sure strokes. For a moment, the horse's ears flattened and its hindquarters bunched. Then, as the crooning voice penetrated its panic, the horse snorted, tossed its head, and came to a standstill, quivering with fright. As the firm stroking and gentle voice continued, the quivering gradually subsided.

Ignoring the protests of his tutor, Jayhan rushed out of the school room and down the stairs. He catapulted from the front door just in time to see the boy slide off the great horse's back and walk over to Beth, who was still sitting on the gravel. The boy held out a hand to help her up.

"Are you all right, ma'am?"

"I'm fine, thank you. I was just waiting for the horse to calm before making any movement in front of him. I'm quite capable of standing up in my own." Fright and irritation made Beth's voice harsher than she intended. She stood up and brushed gravel off her scraped hands.

The boy dropped his head. "Sorry, Ma'am. And sorry about Hoofer."

Suddenly, a great burly man pushed past Jayhan and strode over to the boy, grabbing him by the scruff of his shirt and dragging him away from Beth before bringing his other arm around in an arc, to hit him hard across the back of his head. The boy went sprawling.

"Sasha," he roared. "What do you think you're doing, talking to the patrons? You get back up on that cart and hand me down that sack of potatoes."

The boy pulled himself to his hand and knees, shaking his head in an effort to clear it. As he struggled to stand up, the big man strode towards him, hand raised, ready to hit him again.

"That's enough, Bryson," cracked a harsh voice.

The man stopped in his tracks and turned belligerently.

Dwarfed by him, Beth stood hands on hip, glaring up at him. "That child just saved my life. But even if he hadn't, you have no reason to use him so roughly."

Bryson towered over her, glaring but constrained by his need to sell his goods. "He's mine. I'll do what I like with him."

"If you keep hitting your son around the head like that, his wits will be addled before he is full grown."

The man spat to the side. "He's not my son. No whelp of mine would be so small and scrawny by the age of eight. Sasha's a foundling, and I am looking after him out of the goodness of my heart."

"Cheap labour, more like."

Bryson shrugged. "The boy must earn his keep."

While they talked, Sasha had climbed nimbly up the wheel spokes, onto the top rim of the wheel and from there, onto the tray of the cart where he stood holding a corner of the sack of potatoes, waiting for his master to be ready to catch it. The side of his dark face was grazed from being hurled onto the gravel and a trickle of blood was drying, unheeded, on his cheek. He watched warily, knowing his master would be even angrier after Beth's intervention.

"Then he can earn it with me," said Beth firmly. "I need a new stable lad and this one has a way with horses I have rarely seen."

The burly man spluttered. "You can't just go taking my lad away from me. I've spent months training him up; teaching him how to drive the horse, how to pack up the merchandise and keep the cart in good order. There's a lot in it, you know. Not as easy as you might think, carting merchandise."

"How much?" asked Beth baldly.

Just as the carter opened his mouth to reply, Beth held up her hand. "Whatever you were going to say, halve it. It will save us both a lot of time."

The carter shook his head despondently. "You're a hard woman, Beth. But since my own lad's nearly ready to join me, I won't have to hire someone until I train up a new lad, so ten silver florins should cover it."

"Six," returned Beth promptly

"Nine."

"Seven and the deal is struck."

"Done," said Bryson, spitting on his hand and holding it out to Beth, who grasped it. "I'll be glad to see the last of him," he added spitefully.

A piping voice interrupted them from the top of the cart. "Now, hang on a minute. I'm no slave to be bartered around. I may be a foundling but I'm a free foundling. I've been working day and night for this bloke. Where's *my* money?"

"You don't get none, you halfwit reject," snarled Bryson.

"I'm not a halfwit and I'm not..." Sasha's voice died away.

"Huh. You see. You *are* a bloody reject. Just be glad you've had food and a place to sleep. Now finish unloading that cart."

Sasha, his face tight with resentment, directed his anger into the strength he needed to push the sack of potatoes off the cart into his master's waiting arms. Without another word, he waited sullenly for Bryson to deliver the potatoes inside then handed down each item as required. He avoided Bryson's gaze, and everyone else's. When the cart was empty, he pulled the ropes onto the cart and rolled them into neat coils at the front of the tray.

Jayhan watched the boy standing in front of the coils of rope, arms folded across his chest, a scowl on his face, and suddenly realised Sasha was frightened. No one had told him when he would come to work for Beth and if he went back with Bryson, he was facing another beating, Jayhan guessed. If Sasha stayed now, he was entering a new, uncertain world and although Beth had stood up for him, she had been tetchy to him and aggressive with Bryson and had not stayed to watch the end of the unpacking.

Jayhan walked quickly to the stables and called, "Beth. Bryson's leaving. Are you keeping the boy now?"

He found Beth with her head under her bed. "Tell them to wait. I will be out there in a minute."

Jayhan frowned and peered under the bed next to her. "What are you doing?"

"I need another shilling. It rolled under the bed here and I can't find it." She pushed him back. "Now go and tell Bryson to wait."

"I will." He hesitated. "Beth, I have two florins saved up. It's in my room upstairs. Do you want them? I don't want that boy to go home with Bryson. He's going to beat him again, isn't he?"

Beth pulled head out from under the bed. Cobwebs clung to the front of her hair and she used the back of her hand to wipe them away. "Oh Jayhan. You're a dear. Thanks. Just a loan, mind. I'll get it back to you. Now go and tell them to wait, then run inside and bring the money to me here. Got that?"

Jayhan nodded, pleased to have his offer accepted. He walked quickly to the front of the house and saw Bryson already sitting on the seat of his wagon, ready to leave. "Excuse me Bryson. Beth says, asks, could you wait a minute please. She will be out shortly."

"She'd better be quick. I've got to get back to the store house before dark," Bryson grumbled.

"She will be," said Jayhan as he shot into the house and up the stairs. He dodged past Eloquin and into his bedroom, pushing the door shut behind him with a little too much vigour. He opened the cupboard under his bedside table and took out a cloth drawstring bag full of colourful rocks that he had collected. At the bottom of the bag was another small cavity held shut by another drawstring.

Jayhan emptied the little rocks onto his bed then felt around for the small loop of the drawstring and from there, inserted a finger into the little hole that expanded to reveal the cavity beneath. His fingers closed around the silver florins.

With the florins clutched in one hand, Jayhan threw the door open, ducked past Eloquin who was just about to knock on his door. He muttered an apology over his shoulder as he sped off down the side stairs. He scooted through the kitchen, nearly scattering a bowl of shelled peas, and out through the side door across to the stables.

"Here," he said, panting, as he held his hand out to Beth.

As she took the florins, Beth smiled into his unnervingly pale eyes, noticing only his earnest, kind face. "Well done, young one. Now, off you go, back the way you came. Thank you."

As Jayhan emerged from the stairwell, he saw Eloquin down the other end of the corridor, gesticulating wildly as she told his mother of his behaviour. He slipped unnoticed into the schoolroom, crossing straight to the widow to peer down at the scene below.

Sasha had climbed down from the wagon and was now standing beside Beth as she farewelled Bryson. They watched as Bryson turned the cart and headed for the front gate without a backward glance. Then she placed an arm around the boy's shoulder to steer him towards the stable. Unexpectedly, Jayhan felt a stab of jealousy as he turned from the window and returned to his work table.

When his mother and Eloquin entered a few minutes later, he had already written a sentence about a boy walking his dog and was waiting for his next task.

He smiled cheerily. "Sorry Eloquin. It was important," he said, but refused to say what was important.

Chapter 5

Sasha flinched as he felt Beth's hand come down on his shoulder. With an effort, he tried to relax his muscles under the pressure of her hand, but Beth could still feel the tension in them.

He was trying to appear nonchalant so he only glanced up quickly at the two storey cottage as they walked past. He didn't really see the beauty of the yellow climbing roses or the cosiness of the rooms that could be seen through the diamond panes of the leadlight windows. All he saw were tall whitewashed walls that lay between him and the family who lived there. Somewhere behind those walls were the people who could, if they chose to, make his life hell.

Then he risked a glance up at Beth and found her watching him. Fear knotted his stomach as he quickly dropped his gaze. He had often been belted for cheekiness and he didn't know what passed for cheekiness in his new world. His cheek still throbbed dully from his last beating.

"Come one, young one. I'm not going to eat you," said Beth bracingly. "Let's get that face of yours cleaned up and then we'll think about dinner. I bet you're hungry after all that unloading. That was heavy work for a small boy."

Sasha risked another glance up and saw that she was smiling at him. He nodded but said nothing.

He felt the change in texture under his bare feet as they crossed from gravel onto the brick path leading into the stable. He stared ahead at the well-kept wooden structure, smelling straw and dung and horses.

As they entered, Beth drew him into her office on the left side of the entrance. A wooden chair was pulled up to a large desk scattered with papers against the far wall, while along the right-hand wall was a long rough workbench, which Beth used for repairing and cleaning tack. The walls were hung with spare leather thonging, coils of rope, broken bridles and halters and, along the top of the wall, a row of rosettes and ribbons that nearly reached around three of the four walls. A fire burnt in a small hearth set into the outside wall and two chairs, one upright and the other a rocking chair strewn with knitted rugs, were set on either side of a small wooden table, on which a book and an empty cup of coffee had been left. A heavy black kettle hung over the fire, steam whisping up from its spout.

"Sit there," Beth said, indicating the upright chair nearest the door. She busied herself with pouring water from the kettle into two chipped cups and a bowl. She added coffee and milk to the water in the cups and ground willow bark to the bowl.

She found a clean rag and used it to gently cleanse his wounded cheek with the suspension of willow bark. Sasha held still, lips pressed together, expecting to endure pain. But Beth was gentle and as she pulled away, Sasha let out a soft breath of relief.

A knock on the outside door made Sasha jump but Beth merely asked him to answer it. When he hesitantly opened the door, a young brown-haired blue-eyed maid from the kitchen handed him two steaming plates of what appeared to be beef stew.

"Here y'are, new boy. I'm Rosie, the parlour maid. Don't expect me to bring your food over every night. You can eat with the rest of us in the kitchen tomorrow."

Sasha nodded his head and mumbled his thanks.

When he re-entered the office, he handed a bowl to Beth and sat down, holding the other. He waited until she started eating. When he was sure that the bowl of stew he still held was for him, he picked up his spoon and began to eat. The stew's aroma almost made him giddy. Despite his hunger, he ate it slowly, wringing every last ounce of enjoyment out of its rich flavour. As he scooped the last spoonful slowly into his mouth, he gave a shudder of contentment. He looked up to find Beth's eyes on him, her bowl empty long ago.

He gave a little embarrassed grin. "Oops. But that was so... so amazing."

After a moment, Beth smiled. "Better than Bryson's fare, was it?"

"Oh yes, ma'am. I only ever had bread and cheese, sometimes an apple." He scowled. "Sometimes nothing at all, if he was too tired or drunk."

"Hmm. He didn't clothe you too well, either. We will have to find you some new trousers and a good warm shirt. You'll need boots too. Can't have bare feet round horses. I think young Master Jayhan may have some clothes he's grown out of that would fit you, until we can get you your own." She stood up. "But first, before you dirty new clothes or my stables, you will have a bath."

"*Now?* It's cold and dark and..."

"And you've never had one before, I'm guessing."

"I went swimming in summer, in the river," Sasha said defensively.

"Good for you. Now, there's a big metal horse trough outside. Throw out what's in it, get a bucket of water from the well and rinse it out. Then bring it in here. Once that's done, you can bring two more bucket loads of water from the well and put them in the trough. I will add the rest of the boiling water and by then we should have the makings of a bath."

Sasha stared at her for a few moments with his melting black eyes, then turned on his heel and followed her instructions to the letter.

As she added the hot water to make a shallow lukewarm bath, Beth nodded her approval. "Well done. You have a good memory." She handed him a piece of soap and a clean rag. "Now, undress and hop in."

Sasha baulked. "Not in front of you."

Beth frowned for a moment then shrugged. "Very well, I will give you twenty minutes. But when I come back, you had better have washed yourself thoroughly, including your hair. Otherwise, I'll be doing it for you."

Chapter 6

At dinner that evening, the new stable boy was the main topic of conversation. Sheldrake, Maud, Eloquin and Jayhan were seated around a long mahogany table, being served with discreet efficiency by Clive.

Maud tore off a piece of bread and dunked it into her seafood chowder. "It was a little high-handed of Beth to employ someone without your approval, Sheldrake, don't you think?"

Sheldrake glanced at Clive, Beth's husband, whose face remained impassive, then back at his wife. "I believe the circumstance were unusual. The boy demonstrated quick reactions, intelligence and a remarkable affinity with horses. He acted without hesitation and with some courage to save Beth from that cart horse's hooves."

"And then his master beat him around the head so hard, he could hardly stand up again, just for talking to Beth," interrupted Jayhan hotly. "Of course Beth had to rescue him."

As Clive passed behind him, he felt the weight of something being slipped into his pocket. When he surreptitiously felt in his pocket, his fingers closed around two metal disks. His silver florins had been returned.

"No 'of course' about it. We cannot rescue every well-deserving battered child. We do not have the resources," responded his mother. She shrugged. "However, I understand Beth was prepared to pay for him with her own money."

"She was, although I have naturally reimbursed her, since he will be working for us," said Sheldrake.

"Why did she have to pay for him?" asked Jayhan. "Sasha said he wasn't a slave…but is he free to walk away from here?"

"Our society does not have slaves, Jayhan." Sheldrake's voice developed its didactic tone. "But we do have indentured apprentices, whose masters pay their parents for them in return for their labour. The apprentices can be given a small wage, especially towards the end of their training, but generally they work in exchange for training and board, so that they may eventually become tradesmen in their own right. Bryson would have paid the orphanage for this boy and raised the price because he had given the lad experience, even if carting is not an actual trade."

"But is he free to walk away?" he persisted.

Sheldrake gave a little cough. "Not exactly. His absconding would be broadcast and no one would take him in or give him work. An apprenticeship is a contract of trust, you see." Seeing Jayhan about to raise an objection, he added. "If the boy fled far away, he might be able to start again but he would have no money, no credentials and his chances of survival on the road alone would be vexed. A young lad is easy prey."

"Easy prey for what?"

Sheldrake glanced at him before taking a spoonful of chowder to his mouth. He swallowed unhurriedly before replying, "Other societies trade in slaves. And a child on his own is not safe. There are those among us who would use and abuse a child with no connections."

"Hmph. Like that Bryson, you mean." Aware of his mother's eyes on him, Jayhan scooped a couple of spoonsful of soup into his mouth, careful not to spill it down his chin. When she looked satisfied and returned her attention to her own meal, he added, "Bryson didn't even pay him, you know, and the boy said he should have."

His mother asked for more wine and waited while Clive poured it before replying, "We will house him and feed him and Beth will teach him." As she saw a frown gathering on her son's face, she added hurriedly, "And I suppose we will give him a small wage. After all, a boy needs a bit of spending money, doesn't he, for his days off."

Jayhan let out a breath. "Of course he does."

Sheldrake smiled. "You seem to have taken this child's cause to heart."

"Dad, he saved Beth and I love Beth…and then that carter was so mean to him and…" his voice hitched… "I've never seen anyone be hurt like that before. It was so unfair." He suppressed a sob. "It was awful."

Sheldrake met Maud's eyes across the table as he put his arm around his son's shoulder. "The world is an unkind place for many people, Jayhan. We can't help everyone, but don't worry. We will look after your waif for you."

The boy leaned his head against his father's shoulder. "Thanks."

Chapter 7

Next morning, well before dawn, Sasha sat up suddenly, starting in fright at an unexplained thump. After a moment, he remembered where he was, bedded down in a corner of the loft above the stables. He breathed a sigh of relief, as he realized that the noise would not preface Bryson's entry. He listened carefully, waiting to hear whether the thump would be repeated. After a minute, he heard the sound again and recognised it as a hoof being stamped on a bed of straw.

In an instant, he had thrown off his blankets and was climbing down the wooden ladder into the stables. He grabbed a pocketful of oats then crept quietly along the row of stalls, his bare feet hardly making a sound. He was sure the noise had come from further down. Sure enough, he heard the stamping of restless hooves three stalls from the end on the left hand side.

In the predawn monochrome, he could see a large draught horse filly, deep in her stall, tossing her head, ears back.

"It's all right," Sasha murmured, "What has spooked you, hey? No one else is upset."

Crooning softly, he walked forward and placed his hands on top of the half door of its stall.

"There now. Here I am. Nothing to be scared of." In actual fact, Sasha's heart was hammering in his chest, not because he was frightened by the great horse towering over him but because he didn't know what was spooking her. Was there actually some danger lurking that he couldn't see? Despite his efforts, the filly was still on edge. Sasha decided that something in her stall was upsetting her.

He took a long slow breath. Letting none of his own fear show in his voice or movements, he maintained a stream of soothing drivel as he felt his way to the bolt and carefully pulled it open, slithering in and re-bolting the half door behind himself.

The huge horse stamped her feathered foot and sashayed backwards from him until her rump hit the back of the stall. Sasha caught the flash of white in the semi-darkness as she rolled her eyes. The boy stood very still and waited for her to get used to him. After a few moments he started talking quietly to her again.

Her ears twitched forward at the sound of his voice but then she whickered and tossed her head. Suddenly Sasha realised that whatever was upsetting her was near the front of the stall. Talking all the while, he cast his eyes around, looking for the cause. His eyes lit upon the horse's feedbag which was hanging from a hook next to the door's hinges. He frowned. Was the feedbag moving, ever so slightly?

Heart in mouth, visions of snakes or sharp toothed rats in mind, he crept up to the feed-bag and snatched away the top layer of hay. Two bright golden eyes looked up at him and blinked.

Sasha gave a low chuckle and patted a small ginger cat that lay curled up in the horse's feed bin. Under his hand, Sasha felt the vibration of a contented purr. After a minute, he left the cat and reached up slowly to stroke the filly's neck in long soothing movements. When she was calm, he placed the hand he had used to pat the cat under her nose, all the while stroking her with his other hand. The horse snuffed and snorted, perhaps at the cat smell or perhaps because Sasha's hand did not contain a treat.

Sasha produced the oats from his pocket and gave them to her before walking to the food bin to retrieve the little cat. With the cat curled in the crook of his arm, Sasha walked the few steps to the horse. He presented the cat slowly to the filly, who eyed it askance for a moment before bending her head to sniff it. The cat rubbed its ear against the horse's muzzle. Suddenly, like a flame flickering into life, a connection bloomed between the small cat and the huge horse. The filly snuffled gently and the cat batted the end of her nose. After a few minutes, Sasha sat the cat carefully on the floor in front of the horse and moved slowly backwards to sit himself in the corner of the stall to watch.

When Beth entered the stables an hour later, all but one of the horses popped their heads over the doors of their stalls to greet her. Immediately concerned, Beth crossed to the gap in their ranks and looked into the stall. Sasha was sitting cross-legged in the corner, sound asleep, with a small ginger cat curled up in his lap. Her fractious filly's head was lowered, watching them and from time to time, gently nosing the cat.

Beth was so bemused by the sight that, for a few minutes, she simply leaned on the door and gazed at them. But time was short and there was the day's work to be done, so eventually she cleared her throat and murmured, "Sasha," as quietly as she could.

The boy's eyes flew open as he jerked awake. The filly snorted and flung up her head but as Sasha, with a supreme effort, did not make any further move, the horse lowered her head again and nudged Sasha under the chin.

Sasha grinned and, disentangling one hand from the cat, pushed the horse's big velvety nose away. "Get away from me, you big brute." He placed the cat on the straw next to him and stood up. "There. You can have Apricot to play with. I have to go." He glanced apprehensively at Beth and pulled his forelock. "Sorry ma'am. I didn't mean to go to sleep." He ducked under the horse's head, drew the bolt and slipped out to join her. "I'm late, am I? What do you want me to do? I'll get right onto it. I'll skip lunch to make up the time. Sorry Ma'am." He took a quick breath. "Please don't send me back to old Bryson. I'll do better tomorrow."

"Stop!" Beth held up a hand which made Sasha flinch. She noted the movement but betrayed no response to it. "Stop, Sasha. I will not send you back to Bryson, whatever happens. At the very worst, if things don't work out here, I will find you a new position where I know you will be safe." She put her hand on his shoulder, again ignoring the flinch she felt beneath her fingers. "Now calm down and tell me how you come to sleeping in Flurry's stall?"

"Is that her name? It suits her." When he had given a brief explanation, she asked for more details. He finished by saying, "I supposed I should just have removed Apricot but, you know, Flurry has to start being brave about cats sometime. It's just a pest if she shies at a cat when you're driving her. It could even overturn whatever she's pulling or she could hurt someone. Look what happened with Hoofer."

Beth brow creased. "How old did you say you were?"

Sasha shrugged. "Bryson told you, ma'am."

"You don't talk like an eight-year-old."

Sasha scuffed his foot through wisps of straw that had drifted out into the walkway. "Sorry Ma'am. I didn't mean to be cheeky."

"It was not meant as censure. You seem wise beyond your years, that's all."

Sasha lifted his head and smiled, his face lighting up. "Thanks."

"I am not angry at you for sleeping in. You did well… Better than you know." She dug into her pocket and produced a small leather disk, stamped with a B. She handed it to him and gave his shoulder a final pat. "Now, off you go to the kitchen and give this to Hannah, the cook. Get some breakfast then come back to me for instructions."

"Yes Ma'am. Thank you Ma'am." Sasha couldn't believe his luck. He was still going to have breakfast. He ran as fast as his legs would carry him.

As he scooted into the kitchen, a large, comfortable, middled-aged woman turned from the stove and frowned at him. "No running in my kitchen, young fella."

"Yes Ma'am. Sorry Ma'am. Beth gave me this to give you and said I could have some breakfast." Seeing her frown deepen, he added hastily, "… if it's all right with you."

The cook took the leather disk and put it in her pocket without looking at it. "You're a bit late. The others have already eaten and are off about their jobs." Her face softened when she saw Sasha's face drop. "Jug of milk's still on the table. Get a glass and help yourself. Then sit yourself down and I'll rustle you up some hotcakes and honey. How does that sound?"

Sasha's breath came out in a rush. "Oh. That would be wonderful, Ma'am." Once he had poured himself a large glass of milk and slugged down half of it in one go, he asked, "Did you make the stew we had last night? It was marvellous, Ma'am."

The cook looked at him quizzically. "It wasn't stew, young fella. It was beef and red wine casserole, but I'm glad you liked it."

"My name's Sasha, Ma'am." He beamed at her. "I am going to be working with Beth in the stables, you know."

The cook smiled in amusement. "Yes, I did know. I hear you saved our Beth from the hooves of a plunging stallion yesterday."

Sasha shrugged and looked down, a little embarrassed. "Yes Ma'am. I suppose I did." He drank some more milk, which left him with a white moustache, "Mind you, it was our horse's fault in the first place. Hoover never could abide cats. I wanted to teach him to, but Bryson wouldn't let me near the horse once I'd taken off his harness and rubbed him down."

As he chatted, Sasha peered around the kitchen until his eyes fell on a basket in the corner containing a large tabby cat.

"Another cat!" he exclaimed. "Seems like this place is crawling with them." Immediately he hopped out of his chair and went to pat it. "Hello there. You're a handsome one, aren't you?" he said as he chucked it under the chin.

"Not crawling exactly, but we do have six of them. This one's the grand old man. His name's George. Now come back to the table. Your hotcakes are ready."

"Oops sorry, Ma'am."

"And stop calling me Ma'am. I'm not your mam. My name's Hannah."

A dull red darkened Sasha's cheeks. With none of his previous jauntiness, he came back to the table and sat down quietly. When the cook served him his hotcakes, he forced a smile and said, "Thank you Hannah."

Hannah could have kicked herself as she belatedly remembered where Sasha had come from. She put her arm around his little shoulders, stiff and resistant beneath her touch. "I'm sorry, lad. I didn't mean to be unkind. I know you were only saying Ma'am as a title of respect. I shouldn't have said what I did."

Sasha didn't know what to say, so he stayed silent. After a minute of munching, he said with a shade more warmth in his voice, "These hotcakes are very nice. I've never had them before."

"Good. Now wash up your plate and glass when you've finished. Then you'd best be on your way."

As he was about to open the door to leave, he was nearly bowled over by Rosie who shoved the door from the other side and swept into the kitchen. She took one look at Sasha, sniffed the air and scowled. "How come he gets a late breakfast?'

"Because I say so," stated Hannah baldly, crossing her arms and omitting to mention the leather disk. "My kitchen. I decide."

Rosie flounced. "Fine. But don't expect any favours from me," she said to him as she moved to the cupboard, reaching in to get out a tray.

Sasha looked startled. "No, Ma'am."

"I am not a Ma'am, I'm a Miss."

"Yes Miss."

"You're not Miss to Sasha," said Hannah, thumping her spoon against the edge of a giant pot she was stirring on the stove. "Don't you go getting airs above your station, young lady. If he calls me Hannah, he calls you Rosie and that's the end of it."

Rosie had placed the tray on the bench and was now filling it vehemently with a teapot and cups ready for morning tea.

"And," added Hannah forcefully, "if you break any of that crockery because you're cross, you'll pay for it out of your wages."

Rosie straightened, took a deep breath, not looking at neither of them and continued her work more carefully. Sasha saw her cheeks flame with chagrin and decided that he would be wise to avoid her until she had time to forget that cook had championed him against her. He suspected that might be a very long time.

Chapter 8

It wasn't until late in the afternoon when Jayhan had finished his studies that he could get away to the stables. He was dying to meet the new stable boy and a small, unacknowledged part of him wanted to assert his prior claim to Beth.

With a flash of inspiration, he detoured to the kitchen and wheedled a small basket of rock cakes out of Hannah. He entered the stables, clutching his rock cakes and found Beth in her office, poring over accounts.

She looked up as he entered and smiled. "Hello, young man. I was wondering when you would get here."

He gave a little frown. "Were you?" He held out this arms. "Here. I brought you some afternoon tea."

Her smile broadened as she took the little basket from him and placed it on the bench. "Lovely. I'll put the kettle on."

Once they were settled with the tea and rock cakes, Jayhan finally asked, "So where's Sasha? I thought he would be here."

"He's out cleaning the dung out of the top paddock. He should be finished soon."

Just as Beth finished speaking, Jahan could hear the scrape of iron on paving as a shovel was leant up against the wall. Moments later, Sasha poked his head around the corner of the door jamb. His hair was hanging in untidy strands and his dark brown face glistened with sweat.

Sasha produced a small bunch of wildflowers from behind his back, a shy smile on his face and held them out to Beth. "These are for you. To say thanks for getting me away from Bryson."

"Thank you, Sasha." Beth gave him a warm smile as she took the flowers from him.

To cover his awkwardness, he ran the back of his hand across his forehead and said, "Phew. It's warm out there. What do you want me to do next?"

"That's enough for today." Beth indicated the other occupant of the room. "Come in and meet Jayhan."

Sasha's eyes widened and his dark face flushed with embarrassment as he realised his gesture to Beth had been observed. He straightened up resolutely as he turned to face the boy sitting on the other side of the office. Jayhan and he exchanged stares as they surveyed each other. With undisguised curiosity, Jayhan studied Sasha's dark brown skin and deep liquid brown eyes, noted that Sasha was wearing his own cast off clothes and that they were a bit big for him. At the same time, Sasha's gaze roved over Jayhan's auburn hair, lightly tanned skin before coming to rest, with no overt reaction, on his pale lavender eyes.

Once the inspections were over, Sasha gave a small formal bow and said, "Good afternoon, Master Jayhan. I apologize for interrupting. I didn't realise you were here."

Jayhan felt uncomfortable with the boy addressing him as Master Jayhan but wasn't sure what he was allowed to do about it. He directed a small frown towards Beth, hoping she would understand what he was trying to convey. Beth, who was a bit of a genius with small boys as well as horses, gave a tiny nod and smile in return.

Jayhan relaxed. "Hello. Just call me Jayhan. You're Sasha, aren't you?" He gave a little grin. "Nice flowers. Wish I'd thought of that. I just brought rock cakes." He waved his arm around him. "So, what do you think? Do you think you'll like it here?"

"I do so far. The food's great."

Jayhan blinked. "Is it?" He grinned and proffered the little basket of rock cakes to Sasha. "Here. You'd better have one of these then. I brought them over for afternoon tea."

Just as Sasha reached out a hand, Beth said firmly, "Oh no you don't. Not until you've washed up. Off you go. There's a cake of soap next to the pump in the court yard. Come back when you're clean and then you can have one... and I'll have a cup of tea ready for you as well."

Sasha gave a comical grimace that made Jayhan laugh as he shot off to do Beth's bidding. When he returned, his black hair was slicked down and his hands and face were dripping. He stood in the doorway shaking the excess water off and grinning. "No towel."

Beth threw him a scrappy old towel. "Here, young one. Dry yourself off and sit down. Your tea's there. So's your rock cake."

"Thanks." Once he had dried himself off, and taken his first sip of tea and first bite of rock cake, Sasha let out a long sigh of contentment. He saw Jayhan watching him and sat up straighter in his chair. "Sorry. I'm just a bit tired, that's all." Then he said inconsequentially, "You have very interesting eyes, you know. Just the opposite to mine. Yours are nearly white and mine are nearly black."

"They don't spook you?"

Sasha looked surprised. "Spook me? No. Why would they? I like them." He scrunched his face up as he thought. "I think they are very rare. I've never seen eyes like yours... but that makes them special, not spooky." Suddenly he jumped up and crossed to the chipped jar on Beth's desk that now held the little bouquet he had brought in. He plucked out a tiny pale orchid with a deeper lavender centre and presented it to Jayhan. "Look," he said grinning, "Just like your eyes."

Suddenly Jayhan's eyes filled with tears. "Thanks," he said thickly.

Sasha's face fell. "I didn't mean to upset you." He sent a worried glance at Beth but she just smiled.

"You didn't upset him. You accepted him."

The little boy looked a little confused by this. After a moment, he shrugged and grinned at Jayhan. "Deadly eyes. This orchid is called Pale Death." He chortled and said, "I don't think there is a dark brown orchid but there's a dark brown mushroom called Black Velvet and it is *fatal*.' He spread his arms wide. "So we both have deadly eyes."

For the first time in his life, Jayhan didn't feel a knot of tension as someone commented on his eyes. Sasha was sharing in the menace of his eye colour, even revelling in it. A tiny smile appeared on Jayhan's face. "What about Beth's eyes? They are deep blue."

"Oooh," exclaimed Sasha, "the deadliest of them all. Larkspur flowers are deep blue and *very* poisonous." He gave Beth a cheeky grin. "Much worse than Pale Death."

"You, young sir, are becoming far too comfortable far too fast." Her twinkling eyes belied the severity of her words. "You've only been here a day and you're teasing your boss. Now off you go, the two of you, and play outside. I need some peace and quiet to tackle these accounts."

And so began a friendship that would last their lifetimes. They wandered out past the stables then, by some unspoken mutual agreement, broke into a run.

"Race you," shouted Jayhan. "First to the fence on the other side of the paddock."

Jayhan, full of beans after a day behind his desk, won by a couple of yards. It occurred to neither of them that Sasha might be tired after hours of physical work.

"Cheat!" shouted Sasha joyfully. "You'd already started running when you said "Race you.'"

"No, I didn't."

"Right then. Race you!" yelled Sasha, grabbing a definite head start. "To the tree line."

The tree line, which marked the edge of the forest, was a considerable distance and after a hard run race, both declared roundly that they had won. They caught each other's eyes and laughed before leaning over, gasping for breath. In no time at all they had recovered and Jayhan invited Sasha to come and see a wombat hole he had found.

As they drew near, Jayhan put his finger to his lips and whispered, "Shhh. It's nearly sunset. If we are very quiet, we might see it come out in a bit."

They hunkered down behind a bush about twenty yards from the hole and waited… and waited… and waited. After what seemed like an hour but was actually six minutes, Sasha began to reach his hand out slowly. Jayhan frowned and mimed, "Shh," to which Sasha mouthed back "I know, I know," and continued to move his hand. Jayhan gave an irritated shrug and turned his attention back to the wombat hole.

Minutes passed. Although he could still feel Sasha moving at his side, he had to grudgingly admit that the boy's movements were silent. Soon he felt a gentle dig in the ribs and turned to see Sasha gesturing that he should look at something on the ground while Sasha watched the wombat hole. Jayhan found two faces, made from rubbed lines in the dirt, twigs, leaves and pebbles, smiling up at him. No attempt had been made to define skin colour but one had white quartz eyes while the other's were obsidian. A decorative circle of twigs and leaves surrounded the two faces.

A broad smile split his face and his eyes teared up as the acceptance of this one child brought home to him how lonely he had been. Sasha glanced at him and his eyebrows twitched in concern when he saw the tears. Jayhan waved his hand in a gesture that meant not to worry and kept smiling. He raised his thumb to show he liked the pictures.

Suddenly the faint snapping of a leaf drew Sasha's attention to the hole on the other side of the bushes and he dug Jayhan excitedly, and less gently this time, in the ribs. As they watched, a broad hairy muzzle emerged from the hole and sniffed the air. Beside him,

Jayhan saw Sasha stiffen in consternation then relax as he quickly licked a finger and raised it, feeling the breeze against the wombat side of his finger. They were downwind of it.

Sensing no danger, the rest of the wombat soon followed. For a minute or two, it gave a few desultory scratches in the leaf fall near its hole before trundling off, scratching from time to time with its powerful claws and rootling around with its nose among the detritus and roots, until it disappeared out of sight through the trees.

The boys heaved a sigh of satisfaction.

Chapter 9

"White quartz is very powerful, you know," said Sasha a few days later as, once more, they wandered through the bushland on the other side of the paddocks. The weather was turning cold and they were both rugged up in warm coats and boots.

"So?" Light dawned. "Is that what you used to make my eyes on your drawing?"

Sasha nodded. "Yep. White quartz. Stores and channels energy. Even makes thoughts clearer, stronger somehow."

Jayhan frowned. "How do you know all this stuff?"

Sasha shrugged.

When it was clear that Sasha wasn't going to answer, he asked instead, "So what about the black stone you used for your eyes? Does it have any special powers?"

Sasha bent down and picked a small piece of it up from the ground and began to toss it in his fingers. "Yep. It protects you. Keeps you safe from mean people."

Jayhan eyed him for a moment before saying, "Didn't do much to protect you from that bastard, Bryson."

Sasha stopped tossing the stone and looked at him. "You'd be surprised. My time with him wasn't good but it could have been a lot worse." He gave a little smile. "And look!" he said sweeping his arm around him. "I'm here now, aren't I? Not with him."

"Huh," snorted Jayhan. "That's because you were brave and you're good with horses, not because of some little black rock. Besides, you didn't have a little black rock then. You just had your dark eyes."

In answer, Sasha pulled a silver chain out from inside his shirt. Hanging from it was a polished black stone, held by a small ornate claw of silver. When Jayhan looked closer, he could see a series of lines cut into its surface; a triangle bisected by a long line that continued past its base. As he frowned, Sasha said proudly, "It is my family's symbol; a fire tree."

Jayhan looked puzzled for a moment before his brow cleared and he gave a short laugh. "You have a funny way of speaking sometimes. You mean a *fir* tree, don't you?" He nodded. "I can see now. It does looks like a fir tree."

Sasha huffed impatiently. "No. I don't mean a fir tree. I mean what I said... and my accent isn't funny... It's a *fire* tree. You know, like flames. In summer, it is covered in red and orange blossoms...looks like fire. Get it?"

"All right. Sorry, sorry. We don't have fire trees around here. At least I don't think we do." He thought for a minute. "So where are your family and you from? Somewhere they have fire trees, I'm guessing."

Sasha chortled. "Well done. Quick as a flash."

Jayhan grinned. "Thanks." After a moment, he prompted, "So go on. Where are you from?"

Sasha glanced at him then away. "From across the Najabi desert. From the Eastern Plains that run to the foothills of the Darkstone Mountains."

Jayhan's eyes grew round. "Wow! That is far, far away. How'd you end up here?"

"I don't know." Sasha gave an unhappy little grimace. "I was too young to remember... and no one can tell me."

"Did you ask them?"

"What do you think? Of course I asked them. I asked everyone at Stonehaven orphanage but all they knew was that I was left on the front steps sometime during the night. Old Tom told me that the delivery man found me the next morning lying wrapped in blankets in a very large basket made from woven grasses."

"So how do you know where you come from?"

Sasha looked at him a long moment, waiting to see whether he would figure out something so obvious. "My colouring and the basket," he said finally, "And my amulet."

Suddenly Jayhan stood up and started walking back towards the edge of the bushland. As Sasha caught up with him, Jayhan said, "So you've never seen those fire trees, have you? Someone just told you about them."

"So what?"

"And being dark coloured doesn't mean you have to have come from these Eastern Plains of yours. People with dark skin also come from the Western Islands, Kimora, Pangetti, Booralee. Just like paler skinned people like me come from here, Eskuzor, and Asthania."

"The Eastern Plains and the Darkstone Mountains are *in* Kimora, you idiot. Anyway, what about the basket?"

Jayhan stopped and put his hands on his hips. "What about the basket? Even if it comes from the Eastern Plains... personally I wouldn't have a clue where baskets come from... who's to say someone didn't buy it from the local market to put you in it. Goods travel between lands, you know. So do people for that matter. You could be from anywhere."

Sasha's face puckered as he stamped his foot and yelled, "I didn't know you could be so mean." Tears streamed down his cheeks. "I hate you."

Jayhan was struck dumb. Before he could recover, his little friend took off back the way they had come, dashing his way between sharp-leaved tea trees and clambering over a granite outcrop. Before Jayhan knew what was happening, Sasha was lost from view.

"Hey, Sasha," he yelled. "Come back." He set off in pursuit, muttering to himself, "What did I do? What on earth happened? What's got into him?"

By the time Jayhan reached the other side of the rocky outcrop, Sasha was nowhere in sight. He stopped and listened. A cold breeze crept down into his coat and made him shiver. After a few moments, he thought he heard leaves scrunching to his right. He turned and started in that direction but a wattle bird flew out from a bush almost under his feet and he realised that it was the bird and not Sasha that he had heard.

He grimaced in disappointment and stopped to listen again. The bushland around him seemed deathly quiet but slowly he tuned in to the drone of insects and, as he waited quietly, bird calls started up.

But no sound that he could interpret as being Sasha.

Suddenly he was startled by a pair of rainbow lorikeets, their orange, purple and green plumage flashing in the sunlight as they swept low over his head and disappeared at break-neck speed between the trees, shrieking as they flew.

Maybe Sasha disturbed them, thought Jayhan, heading further still to his right in the direction they had flown from. After a few minutes, he found himself at the edge of the bush but there was no sign of Sasha. He scanned the fields and ran his eyes along the tree line but nothing. Pushing down a confused sense of panic and frustration, Jayhan decided to head for home, hoping that Sasha had returned ahead of him, and if not, to get help looking for him.

By the time he reached Beth's door, it was full dark. He peered in the window and his heart sank as he saw no sign of Sasha. Still, perhaps he had gone inside the house for dinner already. Jayhan knocked and pushed the door open.

"I've lost Sasha," he said in a rush. "Has he come back here?"

Beth's eyes widened in alarm. "No. Not as far as I know. Why isn't he with you?"

Jayhan grimaced. "Tell you the truth, I don't know. He just got upset and ran off. I've been looking for him but I couldn't find him. If he hasn't come back here, I think he's still somewhere in the bush."

Beth grabbed her coat and strode out to join him in the darkness. The wind had picked up and snowflakes were swirling past them. She quickly checked the stables, calling Sasha's name as she ran.

"No. Not here. Where did you last see him?" When Jayhan described the location, she frowned. "The weather is closing in. The ground will freeze tonight. It will be a long, cold, lonely night for him if we don't find him." Seeing that Jayhan was already on the verge of panic, she didn't voice her fear that Sasha might not make it 'til morning. She took a deep breath as she collected her thoughts. "Right. We'll need a couple of horses saddled. You start on that while I round up some helpers. I'll let Maud know what is happening."

Twenty minutes later, two farmhands, Jake and Thompson, Leon the surly coachman and Beth were assembled outside the kitchen door, carrying lanterns. She handed Jayhan a meat pie. "Here. You and I will ride on ahead. Eat this on the way. I know you're probably tired but we need you to show us exactly where you were." She turned to a burly bearded man. "Jake, you two spread out and search the fields on your way to the trees. Jayhan and I will begin looking within the tree line but won't go out of sight until you join us."

Just as they had mounted up, Sheldrake stuck his head out the kitchen door. "Just a minute. Do you have any clothing of Sasha's? Something that carries his scent?"

"Up in the hay loft," replied Beth, nodding at Jayhan to fetch it.

As he returned with Sasha's spare shirt, a huge thickset bloodhound emerged from the kitchen and sniffed at it.

Beth gave a lop-sided grin. "Hello Maud. Good of you to join us. You can lope along next to Jayhan and me, if you like. The boys will meet us at the forest edge."

Chapter 10

Sasha ran through the scrub, furious and distressed all at once. Underlying it all was a sense of panic. He had thought he knew at least something about who he was and where he was from, but Jayhan had taken it all away with a few thoughtless words. He had treated the meagre clues to Sasha's life as an interesting puzzle, casually challenging the scraps of knowledge that Sasha had woven together to create his past. For Jayhan a casual pastime; for Sasha, his whole identity.

As he rounded a corner, a stick rolled under his right foot. He fell heavily, his left leg folding under him. When he tried to rise, his left knee felt jarred but held him. He stood quietly for a moment, his forward impetus broken by his fall. He looked back the way he had come and realised he could no longer see the forest's edge.

Better go back before I get lost, he thought.

But as he moved his right leg forward, his jarred left knee buckled.

"Ow!" he yelped as he just managed to save himself from falling. He stood with his weight distributed carefully between both feet, feeling unable to move.

"I need a stick," he said firmly. He hopped a few steps to a partly fallen dead tree and dragged a dry branch towards him. The bark held it to the tree by a determined thread. He pulled hard and as the bark gave way, he lost his balance and toppled backwards, banging his head on a raised patch of hard earth.

"OW! Again!" He sat up rubbing the back of his head, tears starting to his eyes. For a moment he felt woebegone, but with the determination bred from a hard life, he clamped down on his feelings, gave a defiant sniff and climbed gingerly to his feet.

He grasped the stick in his right hand to give him support as he put his weight on his left leg. After a few practice steps, he nodded his approval and set off back the way he had come. Long shadows striped the ground and he used them to keep his direction as constantly north-west as he could, given that he had to wind between trees, logs and the odd boulder. After twenty minutes, he could just see the last glimmer of evening shining through distant gaps in the trees, showing him the edge of the forest. But even as he watched, the light faded. With his eyes adjusted to the dark, he could still see, but he knew he didn't have long before it would be too dark to keep going.

Sasha tried to hurry but didn't want to risk falling again so his speed barely increased. Even so, he caught his right foot on a root that had grown under his path, making pain flare in his knee. From then on he stepped carefully, using his stick to feel out indistinct variations in the ground's surface. There were no longer any shadows to help him and this area of bush was dry, no moss on the south side of the trees to guide him.

In the distance he heard a dingo howl. He stopped to listen, guessing it was in the opposite direction from habitation. According to his own calculations that was almost right. A dark shape loomed and he realised it was a large boulder he has passed on his way in. Good. He was still heading towards home.

Home? Was it home? It was the closest he had to a home. Maybe after tonight, it wouldn't be any more. His stomach clenched. Oh no! What had he done? He had to get back and explain.

He stopped dead in his tracks. Explain what? That Jayhan had upset him? Would they even understand? And even if they did, would they then turn their anger on Jayhan? He didn't want that. And what would it do to their friendship if he got Jayhan into trouble? Jayhan may be an insensitive idiot, but Sasha still liked him... and he was the only friend Sasha had.

Suddenly a deep throaty howl sounded up ahead.

Sasha's face split with a grin. "Maud! Maud! I'm over here," he yelled. He started to hobble-run and promptly fell over a log and landed in a heap on the ground. "Oh, not again." He pulled a stick away that was jabbing into to his arm, raised himself on one elbow and yelled again. "Maud, over here."

Moments later, an enormous bloodhound bounded up and thumped him back to the ground with huge paws on his chest. Sasha beamed up at her and flung his hands around her neck. "Oh Maud, I'm so glad to see you. I was trying to get back as fast as I could, but my knee is sore and it's dark and..." He sniffed, then before he could stop himself, he was sobbing into the soft warm fur of her neck.

It was not long before Sasha heard voices and saw lights bobbing up and down as the rest of the search party approached. Maud gave a couple of ear-splitting howls, which guided the search party to them.

Sasha drew in a few shuddering breaths, trying to pull himself together before the others arrived, but the streaks from his tears shone on his cheeks in the lamp light. He looked up at them, his arms still round Maud's neck, his hands fondling her long ears.

"I'm sorry. I hurt my knee and couldn't get back fast. I tried. I really did." He sniffed and threatened to dissolve into tears again, scared of what would happen to him. He didn't seem to connect that he was drawing comfort from the mistress of the house while fearing the retribution of her staff.

They all stared at him, speechless.

Finally, Jayhan said, "You do realise that's my mother you're holding?"

Sasha gave a little smile and nodded. "Yes, I know. Maud found me."

Beth frowned. "How did you know it was Maud?"

Sasha looked puzzled. "What wouldn't I? Maud is Maud. You are you. It doesn't matter what shape you are. You're still the same person."

"Did you know Maud was a shapeshifter? I didn't tell you." Beth turned to Jayhan. "Did you?"

"No one told me," interrupted Sasha, before Jayhan could reply. "I didn't know until I heard Maud howling for me."

"Huh. Well, that's very odd. *We* only knew it was Maud because we don't have a bloodhound, so it had to be her." Beth gave herself a little mental shake and became businesslike, "Now that you've found him Maud, we can give you some privacy if you want to concentrate on changing back."

In answer, Maud shook her heavy head, flapping her long ears in Sasha' face before nuzzling him under the chin. Sasha chortled. "Stop it. You're tickling me."

Jayhan watched, feeling a twinge of jealousy. His mother had never been so warm with him.

Finally, Maud heaved herself off Sasha and rose to her feet. Leon, a hefty, broad-backed man, put his hands under Sasha's armpits and lifted him easily to his feet.

"There you are, young fella, me lad," said Leon gruffly. "Do you need a hand walking?"

Beth and Jayhan exchanged looks. Never had they heard Leon say more than a few grudging words.

"Thanks," said Sasha, as Leon handed him his stick. "I think I can manage." He set off, stick in one hand, his other arm draped across Maud's shoulders. Beth held the lantern to light their way. Sasha hobbled along as quickly as he could, not wanting to hold everyone up.

Jayhan came up beside him. "Don't feel you have to rush. It's not far to the horses. You can ride from the forest's edge," he said, eager to be helpful.

Sasha glanced at him, saw the worry in his face and let the residue of his anger melt away. *Just an idiot, not malicious*, he thought.

"Thanks," he said. "I'm glad you came."

Jayhan shrugged, a bit embarrassed, and said in a low voice, meant only for Sasha's ears. "I'm sorry I was unkind. I didn't realise..." He grimaced. "Beth explained to me what I did."

Sasha gave a little chuckle. "Burnt ears, huh?"

For a moment, Jayhan looked confused then realised what Sasha had meant and laughed. "Very burnt ears... most of the way from the house."

"Well, I'm glad you told her what happened. It saved me having to come up with a story to explain why I ran off."

Jayhan frowned across at the great bloodhound padding next to Sasha. "You realise my mother is listening to all of this?" he whispered.

Sasha grinned and patted Maud's back. "Doesn't matter. Whatever I did when I got back would be wrong. Either I would have to lie to cover up for you, or dob on you for being mean... even if you hadn't meant to be." He added hastily seeing Jayhan about to protest. "So, obviously, I would have had to lie."

Suddenly Maud gave a howl, making the boys jump. When they looked at her, they saw she was wagging her tail, although whether it was in appreciation of Sasha's frankness or his choice to shield her son was unclear.

Chapter 11

The next morning Sasha was summoned to confront the family upstairs while they breakfasted. Beth had bound his knee so that he could walk without the aid of a stick, but he still favoured it. Heart hammering, he climbed the polished staircase. He had never been up to the first floor and he was overawed by the richness of the dark wood panelling and the portraits that seem to glower at him as he passed below them.

By the time he reached the top of the staircase, his knee was hurting and he was using the bannister to pull up as much of his weight as he could. He waited a few moments to compose himself before stepping forward to knock on the dining room door.

"Enter," came Sheldrake's voice.

Sasha tried to read what emotion tinged the single word but couldn't. It was neither angry nor welcoming.

Sasha opened the door and stepped in to stand at the foot of the table. The whole room seemed to glare as light from the window reflected off the blindingly white table cloth and bright, silver cutlery. Sheldrake, Maud and Jayhan put down their knives and forks and turned to look at him. Unsure what to do, he bowed to them. He realised his legs were trembling as he put his hands behind his back and waited.

This is it then. They are going to send me on my way. I'm just a big pest. I put all those people out last night. Six people wasted their evening to look for me. Tears sprang to his eyes. *Oh what an idiot I am! Such a nice place; almost a home. And now I've ruined it. I'm not going to beg, though.* He took a deep breath and quelled his tears. *I will just thank them for all they've done for me and leave.*

"Good morning, Sasha," said Maud in a cool voice.

Sasha nodded his head in her direction. "Good morning, Madam." *Madam, not Ma'am,* he thought bitterly. *I learnt that mistake.*

"You are more respectful this morning, young man," she said, appraising him. "I thought you said a person was the same person, no matter what shape they took."

"Yes Madam. We are the same people as yesterday but in different roles today."

Maud gave her head a slight shake and murmured, "Such acumen in one so young," She looked across at Sheldrake. "I believe you have some questions?"

Sheldrake cleared his throat. "I understand, Sasha… that is, Jayhan has told me, I hope you don't mind, that you wear an amulet around your neck that you have had from birth and that gives you some protection. Is that correct?"

Instinctively Sasha's hand flew up to cover the place where the amulet lay against his thin chest. "Yes sir."

"Perhaps Jayhan has mentioned to you that I am an authority on such things and have many in my possession."

"Your pardon, but I do not wish to sell it, sir."

Sheldrake gave a slight smile. "That is well, because I do not wish to buy it."

Sasha looked panic-stricken but stayed silent. If Sheldrake decided to take it from him before turning him away there was nothing he could do about it.

Sheldrake frowned. "Do you think so poorly of me, lad? I would not force it from you. But I would feel honoured if you would trust me enough to show it to me. I might even be able to tell you more about it than you know yourself."

Sasha hesitated only for a moment before pulling the chain from around his neck and handing over the amulet. "I believe it is from the Eastern Plains near the Darkstone Mountains, sir, and bears my family's symbol of a fire tree..." He sent a baleful glare at Jayhan. "but I may be wrong."

Sheldrake glanced at Sasha then Jayhan but said nothing, dropping his eyes to the smooth, black amulet in his hand. "Hmm. Interesting... and beautiful. You are right. This is a symbol of power that is carved into it." He looked up and gave Sasha a surprisingly understanding smile. "I don't think it is a fire tree, however. I think the triangle represents birth, life and death but the line through the middle? I am not sure. I need to research it. Do you mind if I copy this symbol or perhaps keep your amulet for a few days?"

Sasha swallowed. "You may keep it for a short time, although it is my protection, but I must have it back before I go away... sir."

"What? You're leaving us?" demanded Sheldrake. "Jayhan wasn't that unkind to you, was he? I thought you two were friends again."

"No, he wasn't. Yes, we are. I mean..." Sasha's throat ached with unshed tears. *I won't let them see me cry. I won't.* "I thought you called me up here to send me away." There! He had said it and blast it all! Now he *was* crying. "I'm sorry," he mumbled, sniffing furiously.

"Oh for goodness sake!" exclaimed Maud, getting up and coming around the table She put her arm around his shoulder and led him to the table. "Where's Rose? Get this boy a cup of tea. Sit down, Sasha. Here. Have a napkin. Of course we're not sending you away. Oh dear! We must have seemed like judge and jury to you, you poor boy."

Sasha nodded and hid his face in the napkin, unable to shut the floodgates that he had kept so firmly locked. Finally, the thought of how annoyed Rose would be at having to serve him a cup of tea tickled his sense of humour enough to dam the tide. To everyone's surprise, when he raised his head he was grinning. He gave a final sniff and put aside his damp serviette.

"So, was Rose cross?" he asked, as he sipped his tea.

Maud frowned in recollection. "Now that you mention it, she did seem to flounce out of the room."

Sasha gave a satisfied little chuckle and took another sip of his tea.

"So Sasha, do you feel up to continuing our conversation?" asked Sheldrake, helping himself to a now cold slice of toast. "Toast?" he offered as an afterthought.

"Yes please," Sasha took a slice from the toast holder and placed it on the plate near him. Sheldrake handed him the butter and jam as he finished with them. "And yes, especially if it's not about me leaving."

Sheldrake took a bite of jam-laden toast, then setting down the remainder, steepled his fingers. Once he had finished chewing, he asked, "So Sasha, how did you know that the bloodhound was Maud? Most, in fact *all*, of the people I know cannot see through a shape-shifting. Did you just deduce it must be her because we don't usually have a bloodhound and despite what you said, you really did know that Maud is a shape-shifter?"

Sasha's little body stiffened and his eyes glittered. "I am not a liar, sir."

"No need to get huffy. After all, you yourself admitted last night that you would lie to protect Jayhan."

He relaxed a little. "That's not the same at all, sir. I might lie to protect someone. I wouldn't lie to make myself seem cleverer than I am."

Sheldrake nodded slowly. "I see. A nice distinction. So the question still remains; how did you know the bloodhound was Maud?"

There was a lengthy pause as Sasha was munching a piece of toast. He swallowed as fast as he could, nearly choking himself. "Whoops! Sorry sir. I just knew it was Maud. To me, it's the same as seeing you in a different suit on a different day. You're still the same person underneath."

"But you acted differently with my wife?"

Sasha gave a little smile. "So did she. Now it's back to usual." He thought for a moment. "I guess it's like fancy dress. When you're in fancy dress, you act the part and people around you join in. Then tomorrow it's back to normal." Sasha cocked his head. "Does that help?"

"It makes it clear how it seems to you but not how you do it. But I suspect you don't know how," replied Sheldrake. "However, whether you understand it or not, the ability to see through shape-shifting and disguises would be very valuable to me."

"Now Sheldrake," remonstrated Maud, wagging a finger at him. "Don't you go involving this little one in your nefarious doings. He is too young and innocent."

Sheldrake appeared shocked. "Really Maud! I wouldn't put the child in danger. I would arrange things so that he could see the people in disguise without them seeing him. Regardless of whether I use him, I think we should do some training and experimenting in the meantime. If Sasha is agreeable, of course." He turned to the stable boy. "Would you like to join Jayhan in his magic studies, Sasha? While he studies with his tutor in the morning, you can fulfil your duties around the stables then meet us in the afternoon at my workshop. What do you think?"

Sasha looked from Sheldrake to Jayhan, who gave an excited nod. He turned back to Sheldrake, his dark eyes shining. "I would be honoured, sir.... I hope I'm worth your time. I will try my very best."

Sheldrake gave one of his rare smiles. "You are already worth the effort, whether you realise it or not."

Part 2

Chapter 12

BANG!

Jayhan went flying backwards and landed in an untidy heap on the ground. On the bench in Sheldrake's workshop, a beaker of murky grey fluid issued an innocent wisp of smoke but, above it, a thick grey haze wafted near the ceiling.

"Jayhan! What on earth do you think you're doing? You will get us all killed!" roared Sheldrake.

"Jayhan! Are you all right?" cried Sasha, as he ran to kneel beside him.

Jayhan turned a sooty face to Sasha and grinned. "Whoops!"

Sasha heaved a sigh, partly of relief and partly of exasperation. "You idiot! I told you to wait a minute to give it time to work, after you said the incantation. When you said it again, it doubled the force." Once Jayhan had sat up, Sasha helped him get to his feet. "All right?"

"Yes, just grazed my elbow, I think." Jayhan tried to manoeuvre his arm so that he could inspect the damage. He pulled at the tattered hole in the sleeve of his jacket, but frowned in frustration when he couldn't see his elbow. He dabbed at it with his fingers, which came away red and wet. "Yep," he said with some satisfaction. "It's bleeding."

Sheldrake glanced over from where he was concentrating on constructing a knife that could elongate to become a sword. "So, despite the excessive dramatics, did your potion work?"

Jayhan gave a little grimace. He would have liked some sympathy from his father but knew the best he could hope for was to avoid a lecture. *Soldier on until the job is done,* was his father's mantra. He reluctantly lowered his arm, giving his sleeve a shake to put it back in place and wiped his fingers on his trouser leg.

Shrugging off the whole incident, Jayhan turned his attention to the beaker and carefully decanted the grey liquid and a residue of crushed quartz into another beaker, leaving a small rounded oval object in the bottom. He placed a piece of white cloth on the bench then tipped the grey object onto it. Jayhan and Sasha peered closely at it.

"Hmm. Isn't it supposed to be white?" asked Jayhan dubiously.

Sasha used another cloth to wipe it, revealing white beneath the grey. He wet the cloth and tried harder. A stone of iridescent white, with sparkles of red, green and blue shone up at them. A jagged line of black, like a lightning strike, ran down the middle of it.

"Oh look!" breathed Sasha. "It worked. It's turned to opal. It's beautiful."

Jayhan grunted. "Huh. A beautiful marred opal. I wrecked it, didn't I?"

"Well, it's not pure, but I think the black streak looks great."

"Show me," said Sheldrake, not looking up. "Bring it over here."

Jayhan duly presented it on a piece of white cloth to his father and held his breath. Sheldrake finished inserting a tiny piece of metal into his construction and straightened, arching his back against stiffness. Only then did he look at the opal.

He picked it up and held it up to the light, angling it this way and that, so that the colours sparkled. He returned the stone to its place on the white cloth and smiled.

"Well done! Not perfect, but well done."

Jayhan let his breath out in a rush. "Thanks."

Sheldrake's smile broadened. "Son, you could kill yourself, holding your breath like that."

Jayhan grinned. "I didn't realise I was."

Sheldrake looked across at Sasha, who had remained standing at the bench. "Well done to both of you. You are right that the black streak is effective but I want you to be able to create one without. Then you can move onto creating a black opal." He patted Jayhan on the back. "That's enough for today. You can try again tomorrow. Besides, you need to get some antiseptic and a bandage onto that serious wound of yours. Tidy up, then go and see Beth." He gave his son's shoulders a squeeze before sending him off.

Jayhan and Sasha arrived at the stables just as Beth dismounted from a solid brown mare, whose flanks were dark with sweat. Sasha bounded up, took the reins from Beth and stroked the mare along her neck.

"Hello Maud. You look like you need a drink and good rub down." Sasha laughed as Maud tossed her head. "Go on. You know you'd love it. Let's start with a drink and see how you feel then."

Jayhan glanced at Sasha then raised a hand in greeting to the horse. "Hi Mum," he said awkwardly, far less at ease with his mother in other shapes than Sasha was.

As Sasha led Maud to the trough, Jayhan presented his elbow to Beth, who inspected it with due gravity. "I think that definitely needs a bandage. Let's go to my office."

Once he was settled on a chair, Beth dabbed his grazed elbow with a lotion infused with cinnamon bark and thyme.

"There," she said when she'd finished. "Now, you'll have to take your shirt off if you want a bandage."

"Do I need one?"

Beth considered. "Not if you wear that same shirt with the hole in the elbow for a day or two. But if you have to put on a new shirt, your graze may stick to it." She shrugged. "Up to you."

"Hmph. Up to Mum, you mean. If it were up to me, I'd just wear the same shirt."

Beth thought for a moment. "Yep. Better put a bandage on it. Off with your shirt. Anyway," she added, "this will stop it sticking to the table if you lean on it."

Jayhan, secretly delighted to warrant a bandage, took his shirt off with alacrity. While Beth was bandaging his arm, he let his eyes wander around the room, checking out the tack and rosettes, the cobwebs in the corner and the piles of paperwork. Noticing a small stack of books in the corner, he frowned. "Aren't they my old readers? What are they doing here?"

"I borrowed them from Eloquin," said Beth. "I hope you don't mind. I gathered you had finished with them."

"Oh, I don't mind. They're as dull as ditch. Can't think why you'd want to read them, that's all."

Beth finished tying his bandage and patted his arm. "There you are. You'll have to keep your arm out of the bath or get a new bandage if you get it wet. Promise?"

Jayhan nodded abstractedly, still thinking about the books. Suddenly he asked, "Are you teaching Sasha to read?"

Beth grimaced. "Yes, in the evenings after dinner. It's supposed to be a secret."

"Why?"

"Well, partly because Sasha is embarrassed that he can't read."

Jayhan snorted. "I don't know why. I can't read very well myself, not hard books anyway. If he's already up to those books, he's not far behind me. He could do his lessons with me. I'll talk to Mum about it."

"No, Jayhan, don't. That is the other reason he has kept it secret. He is already sharing your tutoring time for magic. He doesn't want to seem as though he is angling to share your academic time as well. After all, he does have to pay his way. He is not, like you, the son of the house."

Jayhan looked troubled. "But that's not fair," he protested.

Beth smiled warmly at him. "No Jayhan, perhaps not. But life is not fair. Sasha would not feel good about having no time to pay his way. He already frets that he is not doing enough in the stables with the time he spends with you and Sheldrake in the afternoons."

"But Dad wants him to do that so he can help in the future. It is like he is a magic apprentice as well as a stable apprentice… and I hadn't thought about it before, but he'll need to be able to read when we start using spell books."

"He will be ready… in his own way and on his own time."

Jayhan brooded for a minute or two. "He works awfully hard, doesn't he? Can I help? What can I do to help?"

"You are a dear boy. You have already helped him by being his friend and accepting him. Don't worry. He is happier now than he ever has been."

Jayhan was not appeased. He would think about it.

Chapter 13

Three weeks later, to the horror of both boys, Sheldrake entered the workshop carrying a small leather book, worn and dog-eared, and announced that it was time for them to start following their own formulae.

"This," he said, "was my first spellcaster's book. It is a primer, if you like." He handed it to Jayhan. "You will have to share, of course, since there is only one. Now today, begin with something simple and innocuous. I want you to make up an antiseptic lotion, probably similar to those Beth uses. Turn to page 4, the recipe is there. Most things you need will be in the labelled jars on the shelves but ask me if you need particular ingredients."

The boys took the book to their place on the bench.

"Well," said Jayhan, "Finding page 4 should be easy enough."

They opened the book and studied the ingredients on page 4. After a couple of minutes, by mutual agreement, they took the book to the shelves so they could match words to labels on jars. Two ingredients stumped them. They whispered together trying to find labels to match but eventually decided they need to ask. Then ensued a heated whispering match about who would ask, both valiantly insisting on taking the fall. Finally, Jayhan won by simply walking over to his father and saying, "We have everything but 'Hone-ee' and 'Thime.'"

Sheldrake looked at him for a long moment before saying mildly. "Well done on the other words. I think you will find honey and thyme in the kitchen. Ask Hannah."

As they walked to the kitchen, Jayhan said disparagingly, "How are we supposed to know that? Why don't they spell them as they say them? Stupid books."

Sasha gave a jaunty laugh. "Yeah, stupid books."

Jayhan glanced at him then threw his hands up. "Right. Confession time." He stopped and faced Sasha. "I saw my readers in Beth's office and she told me about you learning to read. She tried to avoid it but I figured it out myself from seeing the books there. So, if we have to read bloody recipes, it will be better if we both know where we stand. I am not a great reader. In fact, you seem to have nearly caught up to me already, which is just shocking as far as I'm concerned, but ask if you need help and I will try…. Might not succeed, but I will try."

Sasha let out a sigh of relief. "And you won't tell your Dad?"

"No. I've known for a couple of weeks and haven't told him. I completely understand why you wouldn't want to waste your mornings in the library with Eloquin and me. Much more fun mucking out the stables."

"Absolutely," said Sasha, with a relieved smile.

Over the coming months, both boys' reading improved as they used it practically. They realised that Sheldrake wasn't going to bite their heads off if they didn't know particular words and, in fact, would prefer them to check with him if they were uncertain, rather than wreck a potion. Unbeknownst to the boys, Sheldrake was leading them through their little book based on the reading level rather than on the relative difficulty of the potion-making.

"Jayhan, you're nearly ready to continue your research, I would think," said Sheldrake, one sunny afternoon as the boys proudly presented a concoction designed for reducing swelling.

"What research?" asked Sasha.

Jayhan looked puzzled for a moment before his brow cleared. "Oh. I'd almost forgotten about that. I put the books in the back of my wardrobe because they were too hard for me." He explained to Sasha about his search for information about his light-eyed grandmother. He shrugged and gave little self-deprecating smile. "I think the books are probably still too hard for us, but I suppose we could have a try. I'll bring them down tomorrow."

The next afternoon, Sasha walked into Sheldrake's workshop to find a daunting pile of books piled on top of their bench. He glanced at Jayhan who nodded permission. So he reached out, but instead of opening one and attempting to read it, he laid the books side by side along the bench. Then he stood back, surveying his handiwork.

"Hmm. They look pretty old." He looked at his friend and grimaced. "Thick, aren't they?"

"Yep. And full of hard words."

Sasha suppressed a sigh. "So what are we looking for? Stuff about your grandmother?"

"Yep."

"So what was her name? Madison?" Then with a surreptitious glance at Sheldrake, whispered, "How do you spell it? Write it down for me."

Jayhan found a piece of chalk and wrote the name carefully on the bench next to the end of the line of books.

Sasha peered at it then grinned triumphantly. "So all we have to do is start by looking for the name 'Madison' in the books and read in front and behind it."

"If we can read the stuff in front and behind," responded Jayhan gloomily.

Sasha gave him a reproving punch on the arm. "Don't be such a gloomy-guts! I come up with a great idea for cutting down on hundreds of pages of reading and all you can do is whinge."

Feeling Sheldrake's eyes on him, Jayhan forced a smile, worried that either his friend might get into trouble for hitting him or he might get into trouble for sulking, "All right. Good idea, I guess. A good start, anyway." He picked up the nearest book. "So we can take one book each, write down its title and then look through it for Madison's name. Then we just write down the page numbers where her name appears and come back to it when we've gone through all the books. What do you think?"

Sasha smiled. "Great idea." He leaned in and added, "And puts off the time when we have to be able to read them."

"Splendid!" Both boys started, finding Sheldrake suddenly standing right behind them. "Of course, you will do this investigating in your own time. We have more important things to do here." As the boys began to protest, Sheldrake raised his hand. "This is Jayhan's project, not mine. You will do it in your own time or not at all."

"Oh." The colour had risen in Jayhan's face, more from embarrassment than anger. Without a word, he packed up the books and put them in a pile near the door.

"Today," continued Sheldrake, "we will spend some time on investigating Sasha's amulet. Would you mind showing us your amulet again please, Sasha?" When Sasha had pulled it out from beneath his shirt and placed it in Sheldrake's hand, he continued "I have made a copy and have been researching it but now, I want both of you to draw it as accurately as you can. Here, Sasha, have it back."

Sash breathed a sigh of relief as he regained possession of his beloved amulet. "Thank you, sir." He laid the amulet and its chain out, almost reverently, on the bench so that Jayhan and he could copy its markings onto pieces of paper. As soon as they had finished, he put it back on and let the amulet dangle within his shirt, once more out of sight.

Sheldrake walked over to inspect their work and nodded his approval, before handing Sasha an old leatherbound book entitled *Symbols and badges of guilds, sects and dynasties.* "Look through this and see whether you can work out the meaning of your amulet's symbol."

"Do you know, sir, what it means?" asked Sasha.

"Yes, I do now," said Sheldrake, looking over his spectacles at him, "but it has taken some considerable effort to find out. The book I have given you is the product of weeks of searching. I give it to you now so that you can enjoy, as I did, finding the last part of the puzzle. When you have discovered its meaning, we will talk further."

Sasha glanced at him uncertainly, perhaps sensing some undercurrent in his words, but the mage turned away and went back to his own work on the other side of the shed. When he turned his attention to Jayhan, he saw his friend's eyes alight with curiosity.

"Well, come on then," Jayhan said impatiently. "Share."

Sasha smiled at him and placed the book on the bench. "Well, come on then, yourself."

Together, they worked their way through the book, past sections on heraldry, stonemason's marks, insignias, watermarks and even the seals made by signet rings belonging to the more prominent houses in Carrador.

"Look," said Jayhan suddenly. "That's my mum's mark. See? A centaur; half woman, half animal. That's because Mum shape-changes."

"Where's Sheldrake's seal?"

"I don't know. Wait. Yes, I do. Here it is."

Sasha peered down at an angular S within a diamond within a circle. "Hmm. I've seen that before. It's on some of Beth's paperwork." He smiled. "It suits him."

Jayhan tilted his head, thinking about it. "What? No nonsense? With sharp angles? But with an air about him?"

Sasha laughed. "Exactly."

"Come on you two. What are you up to?" came Sheldrake's voice from across the shed.

"Nothing." They chorused, then laughed. Smothering a fit of the giggles, they turned back to the book and flipped a few more pages.

Suddenly, there in front of them was the symbol from Sasha's amulet, although the vertical line only began half way down the triangle, whereas Sash's began at the top point. Beside it was a drawing of a small bush covered in red and yellow flowers.

"Huh! See?" exclaimed Sasha, "It does represent a flame tree."

"Read the small print," said Sheldrake dryly, from the other side of the shed. "One day, missing details might get you killed."

Two heads, one brown, one black, leant over the book, reading the small writing beneath the symbol.

"Oooh. That's tricky' isn't it? Most people wouldn't notice that extra bit of vertical line but it completely changes the meaning. It's like secret code. Amazing," said Jayhan grinning. He looked at Sasha speculatively. "So what does that mean about you, I wonder?"

Sasha shrugged, looking uncomfortable.

"It means," said Sheldrake, right behind them again, in that disconcerting way he had, "that our little friend here is a shaman, from a long line of shamans... and he is, as he told you, from the Eastern Plains, which is indeed from whence this symbol originates."

Jayhan almost winced when he asked the next question. "And how do you know that someone didn't just put the amulet round his neck?" He grimaced at Sasha. "Sorry. Just need to know. Then you can be sure."

Sasha just cocked his head at Sheldrake and waited. In answer, Sheldrake requested him to take off his amulet again. "Just a small demonstration. I won't keep it long this time." He handed it to Jayhan. "Put it on over your head, just as Sasha did."

Glancing at Sasha who gave a small nod of agreement, Jayhan lifted it. But as the silver chain passed above his head, his hands burned and his head felt as though someone were driving spikes into it. He yowled and dropped the amulet. Predicting the reaction, Sheldrake caught it well before it could fall to the floor.

Sasha's eyes grew round. He looked knowingly at Sheldrake. "Is that what happened when you tried to put it on?"

Sheldrake smiled. "Yes. Exactly the same. And I believe the same would happen to anyone other than you."

"Wow. That's wonderful, isn't it?" Sasha beamed. "Something that is really, truly my own and nobody else's."

Sheldrake and Jayhan, who both owned so much, exchanged a glance of shared sympathy for Sasha. The mage put his arm around the boy's shoulders and gave him a squeeze, "Yes. It is rather wonderful, isn't it?" After a pause, he added, "Your amulet has other properties too. Your mother or father, usually the mother, would have passed it on at the moment before her death to the heir of her bloodline... and with it, all the knowledge of generations of shamans."

"But it's supposed to protect you. That's what Old Tom said," protested Sasha. "How could my mother die if she was wearing it?"

"It didn't stop you from hurting your knee," Jayhan pointed out.

"No, but I didn't die and you found me."

Sheldrake was looking thoughtful. "You have raised an interesting point, Sasha. From what I've read, it does indeed protect you. But how much, I don't know. I will see what else I can find out."

"So is that why Sasha can tell it's my mum when she is in different shapes?" asked Jayhan. "Because he is a shaman?"

Sheldrake directed his response to Sasha rather than to his son. "You are not yet a shaman, just as Jayhan is not yet a mage. You both need guidance to develop your potential. However, in your case, Sasha, I believe your amulet is gradually imbuing you with knowledge as you mature. Hopefully, what you learn from me will enhance that." He gave a little smile. "I think those flashes of wisdom that you produce that seem far beyond your years, can be attributed to your connection with the wisdom of the shamans of your ancestry."

"Huh. Not as brilliant as you thought you were," chortled Jayhan.

"Huh yourself. It may the wisdom of my ancestors but it was me who drew on it." Sasha gave a little smile. "At least I have ancestors. That's a good start. Excuse me Sheldrake, sir, do you have any books about the people and shamans I come from? I don't know anything about my family and people, or shamans or anything."

"I do have some books, but more than that, I know of a woman, an ambassador for the Eastern Plains, who resides at the Kimoran Embassy in Highkington. I will see whether she might be willing to talk to you about your people."

"Wow! Really? That would be wonderful. Could Jayhan come too?"

Sheldrake smiled at his enthusiasm. "I'll see what I can do."

On their way out of the workshop, Sasha bent down to pick up one of Jayhan's books to work on, but Jayhan forestalled him.

"No, don't Sasha." Jayhan said awkwardly. "I thought we would be doing it in our magic lesson time. I don't want to you to spend your spare time on these stuffy old books. You have enough to do. It wouldn't be fair."

"But…"

"No. We'll leave it for now," said Jayhan firmly. He managed a smile. "Anyway, we'll be busy learning about shamans, won't we?"

Sasha glanced at him but, reading the determination on his face, subsided.

Later that evening after dinner, Sasha sat down with a jaunty little book, *The cat that lost its tail,* in his hand, ready to read it to Beth, who was sewing an insignia onto a saddle cloth. Instead of reading, he said, "If I could get hold of some of Jayhan's books, I could help him find out about his great grandmother. He's put them away again in his wardrobe, but it won't feel good if we're only looking at my history and not his. I would have said that to him, but he had that stubborn look on and I knew he wouldn't listen… We could make the books into my reading lessons," he suggested hopefully. He cocked his head. "What do you think?"

"I think you two are lucky to have each other as friends. So, just how were you thinking you might get any of these books *out* of Jayhan's wardrobe?"

Sasha gave a little smile. "Clive?"

Beth put down her sewing to look at him. "Now Sasha, Clive is a respectable, trustworthy member of the household…"

"Yes, but it wouldn't be stealing. It would be borrowing... and to be helpful. I'm sure Clive wouldn't mind."

"Clive wouldn't mind what?" asked a third, deeper voice.

Sasha turned melting, dark eyes on the new arrival and beamed. "Hello Clive."

Beth rolled her eyes and resigned herself to the inevitable.

Chapter 14

For another fortnight, Sasha and Jayhan slogged their way through the potions primer that Sheldrake has given them, finally reaching some interesting formulae near the end of the book. They had discovered a potion that changed the pitch of a voice and had smuggled some out to use with great effect on George, the cat in the kitchen, who subsequently sounded more like a mouse for twenty-four hours. Amid gales of laughter, the poor cat had retired in high dudgeon to its bolthole under the house and refused to come out, even to be fed, until his voice had returned to normal.

The following afternoon, as they were about to enter the workshop, Sheldrake appeared in the doorway. "Good afternoon boys. We are having our lesson today out in the back paddock."

He led two intrigued boys past the back of the walled kitchen garden. As they passed the passionfruit vine that covered the red brick wall, Sasha pointed out a small nest.

"Look, Jayhan. A honeyeater's nest."

"How do you know?"

"I just know about birds' nests," said Sasha airily.

Jayhan's eyes widened. "Really?"

Sasha grinned. "What do you think? I saw the honeyeater there this morning."

"Oh." He gave a wry smile. "Fine. So, do you reckon there are eggs in it?"

Sheldrake turned around. "Now boys, you are not to touch that nest. We don't want to scare the parents off, now do we?" As the boys shook their heads, he continued, "Let us talk as we walk. Today I am going to teach you how to discover whether the person or animal you see before you is, in fact, that being's true shape. Am I right in assuming, Sasha, that you can tell what a being's original shape is? For instance, when you saw Maud as a bloodhound, did you know whether human or dog was her true shape... or did you simply know it was Maud? What if you had met her first as a bloodhound and only later as a person?"

Sasha thought about it. "I knew the essence of the bloodhound was Maud," he replied finally, "and I had an image of her human self somewhere inside the bloodhound. But when she is human, I don't see any essence of anything else."

"So you can tell that her original form is human?"

Sasha smiled. "I suppose I can. I hadn't thought about it before."

"So, given that you don't see any essence of anything else inside her, did you know Maud was a shapeshifter when you first met her?"

"No, sir… But I would now. I mean I would know another shapeshifter if I met one." He frowned slightly and glanced at Jayhan standing beside him.

Sheldrake drew his attention back, "And how would you know?"

"She's thicker," said Sasha, then blushed furiously. "Whoops. That didn't come out right. I didn't mean to say that Maud's fat. She's not at all overweight, at least not very, only a little bit tubby. What I mean is that she's…"

"Denser?" suggested Sheldrake, suppressing a smile.

Sasha breathed a sigh of relief. "Yes. Like thick cream instead of thin. Like there are a lot of layers underneath."

"Fascinating." Sheldrake stared at him, clearly entranced by this explanation. They had arrived at the top paddock and Sheldrake pulled himself together to unhitch the gate. Pushing it open, he gestured that they should go in. In front of them was a flock of sheep, idly grazing. A few of them eyed the intruders and moved further away, but most of the sheep ignored them.

"Now," said Sheldrake, "whatever you were going to say, Sasha, and I can guess what it is, keep it to yourself for the moment please."

"I wasn't going to say anything," Sasha protested. "If I gave away which one was Maud, Jayhan couldn't practise, could he?"

Sheldrake gave him a pat on the back. "My apologies for underestimating you." He turned to his son. "Now Jayhan, I want you to figure out which, if any, of these sheep is not in its true form. Here is how you do it." He held his fingers straight out but with the middle finger crooked between them, "This is called, rather melodramatically, the claw of truth. Now you place your fingers, held like this, somewhere on their skin or fleece. If their image is a glamour, you will feel a tingling sensation. Do you understand?"

When his son nodded, Sheldrake suggested that Jayhan try it on Sasha first. Sasha obligingly pushed up his sleeve so that Jayhan could lay his three fingers on his arm.

Jayhan shook his head. "No, nothing."

Sheldrake rubbed his hands together. "Good. So now we know our little friend here is not someone else in disguise."

Sasha frowned. "Of course I'm not," he said indignantly.

Sheldrake gave a slight smile that did not fully appease him. However, Sheldrake's mind was on other things. The mage muttered a few obscure words under his breath and waved his hand to encompass the grazing sheep. "Now Jayhan, I have just placed a gentle spell on the sheep so that they won't fear you, as long as you move slowly and are gentle. One of them, as you have gathered, is Maud. I want you to find out which one."

Jayhan worked his way diligently through eight sheep with no results, but happily, before Sasha could die of boredom, Maud made sure she was next in line. As soon as Jayhan touched her, he sprang back, his eyes widening in shock. "Yikes. That almost stung, it was such a strong tingle."

Maud tossed her head and Sheldrake said calmly, "Touch her again and see whether you can do it without betraying that you have noticed."

Jayhan steeled himself and placed his hand, with its longest finger crooked, gingerly on Maud's woolly shoulder. When he was ready for the sensation, he was quite able to withstand it and could remove his hand with more dignity and less haste.

"Hmm'" he said. "Well, that was interesting." He turned to Sasha. "Are you going to have a try, even if you know anyway?"

Sasha shrugged. "Might as well, I suppose." He placed his hand on Maud's shoulder but nothing happened. He looked disappointed. "Hmph. Doesn't work."

"Never mind. You don't need it anyway." Sheldrake smiled at him. "You're an interesting little character, aren't you? Magical, but in a different way from us. I must see what I can find in the library about shaman magic... and I think we might visit Old Tom and see what he knows."

Chapter 15

Sheldrake and Maud departed for Highkington the next morning, leaving the boys in Beth and Clive's care. Each of them had business in town and the Spring Garden Party was coming up. They took the lumbering old carriage, which was roomy and comfortable, but not at all fashionable. Maud's sumptuous, deep green dress filled most of the interior so that Rose, whom she had brought as her maid, had to ride on top with Leon, the driver. Sheldrake sat across from her, dressed in his usual austere black, although the coat he wore today was exquisitely tailored as befitted a visit to court.

As they watched fields give way to cobbled streets and the stately stone homes of the northern sector, Maud leaned forward and tapped Sheldrake on the knee.

"Now my dear, I will ask Rose to glean what she can from the Kimoran Ambassador's staff. The woman has an excessive number of staff. All show. Quite pointless, in my opinion. However, I shall ensure that she receives an invitation to the King's garden party. Gavin won't mind. He's such a dear boy. So delightfully malleable."

"He's not, you know." Sheldrake smiled at her. "Only where you are concerned. While you get to know Lady Electra, I will look up my network's latest dispatches from Kimora. As I recall, things have been stable there since the current monarch ascended the throne." He frowned. "But I seem to remember some serious unrest preceded her reign. Anyway, I'll also see what anyone knows about shamans and their powers." He nodded at a sprawling mansion whose rooves and chimneys could be seen through the trees of its manicured grounds. "Look! The Academy of Mages. I haven't decided whether we should send Jayhan there or not."

"*You* haven't decided??"

Sheldrake actually winced. "Whoops! I beg your pardon, my dear. Of course we will decide together. I just meant that for my part, I have not yet reached a conclusion."

"Hmm. You only just slipped out of that one." Although Maud's eyes had narrowed, she flipped open a green brocade fan and began to fan herself to hide a smile. "I think his pale eyes will make him the butt of unwanted attention. I suspect that he may prefer to learn from home."

"Perhaps. But he will have to take his place in the world someday and learn to cope with people's reactions to his eyes." Sheldrake gave Maud a wry smile. "And one day, you too will have to come to terms with his eyes. He is a dear boy, if a little impetuous. I have seen him watching you with Sasha when you are in other guises… not with jealousy exactly, but wistfully."

Maud sniffed. "I do not dislike Jayhan, but I don't feel comfortable when those pale eyes turn my way." She threw up her hands. "I know. I'm his mother. I should love him without reservation but, well, I don't. I do love him, but not without reservation." She watched Sheldrake anxiously for his reaction.

The mage patted her knee. "I know, my dear. You are not a cruel woman. I know you do your best."

Outside, the rhythmic hoof beats changed to the sounds of stamping followed by silence. "Ah," said Sheldrake. "We have arrived."

A footman opened the door and handed out Maud, Sheldrake descending behind her. Before them, the broad white marble steps of the palace rose to huge carved wooden doors set into walls of cream sandstone.

Despite the relative cosiness of their own small mansion, Sheldrake and Maud didn't even give the palace's grandeur a second look. They had two adjoining apartments within the palace; one in which they lived whenever they were in town and the other which housed Sheldrake's office and the deceptively small number of staff and records that he allowed the public to see. In reality, the King's Spiders, his network of informants, was spread far and wide, not only through the Kingdom of Carrador, but also through every surrounding country. Maud, to all intents and purposes, was a social butterfly, attending soirees, balls, garden parties and drinking tea or sharing wine with nearly everyone who came to court. Between her servants and herself, very little escaped her, especially since she could, unbeknownst to her acquaintances, change form when it suited her purposes. But while Sheldrake was the gatherer of information, she both gathered and used it. Sheldrake organised the Spiders but Maud decided what and how to tell the king.

For two days they innocuously caught up with business and friends. But on the evening of their third day in town, Sheldrake stood in his study wearing a very worn, grubby brown coat, a rumpled shirt and scuffed shoes below a saggy pair of leggings. A woollen cap hid his black neatly trimmed hair. Jayhan would have gasped in shock. Never had he seen his father look anything other than neat and trim. Beside Sheldrake stood a solid brindle dog of indeterminate parentage, her shoulder on a level with his thigh. Her tail waved gently back and forth as she waited.

Sheldrake pulled out the third book from the fourth shelf of his bookcase and pushed on a seemingly featureless part of the rear panel. After replacing the book, he depressed a rosette in the wooden carving running down the bookcase's left-hand side. With a click, the bookcase swung away from the wall, revealing a flight of stairs disappearing down into the darkness.

"Ready, Maisy?"

The dog wagged her tail and nudged her muzzle under his hand.

After a final glance around his study, he threw his tote bag over his shoulder and stepped onto the landing, Maisy right beside him. Once he had flicked his fingers to produce a floating orb of light, he pulled the bookcase towards him until it clicked back into place.

With the dog trailing behind him, Sheldrake descended the steps to a long passageway which ran under the rear of the palace and the street behind it. They climbed another set of stairs at the other end and minutes later, emerged from an inconspicuous door in a nearby alley. Maisy sniffed the air and the wall, then squatted for a pee while Sheldrake politely looked the other way. They spent the next ten minutes making sure that no one was following them before making their way to the Wayfarer's Inn.

The inn was a cheerful establishment mainly catering to lower-middle and working-class patrons. Merchants, tradesmen and travellers chatted and drank around dark wood tables, creating a genial hum of conversation that conveniently masked any individual discussions that might take place. Rory the barman, a small but very tough man, knew Sheldrake's real identity but always treated him as the down-at-heel travelling salesman he purported to be. He had no idea that Maisy was anything other than a dog but was happy to allow Sheldrake's dog into the bar, provided she behaved herself.

Sheldrake ordered a beer and wove his way through the crowd, slowly so that he could catch snippets of conversations as he passed. As he drew level with the third table, he laid his hand on Maisy's shoulder and moments later, she sat down to have a good scratch. Then she found a few well-trampled morsels, which led her under that particular table. Unnoticed by the patrons deep in conversation, she lay down under the table and put her head on her paws.

Sheldrake continued on his way until he reached a table just inside the far door. An old farmer was already seated there, nursing a pint.

"I heard you were looking for sacks to bag up your wheat," said Sheldrake.

"Only if they are good hessian and good value," came the reply.

Sheldrake's face relaxed into a smile as he sat down. "Good to see you, Kristoff." He leaned in closer. "Why the disguise? Have you struck trouble? Good wig, by the way."

Kristoff shrugged. "A bit. I visited The Hidden Lantern on the other side of town. You know it?"

"I know *of* it but have never been there. Some oddball magic makers group meets there occasionally, as I recall. Any shamans among them?"

For a moment Kristoff ignored the question. "They call themselves the Research Society. From what I saw, they are collectors of information about different types of magic use. A genuine group of enthusiasts, I think, with regular presentations by a variety of magic users from all over the world." He took a pull on his beer. "And yes, they have had shamans present to them in the past but…" Here he leaned in. "when I asked whether there was a shaman I could talk to, the atmosphere changed. They closed ranks, so to speak, and told me that no shamans had visited their Society or the Hidden Lantern for some time. I am certain they were lying."

"Interesting. Go on."

"And when I left, I was followed. I let her tail me until I could duck into a doorway in an alley and get a good look at her. She was a young woman, late twenties, I'd say. Fair hair, brown eyes. I recognised her from the Hidden Lantern. She had been drinking at the bar, near enough to listen, but not a Society member, as far as I could tell." He took a pull on his beer. "I thought of tackling her but that would have given away that I was skilled enough to rumble her and that I had more than a passing interest in shamans. So instead, I threw this dirty old smock over my clothes and donned the wig. Always carry a spare disguise in my tote bag."

Sheldrake gave a brief smile and touched his own tote bag, which lay at his feet beside him.

"Hmph. Of course you do. I suppose you take those things for granted; things I think are clever." Kristoff looked embarrassed.

"You're doing very well, Kristoff. Please, go on."

Kristoff gave a wry smile that acknowledged the praise for the sop it was. "When she gave up looking for me, I followed her. And, to cut a long story short, she ended up at the rear entrance to the Kimoran Embassy."

"Which she entered."

"Exactly." Kristoff pulled out a folded piece of paper. "I sketched her, in case you or one of your contacts knows her."

Sheldrake smiled. "You have done very well. I did not expect this little assignment to become so fraught. It seems we are not the only ones interested in shamans."

Chapter 16

Sheldrake was just cutting the top of his boiled egg when Maud walked in, dressed in a deep red and blue tapestry gown, blue lace around the neckline and cuffs.

Sheldrake smiled. "Good morning, my dear. I do admire those colours on you. Lovely."

Maud smiled in return. "Why, thank you. A cup of tea please," she said to the maid as she sat down. "And perhaps an egg, bacon and a couple of sausages, I think."

"Now Maud," said Sheldrake, as soon as Rose left the room, "you don't need that much. It's the hungry dog aspect still influencing your thoughts."

Maud gave a little frown of annoyance, contemplating Sheldrake's egg as her thoughts moved inward. After a moment she sighed. "Blast you, you're right. Oh well, I shall save what I don't eat and feed it to the next stray dog I see." She gave a little grin. "Did Sasha really say I was tubby?'

"Oh no, my dear. Not completely tubby. Only a little bit tubby." He chortled and nearly spilt his tea. "But he really meant that you were dense." That did it. His tea spattered all down his pristine, white shirt as he succumbed to laughter. "You know," he clarified, "Thick."

Maud crossed her arms in mock admonition, but she couldn't stop a smile from playing around her lips. "Obviously, he means I have depths to me, unlike the shallow, uncomplicated mage sitting across from me."

"Cutting, Maud," said Sheldrake, smiling as he tried to wipe down his besmirched shirt. "Very cutting. Look at this! I'm going to have to change my shirt now."

Rose returned and laid Maud's breakfast out in front of her. Once she had left, Maud continued, "And you were also right about that table last night. I picked up some interesting scraps of information," she dimpled, "and some delicious scraps of beef pie." She laughed at Sheldrake's pained expression. "Ah my dear. You are so easy to tease. Anyway, as you must have gathered, they are merchants recently arrived from Kimora. They were complaining about the increasingly high bribes they now have to pay for their goods to enter the country. Every year it has been getting worse."

"Has it? That does not reflect a strong, ethical regime, does it?"

"No. Unless it is just an isolated pocket of corruption." She grimaced. "Unlikely, I think. Besides, the merchants were talking about unrest among the guilds; forced curfews, higher taxes, raids on guild meetings."

"Anything about shamans?"

Maud shook her head. "No. Perhaps you, or we, should visit Stonehaven Orphanage and talk to Old Tom."

"If you wouldn't mind, my dear, I think your talents might be more useful in becoming acquainted with the Kimoran Ambassador, what's her name?... Lady Electra?"

Maud gave a short laugh. "Sheldrake, there is no point in acting vague around me."

"And," continued Sheldrake repressively, "I wonder if you might infiltrate the Research Society when they next meet. The day after tomorrow, I understand. Kristoff was stonewalled when he asked about shamans and was followed when he left, by a fair-haired woman who returned to the Kimoran embassy."

Maud frowned. "We had better be careful. We don't want our little Sasha being discovered as a shaman until we know why the interest and why the protectiveness."

Sheldrake ate his final piece of toast and wiped his fingers. He glanced towards the door to check that it was closed and leant in a little closer. "And watch young Rose, if you are going to use her. She does not like our little shaman. I don't want her making mischief for him."

"Hmm, good point. Leave it to me. I'll sort it out." She bit a piece of sausage off the end of her fork with relish and waved the remainder in the air as she spoke. "I shall go to the Society as a cat. A mouse would be more subtle but I don't want to risk being eaten by a cat if the Hidden Lantern happens to have a mouser. Much better to fight on equal terms if they do."

"Maud, put the fork down," Sheldrake shook his head, "You do it every time you think about being an animal. Your manners evaporate."

Maud smiled sunnily and returned the fork to her plate. "Oops. The social veneer is thinner when I am not thinking as a human."

Sheldrake left soon afterwards to change his shirt, so Maud was left to eat her sausage as she liked. When Rose returned to clear the table, Maud asked her, "Have you had a chance to talk to any of Lady Electra's servants?"

"No, Ma'am. But my mother's second cousin, Petunia, is stepping out with a footman at the Embassy."

"Indeed? And does this help us?"

Rose finished stacking the breakfast dishes onto an ornately carved wooden tray. "I hope so, ma'am. I am having tea with Petunia this afternoon.... provided you don't need me, of course." She added quickly.

Maud smiled. "I need you to have tea with your mother's second cousin. Well done, Rose."

"Is there anything particular you wish me to ask, ma'am?"

"I don't want your Petunia realising our interest so don't ply her with questions until we are more sure of her discretion." Maud paused for a few moments. "Now Rose, one more thing before you go. I have noticed that you do not seem kindly disposed towards Sasha. Is there a reason for this?"

"No, ma'am," Rose said tartly. "I'm just making sure he knows his place in life."

"Which is?"

"He's a foundling, dependant on the charity of your house and an outdoors servant. He's on the bottom rung in the household and should remember it. That's all."

"Are you aware that he saved Beth's life?"

Rose shrugged. "That's the only reason he's with us at all, instead of where he belongs, with the likes of Bryson."

"I see. So you do not approve of our decision to employ him?"

"It weren't… I mean, wasn't your decision in the first place, ma'am. Beth just went ahead and did it, and you had to back her up."

With a flash of acumen, Maud asked, "And did you have someone else in mind for the stableboy's position?"

"Not my place to say, ma'am."

"Perhaps not, but I am asking you nevertheless."

Rose put down the tray she had been holding during this conversation and wiped her hands nervously on her apron as she gathered her resolve. Then she straightened and said defiantly, "That were… I mean was, my little brother's job, by rights. He was going to start as soon as he turned eight. Ma was depending on that extra money coming in, now that me da's dead."

"Rose," Maud's voice was gentle. "I didn't know your father had died. Why didn't you tell us?"

"Ain't none of your business, that's why. Our business is our own." Rose dropped a quick curtsy and modulated her voice. "Beg pardon, ma'am."

"Then you can hardly expect us to take it into account when we make staffing decisions, now can you?"

Rose dropped her eyes. "No ma'am. Just unlucky, that's all. I knew Beth was thinking about getting a new stable hand and I was going to bring Edgar into work, so Beth could meet him. Sasha got there first."

"Had you arranged this with Beth?"

"Not yet. Wasn't urgent, as far as I knew and Edgar don't… doesn't turn eight until next month." She looked up, her eyes moist with unshed tears, "Like I said, just bad luck. We'll get by. We always have."

Maud patted the chair next to her. "Come and sit down, my dear. The dishes can wait."

Rose wiped her hands again and sat down diffidently next to Maud, her hands clasped tightly in her lap.

"Would you like a cup of tea?' asked Maud, who thought tea was the solution to every emotional issue.

Rose managed a small smile. "No thanks, Ma'am. It'll be stewed by now."

"Oh. Well, never mind." She clasped Rose's stiff hands between her own. "So now that this situation has been brought to my attention - and I wish I had known sooner - I have two things I need to say to you. Firstly, you may tell your brother that he may start work with us the day after his eighth birthday.

Rose frowned fiercely. "We don't want no charity, ma'am."

"I'm sure you don't, my dear. However, Beth will need your Edgar soon because Sasha will be working more directly with Sheldrake as he gets older. Already Sasha is only working for Beth in the mornings. And Clive isn't getting any younger. He needs a young helper to run errands for him."

"Really? Are you sure?"

Maud snorted. "Of course I'm sure. Now secondly, before I let you loose with your mother's second cousin, I need to know that I can trust your complete discretion and your loyalty to our household."

"Of course you can, Ma'am. None of us servants ever gossip about you or your husband. It's part of our employment conditions, right from the start." She gave a little grin. "Not like other households, I can tell you. I expect to hear all sorts of things this afternoon."

"I am pleased to hear that, Rose, and I expected no less. But our household is not just comprised of Sheldrake and me."

"Oh yes, and Jayhan as well," said Rose quickly.

"And you, Rose, and Beth and Clive and all the staff. No one is to be talked about to Petunia."

Rose frowned. "Won't that seem a bit strange?"

Maud thought for a moment. "Yes, true. Well, talk about general things but if you mention any names, make sure what you say is unimportant. Think before you speak. Do you understand?"

Rose nodded slowly, obviously thinking it through.

"And, in particular, say nothing about Sasha."

Rose's eyes widened. "Why not?"

Maud looked at her for a few long seconds. "I am trusting you, Rose. Don't you let me down."

"No ma'am."

"Sheldrake has discovered that Sasha is a shaman; a type of magic-wielder found in other countries but not here. Our initial enquiries about shamans have been met with resistance and until we know why, we want no one to know about Sasha. So don't mention him at all; his age, his colour, how he joined us, nothing. Clear?"

"Yes ma'am."

Maud smiled. "Now, off you go. I look forward to hearing your report."

Chapter 17

Sheldrake descended from his carriage and turned to look at the large, tired old grey building barricaded behind tall iron gates.

"Not very welcoming, is it?" he observed to Leon, who was holding the door for him.

"No sir, although the lawns and gardens seem well kept."

"Hmph. Well, ring that monstrous black bell. Let's see what sort of reception we get."

Leon did as ordered, and the harsh clang brought a small girl, dressed in a well-pressed smock, her fluffy light brown hair pulled into high pigtails, running down the driveway. She peered through the bars of the gate at them and smiled. "Hello." She paused then said, as though the words were unfamiliar, "May I help you?"

Sheldrake smiled and gave a little bow. "Hello young lady. My name is Sheldrake and I would like to speak with Tom, if he is available."

The girl nodded, "Do you mean Old Tom?"

"Yes. I think I do."

"Do you want to know my name?"

"Of course I do," he waved at his driver, "and this is Leon."

"My name is Joanne," she said and beamed.

"Well, Joanne, do you think you could get Tom for us?"

She nodded vigorously, said, "Yes," and shot off back up the driveway.

Sheldrake sent Leon a wry smile and rubbed his gloved hands together as he waited. "It's getting cold, Leon. Winter is closing in early this year."

"Aye sir, the horse dung was steaming this morning."

"Hmm. Perhaps too much information."

Leon snorted with laughter. "Such a delicate stomach you have, sir."

Sheldrake smiled vaguely and was about to make some reply when he spotted a great hulk of a man striding down the driveway. "Good heavens, Leon. Have we offended in some way? I fear we are about to be trounced. Be prepared to make a quick exit."

The huge man reached the gate and looked down at Sheldrake from at least a head taller. He was broad shouldered, deep chested and reached forward to open the gate with hands like hams. Then he smiled and it was as though the sun had come out.

"Good morning gentlemen. What can I do for you?"

Sheldrake let out a breath and dissipated a little spell he had been developing in case of trouble. "Good morning. My name is Sheldrake. I live out of town to the north and have recently employed one of your past children." On closer inspection, Sheldrake could see that the man's face was lined, partly from care but also from kindness and laughter, but not so much that one could think him old. "Would you be Tom?"

Tom's smile broadened. "Yes. Spit it out. Old Tom, they call me. I've been called Old Tom since I was fifteen years old. There used to be another lad here called Tom who was ten years younger than me. So I was Old Tom and he was Young Tom." The side of his mouth lifted in a grimace. "Sadly he died before he could be anything but young. Nice little kid." He pulled the gate wide. "Come on in. Leave the horses there. They'll be fine. No one much comes along this road."

Leon glanced at Sheldrake who gave the merest nod in return. So they both followed Old Tom up the driveway towards the front door.

Long before they reached it, Joanne came bounding up to them and tugged on Sheldrake's coat, "Do you want to see my picture I drew?" Anticipating his answer, she disappeared to return within moments with a scrawled series of lines on a piece of paper.

Sheldrake attempted to look impressed. "Oh well. That's very good, isn't it? Did it yourself, did you?"

Joanne nodded enthusiastically. "And you know what that is?" she asked, pointing at one particular squiggle.

"I would say," cut in Leon, rescuing Sheldrake in the nick of time, "that that is the lantern on the front of the carriage."

"Yes," replied Joanne as though it were the most obvious thing in the world. "I like lanterns a lot. I like carriages, but I *really* like lanterns."

"So I see," enthused Leon.

"Now, Joanne, let our guests be. See if you can organise cups of tea for us."

A few minutes later, they found themselves in a small reception room to the right of the entrance hall, Tom and Sheldrake seated around a polished mahogany table, Leon standing by the door. The chairs and table were of good quality, without being excessively valuable or ostentatious. Everything in the room was clean and well cared for. The walls were hung with portraits of children, exhibiting a wide range of skill in their execution.

Old Tom saw Sheldrake's gaze wandering and said, "Some of our past children have been very fine artists. All of these paintings were done by past residents."

Sheldrake nodded. "Impressive." He gave a little cough. "At least, some of them are impressive."

Old Tom laughed. "Yes. Not all, by any means, but at least they try."

"Is the rest of your establishment as well kept as this lovely room, or is this room kept particularly well to impress visitors?"

Old Tom gave a shout of laughter that made Leon jump. "You don't mince words, do you? What's on your mind? Do you think I'm running a slave labour camp out the back?" He waved his hand. "Help yourselves. You are welcome to tour the place, if you'd like to. In fact, the more people who see this place, the better chance I have of receiving donations to help the little ones."

"I beg your pardon," said Sheldrake stiffly. "I did not mean to offend. I am merely trying to gauge what sort of young life Sasha led. He is a talented young lad."

Old Tom stilled. It was only for a moment, but Sheldrake and Leon were both trained to notice the slightest nuance in people's reactions. "Ah, young Sasha. That is who you have working for you, is it? How did that come about?"

Sheldrake recounted the incident that had led to Sasha changing employers.

Old Tom grimaced. "I am sorry to hear that Bryson treated Sasha so poorly. I had my doubts about Bryson, but he promised to look after Sasha until he could set him up somewhere. And at the time..." He shrugged. "Never mind. I won't place any other children with him."

"I'm pleased to hear it." Sheldrake accepted a cup of tea from Joanna which she had carefully transferred from a large tray held by a small boy.

"This is Mikey," she said, blithely interrupting the conversation. "He is my friend."

Sheldrake inclined his head and Leon murmured a greeting from the doorway. Joanna placed a plate of sultana scones on the table and delivered a cup of tea to Old Tom and one to Leon on the way out.

"Bye," she said cheerily, as she left.

Sheldrake took a sip of his tea before saying, "Sasha seems to have some particular talents, magical talents. And since I am a mage, I have begun to include him in my son's training. However, his type of magic is not familiar to me and I was hoping to find out more about his background, with a view to developing his potential."

"As to Sasha's origins," Old Tom shrugged. "the baby was found wrapped in a blanket inside a woven basket, which was found on the front steps here."

"On the front steps?" asked Sheldrake. "What about the gate, and don't you have a tall stone wall surrounding this building?"

"No. Only on the side facing the street. Behind us are fields of wheat and corn. We also grow our own vegetables. The fences around them are sturdy and high enough to keep the little ones in, but not high enough to keep out adults. We are not a jail. If the older children want to leave, they can choose to do so any time, although I try to make sure they have some future to go to. No wall is high enough to keep an unwilling child in and we have never had issues with marauders."

Sheldrake smiled. "The more I hear and see of this place, the more I like it." He sipped his tea then put it down so that he could pick up a warm scone. He took a bite and spent a moment savouring it. "Hmm. Very good. You must have an accomplished cook here."

"I do, and he teaches the children how to be kitchen hands and chefs. They need training to find work when they leave here."

"Most commendable. And do you keep in touch with the children once they have left?"

Old Tom nodded. "I do. At least I try to. Not all children want to remember where they have come from, but they are always welcome to visit. When we place children in employment, usually at ten years old, we like to visit them within six months to see how they are going."

"So Sasha left early, did he? He's still only eight. And you haven't followed up his progress, as you have others?"

Old Tom stirred his tea, round and round, taking his time. Finally, he raised his eyes and looked directly at Sheldrake. "No, but I would like to. Sasha was always special and always different. They all are, in their own ways, but Sasha more than most. I would love to see Sasha again. Perhaps you will allow me to visit you and we could talk more then."

Sheldrake watched him as he sipped his tea. "And do you know anything of shamans?"

"I have seen nothing of Sasha's magic, if that is what you are asking."

"Not exactly, but it will do." He took a final sip of tea and put down the cup as he rose. "I think we have taken enough of your time. Thank you for hospitality and your cooperation. I shall send you an invitation to call upon us so that you may assure yourself of Sasha's welfare."

Old Tom smiled and nodded at both of them. "It was a pleasure to meet you and to hear that Sasha is safe. I look forward to your invitation."

Chapter 18

As the carriage rolled back towards the centre of Highkington, Sheldrake leant back against the cushioning and reflected on their encounter with Old Tom. The man had seemed friendly enough, but Sheldrake felt sure that he was not being completely honest, or at least not completely open, with him.

Sheldrake lurched suddenly as the carriage took an unexpected turn. As it took another, he heard Leon's boot thump down twice on the roof, a pause then two more thumps. They were being followed.

Sheldrake thumped three times on the roof with the end of his cane. A short time later, the carriage drew to a halt outside a bakery in Tanner's Field, a poorer quarter of town, once redolent with the smells of the tannery but less noisome now that the tannery had moved further out of town. Nevertheless, the narrow twisting street were littered with refuse and, in places used at outdoor urinals, producing their own rank odour.

Sheldrake drew in a breath before exiting the carriage. He descended the steps, ignoring Leon who was holding the door open for him, and made a show of inspecting the array of cakes and buns in the window before entering the bakery. Behind him, Leon went to the horses' heads and made a fuss of them stroking their noses and crooning at them, all the time watching the road behind them.

A solitary horseman trotted around the corner of the previous intersection. His surprise at seeing the coach pulled in to the side, showed in his mount tossing its head as he jabbed on the reins. Recovering himself, he didn't slow but passed the carriage at the same steady trot, touching his hat in greeting to Leon as he passed and turning down the next side laneway. Leon caught a view of a wiry, fair-haired young man, dressed in merchant's clothes that were well-kept but not expensive, in keeping with the quality of the horse.

As soon as the horseman was out of sight, Leon moved. He entered the doorway of a building to the right of the bakery, ran straight down the corridor between doors on either side and emerged into the back yard. He vaulted the back wall and landed in an alley that ran parallel to the main road. Keeping close to the wall, he slipped along the cobblestones until he reached the crowded laneway the horseman had entered. Leon peered cautiously around the right-hand corner and sure enough, there was the horseman, dismounted and appearing to make adjustments to his saddle girth while keeping watch on the road for the carriage to resume its journey. From where the horseman stood, Leon figured he could just see the horses, so would know if the carriage turned around or continued down the street.

He wondered how long the horseman could maintain the pretence before shopkeepers or passersby would begin to notice how long he had been there for so little effect.

Leon threaded through the crowd, slid up behind him and pressed a very sharp knife to the young man's ribs. Even though the lad was significantly taller than him, Leon knew a well-handled blade mattered more than size.

"Now," murmured Leon, "Let's assume I know what I'm doing and that if you move to attack, I will counter you, and at the very least, you will become the centre of attention. Now, ask yourself, is that what you want?" The young man stilled. Leon waited four heartbeats before continuing, "I want you to walk quietly with me across this lane, then down that alley over to our right. If you cooperate, I will not stab you." He glanced at the cloth merchant watching from the nearest window and nodded towards the horse. The merchant, held up her thumb in a gesture of understanding. "Your horse will be here when we return. Karin will mind it."

Leon tensed as he felt the young man take in a deep breath, but whatever he had been going to do, apparently he decided the better of it. Instead he simply nodded and turned to walk in the direction Leon had indicated. Once back in the side alley, Leon guided his charge past the wall he had scaled and ushered him though a gateway in the wall behind the bakery.

"Came like a lamb to slaughter, he did," murmured Leon to someone in the shadows.

A few minutes later, the young man found himself in a dingy room, seated at a table with two men facing him. Leaning his shoulder against the wall inside the door was the dagger-wielding coachman, while seated opposite him was the lean man he had seen entering the carriage. The fact that neither had bothered to disguise themselves worried the young man. Perhaps they weren't planning to let him live. He repressed a shudder and grasped his hands together tightly in his lap, keeping his eyes down.

As though reading his thoughts, the older man said, "There is no point in us disguising ourselves since you already know what we look like. You have, after all, been following us since you left Stonehaven. And whether you live or not will depend on whether we can come to some arrangement. Firstly, what is your name?"

The young man raised a frightened face to look at Sheldrake. "Jon, sir. Sir, I had no plans to harm you."

Sheldrake grunted. "Not directly perhaps. But your information about us may harm us. Had you thought of that?"

The young man half shook his head then dropped his eyes again. "No, not exactly. I'm just supposed to look out for unusual visitors to Stonehaven, find out who they are and report back."

"To whom?"

Jon shrugged. "Dunno." He looked up. "I really don't, sir. It's my brother's job, this. He took ill this morning and asked me to fill in for him. There's a few shillings in it, so I said I would. Didn't know I was risking a knife in my ribs. Seemed straight forward to me at the time."

Leon stood with folded arms against the wall. "That explains why you've been such a rank amateur at tailing us."

Jon shot him a resentful look but didn't say anything.

In the end they decided to let him go, after ringing a promise from him that he would not mention their presence. They plied him with a couple of dire threats and six florins to seal the bargain before Leon led him back to retrieve his horse. Young Jon looked dazed at his good luck at escaping, not only unscathed but richer.

When Leon returned to the room in the back of the bakery, he said, "I can see why you didn't ask him to find out who his brother is working for. He is too wet for words. Would have given the game away."

"Yes. Not cut out for subterfuge, our young Jon." Sheldrake stood up and lifted his long coat from the back of the chair. "But I think we need to know. Set someone to follow the person spying on Stonehaven and see what we can find out, preferably without them knowing that the watcher is being watched."

Just as they turned to leave, the cloth merchant burst into the room, wild-eyed and out of breath.

"He just vanished," she gasped.

"What! Who?" asked Leon, a horrible suspicion forming in his mind.

"The lad whose horse you asked me to keep an eye on. As soon as you walked away up the lane, he mounted his horse and then…" Karin snapped her fingers. "Gone! Right in front of my eyes."

"Gone? You're sure?" pressed Leon. "He didn't just gallop away quickly while you weren't watching."

The cloth merchant put her hands on her hips. "I think I would have heard that," she said caustically. "Anyway I happened to glance up at him just as he disappeared. No doubt, I'm afraid. He simply disappeared."

Leon's hand crashed down on the table, making the other two jump.

"Leon, please," remonstrated Sheldrake mildly.

"We have been taken for a right pair of chumps," fumed Leon. "Too wet? Not cut out for subterfuge? He's a bloody master. We couldn't have been more helpful. Blast! Blast! Blast!"

Karin's face split into a grin.

Part 3

Chapter 19

As Sheldrake and Maud departed for Highkington. Sasha had stood proudly at the horses' heads, waiting until Leon had climbed onto the driver's box, taken the reins and given him a nod. Leon had given him a tiny wave of appreciation that had left Sasha beaming from ear to ear, while Jayhan stood at the front door, waving as his parents left.

When they had disappeared from sight, Jayhan trudged inside to study while Sasha skipped across to Beth, still smiling, and cavorted around her as they headed towards the stables.

"Sasha, stop," said Beth, laughing. "You're like a big puppy. Run up to the top paddock and bring Flurry in for a brush down. That should burn some energy off you."

Completely unabashed, Sasha shot off to do her bidding.

After lunch, Jayhan was at last released and immediately raced to the stables to collect Sasha. Beth looked up as he bounded into her office.

"You don't have magic training, do you, while Sheldrake is away? So Sasha can work in the stables in the afternoons."

Jayhan's face fell ludicrously but he rallied. "Then I will work in the stables too. What can I do?"

Beth thought for a minute. "Fair enough. If you share his work, then you can both finish early. Sasha has just taken Flurry back up to the paddock but when he returns, you can muck out all the stalls together. As soon as you have finished... and mind that you do a good job... you can go off and play."

"Yes!" Jayhan grinned. "Great. Thanks, Beth."

Beth laughed. "You're as bad as each other. Now, if your hands start to get sore using the shovel, put gloves on. You don't want to get blisters or it will hurt worse tomorrow."

Jayhan rushed off to meet Sasha as he walked down the gravelly track from the top paddock. He waved as he got nearer and yelled, "Hi. Beth says I can help you muck out the stables so we can play sooner."

To his surprise, Sasha frowned. "You can't do that. That's my job."

Jayhan hesitated only for a moment before saying, "Well, in exchange, you can help me look through those books about Madison. Deal?"

Sasha glanced sideways at him and smiled. "Already have."

Jayhan boggled. "What? How did you do that?" He waved his hand. "Never mind. Tell me later. So that means I definitely have to help you. So there! No more arguing."

By mid-afternoon, the stables were spotless and Jayhan was exhausted. He propped the shovel against the wall and leaned against the wall next to it. He eyed Sasha as he bounded up, still full of energy. "How do you do it? And you usually do it all on your own. This is only half."

"And I did stuff this morning. I cleaned all the dung out of the top paddock while Flurry was down here, filled the watering troughs, fed them all." Sasha grinned. "Don't worry. You'll get used to it… if you want to keep doing it, that is." He patted Jayhan on the shoulder. "Come on. Beth has some lemonade and scones waiting for us."

Jayhan heaved himself away from the wall. "Yeah, I'll keep doing it. Probably good for me, all this exercise."

"Probably is."

Once they had bolted down their scones and lemonade, Jayhan asked about the progress Sasha had made finding out about Madison.

"I've been through all the books and made a list of the pages where her name appears," Sasha replied, smiling proudly.

"Really? All of them? That's amazing. But how did you get hold of them? I left them in my wardrobe."

Sasha did a little cough. "Well, you have to promise not to tell if I tell you…"

"Of course."

"Clive snuck them out for me, a couple at a time. He put one lot back each time he got the next lot."

Completely unconcerned by Clive's questionable behaviour, Jayhan asked, "So where are the books now?"

"Oh. Back in your wardrobe. I finished going through them all and thought I'd give it a rest for a bit before reading and making notes. That's going to be the hard part."

"I'll say." Jayhan frowned as he thought. "We need to lay them all out again but we can't get into Dad's workshop while he's away and there's not enough room in Beth's office." He grimaced. "It'll have to be the library where I do my lessons, I'm afraid. Do you mind too much?"

"Mind? I'd love to look around your library. It's Eloquin who might mind."

Jayhan blithely waved this objection aside. "Don't worry. She'll just be rapt that I'm spending extra time reading." He pulled a face. "She is so dull."

Firstly, they laid the books out in colour groupings, then from largest to smallest, then in alphabetical order and finally, in chronological order.

Sasha stood back and surveyed their work. "Yep. That makes more sense. So take a book each and compare notes when we've finished?"

"And if we don't understand a word, we write it down and look it up later. Agree?"

"Fine."

They slogged away at it until Jayhan was called for dinner.

Sasha gave him a quick smile. "Whoops. I'd better go too or I'll miss out. See you to-morrow."

They left out the contents of meetings and legal jargon because they had no idea what they meant, but after two days, they had pieced together the main features of Madison's story:

Madison was born in this cottage, just as Jayhan was. Her parents were well-to-do landowners but had their eye on the adjoining property. So, when she was old enough, they arranged a marriage for her with the neighbour's son, Brian, who was, unfortunately, a drunk and a gambler. When he got drunk, which was often, he would come home and beat Madison. One night, according to an eye-witness account by the maid, the husband had slammed Madison against the wall, and as she sank down in fear, he had stalked towards her, anger unabated, a poker in his raised hand. Suddenly, it was as though the extremity of her situation unleashed an inner strength. She raised her head and glared with those pale eyes of hers, straight at her husband. He fell back, clutching his throat and begging her to stop. She said nothing, just kept staring at him as he stumbled out of the room and down the stairs. She didn't kill him, but she hurt and terrified him somehow. From that day forward, her husband stopped drinking and never laid a hand on her again.

But Madison had been controlled and belittled, firstly by her parents and then by her husband. The only person who had loved her without wanting to use her was her nanny, Brenda, who had been dismissed as soon as Madison turned twelve. Now, for the first time in her life, Madison had power and there was no one who could pull on her heartstrings to rein her in. She used a mild form of her power on her servants, just to see what she could do. The eye-witness maid said that when her mistress turned her pale-eyed, power-imbued stare on her, Madison seemed to grow in stature and the need to please her was irresistible. Town officials and other people in the community reported that Madison could dominate a meeting and bend everyone to her point of view by staring them down. Suddenly other people would think their own views valueless in the light of hers. She did not instil fear in them as she had in her husband. Instead, she overwhelmed them.

When Sasha had read the scarps of writing and copied text that comprised this summary, he sat back, looking unconvinced, "She might just have been one of those strong people who can talk people around."

"Yeah, maybe, but what about her husband? She hurt him."

"That's only what the maid said. But maybe this Brian fellow was horrified at what he had been about to do."

"What? And choked on it?" Jayhan snorted. "You're too nice. You always think the best of people."

"Huh. Didn't think much of Bryson."

Jayhan chuckled. "That's the best anyone could think of him."

Sasha scratched his head. "Well, I don't know. She doesn't sound as bad as you thought. Sounds more like someone who just got sick of being pushed around." He smiled at Jayhan. "And no one even mentions her eyes until that maid talked about them."

"True. But people mind about my eyes now. Grownups always pulled back when they see them and then pretend to smile at me. And the kids in the village used to tease me about them. Dad would get angry but they'd just run away laughing. Then one day, I stared back at them and they all looked scared and stopped." Suddenly sombre, Jayhan stood up and started to pack the books into a pile, not looking at Sasha.

Sasha grabbed his arm and pulled him around, staring straight into his pale eyes. "Well, here am I, looking straight into your eyes," he grinned suddenly, "and all I can think of is Pale Death." He laughed and ducked away. "And Black Velvet," he added hastily, chortling.

Jayhan laughed and threw a pencil at him. "You're an idiot. I'm trying to be serious."

"Far too serious." But despite his words, Sasha stopped laughing and said, "Look, if you're really worried about your eyes, why don't we experiment? Maybe you can actually do something with them. That would be exciting, wouldn't it?"

"Huh. I never thought of that." Jayhan placed the last book in the pile. "I'm sick of these old books anyway." He heard his name being called for dinner. His pale eyes were shining with excitement. "All right. Tomorrow. We'll go into the bush and try it out. See you."

Chapter 20

Once they had finished their chores, Beth said they could take ponies to ride along the dirt track to the bushland, on the proviso they only walked and trotted them. "If you do well this time, I will let you canter for a short distance next time."

Jayhan saddled his own pony, Sasha keeping a weather eye on his progress. Once the ponies were saddled up, Sasha led them out into the yard, talking to them and patting their necks as he walked. Tosser, the pony Sasha would ride, was a brown and white mare who tended to toss her head and snap at any unwary person who strayed too close, while Jayhan's dark grey gelding, a gift for his seventh birthday, was quiet and if anything, a bit sluggish. Jayahn had enthusiastically named him Storm, but gradually Jayhan had come to refer to him as Slug. Sasha loved them both dearly. He dutifully helped Jayhan mount and gather his reins, before springing nimbly onto his own mount.

"Show off," said Jayhan with no heat at all.

Sasha just grinned.

They rode past the sheep paddock, the fields beginning to turn gold under the slanting yellow rays of the late afternoon sun. Raucous cries made them look up to see two yellow-crested cockatoos cut and weave their way to land in the branches of a dead gumtree.

Sasha nudged Tosser with his heels and she increased her speed to trot. Jayhan did likewise and Slug grunted and kept walking. Jayhan increased the strength of his kicks but Slug just kept walking.

"Sasha, wait," called Jayhan to his fast disappearing friend.

Sasha pulled in and turned in the saddle, then brought his horse back to Jayhan's side. "Right," he said, "This naughty horse needs stronger persuasion."

He dismounted and, letting the reins drop to signal his horse to stand, rummaged around beside the road until he found a thin stick about the length of his small arm and trimmed the twigs from its sides. He approached Jayhan so that Slug couldn't see what he was doing and handed the stick up to Jayhan. "Here, a switch. Just tap with it. If you hit him too hard with it, he might take off."

Jayhan waited until Sasha had remounted. Once Slug was walking, he kicked and used the stick simultaneously. Slug reluctantly increased his gait to a trot... for forty yards. Then he slowed to a walk and huffed as though he had just galloped for miles.

"Blast him!" exclaimed Jayhan, fast losing patience. "Is he sick, do you think?"

Sasha shook his head. "I'll bet he'd trot if you turned his head towards home. Come on, let's swap for a bit."

Carefully avoiding Tosser's teeth, they swapped horses. Tosser immediately trotted at Jayhan's command, and to Jayhan's annoyance, Slug responded to a kick from Sasha, without even the need for the switch.

As they entered the bushland and shadows from overhanging branches dappled the path ahead of them, disguising possible potholes, they slowed their horses to a walk.

After a few minutes, Jayhan asked, "So what am I doing wrong? You can make Slug do anything you want."

Sasha smiled. "That's what I like about you. No, that's one of the things I like about you. You are happy to accept your... hmm... the things you can't do and want to get better at them. Lots of people would just blame the horse."

Jayhan grinned. "I do the blame the horse. He's a pain in the neck. But obviously that's only part of it. So how come he behaves better for you?"

"To start with, I spend more time with him because I live and mostly work in the stables. I give him treats and pat him and talk to him on the way past." Sasha shrugged. "But mostly, hmm... you have to know you're the one in charge, that your will is stronger." He pulled up at a low branch, lifting it to allow Jayhan to pass before lowering it behind his own head so that he too could pass. "You have to centre yourself and know who you are. Then your horse will feel safe, knowing you're in charge and that you know what you're doing. All the switches in the world won't work as well as believing in yourself."

Jayhan eyed him, "That sounds awfully grown up. Is that Shaman stuff?"

"I dunno. Maybe. Don't care really. It's what I think, wherever it comes from."

They rode in silence for a few minutes until Jayhan asked, "So how do you centre yourself?"

Sasha leant over and patted Jayhan's stomach, just below the ribs. "Here's your centre. Just focus on it. All your power comes from there. If you need to, you can feel power radiating out from there to heal parts of yourself."

"Hmph. You didn't miraculously heal your jarred knee."

"No. It's not that miraculous. Just a bit. If you focus when you're hurt, I think it speeds healing." He gave a shy little smile. "And if you're getting sick, you can focus really hard and usually, but not always, you can send strength to yourself and stop yourself from getting sick."

Jayhan leant forward and patted Tosser's neck as he thought about it. "What if you're already sick?"

"It works to make you better quicker but problem is, you have to be well enough to get the energy up to centre yourself."

Just then, a kookaburra landed in the next tree along, threw its head back and sent forth its laughing call. Tosser shied violently, tossing his head and pulling hard on the reins, striving to break away.

"Centre!" Sasha's voice was low-pitched but loud, cutting through Jayhan's shock.

Jayhan focused on his centre, the world taking a step back. He realised he was keeping a firm, but not panicked, grip on the reins and was talking to Tosser, soothing him with his voice. He felt grounded, his legs melded to the horse's flanks.

Tosser stopped trying to pull away and after giving a few snorts of displeasure, pranced past the tree containing the kookaburra and settled to a calm walk again.

Sasha brought the unruffled Slug up beside him, grinning from ear to ear. "Well done! You handled that amazingly. I was already rehearsing in my mind how I was going to explain to Beth that I had let you ride Tosser who had then bolted with you on board."

Jayhan laughed and patted Tosser on the neck again, far more confident and relaxed. "I get it. I really do. Probably would have taken me ages if I hadn't suddenly had to master it. I didn't have time to think. I just did."

Behind them, the kookaburra's voice rose in laughter echoed by its mate somewhere further to their right, deeper in the bush. Tosser flicked his ear but otherwise didn't react.

"Stop soon?" suggested Sasha.

"All right. What about at the creek? It's not much further."

Another half mile brought them to a small creek, choked with rushes and lined with old river red gums whose limbs twisted and curved and whose hollows provided homes for scores of birds and possums. Even though the nights were cold, today the sun shone warmly and a dragonfly zig-zagged past as they dismounted and untied the food packs that Hannah had provided. They each found a comfortable fork in a tree to sit in while they ate their sandwiches.

"So, how are we going to test your eyes?" asked Sasha.

"Well, I reckon centring would be a good start..." When Sasha nodded his agreement, Jayhan shrugged. "Other than that, I guess I just look at something and ... what?"

"Hmm. I guess you have to decide first what you want to do with it." Sasha took another bite of ham sandwich, chewing for a while before saying, "That Madison great grandmother of yours. She could maybe choke people and scare them." He looked around. "No people out here except me and you're not trying it on me. Don't even think about it. So what can we use?"

"Not horses. A bird?"

Sasha grimaced. "I suppose, if one comes close enough. But you don't want to kill it, do you?"

"Course not. Maybe just try scaring it?"

"Yeah. Good idea. Start with that."

They sat quietly and soon noticed a dozen rainbow lorikeets riffling among the leaves high in the gum tree above them. Three wrens, one of them a brilliant blue, hopped and flew in and around a nearby bush, while a magpie standing in the next tree along, cocked its head to get a better view of them. On the other side of the creek, a white-faced, grey heron picked its way upstream.

"Hardest part will be getting the bird to look at you. Best bet is that magpie. Try it."

Jayhan carefully centred himself, then stared at the magpie. Before he could think of anything scary, let alone think anything at it, the magpie opened its beak and let forth its beautiful warbling song.

Jayhan rolled his eyes. "I don't want to scare it. Listen to it. Nuh. This is hopeless."

Sasha chuckled. "One thing's for sure. You're no evil genius." He swung down from the tree fork and dusted his hands. "Maybe try breaking a rock or a stick with your eyes?"

"What? The rock's going to know I'm looking at it, is it?"

"No. But who's to say what the power is? It might be a physical force of some kind. Maybe Madison's husband choked from a physical pressure on his throat and maybe those people changed their minds because they were scared of what she might do, or because she put some sort of physical pressure that made them feel scared?"

Jayhan jumped down from his perch in the tree and grabbed a stick. "Right. You hold this and I'll try."

"No," said Sasha firmly as he bent down and started to pick up small rocks. "Let's set up the stick between two piles of rocks. Then you can try when I am well away from it."

"Oh. Sorry. Good idea."

They tried everything they could think of for the next hour but nothing interesting happened. Finally, Jayhan gave up.

"Well, that was a bit of a fizzer." He sighed despondently. "I'm hopeless at spellcasting too, you know." He headed towards the horses, leaving Sash to pack up the remains of their lunches to stow them behind their saddles. As an afterthought, he turned back and asked, "Do you want a hand?"

"Not your job," said Sasha shortly. He finished strapping on the little leather luggage rolls, before looking up to meet Jayhan's eyes. "You're not too bad at spellcasting. Just a bit gung-ho sometimes." He gave a little smile. "But you do have a special talent that no one, including you, knows about."

Jayhan's eyes grew round. "Really? What?"

Sasha grinned. "You're a shapeshifter. I realised it when I told Sheldrake how I knew Maud was. You're thicker than other people, sort of layered. Not as much as Maud, but I don't know if that's age or power."

"Oh fantastic! How exciting! Maybe I could become a bird and fly... or a horse and gallop really fast... or a lion stalking across the plains..." Jayhan jumped up and down mimicking the movements of each animal as he thought of them.

Sasha laughed at his antics until he had calmed down enough to listen. "Come on Zoo Man. It's going to be dark soon. Let's head back. You can try out your shape-shifting tomorrow."

As they rode back through the gathering shadows, birdsong quietened as the birds settled for the night. But near the tree line, Sasha pulled his horse up and sat still listening. Jayhan, watching him, did likewise. Sasha gave him a brief smile but continued to listen.

After a couple of minutes, Jayhan asked quietly, "What's up?"

"Not sure. Just seems too quiet, even for this time of day." Sasha shook his head. "Don't know. Just a feeling. Something's not quite right."

Jayhan leaned closer. "Well, if something's not right, shouldn't we get home as fast as we can?"

"Suppose so. Doesn't feel threatening exactly, just... It's like someone is watching us."

Jayhan gave Slug a good kick that urged him into a trot. "Now you're giving me the creeps. Let's go."

Chapter 21

"But Maud, how did he just disappear?" Sheldrake shook his head. "I can't do that. Can you?"

Maud savoured a mouthful of pheasant and leek pie before putting down her knife and fork. When she was quite ready, she replied, "No dear, unless I turned quickly into a small animal like a mouse, but I couldn't make the horse seem to disappear as well."

"Hmm. So no." Sheldrake took a sip of red wine and sighed. "I believe a select number of sorcerers in Eskuzor can translocate, but even they would struggle with the horse, I would think. Still, an outside possibility."

"Perhaps," said Maud slowly, "a shaman can do it. Did he look Kimoran?"

"Not everyone form Kimora is dark, you know, so I don't know whether he looked Kimoran" said Sheldrake irritably. "But who's to say what he can do? Perhaps he can disguise his colouring? After all, if Sasha can see through disguises perhaps he can also disguise himself... but just hasn't tried yet." He cut into his pie with unaccustomed savagery. "Blast it?! He was such a nice, unassuming young man."

Maud smiled sympathetically. "Rather like Sasha then?"

An arrested look came into Sheldrake's eyes. "Very much like Sasha, now that you mention it."

"Now don't go overthinking yourself. Just finish your pie while I tell you what Rose discovered." Once he had nodded, she continued, "Her mother's second cousin is stepping out with a lovely young man, apparently, called Jon."

"JON?" Sheldrake choked on his mouthful.

Maud smiled broadly as she delivered several belts on his back to help him recover. When she was sure he would live, she said, "Yes, Jon. By all accounts, he is tall, fair and handsome, but that may just be a besotted girl's view of him."

"So our tail was also employed by the Kimoran Embassy. Just as Kristoff's was, the other night. Interesting."

Maud gave a little cough, "Not necessarily, my dear, at least not in his capacity as your tail. He did say, if you remember, that he was filling in for his brother."

Sheldrake rolled his eyes. "Which may or may not be true. We are getting nowhere fast."

"I haven't finished." She waited while he let out an exasperated breath and refocused himself. "Rose asked about shamans, hopefully in a way that did not arouse suspicion. The Queen of Kimora is a shaman, apparently, a very powerful one. Many members of her family were also shamans but they seem to have been largely eliminated when she rose to power."

"But presumable there are other shamans outside her family?"

"Yes. But they are strictly monitored. All shamans must be registered by the crown. Unregistered shamans are hunted down, and either imprisoned or killed, depending on the circumstances. They are considered a threat to the crown if they are rogue," Maud gave a little cough, "that is, unregistered."

Sheldrake frowned. "Her jurisdiction does not cover Carrador. Are we to assume the Kimoran government is hunting down shamans within Carrador? Surely the King would not sanction this?"

Maud shrugged. "It would depend on the rationale presented by the Kimoran ambassador. If shamans are indeed dangerous, I can imagine Gavin might be happy to be rid of them."

"This is most disturbing, Maud." Shaking his head, Sheldrake pushed his plate away, suddenly not hungry. "I have become fond of our little Sasha. I don't want anyone hunting him down, but equally I don't want our family endangered by harbouring someone who could grow to be a threat."

"Like Jayhan, you mean?"

"No," snapped Sheldrake. "Just because my pale-eyed grandmother was an evil old woman does not mean Jayhan will be. Powerful perhaps. We shall see. But inherently evil, no." He let out a breath and slowly smiled. "Cunning, Maud. You must like Sasha too, if you're standing up for him. So provided we keep him away from any adverse cultural influences of fellow shamans, there is no reason that Sasha should become dangerous as he grows into his powers."

"Except for mistakes, of course." Maud tilted her head to the side as she thought about it from every angle. "I think that is right. Do you?"

Sheldrake leant forward and took a slow pull on his wine before setting the glass down. "I would like to think so, but in truth, I don't know. Can people be born evil? Or do they perhaps have a tendency towards evil that circumstances nurture?"

"Evil is such a strong word, my dear. And so all encompassing. People are not usually evil, so much as power-hungry, or selfish, or uncaring, vengeful, jealous…"

"Some are just plain sadistic. They enjoy seeing people suffer."

"Yes, that is quite bad, I agree. But other qualities can be equally as destructive."

Sheldrake sighed. "So where does all this leave us? Is Sasha a threat or not? Perhaps shaman magic makes the wielder become obsessed in some way…"

"Before you get carried away, do more research. I am sure there must be books in the great library on shamanism. I thought shamans were supposed to be healers or witch doctors, something along those lines, not malevolent forces. And I think you should gather more information about Kimoran politics."

"All of this, without letting anyone know our interest in shamans."

"Now I must prepare for the King's garden party." Maud rose from the table and added with smirk, "I believe the Kimoran ambassador will be there."

"Well done, my dear. And I have recalled one of my senior agents from Kimora but he will not arrive for several days. Meanwhile, I will visit the library." He put down his napkin and stood up. "Good luck this afternoon and even more so this evening." He grinned. "Try not to get into any cat fights."

Chapter 22

The garden party was held in the rear garden of the palace. Velvety green lawns dotted with majestic river red gums swept down to a small lake. Although most guests tended to stand chatting as they circulated, a few small chairs and tables were provided for those who could not stand for too long. Liveried servants threaded through the throngs bearing trays of drinks and savouries.

Maud drifted artfully through the nobles and distinguished people who had been graced with an invitation, listening briefly to conversations as she passed. She spent a few minutes as part of the group around the King, observing who was intent on speaking to him and why. King Gavin was a slight man in his mid-twenties, his wavy, auburn hair not quite reaching his shoulders. His blue eyes twinkled benignly at those gathered around him. His father had died two years before from pneumonia, contracted after being caught in a torrential thunderstorm during a day of hunting. So Gavin had ascended the throne unexpectedly, and before he felt ready. But as Sheldrake had said, Gavin was no pushover. He listened to people but formed his own opinions and made his own decisions. However, Maud had been his father's advisor and Gavin was wise enough to retain her counsel. He trusted her above anyone to steer him into his new role, knowing she had a perspective that he still lacked. Not wishing to appear dependent, he did not have her always at his side, but he did consult with her from time to time and usually accepted, or at least considered, her advice.

Maud exchanged smiles with him and commented on the success of the party before excusing herself to intercept Lady Electra soon after she had arrived and had been introduced to the mingling crowd.

The Kimoran ambassador wore an exquisitely cut gown with a modest, bowed neckline and billowing skirts in soft shades of orange and yellow, which contrasted beautifully with her rich brown skin. Maud eyed it enviously, thinking that, had she worn it, she would have looked either jaundiced or insipid, or both.

"Lady Electra, how lovely to see you. I wish I could wear those colours. They look stunning on you."

The ambassador raised an eyebrow. "Thank you, but I think the green you are wearing becomes you most admirably. You are Lady Maud, I believe." She accepted a glass of pale green sparkling wine from a passing waiter. Maud nodded but just as she was about to speak, Lady Electra looked her up and down and frowned. "And unless I am much mistaken, you are a shapeshifter."

Maud caught her breath and glanced around quickly to see who was within earshot. Fortunately, the hubbub had covered Electra's pronouncement.

Seeing Maud's reaction, Electra smiled disarmingly. "I beg your pardon. I can see from your reaction that this is not common knowledge. I must assume that the magic wielders in Carrador cannot discern your gift, as I can."

Maud deftly replaced her empty glass with a full one as another waiter passed within reach. By the time she had taken a sip, she had herself well enough in hand to smile in return. "No, it is not generally known. Are you a particular type of magic wielder that you can see it?"

"Of course. I am a shaman, as are many of my countrymen and women. Shamans have an affinity for animals and the more adept shaman are sensitive to their…hmm… I suppose you would call it, essence. Your essence is complex, almost layered." She seemed impressed. "You have the potential to be many things, I would think. Very unusual and very powerful." She leant in closer. "Do not worry, my dear. I will keep your secret. I can imagine it is very useful for one so close to the King."

To her annoyance, Maud felt herself blushing. "You seem to know a lot about me and yet, I barely know you."

Lady Electra laughed. "My dear, you underestimate yourself. You are known far and wide as the power… no, not quite that… as the mind behind the King."

"I do not control the King," said Maud stiffly. "And Gavin has his own mind, thank you very much."

"Of course he does," said the ambassador placatingly. "But you do, I think, exert some significant influence."

Maud glanced around again before saying, "I like to think he heeds my advice from time to time." She took refuge in a sip of wine. This woman was unexpectedly difficult.

Lady Electra raised her eyebrow again, an intimidating gesture. "So why did you wish to meet me?"

Maud choked. In the time it took her to stop coughing, she had come up with a response. "We value the trade that occurs between our two nations. So Sheldrake was concerned to receive reports from some merchants saying that tariffs have risen for goods going into Kimora. Actually, since we are being so devastatingly frank, I will say that I mean bribes, not tariffs. It seems there are some issues with governance and we would like to clarify what this may mean for our trading arrangements with your country. You also have some problems with the guilds, I believe."

"I see. If your husband could supply me with the particular entry port where these bribes were demanded, I can arrange to have the matter investigated." Maud noted with no surprise at all that Lady Electra knew who Sheldrake was. "The unrest among the guilds is more difficult. The Queen has had to enforce strict measures because of ongoing discontent. We believe that someone is behind it, trying to incite the guilds into civil disobedience."

"Really? Any idea who?"

The ambassador shook her head. "No. Not at this stage."

Maud was not sure she believed this but she also knew that she couldn't press. They were discussing internal Kimoran politics, after all. She changed the subject. "And I believe, unlike Carrador, you have a registration process for your magic users. Is the King aware that you are tracking down unregistered shamans within the boundaries of his realm?"

Lady Electra raised those finely arched eyebrows of hers. "Who told you that?"

Maud smiled vaguely. "We, like you, have our sources."

Instead of stalling for time by taking a sip of her drink, Electra simply held up a finger and said calmly, "Just a moment. Let me think."

Impressed, Maud waited.

"Our queen is, not unreasonably, wary of magic users. She came to power by right of her own shamanic magic and although she has now ruled for over ten years, still fears that other shamans may be plotting to overthrow her." Electra gave a gentle shrug. "Hence our interest in unregistered shamans."

"But, is she not the daughter of your previous queen? Wasn't her claim legitimate?"

"Yes, Toriana became the heir after her older sister, the Princess Corinna, and her family were killed by bandits, only weeks before their mother, Queen Suriana, died. It was a very hard time." Electra looked away. When she turned her head back, Maud could see that her eyes were shiny with unshed tears. "I'm sorry. Corinna and I were dear friends. I still mourn her."

"I beg your pardon for upsetting you." When Electra waved this away, Maud continued, "However, we are far from Kimora's seat of power here. Surely it should be safe for anyone at odds with your queen to be in exile here, both from your perspective and theirs?"

The ambassador studied Maud for a long moment. "When a shaman is registered, they are bound to the Queen's service both by oath and by power. This limits what they are able to say or do."

Maud frowned. "Are you saying that a shaman's power needs to be controlled to be safe?"

Electra looked startled. "No. Not at all. A shaman's powers need to be controlled for the Queen to feel safe." She took a little breath. "You missed my point. Perhaps if I remind you that I, too, am a shaman."

"Oh." Maud's brow cleared. "Oh, how dim of me. Can you answer me this, then? Does the King know you are hunting shamans in his realm? Because I give you fair warning, he will soon, for Sheldrake or I intend to inform him."

"I cannot stop you and in fact, do not wi…" Electra gagged suddenly. She swallowed and produced a wan smile. "Ahem, perhaps some bubbles went down the wrong way." Since she had not touched her sparkling wine for several minutes, this was unlikely. "I will prepare our apologies. It was a pleasure meeting you." She gave a formal nod of her head and moved away, leaving Maud gazing thoughtfully after her.

Chapter 23

In strict accordance with the invitations, the garden party ended at four o'clock and carriages bore the invitees away. By a quarter past the hour, the garden was nearly empty. Maud spoke briefly to the King before she left, making a time to see him on the morrow to bring him up to date and to confer with him on any pressing issues.

She returned to her room and rested for a couple of hours before ordering an early dinner. Sheldrake had not yet returned from the library, but she wanted time to check out the area around the Hidden Lantern before entering it later in the evening.

Once darkness had fallen, she retired to her room and produced the image of a cat in her mind: its shape, its movements, its habits, attitudes and tastes. Slowly Maud shimmered into particles and almost disappeared, before coalescing into a rather solid grey cat, sporting white paws and a natty white patch on her chest. She strutted up and down in front of her mirror, conceding that Sasha might be right about her being a little tubby. Nevertheless, she thought herself rather dapper and rubbed appreciatively against the mirror before jumping lightly onto the windowsill, then out into the night.

Maud scampered across roof tops, heading east towards the docks and the Bohemian quarter. As she passed, she peered through windows to see families at dinner, servants preparing trays for their employers, a young man ardently declaring his love for a modest serving girl who looked uncomfortable and... Maud stopped and watched while the girl's protests became more strident and the young man's approach more determined.

Maud spotted a balcony above her, bunched her muscles and leapt. She climbed nimbly up a drainpipe and over the railing. The balcony door was closed but not locked. She leapt up and grasped the handle, pulling it down with her weight and holding on as the door swung open. Maud let herself drop before dashing in and down the stairs. The door to the room was closed and this door had a knob that was not so easy for a cat to open. Inside, she could hear the girl protesting and a thump as something was knocked over.

Maud sat on her haunches and yowled at the top of her voice. In moments, a voice from upstairs demanded to know what was going on. The door to the room was flung open and the young man strode out, glaring for the source of the noise. Maud slipped between his legs and entered the room, while he yelled up the stairs that nothing was wrong, that it was just a tomcat in the alley.

Maud ran straight for the girl who was cowering in the corner beside the fireplace, white with fright, holding up the torn bodice of her dress. Maud clawed her way up the girl's skirts and onto the mantelpiece. When the young man re-entered the room, he was confronted with a grey ball of fury, claws slashing whenever he tried to approach the girl.

Gaining courage from having an ally, the girl grasped the nearby poker. "Keep away, sir." He swayed a little closer, so she raised the poker. "Away, sir. I work here for honest money. I can't afford to lose my job but I will leave, if staying means being your plaything."

Suddenly the fight went out of the young man. He backed into a chair and put his face in his hands. "Oh, no. What am I doing? What was I thinking?" He raised his head and looked at her "And where did that come from?" he asked, pointing at the grey cat that stood on the mantelpiece with back arched. He shook his head. "It doesn't matter. I'm sorry, Larissa. I should never have done that. If you wish to leave the household, I will give you a good reference and will pay to get you settled somewhere else."

Larissa lowered the poker. "I prefer to stay, as long as this doesn't happen again."

The young man shook his head. "It won't. You have my word of honour."

"If you leave the room now, we will say nothing of this."

He stood. "Just a minute. Stay there."

He left and returned a few minutes later with another dress. The cat was still on the mantelpiece but sitting with her tail curled around herself. He held the dress out to Larissa, keeping as far away as he could. "Here. I beg your pardon. I had to enter your room, but you need a change of clothes. I am more sorry than I can say. I do love you, I think." He held his hand up. "but, I know. You don't need to tell me. I have a poor way of showing it." He gave a wistful smile. "Thank you for your forbearance."

With that, he left the room. Maud waited while the girl stroked her and made a fuss of her. When she had had enough, she jumped down and crossed to the window, scratching at the glass.

"Oh. You want to get out, do you?"

Quick as a flash, thought Maud.

Larissa opened the window and Maud slipped into the night.

Ten minutes later, she was slinking along shadows on the opposite side of the road from the Hidden Lantern. Chunky, a fearsome tomcat, so called because he had lost chunks of hair during his long, vicious history of fighting, was the local dominant male but he would only challenge other males, so was no threat to her. Female cats were a different matter, but she had made it clear to those who had met her that she was only in the area for a short time and a specific purpose.

As she rounded the corner, she noted a small low door in the wall of the Hidden Lantern, which presumably led to the cellars for delivery of ales, and a drainpipe leading down from the roof near the corner, past an upper storey window. She jumped the fence into the rear yard and found herself facing a closed back door and an open, street level window. Empty barrels were stacked along the wall of the inn.

She crossed to the wall and leapt lightly up onto a barrel and sat down, her tail curled around her feet listening to the sounds of the night, her ears flicking back and forth. After a few minutes, she took a deep breath, gathered herself and sprang up to the windowsill. She stood balanced on the narrow sill as she listened and looked for people, other cats or, horror of horrors, a dog. The coast seemed clear. A scullery and an open trapdoor with a ladder leading down into the cellars was to her right while straight ahead, she could see a crack of light shining under the door at the end of a dark passageway. After a moment's thought, she jumped down and slunk towards the light. As she neared, she could hear voices but the heavy wood of the door precluded her from hearing what was being said. Her tail twitched in irritation.

Suddenly heavy footsteps approached from the other side. Maud whipped to the hinge side of the door and pressed herself against the wall. The door opened and the inn keeper walked through carrying empty jugs. Maud slid behind him and through the doorway before the heavy door swung shut in his wake.

She found herself in a private parlour, hung with ancient tapestries depicting scenes of war and witchcraft, interspersed with ornate mirrors. Eight men and four women, each wearing a different style of dress, were seated on carved wooden chairs around a large round table. One of the women was dark like Sasha and Maud wondered if she was a shaman. To Maud's immediate left was a heavy sideboard on raised legs. She slunk beneath it and hunkered down to listen.

For a while they discussed mundane things such as the treasurer's report and cost of the venue, which apparently was subject to increase from time to time. Then each magic-user reported on new developments in their field. Maud found it interesting but dry. She would rather see and use magic than hear about it. Finally, a round-faced man in a crimson, embroidered robe said, "Now that we have heard all the reports, I think the next matter on our agenda is two-fold; someone has been watching our proceedings from the bar and another person is asking about shamans."

"And Teleman told me," chimed in the dark woman, nodding at a thin man wearing a ragged, brown linen coat, his beard and moustache long and wispy, "that the person asking about shamans was followed by the watcher from the bar." She huffed, "So now it looks like we have two separate parties interested in shamans."

"Don't worry Yarrow," said the round-faced man, "you know we will not betray your presence nor that of any other shaman who visits us. This society stands for the freedom to develop magical potential. We learn by working together."

Yarrow waved a ring-laden hand. "Thank you for your reassurance Donian, but it is not the Society members I am worried about. I am worried about the watcher from the bar, since we know she is from the Embassy. But even more so, the stranger who enquired concerns me. Where is he from? Clearly not from the Embassy, if she followed him. So who does he represent and what are their intentions?"

"Perhaps he is an ally or simply a researcher of shamans?" suggested Donian. "Perhaps we should have spoken to him."

Certainly would have helped us if you had, thought Maud.

Suddenly a scratching sound attracted her attention and before her eyes, a little mouse scurried out of a hole in the wainscot beside her. It did a doubletake when it saw her, its eyes widening in horror. Without the interception of thought, Maud pounced. The mouse, whose life was on the line, was quicker and scrambled back into the hole. But not fast enough. Maud's claws slammed down, catching the end of its tail. Maud was so intent on keeping her tenuous grip on the tiny bit of tail as she tried to stretch her other paw into the hole that she froze with shock when a hand grabbed her from behind and hauled her out from under the dresser by the scruff of her neck.

Oops.

As she hung in mid-air, staring into the indigo eyes of a finely built man wearing a coat not unlike Sheldrake's, Yarrow exclaimed, "Marvis, be gentle. That cat is a human shapeshifter," she walked around to look into Maud's eyes. "… who has a bit of explaining to do."

The last thing Maud wanted was to shape-change back into human form in front of a roomful of strangers. She focused frantically on the shape and size of a flea. Six legs was a challenge. So too was the size; so small. She felt as though she were changing into a dress six sizes too small for her.

Suddenly, the man's hand closed over thin air.

For an instant, Maud gripped his thumb with her tiny toes then used her multi-jointed legs to push off in a jump that landed her on the shaman's skirts. The next jump took her to the floor and the next, deep under the dresser. She waited for a few moments to draw breath and accustom herself to her new shape, listening to the exclamations and shouts issuing from the magic makers. A huge hand swept in under the dresser, but before anyone could invoke any sort of spell, she was out and under the door in two quick leaps.

She was nearly trampled on by the innkeeper who arrived at the door with filled jugs of ale, just as she emerged. A dollop of foam dropped on her as he paused to open the door and she found herself deep within wet clouds of froth that slowly popped and fizzed around her to become an amber puddle. Before it had time to submerge her, she pushed off from the floor and sprang further down the corridor.

For a while, she just stood there on her chitinous legs, dripping with sticky beer, tired from the unexpected style of exercise and shocked by the nearness of her escape. When her heart stopped hammering and her breathing had slowed, she began to think through her options. Before anything, she needed to get dry.

She jumped her way down the corridor and around the corner until she found an old rag lying discarded against the wall of the scullery. She burrowed into its folds, ruing the pungent smell of hops, until she had wiped off most of the beer. She listened for sounds of the inn keeper returning but from the noise issuing from the room, he was probably being berated for his lack of security.

She drew a couple of centring breaths then imagined her true self in her favourite green gown that she had worn as she shape-changed into the cat form. As she coalesced into her human shape, she swayed and had to prop herself against the wall. She hadn't noticed before how high a human's centre of gravity was. Not a good sign, feeling disoriented in her own body. She usually only shape-changed once a week or less, not three times in a few hours, and not in a tearing hurry.

She steadied herself, shaking her arms to become used to their length and moving her her weight back and forth from one foot to the other until she felt more secure in her body.

Just then, she heard the door open and the inn keeper's footsteps coming down the corridor towards her. Checking her hair briefly in her reflection in the window, she tucked in a few stray wisps, took a deep breath and surged around the corner.

She swept past the inn keeper, saying in her most assured manner, "Bring another glass, would you, when you return with more ale? Thank you so much."

The inn keeper, his hands full of empty jugs, goggled at her as she passed but made no move to stop her.

Maud knocked peremptorily on the door and entered without waiting for a response.

"Good evening," she said, smiling her most brilliant, social smile. "You may remember, we met briefly a few minutes ago." She held up her hand to quell the voices that had begun to speak. "Having listened to the contents of your meeting, I believe an open exchange between you and me is justified. With any luck, I can answer your questions, while you can answer some of mine." She turned her smile on the shaman. "How do you do, Yarrow. My name is Lady Maud Batian and as you can tell, I am a shape-shifter."

They all started talking at once while Maud stood before them, the picture of calm, friendly assurance, saying nothing and simply waiting for them to sort themselves out. Eventually, the man called Donian, who seemed to be their chairman, called them to order. Once they were silent, he turned to Maud and said formally, "Lady Maud, it is an honour to have you here although the manner of your arrival, was," he coughed, a little nervous but determined to do his duty, "somewhat reprehensible."

Maud smiled with unabated cordiality. "It was, wasn't it? However, I did not have to return to face you all and in fact would not have done so, had I decided you to be untrustworthy. I have, you understand, the care of others to consider."

"Indeed, ma'am. Could you be more explicit?"

"Certainly, but firstly may I join you at your table? Do you think another chair could be procured?"

Just then, the rear door opened to reveal the innkeeper lugging a chair in one hand and an extra glass in the other. Maud beamed at him "Oh well done, sir. You have anticipated my need. Thank you very much."

"I will be back shortly with more ale," he said to no one in particular and left.

"Now," said Maud, clasping her hands before her on the table. "Perhaps you would like to hear why I am here."

"I'm sure we would," replied Yarrow dryly.

"It is nothing nefarious, I assure you, and neither was my associate's enquiry about shamans the other day. Sheldrake and I simply want to learn about the powers of shamans."

"Sheldrake?" exclaimed the man with the indigo eyes, whose clothing resembled Sheldrake's. "*The* Sheldrake?"

Maud raised her eyebrows delicately. "Is there another, Marvis? Sheldrake is my husband, as I assumed you would know."

Clearly from the murmurs around the table, not everyone did know.

Yarrow frowned fiercely. "Isn't he, and aren't you, involved in the King's Sp... information service."

"Not I, only Sheldrake. But the King did not commission any investigation into shamans, if that is your fear. And since you people were unresponsive to a straightforward enquiry, I have had to ask elsewhere for the information I am seeking. So today, I had a talk with Lady Electra, the Kimoran ambassador. As you probably know, she is a registered shaman."

Maud paused for a moment, her eyes sweeping around the circle of shocked faces. "Hmm. Before I go any further," she turned again to Yarrow, "are you registered or unregistered? Don't worry. Anything you say to me will remain with me, unless I have your agreement otherwise."

Yarrow drew a deep breath then tilted her chin up in an unconscious defiance. "I am an unregistered, free shaman, ma'am."

"Oh good. That's a relief." Maud smiled around the group, who had all relaxed at her words. "Which is why you need protection. Correct?"

Teleman leant forward and replied tersely. "And not only Yarrow. Any unregistered shaman has our support and protection. If you are harbouring, as I suspect you are, an unregistered shaman, I hope, I sincerely hope, you did not give Lady Electra an inkling of it."

"So too do I," replied Maud. "After our associate was stonewalled by you and followed by the Embassy's agent, I made every effort to disguise the true nature of my enquiry. In fact, I made it clear to her that the King would not look kindly on Kimora chasing unregistered shamans within Carrador's boundaries." She gave a cheeky grin. "And I can assure you I wasn't followed here."

This turned the discussion to her shapeshifting skills which were of great interest to the Society, since they were so rare, particularly to the extent that she commanded them.

Eventually, Yarrow broke across the conversation, asking, "Lady Maud, will you tell us who you are protecting?"

Maud fidgeted with her cuffs then put her hands below table level to hide her tension. "Before we began to make enquiries, we did not realise that he needed protection. Knowing what we do now, I am loath to tell you, but in fairness, I think I must. We recently employed a young lad, who apparently arrived as a baby on the doorstep of Stonehaven Orphanage some eight years ago. He wears an amulet that denotes his origins as a shaman from Kimora." She smiled. "We first became curious about his magic when he saw straight through my shapeshifting," she looked at Yarrow, "as can you."

"Eight years ago? You are sure?" asked Yarrow, suddenly intent.

"Yes, as far as I am aware. Sheldrake visited the orphanage yesterday to check the story and it was just as Sasha had said."

Yarrow leaned back, the tension draining from her. "Oh. No, the timing is wrong. Don't worry. Just someone I'm looking for."

Maud smiled sympathetically. "I gather things have been hard on shamans under this Queen's rule. Is there, as Electra suggests, someone behind the guilds' unrest in Kimora?"

"Many someones, My Lady. Many people, not just shamans, are unhappy with the current monarchy."

"Yarrow, I would not want to put you at risk but if there is any chance that you could find time to teach Sasha a little of his heritage, we would be grateful. We had intended to ask the Kimoran ambassador but..." Yarrow's eyes widened in alarm, but Maud waved a reassuring hand. "But clearly, if we want Sasha to maintain his independence, that is not an option."

"No, it is not," said Yarrow vehemently. "I would be pleased to teach a fellow countryman and shaman. We," she waved her hand to encompass the assembled company, "will find a safe way to communicate with you. Be careful that you are not followed home. Remember that most shamans can see through shapeshifting."

"Hmm. Good point. Is that girl in the bar a shaman, do you think?"

"No. I would know if she were. It is a particular skill I have."

Maud stood up with decision. "To be safe, I will return the way I came." She let her gaze travel around the group. "Have you ever seen a shapeshifter change?"

Amid headshakes and mumbled 'no's, Donian gave a slight laugh, "Except from cat to flea, ma'am. None of our members has that skill."

"I have been impressed by your Society and believe you nurture the development and diversity of magic. So, if you like, for the sake of erudition, I will show you. In return, please tell no one of my particular talent."

Donian stood and gave a small bow. "We would be most honoured, Lady Maud."

"Goodbye then. Please make sure I can get out the back window." With that, she focused her whole being on her grey and white feline counterpart, shimmered and merged into her new shape. She gave a proud "Proww," and rubbed her side against Yarrow who opened the door for her. Without a backward glance, mostly because she was embarrassed, she scampered down the corridor, leapt onto the windowsill and out into the night.

It was nearly midnight when she reached their apartment at the palace. She leapt lightly in the window and slunk quietly across the carpeted lounge room to her bedroom, in an effort not to disturb Sheldrake. She need not have bothered though, because he was seated in an armchair in her room, reading a book. Despite her care, his head rose from the pages as soon as she entered, and his face lit with a relieved smile.

"Ah my dear. You are safely back. I am so glad. I'll get us both a nightcap, shall I?" Not expecting an answer, he rose from his chair and headed for the door, tactfully leaving her to shape-change in private.

When he returned bearing two crystal glasses containing hefty serves of brandy, Maud was sitting up in bed wearing a gold and green silk night gown, with a cream woollen wrap thrown round her shoulders.

"Thank you, Sheldrake. I hope I didn't worry you too much. I have had a very adventurous night." She gave him an entertaining version of events before saying, "I am concerned about our little stable boy's safety. I think we should consider curtailing our visit and return home tomorrow after I have spoken with Gavin. What do you think?"

Sheldrake sipped his brandy, aware that her mind was already made up but happily finding himself in agreement. "I was watched in the library this afternoon; not because it was me but because someone was watching for interest in the section on shamanism. I hope I spotted the woman before she spotted me, but I am not sure. Once I knew she was there, I tried to look as though I was browsing all kinds of magic, shamanism least of all. But I don't know how convincing I was. I agree with you. We must return home and review our security arrangements."

Chapter 24

The next day, happily unaware of any impending danger from the Highkington, Sasha and Jayhan saddled up the ponies as soon as their chores were done and headed off to the bush. This time, Jayhan carefully centred himself and found that he could raise a trot in Slug even heading away from home without the use of a switch; not an enthusiastic trot admittedly, but a trot nonetheless. Slug even managed a short canter but Jayhan had to work hard for every moment of it.

By tacit agreement, they did not speak of magic until they had made their way to the same spot beside the creek that they had stopped at the day before. Dismounting, they climbed into the lower branches of a twisty red gum to eat their sandwiches. Sasha had a whole day of physical labour behind him and was content to eat slowly and relax for a little while, but Jayhan was could hardly contain himself.

As soon as he had swallowed his last bite, Jayhan jumped down and began to pace back and forth below Sasha.

"So, what do you reckon? How do I do this?"

Sasha finished his last bite then leaned back along the branch he was seated on and put his hands behind his head. "No idea."

"Aw, come on. You must have some idea."

"Why? You've had years more magical training then me."

"Yeah but," Jayhan frowned up at him, "But you know about shapeshifters. From being a shaman. Maybe you can concentrate on your amulet and ideas might come about how to shape-change."

Sasha sat up straighter on his branch, held out his amulet on its chain around his neck and peered down at it. "I've never thought of taking in the knowledge from the amulet on purpose. I just let it happen or not. It's worth a try. In fact, maybe I should be trying to draw knowledge from it."

Jayhan, with rare patience, sat down on a nearby log and waited while Sasha concentrated on his amulet.

Firstly, Sasha centred himself. When he felt ready, he studied the bisected triangle symbol on his amulet, running his eyes around the three points which, according to Sheldrake, represented birth, life and death. As he ran his eye down the central stroke, he began to think about Maud and the layers he saw behind her human form. He thought about how she had appeared to him in the shapes of bloodhound, horse and sheep that he had seen her in, her true form clear to him within her outside appearance. Then he thought about her again in her human form and compared it to what he saw in Jayhan.

Something was different. In Maud, Sasha saw a depth and complexity of the other shapes that was lacking in Jayhan. He visualised Maud and Jayhan side by side then he realised the difference. Maud's layers contained a myriad of shapes and colours but Jayhan's contained a wide variety of colours but only slight variations in shape.

With a sinking heart, Sasha looked up at his friend who was waiting so patiently, eager to try out different animal shapes.

"Well?" prompted Jayhan. "How do I do it?"

Sasha shook his head, realising he hadn't even focused on that aspect. "Just a minute. I need a bit longer."

Jayhan huffed but said nothing.

Sasha had never seen Maud shape-change. So he just imagined her as her real self then as the blood hound, cutting back and forth between the two images. Suddenly, from deep within him, the knowledge of how to change welled up. He raised his head, dropped the amulet back onto his chest and leapt down from the tree, to land in front of Jayhan.

Jayhan, who had been amusing himself by watching a large ant struggle to carry away a crumb of bread twice its size, looked up startled.

"I've got it! I know how you change!" Sasha yelled triumphantly. Before Jayhan could replay, Sasha held up his hand. "But..."

"But what?"

"But it's not all good." He winced as he anticipated Jayhan's disappointment. "I don't think you can shapeshift into other animal forms. I think you can only shapeshift into other human forms."

Jayhan's face fell. "Oh." He stood up and scuffed his toe along the ground. "So no flying, or galloping across the plains, after all."

"No, I don't think so. I might be wrong. After all, I'm new to all of this but...no. I'm pretty sure, no."

Jayhan put his hands in his pockets and walked around the edge of the clearing, scuffing his feet through the grasses and leaves, his head bowed. After a while, he sat on a log and said glumly, "Wouldn't you know I'd come up second best?"

"No, I wouldn't know, as it happens. I think you're great." Sasha came to stand in front of him with his arms folded across his chest. "Except that you whinge about yourself too much. Anyway, you still have a special talent most mages lack, even your father. Don't you want to try it out? It could be fun... in a different way." Sasha grinned. "You could pretend to be me and trick Beth."

At that, Jayhan raised his head and looked at Sasha, his eyes narrowing as he thought about it. He gave a lop-sided smile. "Hmph. Not quite as good as flying but hmm, could be fun." Suddenly he smiled, his sunny nature reasserting itself. "And I could become Hannah and pinch whatever I like from the kitchen when she's not there and become Eloquin and tell Mum that I, as in I Jayhan, had done great work and deserve a holiday." He chortled. "So come on then. Tell me how to do it."

Sasha explained how to centre himself then to focus hard on the person he wanted to become, imagining every aspect of their appearance and behaviour, until his real self faded and the image took over.

Jayhan took a deep breath. "All right. I'll try it." He waved his hand. "Go over there somewhere so I don't have you watching me. And look somewhere else. I'll come and show you when I've done it… or at least when I think I've done it."

Ten minutes later, Jayhan blew out a long breath and looked himself up and down before walking over to tap Sasha on the shoulder.

"What do you think?" he asked, torn between embarrassment and amusement.

Sasha turned and found himself staring at himself; dark skin, soft dark brown eyes and curly black hair. After a moment, he cocked his head as he studied particular aspects.

"Well?" pressed Jayhan.

Sasha grinned. "Pretty good. Really good if someone wasn't expecting it."

Jayhan frowned. "What's wrong with it?"

"Well, the face is a bit lopsided. That little mole I have on my cheek is on the wrong side."

Jayhan frowned even harder, then laughed. "No, it's not. You always see yourself in the mirror. And I bet it's not lopsided. It's just the other way around."

"And is my nose really that snubby?"

"It's not snubby. It just turns up a bit at the end."

"Hmph. All right. Come over to the creek and we'll look at our reflections side by side in the water."

Two little Sashas parted the bull rushes and knelt on the muddy bank, staring down into the water, comparing the two reflections. Suddenly the real Sasha grinned and slapped Jayhan on the back. "Well done. That's fantastic, especially for a first time. Let's go home and trick Beth."

They pulled their hoods up as they neared the house and waited until they saw Beth come out of the side door of the stable and walk towards the front garden. As soon as she disappeared around the corner of the building, they trotted their ponies the last hundred yards, flung themselves off and hitched them to the post beside the water trough.

"Quickly," hissed Jayhan. "I can hear her coming back."

They ran quickly down the aisle between the stalls and snuck into her office. Sasha hid behind her comfortable armchair while Jayhan stood near the table ready to look as though he were collecting a curry comb. As she entered, his stomach lurched at his audacity.

"Hello," he said cheerily. "We just got back. I'll just brush down the horses before I put them away."

Beth frowned at him. "Will you now? And where is Jayhan? He is supposed to be learning to look after his own horse."

Whoops. Jayhan waved his hand airily, in what he suddenly realised was one of his own gestures. He hoped Beth wouldn't notice. "I know, but Eloquin called him. Don't know why. He'll probably be back to help me soon."

Beth relaxed a little and asked, "So, did you two enjoy yourselves? Did that lazy horse manage a canter?"

Jayahn grinned. "Yes, for a bit. Jayhan's getting better at managing him, but he's hard work, even for me."

A suppressed snort of laughter issued from behind Beth's chair. Beth whirled around and strode over. "What's going on? Who's here?"

Sasha stood up slowly, grinning his head off. "Hello Beth. Pretty good, hey? Can you tell us apart?"

She thought for a disappointingly short moment before saying, "Well, I would say I have been talking to the false Sasha who was trying to see whether he could trick me. So that means that you're the real Sasha, who is becoming very cheeky for an apprentice, and that naughty ratbag with the curry comb in his hand is Jayhan."

Sasha's smile faltered. "Sorry Beth. I didn't mean to be cheeky."

Beth ruffled his hair. "Don't be silly, Sasha, I'm only joking. You are very clever to have worked out how to do this, all on your own. Your father will be very impressed, Jayhan."

"And with Sasha," said Jayhan, quick to stand up for his friend. "He taught me how to do it."

"When I said you, I meant both of you." Beth put her hands on Sasha's shoulders and looked into his eyes. "Well done, Sasha. You are generous with your growing knowledge."

Sasha smiled up at her, knowing she was trying her best to make up for his lack of parents. "Thanks. You are both really kind to me. Everyone is, except maybe Rose. I trust you a lot." He swallowed. "So, there is something I have to, want to tell you."

And into the fraught silence that followed this pronouncement, walked Sheldrake and Maud.

Part 4

Chapter 25

At first, Sheldrake and Maud only saw Sasha looking earnestly up into Beth's eyes. Feeling the tension, Sheldrake asked, "What's going on?"

"Hello," said Jayhan from the other side of the room, having completely forgotten that he was currently looking like a second Sasha. As soon as he said it, he remembered, blushing and grinning with pride at his accomplishment.

Sheldrake raised his eyebrows so far that they threatened to climb into his hairline. He and Maud looked back and forth between the two Sashas several times, studying them so hard that Jayhan's grin faded and both boys began to feel awkward. Beth let her hands drop from Sasha's shoulders and he walked over to stand, hands behind his back, beside Jayhan. They glanced at each other and a small smile passed between them.

"So is this what you were about to tell Beth? That you have a twin brother? When did he turn up? Does *he* need a job too? What with you, Rose's brother, and now your twin brother, we are going to have a lot of new staff," said Maud, sounding none too pleased.

"No, ma'am," said Jayhan stiffly, miffed on Sasha's behalf. Without conscious effort, he assumed the role of Sasha's fictitious twin brother. "I do not need a job with you. Our family would not wish to cause you any further imposition. I'm sure neither of us would wish to stay where we were unwelcome."

Sasha goggled at him. He dug Jayhan in the ribs, as surreptitiously as he could, hissing, "Shut *up!*"

Jayhan looked at him. "What? She's being mean. I'm just standing up for you."

Sasha rolled his eyes and whispered, a hint of desperation in his voice. "Stop it. *Please.* I can't afford to upset people. I need my job."

Jayhan looked at his mother then at Sasha then back to his mother. "It is easy to be unkind, isn't it, when a person can't answer back."

Maud was turning a dark shade of red.

"That is enough, young man," barked Sheldrake. "You are clearly not cut out for our household. Sasha, however, may remain if he chooses. In fact, I hope he does. We have come to value his work, his knowledge and his good cheer."

Jayhan stared at his father, then remembered who he was and what they were really doing. Slowly he began to laugh. "Whoops! Sorry Dad. Sorry Mum. I just got carried away. I've never been spoken to like that before and I…" he shrugged. "I just didn't like it. That's all."

Sheldrake and Maud goggled.

"Jayhan???" they said in unison.

Jayhan grinned and nodded his head. "Yep. I can shape-shift. But not animals though."

Suddenly Maud clapped her hands, making them both jump. "Well done, Jayhan. Magnificent. Even if you were insolent to your mother."

"And Sasha, we have you to thank for teaching him, I take it?" asked Sheldrake.

Sasha nodded, looking down and scuffing his foot.

"I thought we might. You're a clever little fellow and so is Jayhan. I am most impressed." He rubbed his hands together. "So, before you change back, Jayhan, do you mind if we try a couple of things?"

Maud rolled her eyes. "Sheldrake, we have only just walked in the door. Can't it wait?"

"It could my dear, but it won't take long … and it is so interesting. Don't you think?"

Maud gave a reluctant smile. "Yes, I suppose it is."

"Now," instructed Sheldrake. "Could you both walk outside, muss your hair about, dirty your clothes a bit or something, so we don't know which of you is which. Then come back in and we will try to work out who is who."

"You had better take your pendant off, Sasha, or it will give the game away. Here," said Beth, stretching out her hand. "I will hold it for you."

"And I will turn into a bloodhound. I suspect I will be able to smell the difference," said Maud. "Just a minute."

With that, she retired to a horse's stall to change shape in private while the boys scuttled outside and swapped tops but not pants and mussed their hair.

Once they had reconvened, Sheldrake and Beth went first, debating which was which. In the end, they picked out Sasha because he was still feeling unsure after Jayhan's little sortie and his diffidence reflected in his demeanour. Maud padded in once they had made their choice and after sniffing both, went straight to Sasha. Sasha gave her an uncertain smile and had to have her nose pushed under his hand before he would pat her as he usually did.

Maud retired to resume her true form. When she returned, she came to stand beside Sheldrake, her arms folded. She looked grim. "Sasha, as we entered, you were about to say something of significance to Beth. It was not, as we first thought, that you have a twin. So, what was it?"

Sasha went stock still. He glanced at Beth, standing beside him, and his eyes went to his amulet. Without a word, she proffered it and he placed it around his neck.

"One way the amulet protects me is by hiding who I am," he said. "But I wasn't wearing it when Maud, in her bloodhound form, smelled me and I think she now knows what I am."

"You're a shaman, correct?" asked Sheldrake, frowning.

"Yes, from what you've told me. But I am also… It's hard to explain, but ever since I was a baby, I've had to hide who I am. Old Tom said people were after me and I had to stay hidden. I don't know why."

"Maybe because you are a shaman," suggested Sheldrake. "I gather the Queen of Karoka is hunting down shamans. She either kills them or binds them to her will somehow. Nasty business. I just hope our questions have not alerted anyone to your presence here. In fact, that's why we have returned earlier than we planned. To make sure you are safe."

"It isn't just that, Sheldrake," said Maud quietly. "Is it, Sasha?"

Sasha looked steadfastly at the floor. "No, ma'am, I mean, madam. I was going to tell you. I just had to be sure I could trust you all. Old Tom said so. I never trusted Bryson and the amulet kept me safe, at least mostly." He took a deep breath and raised his head. "I am a girl, not a boy."

Jayhan swivelled so fast to look at Sasha that he nearly fell over. "You're WHAT?" He gaped. "You're a girl? No. Can't be. Really?"

Sasha put her hands on her hips. "And what is wrong with that exactly?"

"Did I say anything was wrong with it? *No.*" Jayhan heaved a breath as his bewilderment threatened to overcome him. "I'm just boggled…" he shook his head from side to side. "and confused… and trying to think about what we've done together …and all that time you didn't trust me…"

Then as his understanding of who Sasha was faltered, so did his shape-shifting. His features blurred and for a moment both Jayhan and Sasha's features intermingled on his face. Then Sasha's features were gone and it was just Jayhan standing there, looking lost and a bit forlorn.

Impulsively, Sasha stepped forward and wrapped her arms around him. "I'm sorry. I truly am. I didn't mean to hurt you. I've been your friend ever since I met you and I still am, I hope."

Jayhan endured the hug for a minute then pushed her away. "We've never been huggy. Why start now?"

Sasha smiled at him. "Because you looked sad, that's all… and I caused it."

"I'm too young to have a girlfriend, you know. I'm only eight."

Sasha rolled her eyes. "Oh for goodness sakes, you idiot. I'm not your girlfriend. I'm your friend who's a girl. Completely different."

"Oh."

"Hmm. And would I be right in guessing that you are also older than we were led to believe?" asked Beth dryly.

Jayhan and Sasha had been so intent on each other's reactions that they had forgotten they were ringed by adults. Sasha's head whipped around to find three sets of adult eyes regarding her. Her cheeks reddened. "I beg your pardon. I forgot you were…that is, Jayhan needed, um…" She stuttered to a stop and frowned. "Er, what did you ask me?"

"How old are you?" asked Maud baldly.

"I am ten years old."

"You're what?" demanded Jayhan. "No wonder you can ride better than me and learn to read better than me and… well, everything better than me."

"Jayhan," interrupted Sheldrake in a tone of mild reproof, "This is not all about you. Please let others have a chance to speak to Sasha."

Jayhan mumbled an apology, then whispered "Cheat!" over his shoulder as he walked to stand, with his arms folded, by the wall and distance himself from the conversation.

Sasha was left standing on her own, facing three very serious adults.

The silence stretched out as Maud, Sheldrake and Beth tried to get their heads around their stable boy being a stable girl.

Eventually Sasha spoke, "Does it matter? I'm sorry I deceived you. I never lied about it because I didn't need to. Do you want me to leave?"

"No," said Sheldrake sharply. "We would not send you out into possible danger when you have… honoured us with your trust," he gave a rueful smile. "even if it has taken you so many months to do so."

Sasha took in a deep breath that hitched on a sob. "Oh good. Because I have nowhere to go, you see. And no one to go to, because Old Tom said it would be too dangerous for me to go back there, to Stonehaven, even though I loved it there." She wrapped her arms around herself. "I had to leave when I was nine. Everyone else could stay until they were at least ten, but not me. I had to leave when I was nine. Someone came and talked to Tom and the next morning, they hid me under the sacking on Bryson's cart and sent me away to live with him. I didn't even get to say goodbye, except to Old Tom."

She looked around in surprise when she felt an arm across her shoulders and found Jayhan standing next to her. He smiled at her, took a breath as though to say something, but then just smiled more warmly. She smiled back, even as tears filled her eyes and coursed down her cheeks. Suddenly Maud and Beth had both encircled her in their arms and Sheldrake even went so far as to pat her on the head and say, "There, there."

After a while she took a deep shuddering breath. "It is such a relief to tell you. It felt so lonely being the only one who knew."

Maud gave her a final squeeze. "We must still keep your gender and age a secret until we know what we are dealing with. I see no need to tell Hannah or Rose. Sheldrake, you may need to tell Leon as he is privy to your investigations and of course, you must tell Clive, Beth. But no one else. For the time being, we will carry on as before. Agreed?"

This last was addressed mainly to Sheldrake, who replied, "Indeed. And we will not broadcast, any more than we have, the fact that you are a shaman, Sasha."

Chapter 26

"I must talk to Leon about security today," said Sheldrake to Maud the next morning, as he rose from the breakfast table, placing his napkin neatly on his side plate. "I have a magical ward around my workshop but perhaps we need one around the whole perimeter. Anyone could walk in off the street."

As if to demonstrate his point, the front doorbell rang. A few minutes later, Clive appeared. "A gentleman has asked to see you. I have put him in the front parlour, while I ascertain your availability. He would not give his name, which I found distinctly odd, but he said you would know him when you saw him." Clive paused. "Do you, in fact, *wish* to see him?"

Sheldrake frowned. "Extremely odd… but intriguing. Yes, I will see him, but I had better take precautions. Ask Leon to join us, would you?"

Clive gave a slight bow, his formality a sure sign that he did not approve of such goings on.

Sheldrake trotted down the stairs and into the parlour, not waiting for Leon before entering. A tall, willowy, young man, dressed very correctly in morning attire, his blond hair neatly pulled back at the nape of his neck, turned at the sound of the door opening. A whimsical smile lit his face.

Sheldrake, who prided himself on being able to maintain a neutral visage, was saved the embarrassment of gaping in astonishment by the young man, who stepped forward and bowed, giving him time to recover.

"Jon, I believe," Sheldrake managed, congratulating himself on the steadiness of his voice.

The young man straightened, his blue eyes shining with laughter. "Indeed, sir. I see you remember me."

"And to what do I owe the pleasure of your company?" asked Sheldrake dryly, waving Jon to a chair.

Suddenly the laughter was gone from the young man's eyes. "You have in your charge, in your employment, a very special person."

Sheldrake saw no point in prevaricating. "Sasha?"

"Indeed. And your enquiries have incited the interest of the Kimoran Embassy."

"Where you, yourself, are employed. Are you here on its behalf?"

Jon inclined his head in acknowledgement of Sheldrake's knowledge. "I am a plainsman from Kimoran and am loyal to the welfare of Kimora but I do not hold with… hmm, how can I put it?… *leashing* shamans."

"I see." Sheldrake heard Leon slip into the room and turned to him. "Were you in time to hear that?"

Leon, his mouth tight with suspicion, nodded shortly and took up residence against the wall.

Sheldrake returned his attention to Jon. "My question remains unanswered. Are you here on behalf of the Embassy?"

Jon stood up abruptly, making Leon straighten, and began to pace. "No, I am not and just be glad I'm not, for Sasha's sake."

"Why were you watching Stonehaven?"

Jon stopped in the window embrasure and studied Sheldrake. "Suffice it to say, that when someone enquired about shamans at the Hidden Lantern, word was carried to the Embassy." His mouth quirked. "Being a footman has its advantages. Generally, I am ignored unless they require me to run an errand. When I heard Marsha's report to Lady Electra, I determined to watch Stonehaven to check whether the enquiry was linked to Sasha. If Old Tom indicated it was, I could then follow you."

"I see. And why follow us?"

"Two reasons. To verify that you were who you said you were to Old Tom. Secondly, to gauge your quality."

Sheldrake raised his eyebrows. "And how did you verify who I am from our encounter?"

Jon gave a sunny smile. "Oh, I continued to follow you after you let me go, watched you return to the palace and asked the guard who you were. Then I rode on out here. I was just approaching the house from the bushland at the back when I saw Sasha and a boy - maybe your son? - riding back to the house. As soon as I had seen that Sasha was all right, I left. I decided it would be better mannered to visit openly through the front door."

Sheldrake exchanged glances with Leon, who looked as though he were restraining himself from throttling the young man. Sheldrake returned his attention to Jon. "And what did you think of my quality?" he asked dryly.

Jon sat down again removing his height advantage, deliberately, Sheldrake suspected. He leaned forward, looking earnestly into the mage's eyes. "I have not yet decided. You are clearly wealthy and can afford an impressive cottage, which is bigger than it looks from the road... I was impressed with your clemency when we last met... Your network and tactics are admirable..."

"Oh very," interrupted Sheldrake, with awful sarcasm. "We were totally bamboozled by you, weren't we? Hardly admirable."

A snort of agreement issued from his coachman.

Jon leant back and grinned. "I shouldn't have let you see me disappear, should I? But I have a playful streak that I just don't seem able to repress. I would have loved to see your faces when Karin reported back to you."

Sheldrake and Leon found themselves at a complete loss. The young man had made complete fools of them, supposedly masters of subterfuge, but was now inviting them to share in his mirth. Finally, Sheldrake demanded, "Do you know what I do?"

"Do you mean as a mage or as the head of the King's Spiders?" asked Jon.

Sheldrake spluttered. "No one knows I am head of the King's Spiders except the King and Maud and a very few trusted agents."

"Lady Electra does, and therefore, so do I." Jon was not smiling now. "Kimora's intelligence service, like any country's, has a vested interest in finding out information such as this."

Sheldrake gave a wry smile. "I suppose they do. After all, I know the identity of the heads of all of their intelligence services." He turned to Leon. "Could you send for tea please?" He turned back to the young man. "So, am I right in inferring that you are particularly concerned for Sasha's welfare, over and above your care for all shamans?"

"Oh yes. I brought Sasha out of the chaos that preceded the current queen's reign and hid h... the baby at Stonehaven."

Sheldrake frowned at Jon's hesitation and wondered how he could broach the question of Sasha's gender without betraying her trust. After a distinct pause, he asked, "Does Sasha know you?"

Jon nodded. "Mostly I have kept away from Stonehaven, but from time to time, I have slipped in to spend a few hours with the child. It was dangerous. The Kimoran Embassy must never know where... Sasha is."

Sheldrake noted that Jon carefully avoided using any pronouns that would give away Sasha's gender. He was becoming increasingly convinced that Jon knew she was a girl.

Clive entered with a silver tray bearing a novelty teapot that was a facsimile of their cottage, a milk jug that resembled Sheldrake's shed, and two quite mundane white cups.

As Clive set down the tray, Sheldrake murmured, "Thank you. An unusual choice of crockery for a new guest??"

"I understand he is playful, sir," replied Clive, completely deadpan.

Sheldrake gave an embarrassed cough and glanced at Jon, whose face, he was relieved to see, was lit with laughter. He returned his attention to his butler. "Hmm. Could you ask Sasha to join us please?"

"Certainly, sir." Clive bowed and retreated with withering dignity.

Jon gave a short laugh. "I see I do not meet with your butler's approval."

"Apparently not. My staff are unnervingly willing to express their views... and I'm afraid I am not the master to quash them." He leant forward and poured a cup of tea for Jon, "I hope you don't take sugar. There seems to be a lack of it on the tray."

"He probably does not deem me worthy of such a luxury."

Sheldrake frowned. "Hmm. But I do. So if you would like some sugar, I will procure it."

"Thank you, but no." Jon accepted the cup with a nod of thanks.

For a few minutes they sat in silence, sipping their tea until a knock sounded on the door. At the sound, Jon put down his teacup and stood up, tense with anticipation.

As the door opened to reveal Beth and Sasha, Sheldrake raised his eyebrows. "Good morning, Beth. Are you being protective or is Sasha feeling unsure?"

Even before Beth could answer, Sasha let out a whoop of joy, ran across the room and catapulted herself into Jon's arms. Jon threw his arms around her, grinning and hugging her tightly.

"Hello, young Sasha." he said, as he held her. "I am glad to see you too. Very glad." He whispered something in her ear, to which she nodded in reply. "Good." He whispered something else and again she nodded. "Oh good. Even better. Old Tom was worried, you know, after Sheldrake visited. He referred to you as a boy, you see."

Sasha pulled out of his embrace enough to smile at the other three. "I only just told them. I haven't been here all that long." She scowled. "And I never told Bryson. He wasn't very nice."

Jon gave Sasha a final hug and let her slide down to stand beside him. "Bryson was rough. Too rough, I gather. I'm sorry, Sasha, that you had to endure him." He looked at Sheldrake. "I heard that Kimoran intelligence was closing in on the orphanages in their search for Sa...for shamans. We had to get her out of there quickly. For all his faults, Bryson is willing to help Kimoran shamans. His wife is from Kimora and her sister is a shaman who refuses to submit to the Queen's will."

"So, did Bryson contrive the accident with Hoofer?" asked Beth.

Jon shook his head. "I doubt it. Bryson hasn't an ounce of magic in him. He would just have seized the opportunity to move Sasha on to a new placement, one with no connection to Stonehaven."

Sasha pouted. "And why didn't you visit me sooner? I haven't seen you for ages." Suddenly her indignation faltered. "I thought you might have forgotten me."

Jon folded his long frame into a crouch so that his blue eyes gazed earnestly into her dark ones.

"No, Sasha," he said quietly. "I would never forget you. You are too important to me... and to Kimora." He took a breath. "Bryson vanished, leaving no word of your whereabouts. I don't know what has happened to him or his family, and until this week, I didn't know what had happened to you either. I have been beside myself with worry." He stroked her hair, ending with his hand under her chin. "Old Tom and I have been trying to track you down but we had to be subtle about it. Other people are seeking you too." After a moment, when he was sure Sasha was no longer upset with him, he looked at Sheldrake and gave a rueful smile. "You have no idea, sir, how welcome your visit to Stonehaven was.

Chapter 27

Upstairs in the library, Jayhan was keeping himself from becoming completely comatose by having one eye on his books and the other watching events in the yard below. As his eyes travelled over the stables, he thought about Sasha and the amazing fact that she was a girl. He looked at Eloquin and tried to imagine Sasha wearing a long flowing dress with her hair long enough to be tied back with a bow. Now he thought about it, Beth didn't wear flowing dresses either. He had seen her in dresses occasionally, but they were unadorned riding habits. Mostly, she wore trousers. Hmm. Now he thought about it, Beth was unusual in that way. Hannah the cook, Rose the maid and Maud all wore skirts or gowns. He wondered how Sasha would go climbing trees in a dress. She might get her skirts snagged and end up hanging upside down. Jayhan gave a little chuckle, which earned him a frown from Eloquin. *Oops. Better look like I'm reading*, he thought.

As he struggled through a tedious book about a family picnic, he saw the tall stranger arrive. The book family was just packing up their picnic and heading home, when he spotted Beth accompanying Sasha across the yard towards the house. Now what was happening? Why was she taking Sasha in to see the stranger? Jumping to the wrong conclusion, Jayhan made a quick apology to Eloquin as he dodged around her, scooted down the stairs and burst into the front parlour.

"You can't take Sasha away. Sh… Sasha's my friend."

Five people turned to stare at him and Jon straightened slowly from where he crouched beside Sasha.

"Shut the door, Jayhan." Sheldrake's voice was like verbal concrete, cold and hard. "Let me introduce you to Jon, to whom you may address your apology."

Watching this interchange, Jon decided that it was Sheldrake's inclination, not his inability to quell, that allowed his staff such leeway.

Jayhan, flushed both from embarrassment and concern for his friend, bowed stiffly. "I beg your pardon, sir, for intruding." Order obeyed, he brought his pale gaze to bear on Jon and continued in a rush, "But please don't take Sasha away. He is happy here and we are happy with him here….and he is my friend."

Jon stared in return but not with the discomfort that usually characterised an adult on their first view of Jayhan's eyes. If anything, he seemed a little stunned. However, he recovered quickly, so quickly that Jayhan wondered whether he had imagined it, and glanced briefly at Sheldrake, Leon and Beth, before returning his gaze to Jayhan. "And you are a good loyal friend who is keeping her secret, but as it was I who suggested that she should masquerade as a boy to keep her safe, her secret is safe with me… and with all of you, I think."

"Yes, it is," replied Sheldrake gravely.

"And does anyone else know of it?" asked Jon.

"My wife, Maud, and Beth's husband, Clive, my butler."

Jon nodded. He looked down at Sasha and placed his fingers under the amulet hanging around her neck, lifting it slightly. For a moment, his hand closed around it before he let it drop back into place. "You have taken this off, haven't you? At least twice." When Sasha nodded, he said, "No one but you can take it off, just as no one but you can wear it. Don't ever take it off again. You and the amulet are the past and future of Kimora, but each without the other is meaningless."

"Well, that's not very nice," protested Jayhan. "Sasha means a lot to us whether she is wearing her amulet or not."

Jon gave a rueful smile. "I beg your pardon. I meant meaningless to Kimora's future. She means a great deal to me also."

"Huh. Should have looked after her better then."

"Jayhan, that is quite enough," interposed Sheldrake sharply. "You are being rude to someone you have just met without knowing anything of the circumstances."

"But…"

Sheldrake's glare would have melted metal. Jayhan subsided into a huff as his father turned to Jon. "I apologize for my son's behaviour." Jayhan found this even more humiliating than having to apologize himself. "However, he is concerned, as are we all, about your intentions regarding Sasha."

Jon looked down at Sasha who was watching his every move. He stroked her hair and smiled at her before replying. "Sasha's welfare matters to me above all else, but I cannot care for her in my current position as footman in the Kimoran Embassy and my… hmm… other activities would also place her at risk. If you are happy to continue having her here, I also would be content."

"So we have passed muster, have we?" asked Sheldrake dryly.

Jon grinned, regaining some of his previous light-heartedness. "Yes. Besides, how could I drag her away from her gallant defender?"

Jayhan reddened and sent a little smile and a shrug to Sasha, who laughed in return.

Sheldrake watched this interchange, feeling a little manoeuvred by Jon's comment. After a moment he sent Jayhan and Sasha out to play, with the promise that Sasha could see Jon again before he left. "In fact, Jon, the decision is not yours alone to make. I think Maud and I need to speak to you in private. Beth, could you send Maud to join us please?" Seeing Leon scowl, clearly reluctant to leave, he added, "Until we have the boundary ward set up, Leon, I would appreciate it if you could keep a close but distant eye on Sasha, if you know what I mean."

Leon's eyes narrowed as he considered whether Sheldrake was fobbing him off. He must have decided there was at least some merit in the request, because after an uncomfortably long pause, he nodded curtly and left in Beth's wake.

It was not long before Maud surged into the room, her green skirts billowing around her. "Ah, here is the young man in question. Jon, I believe."

When Jon nodded, she presented her hand for him to kiss, which he did with a little more flourish than necessary. When he straightened, he smiled at her, "Pleased to make your acquaintance, ma'am."

Maud did not return his smile. She was all business. "Now, you may assume that I know all that has been said, since I was briefed by Beth before entering. So shall we continue as though I had been here all along?" She sank into an armchair, indicating that Jon should also be seated. "I have a question I wish to ask you. When I visited the Research Society, I met a shaman named Yarrow, who seemed excessively interested in the timing of Sasha's arrival at the Orphanage. I assured her that Sasha did indeed arrive there eight years ago, since your friend Old Tom had verified Sasha's story. However, since then, Sasha has changed her story and appears to have arrived at Stonehaven nearly ten years ago." Maud raised her eyebrows. "I presume that Old Tom backed Sasha's original story because Sheldrake had referred to her as a boy." She paused. "Correct?"

Jon, rightly assuming that this was not yet the question she wished to ask, merely nodded and did not attempt to interrupt her flow.

"So, my question is this: Why does it matter that she arrived ten years ago? In fact, what matters so much that you hid her gender and age to cover it up?" Before he could answer, she added firmly, "And you might like to be more explicit about the nature of Sasha's importance to Kimora."

Jon, reeling beneath this barrage, glanced at Sheldrake to find him stifling a smile. Seeing no help from that quarter, the young man hitched a breath and returned his attention to Maud. He stared at her for a moment as he made his decision. "Lady Maud, Sasha is the only surviving daughter of the Queen's elder sister. By rights, Sasha should be on the throne, not Queen Toriana."

Had he been expecting Maud to gasp in amazement, he would have been sorely disappointed. Maud merely nodded. "I thought it must be something like that. It does not seem to me, young man, that you have done a very good job of looking after your liege. Bryson's behaviour towards Sasha was appalling. And then you lost track of her completely. Most unimpressive."

Jon grimaced. "I agree with you, ma'am. I began well, but in the last couple of years, the search for Sasha has intensified and it was a close call when we smuggled her out of Stonehaven. I thought she would be safe at Stonehaven and indeed she was for eight, nearly nine years. But two years ago, the Queen employed a clever, powerful shaman hunter who thought of scouring the orphanages of Carrador and other nearby countries to find her."

"To find Sasha or just any shaman?" asked Sheldrake.

"It is not common knowledge that Sasha survived, but the fact that the amulet has not surfaced suggests that a true descendant of the High Shamanic line still exists. So the Queen's public position is that she is searching for rogue shamans but in actual fact, this shaman hunter has been employed to find Sasha specifically and, even more so, her amulet. Without that amulet, Queen Toriana's right to rule will always be in question. The amulet has been worn by the reigning monarch since time immemorial… and only the rightful Queen can wear it."

Sheldrake and Maud glanced at each.

After a significant pause, Maud said quietly, "You have thrust, or are trying to thrust, a huge responsibility onto us, aren't you, young man?"

"And has it occurred to you," asked Sheldrake, "that we work for the Kingdom of Carrador? How much will it compromise our loyalty to our king to be harbouring a pretender to the Kimoran throne, however legitimate?"

Jon looked from one to the other, visibly shaken. He stood up and moved to the window, looking out over the garden with his back to them. Maud and Sheldrake waited patiently until Jon heaved a breath and turned back to face them. To their shock, they realised his eyes were bright with tears. "If you will not keep her, I don't know what to do." He sniffed and groped in his pocket for a handkerchief. "Sorry about this," he said as he wiped his cheeks. He attempted a wan smile. "You are absolutely right. She is a huge responsibility. I love her dearly but she is a huge responsibility… and as you so clearly pointed out, one I have failed." His tears threatened to overwhelm him again, but he sniffed them away. "But you are also right that she is not *your* responsibility." He took a deep breath and squared his shoulders as he began to think through options. "I could take her to the resistance group. They live in the forests just within the Carradorian border but they are ill-disciplined, bitter and poorly resourced at the moment. I really wanted to protect her from that until she is older and they are better organised." He shrugged. "I suppose I could take to the roads with her. I was only twelve, you know, when I brought her out of Kimora as a baby. That was very hard, but it should be easier to look after both of us now that we are both older." He nodded firmly as this idea took roots. "Yes. That is what I must do. I will leave my post at the Embassy. In time, we will find someone else to infiltrate it." He shrugged again and gave a wan smile. "Besides, Sasha is far more important. Without her, there is no point in gathering information anyway."

"Now, just a minute, young man," interrupted Maud. In her usual response to tears, she had risen and moved to the door to call for more tea. When she turned back, she said, "We didn't say we wouldn't keep her. We are just pointing out the difficulties."

"Oh, but I thought…" Jon frowned at Sheldrake. "Didn't you say it's a conflict of interests?"

Sheldrake waved his hand in irritation. "Yes, I did and it is, or at least it may be. Just let me think it through." He stood up and began to pace back and forth in front of Jon as he thought, waving his forefinger in the air to underline each point. "It would not be politic for King Gavin to be seen as complicit in undermining the reigning monarch of a neighbouring country. The same, of course, applies to us… This only becomes a problem if it becomes apparent that we *know* we are harbouring the pretender to Kimora's throne. So while Sasha's true identity remains hidden, there is no issue. In terms of our personal loyalty to Carrador, I can't see that having Sasha on the throne of Kimora would be counterproductive to Carrador. In fact, the emerging conflict within Kimora is beginning to affect our trading relations with her. So, in the end it may benefit Carrador to have a more stable monarchy in Kimora."

"And Jon, unlike you, we are used to huge responsibilities and have the resources to manage them," added Maud. She glanced again at Sheldrake, who gave a minute nod. "So even though our apprentice turns out to be more of a liability than we expected, we will keep Sasha and do our utmost to protect her."

Jon breathed a huge sigh of relief. "Oh, thank you." Tears sprang to his eyes again.

Maud frowned. "You're not related to Sasha, are you? Your colouring is completely different but you have the same buoyant but fragile air about you."

Jon gave the ghost of a laugh. "Yes. I am her older brother."

Chapter 28

Outside, oblivious to the momentous disclosures taking place in the parlour, Jayhan and Sasha were busy around the back of the stables building a cubby house in a large spotted gum tree on the edge of the front garden. They had gathered planks, old bits of tin and bricks from around the yard and were hauling them up onto a large platform that had been secured with Clive's help in a high fork of the tree.

Sasha caught Jayhan eyeing her thoughtfully as she dragged a large piece of rusty tin from the scrap heap in the middle of the platform to lean it, rather precariously, against the trunk of the tree. She brushed her hands off, ignoring his look, and said, "Quickly. Get some bricks to put against the bottom of it so that it can't slide out."

"Maybe a long solid piece of wood might be better…"

Sasha shrugged and nodded. "And we'll need some long planks to lean against the trunk inside the tin. Otherwise it's going to sag."

"Some long sticks might do."

"No. They'll roll. Planks'd be better, I think."

Their final construction had sticks holding down the tin on the outside and planks holding it up on the inside. They stood back and surveyed their creation.

Jayhan grimaced. "It's not very high, is it? Not high enough to stand up in, I don't think."

Sasha frowned. "No." After a minute of thought, she suggested, "Maybe we should turn the tin around so its long side is going up instead of along, and get another piece to go next to it. What do you reckon?"

"Yeah. Good idea. Maybe two more bits. Except the trunk won't be wide enough to lean all of them against it" Jayhan screwed up his face while he thought. "Hmm. Maybe we can nail a cross beam to the trunk for them to lean on."

Once this suggestion had been implemented, they had created a lean-to that stood about five and a half feet high nearly five feet wide, taking up half of the platform. They ducked inside and looked around.

"Hmm, pretty good," said Sasha. She peered down over the side of the platform. "Maybe we need a back wall… so we don't fall off."

"Yeah. At least a few planks so we can lean against them and maybe hang some cloth from them."

"And one side as well. The other side is where we'll come in and out."

This idea turned out to be fraught with difficulties, since the wood had to be nailed from a position off the platform. Eventually, they spotted Leon lurking near the stables, chopping wood for the lounge room fire, and recruited him to find a ladder and then to help them with building the back and side walls.

His reluctance made Leon surly at first but once he saw what they were doing, he realised his role as Sasha's protector required him to be involved to make sure the structure was strong enough. He decided that Jayhan and Sasha's treehouse building was as much a threat to Sasha's safety as any outside danger could be. However, the two children thought they were doing an excellent job which, in many ways they were, and offered him friendly, helpful suggestions at every opportunity. Leon found this so irritating that eventually he snapped at Jayhan's latest suggestion. "If you know so much, you do it."

Jayhan's face fell as he replied earnestly. "We *are* doing it." He waved his arm to encompass the three of them. "We're all doing it together. If there's anything else you want Sasha or me to do, just tell us. We're busting to help. It was our project in the first place, after all. And then Clive joined in and now you have."

Sasha nodded. "And don't forget, Jayhan and I are experts on cubbies. We make them all the time." She looked up at the treehouse, squinting her eyes against the sun. "This will be the biggest and the best, but it's a bit tricky."

"Well, not the biggest. Remember the one that we built amongst the blackberry bushes down near the creak. The tunnels in it went for miles," objected Jayhan, blithely exaggerating.

"True but this one is definitely the hardest."

"Oh, definitely."

"What's the best cubby you ever made, Leon? Before this one, I mean," asked Sasha.

Despite himself, Leon couldn't resist being dragged into the conversation. Grunts and short answers were met with genuinely interested questions and before he knew it, Leon was waxing lyrical about a particularly grand cubby he had constructed from crates and planks, and had decorated with old pieces of rags. His mother had even given him a cast-off curtain for decoration and let him take his dinner in there for a whole week, by which time he was bored with having no one to talk to at meal time. His story was met with round eyes and an enthusiasm that he had rarely experienced as a child, since his siblings had been much older than him and treated his creations with disdain.

It was almost with regret that he banged the last nail into place and stood back to inspect the new slatted walls. "There," he said gruffly, "That should keep you safe and you can use some old blankets draped over it to keep the wind out when it's cold."

Sasha stood beside him, also surveying the results. "Great job, Leon. That's just what we need." She turned to Jayhan. "What do you think?"

"Yep. Really good."

Then Sasha leaned in and whispered in Jayhan's ear. His face scrunched into a frown and he whispered something back. After an intense minute of whispered discussions, he nodded enthusiastically and looked at Leon, smiling.

Leon scowled, unsure whether they were making fun of him or making up another harebrained scheme. "What are you two up to?"

Sasha beamed. "We are going to call our treehouse the Joosoo Club. See? It has Jayhan's and my initials in Joosoo, and yours and Clive's in Club. Pretty good, hey?"

A slow smile lit Lean's face. He nodded. "I like it. So will Clive."

Sasha and Jayhan swung themselves up through the boughs of the tree, then onto the platform. They walked along the edge of the platform to the open end of their lean-to, then ducked inside.

Sasha nodded and looked around for a few moments before poking her head out and shouting down at their minder. "It's great Leon. You'd really like it up here." Then she put her head on one side and asked Jayhan diffidently. "Do you think we could ask Jon in here for morning tea before he goes?"

Jayhan considered the height of their roof and grimaced, "Well, we could, but he'd have to duck. Maybe if he came straight in and sat down…" He shrugged. "Anyway, he mightn't want to. I wasn't very kind to him before."

"He'll want to," she said firmly. She caught Jayhan glancing speculatively at her again and this time didn't let it pass. "What? What are you looking at?"

"Um, nothing. Um, just wondering what it's like to be a girl?"

Sasha folded her arms. "Don't know what it's like to be a boy so I don't know how it's different. I'm just the same as yesterday before you knew, if you're wondering."

Jayhan reddened. "Sorry. I'm not meaning to be rude. I just want everything to stay the same. You're my best…my *only* friend… Are you going to start wearing dresses?"

Sasha looked horrified. "Of course not. Besides, I'm still supposed to be a boy to everyone outside your family. Remember?" When Jayhan nodded unhappily, she added, "You are my bestest friend too. Even if things change, we will always be friends. Deal?"

She put out her hand and Jayhan grasped it. "Deal!" His face lit in a relieved smile.

"Come on," she said, "Let's go and see whether we can ask Jon to tea."

"Wait a sec." Jayhan swung down through the branches and a few minutes later, returned to the bottom of the tree with four metal buckets. "Chairs!" he pronounced triumphantly, as he proceeded to throw them up to her. "And," he added, as he threw up the fourth one, "A table!"

Chapter 29

Seeing Maud and Sheldrake's incredulous stares, Jon hastened to explain, "In our bloodlines, siblings can have different hair, eye and skin colour from each other. Males tend to be fairer, women darker but not always. Sasha and I are full brother and sister. I may be older but the right to rule passes through the female line. I am not a contender for the throne, no matter what. Sasha is the rightful ruler of Kimora and I will give my last ounce of blood to see that she is."

"Tell us what happened," asked Sheldrake quietly, "how you came to be in Carrador... unless it is too painful for you to recount."

Jon drew a breath. "It is painful but less so, as the years pass. I will tell you."

The tea arrived in the best silver teapot carried by Clive, who bent a reserved but accepting smile upon the young man.

Sheldrake raised his eyebrows at the teapot. "Hmm. You seem to have gone up in the world," he said, as soon as the door closed behind Clive. Once the tea had been poured, Jon and Sheldrake seated themselves once more and Sheldrake nodded for Jon to continue as soon as Clive had left the room.

"Our family was travelling from our estates in Burndale to the capital to celebrate the year's turning. We had camped for the night, and my father and older brother were standing around the campfire talking with the guards when arrows streaked out of the trees. One minute they were standing. The next, they had slumped to the ground. Just like that. I was in the tent with my mother, my little sister, Marina, and the baby, Sasha. My mother had asked for my help to feed and settle Sasha before bed. Sasha was in a travelling cot, a woven basket, against the back wall of the tent and I was beside her in the shadows, rocking the basket to send her to sleep. Through the tent door, we saw the men outside slump to the ground but only my mother knew what it meant.

" 'Stay back,' she whispered urgently to me. A heartbeat later, two huge men... or so they seemed to me... swarmed into the tent. They wore no insignia but my mother knew them. They grabbed Marina by the hair and before anyone could move, they sliced her throat." Jon swallowed before continuing. "One of them growled, 'Now hand over the amulet or your baby dies too.'

"Our mother swept her arm before her in a wide arc, sending her attackers flying in a spray of sparks. But she knew it was only a short reprieve. There were too many of them. She dragged the amulet over her head and threw it to me. 'Protect her with your life, Jon.'

"I caught the amulet and held it over Sasha's head as my mother shouted the words of transfer, 'From Corinna to Sasharia! Karesh!' She flung out her hand, and blue light blazed, turning the amulet red hot in my hand. With a yelp, I dropped it around the baby's neck. 'Now Go, Jon! Go! Don't look back.'"

"My heart hammered in my chest, so hard I thought I might be sick. I drew my dagger and sliced the tent wall. I was so scared, my fingers felt like sausages. Hugging Sasha in the basket to my chest, I threw myself through the gap onto the cold leafy ground outside." Jon gave a lop-sided smile. "For some reason, I have always remembered the leaves. It was autumn and even in the dim light from the lanterns and firelight, I could see they were yellows and red." He gave himself a shake. "Anyway, I shimmered to hide us from view and crept into the woods beyond the firelight. To my horror, I realised I was only a dozen yards away from one of the archers who had killed my father and the guards. So I had to hunker down for ages before the hunters dispersed. I nearly smothered Sasha keeping her quiet."

"What do you mean, you shimmered?" interrupted Sheldrake.

"Oh." Jon grinned and the air around him began to shimmer as it does in the desert on a hot day when travellers see oases that are not truly there. The shimmering increased until suddenly, Jon was gone. "It is my Plainsman heritage," said Jon's voice from the empty chair near the window.

"Can Sasha do that?" demanded Sheldrake.

Jon drifted back into view, shrugging. "I don't know. Shimmering is very rare. Usually it's paired with blonde hair, for some obscure reason. But you never know…"

"Well! What do you know?" exclaimed Sheldrake. "That is truly marvellous! And you can include objects or people or animals with you as well, can you?"

As Jon nodded, Maud cut in, "Sheldrake. Have a little sensitivity. Jon is in the middle of a very distressing story. Discuss his magic at another time, if you don't mind."

Sheldrake grimaced, but his eyes twinkled. "Sorry dear. Your pardon, Jon. Carry on with your tale."

Jon shrugged. "There is not much more to tell. I heard my mother cry out from the tent, then silence. Any servants in the open were cut down and every last one of their tents was fired. They all died, either from fire, sword or arrows." Jon shook his head, his eyes glistening at the memory. "It was terrible, truly terrible."

"And you were only twelve, you say?" asked Maud gently.

Jon nodded. "My mother died alone, facing those men to save Sasha and the amulet and me." A shudder passed the full length of Jon's body. "And there was nothing I could do to save her."

"But you did save Sasha."

"Yes. Only just. By luck, I found where they had picketed their horses. All eyes, even the guards', were on our campsite in the clearing trying to spot Sasha and me, so I was able to sneak behind them and lead a horse away. All I could do was ride hard and hope to find someone to help us. Sasha was starting to whimper with hunger. Eventually, I found a farmhouse in the middle of nowhere and the farmer's wife gave Sasha her pet goat to suckle on. Pretty weird actually, but it worked. She stopped wailing for the first time since we left the carnage. But then the farmer started asking awkward questions and we had to take to the road again. A few times, I found a sheep or goat to suckle her but I had to catch them first. Not easy. By the time we reached Carrador, Sasha hadn't eaten for two days."

"And how did you find Stonehaven?"

Jon shrugged. "Stonehaven is close to the border. I just kept asking people for directions to an orphanage because I knew I couldn't look after Sasha on my own. It was the first one I found."

Maud frowned. "And did you really just leave her on the doorstep? The future Queen of Kimora?"

Jon waved his hand dismissively. "No. Of course I didn't. I took her inside, met Old Tom, had a look-around and then left her in his care. He knew what to do. He'd had babies left there before. He gave me a meal and let me stay for a few days. I couldn't stay for long because I was too old, but he let me visit. Over time, I told him the whole story but we agreed not to tell Sasha who I was or where she was from, until she was old enough to keep secrets." He took a deep breath. "So that's it really." As though expecting their censure, he avoided meeting their eyes, by letting his eyes drop to his teacup as he took a slow sip of his now tepid tea.

"You are an impressive young man," said Sheldrake. "You have dealt with more in your short life than many would in a lifetime."

Jon raised his eyes and lifted one side of his mouth self-deprecatingly. "Not really. You just do what you have to, when you find yourself in a situation."

Sheldrake gave a snort of laughter. "Well, I wish some of my agents could do half as well as you."

"One question, Jon," asked Maud quietly. "Why was your mother wearing the amulet when she was not yet on the throne?"

"My grandmother was very old and knew she only had weeks to live - It's one of the less desirable shaman skills, foreseeing one's own death - and it is customary to pass on the amulet to their successor one moon's travel before their death. So my mother had been given the amulet but did not yet have the protection of the full Royal Guard. If my mother had held onto the amulet, it is unlikely that the warriors could have killed her, but she could not have borne seeing the rest of her children killed and so would have relinquished it. So her last act was a desperate gambit to save Sasha and the amulet from the hands of the usurpers."

"And thanks to you, it worked," said Sheldrake.

Jon laughed. "Thanks to me and the amulet. Never forget the amulet."

A knock sounded on the door and Sheldrake frowned in irritation. "I thought I gave instructions not to be disturbed."

Despite his words, the door opened slowly to reveal Jayhan, Sasha behind his right shoulder, peering in hopefully. "Hello Dad. We were just wondering whether Jon would like to have morning tea with us in our new cubby we just built. Sort of as a sorry present," he added with a flash of inspiration.

Sheldrake glanced at Jon and saw that his face was a picture of indecision, caught between the wish to go with them and the fear that he would offend his hosts.

"And Hannah has made us up a tray with a teapot and cups and milk and fruit scones," piped up Sasha.

Sheldrake smiled. "Well in that case, we can't disappoint Hannah. Jon, I'm afraid you will have to imbibe yet more tea. Perhaps Jayhan can show you the water closet on the way out..."

Part 5

Chapter 30

A week later, Rose sat at the kitchen table shelling peas, her mind on what clothes her brother would need for starting work with Clive. After years of practice, shelling peas was so automatic that she could let her mind wander unfettered as she worked. But suddenly she was called back to the present by the unusual feel of a pea pod in her fingers. She looked down and found the pod she had been about to open was a darker green, less rounded and felt like worn leather rather than the soft flesh of a pea pod. She peered more closely and discerned small letters, MAUD, stamped into it.

"Excuse me, Hannah, I think I have a message for the mistress," said Rose as she stood, ready to deliver the pseudo pea pod.

Hannah looked up from where she was rolling out the pastry for the evening's pie and, spotting the object in Rose's hand, nodded her permission. "Off you go then."

After years in Maud and Sheldrake's service, little oddities were commonplace for both of them.

Rose delivered the pea pod and waited while Maud carefully sliced it open and unfurled the little message contained inside. When she had read it, she looked up at Rose and smiled. "Send Leon to me please. Prepare for an extra person at dinner and make the blue room ready for our guest, should she wish to stay."

"Yes Ma'am." Rose curtsied and headed off to find Leon.

It was a good twenty minutes before Leon presented himself. He entered, wiping his hands on the back of his trousers. "Beg pardon, ma'am. I was down behind the stables, chopping wood and keeping an eye on the little ones."

Maud raised an eyebrow. "I thought we had a magical ward in place right across the front of the property boundary now."

Leon grunted. "We do, but that doesn't stop Sasha and Jayhan from damaging themselves. Yesterday, I hauled them down off the roof where they were about to play hide and seek among the chimney stacks."

"Oh, I see. Well done then." Maud waved the little scroll at Leon. "I have received a communication from Yarrow. She will be waiting in the bar of the Blue Boar at sunset. Since she is a target for shaman hunters, would you go into the village and bring her back here as quickly as possible please? The sun is setting, even as we speak." As Leon was about to leave, she asked, "We have someone checking our front entrance for watchers, don't we?

Are we under surveillance? Because if we are, you will not be able to bring her in through the front gates."

"Yes we do, Ma'am. And no, we are not. All agents are required to inform us as soon as any watchers are sighted."

Maud breathed a sigh of relief. "So far, so good then. It is a little harrowing, having young Sasha with us, much as I am fond of her."

Leon gave her a thin-lipped smile of assurance. "Don't worry ma'am. Between the Spiders and our magical ward, she is safe from outsiders."

Before she could say anything further, Leon left.

An hour later, Maud peered out the window and saw Leon returning with Yarrow, who was wrapped in a non-descript black, woollen cloak covering a drab brown dress.

Maud swept down the stairs and opened the front door to greet her without Clive's interception. "Yarrow! I am so pleased you have come. Leon, take her cloak please. Could you also ask Clive to prepare refreshments and take them to the parlour? We will return shortly. Oh, and let Sheldrake know. I know he is keen to meet Yarrow. Come, my dear. I am sure you are dying to meet Sasha."

Looking a little bewildered, Yarrow was hustled by her hostess to the stables.

Just as they reached the stables, the door burst open and Jayhan rushed out shrieking, "Mum, Mum. Sasha's going to get me." Before anyone could react, a torrent of water sailed out behind him drenching him and splashing the other two. Jayhan pulled up short. "Oops." He grinned as, dripping wet, he performed a neat little bow. "How do you do? I am Jayhan." He looked behind him. "Watch out, Sasha. You're in trouble now. You just wet Mum and a visitor."

"Oh no," whispered Sasha hollowly. In an act of pure courage, she didn't run away but crept forward to face the music. She peered around the side of Jayhan before emerging. She straightened up and squared her shoulders. "I am truly very sorry. I didn't mean to wet you… Would you like a towel?" Without waiting for a response, she disappeared inside and returned with a grubby towel covered in horsehair.

Yarrow held up her hand. "Uh no. We will dry off quickly anyway. It was only a small splash."

Sasha looked anxiously at Maud. "Sorry Madam."

Maud smiled reassuringly. "No harm done. Look Sasha, I have brought someone to meet you. Yarrow is a shaman from Kimora. I told her," said Maud meaningfully, "that I have stable*boy* from Kimora working for me and she offered to tell you about your homeland."

"Wow!" breathed Jayhan. "So do you wear one of those amulets too? With the triangle with the line through it?"

Yarrow frowned. "Yes. How do you know of this?"

"My dad investigated the symbol on Sasha's amulet."

"Jayhan," interposed Maud, "go inside and change. You are dripping wet. When you are presentable, you may join us in the parlour."

Jayhan grimaced. "Yes Mum."

By the time he had achieved world's fastest change of clothes, Sheldrake, Maud and Yarrow were seated comfortably in the parlour. A side table carried an array of cups and the best teapot, waiting for tea to be served. Sasha sat nervously on the edge of a large lounge chair. Without a second thought, Jayhan crossed the room and squeezed in next to her. "Hello," he murmured, "Did I miss anything?"

Sasha frowned and surreptitiously shook her head. "No. Now shush," she whispered.

"I understand," Yarrow was saying to Sheldrake, "that you discovered the meaning of the symbol on Sasha's amulet. Is that how you became aware that he was a shaman?"

"It is. We became interested in his abilities when he was able to see through Maud's shape-changing."

Yarrow nodded. "That is indeed a shaman ability." Her voice held a note of reserve.

"So may we see your amulet?" asked Jayhan eagerly. "Do you wear it always, like Sasha does?"

"Jayhan," admonished Sheldrake. "Yarrow may not wish to show us her amulet. I am beginning to gather that it is a privilege to possess one and that I erred rather grievously in asking to borrow Sasha's."

Yarrow raised her eyebrows. "You *borrowed* it? Took it from him?"

Sheldrake looked a little flustered. "I asked him but, of course, I suppose he felt obliged to say yes, now I think about it." Seeing the severe expression on the shaman's face, he added in a rush. "I was just trying to find out about his origins and his powers... and he wanted to know too. I only kept it for a few days."

"What's done is done," intervened Maud firmly. "And if Sheldrake hadn't worked out that Sasha was a shaman, we wouldn't have known to ask you here to help him."

Yarrow took a breath and with a noticeable effort, relaxed. "True." As a peace offering, she turned to Jayhan. "Let me show my amulet." A chain hung around her neck but its end was deep within her bodice. She pulled it up until a milky grey amulet appeared in her hand. It carried the same symbol as Sasha's.

"Oh, that's pretty. They come in different colours, do they?" asked Jayhan.

Yarrow's brows snapped together. "No. All shaman amulets are crafted from moonstone. All but one."

"Oh," continued Jayhan, oblivious to the frantic efforts of his parents to silence him. "Sasha must have that one, then."

A resounding silence filled the room.

"What?" Jayhan glanced at Sasha beside him. "What? What did I do?"

Sasha shrugged. "I don't know," she murmured. She looked at the severe faces surrounding them and grimaced. "But whatever it is, it's not good."

Yarrow's eyes were wide with shock. She turned to Maud. "Did you lie to me? If you did, I can understand why. But did you?"

"Not exactly," replied Maud. "At the time, I thought I was telling you the truth. I only found out later, you see... last week, in fact."

Yarrow stood up and walked across to Sasha. "You're not a boy, are you?"

Sasha glanced at Maud, who gave a grimace of consent. She returned her gaze to Yarrow. "No madam, I'm not."

"And how old are you?"

Again she glanced at Maud who nodded. "I am ten years old, Madam." She noticed that the shaman was beginning to tremble. "Are you all right?" she asked in concern. "Can I get you some water?"

Yarrow waved away the request. Instead she said quietly. "And may I see your amulet?"

Sasha sent Jayhan a puzzled look before reaching down and withdrawing her amulet from within her jerkin. In her hand, the obsidian amulet pulsed with a dark light. As though in response, Yarrow's amulet shone with clear pale brilliance. At the sight of it, Yarrow sank to one knee.

"Quick Jayhan. Help me hold her up. She's fainting," said Sasha in a panic.

With a child holding each of her arms, Yarrow just knelt there, shaking her head from side to side. In a daze, she said, "No your Highness, I am not fainting. I am kneeling before my rightful Queen."

Sheldrake and Maud rolled their eyes heavenward, as they realized things had gone sadly awry.

Intent on keeping Yarrow upright, Sasha hadn't even register what she had said. Her face screwed up with the effort, she gasped, "Sir, madam, can you help please? She's too heavy for us."

Jayhan, however, had listened to the shaman's pronouncement. He tapped Sasha on the shoulder. "You can let go now. I don't think she's going to fall over. You have a different problem." He leaned closer to Sasha and chortled quietly behind his hand. "Either she's nutty or you're someone you didn't know you were."

"I'm afraid," said Sheldrake, "that your second surmise is right, Jayhan. As you say, Sasha is not aware of who she really is. But Yarrow does know... and so do we."

Jayhan's first reaction was outrage. "You *knew* and didn't tell Sasha?" Then he frowned as he remembered what Yarrow had said. "And Yarrow knows? Are you sure? Because she said..." Jayhan dug Sasha in the ribs. "Were you listening?" When Sasha shook her head, Jayhan said. "Well I think you'd better." He turned to Yarrow. "Could you say that again please?"

Yarrow grasped one of Sasha's hands in her own. "Your Highness, I said that I was kneeling to my rightful Queen."

Sasha just stared at Yarrow, dumbstruck. After a minute, a little frown appeared and she transferred her gaze first to Sheldrake and then Maud. Then she glanced sideways at Jayhan and her little grimace told him that she didn't know what to do.

"Excuse me, Yarrow," said Jayhan. "But it must be getting uncomfortable down there. I think Sasha's had a bit of a shock. She didn't know, you see. She probably needs a cup of tea... or some lemonade, maybe a cake," he added hopefully. "If you could just give her hand back and maybe sit down again..."

Yarrow seemed to come out of a trance. She gave an embarrassed laugh, stood up and moved away to reseat herself in the armchair across the room. She passed her hand across her eyes. "Sorry. Of course. I should have thought. I didn't realize..."

"Well," said Maud, rising to the occasion. "I think discovering your true identity calls for a celebration, don't you, Sasha?" She rose and put her head around the corner of the door. "Clive? Lemonade and cakes, if you please? And perhaps a bottle of champagne."

"So, who is she exactly?" asked Jayhan. "I don't quite get it."

Sheldrake addressed himself to his stable hand. "Sasha, you are the oldest living daughter of Princess Corinna who was heir to the throne of Kimora. As I understand it, Corinna's younger sister, your aunt, tried to kill your whole family but your brother escaped with you to Carrador. Since you were just a baby at the time and could not come forward to challenge her, she seized power on the death of your grandmother. You, however, are the rightful monarch, not she."

"Oh." This was far too much for Sasha to take in. Her head whirled with questions. After a long pause, she said slowly. "So that's why I had to, still have to, hide who I am."

Sheldrake merely nodded, purposely giving her time to think.

After another long pause, she asked, "And is my brother who rescued me still alive?"

"That lovely young man, Jon, is your brother," said Maud.

Sasha's face split into a smile. "Jon's my brother? Oh, I wish I'd known. I wouldn't have felt so all alone... even if he couldn't be with me all the time."

A discreet tap on the door preceded the entrance of Clive, who replaced the unused tea tray with the makings of a celebration.

When everyone's glasses were charged, Sheldrake raised his glass high and proposed a toast. "To Sasha's illustrious identity. The road ahead will not be easy, no matter which course you take, but we will all support you as best we can."

Sasha, her eyes bright with tears, raised her glass and was about to take a sip when Jayhan nudged her, grinning. "You can't toast yourself. Wait a minute, then drink as much as you like."

"Get lost," she said and took a long draft of lemonade.

Chapter 31

Once their tiny celebration was over, Sasha was sent away to have her meal with the servants as usual. Jayhan gave her a little wave as she left and turned to see Yarrow fairly quivering with indignation.

"Come now, Yarrow," said Maud bracingly. "You can either give her consequence or give her safety but not both at the moment. Sasha's future depends on maintaining her disguise as our stableboy. Once you have had an opportunity to change, you shall dine with us this evening and exchange knowledge with Sheldrake. Tomorrow, after Sasha has worked in the stables for the morning, you may share your shaman knowledge with Sasha... and with Jayhan and Sheldrake, during their afternoon magic lessons. The more we know of her powers, the more we can all protect her."

Tight-lipped with displeasure, Yarrow retired to dress for dinner.

When she reappeared, Yarrow was dressed as she had been at the Research Society, resplendent in a loosely fitting black dress, studded with bright stones of many colours and embroidered in swirling patterns around the wrists, neckline and hem. Her black hair, piled on top of her head and held in place by a scarlet scarf, was threaded through with beads. Everything about her shrieked mysticism and magic. Maud admired the woman's flair and was pleased that Yarrow felt at ease enough to display her true colours.

Still unthawed, Yarrow accompanied her hostess up the stairs to the dining room. As she sat down at the white-clothed dining table beside Maud, Yarrow prised her lips apart enough to say, "Shamanism should be women's lore, according to Kimoran custom, which is why I suspected Sasha wasn't a boy. I will not speak of women's business in front of a man and a boy."

Maud smiled charmingly, as though she had just been paid a compliment. "That is entirely up to you, my dear. I think perhaps you should consider however, before you become too huffy, that we have no reason to trust you. We only have your word for it that you are an unregistered shaman. Until we know you better, Sasha will be protected in your company. I'm sure you will concede the need for such precautions."

For a few comical moments, Yarrow simply gobbled. Then she drew a deep breath and let it out slowly. "Forgive me. You are right, of course." Clive serving the soup gave her time to think. Once he had finished and left the room, she said, "Hmm. I can prove that I am not registered. I can speak disparagingly of Queen Torriana and a registered shaman cannot."

Sheldrake sipped his soup. "Ah, pea and ham. One of my favourites." He dabbed his mouth with his serviette before saying mildly, "Although, as a registered shaman, perhaps you might still be able to disparage the Queen, if it were in service of her plans? What do you think?"

Yarrow spluttered and choked on her soup. After a bout of coughing and a drink of water, she sipped her soup in silence for a while. Sheldrake met Maud's eyes across the table and gave a slight smile, content to wait for Yarrow's next gambit. When it came, he was surprised.

"Well," said Yarrow finally. "I have thought hard and cannot think of a way to convince you. The Research Society has accepted me as an unregistered shaman but, as you say, I could be prevaricating as part of service to the Queen. I know how Sasha's obsidian amulet would react to a free and a fettered amulet, which it did. But if *you* don't know, then that will not convince you. Shaman lore is mostly unwritten and passed down by word of mouth. So you will not be able to scour your Carradorian libraries to find it."

"Then Sasha has missed much by losing her mother," murmured Maud.

Encouraged, Yarrow nodded. "Especially *that* mother. Princess Corrina would have known of powers privy only to the direct line of succession. Even Queen Toriana will not know of them."

"And nor will you," finished Sheldrake.

Yarrow shook her head. "No." She took a breath to add something but then thought better of it.

"But, you were going to say, she may learn purely through contact with her amulet," said Sheldrake. He smiled at her obvious surprise. "I learn by observation too, not just through books in Carradorian libraries. Sasha is wise beyond her years and her powers are gradually developing. I may be a mere male, but I have been helping her to tune in to her amulet and to teach her my magical knowledge. She is an adept student, more so than Jayhan, I fear."

"I beg your pardon." Yarrow smiled warmly, as she put down her spoon and leaned back, nodding her thanks as Clive removed her bowl. "I can see that you've been generous with your knowledge while I was planning to be secretive with mine. I do not look down on men. We just have different roles, that's all. But I do thank you for taking Sasha under your wing and nurturing her talent."

He gave an embarrassed glance at Maud before confessing, "I was hoping to use her talents in the Spiders. Not yet, of course. When she was older. Her talent for seeing through shapeshifting and disguises could be most useful." He harrumphed. "Hmm. I may have to rethink that. But," he added hurriedly. "I will continue to teacher her nonetheless."

"In that case, I think it is only fair that I share some of my knowledge with you and your son, and of course you Maud, if you are interested." Yarrow gave a lop-sided smile. "Besides, you will have to guard Sasha against me for the time being." She shrugged. "I suppose I'm grateful that you protect her so well."

Jayhan watched this interchange silently from his place beside his father. He knew enough about kings and queens to know that Sasha wasn't being treated in the right way for someone who should be queen. He understood the need for secrecy, but still thought his parents were being unfair. Although he found Yarrow a little odd, he sympathized with her outrage and was sure she could be trusted. But how to convince his parents? He thought about what she had said about Sasha and her amulet reacting differently to fettered and free shamans and remembered how Sasha had worked out how he could change shapes just by focusing on her amulet. He needed to talk to Sasha.

He shovelled down his dinner and then unusually for him, declined desert and asked to be excused. He thought he had been quite tricky but four pairs of adult eyes, including Clive's, watched him leave the room.

"Hmm, off to see Sasha before bedtime, I'm guessing," said Sheldrake. "Perhaps you could saunter over to see your wife as soon as you have served desert, Clive?"

"Indeed, sir."

To Jayhan's frustration, Sasha had not yet returned from the kitchen when he reached the stables. Beth returned first and Jayhan rushed to hide in one of the stalls, worried that he would be sent off to bed if she spotted him. As she walked down the row of stalls, Beth noted a few shuffles and foot stomps in the straw and with little difficulty traced the cause to a pair of booted feet in the second last stall, easily visible if one bent a little as one walked by. She merely grinned and kept walking.

A few minutes later, Jayhan heard Sasha's light steps and, carefully pulling the bolt so as not to make noise, crept out to meet her. He put his finger to his lips and pointed with his other hand in the direction that Beth had gone. Sasha smiled and nodded, and by unspoken agreement, walked back out the way she had come and headed towards the paddocks. As soon as she was beyond the lights of the house, she turned. Jayhan was at her elbow.

He grinned at her. "Come on. Let's go to our cubby."

They skirted around the back of the stables and using the light of an almost full moon, hoisted themselves up through the branches of the oak to the tree house platform. Jayhan fumbled in the dark looking for the candle and flint they had secreted next to the doorway of the corner of their cubby. Once the candle was alight and carefully placed on their table bucket, they settled themselves on their metal bucket seats.

"So what's up?" asked Sasha.

"What's up?" repeated Jayhan, surprised. "You're what's up. You've had such a bundle of surprises today and then you couldn't even talk to anyone about it." He grinned. "And I knew you'd want to. Aren't you excited?"

Sasha chuckled. "Sort of. I'm very excited about having a brother, especially since it's Jon."

"Yeah, he's pretty good, isn't he?"

Hearing a note of reserve in his voice, Sasha punched him on the shoulder. "Don't worry. I have always loved him, even when I didn't know he was my brother... and Old Tom. But I love you too and I can't play with them as I play with you. Besides," she added grinning, "they all have boring eyes, compared to you."

Jayhan grinned. "That's true, of course." He found a stick and dipped it into the molten wax of the candle then held it into the flame to let the wax drip down again.

"Watch out," said Sasha, as the flame spluttered. "You'll put it out if you're not careful."

"No, I won't," he said, just before everything went dark. "Whoops!"

"Idiot!"

After a bit of scrabbling about in the dark, the flame was re-ignited.

"There. All better again" said Jayhan with an unrepentant smile, picking up a stick to fiddle once more with the candle. As he saw Sasha about to remonstrate with him, he pointed to the flint. "This time I know exactly where the flint is."

Sasha sighed, knowing defeat when she saw it. "Fair enough."

"So what about the queen thing?" asked Jayhan, his eyes intent on the stick and the candle.

"Hmph. Bit odd really, isn't it? I don't feel like a queen. Queens always look so confident and grand and powerful. I don't feel any of those things."

"Well, you're not a queen until you're crowned, I don't think."

"You know what I mean."

"Yes, but at the very least, you're a princess." Jayhan grinned at her. The stick, unsupervised, promptly caught alight. He blew it out and dropped it without a thought for the dry wooden platform underfoot. "Amazing, hey?"

Sasha pouted. "I don't feel like one of them either."

Jayhan looked her up and down, quite unselfconsciously. "No. You don't look like one. Probably the clothes."

"And the boots and no servants, and no palace and…"

Jayhan waved his hand to stop her. "Yes, but I thought a queen or princess would look different from other people up close."

"How exactly? Hidden horns? A royal aura that glows in the dark?"

Jayhan looked pained for a moment before breaking into a grin. "Yeah. Or perfectly neat hair no matter what happens and clothes that stay miraculously clean." Another idea occurred to him. "And hands and face that never need washing and…"

Sasha punched him in the shoulder again. "You're an idiot."

They sat in companionable silence for a while until Sasha broke it by asking, "But you know a king, don't you? Haven't you met King Gavin? What he's like up close?"

Jayhan shrugged. "Oh, but he's just Gavin. He just treats me like everyone else does. Nervous of my eyes and trying to pretend he hasn't noticed them. Mind you, he stopped coming here after he became king. He still sees mum in town but he's busy all the time now."

Sasha scrunched up her nose. "That doesn't sound like much fun… being so busy you can't visit your friends anymore."

"No…" Jayhan trailed off into a thoughtful silence. After a while he glanced at her but didn't say anything.

Sasha rolled her eyes. "Not again, Jayhan! Stop worrying. I already said we will always be friends, no matter what. If it ever turns out that I'm a busy queen then you'll just have to be busy with me, won't you?"

"Yep. Suppose I will." Jayhan leant down and picked up his burnt stick and a couple of leaves he had spotted and threw them out into the darkness. "Tidying up," he said with a little smile.

"Hmm. I wonder if there's a bit of old carpet we could have for our floor?"

"Good idea. We'll ask around tomorrow."

"If we have time. We have that Yarrow lady coming to talk to us in the afternoon." Sasha leaned in close and said quietly, "She's a bit creepy, isn't she?"

"Yes, definitely odd... and," Jayhan added in a conspiratorial whisper "I think she likes you..."

"Stop it, you horrible boy," said Sasha, giving him another thump on the shoulder.

"Ow. That's the third time you've hit me in the same place."

"Serves you right, trying to spook me."

"Mum and dad don't trust her, you know. They think she might be a registered shaman pretending not to be. Yarrow says her amulet shone when it saw your amulet because it is a free amulet, but only she knows if that's true." Jayhan shrugged. "Anyway, *I* reckon, if you concentrated on your amulet, you would know if she were a truly free shaman. What do you think?"

"Hmm. Maybe." Sasha looked unsure. "I'll think about it... but what if I get it wrong?"

"Don't worry, no one's going to leave you alone with her. Dad and I will be with you, even though Yarrow wanted it be just you two." Jayhan chuckled. "Mum made Yarrow very cross about that, but she got over it." He scuffed the toe of his shoe through the dirt on the floor before asking diffidently, "So aren't you angry about having to stay being a stableboy when you're really not?"

"Oh, but I really *am* a stableboy, Jayhan... well, a stable girl. That's my job and my life. All this other stuff is other people's business. I don't know anything about Kimora or this dreadful Aunty-Queen I apparently have, who wants to kill me." Sasha gave an involuntary shudder. "And it doesn't sound to me like I can just wander in and start being a queen. I'm safe and happy here."

Jayhan eyed her, wondering whether she just hadn't had enough time to think it through, but on balance, he decided to let the topic drop.

Chapter 32

The next afternoon found the four of them in Sheldrake's beloved shed. Yarrow was prowling along the benches, scowling at various half-made concoctions, peering at bottles of completed mixtures and running her hands over a scattering of herbs that Sheldrake had left lying about. She strolled over to one of his bookshelves and ran one long red nail along the spines of worn, dusty, little leather books, then flicked her fingernail clean with her thumb. Completely aware of their scrutiny, she finally swirled and looked at them.

"So, Sheldrake," she said condescendingly, "You do indeed have some knowledge of tinctures and remedies. Are you able to heal using only your hands?"

Jayhan could see that it was taking Sheldrake some effort to keep his temper. "No. I wish I could. Tinctures and bandages can only go so far."

"How very true." Yarrow smiled at Sasha. "Now you and I, Your Highness, can heal without the need for these..." she waved her hand around her at the Sheldrake's potions, "...material aids."

Sasha's eyes narrowed. In a hard little voice, she replied, "If, as you say, you value my life, do not call me that. And if you want my friendship, please respect my friends and their skills."

A shocked silence filled the workshop.

Suddenly the wind left Sasha's sails and she looked at Sheldrake in trepidation. "I'm sorry, sir. I should not have presumed to call you my friend."

Sheldrake smiled. "Oh, I think you have just earnt the right."

Yarrow sniffed, put her nose in the air and walked to the other end of the workshop.

Sasha glanced at Jayhan, who was still looking stunned by her outburst, and grimaced. After a minute, she followed Yarrow and tapped her on the arm. "Excuse me, Yarrow. I'm sorry if I upset you." She waited a few seconds but when there was no response, continued, "Could you please show me, us, how you do your healing? My amulet helps me to heal faster, I think, but I don't know how to heal myself straight away or how to heal anyone else. I would really like you to show me, if you would."

Yarrow's stiff shoulders sagged and she turned to face them. Jayhan was shocked to see that her eyes were red-rimmed. She sniffed and wiped her red-nailed fingers under one eye. "It would be my pleasure... Sasha."

Sasha beamed at her. "Oh thank you." She put her hand in Yarrow's as the woman walked back to the waiting man and boy. "Would you like me to hit Jayhan so you have something to heal?" she asked, with a grin in his direction.

Yarrow raised her eyebrows. "Certainly not. Oh. You were joking."

"She's only half joking," muttered Jayhan. "She hits me all the time."

"Only in a friendly way," Sasha assured Yarrow. "So, what else can we heal then?"

"I think we need to work through some basics first. I will explain it to all of you, but I think only Sasha will be able to do it."

Sheldrake smiled. "That's fine. Only Maud can shapeshift and only I can create magical wards. We don't mind knowing of skills that we ourselves do not and cannot possess. It helps us to understand one another."

Yarrow gave a perfunctory smile then looked at Jayhan. "And you can shapeshift into human guises, can't you?" As Jayhan nodded with a shy smile, she added, "And of course you have those marvellous eyes."

"I do?" Jayhan looked like a puppy being offered a bone. "I mean, I know they're unusual, but most people hate them."

"Not me though," piped up Sasha. "I've always liked them."

"And I," murmured Sheldrake in the background.

Yarrow gave a genuine smile. "You see? The people who know you, like them."

"My mum doesn't."

"Oh. Perhaps she fears their power."

"She does," said Sheldrake shortly. "A past relative used their power poorly."

"Ah, but I think those powers are in good hands with this young man, don't you?" Suddenly Yarrow squatted down in front of Jayhan so that her eyes were slightly lower than his. "Poor Jayhan. Here we are talking about your eyes in front of you and not including you. Something that has happened to you all your life, I expect."

Jayhan simply nodded.

"Well you, young man, are very special. Your eyes help you see better in the dark. Have you noticed that?" When Jayhan just shrugged, she smiled. "You would assume everyone else saw things the way you do, wouldn't you?"

He shrugged again and after a moment's thought, nodded. "Sasha and I tried to get my eyes to push things away because we read that Madison flung her husband across the room only by looking at him. But nothing happened."

"You can't just summon the power. It is simply part of you. And if I tell you too much about it, you will become self-conscious and by trying too hard, block it."

Jayhan frowned. "Well, that's annoying."

Yarrow gave a friendly laugh, all attempts at airs and graces forgotten. "Yes, isn't it? Just have faith in yourself and who you are. And most importantly, learn to meet people eye-to-eye, and cope with their reaction. It is they, not you, who have the problem."

Yarrow patted his shoulder then stood up, her dress tinkling as little gems clashed against each other. "And now for you, young lady." She glanced around the windows of the shed and asked Sheldrake, "I know these windows are tarnished but they are still transparent. Is there anyone who might peer in while we work? Are your staff completely trustworthy? I am sorry to seem so untrusting, but I have been in hiding for years."

Sheldrake smiled reassuringly. "My staff are completely trustworthy, but I can place a shield around the shed that stops people from seeing in while you work." He waved his hand, muttering a few words under his breath and surprisingly, the world outside seemed to brighten, rather than fade away. At Yarrow's puzzled expression, he explained. "We can see out better but for them, it is like being in a well-lit room trying to see into the darkness."

"But you can't possibly have lit up all the surroundings..."

Sheldrake laughed. "No indeed. It is just an illusion, but it works for your purposes."

"Thank you, I'm impressed." Yarrow hesitated. "And I'm sorry... for before. I was just trying to align myself with the... with Sasha, and instead I alienated myself. Silly of me, really." She wrung her hands. "It's just, she matters so much to me and I have been looking for her for so long."

The strength of her emotion left everyone feeling a little uncomfortable. Into the silence that followed, she pulled on the cord around her neck and lifted her amulet from within the bodice of her dress. She said nothing but simply held it in the palm of her hand so they could all see it, then focused on Sasha.

After a minute, Jayhan said, "It seems to be giving off light but not a steady light."

"It is pulsing," observed Sheldrake. "It is subtle, but it is there."

"Yes," said Yarrow. "Sheldrake, hold your fingers over the vein in Sasha's wrist... if she doesn't mind."

Sasha obligingly held out her arm and Sheldrake grasped her wrist. He concentrated for a full minute then raised his eyes to Yarrow's. "Your amulet beats in time with Sasha's heart."

Yarrow nodded, tears welling in her eyes. *Oh no,* thought Jayhan *she's going to cry again,* but to his relief, she held herself together. "All amulets are linked to the High Shaman and her amulet. They beat in time to the one true ruler's heart. Now do you see how much Sasharia means to me?"

"And why Toriana can never be accepted as the rightful monarch," finished Sheldrake for her.

Sasha listened but made no comment. Instead, she slowly pulled out her amulet and asked, "Do you mind if I try something?"

"Of course not," said Yarrow.

Sheldrake nodded, "Go ahead."

Sasha grasped her black amulet in front of her. As soon as it appeared, the obsidian began to glow, eliciting a clear, answering light from Yarrow's.

Ignoring the light, Sasha gazed into Yarrow's eyes, focusing on the depths of the shaman as she had focused on Jayhan, when she'd realised he was a shapeshifter. At first, she could not see beyond the surface, so her impressions of Yarrow's character and talents were foggy and unclear. As she tried to penetrate deeper, she found her mind wandering off on tangents or swirling in circular thoughts. Suddenly she realised that Yarrow had made herself inviolate by wrapping herself in cloudy confusion.

Sasha mentally pulled back and gave Yarrow a little smile. "Please?"

At once, the fog cleared and Sasha was swept into the passion and knowledge and skills that lay beneath Yarrow's surface. It was far more complex and diverse than either Jayhan's or Maud's. Sasha allowed herself to whirl among images of ceremonies, herbs, invocations, spells, memories of performing rites, healing, teaching, comforting. She felt the mist within Yarrow trying to reform and push her away but it was too late. Sasha's mind spun more and more wildly as the kaleidoscope of images pressed in on her from all sides. She was drawn into visions of wild chases through the forest, the sound of distant hounds sending terror though her, images of fighting, burning villages, bloodshed and a body swinging under a tree, a noose around its neck.

In her hand, the black amulet roared to life, throwing a pulse of power at Yarrow that sent her flying across the shed to hit her head with a resounding whack against the far bench.

At the same time, a flat oval of unreflective blackness suddenly appeared where Sasha had been standing. They couldn't see her, but Sheldrake and Jayhan both heard her crumple to the floor. They rushed towards her but could not reach her. The area around her felt soft but was impenetrable. When they pushed insistently, their hands began to tingle then burn.

They backed off, hands stinging but undamaged. When they tried to dodge around the patch of blackness, it appeared oval-shaped and apparently two-dimensional from every direction.

"Blast it! We can't get to her," said Sheldrake, shaking his head. "I've never seen anything like this before. It must be a shield of some sort." He turned as he heard a groan. "Yarrow! What did you do to her?" he asked harshly.

Yarrow sat up groggily and put her hand to her head. She brought her hand around to inspect it, but there was no blood on it. She shook her head and winced. "Ow. That hurt." She brought her gaze to bear on the blank oval of blackness, then looked at Sheldrake. "What you are seeing is Sasha's extreme protection. Most of the time, the amulet protects her in subtle ways such as helping her to make everyone believe that she is boy, healing her more quickly when she has been hurt. It can't deflect an unexpected physical attack but the wearer can consciously direct its power in her defence. But this," She nodded at the black patch, then winced again, "this is a full-blown healing shield. It is both protective and healing. It will keep everyone away from her until she is fully recovered."

"But what did you do to her?" demanded Jayhan, still watching the black place where Sasha lay, hidden from view. "You hurt her, didn't you?"

"NO. Well yes, but not intentionally. She learnt too much too fast. The will of her amulet overpowered my defences." She sat on the floor, with her arms wrapped around her knees, making no attempt to get up. "At first I let her into my mind at her request, happy to show her some of my knowledge and skills. By the time I'd decided she had seen enough, the strength of her amulet, or her will, had gained such momentum that I couldn't reinstate my defences. My knowledge and memories streamed into her; the visions, sounds and feelings." Yarrow grimaced. "And some of my memories are filled with fear and horror."

"Oh dear. I see." Sheldrake's face was drawn tight with concern. He pondered for a moment then asked, "Will she recover?"

Yarrow hugged herself closer, tears springing to her eyes. "I hope so. It was so much information for a young girl to take in, especially all at once."

Sheldrake stepped away from the black oval and grasped Jayhan's arm to pull him back too. "And we can do nothing? Just wait?"

"I'm afraid so."

The wait was long.

For two hours, Sasha remained hidden by the strange black oval. Sheldrake sent a reluctant Jayhan, worried he would miss her awakening, off for supplies. Maud and Beth returned in his wake, helping him to bring in trays of tea, lemonade and rock cakes. Then the five of them waited, sustaining themselves with afternoon tea, but not leaving.

Slanting rays of late afternoon sunlight were streaming through the window when, without warning, the oval shrank rapidly and winked out, revealing Sasha lying curled up on her side, apparently asleep. It happened so suddenly that at first, no one moved.

Then Jayhan rushed over to her and knelt down beside her.

"Sasha, Sasha, are you all right?" he murmured. He reached out tentatively and patted her arm. "Sasha?"

Sasha's eyes fluttered then opened. For a moment, her eyes were as black as a fathomless pit, but even as Jayhan drew back in shock, they reverted to their normal dark, liquid brown.

"Phew!" he breathed. "Hello. Are you all right?"

The tapping of nails on the stone floor of the shed made Jayhan look over his shoulder to find himself looking up into the droopy, furry face of his mother. She nudged him aside with her nose and flopped down beside Sasha, putting her heavy bloodhound head and one paw on the girl's chest.

"Oof!" Sasha giggled. "Do you know how heavy you are?" She rolled partly onto her back so that she could use both hands to stroke Maud's long soft ears, then looked at Jayhan. "Hello to you too. Well, your plan worked." The folds around Maud's eyes moved as she looked at her son, still kneeling next to her. A deep growl vibrated in her chest. Sasha giggled again. "That tickles." She stroked Maud's ears soothingly. "Don't get mad at Jayhan. It was his idea for me to look into Yarrow so I could check on her loyalty. It was a good idea and I agreed to it."

"Check on her loyalty, hey?" murmured Sheldrake. "That is an odd way of phrasing it. I presume you mean honesty?"

Sasha's eyes met Yarrow's across the room. "Perhaps. But more than that, I found loyalty." She heaved a deep sigh and glanced out the window. "Is it really that light? I thought more time would have passed." Her gaze took in the presence of Beth and the tea tray. "How long have you been waiting for me?"

"*Ages.*" "Two hours," said Jayhan and Sheldrake simultaneously.

"Oh dear," Sasha gave an impish grin. "I am a troublesome stable boy-girl, aren't I, keeping you all tied up here for the afternoon." She did not, however, sound fearful of being dismissed as she would have previously. In fact, she sounded disconcertingly self-assured.

Her eyes travelled to the tray of cake and lemonade but her self-assurance didn't stretch to asking for some. The look of longing in her eyes was eloquent enough, however, and Beth brought her over a slice of cake and a glass of lemonade.

Sasha smiled. "Thanks. I'm starving. Just keep it away from greedy guts here," she added, gesturing at the huge hound sprawled over her chest. Maud raised her head a little, managed to look even more hangdog than usual and gave a little whine, but Sasha said firmly. "No. I bet you had heaps while you were waiting."

Maud dropped her head even more heavily onto Sasha's chest and heaved a sigh. Sasha laughed. Beth put the plate on the floor next to her hand, out of Maud's reach, and Sasha attempted to eat cake lying down with her head to one side away from Maud. After one awkward bite on which she almost choked, Sasha pleaded, "Come on Maud. Let me up. It's too hard."

After a final heave with her paw that nearly knocked the wind out of Sasha, Maud sat up, towering over the prone girl.

"Thanks Maud," said Sasha, as she sat up, then gasped in shock as Maud reached past her and with one lick of her enormous tongue, polished off the rest of the slice of cake. "MAUD!"

Maud wagged her tail and licked her chops, before wandering away off behind one of the work benches to change. It did not escape Sheldrake's notice, however, that Maud had provided comfort and distraction to Sasha after her ordeal. He mentally saluted her.

Chapter 33

Although Sasha had seen many of Yarrow's memories, the amulet had intervened before she saw everything and she had not had time to fully comprehend the memories she had seen or their implications. So her knowledge was incomplete.

After considerable discussions, it was decided that Yarrow should continue to teach Sasha her heritage and shamanic powers. Sheldrake and Jayhan joined Sasha in these lessons most of the time, although Jayhan's attention tended to flag when the topics under discussion were the history or politics of Kimora.

At the end of the second week, a letter arrived from Jon, asking whether it was safe for him to visit. Sheldrake checked with Leon that their gates were still not under surveillance before sending a reply, inviting him for lunch two days later.

Sasha kept an eye out for him, driving Beth crazy by nipping out between cleaning each stall to check the gate. When he finally arrived, she was caught unawares, hard at work in the third last stall, Flurry's. Sasha had the great draught horse tied on a lead rope to an iron ring in the corridor while her stall was being cleaned and was concentrating on shovelling dirty straw into a big wooden barrow. Suddenly Flurry and the other horses up and down the stalls became restless, tossing their heads or stamping the feet.

"Hello, little sister."

Sasha spun around so fast that her shovelful of straw sprayed around the wall of the stall. She ran out of the stall and flung her arms around him, engulfing him in the smell of horses, straw and dung. "Jon, Jon. You're here, you're here. I've been waiting for you all morning."

"Looks like it," said Jon dryly, hugging her tightly in return even though he knew his clothes would be the worse for it. "Specially dressed for the occasion."

She hugged him even tighter and asked in voice muffled by his jacket, "Why didn't you tell me? I thought I was alone all this time."

Jon stroked the top of her head. "To keep you safe, little one. We have had to be so careful. We still have to be so careful. But now, at least, you're old enough to keep secrets."

"I always was."

A sob issued from the area of his chest and Jon realised Sasha was crying. He kept stroking her hair and hugging her. "I'm sorry, little one. Maybe I should have trusted you more... Maybe I should have done a lot of things differently. But people from Kimora were looking for a brother and sister who had escaped. I had to remove all trace of us. And Sasha," He gave her an extra squeeze which bent her ribs, "I couldn't bear to lose you. You are all I have."

She lifted her tear-stained face at that. "Don't you have a girlfriend, Rose's mother's second cousin?"

For a moment Jon looked taken aback. Then he shook his head. "No. We split up."

"Why?"

"Because I discovered she had been talking about me."

"Oh. That was Maud's fault. She sent Rose off on a fact-finding mission before she approached the embassy about me."

"Just as well she did. I wouldn't have wanted Lady Maud to breeze in and tell Lady Electra about you." He grunted as a big velvety nose nudged him in the back of the head. "Hoy you," he said to Flurry, who was peering at him enquiringly. He disentangled himself from Sasha and turned to stroke the great filly's neck. "She's a beauty, isn't she?'

Sasha beamed with pride. "She's a bit skittish sometimes, but she's better now that she's friends with Apricot."

"Who's Apricot?"

"The little cat who insists on sleeping in Flurry's feedbag."

Jon stroked continued to stroke Fluffy. "You have a little cat friend, do you? You're a funny one then." He looked over Sasha's shoulder at the mess of the third last stall behind her. "So what are we going to do about that?"

Sasha surveyed the stall and grimaced. "I'd better get to and finish it, I suppose. Maybe I'll see you after lunch."

"Hmph. I think I'll give you a hand." So saying, he took off his smudged, pale yellow coat and hung it on the iron ring Flurry was hitched to. "Come on. Let's go."

Just as they finished cleaning out the final stall, Beth came out of her office and walked towards them. There was no coincidence in this at all, as Beth had been keeping a discreet eye on their progress.

"Good morning, Jon. Thanks for your help." She smiled. "You are looking a little less dapper than when you arrived. Would you like to come into my office and sponge down your coat," she inspected him, "… and your shirt before going to lunch? Sasha can bring in a bucket of water."

Jon nodded and thanked her, following her back between the rows of stalls. Every horse watched him, whickering or tossing its head as he passed. Long before he reached Beth's office, he raised his hands in resignation, stopped and went back to the start of the row. He then retraced his steps, this time giving each horse a scratch on the forehead or stroking its neck as he passed.

When Beth turned around to watch, he shrugged and smiled ruefully. "I don't know what it is. Horses are always like this with me. Maybe it's the plainsman heritage."

Once he had greeted every horse, they settled down and were content merely to watch him until he was out of sight in the office.

"Sasha also has a way with horses," said Beth, as she handed him a clean rag, "not perhaps as extreme as yours, but certainly better than most. She wandered into Flurry's stall when she was being skittish, calmed her down and introduced her to little Apricot, the cat. No mean feat… And of course, you know she saved my life by pushing me out of the way of a rearing stallion then hopping onto its back to settle it."

"Did she?" Jon was still smiling, his blue eyes shining with pride, when Sasha entered the office lugging a heavy bucket of water.

Sasha set down the bucket and frowned, "What?"

"I have just been hearing about your heroics."

Sasha's cheeks reddened and she dropped her gaze. "Oh."

"And you, young lady, are going to have a wash and put on your best clothes. You are going up to lunch with Maud and Sheldrake today."

"Oh," said Sasha again, sounding more worried than pleased. She looked up at Beth. "Really? They're all going to be watching how I act."

"Don't worry so much," said Beth bracingly. "Yarrow has been teaching you, hasn't she? And no one is going to be critical."

Jon accepted a sponge and began to wipe the grime off his coat. After a few hard scrubs, he paused and said with a smile, "Just copy me."

Sasha scowled. "I just want to be a stableboy."

"I hear you're very good with horses." Jon turned his coat and studied it critically. "Can you see any more spots I need to clean?"

"No," snapped Sasha with barely a glance at his coat. "I like being a stableboy. In fact, I love it."

"I am pleased to hear it, since it will hopefully to be your lot in life for many years to come." Jon rubbed at another patch of ground-in horse dung then held his coat up for another inspection. "And one day you may rise to become assistant head groom."

"And what would be so bad about that?"

Jon finally raised his eyes from his coat and looked at his little sister. "It would be an honour to rise so high under Beth. I can tell she is a true professional."

"Hmph."

Jon laughed. "You can be a stable boy with good table manners, you know. The two are not mutually exclusive." When she didn't respond, the laughter died on his face. "I was looking forward to your company, but if you do not wish to come to lunch, I will give your apologies. I can drop back over here to see you before I go." He shrugged himself into his jacket and smoothed down the lapels.

Sasha's face reddened. "No. It would be bad manners for me to refuse an invitation when they have done so much for me. I will come. Just wait while I wash and change so we can go over together."

"As you wish," replied Jon, but his voice was cool.

Sasha's eyes swivelled from Jon to Beth and back again, her face taut with worry. "Sorry," she said uncertainly. "I didn't mean to hurt your feelings. Of course I want to have lunch with you. It's not you," she said in a rush. "It's the queen thing. It's pretty weird, you know, suddenly finding out I'm so important to all these people I don't even know." She grimaced. "And it's embarrassing, having everyone watching me practise how to behave as a noblewoman."

"Oh, Sasharia…" Jon took a deep breath then let it out in a long sigh. "I left Kimora when I was twelve. So I remember her, and I care for her and her people. You do not. Second-hand memories from Yarrow are not at all the same. I know that so far you have allowed Yarrow to teach you about Kimora, but if you want no further involvement with your heritage, then that is your choice. I have not, and will not, force you."

"Oh." After a moment, Sasha picked up a flannel, dipped it in the bucket and started to wipe down her arms with it.

"Out you go, Jon," said Beth briskly. "Wait for her at the side door. Sasha needs a better wash than that if she is to be presentable for lunch."

When Sasha re-joined him, she was clean and garbed in fresh leggings and a soft cream shirt covered by a new brushed suede jerkin. "But," she said, as though their conversation hadn't been interrupted, "If I stopped having lessons about Kimora... and stuff, would you still visit me?"

Jon raised his eyebrows at her. "Of course I would. What do you think I am?"

"Sorry. Again. I just thought you cared a lot about this queen thing and saving shamans and maybe only wanted to see me because of your plans to save Kimora. And also that you'd be mad at me," she finished in a little rush.

"Angry? No. Disappointed? Yes. But I would never walk away from you. You are my sister and my..." He shook his head. "Never mind... And yes, my plans are important to me. I have a duty to Kimora that I will not relinquish. But I will simply have to find another way." After a moment, he produced an almost cheery smile and proffered his arm. "Shall we go in to lunch?"

Sash shook her head. "Not yet." She tucked her hand into his arm and asked, "Can we just walk to the paddock and back? It will only take five minutes."

Without a word, Jon turned his footsteps and looked down enquiringly at her as they walked.

"When I was at Stonehaven, I always did my chores as well as I could, to please Old Tom. Even with Bryson, I did my best," She gave a little snort of derision, "although that was partly to avoid being hit and even then, it often didn't work." She threw a resentful glance up at her brother.

"Sorry," he said quietly and squeezed her arm closer to him.

"Hmph. Anyway, then I came here and I tried my hardest from the second I walked in the door. I was desperate not to be sent back to Bryson or to be turned out into the world with no job and nowhere to go." She kicked a little pebble then drew a breath. "Now I just do my best because they are kind to me and have helped me and because," she shrugged, "I guess I expect it of myself."

She stopped walking and withdrew her hand so that she could face him. "So I will do my best for you too, and for all those people."

Jon gave her a little bow of acknowledgement that made her giggle.

"Stop it! I was being serious."

Jon smiled. "So was I."

"Oh..." She shook her head. "And if I do become this queen person, how will I be supposed to act around Beth and Jayhan and Maud and Sheldrake, and how will they act around me and when will it change?"

Jon put his arm around her shoulders and hugged her to his side, chuckling. "You already are this queen person, as you call it. It's a bit overwhelming, is it? With people you know well, it need only change in formal situations. And just remember this. You will always be you, no matter how you act or how those around you act. You will always be you."

"Hmph." She thought for a moment, then tilted her head and smiled up at him. "I suppose that's all right. Tricky, but all right."

He grinned. "Of course, who you are is the rightful Queen of Kimora." She frowned and punched him in the ribs. "Oof!" he gasped playfully, his grin broadening. "But you always were and always will be, whether you knew it or not. Only difference is now you know."

Sasha took a deep breath and prepared herself for the coming ordeal. Well, not quite an ordeal, she corrected herself, a challenge.

As they headed inside, Jon bent down and whispered, "By the way, I have a little surprise in store for you." She glanced at him, but he just gave a secretive little grin and kept walking.

Chapter 34

When they entered the dining room, Jayhan gave her a smile, not of reassurance but of pure, excited welcome. It clearly did not occur to him that she might have reason to be worried. Although this probably sprang as much from his lack of understanding as from his confidence in her, his smile still calmed her.

She smiled back as she followed Clive's gesture to a place halfway down the table between Jayhan and Jon. Eloquin and Yarrow stood behind their chairs opposite her, ready to be seated, while Maud and Sheldrake were standing at either end.

"Good afternoon, Jon and Sasha, and welcome." Maud turned to Eloquin and Yarrow. "Jon knew Sasha at the orphanage, and now works at the Kimoran Embassy."

Yarrow's face tightened. She nodded curtly. "How do you do?"

"It's all right, Maud," said Jon, with a slight smile. "I know of Yarrow's allegiances and her work to help unregistered shamans though my own network. If we can trust her with knowledge of Sasharia, we can trust her with me too."

Maud breathed a sigh of relief and smiled. "Lovely. That will make lunch so much easier. Yarrow, Jon is Sasha's older brother, who brought her out of Kimora after..." She shook her head. "Never mind."

Yarrow gaped in shocked delight. "Oh, Your Highness. Oh, I'm so pleased you're all right. No one knew where you were." She sank into a deep curtsey.

Eloquin, standing beside her, looked a bit panicked as she wondered whether she too should curtsey. She sent a little frown at Maud who gave a slight shake of her head.

Clive discreetly trod to the door and closed it, making sure no other staff could enter until Yarrow had recovered herself.

Jon gave her a warm smile. "I am pleased that you too, as an unregistered shaman, are safe. I have heard of your work. Please rise. You endanger both of us with such gestures." His easy response, in such contrast to Sasha's panic a few weeks before, highlighted the fact that Jon had actually been raised, at least until he was twelve, as a prince while Sasha had no memory of a royal life.

Yarrow scrambled to her feet. "Oh. I'm so sorry. Of course. I should have realised. It's just..." Tears sprang to her eyes, making Jayhan look down firmly so that he didn't roll his eyes.

"Shall we sit down?' invited Jon.

Clive left his self-appointed post by the door and assisted Sasha and Jon to seat themselves, spreading their napkins on their knees, before moving to do the same for Yarrow and Eloquin, while Maud, Sheldrake and Jayhan seated themselves. Sasha, fresh from lessons with Yarrow, suddenly realised that Clive was meticulously giving precedence according to the rank of non-family members, now that it was acknowledged. She felt embarrassed and struggled to meet Eloquin's eyes.

Noticing this, Eloquin leant forward and said quietly, "Sasha, I do like your new jerkin. It looks very soft."

Sasha was forced to look at her and found her smiling warmly at her. "Thanks," she mumbled. Then she stroked the front of her jerkin and grinned in return. "It is soft. I love it. These are the best clothes I have ever owned."

A moment of awkward, sympathetic silence was broken by Jayhan who said blithely, "I bet they are. And if your jerkin's like mine, it has inside pockets. Have a look."

Sasha undid the top three buttons and peered inside. She looked up grinning, "It does too. I hadn't even noticed. That's handy, isn't it?"

The adults around the table collectively relaxed.

It was about then that Sasha noticed another place had been set between Yarrow and Sheldrake. As she pondered this, Clive re-entered the room and announced in a tone dripping with disapproval, "Old Tom, sir."

The huge man followed Clive sheepishly into the room, "I am awfully sorry I'm late... And I seem to have upset your butler. Not quite sure how."

"Old Tom," shouted Sasha and bounced out of her seat and around the table before anyone could object. She threw herself at him and wrapped her arms around his legs, which nearly sent him flying.

Staggering, Old Tom peeled her arms off his legs, grabbed her under her arms and swung her high in the air. "My little Sashakins! I'm so glad to see you. I thought we'd lost you and when I heard bloody Bryson had been mistreating you, well! It's lucky for him he disappeared. That's all I can say." He swung her back down so that she landed neatly on her feet, then looked around the table. "I beg your pardon. How do you all do?" He raised his eyebrows hopefully and Sheldrake rose to the occasion by introducing everyone.

"Lovely to meet you all," said Old Tom as he sat down. "You're looking very dapper, young Jon."

Sasha beamed. "Huh. You should have seen his shirt before Beth sponged it down. He helped me muck out the stalls, you know. And you should have seen the horses! So excited to see him and all demanding to meet him."

"Good gracious," exclaimed Maud. "How inconvenient for you."

Jon laughed. "Yes, it can be."

The first course of potato and leek soup was served by Clive, assisted by Rose, whose nose, Sasha was sure, was more in the air than usual. She did not once meet Sasha's eye.

Jayhan spooned a few mouthfuls without spilling a drop then sighed. "I wish I had such a way with horses. They just put up with me."

"You're getting better," said Sasha. "and let's face it. Slug is well named. Even I have to make an effort to get him going."

Sheldrake's head reared up from his soup. "Slug? I thought you named him Storm."

Jayhan met Sasha's eyes as he gave a little smile, "That was before I got to know him."

"Oh. I see."

The boy grimaced. "Sorry Dad. I know you bought him 'specially for me and I do like him. It's just he's..." Jayhan shrugged, "a slug."

Old Tom smiled at Jayhan with fellow feeling at this remark, showing no reaction to the boy's pale eyes.

Maud frowned. "Sounds like a lazy little pony. I might have a word with him next time I'm a horse."

Jayhan brightened. "Thanks Mum. You never know, that might help." He looked at Sasha who was carefully spooning her soup. He nodded at her. "You're doing well. Soup is the absolute hardest."

Sasha rolled her eyes and promptly clinked her spoon against the edge of her bowl, luckily not spilling any. "You're not supposed to comment, you idiot," she hissed.

"Language, please," said Yarrow.

Sasha's eyes narrowed but she said nothing.

"Of course Sasha is doing well," interposed Old Tom. "We are not savages at Stonehaven. All the children are expected to have impeccable table manners and to be able to hold their own in any company, high or low. I think you will find that Sasha adjusts her behaviour to suit those around her." He gave a slight smile and re-addressed himself to his own soup.

A stunned silence followed, in which everyone but Jon and Old Tom readjusted their view of Sasha.

"Besides, Sasha must be allowed to enjoy our company and the luncheon without the constant scrutiny, both positive and negative, that she is being placed under," said Maud gently but firmly. "We are here to enjoy a meal with Old Tom, Jon and his sister. That is all." She smiled at Jon. "And how are things at the Embassy? I do like your yellow jacket, by the way. Very smart."

"Thank you. Things are much the same. Lady Electra was pleased to be invited to another of the King's garden parties and is becoming better known at court. However, her mother is ailing, and she is becoming a little homesick even though reports of unrest in Kimora are becoming more frequent and more serious." Jon glanced at his sister. "Although she doesn't or can't say it, I think the indiscriminate, vicious reprisals by Queen Toriana have shocked her."

"Can you be more explicit?" asked Sheldrake.

Just as Maud was about to protest, Jon replied for her. "No. Not in front of the little ones. Jayhan is only eight, as I understand it, and Sasha is only a little older. She will have to deal with unpleasantness while she is still young, but now is too soon. If I can protect her for a while longer, I will."

"Of course." Sheldrake motioned for the soup to be cleared away. "Thoughtless of me. Perhaps later."

"Certainly."

Sasha watched and listened but said nothing, giving Clive a quick smile as he removed her bowl. As he turned away with her bowl, he placed his other hand briefly on her back, a gesture which made her glow inside. Seeing it, Old Tom gave her a warm smile.

The next course turned out to be spatchcock. Each plate bore a whole small spatchcock glazed with a spiced apricot sauce and served with long beans, peas and small new potatoes. Sasha repressed a grimace as she contemplated the challenge of dismembering a bony fowl purely with her knife and fork, and spearing peas onto her fork without using her knife or overturned fork to scoop them up and without sending them careening across the table. She looked up to see Rose placing a similar plate in front of Eloquin on the opposite side of the table. As she straightened, Rose looked at her and a fleeting smirk of anticipation crossed her face. Sasha's spirit rose to the challenge. So Rose thought she would make a fool of herself, did she? Not a chance. She could do this. It would be difficult, but she could do it.

Sasha gave a grunt of amusement at herself. The triviality of it struck her. This parade of manners was nothing compared to the trials being endured by shamans in her country of birth. Barely worth the trouble of attempting it… and yet she knew that one day it might matter.

The volume of conversation dimmed as the diners concentrated on dismembering their fowls. Suddenly, a loud clatter next to her preceded a cascade of peas across the table from Jayhan's plate. Maud and Sheldrake frowned while Jayhan grinned sheepishly.

"Whoops. Sorry," he said as he reached out to scoop the peas back onto his plate.

Maud put up her hand. "No. Leave them where they are. Do not compound one error by another. Rose will clean them up before the next course." She studied his innocent little face before calling Rose over. "And Rose, could you procure a few more peas for Master Jayhan please? We wouldn't want him to miss out." She chuckled as he rolled his eyes. "No young man. You will not have your carelessness rewarded by avoiding green vegetables."

Jayhan gave a little huff and returned his attention to his dinner. After a minute or two, when the searchlight of his mother's eyes had moved on, he gave Sasha a little dig in the ribs and when he had her attention, raised his eyebrows in the direction of her meal. In response, she shrugged and gave a little smile. He spotted Eloquin watching her and gave her a guilty grin. To his surprise, she gave a slight smile and spoke to Yarrow, neatly diverting attention away from the two children.

"Do you have any relatives or friends who are still in danger in Kimora?" she asked.

Yarrow finished her mouthful, then picked up her knife and fork, ready to prepare her next mouthful as she answered. "Yes. A whole colony of shamans is living deep within the jungles. I know many of them personally. They are good honest people who use their powers to heal and help. Many of their family members have been hunted down for information. Those family members who are released, are watched and…," she glanced at the children, "harassed, often to the point where they feel forced to leave."

Sensing that Sasha had gone very quiet beside him, Jayhan glanced at her to see a tear trickling down her cheek. He put his hand under the table and squeezed her leg. She gave him a tremulous smile and a sniff, "Yarrow's best friend, Tara, lost her baby," she said sadly, "because they had to travel so hard and fast to escape the Queen's guards. The baby was only a few days old. And a soldier swung at Simeon's dad, but the sword missed his dad and sliced straight through the little boy's leg instead. And now he only has one leg...." She sniffed again, struggling to rein in tears. "Sorry," she added to no one in particular.

Yarrow grimaced. "Don't be sorry. It's I who should be, for allowing you to see my memories. I should have foreseen the danger." She gave a wan smile. "Yes, although she reached the safety of the hidden colony, Tara still grieves for her lost child. And little Simeon... " She shrugged. "He is learning to walk with a peg leg." In an effort to cheer Sasha up, she added, "But when they find out that you are still alive and in possession of the amulet, it will give them hope."

A look of panic crossed Sasha's face. "But I don't know what I'm supposed to do or how to help these people," she exclaimed. "I don't even know them or where they are." She heaved a deep shuddering breath to prevent herself from dissolving into tears and applied herself to the remains of her spitchcock, thus missing the minatory stare Maud sent to Yarrow.

An uncomfortable silence engulfed the table until Jayhan said cheerily, "Well, I know it's a bit tricky, but it's pretty good mattering so much to all these people. I mean, when you were with Bryson, you didn't matter to anybody; at least you didn't think you did. It's got to be better than that."

With her eyes still on her plate, Sasha actually giggled. "Yes it is, isn't it?" She grinned and looked up. "You're right. I've gone from having no one to having heaps of people I belong to. I should stop whingeing, shouldn't I, and just work out what to do."

Jayhan nodded and grinned back at her.

Jon and Yarrow caught each other's eye and a silent message passed between them. This was duly noted by Sheldrake and Maud, who were not so unsubtle as to glance at each other, as each knew the other would have noticed and they could discuss it later.

Chapter 35

Old Tom left shortly after lunch but Jon was able to stay for the afternoon. He was absurdly pleased to be invited to their magic tutorial.

"Jon and I shall go ahead, I think," said Sheldrake, "You three may join us in an hour's time."

They briefly touched on the deteriorating conditions in Kimora as they walked down the path to the shed, but Jon lost the thread of the conversation as he entered Sheldrake's hallowed workshop in the mage's wake. He ran his gaze in awe along the shelves filled with jars of herbs, spices, and strange, unidentifiable substances, but he was particularly taken with the scaled model of Carrador. He studied it for several minutes, asking Sheldrake questions about its accuracy and how the information had been gathered for its construction. He leaned in closer, studying the positioning of minute figures on the model.

Jon looked over his shoulder and asked, "Do these figures represent your agents or areas of concern?" Seeing Sheldrake's face tighten, he gave an apologetic smile. "I beg your pardon. I shouldn't abuse your hospitality by prying, but it is such a wonderful device. It gives you so much better information about the terrain than a flat map does, even a topographical map. It is one thing to see from above that a mountain range is steep or gentle and quite another to be able to see it from every angle. Most impressive."

Despite himself, Sheldrake unbent under the warmth of Jon's enthusiasm. "The miniature figures can represent a variety of things. They can be, as you suggested, hotspots of trouble or my agents. But if, for example, we were considering a particular problem such as improving the transport system, they can represent poor roads that need attention or the way-houses and taverns available for travellers." He gave a little cough. "I had an idea you would be taken with my three-dimensional map. Could I just mention that I don't feel comfortable discussing my work with just anyone... Yarrow, for instance?"

Jon nodded casually. "I wouldn't have mentioned any of this if she were here... or the children. And I thank you for taking me into your confidence by talking to me about this."

Sheldrake's eyes narrowed. "I keep forgetting what an astute young man you are. You have such a disarming manner."

The colour on Jon's cheeks heightened and he shot Sheldrake a sideways glance. Suddenly Sheldrake remembered that this apparently confident young man had had to bring himself up since the age of twelve with no family and no support, except for occasional visits to see Old Tom. On impulse, he put his arm across Jon's shoulders and said warmly, "You are almost as impressive as this map!"

Jon grinned, but his eyes glistened.

"And," continued Sheldrake, on a roll that he worried he might regret later, "you can count on Maud and me to look after you, should you ever need it; not politically, you understand, but personally. Sasha is almost one of the family and so too are you."

All expression fled from Jon's face. He closed his eyes and stood rigid within the circle of Sheldrake's arm. Feeling the tension, Sheldrake gave him an awkward couple of pats on the back and dropped his arm. Finally, Jon mastered himself enough to look at Sheldrake. "I wish someone had said that to me a long, long time ago." He drew a deep, shuddering breath. "But now I have to stay strong, for Sasha, for Kimora."

"You are strong, Jon. Maybe stronger than anyone I have ever met."

"I can't afford to fall apart," said Jon tightly.

Sheldrake shook his head. "Ah Jon, you won't stay fallen apart."

"But the others will be here any minute…" said Jon, trying a last-ditch stand.

"No, they won't. We have plenty of time but just to make sure…" Sheldrake waved his arm and muttered something that Jon didn't hear. Suddenly, a dull click sounded on the other side of the door. "There! My 'Keep out until further notice sign' is now on the door. They will go away when they see it." He patted Jon on the back. "You are safe."

As though a dam had broken, Jon spat out, "I am never safe. I have never been safe since my family died around me. If I remember when I was last safe, it is to remember the family I have lost and to know that safety was an illusion." To Sheldrake's shock, it wasn't sadness that poured out him. It was rage. "That woman destroyed my life, Sasha's life, the lives of countless others. For what? To sit on a big chair and dictate to destroy more lives." He shook his head. "I can't allow her to do that. Not for my own sake or for Sasha's, not even for the true line, but for the sake of the people." He straightened and glared at Sheldrake. "Oh, believe me, I have been sad. I have cried myself to sleep in alleyways, my stomach hurting from hunger. I have sobbed at the loss of my mother, my sister, my father and brother until I retched. I will always carry that grief." He drew a deep breath. "But it is the rage I must control. It is a poison that could leach into my friendships, my judgement and my actions. And I have a duty to my people that I must not jeopardize by marring it with anger."

Sheldrake looked into the intense passion that seemed to contract, even as he watched it, in Jon's blue eyes and saw him, for the first time, as the prince he was born to be. Sheldrake restrained himself from producing a bow of acknowledgement and instead, let out a long breath. "I admire your control. If you ever need someone to discuss your plans with, to make sure they are not too rash, vindictive or vengeful, I am at your disposal."

Jon scrutinized him for a moment, then he too let out a long breath and grinned. "I will take you at face value on that. I know your loyalties lie with Carrador but I have no intentions that threaten her so I can't see that you are being devious in your offer. Thank you."

"If I have any misgivings for Carrador, I undertake to tell you." Sheldrake smiled. "Besides, that is likely to be the quickest way to circumvent any potential issues anyway." He paused and added, "My other offer still stands too. We are here if you need us. I can't do anything about the lonely years behind you but I… and Maud, and Sasha, and Jayhan, and even

Beth, Clive and Leon can be here for you now." He turned and began to fiddle with his map, moving a few pieces around, carefully not looking at Jon. "Then maybe your ruined lives can begin to heal. They will never be the same, even if Sasha regains the throne. And revenge will not repair the damage. But maybe our friendship can help to make them… better."

He heard a sniff and looked up to see Jon standing in the middle of the room with tears trickling down his cheeks. When he met Sheldrake's eyes, he used the palms of his hands to wipe the tears. "Aaah. Now look at me. More than anything, kindness undoes me." He tried to smile, but the tears kept coming. "Blast!" He put his hand over his face and his shoulders shook.

After a brief hesitation, the mage crossed to him and enveloped him in a bear hug. "Sorry about this," said Sheldrake gruffly, "But here is some more kindness. I think Maud would be ordering tea about now." He was rewarded with a watery chuckle amongst the sobs but didn't say anything more for quite some time.

As soon as he felt able to let go of Jon, Sheldrake clicked his fingers, a little flicker of magic that brought Rose knocking on the shed door. With a mischievous glance at Jon, he crossed to the door, opened it just enough to talk to Rose and order tea. When he returned, he was grinning hugely.

Jon chuckled between sniffs. "You two are incorrigible. I may end up drowning in tea!"

"That can only mean you will visit us often. Excellent." The tea arrived and after Sheldrake had poured it and they had spent some time sipping, he asked, "How are you feeling? Ready to face the little ones? And Yarrow?"

When Jon nodded, he removed the sign from his shed door with a wave of his hand. "They should be here in about five minutes, I estimate."

Sure enough, a few minutes later, the door burst open and Jayhan and Sasha tumbled in, eager for Jon to show them his shimmering they had heard about. Yarrow followed them more sedately.

Jon glanced at Sheldrake and Yarrow. "Do you mind if I do it, or will it distract you too much from your study?"

"All magic is our study," replied Sheldrake. "Go ahead."

When Yarrow also nodded her agreement, Jon's form began to waver, the waves in his appearance becoming faster and thinner until, in moments, he disappeared.

"Wow," breathed Jayhan, wide-eyed. "How do you do that?"

A chuckle sounded from where Jon had been standing. "I just think about the light bending past me instead of touching me. I did it slowly so you could watch it happen. It's an inherited ability, I'm told, just as your shape-shifting is."

Sasha stood with her arms crossed, frowning with concentration. "And like being a shaman."

"That's right," agreed Yarrow. "Of course, it is only women who are shamans, whose amulets are passed from mother to daughter down the generations, while it is only men from the royal line who shimmer."

"Why only men?" asked Sasha. "I share the same heritage as Jon."

"Just the way it is," said Yarrow, shrugging.

"Hmph," Sasha did not sound pleased. She walked a few steps and prodded at the last point she had seen him, her hand meeting resistance. "Jon?"

Her brother abruptly reappeared, laughing. "You're tickling me."

She beamed at him, her brown eyes shining. "Could you do that again, holding my hand please?"

"Of course. I can make anything I'm touching disappear too." He offered his hand for her to grasp and the air began to waver around him.

"Me too?" pleaded Jayhan.

Jon grinned and as he took Jayhan's hand, he and the two children instantly shimmered out of sight.

"Wow!" exclaimed Jayhan from out of nowhere. "It's like standing behind a waterfall. Dad, you should have a go."

"I would like to, of course," Sheldrake sounded embarrassed. "But I wouldn't dream of imposing on Jon like that. He is not a funfair ride."

Abruptly the three reappeared. Jon was grinning hugely. "And would you like to try it too, Yarrow?" He didn't wait for her reply, simply letting of the children and grabbing Sheldrake and Yarrow by their arms. The light wavered around them for a few seconds, then they too gradually shimmered out of sight, a little more slowly than the time before. "I told you I like having fun," said Jon.

"Thank you," came Sheldrake's voice gruffly. "This is most interesting."

For a minute there was a silence then a faint sound of shuffling. Suddenly the three adults appeared behind the children and Jon tapped them on their shoulders, making them jump and squawk with surprise.

After a moment, Sheldrake frowned at Jon, whose face had paled. "Have you overdone it, young man?"

"Maybe." He gave Sheldrake a small private smile. "I was a bit wrung out when I started, you know." He shrugged. "But it was worth it. Each shimmering takes effort but staying shimmered does not, at least not to the same extent. Seems that three in a row was a bit much."

"Well, thank you," said Sheldrake warmly. "I really appreciate it. It is such a rare opportunity."

Jon gave a slight bow. "My pleasure."

Sasha snuck her hand into his and smiled up at him. Then she turned to Yarrow and Sheldrake. "So what will we show Jon?"

"Well Jon," asked Sheldrake, "what would be most useful for you to know about?"

The young man thought for a minute before saying quietly, "How to make something that will deaden the pain of wounds and stop them from festering."

The mood of levity that had accompanied the shimmering evaporated.

"A good choice, one which I think all four of us could provide you with. Yarrow, which formula would be easy yet effective, do you think?"

"Basil stops wounds from festering," Jayhan jumped in, eager to help Jon.

Sasha nodded. "And arnica and willow deaden pain."

"So does basil," added Sheldrake. "And it helps reduce swelling. Yarrow?"

"All good suggestions, to which I would add marjoram. Marjoram, like basil, reduces swelling but also speeds healing. In addition to pain relief, arnica reduces swelling and can stave off tiredness."

Jon was looking a little dazed as this barrage of suggestions hit him. "So…?"

Sheldrake smiled. "Definitely basil. And marjoram. Only problem with arnica is that it might keep someone awake when they might do better to sleep."

Yarrow shook her head. "No. It's the arnica leaves that give energy, the roots and flowers that reduce inflammation. So we just don't use the leaves."

"Good point. You can use comfrey on its own for broken bones but it doesn't need to be in the poultice we will give you for general wound treatment." Sheldrake moved to the shelves where he stored his dried herbs. "We have the ingredients here. We'll show you how to make up a poultice of basil, arnica and marjoram, for a start, and give you a jar of it to take away."

"Thanks." Jon smiled. "That will be great and I don't need to be a shaman to use it."

"No, you don't," agreed Yarrow. "A shaman could infuse the wound with healing power above and beyond the scope of this poultice, but this poultice will work quite well on its own."

They spent the next hour deciding on how much of each to include then using the mortar and pestle to crush the herbs into a fine powder. Next, Sasha poured this powder into a jar, leaving a small amount behind.

Indicating the remnants, Yarrow explained, "To treat a wound, you place the crushed herbs in a bowl and add a little water… Thank you Jayhan," she said, as the boy arrived with a small jug of water, "just enough to make it into a paste. Sasha, would you like to show Jon?"

Sasha poured the small quantity of crushed herbs into a bowl and added just a few drops of water. After a bit of stirring, she gingerly added a few more drops of water until a ball of green paste lay in the bottom of the bowl. She looked up at Jon and smiled.

"Your turn, Jayhan," said Yarrow.

Jayhan beamed at Jon before spreading a thin piece of cheesecloth on the bench next to the bowl. Then he tipped the paste onto on half and spread it out until it was about as thick as his little finger. He folded the cheesecloth over and held it up. "Look! This is what you put on the wound. Easy hey?"

Jon nodded. "Once you know how. Well done, you two."

"We'll give you a jar of the crushed dried herbs," said Sheldrake, "and you can add the water to make a poultice when you need it."

A thought occurred to Sasha. "Yarrow, can you infuse these herbs with shaman power to make them work better?"

"Yes, we can. It won't work as well as one of us working directly with the injured person, but it will make a difference." She drew out her amulet.

Jon raised his eyebrows. "That's moonstone, not obsidian like Sasha's."

"And look, Jon," said Sasha, holding out her wrist. "It beats in time with my heart. Amazing, isn't it?"

Jon took her wrist and after a minute, nodded. "Yes. That is amazing." While Yarrow drew her amulet across the mouth of the jar of herbs and muttered a few indistinct phrases, he continued to hold Sasha's wrist, feeling her heart beating in time with the pulsing light from Yarrow's amulet. When Yarrow had finished, he said thoughtfully, "I wonder whether Lady Electra's amulet beats to the rhythm of Sasha's heart, now that her power has been... harnessed?"

Yarrow's eyes narrowed. "Interesting question. I don't know the answer to that, since registered and free shaman naturally don't mix. After all, the registered ones would be bound to report the free ones, wouldn't they?"

"And what would happen," Jon mused, "if a registered shaman came within... I don't know... ten, twenty, one hundred yards of the true monarch's black amulet? Would she sense Sasha's presence?"

Yarrow thought back. "No, I don't think so. I can sense when someone is a shaman but it is a very rare gift. And even I could not tell that the black amulet was in the room until I was shown it. And I was quite close to Sasha by then, only a few feet away."

"And how close were you when your amulet began to pulse like that?"

Yarrow eyes shone with an almost religious fervour. "It always pulses, no matter where I am." She smiled at Sasha in a way that made her squirm inside, although she tried hard to hide it. "That is how I knew, all these years, that our true queen was still alive."

"I see." Jon frowned. "I didn't realise that. Hmm." He fell silent for several minutes, thinking hard.

Jayhan, growing bored, wandered off in search of a ball he had lost last time he had been in there. He spotted amongst it some cobwebs deep under the bench that held the model of Carrador. But as he ducked under the edge of the bench, he knocked a hanging bunch of herbs off its hook and in his momentary fright, reared up, banging his head on the bench. Almost in the same movement, as he turned his head to retreat, he ripped his forehead open on the head of a large nail that had been driven into the underside of the bench.

Jayhan yowled with pain and collapsed onto the floor crying and clutching his forehead. As Sheldrake and Sasha rushed to him, they were alarmed to see blood welling between his fingers.

"Oh Jayhan, what have you done to yourself?" exclaimed Sheldrake, as he sat on the ground, oblivious to the dust, and scooped his son into his arms.

Sasha paled and turned to Yarrow in a panic. "What do we do?"

"We staunch the bleeding, see if it needs stitches and worry about a poultice later." Yarrow grabbed a clean piece of cheese cloth, folded it quickly into a wad and handed it to Sasha. "Here. Hold this firmly on his wound."

For a moment, Sasha looked horrified.

"Do you want me to do it?" asked Yarrow, not unkindly but firmly, more concerned with a quick response than pandering to Sasha's uncertainty.

The girl took a quick breath and shook her head. "No. I'll do it," she said resolutely. Sasha squatted in front of Jayhan. "It's all right Jayhan. Move your hand away and I'll put this on it instead. Okay?"

Jayhan gave a little nod, even though he was still crying, and did as she asked. His whole forehead on one side was a bloody mess. Sasha stifled a dismayed gasp and pressed the wad of cheesecloth onto the area with the most blood. Her stomach felt queasy and she hoped desperately that she wouldn't make matters worse by vomiting.

She felt a hand squeeze her shoulder and looked up to see Jon. Then he leaned past her to wrap a towel around Jayhan's bloodied hand.

"So the blood doesn't go everywhere," he explained briefly, before retreating to the other side of the room.

As Sasha watched, blood seeped into the cloth she was holding, gradually dying it red. Just as she turned in panic, opening her mouth to speak, Yarrow was there, holding out another wad. "Here. Just keep holding it there until the bleeding slows. It will soon, I promise you."

"You see, Jayhan," crooned Sheldrake. "It will be all better soon."

"But it hurts," said Jayhan fractiously, wriggling to sit up straighter.

"Stay still. Of course it does, but it will be better soon." His father moved to ease the weight on his arm. "But you know, I think it may even need a bandage."

"Oh." Jayhan sank back and said, his defences down from the pain, "That's good."

Sheldrake met Sasha's eyes, and despite the gravity of the situation, smiled.

True to Yarrow's prediction, the bleeding did slow and the next wad of cloth did not turn red. Yarrow brought over a basin of warm water and bathed Jayhan's forehead with a clean flannel, revealing a two-inch jagged gash.

Sasha looked on in amazement. "That doesn't look too bad. I thought…" She shook her head, realizing she didn't want Jayhan to know that she'd been scared he might die.

Yarrow smile sympathetically. "That's head wounds for you. They bleed like stink, whether they're severe or superficial." She dabbed Jayhan's forehead. "Doesn't even need stitches." Seeing Jayhan frown, she added hastily, "But it will need a poultice and a bandage, wouldn't you say, Sasha?"

Jayhan, who had his eyes closed, missed the little smile that passed between them.

"Well," said Jon, advancing with the poultice in his hand, "I happen to have something we prepared earlier…"

"Lovely." Yarrow took it from him and placed it over the wound. "Now, Sasha, hold that in place and imagine drawing power from your amulet up your arm, through your hand into the poultice and from there into Jayhan's forehead."

Sasha nodded and concentrated. After a minute Jayhan reported, "It's gone all tingly."

Yarrow nodded her approval. "Good."

He disengaged his hand from the towel Jon had wrapped it in and raised it to place it over Sasha's. "Youch! The tingling just got much worse."

"Perhaps you're pressing too hard," suggested Yarrow.

Jayhan eased the weight off his hand but didn't take it away. After a moment, he shook his head. "Still the same. A bit too tingly."

"Take your hand away completely, Jayhan," ordered Yarrow.

As soon as he removed his hand, the tingling eased. "Huh." After a moment, he replaced his hand on Sasha's. "Yow. Too tingly again."

Sasha was too busy concentrating to think about what was happening, but Sheldrake and Yarrow looked at each other, frowning.

"I think that may be enough, Sasha," said Yarrow. "Remove the poultice, if you please, and we'll have a look."

When Jayhan's forehead was revealed, all that remained of his wound was a neat pink scar.

Sheldrake raised his eyebrows. "Oh dear, Jayhan. I don't think you'll be needing that bandage." He turned to Yarrow. "So what just happened here? Are Sasha's healing powers so powerful? It seemed to me that Jayhan himself played some part in this."

"I agree." Yarrow turned to Jon. "What do you think?"

Jon was about to shrug, when he thought back to his shimmering. Instead he frowned. "Jayhan, do you feel up to trying a bit more shimmering?"

Jayhan felt his forehead, running his fingers over the scar. Reluctantly, he nodded. "I seem to be all better," he said morosely.

Sasha laughed. "That's good, you idiot. If you needed a bandage, you might have had to stay inside until your head healed."

The little boy brightened. "True." He stood up and looked at Jon. "So, what do you want me to do?"

"I'm going to try a little experiment. Sheldrake, can you time this?"

Without a word, Sheldrake drew out his pocket watch.

"First, Sasha." Jon took Sasha's hand. "Ready Sheldrake? Now!" For a few seconds, Jon and Sasha appeared to waver before shimmering out of sight. A minute later, they reappeared. "Okay. Now Jayhan." Sasha stepped back and Jayhan took her place. "Ready Sheldrake? Now!"

Instantly they were gone.

"There we are!" came Jon's voice triumphantly. "Jayhan amplifies other people's magic."

"I didn't even have time to press the knob on my watch the second time," confirmed Sheldrake. "Huh. That is an impressive attribute, Jayhan." The two reappeared, Jayhan pink with pleasure at his father's words. "Hmm. You will have to learn how to control it, though. Some magic would be dangerous if it were magnified. Hmm, yes, very dangerous."

"And who knows what would happen with Mum," said Jayhan cheerily. "She might turn into a wolf instead of a bloodhound."

"Exactly," replied Sheldrake repressively.

They discussed the wonders and possible drawbacks of Jayhan's gift for some time.

Jon had gradually withdrawn from the discussion, lost in his own thoughts. Suddenly he interrupted them by asking Yarrow, "Excuse me. So, you said all the unfettered shamans' amulets beat in time to Sasha's heart, didn't you? Then they must all know the true queen is still alive. Right?" When Yarrow nodded, he continued, "No wonder the resistance is so determined. The shamans *know* Queen Toriana is holding the throne illegally and they will have told their companions."

"Yes, but they didn't know at the start," Yarrow clarified. "When she ascended the throne, Toriana sent out a proclamation saying that she had recovered the amulet. According to her proclamation, a special ceremony had enabled her to wear it, even though her predecessor had not been able to pass it onto her." The shaman unconsciously looked at Sasha as she continued, "But the heart rate generated by the true amulet was high, over one hundred and twenty beats per minute, even when she was sleeping. At first, people thought Toriana's heart rate must be raised by the distress of losing her sister and family. She made good use of that time and swore many shamans to her, using an oath laced with power. But weeks went by and the pulse rate coming from the true amulet remained too high for an adult, sometimes as high as one hundred and sixty beats per minute for extended periods of time." Yarrow drew her gaze from Sasha and began to tidy up, starting by wiping out the mortar. "People began to talk. They watched Toriana. It soon became clear that her moods, exercise and sleeping were not in tune with the heartbeat changes in unsworn shamans' amulets."

Sasha recorked the jars of herbs and placed them back on the shelves. "So," she concluded for Yarrow, "they could tell she wasn't wearing my amulet."

"Aha," said Jon, waggling his forefinger as he put the pieces together. "So that's when the unrest started! Shamans began to refuse to swear allegiance to her and those who had, found they were restricted by her power in what they could say or do."

"And then the shaman hunts began," finished Yarrow sombrely.

Sheldrake glanced at Sasha. "No wonder the Queen, ahem, I mean Toriana, is so determined to find the true amulet and remove her opposition."

Jayhan disentangled himself from his father's arm and wandered over to Sasha. He put a friendly arm across her shoulders. "Don't worry, Sasha. We'll look after you."

"Huh!" she said, a surprised smile on her face. "You're getting quite huggy yourself."

He shrugged sheepishly. "I just figured I'd had a hug when I was upset and you're probably a bit worried and could do with one too." He smiled cheerily at her. "Anyway, I've just had this really good idea."

Sahsa immediately looked worried. "Uh oh."

"No really. It's a great idea, actually."

"Go on," Sasha said, her tone anything but encouraging.

"We should invite Lady Electra out here!" he declared with an air of triumph.

Four voices shouted, "What?" in unison.

Jayhan cringed but when nothing else happened, he gradually straightened and explained. "Well, you see, Yarrow said she couldn't detect Sasha's amulet. Right? So neither will Lady Electra. And if you want to know how Lady Electra's amulet acts, you ask to see it and then you can see whether it's beating in time with Sasha's heart. She doesn't have to see Sasha at all for us to test it out. We can be with Sasha watching through a window." He grinned at their stunned faces. "Mum can ask her out for afternoon tea or something."

Sheldrake was the first to recover. "Very ingenious, son. But do we really need to find out this information?"

Seeing Jayhan's face starting to fall, Jon intervened hastily. "I think so. If we are to have any hope of opposing Toriana, we need to find out how her power binds the registered shamans; whether it only affects the women themselves or their amulets, or both."

"Hmm," muttered Sheldrake, standing up and preparing to leave the shed, "Interesting. Let me think about it. We don't want to rush into anything that may endanger Sasha, now do we?" He patted her on the head as he passed. "I think we have done enough for today. Afternoon teatime," he said firmly.

Part 6

Chapter 36

Jayhan was beside himself with pride and excitement as he waited next to Leon for the first of the carriages to arrive. Jayhan, Leon and Sasha had spent all afternoon setting up lamps in sconces mounted on the gates, house walls and on poles that had been placed at regular intervals along the driveway. He was dressed in a smart frock coat and long pants, his hair brushed and not a speck of dirt on him. His strange pale eyes shone in the glow of the lamplights. Looking down at him, Leon couldn't help smiling, even though he was on edge himself, keeping his eye out for any sign of trouble.

Maud had baulked at simply inviting Lady Electra to dinner or afternoon tea, saying that it would seem too strange on so short an acquaintance to invite her home. Instead, she and Sheldrake had hit upon the notion of Sheldrake's fortieth birthday being the perfect excuse to invite a wide range of dignitaries and friends to a party. Left to his own devices, Sheldrake would not have chosen to celebrate his birthday so publicly, but he was happy to sacrifice his preference to provide a pretext for Lady Electra's visit.

As the coaches rolled in, they disgorged their patrons at the front steps before Leon, with Jayhan standing beside him, directed them to continue on past the house to where Jake and Thompson, the two farmhands, were waiting to show them where to park in the paddock behind the kitchen garden.

Under strict instructions from Beth, Sheldrake, Yarrow, Maud, Leon, Jon and even Jayhan, Sasha was relegated to the loft above the stables while people arrived. She was disconsolate at first, until she discovered a crack in the woodwork that allowed her to peer through to watch the parade of carriages as they passed the stables to the back paddock. Once they passed, she could catch a glimpse of the guests just before they entered the front door.

The days were drawing in and the evening was frosty. Both men and women wore cloaks against the cold. The men's cloaks were mainly black or brown, but the women's cloaks were chosen to set off the colour of the gowns they wore underneath, which in turn were chosen to set off their hair colour and complexion. Sasha had never seen such richly coloured, sumptuous materials. She was dazzled by the clothes, the hairstyles and the jewellery and wished fervently that she could be closer to see them better. She grimaced as she imagined Rose telling her smugly tomorrow what she had missed.

At last, Sasha spotted Jon, resplendent in the deep blue and pale orange of the Kakorian colours, standing at the back of a carriage as it pulled up in front of the house. Even before the carriage had halted, Jon had sprung down, ready to open the carriage door and assist

Lady Electra to alight. Unexpectedly, Sasha felt a surge of resentment that he should have to wait on someone, who, by rights, should be serving him.

Electra did not appear to even notice Jon - she certainly did not acknowledge him - but took a moment to glance around her surroundings, a slight frown on her face. As her eyes swept past Sasha's hiding place, Sasha felt a jolt and her amulet warmed against the chest. Sasha saw Electra's frown deepen as she looked away. The ambassador gave her head a little shake and trod the path to the front door while Jon was left to close the carriage door and remove himself to the kitchen where food would be provided for the waiting servants. Not once did he look up towards Sasha or betray in any way that he knew the layout of Sheldrake and Maud's property.

Once inside, Electra took a moment to adjust to the glare of a shining dome that hung from the ceiling in the hallway. As she squinted against the light, Clive took her cloak from around her shoulders and directed her to Maud and Sheldrake who were waiting to receive her at the foot of the stairs.

She arrived in time to hear Maud saying. "Oh dear, Sheldrake. I told you that your light orb would be too bright. Look! Poor Electra is nearly blinded by it."

Electra, whose eyes were quickly adjusting, waved her hand. "Not at all. It is merely the contrast with outside." She blinked a couple of times, trying to shake off a slight headache, and looked up at the sphere of pure light that Sheldrake had created for the evening. "It is rather wonderful, really. Do you have one in every room?"

Sheldrake gave a little bow. "Thank you. I am pleased with it. But no, it is something in the way of an experiment, so other rooms are lit with candles or lanterns, some of which can be redeployed here if my orb fails." He took her gloved hand and kissed it. "I am pleased that you could join us for the celebrations."

"As too am I," added Maud. "I had wondered whether anyone would bother to come all this way north from Highkington."

Electra raised her eyebrows, but her brown eyes twinkled. "Really, Lady Maud? But surely you are aware that an invitation to your country retreat is the height of social achievement?"

Sheldrake gave a crack of laughter. "Touché, my dear," he said to Maud. "You really say the most absurd things sometimes." He turned back to the ambassador, smiling. "Lady Electra, you're absolutely right. So, congratulations on reaching such dizzying heights."

Electra grinned and dropped a small ironic curtsy. "Thank you."

As she resumed her full height, a small frown line appeared between her eyes which vanished when she saw a short, thick-set, middle-aged gentleman walking with military stiffness from the front door to join them.

"Ah. Colonel... I mean Lord Argyve, how lovely to see you," gushed Maud. "You retired from the military some time ago, didn't you? Are you acquainted with Lady Electra, ambassador for Kimora?" She turned to Electra. "This is Lord Argyve, the Esukorian ambassador."

Electra curtseyed again as Argyve performed a neat bow and smiled at her, before turning to Maud, "Actually, Lady Maud, Electra and I have met on several formal occasions in the capital. Always a pleasure."

"Just Sheldrake and Maud will do here." Maud quirked an eyebrow at Electra. "Well, perhaps you can have a more relaxed chat at our little gathering this evening." She was amused to see Electra frown repressively at her while the colour in her cheeks heightened. Maud smiled mischievously and added, "Argyve, would you mind accompanying Electra through to the ballroom for refreshments? We will join you shortly, once all the guests have arrived."

"Of course. I would be delighted." Argyve proffered his arm, which Electra accepted with a tight smile. As they walked off towards the rear of the house, Maud heard him ask, "Are you all right, my dear?"

Just before they moved out of earshot, she heard Electra reply, "I think so. I just feel a little strange, head-achy. Nothing to worry about. I'm sure it will pass when I've had something to drink."

Maud gave Sheldrake a significant look. "Interesting, don't you think?"

"What? That he called her 'my dear' or that she has a headache?"

"Both." Maud leaned in towards Sheldrake so that they couldn't be overheard. "What do you think of her?"

"She is charming and intelligent. I like her. I hope she doesn't make things too difficult for us if she becomes aware of Sasha's presence, or reacts badly to her amulet."

Maud's face scrunched up with concern. "Oh dear. I hope so too. This is all very fraught, isn't it?"

Sheldrake's face softened. "A little, but we will do our best to bring them all through unscathed."

They had no time to say more as the arrival of new guests kept them busy for the next half hour, meeting and greeting. Once everyone had arrived, Maud and Sheldrake joined them in the ballroom at the rear of the house. A string quartet was playing in the corner, but it was no part of Sheldrake's plan for people to dance. It was a party, not a ball.

Large glass double doors led out onto a terrace at the rear of the house, where braziers had been set up to ward off the cold. Steps led down to a lawn that wandered up to a wire fence. Through it, sheep and couple of horses could be vaguely seen through the gloom, grazing in the home paddock. Already, many people had taken food and drinks outside to sit at the tables near the braziers. Sheldrake and Maud separated and chatted their way from group to group until the clock chimed nine o'clock. Then, with masterful choreography, they casually converged on Electra, who was still, they were pleased to note, in the vicinity of Lord Argyve.

"Hello you two," said Maud cheerily. "And hello Sheldrake. I haven't spoken to any of you all evening. Finally, I have managed to make it round to talk to you. I see you two have been catching up. Lovely."

Argyve frowned and gave a nervous cough. "Ahem. Just so. Electra and I have had trade agreements to discuss."

"Of course you have," said Maud spuriously.

"I hear, Argyve," said Sheldrake, cutting across his wife's teasing. "that you have acquired a high-stepping pair of bays. Did you bring them tonight?"

The ex-colonel gave a wry smile. "No. To be honest, they are a bit showy for a long journey. They impress around town, but they are so busy stepping high they don't seem to step along enough to have stamina over longer distances. I don't think I will keep them."

"Is that right? What a shame." Anyone who knew Sheldrake well would know this was not news to him. "So, are you looking for replacements?"

"Possibly. I am in no hurry, but if a good pair came up," Argyve shrugged, "I might be interested."

"Do they have to be bays or would chestnuts do?" asked Sheldrake. "I have a fine pair of chestnut geldings that I am planning to part with. We bred and trained them ourselves." He smiled. "When I say we, I mean our head groom, Beth. She is an outstanding trainer."

"I would certainly like to see them," responded Argyve. "At your convenience, of course."

Sheldrake glanced around to check that everyone seemed happily engaged in conversation and well attended. "Perhaps we could take a quick stroll to the stables now?"

He looked enquiringly at Maud who said, "We can have a nice cosy chat while the men are gone." Suddenly she frowned and murmuring an apology, raced across the room to where the servants were preparing drinks to hand around.

"Ahem, perhaps not this evening, after all, Agyve" said Sheldrake ruefully. "It would be churlish of us to abandon Electra... as my wife has just done."

Electra smiled cheerily. "Don't worry. I am not offended. I am surprised you have lasted this far into the evening without any hiccoughs. If I may, I would be delighted to accompany you both to the stables. I would love to see your horses. I have a horse stud back home in Kimora, you know."

"Do you indeed? Now why didn't I know that? I must be slipping."

"And," continued Electra, "would you mind if I sent for my footman to meet us there? He has an affinity with horses I have rarely seen."

"Why is he not your head groom then?" asked Argyve.

Electra shook her head regretfully. "I could not replace old Morgan, who has been my family's head groom and coachman since I was a small child. Besides, Jon is tall, athletic and good-looking which, as you must know, are very desirable qualities for a footman who is to be seen up behind one on one's carriage or serving in the dining room and salon. Jon helps with the horses when he has time between his other duties."

"Ah yes, I recall him now," said Argyve, "He is indeed a credit to your turnout. He must be a busy lad then." His mouth turned down, but his eyes twinkled as he said mournfully, "Alas, my Frederick is not even six feet and he's getting a little dumpy. Still, like servant, like master. I am no longshanks myself."

Sheldrake and Electra laughed.

"You are absurd, sir," said Electra. "Shall we stop this nonsense and go for a quick look at your horses?"

"Certainly. I'll send for your footman as we pass the passage to the kitchen." Sheldrake gestured to his right. "Let us go past the stairs and out the front door. The stables are just across the yard from there. Since everyone else is at the back of the house, we won't be commented upon or waylaid."

As they approached the front of the house, Argyve noticed a small furrow reappear in Electra's brow. He didn't comment but gave her arm a slight squeeze.

Chapter 37

It had been a long evening for Sasha, stuck up in the loft. Once everyone had arrived, Jayhan had joined her while Leon had remained downstairs to keep watch. They talked excitedly about the dresses, horses and carriages they had seen.

"Did you see Jon?" Jayhan's pale eyes almost glowed in the gloom. The only light came through the crack in the wood. "He gets to stand up while they're going along. How much fun would that be?" His face fell. "Dad would never let me do that."

"I bet it's cold." When Jayhan shrugged, she added, "And what if it's raining or snowing or really windy? That wouldn't be much fun."

Jayhan glanced at her and conceded defeat. "No, I suppose not. And it'll be freezing by the time they leave tonight." He brightened. "Still it would be great on a sunny day."

A while later, Leon called up, "Jayhan, come down. Hannah has sent you over some party food."

With a quiet whoop. Jayhan almost threw himself down the ladder and landed in front of Leon before he could draw another breath. Leon shook his head, smiling as he handed Jayhan a bulging cloth bag.

"Thanks." The boy's eyes strayed to another cloth bag sitting on the floor beside the door. "What about that one? What's in that?"

"Get away with you," growled Leon with mock ferocity, turning Jayhan by the shoulder and giving him a light tap on the bum to send him back up the ladder. "That's my little bundle of treats."

Jayhan grinned and scuttled back up with his booty.

They ate their way through salmon patties, tiny meatballs, little fruit tarts and an assortment of beautifully decorated tiny cakes, holding each item up to the sliver of light to work out what it was and admire it before eating it.

After their feast, time dragged. They played a few word games, but they couldn't see well enough to play board games or read. Despite entreaties, Leon refused to let them take a light up into the loft in case it attracted attention.

Finally, they heard Leon call softly, "They're on their way."

They peered through the crack to see Sheldrake accompanying a lady in a deep apricot gown, a warm but ornate cloak of velvet green thrown over the top.

"Wow!" whispered Sasha. "She's beautiful. What wonderful colours she's wearing."

"Same colour as you, under all that," observed Jayhan prosaically.

"Well, I think *she's* beautiful too, not just her clothing."

"Yeah. Of course. So are you."

Sasha blinked and looked at him. He just gave a little smile and shrugged.

"Who's that bloke with her?" he asked, completely unfazed by the compliment he had just given her.

"I don't know. Quick. Ask Leon before they get here."

Jayhan shuffled through the straw to the top of the ladder and called down sotto voce, "Leon. Who's that? How does he fit in?"

Leon turned an agitated face upwards and waved frantically with his hand. "Get out of sight."

Jayhan grinned. "I will. I promise. Who is it?"

"I don't know. Well I do. It's some bloke called Argyve who's a friend of Lady Electra. But I have no idea why you father decided to include him except as a pretext for getting the lady over here. He just got it into his head that we needed him." He glanced towards the doorway. "Now shush. Go away."

By the time they were halfway across from the house, Electra was leaning more heavily on Argyve's arm. Jon joined them from the direction of the kitchen and his appearance forestalled Argyve's query of concern. Jon simply nodded at Argyve and fell in behind them without a word, his tall willowy physique contrasting noticeably with Argyve's shorter muscular frame.

As they stepped into the lantern-lit stables, the horses moved restlessly in their stalls as they became aware of Jon amongst them. But he had no attention to spare for them as Electra clasped her hand to her chest, feeling for her amulet. Her breathing was becoming constricted and her movements stiff and uncoordinated. A patina of sweat had broken out on her forehead.

As she passed directly beneath Sasha, a pale blue light pulsed once from beneath Electra's fingers. She saw Argyve step back in surprise.

"What on earth is that?" he demanded. "Are you all right?"

Electra pressed her hand more tightly to her chest. "It is my amulet. I'm not sure what it is doing. Perhaps that is why I'm feeling so..." She glanced down, as the light from her amulet began to pulse erratically, shining right through the bodice of her dress and through her hand. "Oh, look at it! What's happening to me? To it? It should be pulsing in time with the Queen's heart. Maybe she's sick."

She leant heavily against Argyve who held her up as her knees threatened to give way.

"Don't worry, my dear. I have you," he said bracingly. "Perhaps you should give me that amulet until it settles down."

"No," chorused Electra and Jon.

Argyve threw a repressive frown at Jon but addressed himself to his host. "What do you think, Sheldrake? You know about these things. Is it dangerous?"

Before he could answer, a strong firm rhythm began to super-impose itself over the amulet's erratic pulsing.

Electra looked around wildly. "Someone is taking over its rhythm." She stared in horror. "No. It can't be. They all died... My oath..."

Up in the loft, Jayhan whispered fiercely, "That's it. Focus…hard. Breath slow. Think about your heartbeat."

Sasha grasped her amulet in her hand and sent her heartbeat through her obsidian amulet down towards Electra. Suddenly, a vast stream of power sheared through the wooden floor of the loft, leaving a cut a foot long, before spearing down towards Electra. As the black stream coursed into her, Electra's whole body began to glow within a dark transparent cloud. Argyve was clearly unnerved but held onto her stoically. The glow built until, with a low whoomph, it detonated. A blinding flash of light completely obscured Electra. When the light subsided, her limp body was being held up only by Argyve's arms, the amulet's light beating with a strong steady rhythm that could be seen through the material of her gown.

"What on earth is going on?" demanded Argyve, as he laid her on the ground. "Get me something for a pillow," he ordered, his military background re-asserting itself in a crisis. "Find a healer."

Jon rushed into the office and returned with a cushion from Beth's chair, which he placed under her head.

Argyve frowned furiously as his eyes swept around Sheldrake, Jon, Leon and Beth, who had followed Jon out of her office. "What is happening here?" he demanded. "What have you done to her?"

Beth came over to kneel beside him and took Electra's limp wrist in her hand. "I am a healer of sorts although more used to horses than people." She gave Argyve a calming smile. "Her pulse is steady and strong. Jon, dampen a towel and bring it here."

Sheldrake squatted down in front of Argyve, so they were face to face. "I think we owe you an explanation."

Argyve glared at him. "If you have hurt her, an ambassador of Kimora, you will have not only Kimora, but also Eskuzor, to answer to."

"I hope she is not hurt. I think, in actual fact, her mind may be clearer than before. I can't be sure until she wakens, but I believe the magical constraints placed on her by her Queen have been broken."

As Argyve continued to glower at him, Sheldrake went on to explain Queen Toriana's deception of her people. While he was talking, Jon arrived with a damp towel which he placed on Electra's forehead. As yet, she was showing no sign of rousing.

"Hmph," Argyve grumbled. "These bloody royals. For every good one, there's a bad one. At least in Eskuzor, we now have a stable, moral monarchy, but the previous one was a nightmare. Your King Gavin seems pretty good too," he added hastily, suddenly remembering he was an ambassador to their court.

Sheldrake grinned. "Yes, we are fortunate in our monarchies, your country and mine. But Kimora is not."

Electra murmured something but by the time they had focused on her she was quiet again.

"Did you hear what she said?" asked Argyve.

Sheldrake shook his head.

Argyve heaved a sigh of frustration before asking, "So why are you involving yourself in another country's affairs… so blatantly, I mean? And why involve me?"

Instead of answering, Sheldrake stood and walked to the bottom of the ladder. "Come down, you two." He glanced at Argyve with a slight smile before adding, "I have a very kind, wise man I would like you to meet."

In moments the two children had scampered down the ladder and stood neatly at the bottom, hands behind their backs. Covering his surprise at their unusually exemplary behaviour, Sheldrake introduced them, "Children, this is Lord Argyve, previously a colonel in the Eskuzorian army and now their ambassador. This is my son, Jayhan, and this," he concluded with a flourish, "is my stable boy, Sasha, who turned out to be a stable girl, who then turned out to be the rightful Queen of Kimora."

"Good heavens!" Argyve looked thunderstruck but took only a moment to adjust. He rose to his feet and performed a neat bow. "How do you do, ma'am? And young sir." If he had any reaction to Jayhan's eyes, he did not betray it.

Sasha glanced uncertainly at Jayhan before bowing in return. "Pleased to meet you, sir."

Jayhan also bowed. "How do you do?" More used to civil greetings, he promptly looked past Argyve at Electra, lying on the floor, his brow crinkled anxiously. "Is she all right, Beth? She's not going to arrest Sasha, is she?"

Beth shook her head. "I can't answer either of the questions for certain."

"She has no jurisdiction to arrest Sasha within Carrador," said Sheldrake firmly, "and we will continue to keep Sasha safe from their agents who are seeking unregistered shamans."

As he spoke, Sasha slipped past Argyve and knelt beside Electra. She gently drew out Electra's pale amulet and held it in the palm of her hand.

"Birth. Life. Death… Always," she murmured slowly, then placed the amulet back on Electra's chest. Jayhan wondered whether she had learnt those words from Yarrow or just absorbed what to do from the amulet.

Electra's eyelids fluttered. Then she heaved a deep breath and opened her eyes. As she saw Sasha leaning over her, her eyes widened further. "You… You're… Who are you?" She closed her eyes again as confusion overwhelmed her.

Sasha gently stroked her hair. "I am Sasharia."

Electra's eyes shot open again.

"And," Sasha took a little breath for courage, "your liege."

Electra sat up so quickly she nearly head-butted Sasha, who pulled out of the way just in time but remained kneeling beside her. Electra grabbed for her own amulet and held it, feeling its pulsing.

"Give me your wrist," she demanded of Sasha, "And show me your amulet."

Sasha frowned, then looked at Sheldrake for guidance.

"Not the way to speak to your liege, I wouldn't think," murmured Sheldrake quietly.

"Please," snapped Electra.

Sheldrake nodded, so Sasha held out her wrist.

Electra felt Sasha's heartbeat as she watched her own amulet beat time with it. After a minute she shook her head and gazed up at Sasha, before saying more gently, "And your amulet? Please, may I see it?"

Slowly, Sasha withdrew her amulet. Electra's eyes widened at the sight of the obsidian, so different from her own moonstone. As she watched it, the black amulet sent forth a pulse of dark light. Just as Yarrow's had, Electra's amulet shone in response with clear pale brilliance.

Tears spring to her eyes. "And am I right in saying that no one else can wear this?"

Sasha nodded.

"I tried," said Jayhan from the sidelines. "It hurt and wouldn't go over my head."

Electra waved a hand. "So how…?"

"Would you like a chair, ma'am?" asked Leon urbanely, placing one from Beth's office beside her.

"Thank you. I would."

Argyve was instantly at her side, assisting her to rise and deposit herself on the chair.

She smiled at him warmly and thanked him before returning her attention to Sasha, simply waiting expectantly for an answer to her half-asked question.

Sasha stood before her, wringing her hands, not at all sure how to proceed. "Before I tell you, or others do, could I ask what you intend to do about…?" she waved her hand to encompass herself and the others then shrugged, "Well actually, mostly about me, because I understand you are hunting unregistered shamans, and I, of course, am one. In fact," she added with a little grimace, "I think I may be the person the Queen is really looking for … and my amulet, of course."

A look of consternation passed over Electra's face. "Oh my stars! I didn't realize." Straightforward as ever, she said simply, "Give me a moment." She put her hands over her face for what seemed a long time to her onlookers but was probably only two or three minutes. When she emerged, she looked calm, clear and decisive. She looked around at them all, taking her time to assess them; Sasha, Sheldrake, Jayhan, Leon, Beth, Jon and Argyve. Finally, she asked, "And is my life forfeit if I give the wrong answer?"

"Certainly not," said Argyve. "They would have to get through me first."

"No," said Sheldrake calmly. "In fact, I included Argyve in the hope that he would give you independent support. We didn't know how your amulets would react, but we suspected it might be difficult for you… or Sasha." He shrugged, "If you remain determined to hunt down unregistered shamans, we will hide Sasha and inform our king of your renewed intentions. That is all."

"Hmm." Electra turned to Jon. "And are you part of this or an incidental bystander?"

Jon gave a little bow. "I work for the welfare of Kimora, as I always have."

"And that," said Electra tartly, "is no answer at all. But based on its ambiguity, I will assume you are part of this conspiracy."

Jon glanced at Sasha, who said, "You might as well tell her. She won't trust you any more after this anyway."

Electra raised her eyebrows haughtily at Jon. "Well?"

Jon grinned. "I am Sasharia's older brother."

Electra looked for one to the other and back again. "Oh my word!" she said, "I am sitting in the presence of two members of the royal family while they stand." Before anyone could react, she rose to her feet, Argyve's hands supporting her arms from behind. Once standing, she sank into a low curtsey. "Your pardon, Highnesses."

Jon laughed. "You've been doing it to me for years."

Electra rose, her face flushed partly with chagrin and partly with anger. "That is unfair. How could I have known?"

"That was not an admonishment. I merely find it funny. It is I who have chosen to endure it, not you."

"And are any other members of your family still alive?"

The laughter died in Jon's eyes. "No. All were killed. As the killers closed on my mother, she threw the amulet over Sasha's head, invoked the words of transfer and bade me escape with her to safety," he took a deep breath, "which I did."

Electra looked at him. "That breath speaks of months and years of lonely hardship. I am glad you survived it, Your Highness, and saved your sister. And I applaud your courage and ingenuity. How old were you?"

"Twelve."

Electra nodded. "It is no small thing for one so young to achieve such feats and to grow into manhood, alone and unacknowledged. I loved your mother. You have my sincerest thanks and admiration."

Jon's eyes shone with unshed tears which he tried to cover by bowing his appreciation. Sasha stepped over to him and put her arm across his bent shoulders before he straightened. He scooped her up and swung her into the air before settling her in his arms. She beamed up at him and he smiled back. "Hello, little one."

"Hello yourself, big brother. You have to tell me that story sometime, you know... when I'm older," she said in chorus with him saying, "When you're older."

They both laughed. Suddenly they realised everyone was waiting for them and Jon swung Sasha back down to land on her feet.

As though there had been no interruption, Electra said calmly, "I am now free of Toriana's compulsion and I consider myself free of my oath, since it was given under false pretences," said Electra. She went down on one knee. "So I hereby pledge my loyalty to you, Sasharia, and your brother, Jondarian."

Sasha smiled and drew her up. "Thank you. Thank you so much."

Electra smiled in return. "An unexpected pleasure, I assure you." She looked around the group. "So, where to from here?"

"I think," said Sheldrake, "that we have tarried here long enough. We are in the middle of a party after all, of which I am the host. Argyve, could you have a quick look at my chestnuts so that you can at least field any queries and then we had better return. Perhaps you would honour us with a visit in a week or so, Electra? Bring that rascally footman of yours, and perhaps you too would like to join us, Lord Argyle? Let Maud know convenient dates and she will arrange it." He smiled disarmingly. "Then we can give you a more complete story and work out our next steps."

"An excellent plan." Electra smiled and, in an effort to lighten the mood, added, "And just think. I will reach even more dizzying heights of social achievement with a private invitation."

Chapter 38

At the end of the evening, when her coach rolled up to the front door of Sheldrake's house, Jon jumped down as usual to open the door for her. She frowned at him but he merely bowed and handed her in.

"We will discuss this later," she said, obviously uncomfortable.

When they reached her house, he was there to open the door and hand her down.

"Thank you," she said, unlike when she had arrived at Sheldrake's party. "I would like to see you in my study as soon as the horses are settled."

"Certainly ma'am." He bowed, but she thought she caught a twinkle in his eyes.

Half an hour later, he presented himself at the study and knocked discreetly on the door. "Enter."

He did so, closed the door behind him and stood waiting, hands behind his back, as Electra rose from behind her enormous mahogany desk and walked round to stand in front of him.

Electra glanced around the room. "Is this room safe?"

"Nowhere has ever been safe, but with you on my side, this room is now safe."

"Oh Jon! I hope I have not treated you too badly. Please sit down," she said, indicating a straight-backed but padded chair.

Jon glanced at the door before crossing and turning the key quietly in the lock. He gave a lopsided smile as he sat down. "I can't afford to relax, if someone might walk in."

"True. Thoughtless of me. I am not very good at subterfuge. You will have to instruct me." She retreated to her chair behind her desk. She picked up a paperweight and fiddled pointlessly with it before raising her eyes to meet Jon's gaze. "Your Highness, I am most truly sorry if I have ever treated you unkindly. This is making me rethink how I treat all my staff."

Jon grinned. "That is no bad thing. I don't think you have ever been deliberately unkind, but you often take us for granted and at times do not consider our welfare. I remember I developed bronchitis two years ago, after standing behind your carriage on a long drive through a snowy evening. I doubt that you even noticed, except for the inconvenience of finding a replacement until I recovered."

Her face tightened as she remembered how annoyed she had been. She took a breath to apologize but he held up a hand to forestall her. "By the way, please do not use my title, even alone. If you start thinking of me like that, it will slip out at the wrong time. Call me Jon, as you always have." Realizing that Electra was looking stricken, he softened his tone and added, "Besides, you were my mother's friend and would have called me Jon in private anyway, had things not gone awry."

She nodded miserably and heaved in a breath. "Sorry," she whispered, and Jon realised she was trying to hold in tears.

In a moment, he was out of his chair and around the desk, holding her against him with his arm around her shoulders. "Ah, that was too harsh. I too am sorry. You were only fulfilling the role of a grande dame. I knew what I was letting myself in for." He stroked her shoulder, looking down at her. "You've had a hard day, haven't you? Your whole world has turned upside down. The last time that happened to me I lost my whole family except for my baby sister."

Something in her body's reaction alerted him. He squatted down next to her. "Is your family safe?"

Electra drew a shuddering breath. "Only as long as the Queen thinks I am true to her. She keeps shamans' families close."

"Hmm. How does your pledge of loyalty to my sister and me hold up against the safety of your family?"

She pulled away so she could look him in the face. "I knew that risk when I made my pledge."

"I see. Then I am even more honoured by your loyalty than I was before." He smiled at her. "We will not knowingly jeopardize your family. I have no immediate plans to change my current role. Sasha is too young still and we are not ready. And you will no doubt continue as Ambassador. I have watched you, as you know, and I think you are doing an excellent job."

Electra gave a watery smile. "Thank you."

Giving her a final pat on the shoulder, Jon stood up and walked back to his seat. "As long as the Queen remains unaware that your amulet is beating in time with Sasha's heart and not her own, you and your family should be safe. Is there any way she could tell?"

"I don't think so… as long as I follow her orders and don't deride her in front of people who report back to her." A look of distress crossed her face. "Oh dear! What about the hunters of unregistered shaman? I never liked that practice, but I like it even less now I know its real reason. I am supposed to facilitate their operations."

"You don't have to do this alone." Jon chuckled as he waved a hand. "I have been undermining their work for years. Now you will also have Sheldrake's services to misdirect them back into Kimora or elsewhere, plus King Gavin's intended ban, so the hunters will become the hunted."

Electra considered him for a moment. "I never knew you at all, did I? And what are we going to do about *us*?"

"What do you mean?"

"Well, how can I continue to treat you as a servant now that I know who you are?"

"Because by doing so, you will be serving Sasha and me and supporting the cause we all share. And if you don't, and the wrong people find out who I am, my life will be forfeit." Jon leaned forward, all humour gone. "Make no mistake. It may feel like play-acting, but it is incredibly serious. My life depends on it."

Electra was shaken by the intensity in his blue eyes. Suddenly she could see the determination that had brought him through ten lonely, dangerous years of exile. She took a deep breath and said, "You honour me with such trust. I will do everything in my power to justify it. And I will keep your warning in mind to wipe out any self-conscious smile that might threaten to emerge."

Then as quickly as it had come, his intensity lifted, and he smiled. "I must go. Already I will have to field questions about what you wanted with me. Perhaps we could say you wanted my opinion on the chestnuts we saw, in case Argyve does not choose to take them? They are excellent, by the way. I have seen them exercising and working with a light carriage."

"Their looks were certainly impressive." She rose from her seat and gave a nod of respect. "Goodnight Jon. My life, which was never dull, will now be even less so. I look forward to working with you."

"Goodnight, my lady." He gave a small bow, unlocked the door quietly and departed, leaving a very thoughtful ambassador staring at the last place she had seen him.

Chapter 39

All night long, Electra tossed and turned. Her mind, for so long fettered by the Queen's amulet and oath, now felt clear and free to roam. She looked back over past events, reviewing them in light of her knowledge of the Queen's duplicity and again in light of Jon's true identity. She wondered how many agents Jon and the Queen each had working within the embassy, at odds with each other. Did Jon know all of them on both sides? She hoped so.

She felt at sea. So much of what she thought she had known turned out to be false. She considered each of her staff in turn, wondering whose side they were on. Ostensibly they all supported the Queen without question, apparently unaware that Sasha and Jon lived. But she knew unrest was growing in Kimora, presumably fuelled by Jon or his network. Was Jon in charge of that network? How many people knew his true identity?

So many questions. So few answers.

She looked back over the events of the evening and felt embarrassed by the number of times she had shown weakness, shock or tears. She prided herself on her self-control and her ability to remain phlegmatic whatever the situation. This evening, that had all fallen apart. She wondered what Argyve must think of her. She couldn't help liking him. He was a few years older than she, not at all flamboyant as she was, not tall, not slim although muscular, almost stocky. But he was warm despite his military bearing, he was wise, down-to-earth, and completely unflappable in a crisis. And apparently, he had maintained his hold on her while all the world exploded into light.

She realized that Sheldrake had shown rare sense in including Argyve while they turned her view of Kimora upside down. Argyve was uninvolved with both Carrador's and Kimora's politics, independent of both Sasha and Sheldrake. Without him as a solid rock to cling to, she would have felt beset on all sides. But with his strength beside her, she had been able to gather her shattered view of the world into some semblance of order and decide where her loyalty lay without feeling coerced. She wondered whether he was quite so unbiased about Kimora's politics after hearing tonight of the Queen's perfidy. She would like him as an ally, she decided... After a moment, she added, at the very least.

The next morning, she arose full of decision. She needed a way to be able to talk to Jon regularly without arousing the suspicion of the other staff. During the night, the answer had come to her.

Her morning was full of appointments so her plan would have to wait.

All the time that her maid, Jensen, assisted her with choosing her gown and dressing her, Electra wondered whether she was a spy for the Queen or part of Jon's conspiracy or neither. All she could do was to try to act as she had always done.

"Are you well, my lady? You seem very quiet this morning."

Oh dear thought Electra. *This isn't going well already.* She managed a smile. "Quite well, thank you. Just tired after Lord Sheldrake's party last night." *And now I've just said thank you. Would I usually do that? I can't remember.*

Once she had dressed, she took a deep breath before emerging from her bedroom into the likelihood of encountering Jon. Sure enough, there he was, standing outside the dining room, dressed in the embassy's deep blue livery with its pale orange piping, looking straight ahead. Steeling herself, she walked past him without even glancing at him.

Once she was seated at the table, he appeared at her elbow with a fresh pot of tea. He filled her cup, placed the teapot on the table and stepped back. Taking another breath, she resisted the urge to thank him. "I will have the eggs, bacon and tomatoes this morning, I think."

More and more it was being driven home to her, how little she acknowledged or thanked her servants. She found it excruciating having to continue as she had, now that she had become aware of it. She cringed inwardly as she remembered Argyve saying how busy Jon must be, working with the horses on top of his other duties.

When he had placed her breakfast before her, she said, "Let Morgan know that I will want the carriage after lunch. I will require you to accompany me."

"Yes, my lady." Jon gave a slight bow and retreated to stand by the door until required further.

Electra ate her breakfast with no pleasure at all, knowing her prince was standing behind her. Each mouthful was an effort. Several times she came close to throwing down her napkin and sweeping out of the room, but she persevered. When she had finally finished, she chanced a quick glance at Jon on her way out of the dining room, but he looked rigidly straight ahead. She couldn't help feeling chastened but reminded herself it was all an act.

Finally, with her appointments and another excruciating meal under Jon's eyes out of the way, Electra made her way down the front steps of the embassy to where Jon was holding the door of her coach open for her. She gave directions to Morgan the coachman, then nodded at Jon as he handed her in and, giving her no response, took his place at the rear of the carriage.

Forty minutes later, they pulled up outside a large workshop with a swinging sign over the doorway proclaiming it as Conway and Sons, Coachbuilders. As Jon helped her to alight, she said with a mischievous smile, "Jon, I would like you and Morgan to assist me in buying a phaeton."

Jon raised his eyebrows, but merely bowed before walking to the coachman's seat to relay her request.

Morgan scowled as he tied the reins and climbed stiffly down. "I hope she don't think she'll be driving it on her own."

"Why? Not good enough? Surely you trained her to drive horses when she was younger."

"It's just not proper, a young lady gallivanting around on her own."

Jon laughed. "Not so young and probably not planning to gallivant."

Morgan sniffed. "Well, all I can say is, you'd better make sure she takes you with her. Some ladies drive phaetons completely unaccompanied, but I won't hold with that and so I will tell her."

"Morgan, she is more likely to listen to you. You have the advantage of long acquaintance."

This sop to his vanity mollified the old coachman and he entered the coachbuilder's premises with a more open mind.

Lady Electra was already strolling along a line of twelve carriages of various designs by the time that Morgan caught up with her, slightly out of breath. The first four were coaches, designed to be driven by a coachman with the patron seated inside. The fifth was a very perky high-perch phaeton with yellow wheels and only one seat. Electra stopped to look at it, astonished by the small size of its body compared with the size of its enormous wheels.

"My lady, I think something with a double seat and a footman's seat behind might be more suitable," Morgan said repressively. "Then you could take a companion if you chose to or perhaps put a parcel in it if you need to."

Electra looked at him, her eyes dancing, "Do you not approve of this one?" she asked. When Morgan frowned, she smiled and relented. "I think it ridiculous, myself. But I'm sure some young lady will think she is cutting a dash in it. Let us move on." Jon, she noticed, stood back, waiting to be consulted but not offering an opinion.

The seventh vehicle was a red-enamelled phaeton, with a double seat for the driver and passenger, a small seat behind for a groom or footman and a roof that could be folded back. In the style of phaetons, the wheels were large but not ridiculously so. Electra walked around it, admiring the woodwork and the colour of the enamelling.

She turned to Morgan and Jon, "I like it. What do you think?"

Morgan's shoulder relaxed noticeably. "Very good, ma'am."

Jon inspected the groom's seat and grinned at Electra. "Enough room behind the front seat for my long legs," earning himself a frown of disapproval from the old man.

"How many horses will I need, Morgan? These shafts seem designed for one and I would rather have two horse drawing it. What do you think?"

Morgan studied the ends of the shafts. "These are bolted to the body. I think the coachbuilder could easily change the front assembly to cater for two horses."

"Two horses would look smarter, Ma'am," said Jon, "They would last longer and draw your phaeton more quickly. More expensive, of course."

"True, but I might able to procure a matching pair such as those Sheldrake showed me last night."

Jon gave a slight smile. "Let us hope then, that Lord Argyve decides against them."

They were interrupted by the coachbuilder, who had dragged himself away from a work bench at the rear where he had been shaving a long piece of wood. He rubbed the sawdust off his hands on his big leather apron as he approached. "Good morning. I am Conway the Elder. Can I help you or would you like more time to look?"

Morgan explained Electra's wishes and began forceful negotiations with Conway, while Electra retired towards the front of the premises, with Jon trailing behind her.

"Does Morgan know about you?" asked Electra, once they were safely out of earshot.

"No. It would have created a conflict of interest for him. He is fiercely loyal to you but I suspect he would also be loyal to the true line which, while you were restricted by your link with the Queen, would have been in opposition to you."

Electra smiled. "I am glad you did not put him in that position, for his sake as well as yours."

A few minutes later, they saw Conway the Elder return to his work bench while Morgan stomped his way towards them.

"Can we tell him now?" asked Electra. "We can browse between these coaches."

Jon nodded. "From what I know of him, he deserves your trust… and mine. Just a minute, I will skirt behind the coaches just to check no one is working on them. Then I'll position myself where I can see the door, in case someone else arrives or Conway wanders up this way."

Morgan reached Electra, just as Jon disappeared behind the row of carriages. "All done, my lady. Fair price. Should be ready to pick up in two days' time." He frowned. "Where has that flibbertigibbet gone? He shouldn't be wandering off on his own. He's supposed to be attending you."

"Thank you, Morgan. Now come down this row," said Electra, ignoring his little diatribe. "I have something I want to show you." She led him a short way down the aisle between the second and third carriages before turning to him. "Actually, it is something I want to tell you. Just a minute." She put up her hand. "I'm waiting for Jon."

A soon as Jon appeared and took up his position at the front of the row, Electra began, "Morgan, you have always been faithful to me, my family and my wishes."

Suddenly Morgan seemed to deflate. "Ma'am. I know Jon's a natural with horses, but I have much more experience than him. I may be a bit stiff but I'm not too old to do my duties."

Electra looked shocked. Impulsively, she reached out and grasped Morgan's gnarled hands in hers. "No Morgan. I am not planning to dismiss you. Quite the contrary. I am planning to take you into my confidence."

Unconsciously, Morgan straightened. "I see," he said gruffly, sending a less than friendly glare at Jon, who had witnessed his moment of weakness.

"As I was saying, you have always been loyal to me so I think it only fair to inform you of my own change of loyalty so, hopefully, you can continue to support me." Letting go of his hands before it became awkward, Electra hesitated, working out how to broach the subject. "Morgan, I recently, yesterday actually, discovered that two members of the true royal line survived the attack on Princess Corinna's party."

Morgan eyebrows shot together. "But it was announced at the time that they all died. That's what gave Toriana the right to be Queen."

"Exactly, Morgan. As you can understand, this information has far-reaching implications."

"Indeed ma'am. But how do you know it's true? Could be rabble-rousers stirring up trouble."

"Because, Morgan, my amulet's link to the Queen, which has fettered my thoughts and actions for years, was broken yesterday evening by a ten-year-old girl wearing the one true amulet."

For a moment Morgan was thunderstruck. Then his eyes lit with excitement. "The true line is safe! And that scheming woman has no right to rule. I am pleased you are free of her, my lady. I didn't hold with keeping people in line with magic, even before I knew of the Queen's treachery."

"My amulet," she continued, "now beats in time with the rightful queen's heart." She smiled. "The girl's name, you may be able to recall from your knowledge of the royal family, is…"

"Sasharia." he finished for her. "If she is only ten, she must be Sasharia, the youngest princess." His whole face seemed to glow. "This is wonderful news."

"And she was brought out of the chaos of that attack by her twelve-year-old brother who carried a babe in arms across the vastness of Kimora into the safety of Carrador."

"Twelve years old?" Morgan frowned with the effort of remembering. "So now he's be twenty-two? That would have had to be the youngest prince, Prince Jondarian." He shook his head in admiration. "And he managed that at twelve, did he, a soft-bred lad like that? Amazing."

Electra smiled warmly. "Yes, wasn't it?"

At the end of the row, Jon crossed his arms, shifting uncomfortably. He glanced to his left and right. "My lady, we cannot linger too long."

Morgan frowned at him, "It is not up to you, Jon…" He trailed off and turned a look of enquiry at Electra who nodded.

"Yes, Morgan. Jon is Sasharia's older brother."

As he returned his attention to Jon, Morgan's face spread into a grin, an expression rarely seen on the old man's face. "You young scamp! Well done. And fancy that! Me working with a prince all this time. You're such a friendly, helpful sort of character, no one would ever know." Still smiling, he went down on one knee and bowed his head. "Your Highness. It has been a privilege working with you."

With a final glance left and right, Jon came forward, grasped the old man's hands to raise him to his feet and grinned back. "The privilege is all mine, Morgan. You have been a great teacher and mentor for me… and will continue to be, I hope."

"I would be honoured, Sire."

"Just Jon, if you please. We are not out of the woods yet. Queen Toriana would have a vested interest in my demise, should she learn of my continued existence."

"And even more so, your little sister. Is she safe?"

"Yes, I think so," Jon gave a self-deprecating smile. "She is certainly safer now than she has been at some points in her past."

"So you see, Morgan," cut in Electra, "why I need a phaeton. It gives me a safe place to talk to Jon."

"I do, my lady." The old groom chuckled and gave Jon a friendly slap on the shoulder. "And I can also see that I'll have to keep bossing this young one around, just as I always have." He pulled a face. "Shame I can't share the joke with my wife, but I'll be able to one day."

"Wouldn't she support us?" asked Jon.

Morgan gave another chuckle. "Oh yes, she'd support you, but don't tell her until you want it spread all over town."

"Oh, I see." Jon grinned.

Chapter 40

Two weeks after Sheldrake's party, Lady Electra drove out on a sunny afternoon to visit Batian House in her new phaeton, Jon seated behind her. As soon as the phaeton pulled up, Jayhan catapulted out of the front door almost cannoning into Jon, who was holding the door open for Electra to alight.

"Wow!" breathed Jayhan. "What a wonderful red. Can someone take me for a drive around in it? Look how high up it is."

Jon smiled down at him. "Hello rascal. Hop out of the way so her ladyship can alight."

Jayhan turned his face up to Electra who was laughing at his enthusiasm. "Lady Electra, can you take me for a drive before you get down…please?"

"Jayhan!" came a voice of displeasure from behind him.

"Uh oh" whispered Jayhan as he turned. "Yes, Dad?"

"You know what I'm going to say. Now move out of the way and let Electra get down. My word! You are cheeky sometimes."

"Maybe later, young man," said Electra kindly, as she was finally able to descend from her high perch.

Sheldrake nodded approvingly. "Very nice. I can see why Jayhan is so impressed."

Electra nodded, smiling, as she pulled off her gloves. "I'm glad you approve. Did Argyve buy your matched chestnuts?"

"He is still thinking about them. They would look very good between the shafts of your phaeton."

"Yes, wouldn't they?" Jon agreed. "Lady Electra is a skilled whipster so she could handle their spirit. In fact, I think she would enjoy them immensely."

"I'm sure Argyve enjoyed the spectacle of your arrival," said Maud mischievously. "I saw him watching through the parlour window."

"Oh."

"Now Electra," said Sheldrake, as he offered her an arm to lead her into the house, "I have someone I would like you to meet. She is, understandably, rather nervous about seeing you, but she has been of great assistance to Sasha."

"How intriguing."

Once Sheldrake, Maud, Jon and Electra had joined Argyve in the parlour and settled themselves, a knock came on the door.

"Come in," said Sheldrake.

Jayhan and Sasha poked their heads around the corner, then entered to stand either side of Yarrow as she entered. Although she was defiantly wearing her flamboyant clothes and jewellery, she looked, unusually for her, tense and awkward.

"This is Yarrow, my lady," said Jon. "She is worried about meeting you because she has been in hiding as an unregistered shaman for many years now. So she is taking a risk letting you know what she looks like."

Electra rose and walked over to clasp Yarrow's hands. "How do you do, Yarrow? If it is because of your knowledge that Sasha was able to overcome the enchantment that my amulet and I were under, then I thank you."

Yarrow breathed a quiet sigh of relief as she dropped a curtsey.

Sheldrake added, "She has also been teaching Sasha many other aspects of shamanism and about Kimora's history. We have all benefited from her efforts."

Once Yarrow had been guided to a seat and given a cup of tea, Electra asked, "Are there many unregistered shamans in Carrador and Kimora just waiting to rise up against the Queen?"

Yarrow eyes widened in alarm and she didn't answer.

"Don't worry, Yarrow," cut in Jon. "As soon as Lady Electra was freed from the amulet's fetters and realised what Toriana had done, she swore loyalty to Sasharia and me. I have worked for her for four years now and I trust her word." He took a sip of tea then set down his cup. "In answer to your question, the numbers are, of course, uncertain, but in Highkington alone there would be close to one hundred unregistered shamans and perhaps another three hundred spread throughout Carrador. Of course there are the shamans' families and other people who have escaped from persecution in Kimora. I would say that altogether, five thousand Kimoran refugees reside now in Carrador."

Sheldrake frowned. "That is a serious security matter for Carrador."

"Perhaps if we had eyes on taking over Carrador it might be, but all intention is aimed at protecting the people of Kimora." Jon looked puzzled. "But surely you must be aware of the influx of Kimorans into Carrador over the last few years?"

"I think" said Maud, "that we were not previously so clearly aware of the issue with shamans and current Queen. Hmm. In all conscience, I may have to chat to Gavin about it." Seeing the look of consternation on Jon's face, she added quickly, "But no names, I promise you."

Discussion turned to the events of the night of Sheldrake's party. Yarrow listened entranced as she heard how Sasha's amulet had affected Electra's.

"Well done, Sasha," she said at last, "Very well done." Yarrow turned to Electra, "How did you feel? It sounds gruelling. I am sorry you had to go through it."

Electra smiled. "Thank you for your concern. It was very disorienting, frightening; I had no idea what was happening." Her smile broadened. "But such a relief and a delight when I realised the cause."

"The process presents a few problems, though, doesn't it?" said Yarrow thoughtfully. "If your amulet affected a whole group of registered shamans, Sasha, you'd have all of them dropping like flies. Then you'd have to run around saying that phrase, 'Birth Life Death, Always,' to each of them to wake them up."

Sasha glanced at Sheldrake. "What do you think?"

"Why did you say it to Electra?" he asked in return.

Sasha shrugged. "It just came to me. I knew it would comfort her and bring her back more quickly."

"And would she have recovered without it?"

"Yes. But it would have been harder for her." Sasha frowned. "But we're not planning to try it on a big group of shamans, are we? Jon said I have to grow up first and that they, whoever they are, are not ready yet."

"True," said Yarrow. "I suppose I'm just getting ahead of myself." She grimaced. "It's just sad for those people, like Electra, who have been constrained."

"Yes, it is," agreed Electra wholeheartedly. "You have no idea how much more clearly I am thinking now and how my spirits have lifted. It is a terrible thing to do to people. I didn't realise how bad, until I was free of it." Electra glanced at Yarrow then Jon. "Perhaps… What is your status with these refugee groups, Jon? Could you be instated as…" She turned to Yarrow. "Would he be accepted as regent until Sasha is older?"

"No one has any idea who Jon is," said Yarrow. "Sasha would have to be involved for them to accept who he is." She glanced at him but kept her eyes on Electra. "Saying that, he is a leader among them. He comes and goes between groups bringing them news of each other and nurturing a common purpose of looking after any who need help and working towards addressing the injustices within Kimora." She smiled at Jon. "You would make a fine regent."

"Absolutely not," exclaimed Jon. "I did not rescue Sasha all those years ago, just to usurp her." He ran his hand distractedly though his blond hair. "Besides, I will not have her placed in danger, just to verify my identity." He surged to his feet and began pacing. "And not only that, I don't want our people to end up in a bloody conflict with others of our people who are still in Kimora."

Argyve stood up and gripped the young man's shoulder as he strode by, bringing him to a standstill. "Now, Jon," he said quietly but with authority. "Listen to me. You have been carrying too much on your own for too long." He gestured around the room. "This room is full of powerful people. None of us is going to allow your sister to come to harm. Let's work out what you want, then how we can help you achieve it, and when."

Jon lifted his shoulders then dropped them, as he gave a huge sigh. Tears sprang to his eyes. "Thank you," he said thickly. He rubbed the heel of his right hand across his eyes. "Sorry." He felt a little hand in his left hand and looked down to see Sasha staring up at him solemnly.

"Jon, what is a regent? Do they want you to be king, instead of me being queen?"

He squatted down in front of her. "No, little one. Everyone here wants you to be queen… when you're old enough. A regent is someone who rules in the monarch's stead while they are still too young."

"And when I'm old enough, I would still become queen, even if there were a regent?"

Jon nodded. "The regent would step aside."

Sasha squeezed his hand. "Jon, if you could be a regent, we could help people sooner, couldn't we?"

"Yes, but you would have to become known to many people, which would place you in danger."

"She would only have to become known to a small representative group who could tell the others," suggested Maud. "This group would not even have to know where she resides."

"Having a regent would give our people more hope and more focus," pressed Electra. "You can't cajole them into opposing Toriana if there is no viable alternative. I agree with Sasha, if you accept the role of regent, we can begin sooner."

Jon squeezed Sasha's hand before standing up, a little dazed. "You were right, Argyve. There is a lot of power in this room." He looked down at his little sister. "Are you sure about this? It means handing over control until you are..." he frowned. "Hmm, Is it eighteen or sixteen? Electra, do you know?"

"Under Kimoran law, the regent shares the role when the monarch is between the ages of sixteen and eighteen. At eighteen, he or she relinquishes the role entirely, although he or she may stay on as advisor, of course."

Sasha beamed up at him. "Perfectly sure."

Jon shook his head. "Thank you for your confidence in me little one, although I fear you are too young to fully understand the ramifications of what you are agreeing to."

"She knows," said Jayhan, just as naïve as her. "Anyway, the room is full of people she trusts so she knows someone would tell her if they thought it was a bad idea." He grinned at Jon. "I think it's a great idea."

"And I think you must tell Sasha the story of her escape before she meets these representatives of yours," said Maud firmly. "They are bound to ask you and it would be better if she heard it in a place of safety first."

"Me too?" pleaded Jayhan.

Maud looked from one to the other of the children and gave a slight smile. "Yes. You too, but not now. We still have more to discuss."

"However, time for a break, I think," said Argyve decisively. "I need some fresh air," by which he meant the very unfresh air of his pipe.

Chapter 41

A stiff breeze sent the smaller branches of the eucalyptus trees waving, their slender leaves seeming to flow and sparkle in the evening sunshine. The wattle trees among them were heavy with soft yellow pompom flowers. Honeyeaters darted among them, squawking at each other. High in the eucalypts, three sulphur-crested cockatoos swooped in to land, then called raucously, flipping up their crests and stomping along the branches as they settled.

Argyve sat on a bench in a sheltered spot in Sheldrake's front garden, drawing contentedly on his old briar wood pipe, while he contemplated the marvellous fact that here in Carrador, one wattle tree or another would be in flower at every time in the year. He turned his head as a young boy trundled a wheelbarrow around the corner of the stables, propped it under the trees and began to gather the fallen twigs and small branches that littered the lawn.

Argyve watched him for a few minutes then said, "Hello. You're doing a good job there. Are you gathering kindling for the fire?"

The boy nearly jumped out of his skin, making him drop the bundle of sticks he was just about to put in the wheelbarrow. Then he grinned from beneath an unruly thatch of light brown hair, as he saw Argyve sitting there. "Sorry. I didn't see you there. Am I disturbing you? Should I come back later?"

"Certainly not. You are doing a fine job. It is I who would not wish to disturb you."

"Oh." The boy, dressed in good quality brown working shirt and leggings, stared at him with piercing aqua eyes for a moment while he thought about the merit of this point of view. Then he shrugged and went back to work.

Once the boy had filled his wheelbarrow, Argyve asked him "What is your name?"

"I'm Edgar, sir. I'm just new. Started yesterday. My sister is Rose."

Argyve had no idea who Rose was. "Rose, eh?"

"Yes, she works here as a maid.' Edgar smiled proudly and pointed to his chest. "And now I work here too. And I have new clothes and I already had two meals yesterday and two today. The food is great. I've never eaten so much in my life. I wish mum could be here too. She would love the food as well."

"And how old are you?"

"I've just turned eight."

Argyve thought back to when he was eight, scampering around his parents' country mansion; lessons in the morning, sword craft or riding in the afternoons. He hadn't raked up a leaf in his life and, being a lord, he had started in the army as an officer so had only ordered others to gather kindling, never gathered it himself.

Suddenly Edgar's widened in fear and Argyve looked around to see that Jayhan had just entered the garden from the house. Jayhan hesitated in the face of Edgar's expression and dropped his eyes as he walked over to Argyve.

Argyve looked from Edgar to Jayhan and back again. "Now what's all this then? What has Master Jayhan done to you?" He frowned severely at Jayhan. "I hope you have not been abusing your position, Master Jayhan."

Jayhan waved a hand in a denial but kept his head down. "My father has asked you into afternoon tea and promises that they have stopped talking about shamans and amulets and things."

As Jayhan turned to walk away, Argyve said, "Just a moment." He turned to Edgar. "Now don't be afraid, Edgar. Tell me what is wrong."

"No. Please don't, Lord Argyve," pleaded Jayhan. "Just let it be. He will get used to me." When Argyve looked confused, he huffed impatiently and added, "It's my eyes, sir. I haven't done anything to him. He's just scared of my eyes."

"What nonsense!" declared Argyve. "Come here, young man," he ordered Edgar.

For a minute Edgar looked like he might cut and run, but Argyve frowned ferociously at him until finally he edged closer, not daring to look at Jayhan. Once he was standing before him, Argyve said, "Well done. Now, I want you to look into Jayhan's eyes. Jayhan, raise your head and look at Edgar."

Jayhan shrugged a sorry and raised his eyes, his face tight in anticipation of Edgar's reaction. Edgar did, in fact, flinch back but then stopped himself from retreating further.

"I can't help having these eyes, you know," said Jayhan crossly. "I don't think they mean anything. My great grandmother had eyes like mine and she wasn't very popular. That's all. As far as I know. Since everyone was so scared of them, I even tried making my eyes move or push things, but nothing happened." He put his hands on his hips. "Anyway, why didn't Rose tell you I'm not scary?"

"She said, 'Don't worry. As long as you do your work well, you'll be safe.' "

"She what???" Jayhan's face suffused with anger, making Edgar cower. Seeing that he had inadvertently frightened the boy, Jayhan backed away, waving his hands placatingly. "Sorry. I'm not mad at you. You can do as bad a job as you like, and no one here will hurt you…" He gave a wry smile. "But you mightn't keep your job, I s'pose."

"I think," interposed Argyve calmly, "that your sister probably meant your *job* would be safe if you did a good job."

Both boys looked at him then Jayhan returned his attention to Edgar. "Do you think?"

Edgar shrugged. "I don't know. Maybe." He thought for a while and shrugged. "Maybe she thought I was just nervous about the job and didn't realise I was scared of you." Suddenly his serious little face was transformed by a smile. "Sorry. I won't be scared any more, I promise. It's the kids in the village, see? They told me all this stuff about you being a walking corpse. They said you could strike them dead just by looking at them." He shuddered. "They got me really worked up."

"You were very brave to come here to work, in that case," said Argyve gravely.

174

"Yes, you were."

"Had to," Edgar looked down and scuffed his boot along the ground. "Mum's not well and we have to look after the little ones." He looked up and grinned cheekily at Jayhan, "Anyway, except for you, I was looking forward to getting away from the house."

Suddenly a loud voice interrupted them. "Hoy Edgar, where the blazes have you gone? You should have finished long ago. I've been waiting to show you where to stack the kindling. Get your lazy arse over here." Leon strode around the corner into sight.

Jayhan smiled at him. "Hi Leon. Our fault. We're just meeting Edgar."

"Yes. Can't blame him. I ordered him over here. Little matter needed sorting out."

At these words, Leon frowned suspiciously at Edgar but Jayhan just shook his head and said briefly, "Eyes." Despite his best efforts to follow his father's admonishment to stand tall and meet people in the eye, his gaze dropped.

Leon ruffled Edgar's hair sympathetically. "Well, I'm glad we have that sorted then. Come along little fella. Bring that wheelbarrow you've filled and I'll show you where to put the twigs." He gave a nod of respect to Argyve before departing with Edgar trailing behind.

When they had gone, Argyve said, "Now look at me, young man. Let me study these eyes of yours." Taking a deep breath, Jayhan raised his face to find Argyve smiling encouragingly at him. "That's better. Hmm. When you look closely, your eyes are quite beautiful. The colour varies from white to lavender with small streaks of darker purple." He patted Jayhan on the shoulder. "You know, in my country, Eskuzor, there is a greater variety of eye colours. I haven't seen any like yours but the Prince Consort has bright purple eyes."

Jayhan grimaced. "I'm not sure that I want to be beautiful."

Argyve gave a crack of laughter. "Not all of you, young man. Just your eyes."

"And I definitely don't want to be scary."

"Well, Jayhan, No matter how big and scary an animal looks, it is only as frightening as its intention. Even a huge wolf is not frightening if it is sleeping in the sun, after a good meal. If people cannot look at you carefully enough to discern that your intention is to be kind and friendly, then that is their problem, not yours." His smile broadened. "Anyway, there are times in life when it is useful to appear frightening. If my soldiers were up to no good, my appearance in their midst would frighten them into better behaviour." He shrugged. "Though admittedly, it was my position rather than my appearance that frightened them. He grimaced self-deprecatingly. "I'm afraid I don't cut a very fearsome figure."

Jayhan chuckled then tilted his head as he looked the ex-colonel over. "I think you come across as strong and kind and solid as a rock," He coloured. "Whoops! I don't mean solid as in fat. I mean unmoving like a rock to cling to in the middle of a flood."

Argyve turned down the corners of his mouth. "That doesn't sound very dashing."

"That," said Jayhan with a flourish, pleased with himself for using the older man's own phrase. "is because of your intention. I bet you fight really well if you need to. It comes across in your… stillness."

Argyve stood up and rested his arm across Jayhan's shoulder as he started to walk. "Come on. We mustn't keep your father waiting. And in return, I can tell you that you come across as cheerful but with a streak of uncertainty, kind, brave and very perceptive about other people and how to react to them."

"Do I? What's perceptive?"

The older man laughed. "You notice things that other people might not. For instance, you noticed the times Edgar was scared and immediately changed what you were doing to make him feel safer."

Jayhan glanced up at him and grinned. "Well, I noticed that Lady Electra likes you quite a lot, even if you're not dashing."

The colour in Argyve's cheeks darkened. "Goodness, harrumph, um, you don't need to say everything you notice."

"Just thought you might like to know, just in case you didn't know already."

Argyve looked down at him as they rounded the corner of the stables and headed across the driveway into the house. "I didn't think boys your age were interested in romance."

"Oh, I'm not. Not at all. But older people are, aren't you?"

Argyve was saved from answering this by their advent into the parlour where Clive had just produced a tray of fresh tea accompanied by an assortment of tempting cakes and sandwiches. As they entered, Argyve particularly noticed that Electra's face lit up at the sight of him and to his horror, felt his cheeks warming. He hoped desperately that it didn't show.

Part 7

Chapter 42

Jayhan knew when he was being left out of something. As he sat in the library preparing to answer a set of questions about the latest tedious reader, 'Daisy Gets Caught in the Rain', he gazed intermittently out of the window to see Sheldrake and Yarrow talking to Sasha. Then he watched Leon preparing the coach for a journey.

"You know I can read harder books now?" he complained, dragging his attention back inside.

Eloquin smiled at him. "The reader may be easy, but the questions are not."

Jayhan gave a little grunt of disbelief and returned his attention reluctantly to his work. He lifted his brows in surprise when he read the first question: *What ingredients would you use to help the girl get over the cold she caught in the rain?* He grinned as he looked up at his tutor. "Huh! I can answer that."

"I'm sure you can. You can put some of your magic training to use. Full grammatical sentences please." Her eyes twinkled. "Of course, I shall have to take your answer to your father or Yarrow for their opinions on your accuracy."

For the next half hour, he was distracted by actually completing some work so, by the time he looked back out the window, no one was in sight. But if he craned his neck, he could just see the carriage pulled up outside the front door. Someone was going somewhere, and no one had mentioned it to him at breakfast. Unusual.

He asked Eloquin, who had become more approachable over time, but either she didn't know or had been told not to say anything. Determined to find out more from Sasha in the afternoon, he turned back to the last question: *How could the girl have avoided being caught in the rain?* Hmm. Tricky.

Just as he emerged after his morning study session to cross to the stables, the coach, driven by Leon, rumbled slowly past him. He caught a glimpse of Maud, Sheldrake, Yarrow and Sasha inside it before they were past him and heading towards the gate. Outrage surged through him. How could they leave him behind like that? Without a word. Didn't they realise he was Sasha's protector?

Before good sense could intervene, he ran as fast as his small legs would carry him and jumped for the luggage rack at the rear. He just managed to grab it and, for a moment, hung dangling, holding his feet up, before hauling himself up.

Inside the coach, Sheldrake frowned as the coach gave a faint lurch, but only faint because the weight of four passengers softened its movements. "What was that?"

"I told you, dear," said Maud placidly. "The driveway needs attention. There are potholes forming everywhere."

Sheldrake raised his eyebrows. "Well, after that jolt, I shall heed your words."

Outside on the luggage rack, a large trunk took up most of the space but Jayhan was able to shove it over a little so that he could squeeze himself in beside it. He peered over the top of the carriage and spotted the back of Leon's head. Then he realised there was a rear window in the coach, only small and mostly blocked by the trunk, but he would have to stay low to avoid being spotted. Once they stopped, he had no idea what he would do but he had a strong feeling his father would not be happy to see him.

Inside the coach, Sasha peered out the window, her face tight, a small crease between her brows.

Yarrow patted her hand. "It's all right. They are friendly people. You have nothing to worry about. You'll see."

Sasha turned her head to look at the shaman. "I don't see why we couldn't bring Jayhan. We do everything together. He will feel like I've betrayed him."

Maud leaned forward. "Now Sasha, this is adults' business."

"I'm not an adult," protested Sasha, pouting.

"No. Clearly," retorted Maud acerbically. "And once we have handed over the regency to Jon, you will have nothing more directly to do with this rebellion until you are older and better prepared. I wouldn't be risking you outside the gates now, if we didn't have to support Jon. And I'm not risking Jayhan, if I don't have to."

"I still have my doubts about the wisdom of us accompanying Sasha," said Sheldrake, eyeing his wife. "If anyone among them is a spy for the Queen, our presence is like a beacon to Sasha's whereabouts."

"Nonsense, dear. We are merely Carradorian officials representing our king." Maud smiled at Sasha and patted her leg, "And we are the closest thing Sasha has to parents and I won't have her enduring this ordeal without us."

Regardless of whether he continued to think he was right, Sheldrake subsided, merely giving Sasha a rather whimsical smile.

As the minutes turned into slow hours of hunching down out of sight, Jayhan revised his impetuous decision to stow away and wished he could reverse it. The afternoon wore on in a tedious blur of open fields that gradually merged into patches of bush then thick looming forest on either side. Jayhan was glad he had Leon, Sheldrake and Maud with him, even if they didn't know he was there.

The vast forest they were now entering spread from fifteen miles east of Highkington, fifty miles to the border with Kimora, then another sixtty miles beyond. In the west, the trees were mainly eucalyptus, soft grey green leaves hanging in gentle swathes, scrubby wattles interspersed with yellow and red flowered grevilleas filling the space beneath them. As the forest became denser, tall mahogany and myrtle trees reached high, battling against each other to reach the sun light, great sinuous vines trailing from their branches, the screeches of strange birds echoing through the vast canopy. Tree ferns, dense tall grasses and bull rushes competed for the space along the creeks and rivers, where the sunlight could penetrate the canopy.

On the edges of the forest, loggers and farmers ventured in for timber, firewood, herbs, mushrooms and berries. Few people braved the depths of the forest, daunted by tales of travellers being lost, murdered, or robbed and left for dead. Few people dwelt there and those who did were considered strange and insular by those who lived outside.

The main Highkington to Manassa road, affectionately known as Park Lane, speared in a straight line through the forest but travellers then had to turn south, once they reached Kimora, and head across the Eastern Plains to reach the capital. A more direct route between the two capitals ran through the southern part of the forest but only determined or very experienced travellers could find their way along its obscure, narrow pathways. The rest of the forest was a maze of narrow winding tracks that would often end at an impassable tangle of undergrowth, the edge of a deep creek or sheer escarpment, or simply peter out in the middle of nowhere.

Twenty miles east of the forest's edge but still well within Carrador, the Creeping Vine Inn nestled beside Park Lane under a spreading river red gum, providing travellers with food, ale and changes of horses.

And it was outside this inn that Leon finally heaved on the reins, pulling up his team of horses so firmly that the decision about what to do next was taken from Jayhan as the sudden halt threw him from his perch. No one heard his yelp of pain above the jangling of the harnesses, as he landed on the stony ground behind the coach. He picked himself up and dusted himself off, inspecting his sleeve where it had torn at the elbow. He drew a sharp intake of breath when he tried to put weight on his left leg and realised his knee had been jarred by the fall. Suddenly, Jayhan heard Leon's feet on the gravel as the coachman walked along the lefthand side of the coach to open the door for his passengers. Wincing against the pain, Jayhan hobbled as fast as he could to the right, slanting backwards so that whoever was seated on the right couldn't see him. Once around the corner of the inn, he hid behind some beer barrels stacked against the wall. Heart hammering and panting for breath, he peeked back around the corner to watch.

Maud and Yarrow were walking arm in arm towards the inn, with Sasha and Sheldrake bringing up the rear. He could hear Maud saying, "We will have about an hour before Jon arrives. We will take a private parlour so that we don't run into anyone unexpectedly and I'll order some refreshments while we wait. I will change later, once we are out of sight of the inn."

Refreshments! Rats! Almost on cue, his tummy rumbled so loudly he was sure they would be able to hear it from across the yard. But no. No one looked his way. The four of them disappeared inside while Leon led the horses around to the stables on the other side of the inn.

Jayhan slid down against the wall and felt his knee for damage. Not much, he concluded with mixed feelings. He would be fine to walk and run, now that he was over the shock of falling.

He took stock of his surroundings. To his left, the inn stretched to the edge of the forest. Several windows on this side of the inn looked onto the road from Highkington and the yard he was in, so he would have to stay close to the wall and duck under them to gain the cover of the trees undiscovered. Even as he contemplated what to do, he saw another carriage appearing in the distance as it crested the rise in the road. Time to move.

He crept his way along the wall, past another stack of barrels and a woodpile before coming to an open door near the rear of the inn. He paused, listening for sounds of footsteps and when he heard none, peered around the corner. The door led into the kitchens and as he watched, someone moved across the light at the other end of a short corridor. He took a breath and scuttled past, quickly reaching the end of the side wall. A large gum tree stood only feet from the rear of the inn, its huge branches over-hanging its roof. Jayhan took a quick look around the corner then dodged the short distance to hide on the forest side of the tree.

The carriage he had seen in the distance was now pulling up at the inn and disgorging a motley group of men and women, many of them with the same dark colouring as Sasha. Jayhan surmised they were some of the Kimoran refugees. He saw them enter the inn but only twenty minutes later, they re-emerged and headed around the side of the inn straight towards where he was sitting. Jayhan scrambled backwards into the depths of what he now discovered was a rather prickly bush. After a quick re-think, he dodged to the far side of the huge gum tree and jumped for the lowest branch. He missed. He took a few steps back and with strength born of urgency, ran full tilt and threw himself upwards. As his hands grasped the branch, he swung his legs back and forth a couple of times until he had gained enough momentum to swing himself up onto the branch. He only just had time to settle himself when the motley group passed the other side of the tree. He forced himself to stop panting from the exertion and held his breath until they were several trees away. Jayhan frowned. *Why are they heading into those scary woods,* he wondered.

His attention was distracted by the appearance of a large cart on the brow of the far hill. As the cart drew nearer, he could see it was been driven by a woman holding the reins of a downtrodden old mare. Everything about them was grey; the woman's skirts, shawl, and hair. Even the old mare was grey. Two more women and two men were seated on the bare boards of the tray of the cart, leaning against the sides, their legs pulled up in front of them, with their arms wrapped around their knees. *Not very comfortable for a long distance,* thought Jayhan, *but better than a luggage rack shared by a travelling chest.*

Jayhan lost sight of them when they pulled up in front of the inn but could hear the sounds of them greeting other people who must have arrived from the other direction, either by vehicle or on foot. He could not hear any voices that sounded like members of his family's group, so he assumed Jon had not yet arrived. He certainly hadn't seen him.

This latest group of people did not linger but after a bit of chat, headed down beside the inn and took the same path into the forest that the previous group had followed.

For a while, nothing happened. Jayhan flicked away an ant that had begun the long climb up his hand. He noticed the bark felt rough under his legs below the leg line of his short leggings and ran his hand through some long thin leaves that were swaying in the breeze. Jayhan watched the progress of a black, yellow and white honey eater as it flitted in and out of the surrounding wattle trees. A shrieking trio of rainbow lorikeets shot overhead before zig-zagging at insane speeds between trunks and branches to swoop into a controlled landing in a distant tree.

Jayhan heaved a sigh. There was no doubt about it. He was bored. Being a spy was already turning out to be duller than he expected. Finally, a lone rider appeared on the road coming from the direction of Highkington. Jayhan squinted. The sun was starting to drop towards the horizon silhouetting the figure against the sky. Even so, he thought he recognised Jon. But maybe that was just wishful thinking. No. As the rider approached, Jayhan's guess was confirmed. He grinned to himself. Now, at last, his parents and Sasha and Yarrow would do whatever they were here to do. Jayhan guessed it was about making Jon a regent but he couldn't really believe they would leave him out of it when he had been present for so much of the planning.

Jon disappeared from Jayhan's view as he arrived at the front of the inn and by the time Sheldrake, Maud, Yarrow, Sasha and Jon finally emerged, the western sky was streaked with gold and orange. They walked along the side of the inn, just as the other groups had, and headed off along the same path into the trees. But before they were out of sight, they halted while Maud separated from them into a nearby, denser grove of bushes. She re-emerged as a large, grey timber wolf; solidly built, Jayhan observed with an inward smile. He frowned. He had better stay upwind of them. A wolf had a keen sense of smell.

He was just about to climb out of his tree when eight people emerged quietly and walked down the side of the inn. Jayhan found them disquieting. They had an air of constraint about them and kept their voices low. As he listened, he realised with a trill of surprise that even though they were all dressed in men's clothing, two of them were women.

They passed directly beneath him, so that Jayhan could see that they were all dressed in black jackets and trousers, neat and in better repair than many outfits that he had seen pass by. They were more heavily armed than any others; each wore a sword on their left hip and a dagger on the right. Two of them carried what appeared to be long slender staffs, but when Jayhan spotted quivers of arrows on their backs, he realised he was looking at unstrung bows. A frisson of fear trickled down Jayhan's little body. He had heard how Sasha's father and brother had died.

He listened harder. He could just make out the words, "gathering," and "rumours." He thought he might have heard the word "amulet" but that may have been his imagination or expectation. He wasn't sure and now that they were moving into the trees, he couldn't hear them anymore.

Overhead the brilliance of the sunset was intensifying into streaks of deep orange. As dusk settled among the trees, the breeze died down. As soon as they were out of sight, Jayahn slithered down the tree on the side away from the forest, intent on overtaking them. He had to warn Sheldrake.

Suddenly a huge hand clamped down on his shoulder.

Chapter 43

South of the inn, deep in the forest, a motley group of men and women sat in the dark around a campfire, clutching mugs of tea and talking quietly. They were clearly on edge, glancing frequently into the gloom around them, starting at faint noises. Some were well dressed while others wore worn tattered garments that suggested their owners had not been able to replace them for some time. For all that, the quality of clothing did not seem to correlate with differences in rank.

Suddenly, conversation froze as they all looked towards the north where definite sounds of people approaching emanated from the darkness. Some hands reached for weapons lying on the ground beside them.

A large solid man with a full but neatly trimmed beard shook his head and growled, "Nah. Don't bother. We're not surrounded. If this were a raid, they'd come from all sides."

Beside him, a taut young man, his sandy hair sticking out in tufts, brought his hand back onto his lap and flexed his thin fingers nervously. "What about the lookouts? Why haven't they alerted us? They should have alerted us, Argus."

Just then, an older woman dressed in dusty billowing brown skirts walked quickly into the clearing. She glanced at the taut young man. "I'm alerting you now, Shay. Stop fussing. Jon's arrived, that's all," She frowned slightly, "though he has brought a few more people with him than I expected." She shrugged. "Still, I suppose he knows what he's doing."

A minute later Jon entered the clearing, giving a wave of greeting and smiling disarmingly at them. "Thank you all for coming. As Rhoda said, I have brought some people to meet you; people who have your welfare, and that of Kimora, at heart." He cleared his throat and looked a little embarrassed. "They have a proposal to put to you."

Argus raised his eyebrows. "Do they now? And why haven't they come straight out and shown themselves?"

"I am here, Argus," said Yarrow, stepping into the firelight. "And the others will come out to meet you once I have had a chance to tell you about them first." She looked around the circle of faces. "Now, who among you are shamans? I know a few of you who are but possibly not all."

A show of hands indicated that eleven of the twenty-four people seated around the fire were shamans. Only three women weren't. Rhoda didn't raise her hand but said gruffly, "You know I am."

"Now, indulge me for a few minutes," said Yarrow. "Could each of you lift out your amulets and pace them on your hand so that everyone, shamans and non-shamans alike, can see them."

With a few mutterings under their breath and some narrowed eyes and frowns, they complied, making it clear they were not comfortable with the request.

Yarrow also produced her own before beaming at them, "Thank you." She swept her hand to indicate the revealed amulets. "Now, see that they are all gently pulsing in time with each other? Does their light seem a little stronger? Now I would like to present to you.... Sasharia, youngest daughter of Princess Corinna."

There was a collective gasp around the campfire as Sasha came forward from among the trees. Despite entreaties for her to wear a skirt, she had determinedly dressed in her usual leggings, her new leather jerkin worn over a white, neatly pressed shirt. Her only concession was the blue and orange ribbon, the colours of Kimora, which had been threaded through her dark wavy hair. She looked stiff, but otherwise hid her self-consciousness well.

"And," continued Yarrow, "may I also introduce Lord Sheldrake and Lady Maud Batian, who are here in an official capacity representing the Carradorian king's condemnation of the hunting of unregistered shamans within his borders?"

Sheldrake walked to her right with his arm around her shoulder, a great, grey timber wolf padded silently to her left. Murmurs around the fire passed the word from shamans that the wolf was a shapeshifter, although the introduction made that obvious. If anything, that knowledge made the wolf more intimidating since it meant she had the intelligence of a human combined with the strength and potential aggression of a wild predator.

Sasha stood uncertainly in the firelight, Yarrow and Jon, a little further to her left. She glanced at Yarrow for guidance who nodded. At the signal, Sasha drew forth her obsidian amulet. Immediately, her amulet sent forth a pulse of dark light. All around the campfire, the shamans' amulets flared with pale brilliance; some clear, some pale blue, some yellow, one a pale purple.

Excited babble broke out all around the clearing.

"I knew it."

"I knew she must still be alive."

"Oh thank heavens!"

"It's her! You found her."

Then, as the excitement died down, the murmurs began and slowly the volume rose again.

"Where has she been?"

"She's so young still."

"But at least she's here."

"Is it really her?"

"Maybe she stole the amulet?"

Jon raised both his hands in the air. "Please listen," he said quietly and after a few moments, they did. "I can understand both your joy and your scepticism. Let us address your uncertainty so that your pleasure in welcoming back your true monarch can be unrestrained. Would one of you shamans like to come forward to assist us?"

Rhoda glanced around the group and stomped forward. "I'll do it. What d'you want me to do?"

"Firstly, if you wouldn't mind holding out your wrist, Sasha?" He turned to Rhoda. "Feel her pulse and check whether it beats in time with your amulets."

Rhoda looked Sasha in the eyes and tilted her head as if to ask for permission. Sasha nodded. The pulsing of all the amulets quickened as Sasha' nervousness affected her heart rate. Rhoda gently took her wrist in her large seamed hand and concentrated for a full minute, during which Sasha's heart rate calmed and beat of the amulets slowed. Rhoda let go and smiled at her before turning to Jon.

"Anything else?"

"Now I would like you to put on Sasha's amulet. Sasha?"

Sasha removed her amulet and held it out to Rhoda, who looked at it doubtfully.

"Go on," urged Jon. "We'll get a non-shaman to do it too. Argus?"

Rhoda attempted to put the amulet over her head and cried out in pain as the amulet twisted away.

"Perhaps if you take your own amulet off first?" suggested Jon.

Rhoda frowned at him, knowing the outcome before she even tried. Nevertheless, she endured the reaction of Sasha's amulet a second time just to prove the point.

Argus took the amulet from her, then bowed to Sasha and said in his deep baritone, "If you will allow, my lady?"

Sasha's eyes widened at his respectful manner and she nodded quickly. As Argus placed the amulet over the top of his head as though to put it on, his hand burned and pains lanced through his head. With a yell he pulled it away from his head but managed to hold onto it and return it, rather abruptly, to Sasha.

"I think we have seen enough," growled Argus. "I believe, beyond the shadow of a doubt, that our rightful Queen stands before us. Does anyone disagree?"

People shook their heads and a few murmured, "No."

Argus lowered himself to one knee and placed his hand on his heart. "I pledge you loyalty and service, Sasharia, and will do all I can to restore you to your rightful throne."

Behind him, every single person around the campfire rose before going down on one knee, some quite stiffly, all offering pledges of loyalty. Their pledges were not in unison, so the result was ragged but heartfelt.

For a brief moment, Sasha looked panic-stricken but, after a glance at Jon, cleared her throat and said, "Please rise. Thank you. Um, could we sit down and talk to you please?"

A few people grinned but Argus said formally, "Of course. We would be honoured," and waved her to a seat on a log by the fire.

An old bloke, white whiskered and wizened, shifted over and patted the spot he had vacated. "Here y'are, girlie." He gave her a half toothless grin. "Me name's Berren but everyone calls me Beetlebrow. You can too, if you like. I s'pose I should call you Your Highness or some such, but you're a wee young thing and I haven't quite got my head around it yet."

Sasha gave him a nervous smile and sat down. "Thanks."

Maud paced back and forth a few times behind the row of people, deliberately making them nervous, before circling to the front of the log and settling down on the ground at

Sasha's feet, while Sheldrake placed himself at the edge of the clearing near Jon, where he could keep his eye on everyone present.

Sasha noticed a woman in her twenties sitting across the fire from her and wondered how she had kept her long wavy brown hair so lustrous when the rest of her looked so ill kempt. The young woman looked her up and down with hard grey eyes before pronouncing, "Your existence will give us someone to fight for, to right the wrongs and overthrow the tyrant Queen." She flicked a twig into the fire. "But..." she added disparagingly, "you don't look like much of a warrior queen to lead us into battle."

Sasha felt like she'd been slapped in the face. Immediately, many voices around the fire rose to her defence.

"Draya, stop it."

"Don't be rude."

"Draya, mind your mouth."

As the recriminations died down, Sasha took a deep breath and said in a tight brittle voice, her hands held tightly on her lap, "I am ten years old and was brought up in an orphanage. I have been in hiding all my life. First I worked for a carter who beat me almost daily," this elicited a communal intake of breath and Jon, standing in the shadows, winced, "but now I have a job I love, working for a kind and clever family as a stable hand." She took another breath. "I only found out who I was, a couple of months ago. You can be as mean as you like, but it won't change who I am. But it might change whether I want to help you."

Voices came from everywhere; shocked and angry. Sasha glanced at the old bloke next to her who gave her a wink. She responded with the tiniest of smiles as she waited for the tumult to die down. Finally, when they were quiet, she continued as though no one had spoken. "My brother brought me out of Kimora when I was a baby. So, I remember nothing about Kimora. Nothing. Yarrow and my brother have been teaching me about her and explaining all the bad things that this new aunty of mine has been doing. I do not have, as my brother does, the inbred commitment to the Kimoran people, but for his sake and for the sake of what seems right, I will try to develop it." For the first time, she looked directly at Draya. "So don't make it too hard or I might just walk away."

A stunned silence was followed by another babble of voices. Finally, one question made itself heard above all the rest and was then taken up by everyone, "Who is your brother?"

Sasha gave a fond smile and gestured to Jon to come over to her. "Jondarian."

Spontaneous applause and shouts of approbation broke from the group.

"Ah Jon boy. We should have known," growled Argus. "You've done so much for all of us; organising shelter, food, introducing groups to each other. Yes, we should have known."

"Hardly our fault we didn't," snapped Draya. "We didn't even know he was still alive." She held up a hand to prevent another barrage of censure. "But I am glad he is. Really glad. And I'm glad our queen is, too."

"Thanks, Draya," Jon left his place on the clearing's edge and came forward to the fire, his smile diffident at first then broadening into a grin as people gathered around him slapping him on the back, smiling and laughing in delight. For a while, mayhem reigned, people handed out cups of tea while asking how he had escaped, how he'd rescued Sasha and how he'd lived in Carrador as a little boy. It did not seem to occur to any of them to demonstrate their allegiance to him as they had to Sasha, perhaps because they already knew him. Eventually someone remembered that a proposal was to be put to them.

"So come on, Jon, tell us, what is this proposal?" asked Rhoda.

Unaccountably for his onlookers, Jon looked a little embarrassed and turned to Yarrow. "I would rather this came from someone else."

Yarrow smiled understandingly at him, but before she could speak, Sasha said firmly, "I would like Jon to be regent until I come of age. That way, he can lead Kimora as soon as we get rid of my aunt." She shrugged. "Otherwise you will have to wait until I am old enough and know enough to rule myself... which will be ages," she added with a flash of childish language.

With no hesitation, Argus stood up. "I agree."

One after the other, they all stood and repeated his words. Angus glanced around himself and went down on one knee. The others followed his lead and the whole group pledged their faith in Jon, more closely in unison than their previous effort. Then Argus stood up and clapped Jon on the back. "You have earned our trust, young one." He smiled strongly at Sasha, "And you have all the makings of a great leader in the fullness of time."

Sasha blushed and looked down until the old bloke beside her nudged her and whispered, "Hold yer head high, girlie."

She grimaced at him but did as he directed. "Thanks Argus."

Just then, Maud stiffened and raised her snout to the wind, staring into the darkness beyond the clearing. A deep growl emanated from her throat. Around the fire, conversations died.

Sheldrake's eyes snapped to her. "What is it?'

In answer, her growl intensified. Suddenly she was gone, and a peregrine falcon shot out of the clearing, narrowly missing a tree branch, as she disappeared into the night.

"Careful Maud," murmured Sheldrake, as much to himself as to anyone else. He turned to the assembled people, unaware that his shadow loomed high and menacing against the trees behind him, and swept his arm overhead, creating a translucent lilac canopy over them.

"What on earth are you doing?" growled Argus.

Sheldrake looked mildly surprised. "I am merely protecting us. Clearly someone or something is out there. While Maud investigates, I offer you all my protection."

"It's a shield, Argus," explained Rhoda impatiently "Haven't you seen one before?" She grimaced at Sheldrake. "Mages and wizards are not common in Kimora, only shamans."

Sheldrake nodded. "They are not so common in Carrador either, though I believe everyone in Eskuzor is a sorcerer to some degree. Perhaps I should explain. Maud has heard or sniffed people approaching. As a wolf, she can become aware of them much sooner than even your lookouts can. She senses they are a threat so has gone to investigate."

"Yes," growled Argus. "I gathered that much."

"So meanwhile," continued Sheldrake. "I have placed a translucent film of protection over you all, until we know what we are dealing with. Is that acceptable to you or do you feel too threatened by it? I assure you it merely blocks physical and magical attacks. It does nothing to the people within it."

Argus shrugged. "Good idea, I suppose."

"NO!" yelled Shay, his voice high with strain. "I hate being trapped. I can't stand it."

Before anyone realised what was happening, Shay had grabbed a long heavy branch from the woodpile and swung it into the back of Sheldrake's head. It connected with a dull thwack and Sheldrake dropped to the ground. The lilac shield winked out of existence.

"Shay, you idiot!" cried out Rhoda. "What have you done? This man is in the Carradorian government. If you've killed him, you'll hang."

"You bloody fool, Shay," bellowed Argus. "You'll get us all into trouble. He was protecting us."

Shay, wild-eyed, stood over Sheldrake's prone figure, still holding the branch, his breath coming in heaving gasps. Jon walked quietly over to him and held out his hand.

"Come on, Shay" he said gently. "Give me that stick. We don't want any more…"

Shay's eyes flew up to look at him and for a moment it looked as though he was thinking of swinging at Jon. Then he let out a breath and surrendered the branch.

"Good lad. Now sit down quietly by the fire and calm yourself down." Jon looked at Rhoda and Yarrow. "Can you attend to Sheldrake please?" He shook his head. "I hope he's all right." He looked across at Sasha, sitting stiff and frightened beside Beetlebrow, and gestured. "Come over here, little one."

Chapter 44

Jayhan's heart nearly stopped with fright, thinking one of the fighters had returned. The hand propelled him around and he found himself staring into Leon's very grim face. Although this was not good, the alternative was so much worse that he breathed a sigh of relief.

"Oh hi, Leon. Thank goodness you're here. I need you."

"A good spanking is what you need," responded Leon severely.

"NO! Yes, well, maybe. But not now. Did you see those people? Eight of them. Two have bows and arrows and they're following Mum and Dad and everyone. Leon, they might kill them like they did to Sasha's family." His chest began to heave with panic as he worked himself up. "Leon, we have to do something."

"Not we. *I* have to…" Leon looked down into the panic-stricken little face and shook his head in exasperation. "Oh never mind! I haven't got time to make sure you stay here." He grabbed Jayhan's hand, none too gently, and dragged him towards the track through the trees. "Come on."

As Jayhan trotted along beside Leon, struggling to keep up with his captured hand, a little frown appeared between his eyes, "How come you didn't go with them to protect them?"

Leon glanced down at him and said impatiently, "Come on lad. Figure it out."

After a moment, Jayhan's brow cleared. "Oh! To check no one followed."

"Exactly." The family henchman explained between breaths as he jogged along. "I will send a flare up to warn Sheldrake but not while he ad Maud are still travelling within the tree canopy. They might not see it. I'll have to gauge when they have arrived in the clearing and find a gap through the trees to send it up then." He grimaced. "But I didn't expect eight attackers or any of them to be archers.

"We have to stop them, don't we, Leon?"

"Somehow," muttered Leon, tugging on the little boy's hand. "Come on," he said, picking up the pace.

Ten minutes later, the dusk had given way to full darkness, but their eyes had adjusted as the light faded. Nevertheless, it was becoming harder to see the path ahead. Jayhan was out of breath and dragging on Leon's arm.

"Sorry. I can't go as fast as you," he puffed. "I have to rest."

Leon stopped and stood over him, flustered, not knowing what to do. "Ah Jayhan! I have to go. I have to disarm those archers, at the very least. Stay here. Stay out of sight. Keep yourself safe. Please." Without another word, he let go of Jayhan's hand and sped off in pursuit of the attackers, at a much faster pace now that he was unencumbered.

Jayhan sat himself against a tree and waited until Leon had disappeared from view around a bend in the track. He had no intention of staying where he was, but how could he get there in time to be helpful? It didn't cross his mind for a minute that he might make things worse, by getting himself hurt or getting in the way.

He thought about the speed at which Leon could move compared to him and a stunning idea come to him.

He could shapeshift to be Leon... or better still Jon. Jon was even taller and younger, so probably faster. Then another idea occurred to him; maybe he could disguise himself as one of the attackers? No. He needed to know them pretty well to copy them. He'd only caught glimpses of the attackers as they'd passed beneath his tree. No. So, Jon it was.

Once he'd decided, he wasted no time.

He centred himself, focused inward, then visualized Jon as clearly as he could; how he stood, walked, waved his arms around, how he bent down. Slowly the image of Jon took over. For a few seconds, Jayhan nearly panicked and backed out. The differences in size and shape between Jon and him were far greater than the differences between Sasha and him had been. Well, except that she was a girl, but he didn't know that at the time... and now he thought about it, he didn't actually know in any detail, what those differences were. His wandering mind started to lose Jon's image and the sense of strangeness in his body faded.

Remembering the high stakes involved, Jayhan frowned at himself, refocused and prepared himself with grim determination, to accept the changes in his body. He visualized Jon again, ignoring the sensations in his body until, in his mind there was a small thunk as the change was completed.

He waved his hand and found it further away from him than he was used to. His feet looked huge and were on the end of long, proportionally slimmer, legs. It took him a couple of tries before he could grab a bit of his hair to see if it was blond; his hands kept not being where he expected them to be. Got it. Yes, he could see his hair was blond, even in the dark. He grinned.

Right. Time to stand up and get used to his limbs before setting off.

His first discovery was that it took more effort to raise a larger, taller body off the ground and when he straightened, he seemed a lot higher from the ground. His second discovery was that the branch he had been sitting under wasn't as far above him as he anticipated and he found himself entangled in it, his hair caught by small twigs and leaves.

When he brought his hand up to push away the twigs, the weight of his long arm swinging towards him sent him swaying backwards and only the fact that he was tangled in the branch saved him from hitting his head against the trunk or falling over. He grabbed hold of the foliage and after pushing it out of his hair, used it to give him something to hang onto while he took a few tentative steps.

At first, it felt like being on stilts. He stepped back and forth a few times, keeping hold of the tree for balance. Then leaning slightly forward, he took a breath for courage and walked away from the tree in the direction Leon had taken. Being young, fit and reasonably athletic, Jayhan soon got the hang of it and began to stride along with increasing confidence. In fact, it was fun. He realised the moon was rising behind the forest to the east and the path was now easier to see, although streaked with deep shadows of the trees. He began to experiment with jogging and was doing well until his toe hit a raised root on the path and he lurched forward. Unable to right himself quickly enough in his unfamiliar body, he crashed to the ground. This was when he discovered the ground was a lot further away to fall to and hurt more when he landed.

He sat disgruntled in the middle of the path, rubbing his bruised shoulder and inspecting his left hand which was grazed and oozing blood. The breeze had sprung up again and sent a fine cloud of dust into his face. His eyes blurred with tears and for a moment he thought it was maybe all too hard. But he was a determined little fellow and his family was in danger. So he gave a great big sniff and pulled himself together.

Gingerly, he pushed himself up onto his feet again and set off, quickly increasing his pace again to a jog, but this time more alert to the path's undulations and more wary of bumps concealed within the trees' shadows. He was just beginning to lengthen his stride when he rounded a corner to be confronted by a mound in the middle of the path. His momentum almost carried straight him onto it, but he was able to grab hold of a low-slung branch to stop himself in time. As he drew nearer, he could see the lump was a large man sprawled face-down in the middle of the path.

It was Leon.

Filled with dread, Jayhan carefully crouched down beside him. At first, Jayhan just looked at him, taking in his closed eyes and the dark wet patch on the side of his head. After a moment, he slowly reached out a shaky hand to touch Leon's chest. He felt almost giddy with relief when he felt Leon's chest rise and fall beneath his fingers. The movement was faint, but it was there.

Jayhan sat back on his heels and pondered what to do. After a bit of thought, he decided that no one was likely to hurt Leon, any more than he already had been and, in fact, if someone else came along the path and found him, they might be able to help him. On the other hand, if Jayhan tried to move him, he might hurt him more. Jayhan vaguely remembered it could be dangerous to move people with head injuries… or was that back injuries? He gave a faint shrug and decided to leave Leon where he was and tell Sheldrake as soon as he could.

As he leaned his weight forward, ready to stand up, he noticed a slim, smooth, slightly tapered stick poking out from beneath Leon. He pulled it free and found the other end was jagged. After a moment, he rubbed his hand along the tapered end and found a notch. Hmm. So at least Leon had disarmed one archer before being knocked out. One archer left.

Giving Leon a farewell pat on the back, Jayhan unfolded himself to his greater height, taking noticeably longer to straighten. He realised he still had the broken half-bow in his hand. He decided he might as well keep it. It wasn't much, but it was the only weapon he had. With a last glance at Leon, he set off down the track.

After his encounter with Leon's body, Jayhan decided to lope as fast as he could in the low light, on the straight parts of the path, but to creep around the corners in case any of the attackers were lying in wait for him. This had the added advantage of giving him periods of rest. He was nearing the end of a straight section when he thought he heard a voice. He stopped dead and listened. Nothing. Realizing that he had probably been making too much noise, he crept to the side of the path and hid behind a large tree. He stood silently, trying to hear above the hammering of his heart.

There it was. The soft sound of a shoe shuffling on the dirt of the track. Jayhan desperately wanted to peek around the side of the tree and see what was happening but he couldn't risk his pale face and blond hair being visible in the gloom. Anyway, he knew what he would see; one or two of those people creeping back along the track, looking and listening for anyone following them.

After what seemed an eternity, he heard a low murmur of voices and the sound of unguarded footsteps as the rear guard walked back to re-join their companions. Jayhan let out a slow breath of relief. Well, he had caught up with them but now what to do? After a bit of thought he decided to change back to his own familiar body. Less chance of making a noise inadvertently. Less concentration on himself, too, which meant he could focus more on these armed interlopers. He slid down the trunk of the tree until he was seated on the ground, noting but ignoring a couple of sharp rocks under his bottom. Then he closed his eyes and remembered how he felt usually.

The sense of strangeness came and went more quickly this time and his back slid further down the tree as he decreased in size. With a mental thunk, Jayhan was back as his own body. He smiled, enjoying its familiarity, although he realized he was feeling tired after the changes, the concentration and running to catch up. Never mind. Not so tired that he couldn't keep going.

He rose quietly and crept along the side of the path, keeping within the shadows of the trees. Because of the density of the forest, there were only a few patches where the moonlight shone brightly, and he was mostly able to avoid them by keeping to the easterly side of the path. Every now and then, he stopped to listen. Sometimes he caught the sound of lowered voices up ahead.

A short time later, he heard the unmistakable sound of a large group chatting and laughing together, making little effort to lower their volume. Clearly Jayhan and his interloper companions were close to their destination. Jayhan drew up as close to the intruders as he could risk, keeping himself hidden in the undergrowth, but looking for the archer among them. He could only see six of them. Maybe the other two had gone ahead. He hoped the archer was among the remaining six. The interlopers began to spread out, three to the right, three to the left. Then Jayhan spotted the archer. One man had stopped before reaching the deep shadows to string his bow, grunting with the effort of curving the wood enough to slot the string into the notches at either end. The archer straightened and crept forward, until he reached the base of a huge spotted gum tree. Then he began to climb.

Suddenly a peregrine falcon flew in low, angling swiftly to avoid low branches. In a trice it was gone, winging up the track the way they had come. A minute later it was back, swooping low under the tree canopy before gaining height and flying off in the direction of the voices. Jayhan was pretty sure it hadn't seen him, or the archer, but it had seen the other five, at least. He thought the falcon was behaving strangely and he wondered whether, *hoped*, it was his mother.

But even if it were, she had not seen the archer. Jayhan waited until the other five had disappeared into the trees on either side of the path and crept forward, with no clear plan except to follow the archer and stop him if he could. As he drew nearer, he caught glimpses of firelight flickering through the trees. He reached the foot of the spotted gum that the archer had climbed and looked up. He could see no sign of him. Maybe, probably, he had climbed around the other side of the tree nearer to the campsite ahead of them.

The lower branches were within easy reach. Pushing his broken bow into the belt of his leggings, Jayhan swung himself easily up onto a long low branch then stopped to listen. He could hear nothing but the swishing of leaves swaying in the breeze. He eased himself onto his feet and climbed quietly to the next level. Every move he made sounded loud in his ears, but the breeze had quickened, and leaves were rattling all around him, masking the sound of his movement. After he had pulled himself up onto the third level of branches, now about twenty feet off the ground, he peered cautiously around the trunk. There, straight ahead of him, lay the archer, stretched out over a fork in the branches directly over the near side of the clearing, his nocked arrow aimed at Sasha, who was sitting on the other side of the fire. Even as he watched, Sasha moved around the fire to stand beside her brother, bringing herself even more conveniently into range. The bowman adjusted his aim and pulled back the string of his bow, ready to release.

Jayhan had no time to think. He simply threw himself at the bowman, desperate to disrupt his shot. The bowman grunted, there was a loud crack and the two of them fell through the branches to land at Sasha's feet; the archer landing on the broken branches, Jayhan happily cushioned by the archer.

They were immediately surrounded by a circle of drawn knives.

Jayhan didn't care. His only concern was whether the arrow had missed its mark. He blew a sigh of relief when he saw the arrow stuck in the ground three feet from Sasha's side.

But from his new vantage point on the ground, Jayhan could also see his father sprawled on the ground close to him. He did care about that. The crash of their landing seemed to have roused Sheldrake, who lifted his head groggily, struggling to make sense of the vision of his son lying beside him on the back of an unknown black-clad man.

Even though he was feeling jarred by the fall, Jayhan managed to give him a sheepish smile. "Hi Dad."

Sheldrake rolled his eyes and passed out again.

Chapter 45

"Jayhan!" chorused Jon and Sasha, staring at him in astonishment. This was followed by a garble of questions that Jayhan couldn't make out; his mind was so taken up by the sight of his stricken father that he barely registered them.

"What's wrong with Dad?" asked Jayhan in alarm.

"Hit in the head," replied Jon briefly. "A shaman looked at him. I think he'll be all right." He waved his hand. "Worry about him later. Maud's just told us there are five people about to attack us."

Still lying on the prone archer, Jayhan lifted his torso up on his arms, his elbows digging into the back of the man below him, who still hadn't moved. "Seven actually. Eight to start with, all with swords and knives, two of them archers. One's bow is broken, the other one..." he pointed downwards. "Don't know what happened to the other two that Mum didn't see. They disappeared a while ago."

"Where are the sentries?" asked Jon suddenly. "Maud sensed intruders, but we've still had no word from the sentries... or Leon."

"Leon is back on the track. Uncons..." Jayhan couldn't remember the word and settled for, "Like he's sleeping but won't wake up. He broke one of the bows, though."

Jon's eyes widened. "Right. Argus and you three, go and check the sentries. Bring them back if you find them. Come straight back yourselves. We all need to be here together." He looked at the people standing around Jayhan and waved his hand impatiently at them. "Get your knives away from Jayhan. He just saved Sasha's life." He used his foot to gently prod the archer's head, which rolled with sickening ease. "And he's dead. So you don't have to worry about him."

"He's dead?' yelped Jayhan, throwing himself off the dead man as though he'd been scalded.

Despite the gravity of the situation, Jon grinned. His grin faded when he saw the four he had sent off return at a run, panting.

"One's knocked out. The other, Morin, his throat's been slit." The speaker, a young lad with hair and skin dark like Sasha's, looked like he was about to be sick. Sure enough, a moment later, he doubled over and retched.

Jon put his hand briefly on his back but was distracted by the sight of Maud, back in human form, storming across the clearing.

"Uh oh. You're in trouble now, Jayhan," Jon left him to it, turning away to deploy people defensively; some close to Sasha, others around the perimeter.

Jayhan jumped up, staggering from the stiffness in his muscles. "Hi Mum," he tried cheerily, knowing it would be futile.

"And exactly what are you doing here, Jayhan?" his mother growled at him, standing over him with her hands on her hips.

He was tempted to say, "Saving Sasha's life," but instead settled for, "No one said I couldn't come."

This turned out to be a poor response. Maud's face turned an interesting shade of dark pink. "I've brought up an idiot, have I, who can't read the signs that he's not wanted on a trip?"

Jayhan hung his head. "No, Mum."

His mother snorted with exasperation, then suddenly reached forward and grabbed him into a huge hug. "Oh, my wilful little son! What would we have done without you? Sasha would be dead by now, if not for you."

Jayhan's eyes widened in surprise as he was enveloped by his mother. He hugged her back fiercely and mumbled, "Sorry Mum," but they both knew he would do it again.

Sounds of fighting drew them apart. They swung around to see two black-clad fighters, a lithe whip-strong woman and a heavier man, run from the cover of the trees to cut at Jon, who dodged out of the way, drawing his own sword as he backed up. Above him, balanced on the fork of two branches, stood another man waiting for his opportunity to drop on Jon or throw his knife. Jon's actions in ordering men out to search for the lookouts had designated him as leader and it was clear they were targeting him.

Intent on reaching Jon, another intruder was attacking Argus, who barely drew his sword in time to parry the first blow. He was staggering back under the onslaught of an experienced fighter, when suddenly a bulky shadow emerged from the path to grab the intruder from behind and hoist him, sword flailing, away from Argus. It was Leon, battered and bloody, but back in good fighting fettle. Leon wrested the man's sword from him and swung the sword's hilt to connect solidly with the man's temple, dropping him like a stone.

Maud thrust Jayhan aside and started towards the attackers, changing between one step and the next into a snarling mountain lion. She dodged between the fighters and out of the clearing. In three fluid jumps, she reached the height of the assailant in the tree above Jon. With a roar, she lunged at the man balanced in the fork of the tree. The intruder had no chance to turn or to use the sword in his left hand. The knife he held ready in his right hand, clattered to the ground below. The sheer momentum of Maud's leap thrust the intruder from his perch and sent him crashing through the branches to land, broken and unconscious, at Jon's feet. Maud, however, did not fall with him as Jayhan had, but braced herself on the branches and considered her next move. Below her, Jon was so hard-pressed, he could barely afford the time to glance at the man's body as it thudded to earth beside him.

Now, three black-clad figures lay sprawled on the ground, but two were still advancing on Jon while several refugees, sporting deep gashes or clutching bruised or broken limbs, struggled to intervene. Even though the marauders were outnumbered three to one, they were trained and merciless while the refugees were used to eluding capture rather than standing and fighting. Many bore weapons but few really knew how to use them.

Two attackers were still pressing Jon when another man and woman leapt into the clearing, slashing their way towards Jon, aiming to force him, in a pincer movement, towards the edge of the clearing. Draya threw herself into the fray, roaring her own fearsome battle cry as her sword clashed with that of a solidly built man. Her attack was so ferocious that her opponent staggered before regaining his footing and pressing forward again.

Beetlebrow reached down and grabbed a large stone. Squinting his eyes for a moment, he threw it with such uncanny accuracy that he hit the heavy man who had been pressing Jon from the start, in the middle of his forehead. The man's legs folded beneath him.

A second female attacker was holding other defenders at bay, swinging her sword in an arc before her as the man fighting Draya edged his way towards Jon. Suddenly the swordswoman's eyes widened as a pale yellow glow shone up through the neckline of her black clothing. The yellow light began to pulse steadily at first, then randomly, before a new firm rhythm took over. Sweat glistened on the woman's forehead and she staggered.

"She's a shaman," shouted Yarrow. "Sasha, focus on her."

From within her ring of protectors, Sasha concentrated instead on her own heartbeat unitl a swathe of black power speared towards the enemy swordsman, encasing her in a black cloud. Unnerved by what was happening to the shaman, other defenders edged away from her, rather than taking advantage of her distraction. The blackness grew in intensity until, within a blinding flash of light, the woman gasped and crumpled to the ground.

"Wow. Sasharia just broke through the Queen's binding spell. Amazing," yelled Rhoda triumphantly. "That's five down now. Two here. If that boy is right, there's another one somewhere. We're winning. Keep going."

Maud was just bunching her muscles to leap down onto Jon's attacker when a tall wiry man broke cover behind Jon and grabbed him around the neck. Suddenly, Jon felt the coldness of metal against his throat. From either side of Jon, the other two attackers calmly disengaged from their opponents and converged on him. As he stilled, the first assailant stepped forward with cool efficiency and relieved Jon of his sword, then stood close by, ready to help his accomplices, if needed.

"Stop!" the wiry man commanded, "Or he dies."

Everyone froze.

To the refugees' shock, Shay stood up and strode over to join them before turning to face those in the centre of the clearing crowded around Sasha. In a hard, forceful voice, completely different from his usual stressed whine, he ordered, "If you don't want to lose your so-called regent, hand over the girl... and her amulet. We won't hurt her. You have my word. You shamans, line up over there," he added, indicating the base of the gum tree that Jayhan had catapulted out of previously.

Before anyone could move, Jon shouted, "NO! They'll take her back to Toriana, Keep her s..." His voice was strangled off as his attacker applied pressure to his throat, pressing the blade harder until a row of tiny droplets of blood appeared on Jon's neck.

Jayhan's eyes widened in horror and he screamed, "Nooo!"

All heads turned to him, expecting a hysterical little boy. Instead, they saw a fearsome sight. A small figure with ghoulishly white eyes, far whiter than they had been before, shining so brightly that they bathed Jon and the assailants in a sickly pale light. Shay and his henchmen stared at him in stark terror, their bodies frozen rigid with fear.

Yarrow calmly walked over and took the knife from the wiry man's now unresisting hand. "Beetlebrow, Argus and you people, secure these bastards. Draya and Rhoda, secure Shay. Jon, go to your sister where you have more protection. Quickly."

People leapt to do her bidding, completely unaffected by the white light. Within seconds, they had bound Shay's and the assailants' hands and shoved them roughly against a tree where they were secured firmly with lengths of rope.

Maud leapt down from the tree and padded into the clearing. As she passed the prisoners, she growled threateningly at them, her fearsome teeth shining white in the gloom. Then she and everyone else returned their attention to Jayhan.

Yarrow approached him, walking unscathed through the bright light of his eyes, and squatted down in front of him. "It's all right now, little one," she crooned, "We are safe."

Slowly the light faded, leaving behind a rather dazed little boy. He blinked a few times and looked uncertainly at Yarrow. "What happened? Did I hurt them?" His gaze shifted to his mother who was padding slowly towards him. His face crumpled and he sobbed at her, "Oh no! Now you'll hate me, 'cause I'm like my great grandmother."

Maud had no time to respond before Sasha dodged between her minders and threw her arms around Jayhan. "Jayhan, it finally worked. But you didn't throw them backwards. You just frightened them, almost to death. Fantastic!"

"No, it's not," he wailed. "Mum hates me now."

"Mum does not hate you now and never will," said Maud firmly, back in her human form, although a little shaky from so many recent shape changes. She enclosed both of them in her arms. "I am very proud of you and love you very much."

He hiccoughed on a sob and looked up. "Do you? Really? Even though I…" he half-waved a trapped arm, "you know…everything?"

Maud smiled down at him. "Yes, even though, and maybe especially because of, everything."

"Oh." And because he was so young and had been through so much on his own and was so relieved his mother still loved him, he let go and had a good long cry, oblivious to the cheering around him.

Chapter 46

Sheldrake sat on the ground with his back against a log. His head was wrapped in a bandage that secured a poultice to the bruised bump on the back of his head. Earlier, Rhoda had held his head between her hands, easing the pain and apparently healing a hairline skull fracture before applying the bandage. He was still pale and lethargic but was doing his best to get a grip on the situation. Maud was sitting beside him and, in an uncharacteristic display of public affection, held his hand in hers, a gesture that told Jayhan how serious his father's injury had been.

On her left side, Jayhan leaned in against her within the circle of her arm, exhausted but too tense to sleep. Every time his eyes drooped, the memory of the dead man beneath him or Jon with the knife to his throat would jerk him awake again. Each time this happened, his mother would hug him closer or pat his side, soothing him until his tense little body relaxed again.

Only a few yards away, Sasha was curled up on Jon's knee, her head against his shoulder, sound asleep. But from time to time, her limbs would twitch or her eyelids would flutter, as her sleep was disturbed by dark memories. After a particularly noticeable jerk of her leg, Jon looked at the others around the fire and said, "This why I don't want Sasha involved until she is older."

A few of the refugees glanced at each other.

"What?" demanded Jon, his gaze coming to rest on Argus whose left cheek was swollen and bruised.

Argus wrung his hands, looking uncomfortable before he straightened up and said, "Many of us have children who have been through a lot worse than this." He held up a hand to forestall Jon's protest. "Don't worry. I agree with you that we should protect Sasharia from such unpleasantness as much as we can, just as we do with our own children. But..."

"But what, Argus?" Jon pressed, but not unkindly.

"But she has great power, Jon. Power that none of us has. She alone can unleash those poor fettered shamans." He nodded in the direction of the tree where the attackers were being held captive with a dazed shaman sitting amongst them. He waved his hand and subsided. "Just saying, is all."

Jon gazed down at his sister in his arms and stroked her hair. After a minute, he said softly, "Yes she does. And you're right, we will need that power, but not yet. At the very least, we need to build our strength, organise ourselves and plan very, very carefully before we take her anywhere near Toriana." He looked up. "Tonight was the first step towards that. Knowing that Sasharia lives and can break though the binding between Toriana and her shamans will give our cause hope and focus." He gave his self-deprecating grin, "And to a lesser extent, so will I."

"Ah, Jon boy. You've already given us more than hope. You and your sister have given us back our faith in our cause, in our people and in our country," Beetlebrow flicked a stick into the fire. "And what you say makes sense. We can't afford to risk the little princess, not just for her sake, but for the sake of all of us."

"On which topic, how did they know Sasharia was here?" asked Sheldrake quietly as though trying not jolt his head. Even so, he winced slightly as he spoke. "Where is the leak in your organisation?"

Jon glanced around at his companions and grimaced. "Well, Shay obviously. But I don't know how he knew Sasha was going to be here."

"He didn't," said Rhoda flatly. "He and his cutthroats were after shamans. All he knew was that we'd be gathered here and that he could capture several of us at once. He just grabbed the opportunity… or tried to."

"I bet he couldn't believe his luck when Sasharia was introduced to us," added Argus.

Jon nodded. "Toriana wants control of all shamans but more than that, she wants the black amulet in her hand and to make sure Sasha is dead. Only then will her rule be secure. Shay would have been richly rewarded."

"Well, now they will moulder in a Carradorian prison instead," said Maud with relish. "Jon, set some of your people to guard them. We will send soldiers as soon as we can, to take them into custody."

She looked around the clearing, seeing the gouges in the dirt and broken branches strewn on the ground. Two men were digging a grave for the dead archer after Jon's insistence that the man was still Kimoran, serving his country even if misguidedly. Not everyone had agreed with this view, but they had still acquiesced to Jon's request. Another grave was being dug under the overhang of a soft flowing vine for the murdered lookout.

The other unconscious attackers had been dragged close to their comrades, securely tied in preparation for them regaining consciousness. Shamans had checked them over and made sure their injuries were not slowly killing them. Other than that, they were left to heal on their own.

Yarrow followed her gaze and said, "I'm afraid we will have to find a new meeting place if we wish to escape notice. Too many will know of this place now,"

"No great loss," grumbled Beetlebrow. "Wouldn't feel safe here after this, anyway."

Sheldrake glanced at Maud and in response to some unspoken understanding, Maud said, "You realise that the actions of those Kimoran soldiers on Carradorian soil is an act of aggression against our state?"

"But we are not Carradorians," protested Rhoda.

"Sheldrake is indisputably Carradorian, and while you are within our borders, unless you are criminals, which you are not, you are under our protection. I stated explicitly to the Kimoran ambassador that we would not sanction the hunting of shamans within our borders."

"And we now have a foreign regent living within our borders," added Sheldrake.

Maud gave a rueful grimace, knowing they would not like what she was about to say, "I'm afraid I will have to inform King Gavin of tonight's events."

Chapter 47

Sasha wiped her hands nervously down the side of her beautifully tailored tan leggings. In her continued masquerade as a stableboy, she was wearing leggings, a white shirt and her new jerkin. Her palms were sweaty, and her chest heaved with anxious breaths.

Her brother, Jon, stood beside her, tense but in control. His blonde hair was tied back neatly at the nape of his neck and his court dress of grey and yellow accentuated his tall willowy frame. He glanced down as she drew in yet another deep breath, and leant down to say, "Sasha, he won't eat us. You're working yourself up. Breath out and don't breath in for a few moments." He took her hand and squeezed it "Hold it... Okay. Breath in slowly." He smiled encouragingly at her. "Good girl. You'll be fine. Try to breathe normally or you'll start to feel a bit strange."

They were distracted by the huge cream and gold doors gliding open before them. Even though she was only ten years old, Sasha pulled her hand away and straightened herself up.

The footmen who had been standing before them in their red and gold livery, moved aside to reveal an intimidating, rotund, old woman. She was dressed in severe black relieved by two thin lines of colour, one gold, one red, running down either side of her bodice, denoting her as a staff member without being too obvious about it. She glared them up and down, then ushered them through into the King of Carrador's presence, before leaving and closing the doors behind herself.

The room they entered was not the audience chamber but a comfortable sitting room, several arm chairs placed in a loose semi-circle around a small, highly polished wooden desk that had been placed facing into the room so that its occupant could look out the window into the gardens leading down to the lake. Bookcases filled with leather bound books lined three of the walls.

King Gavin was only a year or two older than Jon. His long russet coat and cream shirt were of the finest materials but, given that they were court clothes, not overly ostentatious. He wore his wavy auburn hair a little shorter than many, just resting on his shoulders and he wore no crown or sign of his rank, except for the signet ring on his right ring finger. Gavin was noticeably shorter and slighter than Jon but held himself with an unconscious authority. As they entered, he rose from the desk and walked into the centre of the room to greet them.

Jon's quick eyes noted that no one else was apparently in the room.

Jon and Sasha both bowed neatly from the waist but did not genuflect as one of the king's subjects would have done. A lot of thought had gone into the gesture. They owed the king a gesture of respect for sheltering them within his borders even if, until very recently, he had been unaware of it. On the other hand, they knew Maud had revealed their identities to him, and even if they were not currently officially recognised as the rulers of Kimora, they too were royal. It had been a long, and Sasha thought, tedious discussion.

As they straightened, Gavin inclined his head briefly in recognition of their gesture and status. Maud had reported that the king's blue eyes twinkled benignly at people, but they were not twinkling now. His face looked closed and wary.

"So, we meet at last, even though I am given to understand that you have been within the borders of my kingdom for nearly ten years." The king gestured to the armchairs, as he himself sat in one to the right of his desk that gave him the view of his garden. "Please. Take a seat."

"Thank you, Sire," said Jon, sitting down and crossing his legs, still formal although not obviously nervous.

Sasha chose a chair two away from Jon so that she did not appear too clingy. She did, however, looked ill at ease despite her best efforts, sitting bolt upright on the edge of the chair.

There was a short uncomfortable silence before Jon uncrossed his legs, leaned forward and smiled, not his usual sunny smile but a smile, nevertheless. "I suppose I must apologize to you, Your Majesty, for not coming to you... or your father, sooner. As Maud may have told you, the situation has been vexed. I fled from the slaughter of my family when I was twelve, carrying Sasha, the rightful successor to the throne, as a babe in arms. I was running from betrayal at the highest level. I wasn't running *to* anywhere. It never occurred to me to seek sanctuary from the Carradorian crown. I just hid from everyone." He gestured at Sasha. "I did not even tell my own sister until four months ago. The only person I told in all that time was Old Tom. He's..."

"I know who Old Tom is," interrupted the king, firmly but not unkindly. "Maud has briefed me comprehensively." He glanced outside at the sunlit garden then at Sasha. "Perhaps you two would like to accompany me for a stroll in my garden?"

Sasha's face brightened immediately.

"Of course, Sire," responded Jon stiffly, feeling he had been snubbed.

He rose to his feet and Sasha bounced over to his side as the king opened the French windows leading into the garden and gestured, "This way." As a fresh breeze blew in, he asked, "Not too cold?" When Sasha shook her head, Gavin stepped out onto the broad pale yellow gravel path that led down to the lake and said to her, "Do you think you could race down to that tree by the lake and pick one of those lovely pink flowers for me?"

Sasha stared at him for a moment, but the urge to explore overcame any qualms she might have had that this wasn't what a future queen should be doing.

As Jon joined him, Gavin turned to him. "I believe I was too abrupt. Sasha's worried eyes were distracting me, and I was racking my brains trying to think how to put her at ease." He gave the slightest of bows. "You have my apologies."

Jon took in a long breath and let it out slowly, letting the resentment dissipate. He stared at Gavin for a long moment before breaking into a genuine smile. "I don't know about you,

Sire, but I have no idea how to act in this situation. None of my court training, which was cut short at twelve, prepared me to meet a monarch, while I am both regent of a neighbouring power and, at the same time, an untitled refugee and footman."

Suddenly, Gavin stopped being formal and smiled at him. "No. Neither do I. It is, as you say, a most peculiar set of circumstances. It is really most reprehensible, both on your part and mine, that you have been living, unacknowledged, in fear within my realm all these years." Gavin raised his hand to forestall Jon's protest. "I understand why you didn't approach the throne before. In fact, I doubt that you could have broached the citadel of palace officials to gain an audience without Maud's intercession. But I have been extremely disturbed to discover that such a significant number of foreign agents have been hunting down Kimoran shamans and searching for Sasharia without my knowledge. That degree of interference within my realm is close to a justification for a declaration of war on Kimora. They have no right to hunt down residents of Carrador without my permission."

Whatever Jon had been going to reply was forestalled by Sasha who arrived at a run, flushed and slightly out of breath, bearing a large pink bottlebrush flower. She held it out to the king. "Here you are, Sire. The bush is full of them and there's a wren's nest right in the middle. Did you know that?"

"Thank you." Gavin smiled and accepted the flower. "No, I didn't know. Are there any eggs in it?"

Sasha grimaced. "I don't know. It was too high for me to see."

Gavin pointed to a mass of reeds further along the shore of the lake, "See over there? Inside that clump of reeds is swan's nest. Shall we go and inspect it?"

"Jayhan was right. You are just like other people."

Gavin raised his eyebrows. "Were you expecting horns?"

Sasha giggled. "No. That's just what I asked Jayhan when he thought I should be different if I were a queen."

"Did you indeed? That's a coincidence. Maybe we think the same way because we're related." Gavin veered off the path and walked across the lawn towards the reeds. The grass underfoot was neatly trimmed but damp, glistening in the morning sunshine.

"Are we?" asked Sasha, surprised.

"Yes. We share grandparents on our fathers' side. My father's younger brother married your mother. We are, in fact, cousins."

Jon glanced at Gavin speculatively. "So you believe Sasha's claim to the Kimoran throne?"

"Yes. I trust Maud implicitly. She and Sheldrake would have made very sure of their facts before presenting such a claim." He reached the side of the lake and began to pace along its shore, peering into the reeds, now and again pushing some aside. Then he stopped. "Ah, here we are." He gestured to Sasha then pointed through the reeds.

On a raised piece of land inside the reeds, a black swan sat on a large untidy collection of straw, old reeds and sticks. As they watched, her mate glided through the reeds from the other side and clambered up onto the nest, waggling his tail and shaking out his wings, showing off the panels of white on the underside of his wings.

Sasha smiled up at Gavin. "They're wonderful. I've never seen swans up close before." She chortled, her self-consciousness completely forgotten. "Wait 'til I tell Jayhan. He'll be so jealous."

Now the king's blue eyes did twinkle as he laughed in response. "I gather you two are very good friends."

Jon smiled wryly. "They are almost inseparable. We tried to leave Jayhan behind when we drove into the forest to introduce Sasharia to the Kimoran refugees, but he just stowed away on the back of the coach."

"I told you we shouldn't have left him out. It wasn't fair after he'd been with us for all the planning." Sasha turned earnest dark eyes up to Gavin. "Jayhan said you used to be nervous of his pale eyes, just like everyone else, but you don't need to be. He is brave and strong and kind, and a bit silly at times, well often, but," she shrugged, from her mature standpoint as a ten-year-old, "he *is* only eight. He's not evil."

A faint blush coloured the king's cheeks. "Oh dear. I tried not to show it, you know."

Sasha grinned. "I know. Jayhan told me."

Gavin rolled his eyes.

Jon laughed. "Whether his eyes are unnerving or not to his friends, they hold great power against his enemies. Did Maud tell you how he saved Sasha's life by pure desperate courage and mine with his eyes?"

"No. Maud didn't go into details. She merely told me that eight Kimoran agents had attacked a group of peaceful refugees within the forests to the east, while you, Sasha, Sheldrake and Maud were present. I believe people had gathered so that Sasharia could be introduced to them as their true queen and you could be instated as regent. Am I correct?" When Jon nodded, Gavin added with a hint of censure, "All without my knowledge."

"Again, I apologize," began Jon.

Gavin turned to head back towards the palace. "It is not just you. I am disappointed in Maud. Her loyalty to me should be paramount."

"It is, Sire. As soon as she knew, she told you about the shaman hunters and the number of shamans and refugees living within your borders."

Gavin was implacable. His anger was betrayed by the length of his stride, which made Sasha have to run a bit to keep up. "She did not tell me about you and Sasharia, not until last week."

"Had she considered us a threat, she would have. But when she first employed Sasha, Maud had no knowledge of her true identity and in fact, thought she was a boy."

"But she has known for some time now, I think." Gavin stopped and turned to Jon. "Don't play games with me. We both know that Maud should have informed me of a claimant to the Kimoran throne living within my realm, as soon as she knew. Think as a regent, before you reply."

Jon sighed. "You are right, of course." He frowned as he thought back to a conversation he had had with Maud and Sheldrake. "Sheldrake said it would be... awkward for you or them to be seen as complicit in undermining Toriana. They thought that it would be less problematic if Sasha's identity remained hidden. However, they did think through whether supporting Sasha compromised their loyalty to Carrador and decided that a more stable monarchy in Kimora would, in fact, be in Carrador's best interests, since the unrest in Kimora is affecting your trade relations with her."

Gavin's mouth was set in a thin line. Clearly, he was not impressed by their reasoning. Suddenly he was distracted by a little hand taking hold of his. He looked down to see Sasha gazing up at him with big worried eyes. "Please don't be mad at Maud. I was with a carter who beat me every day before they rescued me and took me on as their stable boy. It was my first good home outside the orphanage. Jon would have left his job and taken me on the road, but Sheldrake and Maud just wanted to keep me safe until they worked out what to do."

"Oh, for goodness sakes," exclaimed Gavin, rolling his eyes in exasperation. "No wonder they wanted to look after you. You both wear your hearts on your sleeves. Whether you intend it or not, you two are a force to be reckoned with." The king shook his head and turned once more for the palace, still holding Sasha's hand. "Come on. Let's go inside and have morning tea."

Chapter 48

When they re-entered the study, they found a low table set out in the middle of the room with freshly brewed tea and coffee, a jug of lemonade and a wonderful variety of little cakes, savoury morsels and sandwiches. Small side tables had been placed near the chairs so that the guests could help themselves and take their booty back to where they chose to sit.

"Wow!" breathed Sasha. She dragged her eyes away to look at the king. "Do you eat this *and* breakfast *and* lunch?"

Gavin laughed. "Not usually to this extent, no. Only when I have very honoured guests."

"Oh." Sasha blushed.

Gavin nodded at the food. "Go on. Help yourself to whatever you want. We'll let you go first."

With great restraint, Sasha did not overload her plate, although she looked longingly at a couple of little jelly cakes she couldn't fit on it, as she headed to her seat.

"Don't worry, "said Gavin, as he chose a bacon and egg tart and a cheese twist for his own plate. "You may come back for more."

Sasha beamed at him as she sat down.

"No wonder so many pictures of kings show them as overweight." Jon smiled at Gavin. "No reflection on you. You look pretty trim."

Gavin smiled and shook his head. "What is it about families? Even though we have never met, we still feel familiar to each other."

Jon looked surprised. "Yes, we do, don't we?"

Once they were seated and Sasha had had a few minutes to take the edge of her hunger, Gavin asked, "So tell me about your heroic little friend Jayhan. I think Maud must have been too modest to blow her own son's trumpet by telling me."

Sasha nearly choked herself trying to quickly finish the mouthful of cream cake she was eating.

Gavin held up his hand. "No rush. Please don't die on my account."

Sasha just managed to swallow rather than spit the cake she was eating as she laughed. She took a big breath and said, "Okay. I'm ready now." She gave her mouth a neat swipe with a serviette then began. "Jayhan followed the bad people from the inn into the forest. He knew two of them had bows and was worried they would shoot us as they had our family." She shot a sympathetic glance at Jon as she said this. She didn't remember her family being killed but she knew he did. "Leon, that's our coachman and Sheldrake's righthand man,

206

discovered Jayhan but told him to stay put while he went ahead to warn Sheldrake. Jayhan didn't, of course. He followed and found Leon unconscious on the path with a broken bow under him.... Which still left one more bowman."

"...and seven other attackers," put it Jon.

"So Jayhan followed them and saw the archer climb a tree. He snuck up after him... Jayhan and I climb trees a lot... and saw him about to shoot an arrow at me." She grinned. "So then he did the only thing he could. He threw himself on the archer and they both fell out of the tree, landing right next to me. Luckily," she added, wiping a bit of cream off her fingers with her napkin, "Jayhan landed on the bad man, who died."

"My word!" exclaimed Gavin who had been listening with rapt attention. "What a brave little lad."

Sasha beamed. "Yes, wasn't he? Mind you, I'd have done the same for him." This was not said to raise herself in Gavin's esteem, but simply as a statement of her friendship with Jayhan.

Gavin understood its intention and turned to Jon. "And how did our fearless young man save your life?"

Jon laughed. "By being terrified. When it looked like an attacker was about to slit my throat, Jayhan screamed out in pure terror and suddenly his eyes blazed forth with an amazing white light that froze our attackers with fear, horror... I'm not sure what... but did not affect any of his friends."

"Extraordinary. So his eyes are something to fear, after all," said the king thoughtfully. "No wonder they seem so uncanny. Can he do this at will or only *in extremis*?"

"I *like* Jayhan's eyes," said Sasha, quick to defend her friend.

"At this stage, he has only done it once, as far as I know," replied Jon, ignoring Sasha's outburst. "I doubt that he can do it at will."

Sasha looked from one to the other and frowned. "Jayhan doesn't like people being frightened of him. So he wouldn't want to, anyway."

Gavin sipped his coffee before setting his cup down, giving her time to calm down. "I think he might want to, if it protected people he cares about. Don't you?" He gestured at the central table. "More cakes?" When Sasha had helped herself to a jelly cake and a small chocolate cupcake, Gavin continued. "So, I have heard a little of your past, although I would be interested to hear a more detailed account of your flight from Kimora, Jon, and something of your life there at another time. Now, I would like you to explain your current living and working arrangements. Sasha?"

"I live at Maud and Sheldrake's and work as a stableboy."

"Light duties, I presume. Only a ruse, a front for visitors?"

Sasha shook her head. "Oh no. I muck out all the stables, clear the horse dung from the paddocks, feed, groom and help exercise the horses. And I'm learning how to mend the tack. Then in the afternoon, I have magic lessons with Lord Sheldrake and Jayhan... *then* Jayhan and I can play."

Gavin looked pole axed. "But Maud and Sheldrake know who you are. How dare they continue to treat you as though you were a servant?"

"Jayhan worried about that too, but they care more about keeping me safe and I agree with them. I love what I do. Besides, they are always kind and polite to me."

"Well, I presume your accommodation at least befits your station?" asked Gavin, slightly mollified.

Sasha grinned. "As a stableboy, yes. I sleep in amongst the hay above the stables. I have a little bed and a wooden crate as a side table and a small cupboard for my clothes and belongings."

The king's face darkened. "That is outrageous. Even if your throne has been stolen from you, you are still royalty and my kin. This cannot be allowed to continue." As Sasha began to protest, he held up his hand and turned his gaze to Jon "And you?"

"As Maud may have mentioned, I work as a footman in the Kimoran Embassy. I serve at table, ride behind the carriage, clean the silverware, horse's tack and carriages, and generally run errands and fetch things as required by Lady Electra. I have a small bedroom in the servant's quarters." He hurried on before Gavin could react. "My position has provided me with a wealth of information about the state of affairs in Kimora."

"Pah! I imagine it has, but at what cost? The humiliation of being in service to someone whom you outrank. Unconscionable!" Gavin leapt out of his chair and strode back and forth across the room, driven by his outrage. He no longer looked amiable and easy-going. He waved his hand and turned to look at them, a severe line cutting between his eyebrows. "You realise this cannot be allowed to continue? I will not have my kin working as mere servants. You will come to the palace and reside here. You will have your own apartment, servants and an allowance."

Far from being delighted, Jon face was tight-lipped and Sasha was clearly dismayed. Jon stood up and waited, stiff-limbed, until he could trust himself to speak. Finally he said, forcing himself to be courteous. "I thank you for your offer. But I did not come here to throw myself, ourselves, on your charity." When Gavin waved away his objection, he continued forcefully, "And I do not feel obliged to follow your dictates nor to act merely to suit your feelings of nicety."

The king put his hands on his hips. "You are in my kingdom. You will do as I say."

Jon realised that Gavin could, in fact, place them under house arrest within the palace, or worse, in the dungeons, if he chose to. He forced himself to calm down. After a long moment, where Gavin's last words hung in the air between them, he said quietly, "Are we to be your servants instead, but with no say in our fates, if we must do as you command?"

"No." Gavin seemed perplexed. He let his hands drop form his hips and walked over to pour himself another cup of coffee, giving himself time to think. "These cups are annoyingly small," he said tetchily to himself. He spoke once more to Jon. "I had thought you would be pleased. I may have phrased it rather more vehemently than I intended, because I was shocked by what you have had to deal with. I do not wish us to be at odds." He sipped his coffee and looked at them over the rim of the cup, noticing the strain in Sasha's eyes, before replacing the cup in its saucer. "I like what I have seen of you two or I would not have extended that invitation." He smiled self-deprecatingly. "I know. It sounded more like a command than an invitation. In fact, it was, which, as you have so carefully pointed out, rather defeats the purpose of delivering you from your servitude." He sat down, indicating that Jon should do likewise, and spoke in a calm but authoritative voice. "Very well. Let us start again and discuss this as equals. You know my thoughts on your immediate future. Let me hear yours. Sasha?"

Sasha knew he was addressing her as a future queen and was imposing on her a greater expectation of mature thought than the less complicated wishes of a ten-year-old. She took a deep breath. "I have only been with Lady Maud and Lord Sheldrake for about six months. Even though I act as their stableboy, I know they care about me and it is the first true home I have ever known. I really need to learn magic, which Sheldrake has organised for me, both from himself and from Yarrow, a shaman from Kimora. Yarrow also teaches me about Kimora, its history, customs and expectations. She is an unregistered shaman and in constant danger from the shaman hunters, so has been living in hiding for years. Beth, the head groom, has taught me reading in the evenings. I suppose I have had little training in numbers other than what I learnt in Stonehaven, the orphanage. In the afternoons, between magic lessons and dinner, Jayhan and I are allowed out to play." She smiled. "With all that, I have learnt to work hard and to make the most of every second. Also, I have recently discovered I have a brother. I have never been happier in my life."

Sasha looked around the room at the ornate cornices, the exquisite furniture and the oil painting on the walls and said, "I can see, though, that there is a whole way of life in a palace that I can't really learn at home. They have all been trying to teach me but when I look around here, I realise that it is not the same as being here. It feels completely different." She glanced at Jon then back to Gavin, her brow puckered in a frown. "But…"

"But she needs the warmth and stability she has found there," finished Jon for her, "At least for the time being, or for some of the time."

"I see." Gavin sipped his coffee. "And you?"

"Ah. Well, things have changed recently for me." When Gavin looked enquiringly at him, Jon continued, "After a little experiment we conducted at Sheldrake's birthday party, Lady Electra's amulet was released from the spell binding her will to Queen Toriana. She is, unbeknownst to Toriana, a free agent… and she knows who Sasha and I are and has sworn her loyalty to us." He gave a little chuckle. "And she now finds it embarrassing having me working for her. But she is bravely, and with some effort, continuing as before, to protect my identity." He grinned. "She has even gone so far as to purchase a phaeton so that she can talk to me without others around, while I act as her footman sitting behind her."

Gavin nodded. "I think I saw it the other day, barrelling up the High St. It has red enamelled panelling, doesn't it? Was that you up behind?"

"Yes. Dashing outfit, isn't it?" He grimaced. "Anyway, I would have to admit it is a bit awkward, now that she knows who I am. And now that she and her coachman support me, I could get most of the updates about Kimora without actually having to be in the Embassy myself."

"So, are you saying you will accept my *offer* after all?"

Jon smiled wryly. "Yes, I believe I will, but," he almost winced, "with two considerations." Gavin merely raised his eyebrows, becoming used to the fact that these two were indeed on a par with him. "I'm afraid my pride dictates that I need to be useful to you in some role so that I am paying my way, at least to some extent…"

"He's good with horses," put in Sasha helpfully.

"He cannot be a stableboy or a groom," said Gavin firmly. "And secondly?"

"Secondly, we need to consider whether I should be residing with you under my own name or incognito; for your safety, for mine and for the future of Kimora."

Gavin stood up and walked over to the window and stood, staring out across the lawns at the lake. After a moment, he looked at Jon over his shoulder and said, "My first instinct was to present you to the world with my support behind you. After all, in normal circumstances, an ousted monarch could live reasonably safely in a foreign court…" He turned to face them "But we have a complication: According to Kimora's constitution, the existence of Sasharia and her amulet actually invalidates Toriana's right to rule. When Kimorans discover they have been duped by a false amulet, they will rise against their false queen. And Toriana's response will be ruthless. Thousands will be killed… and all those spellbound shamans will be compelled to fight on her side." Gavin shook his head. "I don't think either," he glanced at Sasha and amended, "*any* of us wants that."

Jon gave a sigh of relief. "No. No, I'm so glad you see that. We have to keep Sasharia secret until the resistance is better organised and she is older, surer of her power, better trained in court craft and," he threw his hand up, "so many other things." He gave a wan smile. "I have tried to rally our refugees over recent years but until now I have had no recognised status. And well, for the first few years…" His eyes slid away from Gavin's.

Gavin walked over and laid a hand on his shoulder. "Jon, do not blame yourself. I only regret that I could not have helped you sooner. A boy of twelve, alone and penniless on the streets of Highkington…" He shook his head. "It does not bear thinking about." He patted Jon's shoulder bracingly. "I am lost in admiration at what you have achieved; saving Kimora's true monarch, setting up networks," At Jon's look of surprise, Gavin nodded. "Oh yes, I know about them - and your camps of refugees placed strategically though the forest. I'm glad you're not planning to overthrow my throne; you would make a formidable foe."

"Thanks." Jon grinned, his air of gloom dissipating. Then he frowned. "Hmm. It does sound rather intrusive, doesn't it, having all those networks and refugee camps within your borders. I can see why you might have been upset."

The king merely raised his eyebrows.

"If you wish it," said Jon magnanimously, "I will undertake to keep you informed of all developments related to Kimora within your borders."

He looked so much like an eager puppy hoping for praise that Gavin laughed. "Very good of you, I'm sure." He glanced at Sasha who was now roving the bookcases, peering at the spines of the leather-bound books. "Hmm. I think we may be boring our future queen."

She turned quickly, her face reddening with chagrin. "Sorry."

Gavin waved a dismissive hand. "Quite all right. Let me know if you find something you would like to borrow." He poured himself yet another cup of coffee, which was cooler now than most people would drink it. He took a sip as he sat down and didn't seem to mind. "And now to your immediate futures. Having taken your views into account, I intend to introduce Jon to the court as Lord Johnson, my new Minister for Transport. The role will encompass oversight of roads, horses and coaches, about which, Jon, you will already know a great deal, but it will also cover the rivers, coastline and seafaring vessels, about which I suspect you may have to learn." He gave a slight smile. "The role will also give you reason to travel around the kingdom." He took another sip as he waited for a reaction.

Jon's head nodded slowly up and down as he thought about it. Gradually a smile appeared on his face that grew until he was grinning from ear to ear. "That sounds marvellous, sire. But who do I replace, and will my persona bear up under scrutiny?"

"You will replace Sheldrake, as it turns out." At Jon's look of shock, Gavin raised his hand. "No. I am not doing away with Sheldrake's services. It is just that he has been holding that portfolio on top of his own since late last year when the previous Minister died unexpectedly. He will be delighted to be released from it. Sheldrake is also organising your persona." He smiled. "Unbeknownst to you, you own a moderately-sized holding up in the north of the country but have been travelling abroad for several years and have just recently returned."

Jon sat back in his chair, his expression wandering from amazement to suspicion to anger. "You had this all planned with Sheldrake from the start."

Gavin shrugged unapologetically. "Well, yes. I was planning on inviting you to reside in the palace, if you remember, and I had come to the same conclusion as you, that you should hide your identity for the time being. So, there we are."

"Huh." Jon's brow cleared. "Huh, there we are indeed. Thank you."

Gavin smiled. "A pleasure. Sheldrake and I had an enjoyable time inventing your persona. Now all he has to do is create it."

"And me?" asked a small voice from the side, "What about me?"

"You, my young cousin, will stay at Maud and Sheldrake's for another two years, at which time we will review it." As Sasha's face lit up, he raised his hand, "But, you must have a proper bed and bedside table, even if it must be up in the loft. You will need a wardrobe and clothes befitting a young princess, perhaps kept somewhere in the house to protect the expensive court dresses." As she went to protest, he overrode her, "You must learn the ways of court. No one can teach you that while you are dressed as a boy. I am not stipulating that you wear dresses while you are at home, but you will wear them when you come to court." With a flash of acumen, he added, "And tell your little friend that I forbid him from teasing you."

When she had nodded her agreement, he continued, "Over the next two years, you will visit me for several days at least once a month. While you are here, you will learn the ways of court and the nobility. My mother's Lady-in-Waiting has a daughter your age, who may bear you company while you are here. Her name is Lady Teresa." He gave another smile, his eyes crinkling in the corners. "And your name is Lady Natasha."

Sasha smiled back. "Clever. Then I can still be called Sasha?"

Gavin nodded. "And one last thing, which I think you two and your little friend may like above all else." He paused to give his announcement a sense of occasion. "I will employ a master at arms to teach Jayhan and you armed and unarmed combat. He will also provide extra security at Maud and Sheldrake's house while you are there. You, Jon, may join me in my training sessions here and have extra training as you choose and have time for. After all, I have been training for years whereas you, presumably, have not."

"Not formally, no. At least, not since I was twelve." He grinned. "I picked up a few tricks on the streets, but all help will be gratefully received. Thank you."

From there, their conversation turned to less weighty topics until next half an hour later, the indomitable woman in the black gown returned to usher them out.

Chapter 49

The trumpets blared and the huge doors swung slowly open, revealing a small, neatly turned-out boy accompanied by his parents. His father wore a black long coat reaching halfway down his thighs over a deep blue shirt and black breeches while his mother sailed beside him in a sapphire-studded deep emerald gown.

Jayhan, wedged between his parents, trod resolutely down the length of the audience chamber, his eyes lowered to avoid meeting anyone's gaze. When they reached the dais, Maud gave a low graceful curtsey while the two males bowed deeply as they stood before King Gavin whose eyes, once more, were twinkling benignly. Next to him, the herald thumped his gold staff twice on the floor and announced sonorously, "Jayhan Batian, accompanied by his parents, the Lady Maud Batian and Lord Sheldrake Batian."

Maud and Sheldrake stepped back and melted into the crowd of finely dressed lords and ladies on either side, who were looking on with mild curiosity, waiting to see why the small boy had been summoned.

"Look up, Jayhan," said the king softly. He rose and smiled down at Jayhan, resolutely meeting his pale eyes, before sweeping the audience with his gaze. Once he was sure he had everyone's attention, he spoke. "Today we honour a brave hero, who fought, with no thought for his own safety… "

"A bit of thought," muttered Jayhan. "I was scared to death."

"Shh," Sheldrake hissed from the sidelines.

Gavin gave a slight frown and amended, "who, although in fear of his life, persevered against almost impossible odds to stop an archer who had an arrow aimed at his friend. Jayhan Batian launched himself at the archer who was lying, bow string drawn, in the overhanging branches of a tree, sending himself and the archer plummeting twenty feet to the ground, thus saving the life of his friend." Gavin crooked his finger. "Come forward, Jayhan."

Jayhan stepped closer to the king, who took a medal suspended on a gold and red lanyard from a tray held by the herald and placed it over Jayhan's head so that the medal dangled on his small chest.

"Thank you," said Jayhan, beaming up at Gavin, who met his gaze stalwartly, his smile never faltering.

Then, amid the cheers and clapping of the audience, the king placed his hand on Jayhan's shoulder and turned him for all to see. "I give you, Jayhan who, at eight years old, is the youngest recipient of our nation's Star of Courage."

As Jayhan turned, the crowd's applause faltered, and a ripple of unease swept through the lords and ladies as they saw his pale eyes. Gavin felt the boy's chest heave beneath his hand as Jayhan lifted his chin and stared back defiantly. Gavin gave Jayhan's shoulder a reassuring squeeze and said loudly, "I can see you are all stunned by the beauty of Jayhan's pale lavender eyes. They are unique, as far as I know, and are the sign of a kind, brave, loyal friend. If you ever gain his friendship, feel privileged, as I do."

The crowd erupted into renewed applause and Gavin felt the tension drain from Jayhan's shoulders. Jayhan looked up at Gavin, his eyes shiny with tears, and whispered, "Thank you," knowing that for him, this was a far greater reward than the medal.

The Green-Eyed Man
The Dark Amulet Book 2

To all those men and women, who see each other as equal.

Acknowledgement

I would like to thank my sister and editor, Wendy Ealey, my proofreader Neil Gardner, my narrator William Merryn Hill and his wife for eagerly awaiting the next instalments, giving me the impetus to keep writing.

Part 1

Chapter 1

Sheldrake and Maud had been summoned to the palace to confer with the King.

A dour, solid woman in black ushered them into the same study that Jon and Sasha had entered. On this occasion she was not glaring. In fact, she smiled in welcome, but her eyes narrowed briefly in warning.

The King was not pleased.

"Thanks Josie," said Maud casually. "I've brought you a bunch of our lovely bottlebrushes. I'll give them to you after I've seen Gav... His Majesty."

Josie's smile broadened. "Lovely," she murmured as she withdrew.

Maud turned to the King and executed a low curtsey, lower than usual, while Sheldrake bowed, bending one knee. Gavin waited a moment before allowing them to rise, a sure sign of his displeasure. Once he had made his point, he waved them to armchairs and took up his favourite position, seated behind his desk. For a full minute, Gavin scrutinised them without speaking. They waited, knowing it was he who must speak first.

"So," Gavin said at last, picking up a gold pen and tapping it idly on the desktop. "Do I have your complete loyalty?" Then he held up a hand. "No. Don't answer that. Silly question. You're bound to say yes." He grimaced. "I know you finally told me about Jon and Sasha and that we have worked out their future living arrangements, but it preys on my mind that you did not do so straight away and that your loyalties may be compromised by your care for them. I have discovered for myself that they possess a vulnerable charm that is hard to resist. I need your objective reasoning and knowledge to help me decide what to do. Are you able to provide that? And can you explain your actions?"

Maud did not gush with reassuring words. In fact, she spoke with more reserve than usual. "I hope so, Your Majesty. As you say, Sasha and Jon are endearing, aren't they? We have become very fond of Sasha and were stunned, as you may imagine, when we discovered that our recently employed stable boy was actually a stable girl. Then Jon turned up and decided to trust us with the knowledge that Sasha was the rightful, but usurped, Queen of Kimora; a fact he had kept, even from her."

"And that you and he also decided to keep from me," interposed Gavin, with a clear note of censure.

"Ah. Yes." Maud looked uncomfortable

Sheldrake came to her rescue. "But not with the intention of deceiving you, Your Majesty."

"We will come back to that. Go on."

Sheldrake took up the thread. "By this stage, we had already begun to suspect that Sasha was someone out of the ordinary, Sire. People were looking for her, you see." He drew a breath. "And then, on top of all that, Jon told us that he was Sasha's elder brother."

Maud gave a tight smile. "Not something you'd guess, really; with Jon blue-eyed, fair and blond and Sasha the complete antithesis; dark hair, eyes and complexion."

"And we learnt all of this in the space of two days, Sire," said Sheldrake. "It was a lot to take in." He took a deep breath. "Sasha and Jon's identities had far-reaching implications, Sire, for them, for you, for us, for our country and theirs." He sat forward to give his next words emphasis. "But from the moment we knew who Sasha was, we thought through the ramifications of harbouring her, in terms of our loyalty to you and to Carrador. Under no circumstances would we compromise either."

"I am pleased to hear it. I would, however, have preferred to be a party to the consideration of those ramifications." Gavin's voice was not sharp, but his face was still shuttered.

"We were concerned, Sire," countered Sheldrake, "that you would not want to appear complicit in supporting a pretender to a neighbouring throne. So we thought that if you didn't know about it, the issue could be avoided."

Now Gavin did sound annoyed. "Sheldrake, I am quite capable of appearing ignorant of information, if it is politic to do so. I do it all the time." He took a breath to rein himself in, then gave a faint smile. "You have not cornered the market on intrigue, you know."

"I beg your pardon, Sire," said Maud with true contrition, "I believe we have been remiss, but not through any desire to undermine you. You have our undivided loyalty."

Gavin leant back in his straight-backed chair and let out a long breath. "I am pleased to hear that, and I accept your apology. I would never say this in front of my other advisors, but I depend very heavily on you two; you, Sheldrake, for your wealth of knowledge and contacts, and you, Maud, for your wisdom and the way you find patterns in that information to guide me."

Maud smiled warmly at him, the need for formality past. "You are doing well, Gavin. You are a fine king; authoritative, but receptive and fair, or as fair as you can be. Regardless of our loyalty, it is in our own best interests, as citizens of Carrador, to keep you as our sovereign."

Gavin gave a short laugh. "Thanks. Thank you indeed. Coming from you, who rarely praises and never flatters… "

"Oh Gavin," protested Maud. "I'm not that bad, am I?"

"Yes," said Sheldrake baldly. When she looked shocked and perhaps a little hurt, he smiled and added, "But… you are also warm and joyful and a tower of strength in times of trouble."

This was said with such rarely expressed, deep emotion that an awkward silence ensued. It was broken by Gavin who said prosaically, "And she's clever."

Sheldrake let out a little breath of relief. "Naturally. I would not align myself with someone tedious."

Maud looked from one to the other, smiling. "When you two have quite finished…"

"So," said Gavin, bringing them back to business. "As you are aware, my father's younger brother, Alfred, married Crown Princess Corinna, with the intention that he become Prince Consort when she became Queen, thus allying our two nations. Needless to say, that plan died in its infancy when my uncle and Corinna were assassinated. Until recently, I had no idea that my cousins had survived or that Queen Toriana was behind the attack." He paused, tapping the gold pen on his desk, frowning. He looked up suddenly. "Are we sure the Queen is implicated? It wasn't just a random bandit attack, as has been widely believed until now?"

"That is a good question," returned Sheldrake. "Our only source of information about the actual attack is Jon, who was only twelve at the time. He did not say that the attackers were Toriana's men."

"However," continued Maud, "from what he says, the attackers were clearly bent on obtaining the amulet, which is the symbol of authority and source of shamanic power in Kimora. Only a usurper would want that, don't you think?"

"Not an evil, power-hungry shaman?" asked Gavin.

Maud and Sheldrake both looked sceptical.

With a slight smile, Sheldrake answered, "From the information I have gathered, Toriana fits that description pretty well. She has bound shamans to her will using shamanic powers, which has never been done by previous monarchs. She has misled her people into believing that she has the one true amulet. She threatens or imprisons families of shamans, while hunting down those who have not yet been forced into binding their will to hers."

"And she has infiltrated your kingdom to do it."

"I have tried to find witnesses to, or participants in, the attack on Corinna's family." Sheldrake shrugged. "Naturally, no one is talking. But interestingly, within months of Toriana ascending the throne, an elite band of the Queen's warriors was sent by boat along the Kempsey River to quell a disturbance in a western province. Apparently, their boat capsized and all were lost." The spy master leaned forward. "But even more interesting; apparently a freak wave rolled down the river and swept them away."

Gavin looked from one to the other. "So you're saying...?"

"Strong shamans can control the weather, currents and the flow of water," said Sheldrake flatly.

Maud stood up and began to pace around the room. "Gavin, we are dealing with a very evil woman here. We must proceed very, very carefully."

"I see." Gavin stood up and crossed to a small side table that held a forest of cut crystal decanters and an array of glasses. "Drink, anyone? I think I need one."

Gavin poured himself a fine old amber brandy and one for Maud. Then he looked enquiringly at Sheldrake who opted for port.

Once he had handed them their drinks, Gavin sat down, this time in an armchair, an indication that his suspicions of them had been allayed. He idly rolled his brandy around his glass, watching the light playing in the amber liquid. After a minute, he said, "It is uncomfortable for me not to acknowledge my cousins for who they are, but I think we are agreed that the risks are too high if we openly declare that we are hosting them. Sasha doesn't just rival her aunt's rule; the existence of Sasharia wearing the High Shamanic amulet actually invalidates Toriana's right to rule. Toriana needs that amulet and she must force Sasha to say the words of power to pass it on to her."

"The amulet protects Sasha," Sheldrake reminded him.

Gavin sipped his brandy before putting his glass down on a side table. "Perhaps so, though to what extent I think none of us is sure. But it does not protect those around Sasha. All

Toriana would have to do is threaten to kill or maim Jon or Jayhan. Sasha would do anything to protect them. And once Toriana had been given the true amulet, she would kill Sasha. Don't you think?"

Maud felt her blood run cold. An involuntary shudder coursed down her backbone. "And already, a military force has made an incursion within your borders and nearly succeeded in abducting Sasha."

Sheldrake laid a reassuring hand on Maud's arm. "We think they were simply looking for unregistered shamans to take back and force into service with the Queen. They might suspect or hope or dread that Sasha survived the attack on her family but only a very few know for sure. And the only survivors of that attack are safely in your custody, Sire." He stood up and paced to the window, looking out at white cumulus clouds billowing on the horizon beyond the lake. After a few moments, he turned back to face the other two. The lines in his face seemed deeper than before. "The force we tangled with may have been small, but where there is one small force, there may well be more."

"I agree," said Gavin. "Even though we have already made it clear to Toriana, have we not, that her shaman hunters are not welcome within our borders?"

"Yes, Sire, we have," said Maud, tucking her legs up under her as she sipped her brandy, rather reminiscent of a cat. "And I am sure the message has had time to reach her."

The King ruminated while he swirled the brandy in his glass. When he looked up, he had clearly come to a decision. "So not only has she had my uncle killed, she is continuing to hunt people within our borders, despite a clear prohibition from me. Still, I do not want to push Kimora to war with us. It would hurt both of our countries and their people. She may not care about that, but I do. But I do want these incursions to stop. Sheldrake, our borders are already guarded but obviously not well enough. Where are our weaknesses?"

Sheldrake crossed to the large map of Carrador that hung on the study wall. Using it to demonstrate his points, he said, "Two main roads run between our nations, one through the Great Forest and one to the south of it through fields and farms. These both have secure checkpoints that can be placed on high alert. There is also a narrow, twisting, overgrown path in the south of the forest but few people know of it or can even navigate it. However, a skilful elite force is much more likely to cut across the fields or infiltrate through the forest. There we have a problem."

"Couldn't we enlist the aid of the farmers near the borders?" asked Gavin, glancing at Maud for her opinion. "Perhaps offer rewards for information about strangers in the area or put them on a retainer?"

Maud nodded. "Good idea. I think rewards might be more motivating. I suppose you may get some who will try to falsify trails or give false evidence." She looked at Sheldrake "But I presume your spiders could sort the wheat from the chaff, couldn't they?"

Sheldrake looked pained, as she knew he would, at having his agents referred to as spiders, but everyone knew them as the King's Spiders, whether he liked it or not. He sighed. "Yes. Time would be wasted, of course, following up false leads, but overall I think the idea has merit." He shrugged. "It does not, however, solve the problem of incursions through the forest."

Gavin frowned. "No, it doesn't, and the border between our two countries winds through more than a hundred miles of forest." He stood up and walked over to study the map closely. "Most of it follows the Charville River but that is no deterrent. There are many places where the river can be easily crossed... and most of them are deep within the forest, out of view of checkpoints or farmers." The king straightened and looked at Sheldrake. "The stakes are high. We must secure our borders. I'll give you a fortnight to consult and come up with a plan to secure the border within the forest. Meanwhile, we will strengthen our checkpoints and instigate incentives for farmers to be our eyes and ears. Agreed?"

This was a rhetorical question, but Sheldrake and Maud both nodded dutifully and soon afterwards were sent on their way.

Just as Josie was about to close the door behind them, Gavin called them back. "By the way, as agreed, I've arranged for a master at arms to take up residence with you. Don't let his looks belie you. He's good, very good. He will protect and teach Sasha and Jayhan. His name's Stefan." He flashed a knowing smile at Sheldrake. "If you're wanting to do a background check on him, his men call him Stefan Longshanks."

Chapter 2

Stefan arrived two days later.

He walked up to the front gate late in the morning and peered left and right along the low, white-painted picket fence that fronted Batian House. It looked innocuous, but he was not fool enough to enter a mage's house unannounced. He rang the big brass bell that hung on the right-hand side of the gate and waited.

A well-muscled man of above medium height arrived a couple of minutes later and stood looking down at him, studying him and the backpack slung over his shoulders. After a moment, the man said, "Good morning. May I help you?"

Stefan grinned. "I believe you are expecting me. My name's Stefan."

Leon's eyes widened in surprise although he quickly quelled his reaction. Stefan knew he would be wondering at his short, slight stature and gave a mental shrug. "We are indeed. Just a minute." Leon touched a series of points on the gate then lifted the latch and swung the small gate open.

As he stepped through, Stefan nodded his approval. "Magical ward, I'm assuming?"

"It is. I'm Leon, coachman, henchman, general factotum and recently, babysitter."

When Stefan raised his eyebrows in query, Leon gave a short laugh. "Sasha and Jayhan get up to all sorts of tricks and I try to keep an eye on them amongst my other duties."

Stefan nodded. "Pleased to meet you. Sounds like I'll be sharing some of your duties. Well, the babysitting at least."

"It's not onerous. They are friendly and polite, just a bit too adventurous."

Just as they reached the front door, it swung open and a tall, solid butler looked down his nose at him before glancing a query at Leon, who responded by saying, "Stefan, our new master at arms; Clive, our butler."

Clive returned his gaze to Stefan, staring at him poker-faced for a moment, clearly taking his measure. Suddenly he smiled. "I believe the King thinks very highly of you. Welcome to Batian House. Let me take your backpack and I will show you to the salon and inform Maud and Sheldrake of your arrival."

"Thank you. The rest of my equipment should be here later this afternoon."

Left alone in the salon, Stefan studied the portraits on the wall, the dark wood wainscot and the small antique chandelier that hung from the ceiling before walking lightly to the window to gaze out into their lovely cottage garden. A ginger cat was crouched under a grevillea, swivelling its hips as it readied itself to pounce on a lovely little grass parrot.

Stefan tapped the window, distracting the cat and startling the parrot into flight. Giving himself a little satisfied grin, he turned back into the room to find himself being surveyed by the lady of the house.

Maud, a vision in her billowing deep green, swept across the room, beaming and holding her hands out to take his. "How do you do? I see you just saved one of our little parrots. What a good beginning. I am Maud."

"How do you do, Ma'am?"

"No, please call me Maud." The door opened further and Sheldrake, dressed in his customary black coat and breeches over a white shirt, stepped neatly into the room. "And this is Sheldrake."

Stefan disengaged his hands from Maud's and gave a small bow. "How do you do? I have heard a great deal about you both. It is an honour to meet you."

"Your reputation also precedes you," said Sheldrake, smiling. "I believe the King put a lot of thought into your appointment. You are far and away their best marksman, I believe. So, welcome."

Stefan grinned. "You did some research, did you? I thought you might. That's why you two don't look shocked, as Clive and Leon did. You could have warned them." His green eyes twinkled up at them, the top of his light brown hair at the height of Sheldrake's shoulder.

Sheldrake gave a little chuckle. "I want you to spar with Leon before he has had time to take your measure. He is big and strong but lacks a certain subtlety in his approach. I am hoping you may have enough time to train with him too."

"Unarmed combat is my least favourite form of attack, but I will do my best."

His eyes strayed to the door as Clive entered, carrying the best silver teapot on a tray with cups, sugar and milk. As he set it down on a low polished table in the centre of the room, Sheldrake's eyes met his butler's and they shared a private smile. Stefan's brows twitched together, hoping he was not a source of amusement to them.

Maud noticed his disquiet and said, as she moved to pour the tea, "Our best teapot. I see you have already earned Clive's approval."

"Have I? I don't know why. I've only just arrived." Stefan accepted a cup of tea and blew on it to cool it. "Thank you. This will be most welcome. It was a bit further than I expected from the King's palace."

"Good heavens! You didn't walk, did you? It's over twelve miles. Didn't they provide you with a carriage?" asked Sheldrake, shocked.

Stefan waved his hand at the view of the garden through the window. "It's a lovely day for a walk and I saw some beautiful gardens on the way here." He smiled. "I must say yours is one of the best. It will be a pleasure to stay here for a while."

While Sheldrake and Maud were digesting this unexpected side of their new arms master, the sounds of chatter and laughter preceded the precipitous entry of two children, who drew up short at the sight of an unknown visitor. One was clearly the son of the house, dressed in expensive but practical shirt, breeches and jerkin, while the other appeared to be a stable boy, dressed similarly but in rougher plainer clothes. Two pairs of eyes, one piercingly pale and the other meltingly dark brown, stared at him.

Then the children performed neat bows and straightened, smiling.

"How do you do," said Jayhan, on his best behaviour.

"I am well, thank you, young man," responded Stefan. "My name is Stefan."

A slight interrogatory lift on the end of Stefan's words prompted Jayhan to add, "Oops. Sorry. I am Jayhan and this is Sasha."

"Hello. Are you our new master at arms?" asked Sasha. When he nodded, she smiled, "Your eyes are a beautiful colour. I've never seen green eyes before."

Stefan blinked. His face scrunched in thought. "You know, now that you mention it, neither have I. I never thought about it before."

"Then you and Jayhan are both special," pronounced Sasha cheerfully. "His eye colour is unique too."

"When will we have our first training session?" asked Jayhan eagerly.

"Oh yes, we are dying to learn how to fight," added Sasha.

"I am not sure," interrupted Maud, "that badgering someone is the best way to begin an acquaintanceship."

Sasha coloured. "I beg your pardon, Madam. Um, perhaps I had better go. I need to check the poultice on Chester's hock anyway."

"No, Sasha, don't go." Maud's voice had softened as she held an arm out. "Come here." She wrapped her arm across Sasha's shoulders. "I am not cross. I just think Stefan might like a little time to get settled and find his bearings first." She smiled down at Sasha. "After lunch, perhaps you two would like to show Stefan around the farm and the stable and some of your favourite places in the bush?"

Sasha and Jayhan's faces lit up. Maud hoped that Stefan had not been planning on having a formal relationship with the children because she doubted he would be able to maintain it by the end of the afternoon. But from what she had seen of him, he did not seem very formal or stringent.

"Sasha, have your ponies saddled up and ready after lunch. Who do you think for Stefan?"

Stefan cut apologetically into her thoughts as Sasha was running her mind along the row of horses in the stable. "If you don't mind, something not too big and not too mettlesome. I like quiet, gentle horses."

Everyone looked at him in surprise, their view of an arms master undergoing yet another revision. He just shrugged and gave an embarrassed smile.

Maud glanced at Sasha. "I think we'll give him Maisy."

Sasha's eyes widened. "Really?"

Maud sighed in exasperation at Sasha's lack of duplicity. "Yes. Really. She needs the exercise." Narrowing her eyes, she added dryly, "Apparently she is getting a little tubby."

"Oh, not tubby, madam. Just a little… hm… solid?" Sasha winced and looked beseechingly at Jayhan, who just chuckled and didn't help at all.

Stefan watched this interchange, feeling once more that he was missing something. He frowned. "Well, I hope this horse is not so broad that I won't be able to straddle her. I don't have very long legs, you know."

This sent Jayhan and Sasha off into gales of laughter. Maud frowned repressively at them before saying, "Don't worry. They're not laughing at you. They're laughing at the thought of Maisy being that fat. She's not at all, as you will see," she folded her arms and added firmly, "and she has a wonderful temperament."

Stefan was at a loss to see why this sent the two little miscreants off into renewed laughter. Sheldrake was unimpressed with their lack of manners and shooed them out with a flea in their ear, before apologizing on their behalf.

On the surface, Stefan accepted the apology but underneath, he was wondering whether he was about to endure yet another repetition of the teasing and bullying he had faced over the years because of his size. It was not a promising beginning.

Chapter 3

After lunch, Maud excused herself, saying she wanted to check that the horses were ready. So Stefan was a little surprised when she wasn't there to see them off on their tour around the property.

"Hello," said Jayhan when he saw Stefan approaching. "I'm sorry we got the giggles. I promise it wasn't about you." He indicated a beautiful, quiet, grey pony. "This is my pony, Slug." He shrugged. "I called him Storm when I first got him but..."

Stefan grinned. "He sounds perfect for me."

Jayhan smiled back. "That's what *I* thought, but Mum wants you to ride Maisy." He nodded at a solid, dark brown mare that Sasha was just leading out of the stables. "She's not much bigger than Slug but she is definitely kinder. Slug's a pain. I have to turn myself inside out to make him trot and when he canters, he acts like I'm trying to kill him. He's a lazy little layabout. We're hoping Maisy might be able to sort him out."

Seeing Stefan's confusion, Sasha stepped in. "You know, like dogs affect each other's behaviour sometimes. If the other two horses keep up a good pace, maybe he won't want to be left behind."

Stefan looked dubiously at Maisy standing stolidly beside Sasha. "I hope she doesn't keep up too good a pace." He walked up to her and, just as Sasha was about to offer to give him a leg up, leapt lightly into the saddle. He took the reins from her and gathered them, holding them lightly but firmly.

Sasha frowned at him. "I thought you couldn't ride."

"I didn't say that. I just said I like placid horses."

"Huh." Sasha swung herself up with practised ease onto her wilful little pony. "This is Tosser," she said, as her pony promptly lived up to his name by tossing his head and trying to nip Slug.

They walked their horses down the gravel road between the fields, with Jayhan and Sasha pointing out particular trees with bird's nests in them, waving vaguely at the mob of sheep, introducing the farmhands, Jake and Thompson, to Stefan, and telling him about their tree house and the various adventures they had had together. Stefan's apprehension that he might have to deal with being the butt of their teasing lessened. He wasn't afraid of the possibility; it just wearied him.

As they neared the bushland behind the paddocks, Sasha asked, "Do you mind if we canter for a short while, just to the tree line so Mau... Maisy can try to sort out Slug?"

"Go on then," said Stefan. "Come on Maisy, a canter if you please." He pressed with his legs, increasing the pressure until the horse beneath him responded, changing straight from a walk to a canter. She had a rocking horse gait which Stefan found very comfortable. As he came up alongside Jayhan who was kicking Slug futilely, Maisy turned her head and nudged Slug sharply in his side behind the saddle. Slug kicked out a back leg then forced himself into a bone-shattering trot, but no more. Maisy cantered ahead then slewed into his path, forcing him to skid to a halt. Jayhan jerked forward in the saddle, nearly going over his stubborn little pony's head. On Maisy's back, Stefan sat firmly despite the sudden change in direction and made no move to direct her. Maisy tossed her head up and down, baring her teeth and even snapping a couple of times.

Slug backed up, the whites of his eyes showing. Maisy snorted, then swung around abruptly and bolted up the road towards the bushland. Sasha put her heels to her feisty little pony and bolted after her.

Even though he was being carried at a full gallop, Stefan looped the reins over the pommel of the saddle before letting go of them entirely. Then he looked back over his shoulder, completely unconcerned at the pace, to see Slug galloping after them, his tail flicking in irritation. He leaned forward and patted Maisy on the shoulder. "Well done. You got that naughty little bag-o-bones moving."

Then as the bushland loomed, he leaned even further forward and whispered into her ear, "And now I would like you to pull up." Her ear flicked back and forth. For a moment, he felt her muscles bunch as she actually increased her pace. Stefan chuckled. He leant over again. "Now please, or I will have to use the reins." Immediately, he felt the drumming lessen as her hooves hit the ground less forcefully and she gradually slowed to a stop. Stefan chuckled again. "I don't know exactly what is going on, but you are no ordinary horse. I thought you might understand me. Usually, I teach my horses to respond to my voice, but you already do so with no training of mine. Interesting."

Sasha and Jayhan caught up with them and pulled up their ponies. Tosser was, predictably, tossing his head with the excitement of a good run. Slug just stood there as placid and boring as ever, although Jayhan was a bit breathless. His face was glowing as he praised Slug and gave him a hearty pat on the shoulder.

"That was better," he said enthusiastically. "So do you want to come and see our creek? It's not too far."

They had stopped fifty yards short of the bushland and Stefan ran his eyes along the fence line to the left and right of him before asking, "Isn't there a magical ward at the rear of the property?"

Jayhan shrugged. "I don't know. Maybe. This isn't the end of our place though. We have two hundred acres of bush out the back here. Miles more land than we have with sheep on it."

"It makes a great playground," said Sasha, grinning. "Maud and Sheldrake wanted to save some of the bushland before all the houses from Highkington took over. The outskirts of the city aren't here yet. We are still quite a way out of town, but the city is growing."

"Huh. That's good." Stefan let his gaze travel across the canopy of eucalypts, their leaves glistening in the sunlight and then lowered his gaze to the grevilleas and wattle growing between them, little gold pompoms and red intricate flowers dotted amongst their foliage.

He watched a little family of blue wrens darting across the grass near the bushes at the edge of the forest and nodded at the brown wrens. "You know the duller brown ones are called Jenny wrens? And only the males have that glorious blue? Sad for the ladies really, isn't it?"

"I suppose so," said Sasha dubiously.

Stefan stored away the knowledge that Sasha wasn't totally pleased about her future role as a lady of the court but didn't comment. Instead, he said, "I come from the forest myself, you know. I grew up among trees and bushes and birds and animals. I'm glad someone wants to look after them. Let's go and see your creek."

As they urged their horses into motion, Sasha asked, "Which forest do you come from?" As soon as she asked, she realised she probably wouldn't know it anyway. But surprisingly, she did.

"The Great Forest, the forest between Carrador and Kimora. My parents own an inn deep in the forest called..."

"The Creeping Vine," chorused Jayhan and Sasha.

Stefan was surprised. "You know it?"

They nodded enthusiastically but then fell silent, glancing at each other.

For a few minutes they walked on in silence before Stefan reined up. He leaned forward and asked quietly in Maisy's ear, "Can you hear or smell anything untoward in our surroundings? Is this a safe place for me to talk to these two?" Maisy did not respond but her ears flicked back and forth. "If all is clear, stamp your front left hoof."

Maisy stamped her front left hoof and Stefan patted her shoulder in thanks.

"Excellent horse you have here," he said conversationally to the children. "Now, before we go any further, let's sort out our trust levels. You don't have to tell me about Maisy here, but I can see you're worried what you can and can't tell me. Given your situation, Your Highness," he said with a twinkle in his eyes and a slight bow to Sasha from the saddle, "I applaud your caution. I know who and what you are, Sasharia, and I know you, Jayhan, received a medal for saving her life. Not only that, I have also been told about the extraordinary power of your eyes, Jayhan, and the extraordinary power of your amulet, Sasha." He grinned at them. "I don't know everything, but I know enough that you can trust me with the rest when the time is right and it is relevant."

Both children let out a sigh of relief and smiled.

"So your inn, The Creeping Vine," began Sasha, "is where we all met before we went into the forest to tell a small group of refugees that I... well, tell them who I am and that Jon is to be regent for me until I come of age."

"And that's where the attackers came and nearly hurt Sasha," added Jayhan. "In the forest, not at the inn, although they did stay at the inn before going into the forest." Catching an irritated frown from Sasha, he gave a lop-sided smile. "Okay. I'll shut up now."

"Aha!" said Stefan, ignoring the last little interchange. "Well fancy that! Then you probably met my father – he's the innkeeper – and one or two of my brothers."

Sasha thought back. "The innkeeper was nice; big and round and cheery. I think I saw one other man working there. Yes, he looked quite a lot like the innkeeper, now you mention it. Both had pale faces but black hair. I don't remember what colour their eyes were, but not green. I would have remembered if they were green." She hesitated then added, "They were a bit taller than you, I think."

"Yes. A lot taller than me, actually. A good six inches." Stefan gave a rueful grimace. "I'm the runt of the family, I'm afraid."

"Who else is in your family?" asked Jayhan. Maisy sidled and grunted, making him add hastily, "if you don't mind telling us."

"No, I don't mind telling you, but we might as well keep walking now that we've cleared the air a little bit." When the other two horses moved forward, Maisy fell into step beside them with no instruction from Stefan. He noted it but kept to the topic under discussion. "I have two older brothers and an older sister and I also have two younger brothers. They all look alike… well, similar, and none of them looks like me. Even my sister, Marjorie, is taller than me."

"Do you mind?" asked Sasha kindly.

Stefan smiled at her. "Thank you for asking. No, I don't mind how I look or how I'm built, but I did get sick of being the brunt of the family's jokes and being bullied by my bigger, stronger brothers." He shrugged. "I guess that is part of the reason I became so good at fighting."

"What? For revenge?" asked Jayhan, a hint of eagerness in his voice.

"No, young sir." He reached over and ruffled Jayhan's hair. "Not for revenge. To protect myself."

"Oh." Jayhan thought about it for a minute. "Hmm. I can see that if you tried to take revenge on them, there'd be five against one coming back at you even worse."

"No, they didn't usually gang up on me. Usually just one or two poked fun at me or sometimes started to get physical. Sometimes the ones not involved would even tell them to lay off. Mostly they thought they were being funny. But if anyone outside the family picked on me…" Stefan gave a short laugh. "Well, you don't pick on the Vine family; that's all there is to it."

Jayhan considered him. "So would you protect your sister or brothers if they needed it, even after they treated you badly?"

"In a heartbeat," said Stefan.

Chapter 4

Sasha, Jayhan and Stefan met at mid-morning the next day in the space behind the stables where Leon kept piles of gravel, soil and sand, stacks of firewood, scrap pieces of metal and wood and some of his tools. He had cleared a roughly circular sandy patch in the middle to use for fighting practice until they could set up an area in one of the paddocks and was now sitting on a pile of firewood watching to see what they would do.

Maud and Sheldrake also wandered over to watch and, rather to the mage's surprise, so did the rest of their household; Eloquin the governess, Clive the butler, Clive's wife Beth who was also the head groom, Rosie the maid, her little brother Edgar and even Hannah, the cook. At the last minute, even Jake and Thompson, the farmhands, came running to join them, wiping their hands on their breeches and looking a little sheepish.

Stefan stood in the middle of the sandy patch, hands on hips and gradually turned a full circle to observe his audience. Eventually he said, "You do know I am not an entertainer?"

This produced murmurs among his audience but failed to move any of them.

"Please, sir," said Rosie, "we'd like to see what you do. We're all very excited to have an arms master in our household. We promise we won't come every morning." She glanced at Sheldrake. "Anyway the master won't let us. We usually have lots to do, you know."

Stefan turned a puzzled frown to Sheldrake, who looked just as bemused as he did. "Huh. Very well. Well, I can't do this alone. So, who would like to shoot some arrows?" A forest of hands went up, making Stefan laugh. "You're an enthusiastic lot, I'll give you that. Leon and Beth, can we set up a hay bale as a target? I don't want to blunt my arrows by shooting into a tree or the side of the stables."

He reached down and rummaged in his big tote bag, which had arrived by coach several hours after him. He withdrew four bows and set about stringing them as he spoke, pausing occasionally for grunts of effort. "We will begin with each of you trying to draw back each bow so that the string is level with your right ear, unless you're left-handed, in which case it will be your left ear."

He demonstrated with the first strung bow before setting it down and moving on to stringing the second as he spoke. "The stronger the bow, the greater the distance you will be able to shoot. However, if the bow is too difficult for you, your accuracy is likely to be affected. So it is a balance. You can also increase your distance to some extent by angling your bow upwards, but that requires more practice and accuracy." He grinned. "Then of course, there is the wind to consider." He glanced around. "But there is little wind this morning and we are in a sheltered spot here, so that won't be a factor we have to worry about today."

When he had the bows all strung, he lined them up on the ground and asked, "Okay, who's first?"

Rather to his surprise, Sasha and Jayhan hung back and allowed the servants to have first shot. When Stefan looked enquiringly at them, Jayhan shrugged and said quietly, "We will be training with you often, whereas they will not have the same chance. So it is better to give them the most time today."

"Well said, young man. However, I do want you to try the bows today so that I can order one to suit you."

Jayhan's eyes widened. "My own bow?"

Stefan smiled. "Yes. On the King's orders. Once he decides to act, there are no half measures. You too, Sasha... and Leon."

Only Leon and Jake could draw back the full-sized bow, but Sheldrake, Thompson, Clive and Beth could draw the second largest to Stefan's satisfaction, while Hannah, Rosie and Maud could manage the third largest. Much to their disgust, Jayhan, Edgar and Sasha were only able to convincingly draw back the string on the smallest bow.

"Don't look so disappointed," chided Stefan. "These are not the smallest bows in existence; only the smallest bows I thought worth bringing with me." When this did not console them, he added, "Once you have mastered a bow of this size, you will naturally graduate to a larger one as you grow older and your arm strengthens. Anyway, small bows are much handier for carrying around. I often use a small bow even now, when I am travelling light."

With the bows chosen, he set up the targets and, using the small bow, gave a demonstration of how to hold and aim an arrow. Then everyone took turns in using the correct bow for their strength. Their lack of skill led to high hilarity as many of the arrows missed the hay bale altogether, skidding along the ground or sailing over the fence into long grass in the adjoining paddock. Stefan made a mental note to enlist the children in a treasure hunt for the arrows hidden in the grass, knowing they would not be easily found.

When they had tired of this, Hannah and Rosie enlisted Jake and Thompson. The four of them slipped away to the kitchen, returning shortly afterwards with trays of lemonade and sandwiches.

"Thank you, Hannah," said Sheldrake. "Do we have time for more? When do you need to start dinner?"

"If this counts for lunch, sir, I could spare another couple of hours." Hannah gave a warm smile. "It's like a holiday, isn't it, sir? A rare thing indeed."

Sheldrake gave a little shake of his head and smiled in return. "I don't know what's come over me. A new member of the household does not usually warrant such attention." He heaved a contented sigh. "But it is enjoyable for a change and I hope that every staff member can spend some time with Stefan learning at least the rudiments of self-defence."

Hannah glanced at him, worried. "Are you expecting trouble, sir?"

"I hope not. No, I don't think so, but I hope not anyway."

This did little to reassure his cook, who determined to speak further at a later date with Maud. After the archery came sword play, using wooden practice swords that Stefan drew from his apparently bottomless tote bag. He only had six of them, so he paired up people of similar strength and let the others watch as he took them through the rudiments of stance, grip, basic thrusts and parries. Then they swapped so that everyone had a turn.

In the middle of the afternoon, after another refreshment break, he introduced hand-to-hand fighting. He was so quick, lively and encouraging that no one grew weary of the lessons.

He began by standing with his arms loosely at his side and inviting Beth and Maud to lift him up. They did this with relative ease and lowered him back to the ground looking a little puzzled. Then he bent his knees slightly, held his arms crooked before him and focused hard. When he repeated the request to lift him, Maud and Beth stepped forward confidently but found it took everything they had to shift him even slightly. Lifting him into the air was out of the question. After a few minutes of strenuous effort, they stood back puffing and grinning.

"Are you using magic?" demanded Sheldrake.

Stefan laughed. "No. Not at all. You can all do it. Pair up and try it. On the second try, imagine yourself as a tree rooted into the ground, your weight low, heavy and connected to the earth. You'll see."

Once they had all tried this to their satisfaction, he asked Rosie and Hannah to step forward to demonstrate fighting techniques. He used them as models to explain low and high blocks and the use of fingers in the eyes and a kick to the crotch, all in slow motion and not connecting.

"These last two are fighting dirty," he explained cheerfully. "But if you ever find yourself in a position where you have to fight, don't pussyfoot around. Fight fiercely and fight dirty. For now, let's just practise the low and high blocks in pairs. One person, try to attack; the other, block. Three minutes, then swap. I don't want to hear any sounds of flesh connecting with flesh. This is just shadow fighting to get the hang of it. All right?"

When they had finished, Stefan gave them a flourishing bow and said firmly. "And that is it for today. You have all done remarkably well. You must be exhausted, but I hope you have learnt something and if you wish it, I can organise further training for you around your other duties."

A ragged round of applause greeted this pronouncement, but a couple of voices were raised in protest that they hadn't seen Stefan fight. Then Jake urged Stefan to challenge Leon while others urged Leon on. Sheldrake watched with his arms folded, a gleam of anticipation in his eye.

Leon stepped up to Stefan, whose head barely reached his shoulder. But instead of squaring off against him, he put his arm across the smaller man's shoulders and turned to the onlookers. "I may look big and bovine, but that doesn't make me totally stupid." He shot a speaking glance at Sheldrake as he said this. "Stefan didn't become a master-at-arms without being an accomplished fighter. I'm more of a street brawler myself, but I have nothing to prove and neither does Stefan. I have no doubt he'd wipe the floor with me, but I would rather he taught me how to do that, than have him do it to me now."

Although a couple of them were still disappointed, they knew an impasse when they saw one and the rest chuckled quietly and left, well satisfied with the day's activities. As the crowd dispersed, Stefan smiled up at him. "You know, it is a nice change, not having to prove myself."

Leon gave him a slow smile in return, clapping him on the shoulder and removing his arm. "Even if I could beat you, which maybe I can and maybe I can't, I wouldn't do it to a newcomer, just to satisfy this lot." He shrugged. "Besides, what's in it for me? If I win, I look like a bully; if I lose, I look like a fool."

Stefan raised his eyebrows. "You could do it to let me show off... "

Leon scratched his chin. "You know, I didn't think of that. Do you want to?"

A derisive snort of laughter was his answer.

Chapter 5

Just as the family were finishing their dinner, a knock sounded on the dining room door and Clive popped his head in to say that Stefan had asked to see Sheldrake.

Sheldrake wiped his mouth neatly with his napkin before informing Clive that they would see him in the salon in fifteen minutes. "And bring down the fine Montreyan port that Argyve gave me the other week." He smiled at Maud. "Will you be joining us, my dear?"

"I will. I don't want Stefan to get into the way of only conferring with you, do I? Besides, I want some of that port."

They finished their coffee, bid Jayhan and Eloquin goodnight and made their way downstairs. They came upon Stefan in the hallway, squatting down, intent on scratching a large tortoiseshell cat under the chin. The cat was purring its appreciation and pressing itself up against his knees.

"You asked to see me?" asked Sheldrake dryly.

Stefan turned his head but did not immediately stand up. "Oh, hello. You are wonderfully punctual. Good to know."

"That cat is George and he knows he should be in the kitchen," said Maud, with an edge to her voice that George ignored.

Stefan gave him a final stroke and stood up. "He must have followed me in. Would you like me to take him back before we get started?"

"No," said Maud, sailing past Sheldrake who was holding the door open for her. "He'll wander back when he's ready."

Sheldrake and Maud arrayed themselves in armchairs before him and waved him to another. Stefan sat down neatly and attempted a smile. He was just about to speak when Clive arrived to deliver a tray bearing a cut glass decanter of a dark ruby port and three glasses. Stefan looked a bit startled. After all, he had eaten his dinner earlier with the servants in the kitchen.

"Don't worry," said Maud kindly, "we won't force port on you every time you want to see one or both of us. It is our custom to have a quiet drink after dinner and we thought you might like one after you did such an excellent job with the staff today."

"Besides," Sheldrake added shrewdly, "I suspect you have quite a bit you need to discuss with us, now that you've seen the place."

Stefan accepted a port from Clive and nodded his thanks. "I do." He waited until Clive left, then began, "Firstly, I need to know who among your staff knows Sasha's true identity. I'm feeling my way in the dark, not knowing who I can say what to."

"Oh, of course you are. So silly of us not to have thought of that." Maud rolled her port in her glass, enjoying the blood red light that shone through it. "Leon, Clive and Beth know. Eloquin also knows, since she dines with us, but she is not as involved as the other three. Hannah, Rosie and Edgar and the farmhands don't know."

"And why is that?" asked Stefan. "Are they untrustworthy? I thought your staff were particularly recruited for their discretion. Unlike other households, none of them is ever heard to gossip or let slip information about you or the household's affairs."

Sheldrake took a sip of his port, allowing the silence to linger. "You are correct. Sasha's revelations are relatively new to us and I suppose we are still feeling our way. Edgar only started with us a few weeks ago and Rose, his older sister, has always shown an antipathy towards Sasha, which concerns us."

"And we are not convinced of their acting skills, if we are trying to maintain Sasha's deception of being a boy when outsiders come to visit," added Maud. "We decided the fewer who knew the better…" Her tone indicated that it was open for discussion.

Stefan looked into his port, then took a little sip. His face lit up. "Oh, very nice." He did not seem to have an obsequious bone in his body. After a moment he asked, "What does Leon think?"

"We didn't ask him," replied Sheldrake.

"Ahuh. Or Clive or Beth?"

Sheldrake frowned. "No."

Stefan cocked his head to one side. "Is it worth me venturing an opinion? I don't want to waste your time… or mine, if it comes to that."

Maud and Sheldrake exchanged a glance.

"You are very cocksure, young man," said Sheldrake repressively.

Stefan just grinned. "No, I just like to be clear. If you don't want my opinion, I won't give it. After all, you haven't asked anyone else's."

"We are the master and mistress of this house, Stefan. It is our decision," said Maud firmly.

Stefan restrained himself from saying that was obvious and merely said, "Of course."

"Go on then," urged Sheldrake, leaning forward. "Tell us what you think."

Stefan leapt lightly to his feet and took up a position in front of the window before turning to address them. "I think you are both very clever, can command magical powers although I am not sure what they are yet, you have great influence at court and are kind to your staff and people you know."

"But?" asked Sheldrake dryly.

Stefan gave a grunt of laughter. "But… I think perhaps you underestimate people… in particular, your staff." Before they could respond, he waved his hand. "A simple example is Leon, who knows you think he's not clever… hence the remark about being big and bovine… but he took all of two seconds to overcome his surprise at my size when we first met. I was never going to catch him before he had my measure. His fighting technique may be unsubtle... I haven't seen it, I'm just going by what he said... but he knows his limitations, which is worth its weight in gold..." He paused. "Shall I go on?"

"Please do," said Sheldrake, in a tone that did not bode well for Stefan's future with them.

"From what I saw today, Hannah has remarkable hand-eye coordination, even though her girth means she mightn't be able to move very fast. Rose is very competitive and, given a chance, would strive to develop her fighting skills." Stefan nodded. "You're right, though. She does resent Sasha. Perhaps she is aware that he/she is getting special treatment and doesn't know why. You see? Competitive... and hierarchical. She firmly believes that indoor servants should be given precedence over outdoor servants."

He crossed to the table where he had left his port, picked it up and sipped it, taking a moment to savour it, before continuing, "Jake is enthusiastic but clumsy. He does what he thinks a bloke should do, without thinking it through. Now, he really *isn't* the sharpest tool in the shed and he was the one goading Leon to fight me. Luckily, he will follow Thompson if Thompson leads, and Thompson is sensible and quietly competent. He has trained with a bow at some time in the past and was better with the sword than anyone but Leon. Beth has excellent reflexes and anticipation; you could see that from the blocking exercises. Clive lacks confidence in himself but may be good if he trusts his instincts. Same with Edgar."

"My word," breathed Maud, "the amount you learnt in one morning."

Stefan gave a self-deprecating shrug. "That's my job, training people. If I don't know where they're starting from, how can I know what to teach them?"

"And what about Sasha and Jayhan?" asked Maud.

"Oh!" Stefan grinned. "They are full of energy and enthusiasm. Jayhan curbed his natural impetuousness to let your staff have first turn. Impressive in one so young. Made Rose a bit uncomfortable, though. They are both quick and agile but Jayhan has a tendency to get carried away and fall over his own feet, so to speak."

Sheldrake chuckled. "A masterful description of my son."

"And what about Sheldrake and me?" asked Maud.

Stefan shook his head. "I have no idea. You both masked your strengths."

After a considering silence, Sheldrake stood up and crossed to the tray where the decanter stood. With a wag of the decanter, he offered Stefan another, before pouring another for Maud and himself. Stefan took this as a hopeful sign that they weren't about to toss him out on his ear.

Sheldrake sat down, leaned back and crossed his legs, all aimed, Stefan suspected, at keeping him in suspense. "And what," asked Sheldrake, "is your opinion about informing all the staff about Sasha?"

Stefan hid his satisfaction at being asked and answered matter-of-factly, "I would consult with Beth, Clive and Leon before making a decision, because they know your staff better than I do. But from my short acquaintance with them, I think that if you include them and train them, you more than double the defences around Sasha. An hour, even half an hour, a day would improve their fighting skills immeasurably."

"But what about the risk of them spreading the word about Sasha, especially Edgar?" asked Maud.

"You're right," Stefan answered, skipping a few lines in the conversation, "I think Rose will change her attitude if she understands why. Edgar would be well-intentioned, but his little mouth might run away with him in the village or with his mother. Jake could also be a problem if he felt the need to brag after a few pints in the pub." He looked at Sheldrake, "Any suggestions, Master Mage?"

Sheldrake frowned at his casual tone, but bent his mind to it nevertheless. He sipped his port and gazed into it, then looked around the room and generally kept the other two waiting for a good five minutes. At last he said slowly, "If and only if they are willing, I could bind them from using particular words; for instance Queen, Kimora, amulet, shaman."

Instead of being impressed, Stefan gave it his consideration and then said dubiously, "But you could say those, hmm, concepts without saying the actual words, couldn't you? A female leader from a neighbouring country, for instance?"

Sheldrake stared at him icily. "I thought that by the time they came up with an alternative like that, they would have remembered to keep the secret."

"True. Good point," said Stefan, completely unfazed by Sheldrake's obvious dislike of having his ideas vetted. "Any other ideas?"

Maud smothered a laugh as Sheldrake's eyes nearly bulged out of his head in outrage.

"You know," continued Stefan, aware of, but unmoved by, Sheldrake's reaction, "it's a bit tough for a little boy not to be able to talk to his mum. Who else is in their family? Could his mother be trusted to keep this secret?"

Maud thought for a minute, keeping a weather eye on Sheldrake. "I think there are a couple of younger children, too. Their father died a few years ago. I know nothing about the woman but I suppose we could find out easily enough. Sheldrake's network could tap into the village gossip."

"Hmm." Stefan thought for a moment before turning to the mage. "Sheldrake, if Edgar's mother passed the vetting process, is there a way for her to temporarily override, then re-instigate your spell? After all, we'd still want it in place while he's on his way home and when he went out to play with other village children, wouldn't we?"

Sheldrake's mouth quirked in a half smile. He was beginning to get used to Stefan's equal-to-equal approach. He nodded. "Yes, I think I can do that. It will be an interesting little exercise for me."

"The other thing to consider," continued Stefan, "is that Sasha's gender is going to become harder to conceal as she gets older, especially if the King expects her to dress for court before she leaves here. Your staff are bound to find out."

Maud sighed. "You are absolutely right. I hadn't really thought about it yet, but it would be ludicrous to think we could hoodwink our staff for long. Her first visit to court is next week and I have brought three dresses from town for her to try on. We will tell them tomorrow evening. We already have an important meeting scheduled for tomorrow morning. I would like you and Leon to attend both meetings, if you please."

Just as Stefan was about to take his leave, a discreet knock on the door was followed by the advent of Clive bearing a letter on a tray.

"I beg your pardon, sir, but this has just arrived from the King. Apparently, it is urgent."

"Thank you." Sheldrake tore open the envelope and scanned its contents. He glanced up at Stefan and Maud, also noticing in his periphery vision that Clive was trying to make himself inconspicuous by the door and had not left immediately as he normally would. "The shaman and two of the men who attacked us in the forest have escaped. The other six are still in custody."

Maud had paled with shock. "Oh, Sheldrake! If that man gets back to Toriana, she will know that Sasha still lives and of her association with us."

Sheldrake nodded grimly. "Send Leon to me," he ordered Clive, without even looking at him. "And with the heightened risk, I think we must tell the staff about Sasha first thing in the morning. I think we can squeeze it in before our meeting with Jon, Electra, Argyve and Yarrow."

Chapter 6

As soon as the light streamed in through his window, Jayhan jumped out of bed, dressed quickly and sped out the door, jumping down the stairs four at a time and nearly crashing into Clive who was carrying a tray of glassware along the downstairs corridor.

"Oops, sorry, Clive," he said cheerily as he dashed down the side corridor, through the kitchen, skilfully dodging Rose who was carrying a stack of plates to the sink clearing up after the servants' breakfast, and across to the stables. Hannah shook her head in fond exasperation in his wake.

Sasha was already working, filling the horses' feedbags before getting started on mucking out the stalls. Without a word, Jayhan grabbed an armful of hay and delivered it to Slug, then a cup of oats. "This much?" he asked, holding the tin cup up for inspection.

Sasha nodded.

"What bout Tosser? Same?"

"No. A bit less. Maybe two thirds."

Once they were in rhythm with their work, Jayhan asked casually, "When do you first have to dress up to go the palace?"

Sasha came out of stall and scowled at him. "I have to try on the dresses tomorrow morning so there is time to alter them before next week. Why?"

Jayhan grinned. "Because I want to see you in a dress."

Sasha put her hands on her hips and said primly, "King Gavin said to tell you that he orders you not to tease me."

This did not have the effect she wanted. Jayhan exploded with laughter as he grabbed an armful of hay for another horse further down the line.

"What is so funny?" demanded Sasha.

"Who's going to tell him? You? Mum? You can handle yourself perfectly well without getting help from him."

"I'll have to tell him if he asks."

"Depends how you tell him, doesn't it? You can make it sound mean or you can make it sound fun." Jayhan smiled broadly at her. "When have you ever known me to be mean, at least, mean on purpose?"

Sasha did not smile back. "Jayhan, I'm really worried about this. I'm going to feel like an idiot in a big swishing dress."

"Didn't you ever wear dresses in the orphanage?"

"No, I've been pretending to be a boy for most of my life."

Jayhan stood stock still as he tried to imagine what it would feel like to wear a dress. After a moment he shook his head. "Yep. Pretty tricky."

Beth interrupted his reverie as she entered the stables. "Sasha, the top paddock has recovered. Take Flurry, Tosser, Slug and I think, the two bays, up there to graze. You can go with her, Jayhan, but you'll have to go straight from there to breakfast or you'll be late. Sasha, you can finish feeding the others when you get back."

Inevitably, Jayhan turned up late for breakfast, cheeks flushed from the cold morning air and emanating a faint odour of horse dung. His mother immediately ordered him from the table to wash and present himself to her for inspection before sitting down again.

They had barely finished their meals and Sheldrake was still drinking his tea when Clive entered and announced, "Unfortunately it is raining, sir, so the staff are assembled in the stables awaiting your arrival, rather than out in the courtyard."

Jayhan looked in surprise at Maud. "What's going on, Mum?"

"If you wipe away the egg from around your mouth, you may come with us and find out. You come too, Eloquin," Maud added.

As Maud and Sheldrake entered the stables, Jayhan ran ahead and joined Sasha and Edgar where they were standing off to one side so that they could see past the adults. He noticed Leon conferring with Stefan near the front of the group and wondered idly whether Stefan really could beat Leon in a fight. Then his eyes shifted to his father as he began to speak.

"Thank you all for making the time to meet this morning. I will be brief and answer any questions you may have afterwards." He raised his arm in Sasha's direction. "Sasha, come here please."

Sasha, with a feeling of foreboding, obeyed.

Sheldrake continued, "Some of you already know this but I have decided it is only fair that you all know. Firstly, Sasha is female, not a boy," he paused for the intakes of breath and asides to subside, "but more importantly, she is the rightful holder of the Kimoran throne."

Amidst exclamations of shock and astonishment, Sasha crept closer to Maud's side. Maud looked down and, realising the girl was trembling, put an arm around her shoulders. Jayhan saw Rose, white with shock, both hands held up to her mouth. He could tell she was reviewing her behaviour towards Sasha and finding it wanting. He gave a little snort of derision; it shouldn't take a revelation like this to make a person behave with consideration.

Sheldrake held up his hand and when the talking stopped, said, "The current ruler of Kimora is Sasha's aunt, but she is the younger sister. Sasha's mother was the legitimate heir. Ten years ago, Toriana attempted to wipe out her elder sister's entire family. She almost succeeded. But in a last desperate effort, Sasha's mother flung the symbol of power to Sasha, her last surviving daughter, and thrust onto her twelve-year-old son the task of escaping with her, while she held back the attackers and faced her death. Queen Toriana sits uneasily on the throne, unable to find the amulet to legitimize her rule and unsure whether Sasha, the true queen, has survived."

Maud gave Sasha a little prod and bent over to whisper, "Come on now, you're a queen. Look up and be proud." When this produced little more than a couple of quick glances, Maud added, "Look at Jayhan or Leon then, but keep your eyes up."

Reluctantly Sasha raised her head and stared fixedly at Leon, her face muscles taut. Leon gave her a big wink and smiled. Immediately she relaxed and smiled back, realising she had been needlessly working herself up.

"Hmm," Hannah stood with her hands crossed comfortably over her belly. "So would I be right in saying that Jon is her brother? And that Sasha has only recently discovered her identity?" She thought for a moment. "Let me see, I'd say it was when Yarrow was visiting and I sent up the champagne and lemonade and cakes a few weeks ago?"

Sasha nodded and grinned at her.

Further back, Edgar leaned over and whispered in Jayhan's ear, "So do I have to call her Ma'am or miss or something now?"

"No, 'course not. She'd hate it if you did that."

Edgar straightened up, reassured.

His sister, however, was tying herself in knots. Rose was wringing her hands and curt-seying all at once. "I'm sorry, Your Highness, Your Grace... What do I call her?" she asked in a frantic aside to Hannah, who just glanced derisively at her and shrugged. "Anyway, Your... maybe it's Your Majesty... Yes, that's it... Your Majesty, I am truly sorry that I have not been treating you as befits your station. I didn't know, you see. No one told me. When I think of all those times I have been less respectful than I should... But I would never have behaved like that if I had *known...*"

Stefan shook his head and mouthed to Sheldrake, "See? Total snob."

If Sasha could have stumbled backwards and disappeared, she would have. Rose was making her feel so uncomfortable. She glanced up at Maud but one look at her face told her that she was being expected to manage this herself. She took a deep breath and held up her hand. "Rose. Stop." Startled, Rose froze mid-sentence. Sasha thought furiously and finally said, "Rose, my aunt is still looking for me. I have to stay in disguise to be safe. The best thing you can do to help me is to treat all of the outside staff, Beth, Leon, Edgar and me, the same way." She gave a slight smile at Leon and Beth. "Actually, Leon and Beth are senior to me so they should be treated with greater respect, but Edgar and I are the same." She saw Stefan raising his eyebrows at her and added hastily. "And Stefan, he's senior too."

To Sasha's relief, Maud took over and told them who else knew of Sasha's true identity and explained about Sasha's upcoming visits to the palace. "And to answer your question from yesterday, Hannah, if any of Toriana's agents gets wind of Sasha's presence here, Sasha and possibly all of us, could be in danger. As more people become aware of her identity, the risk increases... and we have just heard that three of the people who attacked Sasha and Jon in the forest two weeks ago have escaped from custody."

"They'll have to get though me first if they want to hurt my little Sasha," said Hannah, still standing with her hands held loosely over her round stomach, but suddenly looking like an immovable obstacle. She turned her gaze to Stefan. "You'd better come into my kitchen and teach us how we can use what we have to hand, to fight off intruders. There's no supposing we'll have time to nip out and grab one of your weapons."

Stefan smiled and gave her slight bow. "It would be my pleasure. And all of you are welcome to work with me to improve your fighting skills so that we are better able to defend ourselves. Sheldrake and Maud are happy to consider half an hour a day of arms training as part of your duties rather than expecting you to do it in your spare time. You can also do this in a block of one hour every second day, if that suits you better."

"What if we want to do more?" asked Jake.

"I am also happy to train you in your own time."

"Great. Thanks."

Sheldrake looked around the staff gathered there, all willing to share the risk without any objections. His plan to ask them to bind their words withered. Instead, he said, "I am proud to have such a loyal courageous staff and although it may be difficult to hold our secret when other people visit here or when you are out in the village, I have complete faith in your ability to do so. The more time you spend treating Sasha as you always have, even though you now know her identity, the easier it will be. If there are no further questions, you may return to your duties. Thank you."

Chapter 7

The Kimoran ambassador's dashing red high-perch phaeton swept into the driveway of Batian House and was brought to a neat halt just outside the front door by its driver, Lady Electra.

"Well done, my lady," said Jon cheerily, as he hopped down from behind the driver's seat and opened the door for her. Jon, dressed in the blue and orange livery of a Kimoran footman, looked up at her with laughing eyes as he held out his hand for her to steady herself as she stepped down from the high phaeton.

Her eyes narrowed as she stepped primly past him to greet Maud who had just arrived in time to see her in. Maud smiled at Electra's fixed expression. "You may relax, Electra. All of our staff now know Jon and Sasha's identities. So you don't have to continue to pretend to be his mistress."

Electra sagged with relief. "It is difficult, you know, but I am happy to do whatever it takes to keep them both safe. Jon has already taken up his new identity as Lord Johnson, Minister for Transport, but we have kept up the pretence that he is still my footman for a few weeks so that his departure is not so abrupt that it might arouse suspicion. Our story is that he will be leaving me at the end of this week to live closer to his aging mother in the south of the country."

She entered the salon with Maud to find Yarrow, teacher of all things shamanic and Kimoran, Sheldrake and Lord Argyve, the Eskuzorian ambassador, already waiting for them. She seated herself neatly on the sofa, a short distance from Argyve.

Jon entered a few minutes later, having divested himself of his livery and now wearing a plain tan coat. "That's better," he said, grinning at her.

Two voices could be heard approaching down the corridor. As they drew closer, the voice with a gentle lilt was asking, "But how high does it extend? And how strong is it? Could another mage or a shaman overturn it?"

"And this, if I'm not mistaken," said Sheldrake dryly, holding out his hand in introduction as Stefan walked in the door, "is our new master at arms, Stefan." He almost added Longshanks then decided he did not yet know Stefan well enough to use his nickname. "And Leon, of course."

Stefan waved a cheery hand in greeting then stopped himself, said, "Oops," and gave a bow, from which he rose, grinning. He noticed a stocky gentleman sitting next to the curricle driver staring at him in puzzled surprise. Did he know him from somewhere else? Stefan didn't think so.

His attention was drawn back to Sheldrake who was shaking his head dolefully and saying, "And he seems to have no inherent sense of what is due one's status. He just tries to remember the niceties from time to time."

"Not surprising," muttered Argyve to himself, so quietly that no one was sure what they had heard.

"I beg your pardon?" asked Sheldrake.

Argyve blinked, as though pulling himself together. "Don't worry." He took a breath and smiled formally. "How do you do? I'm Lord Argyve, Ambassador from Eskuzor."

Before Stefan could respond, he was distracted by Jon striding forward and giving a bow to Stefan in return. "Pleased to meet you. I've heard a lot about you from Stavros. I've only met him once so far, but he is going to be *my* master at arms when I move to the palace." He looked down at Stefan, his eyes twinkling. "He said to me that since I was so tall, it was surprising they hadn't assigned Stefan Longshanks to train me." He chuckled. "Cheeky bugger, isn't he? I don't know how you put up with him."

"You'd be surprised what I have to put up with." Stefan decided instantly that he liked this tall, blonde young man.

Jon gave him a friendly smile. "Well, you won't have to put up with it from me. I'm Jon, by the way, Johnson at court. Jondarian's my real name but everyone just calls me Jon." He went on to introduce Yarrow and Electra.

"And these are the people, Stefan," said Sheldrake, "who know Sasha's true identity and are working together to secure her future. Beth and Clive have both known as long as Maud and I have, but they prefer just to give her the friendship and support of co-workers and leave the shamanism and the politics to others." He indicated the lounge chairs and sofa. "Do be seated, everyone. Clive will be in shortly with tea."

Leon stationed himself inside the door, but the others, including Stefan, seated themselves as Sheldrake continued, "The King has tasked me with protecting our borders against these raiding parties from Kimora. I think we have the roads and farmlands reasonably well covered by the farmers being rewarded for any reported sightings, but the Great Forest presents us with a problem."

"You come from that area, don't you, Stefan?" asked Maud. "Doesn't your father own the Creeping Vine?"

Stefan's eyebrows flicked together briefly. "How did you know that? Oh, that's right. We were talking about it on the ride. Sasha must have told you." He glanced at Sheldrake. "Is that it, or was it a background check?"

Sheldrake smiled and said in a neutral tone that begged the question, "I gathered *my* knowledge from a background check."

"Hmm. Am I missing something here?" demanded Stefan, quickly on the defensive.

Suddenly Maud grinned at him. "Maisy and I have a strong connection."

"Maisy? The horse? Can you talk to horses?"

Maud shook her head. "No. I *am* the horse. I'm a shapeshifter, Stefan."

Then she blushed and he blushed and everyone else laughed.

Discomforted, Stefan bounced out of his chair and strode to the window, peering out into the morning's sunlight with his back to the room. As the laughter died, he turned on his heel to face them and put his hands on his hips. Taking a deep breath to overcome his chagrin, he said, "Well, you're a pretty good horse. That's all I can say."

Amid relieved laughter, Maud smiled at him. "Thank you. As you know, Sasha thinks I'm a bit solid."

His face cleared. "Oh, so that's why you all laughed when I said I was worried that Maisy might be too broad for me."

"And now that I know you better, I have told you about my shapeshifting, so that you are not at a disadvantage. Very few people know about it."

Stefan gave a little bow. "Then I am honoured." He sent a quick glance around the room and, with no further ado, returned to the question Maud had asked him. "Yes, I am from the Great Forest. My family have owned and run the Creeping Vine for generations."

"Your family owns an inn, do they?" asked Argyve, looking puzzled.

Stefan frowned at him. "Yes. That's what I just said." When Argyve lapsed into a thoughtful silence, he continued, "I'm not sure how keen my father would be on shopping his customers, though. Taverns work on the premise that anyone and everyone is welcome."

"He would allow one of our agents in there though, wouldn't he? Based on the same premise…" Sheldrake looked to the door, as Leon held it open for Clive to enter with a tray full of crockery and the large silver teapot. Once he had set it down on the low table in the middle of the room and begun to pour and hand out cups of tea, Sheldrake renewed his query with a lift of his eyebrows.

"Of course he would. He just lets his patrons get on with their own schemes and dreams, unless they become raucous or violent. Then he boots them out 'til they settle down." Stefan accepted a cup of tea with a nod of thanks and sat down again. "He would also talk to you about what he'd seen, if you asked him. He doesn't cover up for people but equally he won't come looking for you to tell you and he definitely wouldn't accept payment for information."

Sheldrake nodded. "We can work with that."

Stefan shrugged. "It still only covers people who emerge onto the road at the Inn. It won't help you intercept anyone who stays deep within the forest."

"Have you spent much time in the forest yourself?" asked Electra, aware that Argyve tensed at her question.

"I spent all my childhood there. I loved it; much more than my brothers and sister. If anyone wanted herbs, mushrooms or firewood, I would be the first to volunteer. Anything to get out into the trees and among the ferns and bushes." Stefan stopped talking to blow on his tea and take a sip. While he sipped, he glanced at Lord Argyve who couldn't seem to keep his eyes off him.

"So you know this forest pretty well, do you?" asked Jon. "Do you know all the trails through it?"

Stefan nearly choked on his tea. "Know all the trails?" he asked incredulously. "Have you any idea how vast the Great Forest is? Behind our inn, the forest stretches for seventy miles to the south. On the other side of Park Lane, it stretches over one hundred miles to the north into Eskuzor. Our inn is twenty miles from the farmlands that lead to Highkington and ninety miles from where the forest peters out inside Kimora." He gave a quirky smile. "Mind you, it is only thirty miles to Carrador's border from our inn. I know most of that pretty well, and I have explored several other trails, but the whole forest is over fifteen hundred square miles."

The room fell into a gloomy silence until suddenly Sheldrake set down his cup and sat forward. "We are looking at this wrongly. We don't have to cover fifteen hundred square miles. We just need to cover a thin strip where the border is, mainly along the Charville River."

"And just a thin strip one hundred and sixty miles long," said Argyve heavily, who was finally focused on something other than Stefan. "Probably a lot longer, if I know anything about rivers."

"We don't have to follow the exact path of the river," snapped Sheldrake testily.

"Still a long way," said Argyve.

Sheldrake ran a hand through his neat black hair, a testament to the stress he was feeling with having to come up with a solution in such a short timeframe.

"Now, now, dear," Maud crooned. "You know we will think of something in the end."

He shook his head. "It's not feasible. How far apart do guards stand?

Argyve did not rush with his answer. His brow furrowed as he thought about it.

"But doesn't it..?" began Stefan, but was stopped by Argyve's raised hand.

"Yes, young man, it does depend on the terrain. On a flat, treeless plain, you could space guards up to two hundred yards apart, possibly even further. In a dense forest, you might need guards every... hmm... hundred yards. At least every hundred yards, possibly even closer. What do you think, Stefan?" Finally Argyve seemed to have stopped staring at him as though he had two heads.

"I'd say fifty yards in the densest areas. Even then they would have to keep watch at ground level while, at the same time, look for movement in the trees above them. Still, some parts of the river would be uncrossable. So you wouldn't need guards stationed there." Stefan started counting off on his fingers. "Well, let's say, for argument's sake, that you need an average of one guard every hundred yards. That means about eighteen guards per mile. So for one hundred and ten miles you'd need about nineteen hundred and eighty, let's round it up to two thousand soldiers guarding the border through the forest in each shift. So at least six thousand men, I'd say, if they each stood guard for a total of eight hours a day, not in one shift of course. Then you'd need officers, mess staff...."

Sheldrake waved his hand. "All right, all right. Enough. That plan obviously requires far too many resources."

"A magical barrier?" suggested Yarrow. The mirrors on her dress twinkled as she leaned forward to put her cup down. "Like the one you have here?"

Sheldrake and Leon's eyes met, before Sheldrake gave an embarrassed shrug. "The barrier we have across the front of this property will alert me if someone tries to enter uninvited. It's a plain, straight fence line. We haven't actually got around to trying to erect a barrier through or around the land out the back. I'm not sure," he gave a self-conscious cough, "well, actually I *am* sure that I couldn't create one around or through the whole bushland out the back, let alone over so vast a distance as the border between Carrador and Kimora."

The room lapsed into another thoughtful silence.

Then Argyve harrumphed. "I might have an idea. It's a long shot, but it might help."

All eyes turned to him.

"In Eskuzor, we have vast forests in the middle of our country that run across the mountains then south across our borders with Carrador. A few years ago, wide lines of forest sprang up across the land so that if you wanted to, you could travel from one end of the country to the other without leaving the woodlands."

"Yes…?" prompted Maud, in a tone that implied she didn't see where this was going.

"Well, we have our Forest Guardian to thank for that. When I say *thank*, I'm not sure all the farmers were delighted to lose some of their pastures to forest, but the benefits are that our borders are almost inviolable." He looked around the room and gave a smile that carried a hint of pride. "You probably don't realise this, but visitors to our kingdom are welcome if they travel along the roads but if they try to enter through the forest, our soldiers are alerted to apprehend and question the intruders. Sometimes those trying to enter through the forests are allowed in and sometimes they are not, depending on their motives. High Lord Tarkyn, through his network, becomes quickly aware that there are interlopers in the forests. Maybe he could help us to set up a similar system between Carrador and Kimora."

Maud leant forward, clasping her hands tightly in her lap. "This sounds very promising, Argyve. Two questions, though: What do these corridors of forest have to do with protecting the borders? Secondly, why would High Lord Tarkyn help us – or, to be more exact, help Sasha?"

Argyve gave an embarrassed grimace. "I know the reason for the forest corridors but I'm afraid it's a state secret. As to the second, I'm not sure that he will help us. I can only ask. It is two days' ride to the border. From there, the message can be sent to him very quickly to wherever he is in Eskuzor. If he chooses to respond, he can be here within another day or the messenger can ride back with the message of refusal." He gave a private little smile. "But I think I may be able to persuade him."

Part 2

Chapter 8

Argyve entered the library upstairs, intent on writing a letter for High Lord Tarkyn.

Jayhan looked up from his labours with multiplication and beamed at him. "Hello. What are you doing here?"

Argyve glanced apologetically at Eloquin, "I have come to write an important letter. I will try not to disturb you."

"Don't worry," said Eloquin, "Jayhan is already champing at the bit. He knows that when he has finished the ten questions I have given him, he can go."

Unfortunately, Jayhan immediately interpreted this to mean he could chat to Argyve as long as he liked, provided he did the ten questions before he left the room. "There's a little writing desk in the corner. It a special desk, called an escr... escritoire, with lots of little drawers full of pens and paper and things." He pulled his mouth down. "I don't get to use it much because Mum and Dad say I mess it up, but I expect they'd let you."

Argyve chuckled. "I expect they would."

He crossed to the escritoire, sat down on the cushion of a beautifully carved chair and extracted pen and paper. He picked up the pen, ready to begin his missive.

"Who are you writing to?" asked Jayhan, multiplication temporarily forgotten.

"Someone you don't know; High Lord Tarkyn."

"Oh." Jayhan managed not to make it a question while at the same time showing he was interested in knowing more.

Argyve began to write.

After a minute during which all that could be heard was Argyve's pen scratching across the paper, Jayhan's voice piped up again. "Lord Argyve, what is a High Lord? We only have lords, kings and queens, princes and princesses, don't we?"

Argyve put the pen down, accepting defeat. He smiled at Eloquin to include her. "This may be of interest to you, too. I was there when Prince Tarkyn's older twin brothers died. As far as we knew, Prince Tarkyn had suddenly become our king and was treated as such. However, the populace was unaware that Prince Tarkyn had a sister, who was older than he but younger than the twins. She had been exiled as a baby because her magic was rogue."

"Rogue?" asked Eloquin who, despite her duty to keep Jayhan focused, had become interested in the conversation.

"Uncontrolled and dangerous." When she had nodded, Argyve continued. "She had trained hard in exile and, as a young woman, was now not only in control of her magic but had developed to become a powerful wizard; what you would call a mage here."

Jayhan looked puzzled. "So why's he called a High Lord? Don't get it still."

Argyve held up his hand. "Patience, young man, I am coming to that... The Eskuzorian rule of succession is absolute primogenitor. In other words, the eldest child, regardless of gender, inherits the throne. Prince... King Tarkyn had only recently become aware of his sister's existence himself. But even though he had the backing of both the northern and southern armies and the whole population, he stepped aside and gave Navira the throne."

Jayhan's face scrunched up. "But that's right, isn't it? That was the right thing to do."

"Yes, but not everyone with power does the right thing. Anyway, in an agreement between them, Prince Tarkyn assumed the title of High Lord Tarkyn, Guardian of Eskuzor with powers to veto the monarchy's decision, in exchange for allowing Navira the throne."

Eloquin blinked. "But doesn't that effectively make him the ruler?"

"No. I suppose it could if he overused it, but High Lord Tarkyn is our watchdog, so to speak. By keeping himself aloof from court politics, he ensures that our monarchy is fair and informs Queen Navira and her Prince Consort Danton of issues arising around the kingdom. In many ways, his role is similar to that held by Maud and Sheldrake, except that he has the power to enforce his opinions if he chooses to."

"That is a most unusual set-up," said Eloquin, as she packed up a stack of papers. "I have not heard of its like in any other country."

"It is unusual, but I believe it is sound and will provide stability for our country for generations to come." Argyve hesitated, knowing he might release a barrage of questions and readying himself to stem it. "Since he is a true Guardian of the Forest, High Lord Tarkyn will live through the reigns of several monarchs." As Jayhan opened his mouth to ask another question, Argyve raised his hand. "And now, I must have this letter written before lunch. If you want to know more, you might like to research Forest Guardians as part of your studies."

As Argyve turned resolutely back to his letter, Eloquin raised an eyebrow at Jayhan who returned reluctantly to his arithmetic, determined to ask his father about Forest Guardians later.

Chapter 9

As he laboriously finished his last multiplication, Jayhan realised Eloquin was hovering anxiously at his elbow. He looked up. "May I go?"

"Just a minute. I'll have to check them first." She ran her eye quickly down the line of sums and gave a relieved smile. "Thank goodness! You got them all right. And now, I have to go." When Jayhan looked puzzled at her haste, she said, "Remember? Maud and I are helping Sasha to put on a gown for the first time."

"Can I come too?"

"No, Jayhan. You can see her when she's ready. We will bring her down to the salon, just before lunch. So you can see her then." She wagged her finger at him. "And I don't want any witticisms from you. She will be very nervous. Be the kind friend I know you are."

She left behind a very thoughtful-looking Jayhan. If she hadn't been so preoccupied, this might have worried her more, but as it was, she sped along the corridor to Maud's dressing room, where Maud and Rose had hung up the three dresses on hooks around the room and were already talking to Sasha about which one she would like to wear first. Sasha looked up at her arrival, a pleading, trapped expression on her face.

Eloquin smiled reassuringly at her. "Hello, Sasha. It's a big day for you, isn't it? These are beautiful gowns, aren't they? I wish I could afford gowns of this quality." She walked over to a soft green dress embroidered in blue silk and finished with white lace at the neckline and cuffs. "Look at these pretty blue birds," she said, running her hand over the embroidery.

"It would look good on you," said Sasha. "It would be wishy-washy on me." She coloured as she realised that what she said could be construed as an insult. "I don't mean you're wishy-washy. It's just I'm used to tan and black and brown; strong colours." She waved her hand in despair at the next gown, which was a white frothy creation. "I mean, look at this. Can you even imagine me in this?"

Eloquin glanced at Maud, who was looking harassed and Rose, who was trying not to appear flustered.

Sasha walked to the last of the three and waved her hand at it dramatically. "And this one? *Me*? It's pink with ribbons and revolting little white dogs with umbrellas on it. Honestly, whoever sent these dresses knows nothing about me. No one asked my opinion. No one cared what I thought." Her voice choked up. "Is this going to be my life from now on? People forcing me to be someone else?" Tears overcame her and she sank to the floor against the wall, pulling her knees up to her chest and wrapping her arms around her head and knees.

"Oh dear," said Maud, totally flustered. "Rose, you'd better bring her a cup of tea."

Rose fled thankfully. As she left, Jayhan slipped in the door.

"What are you doing to her?" he demanded.

Maud rolled her eyes. "Nothing, Jayhan. She just doesn't like the dresses."

Jayhan plopped himself on the floor next to Sasha and put his arm around her while he studied the dresses. A variety of expressions, mostly, but not all, of distaste, crossed his face as he considered each one. "So why has that made her sad?"

"She thinks she will be forced to be someone she's not."

"Oh. Well, that's silly. How can anyone make you, Sasha? They can't force you screaming and crying down the stairs in a dress you hate." He smiled at his mother. "Anyway, they wouldn't want to. Mum likes you a lot. She's not trying to be mean to you."

Eloquin and Maud looked at him with new respect.

"You know," he said into her ear, "these are just practice dresses, to get the hang of wearing them. You can tell, because they are all dull colours; you know, just like the scruffy saddle you use at home, not the beautiful new saddle you'd use for a show. I bet if you asked, they would try to find dresses you like for when you go out in *real* public."

Sasha sniffed and raised her head a little. "Do you think so?"

"Oh, definitely," he answered, winging it and raising his eyebrows at his mother for confirmation.

"Of course we will, Sasha," said Maud throwing a relieved glance at Eloquin. "What sort of colours do you like; besides black, brown and tan?"

"I love Lady Electra's dresses." Sasha sat up and wiped her nose on her sleeve, making Maud glad she had not yet donned one of the gowns. "She wears beautiful bright colours; oranges, yellows, reds. I like your dresses too. I really like tan, dark green, blue and brown. I *hate* pastel colours," she added with a venomous look at the gowns and received an admonitory dig in the ribs from Jayhan. She glared at him but turned her attention to Maud when she spoke.

"You see, Sasha, girls and young women generally wear paler colours. It just seems to be the fashion." As Sasha's face tightened, Maud hastened to add, "But I can see we may have to help you to start a new trend instead."

Rose arrived with a single large mug of tea and handed it to Sasha with a quick curtsey.

Sasha smiled at her from her tear-streaked face. "Thanks. Sorry to put you to the bother." She had had time to think about Jayhan's jab in the ribs. "And sorry I'm being a pain. I know you're just trying to help but… it's hard."

"I think the pale green one is the best," pronounced Jayhan suddenly. "Obviously the pink one is disgusting but the white one might look good against your dark skin, even if it is a bit frilly." Sasha looked at him in amazement. "Go on," he urged. "Pick one and try it on. Just think of it as an old saddle."

Rose, who had missed his earlier comments, looked scandalized.

Jayhan hopped to his feet. "By the way, I think Sasha might like the green one better if it had dark blue around the edges, instead of the white lace, though the white lace would look good against her skin. See you later, Sasha." He grinned and walked out, leaving four astonished women in his wake.

It was nearly an hour later that Sasha emerged warily and, under instruction from Maud, descended the stairs and entered the salon where the others were still chatting among themselves. They looked towards the door as it opened and beheld Sasha, head held high, but dark eyes anxious, as she walked carefully into view in the soft green gown, now trimmed with blue material that matched the embroidery, cut from one of Maud's favourite scarves. With her hair brushed and pinned into soft dark waves, she had been transformed into a young lady of fashion. Everyone clapped and smiled at her. She gave an uncertain smile in return and performed a stiff curtsey.

Jon came forward and held out his hand. "You look lovely, sister mine. You always look lovely, but especially today."

Sasha took his hand and felt her way into the room, carefully placing each foot so that she didn't trip on the skirts, even though they were only ankle length. When she was safely seated, she had time to relax a little and look around the room. "Where's Jayhan?" she asked, experiencing a pang of disappointment.

Sheldrake looked around. "He was here. I don't know where he has shot off to. I'm sure he'll be back. He'll be sorry to have missed your entrance."

Suddenly they heard through the door a series of thumps, a smothered oath, then a louder thump followed by a ringing clang. Sheldrake strode to the door and opened it. Clive was picking himself up and retrieving a silver tray that had landed somewhere further down the corridor. A white heap lay at his feet and seemed to be emitting groans of pain. It moved and resolved itself into Jayhan surrounded by layers of white lace. He dragged himself to his feet, grimacing as he took his weight on his left leg. "Ow." He looked up at everyone then straightened and grinned sheepishly. "Well, that wasn't quite the entrance I planned. I was going to help Sasha get used to old saddles, you see," he explained, to the mystification of everyone but Maud and Eloquin.

"Jayhan, you are wearing a dress, not a saddle. A very frilly dress, I might add." Sheldrake shook his head. "I would have thought you could play dress-ups when we did not have a house full of visitors."

Clive put an arm under Jayhan's elbow and guided him through the crowd into the salon. "Here, young one, sit down a minute. You took quite a tumble there." As Jayhan tripped again, Clive said calmly, "I believe you trip less if you lift your skirts. That is possibly how you fell down the stairs in the first place."

"Ow. Thanks, Clive. It's a bit long for me, actually. I keep stepping on it."

Sasha walked over and surveyed him critically. "White is a little bright for you but I'm glad you didn't wear the pink." Then she giggled. "You're an idiot, Jayhan. But the nicest idiot I've ever known."

He grinned back at her. "Thanks. I think."

Ignoring his sore leg, Jayahn pulled himself out of his chair and, for the next few minutes, Jayhan and Sasha joyously paraded in their dresses, sashaying back and forth, tripping and striking poses, both laughing uproariously as they thought of new ways to pretend to be ladies of fashion. Maud and Electra, who both *were* ladies of fashion, applauded and provided suggestions and laughed with the rest of them.

By the time they had safely negotiated their way up the stairs and sat down to lunch, Sasha had forgotten her stiffness and was chatting and laughing quite unselfconsciously.

Maud leaned in and whispered to Sheldrake, "You realise your son is a genius, don't you?"

Sheldrake raised his eyebrows, watched the two children for a minute, then smiled.

Chapter 10

As the road curved to the left, the setting sun shone directly into the face of a tired, lanky young man dressed in the blue and red of Eskuzor. He squinted against the light and slowed his pace, knowing the road would return to its northerly bearing in another mile. He might as well take the opportunity to rest his horse, since to ride breakneck, blinded by the sunlight, was idiocy. He knew riders who did it, but he wasn't one of them.

He leaned forward in the saddle and patted the roan horse's neck. He didn't know her very well, although he had ridden her a few times in the past. He vaguely remembered that her name was Patsy. She was one of the many horses who lived in the posthouses on the highway route from Highkington to Montreya.

Jackson had been riding since lunchtime yesterday. He had ridden for six hours yesterday, staying the night at the waystation in the tiny village of Creekside. At dawn, he had been in the saddle and on his way again. An hour ago, he had passed the left-hand turn that would have taken him to the small kingdom of Farenz that ran along the coast in the northwest corner of Carrador, just south of Eskuzor. It meant he was getting close to Eskuzor's border.

The horse he was currently riding was his eighth for the day. She was reasonably fresh; he was close to exhaustion. As she walked quietly down the road, he unstoppered his drinking flask and took a long draught before waving to a traveller driving an old cart laden with firewood in the other direction. Then he rummaged in the hessian bag slung over his shoulder and pulled out a wad of dried beef and an apple, which he munched as the corner in the road drew closer. By the time the road swung back to the north, he felt revived enough to push through the final miles to the border.

When he finally reached the border post, twenty miles south of the Eskuzorian city of Montreya, Jackson nodded in greeting to the Carradorian guards before riding over the border to stop at the Eskuzorian guard station. Here he dismounted and tied his horse to the hitching rail. One of the border guards, a casual fellow with dirty blonde hair that had evaded all of its owner's half-hearted attempts to tame it, walked over to talk to him.

Seeing Jackson's sweat-streaked face, he asked, "Urgent?"

The messenger nodded. "And for High Lord Tarkyn's personal attention."

"Really? We have a specific protocol for that. Come inside and have a coffee. I'll send Markos into the woods with it."

Jackson smiled with relief and handed the guard a slightly bulging envelope. "Thanks, Sandy. Lord Agyve said you had a system for sending urgent messages to the High Lord.

Saves me the extra ride. Usually I just keep going until it is delivered into the recipient's hand. This is all new for me."

Sandy looked at the envelope in his hand and shook his head. "Funny how their messages are always flat and ours are rolled into canisters."

Jackson shrugged. "As long as they fit in my jacket or bag, I don't mind which way they pack them."

He followed Sandy into the little guardhouse and watched as he handed the envelope to an older man who was not in uniform. Jackson frowned a query at Sandy.

"This is Markos. He is a retired teacher. When an urgent letter arrives, he walks out into the woodlands, down that path," Sandy indicated the path out the window, "until he reaches the old oak. A large brass bell is strapped to the trunk of the tree, but the tongue is fastened so that the bell is silent when the wind blows. When he wants to send an urgent message to High Lord Taykyn, he unfastens the tongue and rings the bell three times. Then he waits. After forty minutes, he reads the letter out loud word for word, pausing after each sentence."

Markos did not wait to hear the end of an explanation he already knew, but gave a curt wave before heading out into the gloom of the forest.

Sandy poured coffee into a battered tin cup from a pot on an iron stove and handed it to Jackson. "Sugar?" When Jackson shook his head, he continued, "If the matter is not urgent, Markos simply leaves the letter in the wooden box at the base of the oak. By the next morning, it is gone. The replies come to us by carrier pigeon. We have cotes here that the pigeons fly back to. From time to time, we send a crate of our pigeons to various places around the kingdom so that when they need to send us a message, they can use a pigeon to carry it."

Jackson frowned. "Why don't you just use pigeons yourself to contact Lord Tarkyn?"

"We do use pigeons for messages to Montreya that they can then relay further afield. But no one can be sure where the High Lord will be, so that doesn't work for him. But somehow, the messages left or read at the old oak always find him."

An hour later, Markos returned. "Done," he said shortly.

"Thanks. Aren't you worried walking through the woods on your own at night? What about wolves and mountain lions and bandits?" asked Jackson, as the older man walked through the door and sloughed off his coat.

Markos shook his head. "No. Lord Tarkyn has placed some sort of protection on the area around the old oak and the path between here and there. Never have any trouble." He gave a throaty chuckle. "I once saw a wolf. It saw me too but it just paused, blinked at me then went on its way."

"Huh." Jackson crossed to the stove and scooped some stew from a big saucepan into a bowl and handed it to the old man. "Here. It's good. Your Sandy's a good cook," he grinned, "much to my surprise!" and scooted out of the way laughing, as Sandy swung his booted foot at him.

Chapter 11

Sandy was just about to go out and let the other guard, Warren, come in for some dinner, when they heard a thump on the ground behind the guardhouse on the forest's edge. The three of them rushed out and found a pale young man sprawled on the ground beside a lavender bush, his long black hair half covering his face. The man groaned and dragged himself into a sitting position, wrapping his arms around his knees. His nondescript soft brown shirt and leggings did not seem any the worse for wear, although not warm enough to stop him from shivering against the misty cold that was seeping through the trees. When he had regained a little strength, he dragged his huge wolfskin cloak around his shoulders.

"High Lord Tarkyn!" exclaimed Markos, bowing deeply.

The man in question raised his head and Jackson found bright amber eyes glaring at him through the rays of light from the guardhouse window. "I have you to thank for this, do I?" he croaked.

"Sorry?" Jackson had no idea what he had done. "I beg your pardon," he said hastily, bowing as the older man had done.

Prince Tarkyn, High Lord of Eskuzor, moved his focus to Sandy who bowed, then said, "Just a minute," and raced back indoors, leaving Jackson gaping in astonishment.

Sandy reappeared less than a minute later with a cup of water, which he proffered.

"Thank you." Tarkyn reached out and grasped the cup, downing its contents in one draught. He breathed out and wiped his hand across his mouth. "Ah. That's better."

As Tarkyn hoisted himself to his feet, Jackson's gaze travelled from near ground level to well above his own height. This man was tall.

"So Markos, where is this envelope?" asked Tarkyn, "Did you bring it back with you or leave it at the foot of the oak?"

"I left the letter and brought back the envelope and its other contents, my lord." Markos reached into his pocket, withdrew the envelope and handed it to the High Lord.

"Good man." Tarkyn opened it and peered inside. "Hmm. A gumnut." Unexpectedly, he smiled at Jackson. "Let's hope they know what they're doing."

Jackson was so totally confused by now that he just blinked.

Tarkyn chuckled. "When I translocate, I focus on an object, which returns me to the place where the object was created. To come here, I focused on a piece of lavender that originated on that bush in the guardhouse garden."

Jackson glanced at the lavender bush then frowned. "And are you going to use a gumnut to translocate again? Isn't it a bit dangerous to land high up in a eucalyptus tree? They are very tall. Even more dangerous, if it makes you feel sick."

"Yes, very. So I am hoping that this gumnut comes from a low branch. I think Lord Argyve knows the story of when I translocated into the high branches of an oak tree and plummeted twenty feet to the ground. I hope so." He grimaced. "I must admit I would feel more confident with a grevillea flower or leaf."

"Very prickly, landing in most grevilleas, Sire, I would think," offered Jackson.

Tarkyn gave a grunt of laughter. "Good point... What is your name? I know the other two, but you are new to me."

"I am Jackson, Sire, the messenger who brought the envelope and its contents from High-kington."

"And when did you leave?"

"Two hours after noon yesterday, Sire. I rode until dusk, then have ridden since first light this morning."

"Oh, my word! And here I am keeping you standing out here in the dark. You must be near to dropping."

Jackson smiled. "A bit tired, Sire." His smile broadened. "But my interest in your novel mode of travel is managing to battle off my weariness. I have not seen a translocation before."

"You have an unusual turn of phrase, Jackson," said Tarkyn as he made his way into the guardhouse, ducking his head to get through the doorway.

"My mother is a librarian," replied Jackson, by way of explanation. As he followed him in, he hesitated then asked, "Would you like some stew or are you still feeling a bit crook?"

"Crook?"

Jackson grinned. "A word I picked up in Carrador."

Tarkyn raised his eyebrows. "Hm. Well, I was feeling very *crook* but I'm nearly back to normal now. However, I won't have any stew, thank you."

While Tarkyn sat down at the table and sipped his water, Jackson muttered to Sandy, "Do we have anything better to offer His Highness?"

"I heard that," interrupted Tarkyn. "Now, don't be rude to Sandy. He makes excellent stews."

Jackson's face coloured. "Oh, but I thought..."

"I am happy to eat any well-prepared food," the High Lord smiled, "as long as I don't have to prepare it myself. I am not eating because I intend to translocate again very shortly, and I don't want to vomit Sandy's stew up all over Lord Sheldrake's front lawn."

"Oh, good decision in that case... Sire."

Tarkyn noted the hesitation. "Independent sort of a character, aren't you?"

Jackson grimaced. "I don't mean to be, Sire, but I spend a lot of my time on my own between one place and another. I'm pretty good at protocol when I'm picking up or delivering messages, but that's about as far as it goes. The rest of the time I don't have to answer to anyone."

The High Lord considered him; the messenger's neat brown hair held back firmly in a queue with only a few wisps around his face after hours of riding, his clothes and boots well cared for under the patina of dust that covered them and his loose-limbed frame that moved with the grace of a born athlete. Tarkyn drummed his fingers on the table. "What are your current plans?"

Jackson looked surprised. "Mine? I was going to stay the night here, then head back to Lord Argyve tomorrow, carrying the dispatches that have been waiting here for delivery. On my return, he wanted me to confirm that I had delivered his message and that it had been passed on," he grinned, "but I guess your appearance will confirm it, long before I get back."

"Would you like to come with me? I could give you a lift back, so to speak." Jackson's eyes widened. It seemed to be with excitement but, when he did not respond straightaway, Tarkyn thought perhaps he had been mistaken and it was fear that he was seeing, so he added, "It can be uncomfortable for a few minutes, nauseating, but it passes as you have just seen. You don't have to come, though. It was not a command."

"No, I would love to come, Sire. It would be an honour. No, I was just thinking through my responsibilities before I replied." Jackson looked over at Sandy. "Could you mind the horse? I was going to ride her back tomorrow but the next post rider through can take her back to her stables, if that's all right with you."

Sandy grinned at him. "I would be a surly bugger to stand in the way of a chance like this. Of course I'll mind the horse."

Tarkyn smiled at them. "Translocating is not an experience I hanker after. I do it as rarely as possible. Oh, and just so that you know, Jackson, this particular ability of mine is close to being a state secret. Only a few trusted people know, so please don't broadcast it."

Jackson considered for a moment then nodded.

Tarkyn frowned. "Were you deciding whether to accede to my request?"

"No, of course not. You're the High Lord. I was just thinking through the reasons for it, the tactical advantages of having such a skill up your sleeve, instead of out in the open."

"Hmm. I think I will ask Lord Argyve to re-assign you to be my aide-de-camp while I am in Carrador. Would you be happy with that?"

"It's not up to me, but since you are asking," he paused while he thought about it, "I think it would be a very interesting experience. Much as I like the long stretches of solitary riding, I think I will enjoy being in your company."

Rather to Jackson's surprise, the High Lord coloured a little. "Thank you. Likewise. That, among other reasons, is why I asked."

"Huh." Jackson smiled and bowed. "I am honoured, Sire."

Tarkyn stood up, crossed to the water barrel and refilled his glass. Once he had finished drinking, he turned to Jackson. "Right. Shall we go?"

"Just a minute. I need to get my kit."

"No kit, I'm afraid. You can probably bring a small satchel slung over your shoulder with the dispatches and a few other things. We'll have to procure you spare uniforms in Highkington."

"Uh-huh."

Tarkyn smiled as he watched the now familiar sight of Jackson thinking something through.

"Right," said Jackson. "Back in a minute."

When he returned, he had washed the grime off his hands and face, brushed the dust from his boots and uniform and retied his hair so that the flyaway wisps had been recaptured. He had a small canvas bag slung across his shoulders. He bowed. "Ready, Sire."

Tarkyn raised his eyebrows. "Impressive transformation in so short a time."

"Thank you, Sire. If I am to be your offsider, I have to do you as proud as I can."

High Lord Tarkyn walked over and clapped his arm across Jackson's shoulders. "You are a gem among men. I am glad our paths have crossed. Let's go outside for this."

Sandy and Markos trooped out behind them as they returned to the spot next to the lavender bush where Tarkyn had first appeared.

"Do you have to be in the same place for the next translocation that you arrived in from the last?" asked Jackson.

"No. We just have more room to manoeuvre out here. Now Jackson, I will have to hold onto you very firmly to pull you through with me. The last time I did this, I was rescuing someone who was injured so he wasn't conscious enough to object to me putting my arms around him." Tarkyn grinned. "You are. So I hope you can manage a little indignity."

"I'll cope."

"Now I think about it, it would be much easier for me if you hold onto me too, then I won't have to hold on so hard. Last time, it nearly dragged my arms out of their sockets."

Jackson frowned. "Are you sure you want to do this, Sire?"

Tarkyn waved his hand airily. "Oh yes. Definitely. A bit of pain and discomfort never hurt anyone." Seeing three bemused faces around him, he added, "I did say 'a bit'. Never mind." He pulled the gumnut out of his pocket and held it firmly in one hand. "So Jackson, stand in front of me, wrap your arms around me and link your hands behind me. I will link mine over the top of yours because I must be able to see this little gumnut."

They manoeuvred into position, which felt uncomfortably intimate. Tarkyn peered over Jackson's shoulder at the gumnut held in his linked hands. "Goodbye, you two," he said to Sandy and Markos, then intoned, *"Maya Mureva Araya! Ka Mureva Araya!"* and the two of them faded from sight.

Chapter 12

Jackson felt as though he were being sucked through a warp in space. He seemed to fold him in on himself until he was almost gone, then expand suddenly to land with a jolt, tangled in Prince Tarkyn's arms. A rush of nausea welled inside him and he flailed to disentangle himself, pushing Tarkyn away unceremoniously, just in time to turn his head and vomit on the lawn.

"Aaah. Now I'm the one vomiting on Lord Argyve's front lawn. I feel horrible."

When he looked, he saw Tarkyn lying on his back, propped on his elbows with his head back. After a minute, Tarkyn shuddered and lifted his head. "You do know it is a capital offence to assault me?" he said, with an edge to his voice.

Jackson's stomach lurched, from fear not nausea this time. This new assignment might be harder than he thought or worse still, very short-lived. "I did my best," he replied levelly. "It was the lesser of two assaults, in my opinion. Better to be pushed than to be spewed on."

Tarkyn's eyes twinkled in response, his irritation dissipating. "How true. For future reference, I give you permission to lay hands on me, provided you are not genuinely planning to harm me."

Jackson breathed a sigh of relief. "You really scared me. I'm not used to dealing with royalty. You'd better let me know what else might get me into strife."

Tarkyn sat up, the laughter gone from his eyes. "I will, but we have at least established the most important ground rule… and very few people have been given that permission." He stood up. "I think we are both a little tetchy from the translocation. Being nauseated makes one a little short-tempered, I find."

He put his hand out for Jackson to pull himself up, a clear gesture of reconciliation.

Jackson's mouth quirked into a smile as he accepted the proffered hand. "Thank you. And thank you for your trust."

Now that they had recovered, they took time to look around themselves. They were standing next to a young gumtree, only a few feet high, clearly the source of the gumnut. Much larger eucalypts stood close by, towering into the night sky. The light from inside the house spilled across the cultivated lawn beneath their feet and partly lit the towering gums and the garden beds of shrubs behind them that lined the front wall of the stables.

They spun around at the sound of scrabbling and saw two legs appear high up in one of the gum trees. Moments later, the rest of a small person appeared, climbing down a wooden ladder. Then another appeared, to follow the first. Soon Tarkyn and Jackson were looking down at two children, both dressed in leggings and jerkins. The boy whose clothes were of better quality, had unnervingly pale eyes while the other's eyes were liquid brown.

The boy with the pale eyes bowed. "Hello. You must be Prince... High Lord Tarkyn. I am Jayhan Batian and this is Sasha." He grinned. "We've been watching out for you, although we weren't sure you'd arrive today or even come at all."

"But it gave us a great excuse to be in our cubby in the dark." Sasha glanced at Jayhan, then bowed too. "Oops."

Tarkyn gestured to his companion. "This is Jackson, the messenger who rode all the way to the border to contact me."

"Hello," said Sasha. "You must like horses if you do all that riding. So do I. I'm the stable... boy, you know."

Tarkyn raised his eyebrows. "Are you indeed?"

In the face of his sceptical tone, Jayhan rushed into the breech. "You two looked very funny all tangled up on the lawn. Just as well you didn't land in the salon. You'd have knocked everything over."

"Which is no doubt why Lord Argyve chose the lawn for our arrival," replied Tarkyn.

A certain dryness in this remark made Jayhan squint anxiously up at him. "I didn't mean to be rude. Sorry if I was. Would you like to come inside? My parents are dying to meet you."

Tarkyn couldn't help smiling, although he was by no means relaxed. "Thank you. Lead the way."

As they walked across the lawn to the house, carefully avoiding the little pile of regurgitated stew, Jayhan said, "Just a minute," and disappeared ahead of them. Tarkyn looked enquiringly at Sasha who shrugged her lack of answer. For a couple of minutes, they stood irresolutely outside the front door, waiting for Jayhan to return.

Losing patience, Tarkyn said, "I think we will knock," just as the front door swung open to reveal Clive, with Jayhan hopping from one leg to the other and smiling in satisfaction in the background.

Clive gave a deep bow. "This way, if you please, Your Highness. Would you like me to take your cloak?"

"Thank you, but I will keep it until I am warmer."

"Have you eaten, Sire? Dinner is ready to be served, pending your arrival."

Tarkyn raised his eyebrows. "Really? And what if I had chosen not to come?"

"Lord Sheldrake and Lady Maud would have become increasingly hungry until later this evening. I suspect they would have requested the occasional refreshment, Sire." Clive gave a slight smile. "The same would apply if you had already eaten."

The High Lord laughed. "For their sakes, I am pleased to say that I would indeed like to dine with them, although not straight away. My stomach needs time to settle."

Clive raised his eyebrows very delicately in Jackson's direction.

"My aide-de-camp, Jackson, will of course be joining us... and I suspect his stomach needs even more time to settle."

"Very good, Sire." Clive opened the door to the salon and entered first, announcing, "His Royal Highness, Prince Tarkyn, High Lord of Eskuzor, and Jackson, aide-de-camp to His Highness." Once Tarkyn had entered, Clive introduced Sheldrake and Maud to him.

Sheldrake was rooted to the spot with astonishment. "Good Lord! You actually came. Lord Argyve was right. He said he'd written something that might interest you enough to come. And here you are!" He suddenly remembered his manners and gave a deep bow. When he straightened, he said, "Very pleased to meet you, Your Highness."

In contrast, Maud surged forward and performed an elegant curtsey. As she rose, she said, "Oh, you poor man. You're freezing. Come to the fire."

In the face of such effusion, mistaking warmth for sycophantry, Tarkyn took an involuntary step backwards, made obvious by the fact that his wolfskin cloak swayed forwards. He nearly cannoned into Jackson who had entered the room behind him.

"You too," she added to Jackson. "What would you like to drink?"

"Water," they chorused.

"Oh." Maud motioned to Clive, who withdrew. "Anything else?"

"Tea for me," said Tarkyn.

"A brandy?" Jackson glanced uncertainly at Tarkyn, unsure whether he should drink on duty.

Tarkyn smiled. "If that's what your stomach feels like, by all means."

"I am sorry I missed your arrival. I would dearly love to see a translocation," said Sheldrake. "I wandered out onto the lawn from time to time but really, I don't have the patience required to wait around for hours on the off-chance that you'd decide to come."

"No. Neither do I. If it makes you feel any better, I don't think you missed much," Tarkyn replied, accepting a glass of water from Clive and pausing to down it. "I believe I just appear out of nowhere from the bystander's point of view."

"Really? This is most interesting. And how do you experience it?"

"Now Sheldrake," protested Maud. "Leave Lord Tarkyn alone. He hasn't even had time to take in his surroundings and you are already badgering him about magic. Have some compassion." Maud turned to Tarkyn. "He's a mage, you see. I believe you call them wizards. Anyway, he can be a little obsessive about magic."

Sheldrake frowned. "Not at all. I am an enthusiastic, passionate scholar." Suddenly, his austere face relaxed into a grin. "Your pardon, Your Highness. Maud is right, of course. Do not feel obliged to answer my question."

Tarkyn raised his eyebrows, tacitly reminding them that he had no obligation to them whatsoever. Once he had made his point, he replied to the original question. "From *my* point of view, I must relinquish my existence for a few seconds then come back to myself somewhere else. It is a sickening experience both mentally and physically. Before I say the incantation, I must focus on an object that originates from the place I wish to go. You must be very specific with the origin of the object. Someone once gave me an acorn they had found on the forest floor but it had originated from high in the oak tree. Disastrous."

Clive arrived with the tea for Tarkyn. As he set it down, he asked, "When would you like to dine, Your Highness? Hannah needs time to prepare."

Tarkyn was not yet feeling particularly hungry, but one glance at the dark shadows beneath his new aide-de-camp's eyes told him that Jackson needed to retire soon. "Does half an hour seem reasonable?"

"Perfectly, Sire."

Tarkyn held up a hand. "Before you go, what happened to the children? They did not follow us in here."

"They were under strict instructions to show you in, then to make themselves scarce, Sire."

"I see. For future reference, I am very fond of children. I have a niece, an adopted ten-year-old son and now, my own daughter who is just two years old. So do not feel you have to shield me from them unless, of course, we are discussing state matters."

Standing in front of the fire, towering above them in his long wolfskin cloak, the High Lord did not seem at all the sort of person to enjoy the company of children, but Clive bowed and with a glance at Maud, suggested, "Perhaps you would like to see them before they go to bed?"

"No, tomorrow will be soon enough." Tarkyn's gaze travelled from Maud to Sheldrake then settled back on Maud, rather to Sheldrake's chagrin. "I must see King Gavin tomorrow, Lady Maud. It would be discourteous to be in his kingdom without making myself known. From what I hear, I believe you can arrange that." Sheldrake was a little mollified when Tarkyn then turned to him. "And I believe you and I hold similar roles, Lord Sheldrake, at least in terms of being the centre of our country's intelligence network. Your role, of course, is not so widely known as my own. Lady Maud, as I understand it, decides what the King needs to know and the King makes the final decisions under advisement from her... and you. Is that about right?"

"It is," said Sheldrake shortly, not liking a foreigner being so clear about Carrador's secret power structure.

Tarkyn smiled. "Whereas I perform both your roles and leave the decision-making to my sister, Queen Navira and her Prince Consort Danton, who happens to be my best friend."

"But you have the power to overturn their decisions if you feel the need to. Correct?" asked Sheldrake.

Now it was Tarkyn's turn to frown. "Yes, I do, but I am hoping the need will never arise. If, through my network, I discover some aspect of Eskuzor's functioning that worries me, I make them aware of it and its implications. We discuss it and then I leave them to work out what they want to do about it. If it remains unresolved, I repeat the process. Our current monarch is both clever and well-intentioned. So, I do not anticipate the need to pull rank." Suddenly he grinned. "But it is a great comfort to me that I have the option."

A chuckle, quickly suppressed, came from Jackson standing beside him at the fire.

Tarkyn looked around at him quizzically. "I'm glad you find me amusing, Jackson."

Jackson was not sure whether this was sarcastic or not. "Sorry, Sire. It's just... most people are comforted by a hot toddy or a grandson who visits them, not by the power of veto over a queen. Just a bit different, Sire, that's all."

Tarkyn raised his eyebrows then, to his aide-de-camp's relief, laughed. "Yes. It is a bit, isn't it?"

"And can I just say, Sire, that I understand exactly why you think it's a comfort? You had to work so hard with so few people behind you to prevent the war between your brothers. It is also a comfort to us that you will be there through the next several generations to protect us. The whole nation regards you in the highest esteem, almost reverence, for what you did to stabilise our country." He smiled warmly at his liege. "As do I."

Much to Maud and Sheldrake's amusement, Tarkyn turned a delicate shade of pink and harrumphed. "Thank you, Jackson."

Partly to rescue Tarkyn from his embarrassment, Sheldrake frowned and asked, "Through several generations?"

Tarkyn nodded, relieved to move the conversation on. "I'm afraid so. Were you aware that I am a guardian of the forest, once known as the Guardian of Eskuzor in the time when forests covered the whole country? It means, among other things, that I will live for three or four hundred years, overseeing the monarchy and wellbeing of Eskuzor." He gave a grimace. "Not actually something I am looking forward to; seeing all my friends and family die around me while I live on."

"How old are you now?" asked Maud.

"Twenty-three."

She frowned with worry. "Hmm. That is tough. People yearn for longevity but… Hmm."

Luckily Clive arrived, carrying a tray which bore the best silver tea set, a brandy decanter and a couple of glasses.

"Ah, good," said Tarkyn, dispelling the morose silence. "You can take my cloak while you are here. I am well and truly warm now."

"Ah, good," said Maud at the same time. "I think Lord Tarkyn needs a cup of tea." She smiled warmly at Tarkyn. "And when you are ready, we will explain our particular need for border security."

Chapter 13

The next morning, while Sheldrake and Maud slept on, the High Lord broke with his usual practice and rose with the dawn. He dressed quickly, then wrote a note which he slipped under the door of his aide-de-camp before making his way downstairs and across to the practice yard behind the stables.

Stefan came out of the shed bearing an armful of wooden swords in preparation for the morning's practice. He stopped in surprise as he saw a tall stranger leaning with his elbows on the top rail of the newly constructed post and rail fence that surrounded their little arena. The stranger was watching him intently.

"Hello," said Stefan cheerily. "You're new. I haven't seen you before." He put down the wooden swords in a pile just outside the arena, but when he straightened, he was frowning. "Now, just a minute. Are you this High Lord that Argyve said he might be able to recruit?"

Tarkyn suppressed a grin at the man's casual disregard of rank and merely nodded. "I am."

"Uh. Hmm." Stefan produced a low bow but was already talking as he straightened. "How do you do? You got here quickly. You're an early riser, aren't you? Unusual in a nobleman. Were you wanting to join in with our practice?"

Tarkyn smiled. "I am a prince of the royal house of Tamadil, not simply a nobleman, but you are right; I am not by nature an early riser. Today I made the effort, so that I could see you before leaving to meet your king this morning."

"Well, I'm sure I should feel honoured by your more than noble effort," responded Stefan with a cheeky chuckle, "except that I have no idea why you would want to see me. I have won many tournaments, but I doubt my reputation has passed the borders of Carrador."

Tarkyn chuckled. "I, too, am a tournament champion and I agree. I doubt my reputation has passed the borders of Carrador, at least not in that capacity."

Stefan's interest quickened. "Really? What's your favourite event? Mine is archery. Not too keen on wrestling."

"I'm afraid mine is the magical event: shafts and shields of power."

"Oh, I see. Fascinating! You might be able to spar or train with Sheldrake then."

"Perhaps, but that is not why I am here." Tarkyn shifted his weight. "I understand that your family owns an inn deep in the Great Forest. I would like to stay at this inn with my new aide-de-camp, Jackson, and you. I need to investigate some aspects of the forest, partly in pursuit of your king's wish to better secure your borders, but also for reasons of my own. I believe you know the forest like few others."

269

"Stars above! You get straight to the point, don't you?" Stefan began to sort through the swords, leaning them against the middle railing in order of size. Once he had lined them up, he looked up. "I would be happy to accompany you, but I have been assigned to Lord Sheldrake's household, specifically to protect and equip them against possible attack."

"If I particularly requested you, the King could provide a stand-in for the time you are gone, couldn't he?"

Stefan scratched his head. "Yes, I suppose so, although I don't want my new position here jeopardized. I really like it here and the work is important. Just a minute." Stefan disappeared into the shed and returned with an armful of bows, which he dumped at a spot fifty yards from a target painted on the wall of the barn.

Tarkyn watched while he sorted them by size before saying, "I can make sure your position is secure. I am, after all, conferring a favour on your king by assisting him."

"There are other arms men with knowledge of the forests," said Stefan slowly. He straightened to look the High Lord in the eye, "but somehow I don't think you want them, do you?" Before Tarkyn could reply, he continued, "Lord Argyve told you about me in his letter, didn't he?" He shook his head. "Something odd is going on here. Lord Argyve couldn't take his eyes off me when we first met. He settled down after a while, but now he's written about me to someone from another land. This doesn't feel right."

"He was surprised to see someone with green eyes," said Tarkyn.

Stefan put his hands on his hips and cocked his head. "Really? And did he mention Jayhan's even more astonishing eye colour?"

Tarkyn stared at him for a long minute, his amber eyes gleaming in the first rays of the sun as it rose between the trees. Finally, he lifted his weight off his elbows and straightened up, letting out a long sigh. "No, he didn't. Of course, he has known Jayhan for some time, so his eyes are not novel to him whereas yours are, but..." Tarkyn shrugged. "I am hopeless at prevaricating, so I won't lie to you. You present a conundrum to Lord Argyve and to me, but until I know more, I can't tell you why. However," he added with a lop-sided smile, "I will tell you that, more than anything else, it was concern for your welfare that made me accede to Argyve's request for me to come to Carrador... So, will you come?"

Stefan puffed out his cheeks and blew out a long breath. "Well, now I really do feel honoured, even if I don't understand what is going on. The fact that you have put in so much effort on my behalf demands respect. I will come with you."

Chapter 14

To Tarkyn's irritation but not surprise, King Gavin insisted on a formal welcome the following day, followed by a long, tedious luncheon peopled by every person of power and influence who could be mustered on such short notice. Jackson had proved himself to be an invaluable aide-de-camp by procuring formal attire in deep blue for the High Lord, which he presented with a proud smile, halfway through the morning.

"Thank you, Jackson," said Tarkyn, "you are a wonder."

"Lady Maud is the wonder. I just enlisted her help." Jackson gave a worried frown. "I don't know much about these things, but aren't you supposed to wear a sash and a star-shaped brooch to show your rank, if it's formal?"

Tarkyn reached into his pocket and casually produced a rather crumpled deep blue sash bordered with a thin line of red from his pocket. He rummaged around deeper in the pocket until he withdrew a small black velvet bag. From this, he produced a diamond-studded silver star as big as Jackson's palm. An indigo sapphire nestled in its centre. Jackson just stared, his mouth hanging open.

"Get this ironed for me, would you?" said Tarkyn, smiling at his reaction. "This is the sash and Order of Tamadil. I keep them with me always, but rarely wear them. They really wouldn't look right on my light brown forest garb."

Jackson recovered himself enough to produce a weak chuckle. "No, Sire, I'm sure they wouldn't. Not to mention the fact that the star is likely to get snagged in the undergrowth."

"Exactly." Tarkyn grinned and motioned him away.

A transformed Tarkyn, wearing the deep blue frock coat and breeches in the style currently favoured by Carradorian nobility, with the sash and Order of Tamadil worn across his white shirt proclaiming his royal status, his long black hair confined by an ebony clip at the base of his neck, exited the carriage and trod up the steps of the palace to be greeted by King Gavin, who was wearing the red and gold uniform of Commander of the Carradorian armed forces.

Tarkyn stopped one step below Gavin where he could meet the monarch eye to eye. Tarkyn held out his right arm and they grasped each other's arms in greeting, making it clear that they held equal status. A formal round of introductions and the luncheon followed, so that it was not until mid-afternoon that Tarkyn found himself alone with the King in his study overlooking the rear gardens of the palace.

Gavin threw himself into an armchair and gestured to Tarkyn to do likewise. "Thank goodness that is all over. I'm sorry I put you through it, but too many noses would have been out of joint if people found out you'd been here without invitations being issued. Thank you for coming to assist us." He took a deep breath and smiled before continuing more slowly. "So, now perhaps you can tell me how and why you plan to help us secure our borders within the forests."

"Firstly, because your problem is also our problem. Many of these Kimoran refugees are cutting through your forests and travelling further into Eskuzor." The High Lord leaned forward as he spoke. "Now, we are willing to accept refugees, but we are not willing to allow in members of the Kimoran specialist forces who are acting without our official sanction. In fact, even if they sought it, I doubt we would give it. Once refugees cross into Eskuzor, it is up to our authorities to judge their right to stay. If Kimora is seeking a particular criminal, their courts have to file an extradition request, which we will consider on its merits."

"I agree entirely," said Gavin. "I consider the presence of Kimoran armed forces within my borders as tantamount to a declaration of war, especially when I have already made my objections known to the Kimoran queen." He shrugged. "But I do not want a war. I value my people more than that. But I must find a way to stop the infiltration of these foreign troops."

Tarkyn leaned back and smiled. "My brothers were willing to throw lives away for their own ends, but I have never seen Eskuzor's people as tools to use to resolve conflict. I am very glad you feel the same way."

Gavin stood up and offered Tarkyn a drink. When he had poured a brandy for himself and a white wine for Tarkyn, he resumed his seat. "I understand from Maud that Lord Argyve has said you have a way of stopping these people infiltrating your kingdom through your forests. Is that so?"

Tarkyn nodded. "Absolutely. We seek out and deport or imprison any Kimoran military personnel who cross our borders."

"How?"

"Ah. Now this is where it becomes tricky. Very tricky." Tarkyn took a sip of wine, mainly to give Gavin time to prepare himself to face a possible issue. "I can give you two choices. Either I attempt to implement measures to keep you notified of infiltrators passing through your forests, but don't tell you how…"

"Or…"

"Or you must swear an oath of secrecy and non-intervention. If you do this, I will tell you all."

Gavin's eyes narrowed.

"Either way," said Tarkyn, "I will try to help you if you let me."

"What is your other reason for offering your assistance? You did say, 'Firstly.' "

Tarkyn smiled. "So I did. Unfortunately, the second reason requires your oath before I can divulge it. However, I can give you *my* oath that it is not to your nation's detriment."

Gavin sprang to his feet and began to pace. "I have no problem with swearing secrecy. After all, my position is fraught with state secrets. But swearing not to intervene in something within my borders…" He shook his head. "How can I swear that, when I might need to intervene to support people or save lives?"

Tarkyn looked at him and scratched his ear as he tried to find a way through. "My father, King Markazon, was generally a good king. He tried to be just, he never led our people to war and he did not tax them excessively. But he was autocratic, and unswerving in his belief that all his subjects owed him unquestioning loyalty and obedience."

"Yes? I hope that I, too, fit that description," said Gavin, a note of hauteur entering his voice.

Tarkyn smiled up at him. "You do, I suppose, but you are not fearsome like my father was. Your people are relaxed around you in a way my father's people never were. And all credit to you." He raised his glass in acknowledgement before taking a sip of his wine. "Anyway, there was one group of independent but innocuous people to whom my father did something very wrong. He forced their allegiance by making them swear an oath, bound by sorcery to the wellbeing of their... home area. If any of them were disloyal or disobedient, the homes and livelihood of all of them would be destroyed."

Gavin raised his eyebrows and let out a whistle. "That was excessive. Why was he so harsh in that instance?"

"Because they had been dwelling within his kingdom without his knowledge and without having given their allegiance."

"Still harsh, I think." Gavin sat down again and picked up his glass. "Surely that would have made them feel resentful, not loyal."

Tarkyn chuckled. "Yes, very resentful. I had to bear the brunt of it."

"So, in your convoluted way, are you saying that I have a group of people living in my kingdom who have not acknowledged my sovereignty?" The Carradorian King was no fool. "And," he added, thinking back to the beginning of their conversation, "you don't want me to interfere with them or demand their fealty."

Tarkyn gave a relieved smile "Yes. And to never let others know of their existence, if indeed they do exist."

Gavin blinked. "*If* they exist?"

"Yes. They exist in Eskuzor but I don't know about Carrador, except for one small, compelling piece of evidence that they do. Before I tell you any more, will you at least swear to keep their existence secret, in both our countries?"

Gavin nodded decisively. "I give you my oath to keep these people's existence secret and I can also assure you that I will not force sorcery on them."

Tarkyn let out a long breath, "They are known as the woodfolk and live deep within the forests of Eskuzor. It is they who give us early warning of infiltration by undesirables from Kimora. Until sixteen years ago, no one of non-woodfolk blood knew of their existence. Even now, very few sorcerers know of their existence, even though they relay messages throughout the kingdom and guard our forested borders."

"How extraordinary. And you say they are innocuous? Does that mean they are weak, or unwarlike?"

Tarkyn shook his head. "Oh, they are by no means weak. It was they who helped me to stymie a small army without killing anyone and eventually to prevent civil war. They are quick, deadly, virtually invisible and skilled far beyond your own troops." Tarkyn laughed. "Don't look so worried! Given a choice, they will melt away rather than hurt anyone."

The little frown of worry on Gavin's forehead did not dissipate. "So what was your second reason?"

"I care very deeply for the woodfolk. I have been made an honorary member of their nation and, after a rough beginning, they have accepted me as their liege lord." Tarkyn smiled warmly. "I am married to a feisty woodwoman. When I say feisty, I mean she hunts, is rostered onto guard duty, uses a bow and arrow and slingshot as well as any woodman, as do all woodwomen."

"Hmm. There go my matrimonial plans for my younger sister," said Gavin regretfully, but with a twinkle in his grey eyes.

Tarkyn grinned. "I'm afraid so. Few people know I am married because of the secrecy surrounding the woodfolk."

"Ah. Of course."

"My two-year-old daughter is half woodfolk and so is my ten-year-old ward. But that is beside the point. What is to the point is the fact that all woodfolk are generally a little shorter than us, have green eyes and light brown hair. No other people that I know of have green eyes."

Gavin's eyes widened. "Stefan! Lord Argyve wrote to you of Stefan."

"You are very quick. It is a pleasure talking to you."

"Does Stefan know?"

Tarkyn shook his head. "I can't say for sure because Carradorian woodfolk, if they exist, may behave quite differently from those in Eskuzor. However, since you clearly know of only one person with green eyes, I would say they also maintain the secrecy of their existence and so presumably he has no idea who he is."

"Huh! No wonder you were intrigued enough to come here. Stefan's presence amongst men and sorcerers sounds like a complete anomaly." Gavin gave a little smile. "You know, of course, that he is by far the best archer we have ever had."

"He did mention he had won several tournaments. It just provides more evidence that he is indeed a woodman."

"So, your plan?"

"Hazy at best. Somehow, I have to make contact with a nation of woodfolk who do not wish to be known and then enlist their aid on your behalf." Tarkyn hesitated. "I have asked several of my woodfolk to meet me in your Great Forest. I hope you don't mind. But I will need all the help I can get."

"They are welcome. In fact, I would like to meet them at some stage, if that is at all possible."

"And of course, I will need Stefan. Could you replace him temporarily, but only temporarily? He is worried about losing his new position."

"Anything else?" asked the king, his tone becoming dry.

Tarkyn laughed disarmingly. "Not at the moment, thank you. The woodfolk are forever berating me for being too autocratic, so I will not take it in bad part if you do the same."

Chapter 15

The day after Tarkyn's meeting with the King, the gate to Batian House opened again and the family coach, driven by Leon, rolled out, headed for the Royal Palace in Highkington. It was accompanied by a small company of the King's Guard which had been provided to ensure Sasha's safety in the absence of her parents and the arms master.

Inside, Sasha, wearing a teal blue gown trimmed in pale orange, sat opposite Jayhan, who was wearing his best breeches and jacket. Neither of them looked at ease.

Sasha pushed back an unruly stand of hair and sighed. "I know I need to go to the palace and learn all this etiquette stuff, but I really don't want to."

"Huh! You reckon you've got problems. Everyone's going to stare at my eyes."

Sasha laughed, not unkindly. "No, they're not. You and your eyes are famous now, after you received that award."

"Exactly."

She leant over and dug him in the ribs. "Stop being a grumpy-boots. The King did the best he could to make everyone admire your eyes instead of being spooked by them. They'll get used to them." She gave a discontented huff. "At least you know how to act at court. You've been going there all your life."

"Not often. Mostly Mum and Dad leave me at home when they go." He shrugged. "But I guess I know it better than you."

"I'm glad Maud finally let you come too. It will be much better with you there."

"And we'll see Jon and maybe Electra."

Sasha nodded. "And I bet the Royal Stables are worth a visit."

Suddenly Jayhan's bad humour dissipated and he grinned. "If you're allowed near them in your fancy dresses."

"Just watch me." Sasha leaned forward so she could watch the Royal Guards riding beside them. After a few minutes, she gave a gusty sigh. "I wish I could be a Royal Guard. Look at those beautiful saddlecloths! All hand-stitched. And the saddles. Look at the quality of the leather."

"Not to mention the horses," said Jayhan dryly.

"Of course, the horses." She crossed her arms, straight away on the defensive. "Not as good as our horses, obviously."

Jayhan chuckled.

Suddenly, Sasha's attention was caught by a scruffy man who looked somehow familiar, skulking on the far side of the road. She craned her neck for a better look, but her view was blocked by the guards' horses. She turned to Jayhan. "I saw someone watching us."

Jayhan was not impressed. "Of course you did. Lots of people will be watching us go past with all these Guards around us. I'd be watching if I were out there."

"Hmm. No. Not the same. This man ducked into an alley as we came closer."

Jayhan chewed on his lip for a moment as he thought. "Ducked? Didn't just happen to be going that way?" When Sasha looked ready to hit him, he threw up his hands. "Okay. Okay. Just checking." He glanced up at the ceiling of the carriage. "Dad taps the ceiling with his cane if he thinks someone is following." He grimaced. "But I don't really want to make a fuss in front of all these guards. Do you think the person was following us? We're going slowly enough for someone to follow on foot if they run a bit."

Sasha shook her head. "I have no idea. I only caught a glimpse of him."

"Probably nothing."

"Probably."

Neither of them sounded convinced.

After a minute Jayhan suggested, "We'll tell Leon when we get there, just in case."

Sasha nodded. "Yeah, good idea."

But as the journey progressed, many people and houses of interest caught their interest and by the time they drew up at the steps of the palace, they were so preoccupied with preparing themselves to face the stares and expectations that they had forgotten all about it.

They looked out to see two rows of liveried servants lining the steps up to the great doors at the top. Sasha's heart thumped hard. She had not received this treatment last time when she had visited the king with her brother. Clearly, they were being given a formal welcome.

To their relief, Jon came running down the stairs to greet them, just as the door to the carriage was opened by a poker-faced, liveried footman. Sasha politely inclined her head, smiled her thanks and stepped forward primly into the waiting arms of her brother who grabbed her and twirled her around, lifting her feet off the ground and bringing a reluctant grin to her face.

"Jon!" she said repressively, as she was returned to earth. "I am supposed to be learning to be dignified."

Seeing Jayhan standing to one side, trying not to look envious, Jon ignored her and took hold of him, twirling him around in the air until he shrieked with laughter.

"Come on," said Jon, holding out a hand to each of them.

"What will all these servants think of us?" whispered Sasha, as they proceeded up the stairs between the two rows of expressionless servants.

"If they are kind," said Jon in a voice loud enough to be heard by the staff, "they will be pleased that you have been given a warm welcome. If they are judgemental, they are not worth worrying about. They are people, just like us." He smiled. "Remember? I have been a footman for years. I know what I am talking about."

Jayhan, who was not as overwhelmed as Sasha, noticed barely suppressed smiles on the faces of several people they passed.

At the top of the stairs, however, stood the King's stern steward, dressed in black bombazine, her hands linked on her stomach. She was not smiling.

Although the children quailed inwardly, she had no effect on Jon, who smiled sunnily at her. "Good afternoon, Josie. You have met Lady Natasha before, I believe," he said, carefully using Sasha's new pseudonym, "but have you met Lord Jayhan? He has been here several times with his parents and, of course, for the presentation of his Star of Courage, but I'm not sure whether your paths have crossed."

Josie bosom heaved. "Lord Johnson," she began, "You know my views on unruly children."

Jon raised his eyebrows. "Actually, I don't, but I can imagine." He shrugged. "However, I struggle to see their relevance at the moment." Josie pursed her lips and her face darkened but before she could say anything further, Jon asked, "So, are you here to usher the children to their rooms or to see Gavin? He will be delighted to hear how welcoming you have been to his little cousin and her friend."

Josie glared at him for several long seconds. "You are very cheeky, young man. We clearly have different views on what constitutes a welcome. I have spent most of the morning making sure the children's rooms are warm, comfortable and, I hope, welcoming for their arrival. And what have you done?"

Jon grinned. "Nothing at all. Just run down the steps and hugged them."

"Good," she said tartly. "So between us, we have covered everything."

Jon gave a slight bow. "I stand corrected, ma'am."

Josie quirked an eyebrow at him, the faintest hint of a smile on her lips, before whirling and beckoning with her finger for them to follow. "This way, children."

Jayhan's room opened off the lounge room of his parents' apartment and was much as he had last seen it, although there were biscuits and a mug of lemonade waiting for him in the dining room and a cheery fire in his bedroom. Once he had had a cursory look around and fiddled with a few of his toys, they continued on to inspect Sasha's new room.

Sasha approached with trepidation. All the way to the palace, she had been envisaging swathes of pink and white lace, which would make her feel ill at ease and nauseous. Instead, as she walked past Josie through the doorway, she found herself in a room painted oyster grey with stained wood trim, hung with paintings of horses. Her bed covers were in soft but warm autumn colours. The room was large; larger than the kitchen at Batian House and, besides the three-quarter-sized bed, contained a dressing table, a small bookcase, two armchairs and a round table with four chairs. A doorway that Sasha had not yet noticed, led to a walk-in wardrobe and a private bathroom.

Sasha gasped in wonder and turned to Josie, a great smile blooming on her face. "Oh, thank you so much. This is…" Tears sprang to her eyes. "Oh, it's just what I always… so much more than I've ever wanted. It's wonderful."

She scanned the books, noting that they ranged from stories to heavy tomes of heraldry, history and court etiquette. Aware that Jon and Jayhan were waiting for her, she dragged her eyes away, then noticed the huge bunch of wildflowers in a large vase on the dressing table and a tray loaded with milk and cookies that waited for her on the table. In a daze, she crossed to the window and found herself looking out over the lake in the back garden.

For a minute she stood there trying to fight the tears that were threatening to overwhelm her. With a supreme effort, she swallowed and managed to say thickly, "Look, Jayhan. Come here. You can see the swan's nest from up here."

Jayhan, who was no fool, walked up next to her and casually put his arm around her waist. She gave a watery giggle and murmured, "I thought you weren't huggy."

"I'm not usually," he said gruffly. "Just sometimes."

In the doorway, Jon smiled down at Josie, who was watching them with an air of satisfaction. "Well done, Josie. Well done."

Chapter 16

Two days later, Tarkyn, Jackson, Stefan and Sheldrake rode out early from Batian House towards the Great Forest. Maud had insisted they wait long enough to ensure that no panic-stricken messages were being sent home from the palace.

Jackson rode a strong but well-mannered chestnut gelding who had been named Bosco for reasons no one could remember. Stefan was riding Slinky, a tall, narrow-backed mare whose ebony coat gleamed in the sunlight, while Tarkyn had been mounted on the frisky young Clydesdale, Flurry. Even though her main work would be as a plough horse, Beth thought Flurry was best suited to Tarkyn's weight and wanted her to get used to being ridden. She had been training her as a saddle horse around the farm, with Jon in mind as her rider, but this was Flurry's first foray further afield. Beth had insisted that Tarkyn spend an hour with her while she watched him critically to check that he was up to the task of riding her.

To Stefan's private amusement, Sheldrake was mounted on Maisy.

The morning was crisp and clear, and dew still glittered on the roadside grasses. Few travellers were out and about this early, but a steady trickle of carts laden for market passed them from the opposite direction, heading towards Highkington. As the road narrowed over a one-lane bridge, they found their way blocked by an old woman trying to persuade her mule to step onto the rickety boards of the bridge on the far side of the stream.

Realising she was holding up a prestigious group of riders, the old lady became flustered and consequently more aggressive with her mule, which in turn became frightened, confused and even more stubborn.

While the others waited, Tarkyn dismounted and led his huge draught horse onto the bridge. As he approached the old woman, she seemed to calm down, as did the mule. He left Flurry in the middle of the bridge, where she stood quietly, waiting for him. Then he approached the mule, stroked its neck reassuringly and led it, unresisting, onto the rickety bridge. Once the mule and cart were both moving across the bridge, Tarkyn walked ahead of them to Flurry, mounted and wheeled her, riding back to wait with the others, while the old woman completed her crossing.

Sheldrake nodded his appreciation. "Beth will be very impressed to hear how well Flurry behaved. You certainly have a way with her."

"Thanks." Tarkyn smiled. "But I am a forest guardian, after all."

Because he was concentrating on making sure that Maisy found her way safely across the loose boards, Sheldrake didn't really take in what Tarkyn had said and so did not pursue it.

Once across the bridge, Tarkyn rode beside Sheldrake, exchanging desultory comments on the scenery they passed, and listening while Sheldrake explained the route they were taking and the breadth and direction of the border within the great Forest.

Eventually Tarkyn held up his hand. "Much as I would like to gain an appreciation of the area, I have absolutely no sense of direction so you will need to make sure Jackson understands everything we need to know as well, so he can haul me back if we head off in the wrong direction."

Sheldrake chuckled. "Right. I'll remember that."

Houses soon gave way to fields and the quality of the road deteriorated as they drew further away from the city. Gravel, sharp stones and runnels across the road made the horses pick their way more slowly.

"I don't remember the road being so bad when we came through here a few weeks ago," muttered Sheldrake.

"I think heavy rain last week washed away the surface, sir," suggested Stefan.

Sheldrake smiled. "We'll have to let Jon know. He's the new Minister for Transport. Happily, it is no longer my problem."

Suddenly, Tarkyn jerked upright as though he had been hit. Even as he drew Flurry up, his hands not touching the reins, Sheldrake had thrown a translucent lilac dome of protection over all four horses and riders.

"Thanks," said Tarkyn. "But I was not reacting to danger. As far as I know, there is none." He swung down from the saddle. "Keep your horse still, Jackson," he ordered, walking over to him.

"What's wrong?" Jackson glanced around, checking for possible hazards.

"Nothing drastic," Tarkyn assured him, "I just need to check your horse's hooves. He hurt his hind right hoof on a sharp stone back there and I think it may have become lodged. Stay mounted. I'll just check."

Watched by a rather bemused Jackson, Tarkyn walked behind Bosco and lifted his hoof. Sure enough, a sharp stone was jammed between the frog and the shoe, digging into the sole of the hoof. Tarkyn pulled out his knife and flicked away the offending rock. The sole below was red and, to Tarkyn's forest guardian senses, radiating pain.

"Just sit still a minute," he instructed Jackson. "I need to heal him."

Tarkyn focused inside himself, drew forth his *esse* and sent his power into the horse. After a long minute, he let go of the hoof and straightened. He gave the gelding a pat on the rump and returned to his own horse.

As he mounted, Sheldrake's eyes were alight with curiosity. "What just happened? What did you do?"

Tarkyn smiled. "I told you before, I'm a forest guardian. I pick up the feelings of people and animals, also the mental images of horses, other animals and some people. So when Jackson's gelding hit that stone, I felt his wave of pain. I sent him a query; no words, I'm afraid, just images and impressions. He showed me that his hoof was hurt." He shrugged. "So then I healed it straight away before it could get any worse and send the horse lame."

"Is that how you handled that mule on the bridge?"

"It is. I sent out waves of calm and reassurance to the woman and the mule. Then I rode Flurry onto the bridge to show the mule that it would hold his weight. Once the mule was calm, I could send it images of the cart and itself safely crossing the bridge." Tarkyn grinned. "By the way, Flurry tells me that Maisy is your wife... using images, of course."

Sheldrake and Stefan both laughed, while Jackson frowned in confusion. "Really? What? Maisy is really Lady Maud?"

Maisy sashayed sideways then did a little buck,

"She's embarrassed," explained Tarkyn kindly. "Yes, this lovely little mare is Lady Maud... but you mustn't tell other people, Jackson. Closely kept secret apparently."

Soon after the road entered the forest, Sheldrake swapped places with Stefan so that he could re-explain the geography and terrain of the Great Forest to Jackson, leaving Stefan to ride beside Tarkyn.

For a time they rode in silence; the only sounds the creaking of their saddles, the occasional chirruping of birds hidden in the bushes along verge of the road and the indecipherable voices of Sheldrake and Jackson behind them.

Stefan caught Tarkyn glancing sideways at him a couple of times. On the third time he demanded, "What?"

Tarkyn gave a sheepish grin. "I was wondering whether you might be able to receive my mind-images. Only a few people can, and you may be one of them."

Stefan's eyes narrowed as he thought about it. Eventually he asked, "Why me? Why not Lord Sheldrake? He's a trained mage, after all."

"It is not to do with magical power. No sorcerer I know of, other than me, has the ability to send and receive mind messages."

"Aha. This has something to do with that conundrum I apparently present to you and Lord Argyve, doesn't it?"

Tarkyn nodded. "I could try to push into your thoughts without your permission but firstly that would be bad manners and secondly, it might confuse or even frighten you if you didn't know what was happening. So I won't do that." He looked hopefully at Stefan. "But would you like to try?"

Stefan chuckled. "How could I resist such an entreaty? Besides, it will help to pass the time and may be interesting. Go on then."

"Maybe I'll tell you a bit about it first." As he spoke, Tarkyn was scanning the sky and trees for a bird he might be able to connect with. "If you have this ability, you can receive and send mental images of memories, ideas, what you are currently seeing and mental images from a third party."

"What do you mean, from a third party?"

For a moment, Tarkyn was a little distracted as he had just spotted a large white parrot perched high in a gum tree ahead of them on their left. "Hmm? Oh, I mean that I could connect with another person or a bird or animal then share their images with you." He pointed up into the tree. "What is that bird? We don't have them in Eskuzor."

Stefan squinted up into the tree. "That? That is a sulphured-crested cockatoo. Wait 'til it squawks. They have the most raucous cries. They are cheeky and very smart. I love them."

"Do you?" Tarkyn smiled. "Perhaps we could start with it then. I will connect with the bird, then try to connect you to its images. What do you think?"

"Yeah. Great. That would be wonderful if you could do it." Stefan grinned with the excitement of a little child. "Though I only half know what you're talking about."

"Hold onto your pommel... and it might help if you focus on the bird. I'm not sure."

"I can ride, you know," said Stefan defensively. "I don't need to hold onto the pommel if the horse becomes skittish."

"Of course you don't. It's to make sure you don't fall off while the horse is walking quietly." Tarkyn shrugged. "Up to you. But if you fall off, don't say I didn't warn you."

Stefan frowned but on balance, decided to follow Tarkyn's advice. Once he had overcome his pride enough to take a firm grip on the pommel, he focused his attention on the sulphur-crested cockatoo, aware at the same time of Tarkyn riding beside him, outwardly appearing to do nothing.

The first sign of anything unusual was the cockatoo shrieking, raising its crest and bobbing its head up and down. It pranced up and down the branch, bobbing its head and spreading its wings. Beside Stefan, Tarkyn laughed. "I can see why you like them. This one is a real character, isn't she?" For a minute he said nothing, then, "Right. Now I am going to try to connect to you."

One moment, Stefan was watching the cockatoo in the tree, with his peripheral vision on the road and Tarkyn. The next moment, he was looking down at four horsemen far below him on the road. With a sickening lurch, he travelled with the bird as she took off and began to swerve and sway her way down until she landed on a short, stunted tree fifty yards in front of the horsemen, studying them with intense curiosity. He felt her raise her crest and shriek in greeting, bobbing along the small branch, clearly excited by the connection she felt with the tall man on the huge horse. After a little dance, she took off once more and came swooping in, to land on Tarkyn's head. There she bobbed up and down a couple more times, shrieking and flapping her wings, blithely digging her claws into Tarkyn's scalp.

"Enough!" said Tarkyn firmly, breaking the connection to Stefan while at the same time reaching up to stroke the over-excited cocky. He sent out waves of calm and gratitude to the cocky, who hopped onto his hand and rode it down as he brought it to rest on the saddle before him. She raised her crest a few more times but refrained from shrieking or bobbing, just making little comfortable grinding sounds with her beak.

Tarkyn turned to find Stefan looking dazed and a little green, his knuckles white from his hands clenching the pommel. "Looks like you can receive mind images then," he said, then peered at him in concern. "Are you all right? It is a shock for people who are familiar with mind images when they first look through the eyes of a bird, now I think about it. Hmm. Perhaps I should have started with something stationary."

"Maybe," croaked Stefan. He prised his fingers from the pommel, attempted a grin which went sadly crooked, and blinked. He wiped his hand across his face and took a deep breath. "That was absolutely amazing but very disconcerting... but amazing. Phew. I'm glad I held onto the pommel. No way could I have kept my balance otherwise."

Tarkyn chuckled. "I remember showing something similar to a group of people without warning them; half of them fell over."

Just then Sheldrake and Jackson came trotting up and stopped either side of them.

"What's going on?" asked Sheldrake, frowning. "You asked that cockatoo to come down, didn't you, with your forest guardian skills? And why is Stefan looking like a stunned mullet?"

"Careful," murmured Tarkyn, gently stroking the cocky's head. "You'll frighten our little friend here. She has been very brave to come down amongst us, as it is."

Jackson grinned. "She has, hasn't she? What a cutie." He manoeuvred his horse around behind Tarkyn's, bringing Bosco up beside Stefan. He leaned across to Stefan, handing him his waterbag. "Here. Drink this. You look like you've seen a ghost."

Stefan shot him a grateful glance as he accepted the waterbag. He didn't feel he had the coordination at the moment to reach his own waterbag, tied behind him with his saddlebags. After a long draft, he wiped his mouth, re-corked the waterbag and handed it back. "Thanks."

Jackson just nodded, not pressing Stefan to answer any questions, and retied his waterbag to his saddle.

When he was sure the cockatoo was happy where she was, Tarkyn answered Sheldrake's question. "I shared images with this bird and then connected with Stefan to see whether he could receive mind images. It turns out he can. He is looking sickly because his mind followed the cocky on her zig-zaggy course down," he chuckled, "and he's not used to flying."

"Really?" Sheldrake was agog with interest. "Do you think I could do it too?" A restive stamp from Maisy beneath him reminded him of his obligation to his staff member, making him add, "How are you, Stefan? Should we rest for a while, do you think?"

Stefan had recovered enough to appreciate the interaction between Sheldrake and Maud. He smiled and shook his head. "No. I am happy to sit quietly on Slinky for a while. I don't mind whether we're stationary or moving."

Tarkyn gave the cockatoo a final stroke and sent her on her way before saying, "I can try. Do you want to try too, Jackson?"

Jackson shrugged, trying to look nonchalant. "It could be interesting."

"Right. I will try to connect with your minds." Tarkyn glanced at Stefan and raised his eyebrows slightly in a conspiratorial sign that he thought this would be a waste of time. "If I do, I will replay the cockatoo's mind-images of her flight down into that little tree over there. Just close your eyes and think about joining your thoughts to mine."

After several minutes of effort, neither Sheldrake nor Jackson received any mind images. Eventually, Tarkyn gave up. "No. I'm sorry. I did try but I can't connect with either of you. I didn't really think I would be able to, but I did try." He smiled ruefully. "I'm afraid there is a good chance you will pick up on some of my emotions whether I want you to or not, but not images, apparently." He gathered his reins and urged Flurry forward. "Let's move on, shall we?" Seeing Sheldrake's crestfallen expression, he added, "It is a very rare gift. If you like, I will try again later once we have arrived at the inn, but it is unlikely to work."

Sheldrake brought Maisy alongside Flurry as they resumed their journey. "But you were fairly certain, weren't you, that Stefan would have that gift?"

Tarkyn glanced at him briefly. "Yes."

"But you won't tell me why?"

"Not yet. Not until I tell him why first and I'm not ready to do that yet, either."

Sheldrake gave a grimace of frustration.

Tarkyn laughed. "And I will annoy you further by telling you that I can share images with your wife… at least I can while she is a horse. I haven't tried when she is her human self." He smiled. "I didn't share the bird's images with her in case she fell over and took you with her. Probably would be all right on four legs, but you never know."

To Tarkyn's surprise, this had the effect of engaging Sheldrake's natural curiosity, distracting him from his disappointment. "That's interesting. We'll have to experiment, won't we?"

As they rode further from Highkington, the stream of travellers coming from the Great Forest dwindled and for the rest of the journey, nothing untoward happened. They arrived at the Creeping Vine Inn by mid-afternoon. The inn was a sturdy, two-storey cottage-style building, white-washed under a thatched roof. At the sound of their arrival, a broad-shouldered man a few years older than the younger three travellers walked out of the inn to greet them. His pale skin contrasted with his thick black hair and pale blue eyes. He ran his eyes over them and smiled broadly when he saw Stefan among them.

"Stefan, my man! What a great surprise to see you." He strode up to Stefan's pony, grabbed him bodily and whirled him out of the saddle to stand him on the ground before him. "Dad will be pleased as punch! Who are your friends?"

Stefan, whose head barely cleared his shoulder, slapped him on the back, obviously used to this boisterous treatment. "Hello, you big bear. It's great to see you too." He turned to make the introductions, waving his hand to indicate each of his companions, "This is Prince Tarkyn, High Lord of Eskuzor, Lord Sheldrake whom I believe you have already met, and Jackson, aide-de-camp for Lord Tarkyn." Then he indicated his brother. "And this is Anton, my eldest brother."

"Excellent company you're keeping." Anton put his fingers to his mouth and let forth a loud whistle that brought two younger versions of himself running from the stables. Stefan grinned and hugged each of them in turn before turning to introduce them too. "And this is Javier and this is Marin."

"Pleased to meet you all," said Sheldrake, smiling. "We didn't get a welcome like this last time we came."

Stefan laughed. "You didn't have me with you."

As the other three dismounted, Anton said to his brothers, "Right you two, take their horses, give them a good rub down, feed and water. You can come in and see Stefan as soon as you've finished."

Tarkyn frowned a query at Sheldrake, who gave a conspiratorial little smile and said to the boys, "Maisy loves oats, but if you don't mind, don't tie any of our horses up. They are well behaved and happy to stand calmly in the stalls." He gave a Maisy a cheery pat on the rump before turning to walk inside.

"Fair enough." Marin grinned and took Maisy's and Slinky's reins, clicking his tongue to encourage the horses to follow him, while Javier led the other two.

Tarkyn nodded at Jackson. "Go with them please, unload the horses, take our bags up to our room and meet us in the bar."

Jackson who, like Tarkyn, was concerned for Maud in her horse's guise, obeyed with alacrity.

The travellers entered the inn in order of precedence. As protocol demanded, the lords entered first while Stefan's brother, as host, entered last with his arm firmly around Stefan's shoulders. As soon as they were inside, Anton bellowed, "Hey, Da, look what the cat dragged in."

The rotund innkeeper gave a perfunctory bow to the two lords before surging past them to envelope Stefan in a huge bear hug. The small arms master was almost lost to sight. Shortly, a couple of smothered squawks signalled Stefan's need for air so, with a solid slap to his back, his father let him go and held him out at arms' length to look him over. "Stefan, my son, you haven't grown any, but you're looking fine, very fine."

"Hi, Da. You're looking pretty good yourself. Haven't got any thinner though."

His father roared with laughter. "Cheeky boy! Ah, your mother will be pleased to see you. We haven't seen you these many months, busy as you are in the big city." He gave Stefan a push in the direction of the kitchen and turned to the others of his party.

Stefan gave an embarrassed smile and shrugged at his companions as he made his way through a door behind the bar, but the quickness of his gait belied his apparent reluctance.

The Innkeeper beamed. "Welcome, gents. Any friend of my son's is a friend of mine. Come in, come in and sit down. What can I get you?"

Tarkyn ordered tankards of ale for Sheldrake, Jackson and himself. Jackson re-joined them soon after and once the three of them were settled with the ale in front of them, the innkeeper, whose name turned out to be Ivan, chatted to them for nearly twenty minutes before the demands of other customers called him away. A group of merchants from Kimora, five women and three men, had entered, and they were hungry and thirsty after their long trip while at the bar, a few local foresters had drained their glasses and were waiting patiently for Ivan's return.

Sheldrake swept his eyes across the bar's inhabitants, noting a scruffy young couple who appeared to be celebrating something, various other workers, both male and female, and an unobtrusive woman in the corner, knitting while she sipped her ale. He made no comment but turned instead to Tarkyn. "So here we are, my lord. What is our next move?"

Tarkyn looked pensive. "Hmm. Stefan is well loved by his family, I think. I will need to speak privately with Stefan's parents. It will have to be after the inn has shut for the evening. Can you organise that please, Jackson? Meanwhile, let us have a good dinner and settle into our rooms." Suddenly he grinned. "Sheldrake, I believe your wife is about to join us."

Sheldrake was unperturbed. "I was expecting her sooner or later."

Sure enough, five minutes later, the front door opened and Maud surged in, dressed in her favourite green gown. Jackson jumped up to pull out a chair for her. She smiled graciously and sat down. "I'll have a large tankard of ale too, if you please. I have earned it, I think."

"I'll say," said Jackson appreciatively. "I couldn't walk that far in one day, let alone carrying someone."

Maud laughed. "I couldn't either, in human form."

Jackson signalled and a tall, big-boned woman with dark hair pulled back into a bushy ponytail walked straight over to them and smiled a welcome. "Hello. I'm Marjorie. You're Stefan's friends, aren't you? Welcome. What can I get you?"

"An ale for Maud here, please," replied Tarkyn, smiling in return. "You're Stefan's sister, I take it. You have the same look as Anton, Javier and Marin."

Marjorie frowned. "Big and strong, you mean. Now, don't you go picking on Stefan. He can't help it if he's a bit smaller than the rest of us. He's the deadliest shot this side of the border."

Tarkyn raised his eyebrows in surprise and held his hands up in a placating gesture. "I was casting no aspersions at all. Stefan is clearly a force to be reckoned with."

Marjorie beamed at him. "Yes, he is, isn't he? Sorry. It's just we have been defending him since he was a little 'un, as in *very* little 'un, from the slurs of customers. Kind of comes naturally to jump to his defence."

"But it's all right for you to take a little dig at him."

She waved her hand. "O' course. He's family."

"U-huh. And do you think we'll ever get to see him again?" asked Tarkyn.

Marjorie laughed. "Not unless you really need him. The boys came in from the stables to see him but then that Kimoran lot arrived, so they had to go back out again. And Karl is coming in with supplies on his way through to his own cot. He should be here in half an hour or so. He lives a bit away from us now that he's married. He's set up his own business, you know, selling herbs and plants from the forest. Doing well. And o' course Ma hasn't stopped fussing over Stefan since he got here. We haven't seen him for more than a half a year, you know."

"Right. Thanks. In that case, I think we'll order more ale and dinner, if you please." Tarkyn settled back, preparing for a long but pleasant evening and the strong possibility that he would not get the chance to see Stefan's parents until the following day. In fact, as soon as Marjorie left, he leaned over to Jackson and said, "Don't worry about organising that meeting. I think today is too soon. Some things should not be rushed."

Part 3

Chapter 17

Stefan had remembered himself enough to present himself to Lord Sheldrake, late in the evening and notably worse for wear, to enquire when he might be needed. Sheldrake kindly suggested that lunchtime tomorrow would be soon enough and that he could spend the intervening time with his family.

When Tarkyn arose the next morning for a late breakfast, he found Sheldrake and Jackson waiting for him in the deserted bar of the tavern, drinking coffee. Other customers had already left, either going home the previous night or heading off earlier that morning for their destinations.

"Have you two eaten yet?"

"About two hours ago," responded Sheldrake dryly. "I have been out for a short walk but since we don't know why we are here, we have resorted to drinking coffee until you arrived."

Tarkyn smiled, quite unrepentant. "And where is Maud?"

Sheldrake's eyes shifted. "Oh, around somewhere."

"By which I gather she is currently reconnoitring for you. A very handy asset for your information-gathering toolbox, as long," a slight edge developed in Tarkyn's voice, "as it is not used to gather information about me." Tarkyn said nothing more as he sat down and poured himself a coffee from the pot in the middle of the table. He let his mind wander up the stairs to the corridor where his room was situated. A fluffy, grey cat was running along next to the wall in short bursts, stopping now and then to peer around and sniff the air. Tarkyn's mind nudged the cat's and connected. Not only did he become aware of the cat's view of the corridor, he also recognised the mind as Maud's, intent on finding a way into his room.

In that moment of recognition, two things happened simultaneously.

The fluffy grey cat's back arched, her hair standing on end, as she hissed at the image of Tarkyn in her mind, while downstairs, Sheldrake and Jackson clutched at the table, as the ground beneath the Creeping Vine Inn shuddered. Bottles rocked on shelves behind the bar and one picture fell off the wall. Ivan nearly lost his balance and grabbed at the bar to save himself.

Sheldrake's eyes widened. "What was that?"

"Earthquake," muttered Jackson, his body tense as he waited to see whether it would settle or get worse.

Tarkyn rose from the table and stood staring down at Sheldrake, his mouth thinned with anger. After a moment he took a breath and said, "That was not an earthquake. That was my outrage. Just be glad that I have learnt to control my feelings, at least to some extent."

Leaving behind him two shaken men, he turned and strode out of the inn.

Once outside, he stood for several minutes until his rational mind gradually overcame his initial reaction. As an information-gatherer himself, Tarkyn could understand that Sheldrake wanted to know more about him, a powerful mage from another country who was not being open about all of his motives for being in Carrador. He could not expect them to trust him implicitly after so short an acquaintance. He remembered wryly when Danton, his lifelong friend and now his brother-in-law, had said that integrity tended to shine most strongly out of the most accomplished con artists.

He gave a grunt of laughter at himself. He was no con artist, witnessed by the fact that he hadn't kept quiet about his ulterior motive. Mentally forgiving Sheldrake and resolving to apologize both to him and the innkeeper, he walked down the side of the inn and into the forest behind it.

He let his senses range, trying to discover whether any of his Eskuzorian woodfolk had arrived. Tarkyn himself had used translocation to travel almost instantaneously to the border then to Sheldrake's, while his woodfolk friends would have had to walk the whole way. Using Sheldrake and Jackson's knowledge, he had sent mental images of the Creeping Vine's location so that they could cut through forest directly from Eskuzor to reach here, but his geographical skills were suspect, to say the least, so he hoped he had not misdirected them.

Suddenly a raucous cry split the air as a great mountain eagle came into view above the trees. Her huge black and gold wings beat the air as she glided overhead and disappeared slowly out of sight above the canopy. Tarkyn almost jumped up and down with excitement. He sent her a mental wave of greeting and waited until she reappeared above the forest road and, with harsh cry, glided down and around, heading at speed towards Tarkyn to land on his shoulder, her powerful talons gripping the leather shoulder pads on his shirt. Despite all his past experience, Tarkyn still staggered under her weight. She shuffled around, her tail brushing across his face and filling his mouth with down and feathers as she turned to face forward.

"Blasted bird!" protested Tarkyn. "Why don't you turn the other way?" The eagle just cocked her head at his tone then gently ran her wickedly sharp beak along strands of his long black hair. Tarkyn lifted his hand up to stroke her. "Yes. All right. I'm glad to see you too, even if you do a weigh a ton." He gave the eagle an image of his woodfolk bloodbrother, Waterstone, accompanied by a sense of query.

In return he received an image of five adult woodfolk and three youngsters threading their way through dense forest. He queried how far away and was given an image of the sun setting, then directly above him.

"A day and a half away, I think." Tarkyn turned and headed back inside, the great eagle bouncing gently on his shoulder with every stride. "I had better speak to Stefan's parents."

As he entered the inn, he saw Maud, back in human form, with Sheldrake and Jackson seated around the remains of their rolls and tea, in the middle of a heated discussion. A look of relief passed over Jackson's face when he saw Tarkyn. Then his eyes widened in amazement as he spotted the eagle riding Tarkyn's shoulder. A murmur ran though the patrons in the bar.

Tarkyn walked over to the table and sat down. The three at the table could not take their eyes off the eagle.

"What a beauty. Is that why you have leather pads on your shirt?" asked Jackson.

Tarkyn gave a rueful nod. "Yes. She lands on me, whether I want her or not, and she leaves deep gouges in my shoulder if I don't wear the leather pads." He transferred his attention to Sheldrake. "I apologize for the mini-quake. I did not intend it. I understand your suspicion but can only reiterate that I intend no harm. If I did, I would not have announced my presence to you, when I first arrived."

Sheldrake and Maud glanced at each other, clearly embarrassed. Sheldrake cleared his throat. "I don't know what to say."

Tarkyn gave a short laugh. "I know what you want to say; that you're sorry you were caught but not really sorry that you were investigating me. It is, after all, your job. At least you have spared me an empty apology."

Sheldrake frowned and took refuge in sipping his tea.

"It is, of course, a diplomatic disaster to offend a visiting head of state." Tarkyn let that little pearl hang in the air for a few moments before reaching into his pocket and slapping a key on the table. "Here. If you want to search my room, be my guest. I have been outside, so I have not had the opportunity to remove any incriminating evidence. So help yourselves." Without waiting for a response, he turned to Jackson. "Have you asked Stefan's parents to make time to see me?"

Jackson nodded, glad to move on to a new topic. "Once the breakfasts have been served and cleared away, they can meet with you for a short time before they have to start preparing for lunch. Mornings are usually slow in the bar, I gather. Anyway, I think their kids can cover for them if need be."

"Thank you. I believe there is a private parlour we could meet in.'

Jackson nodded again. "I have already booked it."

Tarkyn smiled. "Well done. I can see your talents have been wasted as a messenger."

There was a pause before Jackson said slowly, "Not wasted, Sire. Just in abeyance, while I used a different set of talents for a different important role."

Aware of the censure in the remark, Sheldrake watched the High Lord for his reaction. Tarkyn stared at Jackson for a long moment, then stood and with a nod at the other two, walked out, the huge eagle bobbing gently on his shoulder.

"You're pushing the boundaries, young man," said Sheldrake. "That was an ungracious way to receive a compliment, even if you do, presumably, have strong views about messengers being undervalued."

Jackson coloured a little but when he started to protest, Maud added, "No matter how valuable messengers are, and I agree, we couldn't do without them, you did not pick your time well to ram that down Lord Tarkyn's throat. If he has to monitor everything he says to you, you will find yourself with a very aloof liege, which would be a shame. He seems to like you and always treats you with respect and courtesy. But don't forget; despite his power, he is still a stranger in a land strange to him. Your role is to support him, not just practically."

"Thank you for your advice." Jackson stood up and gave a small ironic bow. "It is also a shame that you two have shown yourselves to be neither trusting nor trustworthy."

As he walked out, Maud said, so quietly that he didn't hear her, "That's better, young man."

Word of the eagle had spread quickly, and Jackson walked out to find Tarkyn surrounded by a small crowd, two of Stefan's brothers among them, eagerly seeking a closer look at the eagle on his shoulder.

The eagle was not happy. She squawked from time to time, spreading and flapping her wings, each time hitting Tarkyn on his head and digging her talons into his shoulder. People were pressing so close that it would be hard for him to raise a shield. Amidst his efforts to keep his eagle calm, Tarkyn had thought of using a spell to immobilize the crowd but was vaguely concerned that it could be construed as a hostile act. So, he was currently contemplating levitating the eagle and himself above the crowd, even though he was loath to provide even more entertainment.

Jackson knew none of this but could see that Tarkyn was feeling harassed. Without hesitation and admittedly, with no thought for the eagle's reaction, Jackson put his fingers to his mouth and let forth a piercing whistle, which the eagle answered with an ear-splitting shriek but other than that, seemed to calm down a little.

"Move back please," ordered Jackson firmly. "You are upsetting His Highness and the eagle. You do realise that touching High Lord Tarkyn constitutes a capital offence." He had no idea whether the same applied to Carradorians as to Eskuzorians but he guessed no one in the crowd knew either. "And mountain eagles are known for their ferocity. I'm amazed she has attacked no one so far and can only assume His Highness has been battling with her to protect you all."

The crowd backed away and even from a distance, Jackson could see Tarkyn heave a sigh of relief. He met Jackson's eyes and gave a nod of thanks before addressing the crowd. "Bird is a wild eagle. She will only let one other person and me, touch her. Jackson is right. She will go for you if you come too close. It was taking everything I had to keep her from attacking those closest to me. I'm surprised she stayed so long. I would have expected her to fly away. Perhaps she thought she was protecting me."

As though in answer, Bird launched off Tarkyn, driving herself upwards with slow beats of her wings. Once she had gained enough height, she swooped down and glided over the crowd, a mere foot above their heads, making them duck in panic. Then she let out a satisfied shriek and returned to Tarkyn's shoulder. Jackson, standing a little further away, chuckled in appreciation.

Gradually, as the novelty wore off and nothing new happened, the crowd dispersed. Tarkyn gave Bird a reassuring stroke before walking towards the west side of the inn, away from the people and the stables. Without a word, Jackson fell in beside him.

As they neared the huge gum tree at the rear of the inn where Jayhan had hidden, Tarkyn said, a new note of formality in his voice. "Thank you for your intercedence." He turned his attention to the eagle and said in a more friendly tone, "Go on, Bird. Go up in the tree for a while. My shoulder is getting tired."

The eagle responded by preening his hair for a few seconds just to make sure he knew she was the one making the choice, then launched herself up into the tree.

Jackson glanced at him and could see that he was, as Maud had predicted, less relaxed with him. "I'm sorry, Sire," he said in a rush. "I'm sorry I sniped at you before." He ran a hand over his forehead. "I suppose… It's just that I had been sitting with Maud and Sheldrake who were feeling… hmm… anxious, quite deservedly, I might say, about how you would behave towards them when you returned. It was very tense and I guess I was on edge and snapped at you, the last person who deserved it. So, I'm sorry."

Tarkyn turned and looked at him, keeping him waiting while he decided on his response. Finally, he smiled. "That was a very handsome apology, which I accept. Can we enter the private parlour via this side door? Then I can avoid Sheldrake and Maud for a while." He gave a slight smile. "I have forgiven them too, but I'll let them sweat a bit longer."

Jackson grinned in relief. "Yes, we can. Come this way."

Chapter 18

He led them through the door along the corridor and into the kitchen, where Vera, Stefan's mother, looked up from a large slab of dough she was kneading. A look of surprise crossed her face when she registered that it was not one of her children entering. She stopped what she was doing and dropped a curtsey.

"Good morning, my lord. Are you waiting for me? I'll just finish this, if you don't mind, and be along in a few minutes. I need to get it into the oven, ready for lunch."

Marjorie and Marin smiled at them from the other side of the kitchen where they were cutting up a bunch of carrots.

"Keep her as long as you like," said Marjorie. "She could do with a morning off. Shall I bring you some tea or coffee while you're waiting?"

Tarkyn nodded. "Yes please. Enough for the four of us."

Jackson led him out of the internal kitchen door into a short passageway on the lefthand side of the bar. A door in the oak panelling on their left opened into a good-sized private parlour, decorated with whitewashed walls and dark panelling in a similar fashion to the public bar, but with more comfortable lounge chairs placed around a polished, unscratched table in the middle and a few armchairs around the walls. The window looked out at the gum tree so that Tarkyn could see Bird perched patiently in one of the higher branches.

Not long after they had seated themselves, Ivan and Vera arrived, Ivan bearing a tray full of pots, cups, plates and freshly baked scones filled with jam and cream.

"Oh, well done. This looks excellent," said Tarkyn. He gestured to the other chairs. "Do take a seat."

Jackson suddenly realised that, for some reason, Tarkyn was nervous.

Once everyone was settled, Ivan opened the proceedings by saying, "You asked to see us, my lord."

Tarkyn gave a slight cough. "Uh yes. It is about your son, Stefan."

Ivan frowned. "What about him? He's not in any sort of trouble, is he?"

Tarkyn waved his hand. "No. Nothing like that. From everything I have seen, he is very well respected."

"So, what then?"

"Well, this is very awkward, but I was wondering whether Stefan is really your son?"

Ivan scowled. "Now, don't you go picking on him because he's smaller. He's worth his weight in gold, he is."

"I know he is. I've just said that he's well respected. No. It is not just his size. It is also his eye and hair colouring." Tarkyn leaned forward. "Is he your biological son? I ask because I have several particular friends who look just like him."

Ivan and Vera exchanged looks. Jackson saw them clasp hands. Ivan squeezed Vera's hand and very slightly raised his eyebrows at her. When she squeezed his hand back, Ivan turned resolutely towards Tarkyn. "Stefan is as much our son as any of the others but you're right; he is not our biological son."

"There was a terrible flood, you see," said Vera in a rush, as though anxious to explain themselves. "Anton was out walking in the forest down by the river, looking to see what the river had swept up onto its shores and to see how much damage it had done. We warned him to be careful, but the flood waters had mostly subsided by then." She waved her hand in the air. "Anyway, he thought he heard a cat or a kitten mewling but when he looked for the source of the sound, he found a baby, maybe two months old, wrapped in a shoulder sling that had caught on the branches of a sunken log. The current must have pushed the child past the log, then the sling had snagged on the branches and held him firm while the water subsided. It was a miracle he survived. We looked all along the banks of the river for any sign of the mother, but there was nothing." She shrugged. "As fate would have it, I'd just lost a newborn child so recently that I was still producing milk." Her eyes shone with the tears of an old grief. "So we brought him home."

"And he's been our son ever since." Ivan scowled again. "And he always will be, no matter what."

"Thank you for telling us his story." Tarkyn studied Vera's strained face and asked, unknowingly echoing Maud, "Would you like some tea?"

When she nodded, he reached for the teapot but was forestalled by Ivan who growled, "I'll do it."

Once she had taken a few sips and settled down a little, Tarkyn asked, "Does Stefan know? Who, other than Anton, knows? Or was he too young to remember?"

"Anton, Karl and Marjorie knew, but I think we all more or less forgot." Ivan sighed. "We never spoke of it. We just accepted him as part of the family."

"So does Stefan know?" pressed Tarkyn, as gently as he could.

Ivan frowned and shook his head uncertainly. "Not as far as I know. I suppose one of the older ones could have told him when they were teasing him, but I think he would have come to us, if they did."

"They'd tease him about his size and push him around a bit but they all did that to each other, including Marjorie at one time or another," said Vera. "They never *really* hurt each other, I don't think."

Tarkyn thought about his own biological brothers who had conspired to imprison or hang him. Then he thought of his woodfolk blood brothers who might tease or disagree with him but would support him to the ends of the earth. He smiled. "I am glad Stefan has grown up in such a warm, kind, if somewhat boisterous family."

Ivan chuckled. "That he has." He took a ruminative sip of his tea. "But he's given us back full measure, you know. He's great with the horses, the chooks, the cow. He's the best of them at finding mushrooms and herbs in the woods. He's the most accurate of us when we go hunting. And now he's making a name for himself in the big city." He shook his head. "He used to be the worst at rough and rumble but he worked at it, and now I wouldn't take him on in a fight, if I didn't have to." Suddenly Ivan's scowl re-emerged. "So what do you want with him? I'm not a fool. This hasn't been idle curiosity. You're up to something."

"Yes and no. I can probably manage without Stefan's help in my endeavours on Carrador's behalf. My main motivation is Stefan's welfare." Tarkyn glanced at Vera before meeting Ivan's eyes. "But before we go any further, I must ask you to take an oath to keep a secret." He half-turned to Jackson. "You too."

"We are not going to keep secrets from our family, especially when we don't know what they are," said Vera firmly.

"No, I wouldn't expect you to." Tarkyn gave a wry smile. "Your family is far too close for that to work, although the choice is yours whether you tell them of it. They, too, including Stefan, will have to be sworn to secrecy. If it helps, it is about his heritage."

Vera and Ivan looked at each other, then Ivan asked, his scowl firmly fixed on his face. "Why? Is there something disgraceful about his heritage?"

Tarkyn looked startled. "No. Not at all. It is a heritage to be proud of, but I cannot say more without your oath."

"Give us a minute," grumbled Ivan, turning to his wife. "What do you think?"

"Stefan's heritage has never been anything we discussed with outsiders or patrons, except to defend him as a family member."

"So we'd only talk within the family about it, anyway, wouldn't we? Hmm. But what if this heritage posed a threat of some kind? We might want to warn people of it." Ivan turned to Tarkyn. "Well?"

"I know more of Stefan's heritage than any man or sorcerer alive, and I do not believe that there is, or will be, any threat."

Ivan's eyes narrowed as he surveyed Tarkyn, clearly assessing the value of his word, an impertinence the High Lord endured in silence. "And what about Karl's spouse and children when he has them?" he demanded at last.

Tarkyn grimaced, waving his hand in a helpless gesture. "I don't know. I suppose his spouse would have to know but perhaps it will be old, irrelevant history, just as the truth of Stefan's birth is now, by the time the children are old enough to listen in on conversations."

Vera placed her hand on her husband's arm. "Ivan, I would like to know where Stefan came from. I am willing to take the chance."

Ivan grunted. "Very well. But," he said belligerently to Tarkyn, "I am not necessarily going to allow you to tell Stefan."

Tarkyn eyes glinted dangerously. "I do not need your permission. Stefan is a grown man. I could have gone straight to him but I have come to you first, to make sure that my surmises were facts and to discuss with you the wisdom of telling him of his true heritage. Do not push me too far, Ivan. I do not take orders from anyone, either in Carrador or in Eskuzor."

Vera squeezed Ivan's arm in warning, but the landlord shook her off. "Get off me. I will protect my family, no matter what the cost."

"The cost," said Tarkyn evenly, "is being civil to me. That, at least, will give you a say in what I do."

The two men glared at each other, while Vera and Jackson watched in trepidation. Outside, the mountain eagle screeched her disquiet to the surrounding trees. The sound pulled Tarkyn out of his anger. Suddenly he smiled. "Now look what you've done. You've upset Bird. If you're not careful, you'll have every raptor for miles around circling your inn and swooping down on your customers."

Ivan frowned, confused by the sudden change in atmosphere. "Is that a threat?" he asked uncertainly.

Tarkyn laughed. "Not at all. I don't control the raptors… but they do look after me. Even when Bird is off somewhere hunting, if you look, you will always see at least one hawk, or eagle or owl, or some other raptor, watching me from a nearby tree."

Ivan stared at him, perplexed. "I am dealing with things beyond my ken. I will take your oath, but can I ask you, please, to be kind to my Stefan? We love him dearly and do not want him distressed."

"Neither do I," said Tarkyn. "That is why I came to you first."

Once all three were sworn to secrecy, Tarkyn told them about the woodfolk, just as he had told the king.

"So," concluded Tarkyn, "I do not know if woodfolk inhabit your woodlands, but Stefan's existence implies that they do. A small group of Eskuzorian woodfolk, my family included, are even now on their way to rendezvous with me here… well, out in the forest somewhere near here. I can introduce Stefan to them, but…" He leaned forward and spoke earnestly. "I think it is important for any man to know his antecedences. For Stefan, it would make his stature, colouring and skills make sense. My woodfolk could teach him a whole new set of skills that the rest of us could not accomplish. I know he is sensitive about his size. I have seen him become defensive about chance remarks, not even directed at him. Now, he could understand the reason for it and maybe be proud of it." He leaned back again. "But he would also lose. He would lose the certainty of being a member of your family." He held a hand up to forestall their protests. "I know you will not reject him, but how will he feel when all his assumptions come tumbling down?"

Vera wrung her hands. "Oh dear! Maybe we should have told him. We never dreamt his true mother or family or whatever might turn up. Silly, really. It was always a possibility, when you think about it."

"Are you giving us the choice whether to tell him?" growled Ivan.

"Honestly, I don't know. I am talking it through with you so that we can decide together. At the very least, I want to know your views." Tarkyn threw his hands up. "You do not know these people as I do. To become an honorary woodman was the greatest honour of my life… and I have had many honours, being the son of a king. It would be a terrible shame for someone to live his life, ignorant of the wonderful people he belonged to."

Ivan heaved a great sigh. "I hope we don't lose him. He will be more like them than us, from what you're saying. And he will be angry at us for not telling us." Tears sprang to his eyes. "I love that boy. I don't want to lose him."

"Are you saying we should tell him?" asked Tarkyn.

Ivan nodded miserably. "How can I say I love him if I don't let him be who he really is?"

"Who he really is, and has always been, is part of our family," said Vera, threading her arm under his and around his back, to pull him close. "Even if he forgets that for a while, he will come back to it."

Tarkyn put his elbows on the table and ran his hands through his hair. "Whew. I knew this would be hard. I'm glad you have agreed."

Unasked, Jackson filled his teacup, added milk and handed it to him. Tarkyn took a long swallow and let the tension leech from him.

"So now what? Who tells him?" asked Jackson, voicing the question they all were thinking.

With Vera's arm still across his back, Ivan put his arm across her shoulders, presenting a solid front. "We will tell him. He is our son. It is our responsibility. We will tell him."

"I applaud your courage," said Tarkyn. "When will you tell him? It is entirely up to you. I only ask to make sure I don't say anything before you do."

"We will tell him now, before the midday rush," said Ivan heavily. He waved his free hand at them. "You go. Tell Stefan to come here. We will talk to him now."

Tarkyn stood and gave them a slight bow, as a gesture of respect for what they were about to do and left the room.

Chapter 19

As they stood in the corridor outside, Jackson raised his eyebrows in query and Tarkyn gave a slight nod before continuing into the public bar.

Maud and Sheldrake were the only patrons still in the bar. Those who had stayed the night had moved on and the lunchtime crowd had not yet arrived. They watched Tarkyn as he approached, cautious of his grave expression.

He gave them a slight smile, which Maud thought looked strained. "I am sorry for keeping you waiting," he said. "It is a beautiful morning outside. Would you like to come for a walk with me, perhaps along the road in the direction of Kimora?" After a tiny pause, he couldn't help adding, "If you have finished with my room, of course," and grinned.

"Yes to both," said Maud with great aplomb, as she rose from the table to join him.

Sheldrake frowned at her, as he, too, rose from the table. "Maud. You know we didn't…"

Maud laughed. "So does he."

"I could be bluffing," suggested Tarkyn, as they walked through the door into the morning sunshine.

Maud shook her head, squinting against the light. "No. I doubt that you could. Too honest and from the earthquake we all felt, I suspect your feelings would give you away if you tried." She held out her hand. "Here is your key."

They walked along the front of the inn but as they approached the stables, a thought struck Tarkyn, making him turn to Maud. "How do you explain to the stableboys the disappearance of the brown mare Sheldrake rode in on?"

Maud smiled. "We don't. We just take them into our confidence. There are a few hostelries up and down the country that we frequent for one reason or another. They all know."

Sheldrake gave a tight smile. "We tried at first to make up cover stories, but even if we could get away with it once, it pushes people's credulity too far for me to lose my horse every time I come to a particular inn." He shrugged. "So Maud's secret is only a secret in certain circles."

As they passed the stables, Javier gave them a nod and a smile from where he was pitching fresh straw into a wheelbarrow ready to take inside to freshen up the stalls.

Once they were past and had forest on either side of the road, Tarkyn finally swore them to secrecy and filled them in on the overall plan.

"I wasn't going to tell you until I had spoken to Stefan but I've talked to his parents and they are speaking to him instead." He told them what was happening, even now, back in the private parlour of the inn and grimaced. "And I think he may need support from all of us over the coming days."

"Oh, the poor boy." Maud's face creased with concern. "Do they have a dog?"

Tarkyn frowned in confusion. "Sorry?"

Sheldrake gave a dry chuckle. "Maud wants to comfort him, give him something to pat."

Tarkyn's face cleared. "Oh, I see. Might be a good idea. I'd like someone to keep an eye on him afterwards. He'll probably work out it's you, though."

Maud gave him her warm smile. "Even if he does, it might be good for him to have someone outside the family to talk to or be with."

"Now Maud," said Sheldrake, "Don't go rushing in. See how he goes."

"Yes, dear."

Tarkyn smiled, understanding full well that Maud would do as she saw fit.

Chapter 20

Stefan entered the private parlour, cheerful and unsuspecting. "Hallo. This is nice; having a bit of time to catch up without the others around. How have you been? You both look well. I've missed you, you know. No one to tell me off if I forget to comb my hair. No one giving me big bear hugs. It's great to be home, even if it's just for a few days."

"Sit down, son," said Ivan heavily, at the same time as Vera said with forced cheerfulness, "It is lovely to see you again, too."

Stefan sat down slowly, looking from one to the other. "What's up?"

Ivan leaned forward and spread his hands on the table. "First of all, Stefan, son, let me say that we both love you with all our hearts and," he hesitated, "you are and always will be a loved, valued member of this family."

"Dad, what's wrong? You're scaring me now."

Ivan glanced at Vera, a plea in his eyes, to which Vera responded.

"Um, Stefan. Thirty-four years ago, there was a big flood."

Stefan nodded. "Yes, I know. You can still see the high-water mark. There hasn't been as big a flood since." He frowned. "So?"

"Well, you know how Anton likes to go rummaging around looking for things? Well, that's what he did after the flood."

Stefan gave a cautious smile. "I bet he did. He would have loved the junk that was chucked up by a flood."

Ivan grimaced. "Unfortunate choice of words," he said. "Junk can sometimes turn out to be very precious."

Stefan shrugged. "I suppose so. Everyone looks for that rare, overlooked treasure."

There was a short awkward silence.

Then Vera began again. "Well Stefan, you were that rare, overlooked treasure."

Stefan's eyebrows came together in a ferocious frown. "What! What are you saying?"

"Anton found you. After the flood. Caught in the branches of a log." Vera wrung her hands, fearful of his reaction. "And he brought you home and you have been our son ever since." She quailed before his thunderstruck expression. "And we love you. We always have and always will. We'd almost forgotten where…"

She trailed off as she realised that Stefan wasn't listening anymore. His eyes had glazed over with shock. Ivan and Vera looked at each other. Then she rose and moved around the table to hug Stefan. She was prevented by his raised hand. She returned to her chair and subsided into it.

They waited in silence for several long minutes before Stefan's vision cleared. "Kind of you to look after me for all those years," he said cuttingly.

"No, Stefan," rumbled Ivan. "It wasn't like that. We truly think of you as our son."

"So why tell me then?" Before they could answer, he rolled his eyes. "Wait on. It's that bloody High Lord, isn't it? I don't know what's going on, but he and that ambassador have been taking an inordinate interest in me. Did he make you tell me?" He looked ready to go out and throttle Tarkyn.

"Not exactly. No," said Vera carefully. "But he made us realise that we were depriving you of your heritage. We never knew anything about it 'til he came. Never cared, really."

"And is it worth losing my family for?" stormed Stefan.

Ivan's face creased with worry. He looked like he might cry. "You haven't lost your family, lad. We're all still here and still love you."

Stefan stared at him. "No. You haven't lost *your* family. I have. I'm an outsider among you." Suddenly he threw back his chair, toppling it onto the ground, and pushed past them out of the room.

The words, "No, son!" rang in his ears as he slammed the door behind him.

Ivan and Vera sat in shattered silence then sought the refuge of each other's arms.

Stefan strode blindly through the kitchen, not even noticing Marjorie and Javier, his mind overwhelmed. He blundered outside and ran until he made the cover of the trees. Then he slowed, walking fast along a narrow path overhung with swaying lemon-scented eucalypts. Although he didn't consciously notice the bush around him, its shadows and soft greens salved his soul. He walked until the path he had chosen narrowed into a climb over tumbled rocks that he scrambled up until he reached a sheltered spot on the top of the hill, hidden among the granite boulders, a scraggly old she-oak giving it shade.

He threw himself down on the grass against a boulder. His chest was heaving with exertion and emotion, but he was so confused he didn't know whether he was angry or sad. He put his elbows on his knees and wrapped his arms around his head, trying to hide from the world. An hour ago, it had been a beautiful morning. He had been bouncing with joy at being home. Now, he didn't know where to put himself.

All those times he had played with his siblings. Had they known? They never said anything. All those times he had struggled to keep up with them, trying to be like them, when all the time he looked different. All those years waiting to grow taller as they did, realising in the end that it wasn't going to happen.

As time went on, he uncurled enough to sit up straight against the rock, but his arms were still folded across his knees. When he had thought and thought through the past, the questions started: Who was he? Where did he come from? Why did it matter to a foreign prince?

An hour, two hours passed; he didn't know. He was dragged out of his inward turmoil by the sound of boots on stone coming up the side of the hill. A minute later, Anton's head appeared above the rocks.

Stefan scowled at him, but Anton just smiled. "Hello, little brother. I thought I'd find you here."

Stefan wanted to say that he wasn't his brother but knew it would sound petulant. Instead he just grunted.

Anton swung himself over the last boulder and sat down next to him. "So you must be feeling pretty shitty then. I keep trying to imagine what it must feel like to suddenly find out I'm not who I thought I was." He shook his head. "I tried but I can't. My mind baulks at the thought. So I guess you're feeling crap."

Stefan tried to say, "U-huh," but his breath caught in his throat and after a shallow cough, he just managed, "Yep."

"We older ones, me, Karl and Marjorie, we always knew," he shrugged, "but we just forgot. Once Mum held you in her arms, the past was gone. You were just the new baby." His eyes slid sideways to study Stefan's set face. After a minute, he tried again. "Anyway, think of it this way. You'll always have us. You know that: I'm your brother, you're mine. Nothing will ever change that. But now you might have a lot of new people, as well as us, to belong to." He gave a lop-sided smile. "But I hope they're not too nice, whoever they are, because no matter what, they have to come second. You belong to us."

Finally Stefan looked up and met his brother's eyes. Tears sprang to his eyes and as Anton grabbed him and pulled him against his chest, the sobs came.

Chapter 21

Not surprisingly, Stefan missed his appointment with Sheldrake at lunchtime. Dinner that evening was fraught as Tarkyn sat with Sheldrake, Maud and Jackson, watching the door from the kitchen for any sign of the arms master.

Marjorie served their food in severe silence, clearly blaming Tarkyn for Stefan's distress. As she came to clear the dishes away, Tarkyn said to her, "If Stefan wants to know more about where he came from, I am available any time to talk to him and some people he might like to meet are arriving here around midday tomorrow."

"He's not meeting anyone, without one of us with him."

Tarkyn nodded mildly. "As long as you are sworn to secrecy, any of you is welcome to accompany him."

"And where is Stefan now?" asked Maud.

Marjorie transferred her glare to Maud. "In his room. Not talking to anyone. Not even Anton. So, well done. I hope you're pleased."

Tarkyn went to stand up. "Perhaps I will..."

"No, you bloody won't. You leave him alone. You've done enough damage."

After she had flounced off, bearing their dirty dishes, Sheldrake blew out a long breath. "We are truly personae non gratae, aren't we?"

Tarkyn grimaced. "I'm sorry I dragged you into this."

"No need to apologize," replied Sheldrake. "You are, after all, trying to solve a problem for Carrador."

"Yes, but... I didn't actually have to involve Stefan in my efforts to contact Carradorian woodfolk. Although he is suffering now, it is for his sake that I came... well, and curiosity; to find out why a woodman was living among men and sorcerers." Tarkyn ran his hand through his hair. "But it's harrowing, isn't it?" He let his eyes roam around the bar, thinking how Stefan's sense of belonging here had been shaken.

Sheldrake leaned in closer and murmured, "See that couple over there in the corner? They are young local farmers. Just starting out in the world. Need a bit of extra cash. So they keep an eye on things for me." He moved his gaze to watch a group of three older men at the bar, so that no one noticed his particular interest in the couple in the corner. "They don't know who I am, of course. We keep in contact through notes and letters, sent with traders and passing messengers to my agent on the outskirts of Highkington. If something really urgent came up, I would expect one of them to get on a horse and ride like the wind to deliver the message."

"Huh." Tarkyn turned to smile at him. "Apology accepted."

The startled look on Sheldrake's face made Jackson chuckle. "Maybe you do trust him after all."

It was about then that they noticed Maud was no longer with them.

Outside, a fluffy grey cat was running along next to the wall, looking for a bedroom with lamplight shining through its window. At this hour, darkness had drawn in, but everyone was downstairs either eating or working. Only Stefan would be in his room. But would he have lit his lantern?

Along the western wall, all the windows were dark. Maud's heart sank. How could she find him? None of the family were going to tell her. She scurried past the entrance to the kitchen to the end of the wall and turned the corner. She gave a happy little 'prow' as she spotted a single shaft of lamplight coming from a window halfway along the back wall.

Now, how to climb up?

She surveyed the back wall. A drainpipe ran down the corner of the wall and guttering ran along the top. A straggly passionfruit vine clung to parts of the wall but not up as high as the first floor and it finished closer to the window next to Stefan's.

That will have to do, she decided.

Without waiting for thoughts to undermine her courage, she leapt onto the vine and clawed her way up to the top of it. Then, gathering her hind legs beneath her, she leapt the extra height onto the windowsill of the next-door window. The sill was narrow, and she was facing the wrong way. She had to arch her back until she was short enough to turn. Then she measured the distance, took three running steps and threw herself at the distant windowsill. She just managed to grab the edge of it with her front claws. It looked easy when she watched other cats but in actual fact, her arms were screaming with the strain of holding her whole body weight while her back legs scrabbled futilely in the air for purchase. With an almighty contraction of her front legs, she heaved herself up until her hind legs could latch onto the edge of the sill. She pulled herself up onto the ledge using all four legs, and lay there gasping for breath, shocked with how close she had come to disaster. Funny. She never saw other cats lying gasping for breath after a manoeuvre like that. They just carried on without giving such an astonishing feat of strength and agility a second thought.

When Maud had recovered enough to stand and investigate the windowsill, she realised that the window was shut. Blast! She should have checked that. She rubbed herself along the windowpane and produced a piteous miaow. Then she sat down and miaowed again. Nothing. She scratched at the window, sticking out her claws for maximum effect. Still nothing. She scratched a few more times then sat down and produced a really heart-rending yowl.

The window slammed upwards and Stefan shoved his head out, nearly knocking her off the sill.

She dug in with her claws then pushed towards his head and rubbed against his cheek. "Prowww?"

Stefan frowned. "Hello. What are you doing up here? You're a clever puss. You're new since I last came. Do you think I have something for you to eat?" He picked her up and brought her inside, stroking her as he walked. "Come on, come in here out of the cold. It's too dangerous for little cats to be so high up. Yes, I know you're a good climber. You must be, to have made it up here but it's pretty tricky out there." He held her against him as he reached over and pulled down the window. "There. You see? No more going outside on windowsills. Too dangerous for a little puss."

In truth, Maud had to agree. As he stroked her, she started to purr, encouraging him to hold her and stroke her more. In the corner of the room lay a plate containing his half-eaten dinner. He took her over to it and put her down in front of it.

"Look," he said gently, "here's a bit of chicken you might like. And here's a bit of cheese on the vegetables. See? You can have the chicken while I pull some of the cheese off the vegetables for you." Luckily Maud was not at all squeamish about eating someone else's leftovers. "There's a good puss. You were just hungry, weren't you?"

Not at all, thought Maud, *but this chicken is very tasty.* Once she had eaten her fill, she sat and cleaned herself meticulously. While she held her hind leg at a ridiculous angle, Stefan retreated to his bed and sat watching her for a while before lying down, lacing his hands behind his head.

When she had finished her ablutions, she jumped lightly on top of him and started kneading his chest. He reached one hand down to stroke her and after a minute, began to talk, "The world's gone mad, you know, little cat. Everything I knew is gone; blown away like a dandelion in the wind. I have to start all over again. Learn my life again from the beginning, from my first memories." He kept stroking her as he talked. "I have to be methodical, start at the beginning and work up through my ages. But it's hard, little cat. It's hard. All sorts of later memories keep intruding, shoving their way into my mind when I'm not up to them yet. I have to push them aside. They have to wait until I've worked through the years before them." He sat up, holding her to his chest as he changed position. When he let her go, she curled up in his lap, purring loudly. He smiled. "Life's so simple for you. You just eat, sleep, play and sleep some more."

Little do you know, thought Maud.

His smile faded. "But life is hard, little cat. Oh, suddenly so hard." He drifted off into a reverie, so she batted his hand until he started stroking her again.

After a while he said, "Anton's always been a rock for me. So have Mum and Dad but that was their job, if you know what I mean. Maybe it's because he found me, not just because he's the eldest." He gave a humourless laugh. "See, cat, what I mean? Every little thing has to be re-examined from a new perspective. Oh, my brain is so tired. I've done nothing but think all day. I'm nearly there, little cat. I'm up to when I left home when I was twenty. Trouble is, younger memories that I forgot to consider are intruding now, so I guess I won't be able to cover everything. But if I get most of it in order, I think I'll be able to face them tomorrow." He sighed. "But I'm too tired now. I have to sleep."

With an effort, he got himself off the bed and crossed to the door, where he stood uncertainly. "What am I going to do with you? I like having you in here, but you'll probably piss on the floor before morning. I don't want to leave the door open because I'm not ready to see anyone yet. No. I think you'll have to go," he said regretfully and, after listening a minute, opened the door and tossed her gently into the corridor. "Goodnight little one."

Chapter 22

Next morning, breakfast came and went with no sign of Stefan. By mid-morning, even Anton, who thought he understood why Stefan needed time alone, was becoming anxious. Maud was unable to reassure anyone in the family without giving away what she had done and on balance, she thought that would be counterproductive.

Finally, an hour before noon, Stefan shoved up his window and yelled down at Javier, who was crossing the back yard. "Send Mum and Dad up, will you?"

Javier shot into the inn with a big smile on his face. "Mum, Dad, quick! Upstairs now! He wants to see you."

With no thought of standing on their pride or objecting to being ordered about, Vera and Ivan wiped their hands on their respective aprons and rushed up the stairs. Stefan was waiting for them at the door of his room and dragged them inside. He threw his arms around them both and for some time they just stood in each other's embrace.

Eventually he pulled back and said, "I've been through every single memory that I can think of. You have always treated me the same as the others," he gave a little chuckle, "except that I escaped the hand-me-downs, 'cause they were always too big. I love you and I know you love me." He gave a wry smile that was underpinned with sadness. "I feel like a spinning coin. One side of me feels safe and knows I'm a loved member of the family. The other side is on the verge of panic, alone, not knowing who I am." He took a deep breath. "But the safe side is keeping the other side together…just."

"Oh, I hope we've done the right thing, telling you," said Vera. "I hope, in the end, it is worth what you, and we, are going through now."

Ivan frowned anxiously at him. "Are you ready to come down now, son? Don't worry if you're not. We won't let anyone rush you."

"Yeah, I'm ready." They walked along the corridor with Stefan in the middle, his arms around both of them. "You know Anton came and found me yesterday?"

His father nodded. "Yes, we know. He's a good lad, isn't he? I think we all knew where you'd gone, but I knew he'd be the best one to go after you."

As they reached the top of the stairs, they let each other go as there was not room to walk three abreast down the stairs. Stefan went first, with his father's heavy hand on his shoulder to steady him. His siblings were clustered around the base of the stairs waiting for him, to drag him into a suffocating bear hug the second his feet touched the floor of the bar.

When they finally released their grip, Stefan was laughing. "Get off me, you great galoots. Can't you see I'm smaller than you?"

This led to joyous shouts, with Stefan being hoisted into the air and carried around the bar, much to the entertainment of those patrons who had already drifted in.

"Oh, my word," said Sheldrake dryly, watching from the side. "They really are a very demonstrative family, aren't they?"

"Yes. Delightful, I think," said his wife, smiling warmly in appreciation.

Sheldrake frowned at her. "Do you really think so?"

"Absolutely, dear."

Like a plague of locusts, the noisy family, including Vera and Ivan, processed their way out into the kitchen, still with Stefan on high, leaving those in the suddenly quiet bar to fend for themselves. No one took advantage of the situation, but just helped themselves to what they needed and left the money on the counter.

Tarkyn, who was feeling bad about the whole situation, had removed himself from the bar room and was standing near the tree line at the back of the inn, gazing into the forest. His eagle, sensing he was upset, was sitting on his shoulder, preening his hair. Tarkyn was absently stroking the long feathers of her wings, as he waited, both for news of Stefan and the arrival of his woodfolk.

Raucous laughter split the air behind him as the whole Vine family erupted out of the back door, Stefan in their midst. Tarkyn turned swiftly at the noise, nearly unseating Bird. His relieved pleasure at seeing Stefan once more connected with his family washed across the yard, but in the mayhem, no one but Stefan noticed it. He frowned then looked over at Tarkyn and cocked his head. Tarkyn smiled and nodded. Stefan stared at him a moment longer before pointedly turning his back on him and returning his attention to his family.

Not forgiven yet then, thought Tarkyn, repressing a flash of anger. *It is hard being in a foreign land. I would never accept that level of discourtesy in Eskuzor.*

Jackson, who had been sitting on a bench outside the kitchen door to keep a weather eye on his liege, had been nearly swamped by joyous Vines. He noticed the interchange and, skirting around the family, strolled over to talk to Tarkyn.

"Give him time, Sire. He is not naturally a discourteous man."

Tarkyn grunted. "No, at least he hasn't been until now. Perhaps this will change him. I almost wish I hadn't interfered. He seemed quite happy as he was."

"He seems happy now."

"No, he's not. You watch him." After a few minutes, Tarkyn pointed out, "See? Now and then his face stiffens and sometimes his eyes glisten with unshed tears. Then he pulls himself out of it. I don't know whether his family are noticing, but if so, they are pretending not to."

Gradually the family settled and various members drifted off to return to their duties, until only Marjorie and Anton remained standing with Stefan. They talked among themselves for several minutes until, in a concerted move, they turned and walked over to Tarkyn.

"All right then," said Anton, an edge in his voice. "Time for you to justify what you have done."

Bird ruffled her feathers and snaked her wicked beak towards him at his tone. Tarkyn placed a calming hand on her back but glared at Anton for a moment, unimpressed with his attitude even though he understood its reason. "I will." He raised his index finger. "But first, you need to realise to whom you are speaking. Your King Gavin and I are equals and I am here with his blessing. I have not demanded obeisance every time you approached me, but I cannot abide belligerence towards me."

Marjorie smiled slightly. "I'll translate for you, brother. He's saying, 'Back off.'"

Tarkyn gave a surprised frown and turned to Jackson. "Is my speech usually too florid?"

"No, Sire. And I think you were saying a little more than that."

Marjorie hesitated then dropped a shallow curtsey. "I beg your pardon, Your Highness. I did not intend to be disrespectful."

"No, you were not. It was your brother who erred. But enough of this. I do not want to labour the point any further. I came to Carrador to assist your king, but also to help Stefan." He grimaced. "So far, I have only hurt him, for which I am truly sorry. I do hope that when you meet his kindred, if you choose to, you will agree that it was worth it."

"Tell us about them," asked Anton, his tone no longer abrasive, "please."

"It would be my pleasure." Tarkyn took a breath then gave a quirky smile. "I suppose the first thing I should tell you is that I admire these people so much, I have married one of them. Her name is Lapping Water and she has the same colouring as you, Stefan, although her hair is straight and glossy and falls down her back almost to her waist. I have two blood brothers, Waterstone and Ancient Oak, and a thirteen-year-old niece called Sparrow." Suddenly his aloofness had vanished and he was grinning. "They too share your colouring. These people, collectively, are known as woodfolk. I know nothing about them in Carrador, except for your existence, Stefan. But in Eskuzor, they live within the forest, unknown to the general population... hence the oaths of secrecy I insisted on... and I am their liege lord and protector."

His whole face was alive. After a moment he chuckled. "Mind you, they don't really need my protection and they would take issue with me, if I said they did."

Stefan was standing with his arms crossed, trying to remain unaffected by Tarkyn's enthusiasm. "Uh-huh. So are these some sort of tribal people who live among the trees? Do they wear clothes? What are their houses like?"

Tarkyn frowned. "They are not tribal. They have different communities but people are free to swap between them at will. They wear the same clothes as I," he said, brushing his hand down the light brown of his shirt, "designed to blend into the forest. Except for the Forestals and Mountainfolk, woodfolk tend to be itinerant and live in shelters that can be quickly built and hidden. My family belongs to the Wanderers."

Seeing Stefan's continued resistance, Tarkyn added, "Perhaps it would be better if you just met some of them and formed your own opinions. I can tell you of their special talents that you share with them and I can describe why I like them. But against a closed mind, nothing will work. If anything, trying to persuade you will just stiffen your resistance."

"They don't sound too bad, Stefan," offered Marjorie. "Might be worth giving them a go. We'll come with you, then we can all see what we think."

"Yeah Stefan," drawled Anton. "Anyway, after all this, how could you live, not knowing where you really come from? Speaking for myself, I'm dying of curiosity."

Stefan swung out his arm and thumped Anton backhand across the chest, making him grin. "All right," he said. "I will agree to meet them. But that's all."

Tarkyn spread his hands placatingly. "There *is* nothing else, Stefan. I don't expect you to rush off and live with them. My greatest hope is that you learn more of who you are and maybe learn some of their skills. You already have a rich, successful life outside the forest. Why would you want to leave it?"

"Hmph. You destroy my peace of mind just for this?" he demanded.

Tarkyn put his head on one side as he considered the arms master. "You are a strong competitor. Don't you want to be the best you can be, even if it is hard and takes work?" When Stefan re-folded his arms and thinned his lips, Tarkyn threw his arms up. "Oh, stars! What am I doing? I just said I wouldn't badger you, and I won't. It is close to noon. I'm off into the forest to be ready to meet them when they arrive. Do as you choose, Stefan."

As the High Lord swivelled on his heel and headed for the trees, Jackson asked, "May I come?"

"Certainly." Tarkyn glanced over his shoulder as though he might say more but after some thought he just repeated, "Certainly."

They walked out of the noon sunlight into the dappled shadows of the trees. A soft breeze brushed through the branches above them, lazily waving the leaves.

Suddenly Tarkyn smiled at Jackson. "Waterstone just sent me an image. They've arrived." He tapped Bird on the shoulder. "Go on. Up you go and find them. Then come back and show me the way."

The three Vines, hot on their heels, watched with interest as the eagle took to the skies, screeching as she disappeared towards the north above the trees. A few minutes later they heard her screeching to the west. For a moment, Tarkyn's eyes went out of focus before he turned to Stefan. "May I share this image with you? You will know better where we need to go."

Stefan glanced at Marjorie and Anton, scrunching his face in embarrassment.

Anton's eyes grew round. "Can you send mind messages? Wowee. You lucky thing." He nodded. "Go on then. Help the High Lord."

"Just put your arm on my shoulder to steady me, Anton. Last time I nearly fell off my horse."

"Ooh. Interesting."

Stefan rolled his eyes then looked at Tarkyn. "Go on then."

Instantly, an image of trees sweeping past below him appeared in Stefan's mind. If not for Anton's hand on his shoulder, he would have pitched forward. A small clearing appeared in the dense canopy and Stefan could see several figures waving up at the eagle. They were too far below the eagle to see details, but he could make out their light brown hair. With another shriek, the eagle wheeled down lower before thrusting upwards with her great wings and swinging in an arc. The next thing Stefan knew, she was swooping in from behind Tarkyn, aiming to land on his shoulder.

"Watch out," yelled Stefan involuntarily. "Here she comes."

Tarkyn glanced over his shoulder and braced himself just in time to save himself from being catapulted forward by the force of her landing.

"Thanks," said Tarkyn, chuckling. "You forgot that you were seeing that image through me. But thanks." He reached up and stroked Bird. "And you, young lady, are a menace." Once she was settled, he returned his attention to Stefan. "So, do you know where they are?"

"Yes. Don't you?"

Tarkyn shook his head. "Not really. Maybe over that way somewhere," he said, waving his hand vaguely.

Stefan smothered a laugh. "Follow me." He looked at Marjorie and Anton. "They're up near the grand old gum, close to the creek."

Stefan led them out onto the road and headed left towards Highkington for several hundred yards, before cutting back into scrub on the south side of the road along a very narrow path that wound tightly through thickets of tea tree and wattle. Ten minutes later, they came to a clearing beside a huge, gnarled old gum tree.

The clearing was deserted.

Stefan turned to Tarkyn, a look of confusion on his face. "I'm sure this is where I saw them."

Tarkyn smiled. "Don't worry. They're here." He gestured to his companions and introduced them to apparently thin air. "I would like you to meet Anton and Marjorie Vine, whose family runs an inn just down the road. Stefan here, who you can see is a woodman, has been a family member at the inn since he was born. And this is Jackson, my new aide-de-camp. He is Eskuzorian, so no doubt he has some sorcerous powers, but we haven't discussed what they are."

Anton, Marjorie and Stefan all turned their heads to look in astonishment at Jackson.

"Are you a sorcerer?" asked Marjorie, awe-struck.

"Yes," replied Jackson casually. "It's no big deal. Everyone in Eskuzor is." He nodded at Tarkyn. "But no one comes near the power of His Highness, except maybe his sister."

"Excuse me," interrupted Tarkyn, "I am in the middle of introductions. So, as I was about to say, these four and the other members of Stefan's family have been sworn to keep your existence secret, as have a couple of others, but I'll talk to you about them later."

A sound like driving rain on damp earth on their right resolved into a cocky voice. "That's all right then." A young green-eyed man with shoulder-length, light brown hair stood there, hands on hips, grinning at Tarkyn. "Hello. That was a long trip and no mistake. We've never before come further south than the swamps south of the mountains." He nodded at the others. "Hello, Tarkyn's friends. I'm Rainstorm."

Anton frowned. "Where did you come from?"

Rainstorm pointed. "Over behind that tree."

As he pointed to a tree behind him, a woodwoman holding a small child by the hand appeared next to Tarkyn. "Hello everyone," she said in a mellow voice, "I am Lapping Water." She indicated the little girl, "and this is Gurgling Brook." She gave a soft laugh. "She probably won't always sound like a gurgling brook, but she does now when she laughs."

"Dada," burbled the little girl with a wide grin, pulling away from Lapping Water and reaching up with small hands. Tarkyn grinned and in one fluid motion, scooped her into his arms. She turned and waved her hand. "Look, new peoples."

Stefan studied Rainstorm and Lapping Water with a sinking heart. Until now, some part of him had hoped that it was all a big mistake, just some sort of aberration amongst the Vine genes as he'd always thought. But one look at these two woodfolk was enough to show him his true origins. Despite himself, he felt an instant kinship, which he immediately quelled.

Hugging his daughter, Tarkyn looked around. "And where are Waterstone, Sparrow and Autumn Leaves?"

Lapping Water gave a warm smile. "Waterstone, Sparrow and Autumn Leaves currently have arrows trained on you until they are sure we are safe with you. They'll be down in a minute, I expect." Even as she finished speaking, two woodmen and a teenaged woodwoman appeared beside Lapping Water. "Here they are now."

When they had introduced themselves, Waterstone eyed Stefan curiously. "So you're a woodman, are you? You certainly look like one. But what are you doing living out in the open? For us in Eskuzor, we are exiled if we reveal our presence or the existence of our kin."

"I don't know if I'm a woodman." Stefan folded his arms defensively. "Only Lord Tarkyn says I am and only because of my green eyes."

"I checked," put in Tarkyn. "He can receive my mind images."

Waterstone's green eyes twinkled, and clear words formed in Stefan's mind. *You're not happy about this, are you?* He nodded at Marjorie and Anton without saying anything out loud and new words formed in the arms master's mind. *So are these your blood sister and blood brother?*

I grew up with them. Anton found me after a flood. I only found out yesterday that they are not my true family. Unbidden, tears sprang to Stefan's eyes. Suddenly he realised that he was mindtalking.

Ah, you poor old bugger. That must be dreadfully hard.

Anton frowned. "What's going on? Why has everyone gone quiet?"

Waterstone indicated Anton and spoke out loud. "They still seem to want to look after you. So that's good." His smile broadened and he spoke to Anton, "Just mindtalking with your brother. For your information, your Stefan can converse with us using words or images. Tarkyn can only use images but he can use them with animals as well."

Suddenly Tarkyn frowned. "Where's Midnight?"

In answer, leaves rustled above them. "Uh-oh," said Tarkyn and thrust Gurgling Brook into Lapping Water's arms just in time as Midnight leapt down, confident that Tarkyn would catch him. Tarkyn staggered back under the significant weight of a ten-year-old boy. Bird screeched and thrust herself upward in high dudgeon. Gurgling Brook squealed with laughter.

"Midnight," scolded Tarkyn. "You're too big now. Be kind to me."

In answer, the boy, whose hair was a darker brown and eyes were a deeper green, beamed up at him and threw his hands around Tarkyn's neck. Tarkyn hugged him back before sliding him to the ground. "And this," he said to his companions, "is Midnight. He's deaf, so can't introduce himself but he can share images, Stefan."

"Cup of tea?" asked Autumn Leaves urbanely. "Just a jiffy and we'll get a fire going. Rainstorm, where's the kettle?"

"I'll get wood," said Lapping Water. "You mind little madam, Tarkyn. I love her, but I have had her undiluted for over a week now."

"Delighted," said Tarkyn, holding his arms wide for the little girl to run into.

Twenty minutes later, they were all seated on the ground around a small but efficient fire. There were not enough cups, so they shared one cup between two.

"Stefan is a very good archer, you know," said Tarkyn, in an effort to start a conversation.

"Are you?" Rainstorm smiled. "Well, our very best archer is Thunder Storm, but he's not here. Lapping Water is probably next best. Maybe you'd like to compete with her sometime? What about slingshots? How are you with them?"

Stefan raised his eyebrows. "Slingshots? Haven't used them since I was a kid." He turned to Lapping Water. "Are you really the best archer here?"

She shrugged. "Probably."

"Okay. Let's set up some targets," said Stefan eagerly.

"I'll do it," said Rainstorm, springing to his feet. He peered around the clearing then walked through a narrow gap in the trees. After one hundred and twenty yards, he stopped at a thin tree and picked up a bit of clay. *"Will this do?"* he asked silently.

"Good Start," replied Lapping Water.

Rainstorm drew three sets of concentric circles down the trunk of the tree. The widest circle was only six inches in diameter. He stepped lightly back to the firesite, his feet leaving no trail. "Okay. Who's in?"

After a noisy discussion, everyone but Tarkyn and Gurgling Brook decided to have a go. When Anton asked why he refused, Tarkyn held up his hand. "I only use magic. Can't be bothered learning to use physical weapons when I have them inbuilt."

Anton raised his eyebrows. "Right. Fair enough."

"Everybody ready? Rules are: Three arrows. State which targets you're going for before firing." Rainstorm looked around. "Are you happy enough with our bows, Stefan? I gather you're a bit of an expert in arms."

"Your bows and your arrows are of excellent quality."

"Thanks." Rainstorm gave a broad smile. "I made the bow you've chosen myself." He gave a self-deprecating shrug. "My family are Forestals, specialize in craftwork. My dad still isn't sure whether I'm much of a craftsman."

Stefan was beginning to thaw. "Well, I'm impressed."

It soon became apparent that only Stefan was a match for any of the woodfolk. Anton's accuracy deteriorated under the strain of shooting so far; one arrow missed entirely, one scraped the edge of the tree and one didn't quite make the distance. Sparrow hit targets with two arrows and missed the tree completely with the third. Although only thirteen years old, she was clearly disappointed with her performance. Marjorie was a fair shot but knew she couldn't make the distance so stood thirty yards closer to the target so she could at least demonstrate that she could aim. Jackson was outright terrible, much to everyone's enjoyment, but Lapping Water trumped the field by hitting dead centre of each of the three bullseyes so fast that the first arrow had not stopped quivering before the third had hit its target.

Stefan's eyes widened in appreciation. "And you say this Thunder Storm is even better. I can't see how he could be."

Lapping Water smiled, completely unmoved by her performance. "Because it is much harder to use slingshots so accurately that you can knock out a man and know you haven't killed him. You need finesse as well as accuracy for that. Much harder."

"Thunder Storm can hit eight stones set up on a log so that they all rock gently at the same time, but none of them falls," said Rainstorm proudly.

"We all aspire towards that feat." Lapping Water's soft green eyes twinkled at Stefan. "We try not to kill people, you see, and the stones from slingshots leave no trace that we have been there, whereas arrows are a dead giveaway."

Just as Stefan and his family were digesting this information, they were interrupted by the sound of footsteps tramping through undergrowth on the path leading from the road. In the blink of an eye, the woodfolk were gone. Stefan, Marjorie, Anton and Jackson looked around, bewildered. Tarkyn smiled and showed them Gurgling Brook still seated on his lap. "She can't do it yet without her mother's help and I can't do it at all."

"Do what?" asked Stefan.

"Hmm. I call it flicking. I don't know that it has a name. Anyway, they just think themselves somewhere else, somewhere in sight… and they're there."

While they were digesting this, Javier and Marin pushed their way into the clearing.

"Hello, all. Couldn't get away 'til now," said Marin. "Had to help with lunch." This was said with no rancour at all at the three who could have been helping too.

"Yes. Followed your tracks and here we are. What's happening?"

A chuckle formed in Stefan's mind and he recognized Rainstorm's voice. *"My goodness! You are the odd one out. They're all as like as peas in a pod."*

Stefan was starting to get used to this. *"They've both taken the oath too."*

"Oh good." Rainstorm appeared beside Stefan, grinning, making Javier and Marin jump back in surprise. "Hello. I'm Rainstorm."

They stared and Javier said, "You must be Stefan's real brother. You look just like him."

Rainstorm turned and studied Stefan. "No, I don't. I don't look anything like him at all."

Tarkyn laughed. "No, he doesn't, but it takes a while to notice the differences."

The rest of the woodfolk appeared around them, alarming Javier and Marin so much that they found themselves instinctively standing back to back.

Waterstone waved his hands disarmingly. "Settle down. No one's going to hurt you." He introduced himself and the others, adding, "As far as we know, none of us is related to Stefan here. We're all from Eskuzor." He looked around into the surrounding trees. "But I wouldn't mind betting that some woodfolk in these forests are related to him."

Chapter 23

By the end of the second day, Sasha was beginning to settle into palace life, secure in the knowledge that it was only temporary. She was introduced to Lady Teresa, daughter of the Queen Mother's Lady-in-Waiting, Lady Charlotte. At first, both Jayhan and she found Teresa insipid and too compliant but as Teresa got to know them and trust that they wouldn't go rushing off to report on her, she revealed a quietly irreverent sense of humour.

Teresa was kind and patient as Sasha was given intensive lessons in court etiquette and particularly in dining: using the proper utensils at the proper times, knowing to whom she could speak at the dinner table and learning which topics were acceptable for conversation. Sasha tried her best and brought her fearsome memory to bear so that she quickly mastered most of the requirements. However, she baulked at the expected treatment of servants who poured her drinks and served her food. It was impressed upon her that she could only acknowledge them if she were not engaged in conversation. Apparently, it was important to ignore servants while she was conversing with another diner. Otherwise she would be indicating that she placed the worth of the servant above the worth of her fellow diner, to whom she should be giving her undivided attention. Sasha thought this was complete nonsense and refused point blank to comply with it. All the arguments in the world would not convince her.

Josie and Charlotte were relieved that Gavin was elsewhere in the kingdom for the next few weeks and would not see Sasha until next time she came, as it gave them time to polish her manners without having to apply too much pressure. They did not meet her head-on. Instead, they organised a dinner and invited Lord Argyve, Lady Electra, Jon, and Bert, their head horse trainer.

Bert was laconic, had a healthy disrespect for everyone not directly involved with horses and did not suffer fools gladly. Knowing Sasha's love of horses, they had seated Bert next to her and then watched as a constant stream of servants offered a selection of entrees, drinks, platters of meat, several types of vegetables each offered by a different servant, gravy and sauces. Time and again, Sasha had to break off her conversation with Bert to acknowledge each servant. Eventually, annoyed by the constant interruptions, Bert lapsed into silence and addressed himself exclusively to his food.

Feeling flustered and disappointed that she had not had a chance to talk more with Bert, Sasha retired as soon as good manners would allow, retreating to her room to think.

The next morning, she rose with the dawn, donned a jerkin and breeches and trotted downstairs to the kitchens where, as she expected, she found the servants having their breakfast before preparing to serve those of their masters and mistresses.

Conversations ceased as she entered the room. This did not rattle her as she knew how things worked in the servants' domain.

"Good morning, my lady," said the butler, Stevenson, who was seated at the head of the table. "Can we be of assistance?"

Sasha smiled. "Yes. I hope so." She indicated the huge teapot in the middle of the table. "Would you mind if I sat down and joined you for a cup of tea? You don't have to stand on ceremony, you know. I have been working as a stable boy for the Batians and am used to eating with their servants in the kitchen." She grimaced. "It's quite hard, actually, waiting for the later breakfast time. I'm usually starving and it's such a waste of the morning." She squeezed onto the bench between a maid and a footman and accepted a cup of tea. "Thanks. Still, I suppose I can just do more things before breakfast, can't I?"

"And to what do we owe this visit, Ma'am?" persisted the butler. "We do have to get on shortly."

"Sorry. Um, well, I have this problem, you see. At these dinners they have, I'm not supposed to thank you when you give me drinks and food and stuff. Well, I insisted that I should be able to and that's what I want to do, but last night…" she shrugged, "with all those different courses and different choices, it was a nightmare. And I ended up annoying Bert whom I would have loved to talk to, and it all went wrong, really. Any ideas? I really don't want to be rude to you and ignore you."

This gave rise to some animated responses and quite a few poorly suppressed laughs. Sasha could feel her face going hot. Perhaps this had been a bad idea. When the butler held up his hand to silence them, Sasha said sharply, "I don't think it's funny that I want to be respectful to you. If you're laughing because you think I should treat you with disdain, you need to look at your values."

"Lady Natasha," said Stevenson, "I thank you for your concern. In some cases, you are right; the people we serve ignore us, take us for granted and never thank us. However, in some circumstances, we are trying to be as inconspicuous as possible. If we attract too much attention to ourselves, we have failed to do our job well. So, in situations like last night, you are helping us to perform our duties well if you let us blend in, so to speak. You are welcome to thank us beforehand or later if you choose but during the meal, it may be … hmm… counterproductive for both you and us."

Sasha frowned furiously while she thought about it. Then she gave a cheery smile. "So, it's all right if I don't thank you all the time? You won't feel hurt or resentful or think I'm being mean or haughty?"

This time the laughter around the table was friendlier.

"No," said a portly fellow with a pencil-thin moustache. "Think of it as a play where we're all actors with roles we have to perform." He smiled around the table. "And we all know how you feel now… and speaking for myself, I'm glad you didn't just come into the palace and follow all those rules without thinking about them."

Sasha smiled. "Thanks. And if any of you ever need help, just let me know and I'll see what I can do." She extricated herself from her squashed position on the bench and headed out towards the stables, unaware that she had just won the hearts of the palace staff.

She walked until she found the cottage she was looking for in a small fenced-off garden a hundred metres from the back of the stables. She glanced at the green wooden door with its arched top and the darkened leadlight windows and wondered if perhaps Bert was not yet up. She knew he lived here alone and did not breakfast with the others, being of a higher status. His loss, she thought. After some hesitation, Sasha took a breath and knocked firmly on the door.

Almost immediately the door opened and Bert, dressed and ready to emerge, appeared in the doorway. His eyebrows rose in surprise as he surveyed her in her jerkin and breeches. "Good morning, young lady. And what can I do for you? Unusual wear for horse riding. Don't you have a riding habit?"

"Hello. I wasn't planning on going riding just now. I came to talk to you but I thought you might be busy so I thought I could help so you'd have time to talk."

"Help with what?"

"Mucking out the stables?"

Bert laughed. "I don't muck out the stables. I have stableboys for that. And the grooms prepare the horses for riding or carriage work. I just train them."

"Oh. I see." She frowned at him. "Is that enough to do?"

"How many horses do you have in Lord Batian's stables? Twenty?"

"Not quite."

"I have over two hundred horses to train up. I train all the horses for the King's Guard as well as the riding and carriage horses for all the nobility who stay here, the horses for our own carts and the king's own horses, of course. There's a constant turnover."

Sasha's eyes widened. "Wow. What a wonderful job."

"It is." He raised an eyebrow, still not thawing. "Now, what did you want to talk to me about?"

Sasha looked down and scuffed her foot. "I wanted to say sorry for last night. I really wanted to talk to you but never found the time. It was very complicated with all those dishes. There didn't seem to be time for anything else. But while I was trying to be kind to the servants, I think I may have been rude to you. So, I'm sorry." She took a breath and looked up, meeting his eyes.

To her relief, he was smiling. "Apology accepted. You're a good girl to come and talk to me about it. I was a bit fed up by the end of the night, to tell you the truth." He closed the door behind him and began to walk towards the stables. "I hear you and your brother have quite a way with horses. You should come down sometime, meet some of the staff and the horses and watch me training… if you'd like to."

Sasha grinned. "I'd love to. Maybe not for a few days. I have to spend most of my time in dresses at the moment, to get used to it. Jayhan and I are allowed to play in the lake garden in the afternoons, but I still have to wear a dress." She rolled her eyes. "Makes tree-climbing difficult, I can tell you."

Bert chuckled. "I expect... I hope... you'll get used to it." He nodded in the direction from which she had come. "You'd better get back up to the palace and into harness, before they notice you wearing your breeches again."

"Yes, I suppose so." Sasha sighed. "It's not much fun, you know. I miss being with horses."

As it turned out, she wouldn't get much time to get used to her dresses.

Chapter 24

Each afternoon, Jayhan and Sasha ventured further and further afield in their exploration of the gardens, although always within the walls of the palace. Teresa had spent most of her life indoors, painting or embroidering or playing her flute, but after a couple of days of intense cajoling, she tentatively joined them.

Teresa clearly felt out of her element and while they pushed through the reeds to see the swan's nest, she would hang back standing uncertainly on the lawn, waiting for them to return and tell her what they had found. Jayhan and Sasha didn't mind. In fact they liked telling her all their adventures and discoveries. Twice they had slipped into the muddy mire at the edge of the lake while they were trying to sneak closer through the reeds to spy on the swans. Teresa delighted them by squealing in horror at the state of their clothing, the mud and reeds clinging to their shoes, the hem of Sasha's dress and the lower half of Jayhan's breeches.

After the second time that Sasha trooped back inside wearing ruined court slippers, Josie had compromised and allowed her to wear sturdy boots under her gown. Her gown could be washed but the fine satin of the slippers became stained beyond repair.

Around the other side of the lake, Jayhan and Sasha, with Teresa in tow, discovered a large gardening shed, piles of soil and gravel and a variety of interesting tools, all screened by a dense stand of wattle trees and grevilleas. None of these fascinations could be seen from the palace, which gave Jayhan and Sasha the great delight of having discovered a secret place. Of course, it was not an exciting secret place to the gardeners, who based all of their operations from there. It was, however, the gardeners' safe haven and they were not pleased by the intrusion of 'high-born folk from the palace.'

Feeling their antipathy, Teresa hung back, standing uncertainly at the edge of the bushes, her hands clasped over her delicate, perfectly clean, pale grey gown. She watched, half in admiration and half in trepidation, as Sasha and Jayhan trotted confidently up to a surly older woman who was seated on a sawn-off stump, smoking a pipe. The woman eyed them as they approached but offered no greeting.

Unperturbed, Sasha beamed at her. "Hello. Isn't the swan's nest marvellous? And there's a nest in the bottle brush at the edge of the lake near the entrance to the king's study. Are there any eggs in it? It's too high for me to see. Any other nests you know of?"

The woman scowled at her, then reluctantly removed her pipe from her mouth. After a noticeable pause, she growled, "Now don't you go disturbing those nests. This garden gives the birds a safe place to rear their young and we don't need the likes of you disturbing them."

Rather to Jayhan's surprise, Sasha drew herself up and answered, "Firstly, Jayhan and I love watching birds and would never hurt them. Secondly, what exactly do you mean by 'the likes of you'?"

For a moment, the woman looked startled before arranging her features back into a scowl. "I mean young visiting nobles with a care for nothing but their own entertainment." She put her pipe back into her mouth and drew on it with an air of finality.

Sasha glanced at Jayhan, who could see a myriad of responses flitting through her head and wondered what she would say. He thought she would point out that she had been, or was, a stable boy, but she didn't. "Fair enough," she said. "I can see we must seem that way to you. So, what can we do to help?"

The woman took her pipe out of her mouth and tapped the bowl against the side of the stump, sending a dark wad of tobacco to join a little pile at the bottom of the stump. "Ooh, there's plenty you could do, but if you go getting yourself dirty on my account, Josie will have my guts for garters."

"No, she won't," said Sasha confidently. "She's used to us getting dirty in the afternoons."

"Huh. Is that right?" The woman brushed a dirt-ingrained hand through her grey curly hair while she thought. Her fingers found a leaf trapped in the curls and she pulled it out, inspected it then flicked it away, frowning in irritation. She focused on Sasha and Jayhan again. "Well, as it happens, young Dave has been off sick for the last couple of days and I'm behind with planting these little seedlings. A new bloke started this morning but we're still way behind. He and the others are off trimming hedges and weeding at the moment." She pointed the stem of her pipe at a cluster of small potted plants. "Look at these poor seedlings. They're already too big for their pots." Her gaze travelled to Teresa standing hesitantly at the gap in the screen of shrubbery. "What about her? Does she want to join you?"

"I don't know," said Jayhan. "I'll go and ask her." A minute later, he was back. "No. She could see you didn't want us here. She worries a lot about etiquette and things, you know."

"Huh." The woman gave her pipe another thump, cleaned out the bowl with her little finger then stood up and stomped over to Teresa. Jayhan and Sasha watched her give a nod of respect to Lady Teresa that she had not given to them. Then they talked for a while before the gardener returned to them, Teresa walking by her side.

"Hello," said Sasha brightly, smiling a welcome. "We're going to learn how to plant little plants. Are you going to do it too?"

Teresa glanced down at her soft, manicured, white hands then back up at Sasha. She gave gentle smile. "No. But I'll watch."

"We do have gloves you can use," suggested the gardener.

"No thank you, Kate," Teresa's voice was gentle but firm.

Jayhan stared at her a moment longer, then shrugged. "Right. Let's go."

Kate disappeared into the shed and returned with a kitchen chair that she placed near her stump. "Here you are, Your Ladyship." She studied the chair, frowning at the smears of dirt on it. "Just a moment," she said, disappearing into the shed and returning with a rag that she used to wipe the seat. She shrugged. "Best we can do, I'm afraid."

"Thank you." Teresa sat down primly and folded her hands in her lap. An unexpected twinkle in her eyes made the other two children realise that she knew what they were thinking but didn't mind.

Kate showed them where she wanted the seedlings planted, how to dig the holes with the trowels she provided them and how much fertilizer to put in each hole. Then she gave them each a big bucket filled with water and showed them how to soak each plant and fill each hole with water before taking the seedling from its pot, placing it carefully in its new home and pressing the soil in around it.

"There's a mound of compost around the side of the shed. Take that wheelbarrow and fill it, then come back here for the plants and the buckets of water." She sat down on her stump and drew out her pipe again. "Off you go. See you shortly."

She pulled out a small pouch of tobacco from the pocket of her breeches, untangled a few strands, rolled them between her fingers into a rough sphere then pressed the little ball of tobacco into the bowl of her pipe.

"My father has a pipe," offered Teresa. "It has pretty carvings on it, birds mostly."

Kate nodded and continued to poke and prod with her fingers in the bowl of the pipe until she was satisfied that it was pressed in firmly enough to burn slowly, but not so firmly that it wouldn't light. "Does he now? Do you like the smell of the tobacco?"

Teresa scrunched up her nose in thought. "I think so. It just smells like my father and I like him, so I suppose I like the smell." As Kate's pipe caught alight and a tendril of smoke snaked towards her, she added, "His pipe smells more… hmm… sweet? Or scented."

"His tobacco has probably been soaked in some special liqueur." She drew on her pipe. "Costs more, of course."

They lapsed into silence and time passed. Still no sign of Jayhan and Sasha. After another five minutes, Kate took a last draw on her pipe and stood up. "Blast those children. What tricks are they getting up to? It does not take this long to fill a wheelbarrow, even for children."

Teresa watched her stomp around the corner of the shed, glad that Kate was bent on confronting her friends rather than her. A minute later she heard Kate roar, "Jayhan! Natasha! Come out this instant. My nursery is not your playground for playing hide and seek. You haven't even started filling the wheelbarrow." Teresa heard an unladylike snort. "Huh! And to think I wasted my time teaching you how to plant seedlings. You won't be back around this side of the lake again in a hurry."

As Teresa listened, a frown gathered on her face. Her new friends were adventurous and lively, but she had not seen them being deliberately rude. It seemed out of character for them to leave Kate waiting for them. With her usual grace and lack of haste, she stood up and walked around the corner to join the irate gardener. "Excuse me, Kate."

Kate turned her angry glare on her. "Now what? Your two friends have snuck off. Looks like they didn't like the idea of a bit of hard work, after all."

Teresa shook her head, an anxious ball forming in the pit of her stomach. "No. That's just it. I don't think they'd run off on you. They're not like that. Lady Natasha works in a stable when she is not here in the palace and by everything I hear, she loves the hard work and strives hard to please the head groom."

Kate looked thunderstruck. "Good heavens! Does she?" She glanced around, seeing the empty wheelbarrow, still with the shovels lying in it. She frowned and took a closer look. The shovels, which were kept pristine, had damp bits of compost clinging to them. Her gaze travelled to the compost heap where darker moist hollows gave evidence that it had been recently disturbed. Enough to fill at least two wheelbarrows had been removed since the last shower of rain. Struggling to interpret what had happened or was happening, she broadened her gaze to take in the castle walls that towered several hundred yards away and the dirt paths leading from the stables, her gardening area and the kitchens that provided egress for supplies and removal of waste. The three paths converged into a single lane that led through the rear gate of the castle, past the palace guards and out into the working area of Highkington.

Even as she watched, a wooden cart piled high with rubbish, old straw and dirt trundled past the guards and out into the world beyond.

A jolt of shock ran through her. "Guards!" she yelled, but she was far from the nearest guard station. She turned to Teresa. "Run! Run to that gatehouse and alert the guards. You'll be faster than me. Gammy leg. I'll be right behind you."

Teresa didn't hesitate. She picked up her skirts and raced down the dirt path, in a display of athleticism that would have surprised her new friends. As she neared the guards standing on either side of the gates, she shouted, "Help! We need help. Get your captain!"

The guards glanced at each other but before they could respond, Kate roared from further away. "You heard her! Do what she says. This is an emergency. We need someone to get after that cart that just went through here."

The righthand guard fled indoors to send a message through. Moments later, he reappeared and took up his position again at the gate. "We can't leave our posts, but others are coming."

As she limped up, Kate muttered to Teresa, "You'd better be right about your friends."

"I agree," said Teresa. She glanced at Kate and gave a tense smile. "But it would actually be better if I were wrong."

The Captain of the Guard arrived, hastily buttoning the top button of his jacket. He nodded at Kate. "Explain."

"Two children have disappeared from around the side of my shed. Lady Teresa assures me they would not have run off. A cart bearing rubbish has just passed through these gates. I have enough compost missing to cover them both in that cart."

"And," added Teresa, "Lady Natasha is the king's cousin."

Kate paled. "Oh lord. Is she?"

Captain Bryant didn't debate. He turned and delivered a string of orders. The guards were questioned briefly but they had not been watching the path taken by the cart. Guards patrolling the tops of the walls were also questioned and one reported seeing the cart turn to the left at the second intersecting road.

Within minutes, twenty guardsmen had run through the gates, splitting into smaller groups that headed in different directions once they had reached the left-hand turn taken by the cart. Fifteen minutes later, a squad of twenty riders clattered through the gates to join and widen the search. Several guards prowled around Kate's shed, in case the children were hiding or were being held somewhere within the grounds.

Ten minutes later, Josie came puffing up, a train of servants in her wake. She demanded a report then sent servants off to inform the king, Sheldrake, Lord Jon and Lady Electra. She turned to the captain, "My staff are at your disposal to assist you in whatever way we can."

The guards on the gate were replaced, so they could be questioned more closely. They were both tense at having allowed an abduction to occur right under their noses, but anxious to help.

Samar, an older man who was looking forward to retirement in the spring, sat stiffly in a small room inside the gatehouse, helmet in hand, facing his captain. "We know the blokes who drive the carts in and out. We've been watching them for years. We even know the carts. That cart's left wheel has a lump in the metal rim that thumps each time it touches the ground. The bloke who drives it, his name is Rob." He glanced at his fellow guard. "We call him Rob Rubbish amongst ourselves, though he brings in clean hay, gardening supplies like gravel and such. We often inspect his cart to make sure it's clean when it comes back in. We don't look so hard when he's on his way out." A faint flush coloured the man's cheeks and he moved uncomfortably.

"And was the driver today Rob... Rubbish?" asked the captain, betraying no annoyance at their confessed error.

"Yeah. Same bloke as always."

"Did he speak to you?"

Samar shook his head. "No. Never does, unless he has to. Just drove on through, same as always."

The Captain thought for a moment. "Was anything about him different?"

The guards thought for a few moments. Then Samar scratched his beard and said slowly. "Well, he had his scarf wrapped around his face. But he gave a throaty cough and we, *I*, just assumed he had a cold. Not the first time. He's not the fittest character I know."

"Was the cart stacked high? Could someone having been hiding behind him, threatening him in some way?"

Garth, the younger guard, chimed in. "Yeah, maybe. He didn't seem tense though. It was pretty loaded up. There was a lot of old carpet and rubbish from one of the rooms they had redecorated, plus old straw and a pile of dirt."

"What colour was the dirt?" asked the captain.

Garth frowned at the unexpected question. "What?"

Samar responded before the captain could become impatient. "It was dark brown, sir, full of little bits, you know, bits of leaves, twigs, stuff like that."

The captain's blood chilled in his veins.

The abandoned cart was found an hour later.

Part 4

Chapter 25

Five pairs of green eyes lit in horror at Anton's invitation for the woodfolk to return with them to the Creeping Vine for dinner. The afternoon sun was sending slanted shafts of light through the trees of the Great Forest, which had reminded the four Vines that they would soon be needed at the inn for the evening rush and prompted the invitation.

"Sorry," said Waterstone, seeing him stiffen. "Your inn looks very nice... um, solid, from what Tarkyn has shown us and from the very little we know of inns. But none of us has ever been inside a building." He shrugged. "Besides, we are sworn to protect the secrecy of our kin, just as you now are. We would be exiled, condemned to a solitary existence, if we betrayed the existence of woodfolk by appearing in public."

Anton's eyes narrowed. "And what would happen to us if we betrayed your secret?"

Waterstone stared at him, hesitant to jeopardise their new relationship.

"We'd kill you," said Rainstorm matter-of-factly from the side, then grinned at their shocked faces.

Marjorie's eyes were wide. "Really?" When Rainstorm shrugged and nodded, she grew angry. "That is not funny. It's frightening."

Rainstorm spread his hands. "Why? I presume you are all trustworthy or Tarkyn would never have told you. So the issue will never arise."

"But what if some people who had visited the inn started talking as though we had told them when we really hadn't?" she asked. "What happens if you mistakenly think we have told someone?"

"Fair question," said Autumn Leaves, as he refilled the kettle and set it on the fire. When he was sure it was balanced, he looked over his shoulder at them. "If we didn't see or hear you directly telling someone, we would give you the chance to explain."

Stefan snorted. "Well, obviously we might lie to you if we had told someone and our life was on the line. So how could you believe we were telling the truth?"

Waterstone glanced at Tarkyn before saying, "If Tarkyn allowed it and you were willing, we could use our mindpower to overcome your will. Then if we asked for the truth, you would be unable to lie to us."

Anton rolled his eyes at Stefan. "These people of yours are a nightmare. Kill us or subvert our will without a second thought, just for talking about them."

"They are not my people," Stefan said in a hard voice. "I would never act like that." He turned to glare at Tarkyn. "What have you forced us into?"

Before Tarkyn could reply, Lapping Water rounded on Stefan. "Don't judge until you know what you are talking about. Imagine living in a land filled with sorcerers who are bigger, more powerful and more aggressive than you. Would you want your existence paraded around if you could keep safe by staying separate from them?"

Tarkyn and Jackson both frowned and chorused from opposite sides of the clearing, "We're not all bad."

Lapping Water's anger melted, and she grinned at Tarkyn. "Of course you're not. I married you... without coercion," she added hastily. She walked over to him and wrapped her arm around his waist. He re-adjusted Gurgling Brook's position in his arms so that he could put his arm around his wife's shoulders and gave her a wry smile.

"Oh yes. I can vouch for that," said Rainstorm cheerily. "Ancient Oak... that's Waterstone's brother... and I spent weeks trying to get Tarkyn and Lapping Water together."

The Vines watched this interchange in some bemusement.

"If you're trying to reassure us, it isn't working," objected Marjorie after a moment. "You're saying that sorcerers are even worse than you. That is no comfort at all. And you say you keep secret and separate from them and yet you have married one. Pardon me if I'm confused."

Waterstone's calm voice made itself heard. "I will explain." Everyone fell silent and listened. "We have a tradition of secrecy that stretches back for hundreds of years. Fifteen years ago, our existence was discovered by Tarkyn's father, King Markazon of Eskuzor. He forced us to swear allegiance to him and for that allegiance to transfer to Tarkyn after his death." Seeing them frown and cast considering glances at Tarkyn, he added hastily, "It was never Tarkyn's fault. If you want to know more, I will tell you over the days to come, but for now, I will remain brief. Before King Markazon, we had never encountered another sorcerer. Then, four years ago, Tarkyn was exiled by his brothers, unjustly I might add, and ended up in the forest living among us. Because we were oathbound, we had to accept him as our liege. At first, we resented his presence among us," he glanced at Tarkyn, giving him a rueful smile, "... a lot. We have never had leaders even amongst ourselves, let alone accepting an outsider as our ruler. But slowly, a few of us came to know him better."

At this point Gurgling Brook began to grizzle, tired of being held immobile in Tarkyn's arms for so long. Tarkyn let her down and glanced at Midnight as he sent him a mind message. Midnight looked up from where he was squatted drawing the Vine family members in the dust of the clearing and gave a shrug and a smile before trotting over to take Gurgling Brook's hand and lead her to his drawing. He gave her a stick which she proceeded to smack the ground with, rather than draw, entertaining herself by hitting a variety of leaves, pebbles and the earth and listening to the different sounds. The point of this was, of course, lost on Midnight, who couldn't hear any of the wondrous noises she was creating, but he left her to it and went back to his drawing.

Once Tarkyn was sure she was settled, he continued Waterstone's story. "And because of their association with me, these woodfolk met my friend Danton, who came to look for me in exile and various other sorcerers who became entangled in my, *our*, cause to prevent civil war between my brothers."

"So," concluded Waterstone, "since Tarkyn's arrival among us, we have accepted," here he paused and counted on his fingers, "I'd say nearly twenty sorcerers knowing about us."

"Plus those from the Lost Forest," added Tarkyn. "There must be a couple of hundred of them."

"Yes, but they don't count because if they ever broke the oath of secrecy, everyone would think they're talking about fictitious people in the mythical Lost Forest," said Rainfall promptly.

"Even now," interposed Lapping Water, "although we work with the Royal Family to carry information the length and breadth of the kingdom, our existence is a state secret. Very few sorcerers know of us, and, as far as I know, neither do any of the people in Carrador who aren't sorcerers or woodfolk." A little frown appeared between her eyes. "What *do* you call your people?"

"People," answered Anton dryly.

"Oh." Suddenly Lapping Water grinned, easing some of the tension, since her grin was not cocky as Rainstorm's had been and reflected genuine amusement.

"They are not here to kill you," said Tarkyn, letting his authority enter his voice. "In fact, they are bestowing a great honour on you by allowing you to learn of their existence and to meet some of them."

Autumn Leaves was checking the kettle, but when he realised it was not yet simmering, he straightened to look at the Vines. "You don't understand the significance of this meeting. Our whole Eskuzorian woodfolk nation held widespread discussions before deciding that we could make ourselves known to you and we have walked over a hundred miles to reach you." He nodded at the arms master. "And it was mainly for your sake, Stefan, that we did."

Stefan's face reddened and he dropped his gaze to the ground, scuffing his foot until he had left a small furrow in the soft orange dirt. Everyone watched but said nothing. Then he heaved a breath and lifted his head. "I apologize for my harsh words earlier. You were right, Lapping Water. I did judge too hastily." But he looked on the edge of panic.

"Steady, my friend," came Waterstone's voice in his head. *"We may have taken great pains to come to this point, but we have no expectations of you. We also wanted to know, for our own sakes, why a woodman was living among outsiders and what this means for us."*

"If you walk away, we will understand," Lapping Water gave a warm smile. *"But we would love to…"* She shook her head and spoke aloud. "You have had enough for today. Go home to your family and your inn. Perhaps, if you wish it, we will see you tomorrow."

Anton glanced at his siblings before striding forward to wrap a sure arm around his brother's shoulders. Studying Stefan's face, he said, "You're overwhelmed, aren't you? All this care and attention from these people and from us, your family." The emphasis on the last words conveyed a distinct message.

He lifted his head to stare a challenge at the woodfolk but found himself looking at an empty clearing. Other than the Vines, only Tarkyn remained. As he watched, Tarkyn crossed to the fire and lifted the kettle out of the flames.

"Kettle's boiled," said Tarkyn, as he turned and headed out of the clearing in the direction of the road. "I'll be back later."

Feeling a little wrong-footed, the Vines followed.

Chapter 26

Hidden within the trees, the woodfolk watched the Vines depart then listened until their footsteps along the path had faded. In the distance they could hear the faint sounds of a carriage's wheels crunching along the gravel of the road.

"Right," said Waterstone. "Let's move deeper into the forest. This firesite is too close to that road for my taste."

"I agree." Autumn Leaves swung down out of the trees and set about making cups of tea. "Might as well drink this first, now that the kettle is boiled. Then we'll head off."

Autumn Leaves realised that Midnight was standing next to him looking forlornly along the way Tarkyn had gone, tears in his bright green eyes. The solid woodman crouched down next to the little boy and tried to reassure him, using images, that Tarkyn would be back for him soon.

"Poor little fella," said Rainstorm sympathetically, "He's been so brave being away from Tarkyn for so long." He had stayed where he was, standing on a thin branch twelve feet above the ground. "Tarkyn's eagle has followed him back to the inn, so we've lost our temporary lookout. I'll keep watch until we leave."

"Thanks, Rainstorm. I'll send Midnight up with a cup of tea for you. Maybe having something to do will cheer him up."

"I'm not surprised he's upset," said Rainstorm. "It wasn't a very friendly meeting, one way and another."

"I think you could have been a bit more tactful, rather than just blatantly telling them we'd kill them," said Waterstone, as he accepted a cup of tea from Autumn Leaves.

"It shouldn't have come as a shock to them," objected Rainstorm. "What did they think the oath 'I vow not to reveal the presence of woodfolk on pain of death,' meant?" After a moment, Rainstorm gave a wry smile. "All right. I take your point, though it had to be said somehow, once they'd asked the question."

"True."

Half an hour later, they left the clearing and walked quietly south, leaving no sign of their passing. They were all on edge. This bushland with its swaying gums and yellow-studded wattles was sparser than the oaks, elms and beeches of their native forests. A black-tailed wallaby startled them as it broke cover and hopped off between the trees. Overhead, three pink and grey galahs chirruped at each other from the boughs of a large eucalyptus tree and a pair of green, purple and orange rainbow lorikeets raced through the trees, twisting and zigzagging between branches at breakneck speed, tweeting loudly as they passed, before coming to land neatly on a branch a little way ahead of them, next to a hollow in the tree's trunk.

As the woodfolk drew deeper into the forest, the vegetation changed again to myrtle and mahogany, with curling tree ferns clustered in the valleys and long vines swinging between trees. It was breathtakingly beautiful but totally alien for the woodfolk from Eskuzor. More than that, Stefan's existence implied that another nation of woodfolk lived within these woods and they had no idea how these people would react to unknown intruders in their traditional forests. As evening approached, the birds settled and fell silent, adding to their sense of unease.

Sparrow pointed to a thick cluster of tree ferns that shaded a running creek and stood close to a space beneath a grand old mahogany. "Camp here?" she suggested. "It's getting dark. We don't want to be too far from Tarkyn. We've hardly had a chance to talk to him." She grimaced. "And he'll never be able to find us, even if we send him images."

"True." Lapping Water studied the area. "Yes, this looks good." She glanced up at the dense canopy above her and realized that his eagle would not be able to see them from above. She gave a rueful smile. "I think Tarkyn needed those people to help him find the last firesite, even when Bird had shown him where it was. He really is a navigational nightmare."

Sparrow was about to let her pack slide from her shoulders, indicating to Midnight that they were stopping, when suddenly, Waterstone stilled. He sent a sharp warning to the others. They all stopped moving and listened. Slowly, they crept together into a defensive circle around Gurgling Brook, facing outwards, bows in hand, arrows nocked.

"I wish there were more of us," murmured Lapping Water in mind speech.

Waterstone scanned the surrounding trees. *"There could never be more of us than a whole nation of woodfolk, unless we were mounting a war, which we are not and never have. Let's just hope that our small number shows that we're not a threat."*

"PUT DOWN YOUR WEAPONS AND WE WILL REVEAL OURSELVES."

"Stars above!" breathed Rainstorm out aloud. "Who on earth yells in mind talking?"

"I don't know," muttered Waterstone, "but we'd better do as requested."

"We could flick out of sight," suggested Sparrow, keeping her message strictly to her companions.

"It would be tricky," replied Autumn Leaves, *"if they're woodfolk like us."* He grimaced. *"We'll keep it as a last resort. Let's see how this goes."*

Slowly, the little group of Eskuzorian woodfolk lowered their bows and placed them carefully on the ground. They made no move to remove their knives or slingshots from their belts, hoping to keep themselves at least minimally armed.

Suddenly, more than twenty woodfolk appeared in front of them. They were not holding weapons at the ready, but Waterstone had no doubt that archers would have arrows trained on them from the trees around them.

Waterstone and his companions studied the Carradorian woodfolk. They too had green eyes but their hair was a few shades darker, something they had not noticed about Stefan, and their clothes were a deeper brown tinged with green. Waterstone considered their surroundings, deep within the rainforest, and decided that the differences in their appearance reflected the differences in their environments.

"How do you do?" said Waterstone politely. "We are pleased to meet you. I am Waterstone."

"Well, we are not pleased to meet you," returned a thickset woodwoman with a severe face and eyes glittering with anger.

"I suppose it is understandable," said Lapping Water mildly. "After all, we would be concerned if completely new woodfolk appeared in our own forests. I am Lapping Water," there was a pause, "… and you are?"

It was customary for all woodfolk to introduce themselves the first time they spoke. Not to do so was the height of rudeness. But perhaps customs were different here.

For a moment, the tight-faced woman glared at her, not pleased to be prompted. Then she said grandly, "I am Red Gum."

"What sound does Red Gum make?" asked Sparrow, puzzled. She waved her hand to indicate her companions. "We are all named for sounds of the forest."

"We are named for things found in the forest, not for their sounds," she replied, her tone of voice implying that she thought being named for sounds was ridiculous.

A mousy little woman next to her said diffidently. "Red Gum is named after a huge, strong, river red gum." She gave a timorous smile. "I am Grevillea."

"Grevillea?" asked Lapping Water. "What is Grevillea?"

"You may have seen them a few miles back. They are small bushes sprinkled with complicated red or yellow flowers. Their flowers are very beautiful."

"That is enough, Grevillea," interrupted Red Gum. "We are displeased with these people. We have seen them conversing with outsiders."

The Eskuzorian woodfolk exchanged glances, knowing this was going to be difficult.

"Yes, indeed we have. You have clearly flouted woodfolk law," said a wizened old man at the rear of them, whose long, bright white beard looked like it would make camouflage difficult. He sounded almost apologetic. "So, poor welcome though it is, you will have to begin your acquaintance with us by standing trial for betraying our presence to outsiders." Although his words were harsh, his tone was not and he added courteously, "I am Sphagnum Moss."

"Surely they should be given a chance to explain, grandfather?" demanded a young woodwoman, standing beside Sphagnum Moss. "I am Tree Fern."

Red Gum glared at her and then huffed impatiently. "That is why we hold a trial, dear."

"I agree. I am Spinifex," said a stern, stringy man in his fifties. He waved his hand, "Secure them."

In a concerted agreement of thought and a blur of movement, Waterstone and his companions grabbed their weapons and flicked into hiding. Lapping Water and Autumn Leaves found themselves beside two of the hidden archers, but before the archers could react, Lapping Water and Autumn Leaves flicked again to trees further away, then up into the higher boughs.

Midnight, a forest guardian just as Tarkyn was, reached out with his mind into the surrounding area, alerting every bird within a four-hundred-yard radius that he and his woodfolk companions were in trouble. In answer, out of every nest and from every perch, parrots, bowerbirds, birds of prey and tiny scrub wrens and songbirds swooped down into the clearing they had just left.

Brightly coloured parrots, irritable because they had been disturbed just as they were settling for the night, zoomed between and around the Carradorian woodfolk, shrieking. Owls and hawks circled overhead or perched in overhanging boughs, glaring down. Five sulphur-crested cockatoos swept into the lower branches of a myrtle, shrieking and strutting back and forth along the branches, bobbing their heads and raising their crests in outrage.

The archers in the trees were beset by little birds buzzing around their heads and landing on their heads, shoulders or arms. There was no way they could take aim and fire. And while the woodfolk on the ground were occupied with using their hands to alternately block out the excessive noise and/or to fend off the swarming birds, the Eskuzorian woodfolk flicked and flicked until they were far from these woodfolk and their threats of imprisonment and exile.

They mentally coordinated their mad dash, keeping their communication strictly between themselves. Autumn Leaves stayed close to Lapping Water, keeping an eye on Gurgling Brook and making sure Lapping Water was able to keep up, since she was flicking for two. Waterstone made sure Midnight was close to him, giving him a congratulatory pat on the back between flicks. Without conscious intention, they soon found themselves in the eucalypts near the rear of the Vine Inn.

After a short conference, they sent out an urgent mind message to Tarkyn.

Chapter 27

Stefan was seated near the end of the bar, away from the other drinkers, working his way stolidly through tankards of ale and talking in a low voice to his father when he was not otherwise engaged in serving customers. He was also keeping a weather eye on the little table of two sorcerers, a mage and a shapeshifter.

"When can we meet them?" Sheldrake was asking, sipping from his fourth glass of wine. He leaned forward, his eyes lit with alcohol and enthusiasm. "They sound fascinating. I can't wait to meet them."

Stefan frowned but Maud, oblivious to his gaze, just smiled and shook her head. "Please excuse my husband, Lord Tarkyn. He doesn't mean to make them sound like scientific specimens. Believe me, he uses all of us, even my son and me, to further his knowledge of magic."

Sheldrake took Maud's hint, realising he was becoming too intense. He leaned back in his chair, making a conscious effort to relax. Stefan saw him glance around the inn's dining room, relieved to see that no one was watching them. Until his eyes met Stefan's.

Stefan rose a little unsteadily from the bar and dragged a chair over with one hand while holding his tankard in the other, then plonked himself down at their table.

Maud raised her eyebrows at Sheldrake as though to say, *Now see what you've done.*

Jackson shifted along to make room for him and smiled warily at him. "Hello. How are you doing?"

Stefan thumped his tankard on the table with rather more force than he intended and gave a jerk of surprise at the sound it made. "I'm fine. Never better," he added sarcastically. He leaned forward and stared owlishly at Sheldrake. Then he spoke in a low, intense voice. "Now you'd better watch yourself, my lord. You're just lucky it was only me that heard you. That oath you took? Pain of death. You hear me? Pain of death." He shook his head. "They're not kidding, either. They're trained killers. Kill you, quick as look at you, if you put a foot out of line."

"They're not like that," protested Tarkyn.

"Oh yes, they are," insisted Stefan. He knew he was a bit drunk, but he also knew he was right. He vaguely wondered if one was causing the other. "And deadly? You think I'm good? Well, they're better. Specially that woodwoman. What's her name?"

Tarkyn glanced around to make sure they could not be overheard. "That woodwoman," he said quietly, his voice taut with anger, "is my wife, Lapping Water."

Stefan stared at him. "Sorry. Didn't mean to be rude. Just forgot her name, that's all. She's the best marks… person I've ever seen and she's beautiful and self-assured but in a quiet, not in-your-face way. No wonder you love her. She's impressive."

Tarkyn couldn't help smiling and Stefan breathed a little sigh of relief. This man was not one to be crossed unnecessarily.

"She is, isn't she?" said Tarkyn. "I was raised knowing that I was supposed to marry a foreign princess for the good of the kingdom. Your King Gavin was hoping I'd marry his younger sister." He grinned. "But I threw those expectations to the wind by marrying Lapping Water instead." He gave a quirky grimace. "No one outside a very select group knows, of course. So the general public will gradually decide that I am a confirmed bachelor."

The other three chuckled quietly. Stefan smiled along with the rest but suspected they were all revisiting their knowledge that the man with whom they were sharing their table far outranked them. A less comfortable silence followed, during which Stefan contemplated the High Lord, realizing how generous Tarkyn had been with his time in his care for his woodfolk, for the people of Carrador to whom he owed no allegiance, and for Stefan himself.

"I understand why they're so deadly about being secret," Stefan conceded, "at least in Eskuzor. I mean, sorcerers are a force to be reckoned with and imagine a whole country of them! I'd be keeping myself well clear of them too." He shrugged. "Not so sure about the need in Carrador. Not many mages here, and the rest of us… of *them* are pretty ordinary." He heaved a deep sigh and glanced quickly at Tarkyn then away. He leaned his cheek on his hand, looking miserable. "I don't belong anywhere anymore."

Everyone around the table quelled their need to rush in and reassure him, realising he would know all the arguments. But after a minute, Sheldrake couldn't help himself. "You know, Stefan, you belong in more places than most people. Firstly, you belong with us, as our arms master to protect that little girl, Sasha. Just that, on its own, is important. You belong to the King's armed forces. You belong in this tavern and to the Vine family and lastly, you belong to an amazing, mystical group of people with exceptional powers."

Without taking his head off his hand, he swivelled his eyes to look at Sheldrake. His mouth quirked in the beginnings of a smile. "Hmph."

"If you're looking for someone who really didn't belong anywhere, look at Jon when he first came to Carrador," continued Sheldrake. "His whole family had been killed and he brought Sasha into Carrador and had to leave her in an orphanage because at twelve, he was too young to look after her but too old to stay in the orphanage. So he lived alone on the streets of Highkington for years."

"Sheldrake," said Maud reprovingly. "It does not help people to know that someone is worse off than themselves. Stefan has every reason to feel dislocated at the moment."

Jackson gave Stefan a pat on the back. "You belong in too many places, don't you? Not too few. Pretty confusing, I expect."

Stefan pulled himself upright and crossed his arms instead, still defensive but thawing. "Yep."

Suddenly he saw Tarkyn sit up and frown. When Sheldrake began to ask what was wrong, Tarkyn held up a hand to forestall him. After a minute of silence, his frown did not lessen but he became aware again of the people seated at the table with him. "My woodfolk are in trouble. So much so, that they have come close to the rear of the inn and want me to join them straight away." He took a deep breath, forcing himself to appear relaxed and to move slowly as he stood and said in a carrying voice. "Would anyone care to join me for an evening stroll?"

"That would be quite delightful," said Maud at her societal best.

Sheldrake sent him one penetrating glance and stood up. "I too would enjoy some fresh air before turning in."

"Jackson, meet us outside with our cloaks if you wouldn't mind," said Tarkyn, giving his aide de camp a reason to accompany them. "And Stefan, would you come with us so that we don't get lost? None of us knows the area very well..." Just as Stefan was thinking that he didn't want to see the woodfolk again so soon, the High Lord added, "if you wouldn't mind, that is. I am sure we can manage if you have other calls on your time."

And that concession was enough to make Stefan change his mind. Despite himself, Stefan smiled. "Thank you for your consideration but I think I can spare the time." He stood up, took a few breaths and became more focused than he had been. He realised that they would draw less attention to themselves if they did not all troop out past the bar, through the kitchen and directly to the back of the inn so he indicated the front door. "This way, if you please."

As Tarkyn nodded his thanks and preceded him through the front door, Stefan took the opportunity to catch his father's eye and indicate that he was going out for a while. Once outside, he found Tarkyn waiting impatiently, hopping from one foot to the other until Jackson joined them.

"Right. Let's go." Tarkyn turned to the arms master. "Once we get around the back, I will transmit the images of where they are, so that you can work out where to direct us to."

But when he was given the images, Stefan shook his head. "I don't recognise it in the dark. It could be one of several locations and I presume we don't have time for trial and error."

"No, we don't." Tarkyn turned to Maud. "What about you? Any ideas?"

"An owl could scan the forest and find them, but I'd need some idea of direction. A blood-hound could follow their scent, but they didn't start from here."

"Hmm. Don't worry," said Tarkyn after a bit of thought. "I'll ask Midnight to send an animal."

"You'll what?" asked Sheldrake.

Tarkyn held up his hand. "Just a minute." After a noticeable pause, he smiled. "Midnight is a forest guardian, just as I am. But, unlike me, he is half woodman, half sorcerer. He has located an animal and has directed it to come towards the light of the inn. He will be able to see through its eyes. When it sees us, he will ask it to stop and we will be able to follow it back to my woodfolk."

Sheldrake raised his eyebrows. "Impressive. And these are woodfolk skills, I take it?"

"No. Not at all. Woodfolk cannot direct animals they don't know any better than sorcerers or outsiders can. No. It is a forest guardian ability. Far more rare. As far as I know, Midnight and I are the only forest guardians alive today."

Minutes later, a rat-like creature about a foot long, with small ears, an extremely pointy nose, and a long, skinny tail, hopped like a rabbit into the shadows at the edge of the light that was being shed by the inn's windows and sat on its haunches, quivering with fright. Now and then, it would let out a worried chuff-chuff noise.

"Our guide has arrived," said Tarkyn. He peered closer. "What on earth is it?"

Maud smiled. "It's a bandicoot. Cute, isn't it?"

"Really? A bandicoot? Surely you're making that up. That's the funniest name I've ever heard."

"Perhaps we should just follow the brave little creature and stop casting aspersions on its name," suggested Maud acerbically.

"Oh. I beg your pardon," said Tarkyn stiffly. Stefan smiled, seeing that Tarkyn had suddenly remembered that he was a guest in a foreign land. Without another word, the High Lord walked carefully towards the bandicoot and squatted down in front of it, sending it waves of reassurance. He gave it an image of Midnight with a request to go to him. Immediately, the bandicoot shot off with such incredible speed that it was impossible to keep track of it, especially in the gloom. Tarkyn had to ask it to wait for them. With an impatient whuff-whuff, it sat back on its haunches until the five of them came up closer to it. Then it hopped off at a more moderate rate, occasionally darting sideways to grab a spider, worm or insect it spotted as it passed.

Ten minutes later, the bandicoot led them to Midnight, who was standing by himself in front of a huge, spreading gum tree. As soon as he saw Tarkyn, his face split into a grin and he ran forward to meet him. Tarkyn was shocked by how close his woodfolk had chosen to come to the dwelling of an outsider.

"It's all right," called Tarkyn quietly, sending a matching mental image of Sheldrake and Maud standing, hand on heart. "These two have taken the oath too." He sent a message of thanks to the bandicoot who scuttled off into the undergrowth.

While the other three woodfolk climbed down out of the great eucalyptus tree, less nimbly than usual, Lapping Water, holding Gurgling Brook's hand, flickered rather than flicked to stand beside him and flung her other arm around him, almost sobbing with relief. "Oh, am I glad to see you!"

"We all are," said Waterstone tensely. "Please, put up your shield. Now."

Stefan watched a wave of annoyance cross Tarkyn's face at Waterstone's peremptory tone. Quelling it, Tarkyn immediately waved his hand, encompassing all eleven of them in a translucent dome, demanding as he did so, "What's happened? What's wrong?"

"The local woodfolk saw us associating with outsiders. They're not happy. We had to get away from them before they constrained us and put us on trial. "

"And even though we haven't left tracks," added Autumn Leaves tightly, "it won't be long before they find us."

"No, of course not. It's their home territory, after all." Tarkyn hesitated. "Do you want light or should you stay hidden?" he asked.

Waterstone shrugged, "Now we're protected, it doesn't matter much. They'll find us sooner or later."

Tarkyn nodded and created an orb of light in the palm of his hand, which he threw gently into the air, leaving it hanging above them.

Stefan was impressed with his magical facility and caught Sheldrake raising his eyebrows at Maud in a silent exchange of admiration at a feat that Tarkyn clearly took for granted. He watched Sheldrake examining the bronze sheen of the dome that surrounded them. Then he saw the mage turn his attention to these people, slight of stature and green-eyed who, even with the variation in shades and styles of their light brown hair, were so like himself. He wondered what Sheldrake thought of them and was surprised to find himself ready to spring to their defence as he saw Sheldrake frowning at them. Then he followed Sheldrake's gaze and saw what the mage was seeing; the woodfolk were close to exhaustion. In fact, as he looked closer, they seemed almost transparent.

"Are you all right?" asked Sheldrake in some concern. Remembering what Tarkyn told him of woodfolk customs, he added hurriedly, "I am Sheldrake."

"How do you do? Sorry. I should have introduced myself. I am Waterstone, Tarkyn's brother."

Sheldrake gave a slight smile. "I believe you had, and presumably still have, more urgent matters on your mind. I repeat, 'Are you well?'"

"Not really," replied Lapping Water, giving her name. "We have travelled constantly since you last saw us, and for the last hour, we have flicked as fast as we know how, in a zig-zag, trying desperately to throw off pursuit." She sagged against Tarkyn's side.

"We have never flicked so fast so often. Usually we only do it once, to get out of sight," said Autumn Leaves. "But it's easy to evade outsiders. Far harder to evade other woodfolk. We are in serious trouble. I am Autumn Leaves."

Listening to the tiredness and underlying panic in their voices, Stefan revised his opinion of their invincibility. Little did he know it, but Tarkyn was also concerned by their sudden vulnerability.

"I'm sorry we took so long," said Tarkyn. "We had to make an unhurried exit from the inn to allay suspicion. Otherwise, twenty people might have followed us to see what was happening." He studied their drawn faces. "Have you eaten?" When they shook their heads, he turned to Jackson. "Can you hold a shield for long enough to get to the inn and back?"

Jackson nodded.

"Excuse me," Stefan interrupted. "I can understand you're concerned for these woodfolk, my lord, but what about my family? These woodfolk may come after my family because they know about woodfolk. Isn't that right?"

After an uncomfortable silence, Rainstorm answered, "Yes, it is." He shrugged. "I doubt they will go too close to your inn, but they could shoot from within the tree line, possibly."

"Yes, you will certainly have to warn them, Jackson," said Waterstone calmly, "but there are actually several precautions they can take. I doubt these woodfolk would try to kill them where other people could see it or discover it. If they did, it would trigger a manhunt into the forest and that is the last thing they'd want. Also, they will not enter your buildings."

"So, if they stay with other people or keep clear of windows when no one is around, they should be safe enough," added Rainstorm. He shrugged. "It's not ideal but with any luck, we'll soon be able to sort this out with your local woodfolk." He caught Stefan considering him and gave him a crooked smile. "Sorry we got you all into this. Our little group is used to sorcerers and outsiders. Other woodfolk are not, not even most of the Eskuzorian woodfolk. If it is any comfort to you, we seem to be in as much danger as you are."

"No, it's not. I don't want you hurt either, especially since you were just trying to befriend me."

Rainstorm wasn't sure how to take this. He was glad that Stefan at least liked them enough not to want them hurt, but on the other hand, he had said 'trying to befriend', as though they had not succeeded. He glanced away, feeling a little hurt, and focused instead on Jackson.

"So," he said cheerily to cover his uncertainty, "will you stay at the inn or return to us once you have warned them?"

"Or bring them back with you?" asked Tarkyn.

Stefan shook his head. "No, my lord. The inn won't run itself and we have three other overnight guests to cater for, besides you four. I think Rainstorm has outlined enough precautions for my family to remain safely at the inn for the time being. They might need you to shield them, Jackson, to go outside and bring in supplies of wood and water though."

"Jackson," asked Tarkyn, "Can you make your shield large enough for two?"

Jackson smiled. "Shielding is my strength, sire. I can make very large shields for long periods of time."

Tarkyn smiled in return. "Excellent. A very useful skill." He thought for a moment then turned to Stefan.

Even as Tarkyn drew breath to speak again, Stefan knew what was coming and preempted him. "Yes, I'll go with him and help him to bring back food, drink and other supplies." Unlike the woodfolk, Stefan was used to taking orders and took no exception to Tarkyn's unspoken request. Instead, rising to the occasion as host, he asked Waterstone, "Anything you'd like in particular?"

Waterstone gave a tired smile. "I'd kill for a good glass of wine at the moment." He frowned at his poor choice of words. "Not literally, of course."

Stefan actually grinned. "Of course not." He looked around at the others. "Anyone else?" but no one else had particular requests.

"Thanks, Stefan... and Jackson," said Tarkyn. "While you get supplies, I'll be helping my friends to recover."

Tarkyn lifted the edge of his shield in one corner and they slipped out to head back towards the inn. Even as they walked away, Tarkyn positioned himself against the eucalypt and began to draw on its strength to transmit into each of the exhausted woodfolk.

"Right," Stefan heard him say to the woodfolk, "Tell me all about it."

Jackson did not have the same facility with producing luminescence so, as they drew away from the woodfolk's firesite, they had to make their way by the light of a three-quarter moon that kept drifting behind clouds. To those still watching them from within Tarkyn's shield, the two of them disappeared into the gloom even before they turned the first bend in the path, with Jackson's dark burgundy shield barely visible in the moonlight.

Still, the path was well worn, and Stefan was very familiar with it. As they rounded the bend, their eyes became adjusted to the low light and Stefan was able to warn Jackson of protruding roots and soggy puddles.

Suddenly, something clattered against the outside of Jackson's shield. Instinctively they ducked then froze, waiting for a further attack. Hearts pounding, they peered into the darkness. After a few moments, they straightened slowly.

Jackson grinned sheepishly. "They can't hurt us through this shield, you know. I don't know why I ducked."

"Instinct," said Stefan, the arms master. "Very wise, even if unnecessary."

The two of them retraced their steps for a few paces and searched the ground for a missile but could find nothing.

"Keep walking, I think," suggested Jackson uncertainly.

Even as he finished speaking, four more objects clattered on the outside of his shield. They stiffened but this time did not duck. Stefan's keen eyes followed the trajectory of an object as it hit the shield and bounced off, but when they moved to where he indicated it had landed, they could see nothing untoward on the dirt of the path.

Stefan frowned and squatted to pick up a few stones "They must be using slingshots. That missile could be any one of these."

By unconscious agreement, they broke into a run, but before long, Jackson tripped on a raised root in the middle of the path and for a moment, his shield wavered as he recovered his balance.

He pulled up, taking a deep breath. "Wait. It's better for me to go more slowly and focus on keeping my shield in place. We will only be a few minutes later in warning your family, but at least we'll make sure we get there."

Stefan nodded in the dark, realised his nod couldn't be seen and said briefly. "I agree."

A few more missiles hit the outside of the shield as they walked, but their frequency tapered off as Stefan and Jackson came into sight of the inn.

As they stepped into the light shining forth from the windows of the inn, Jackson let out a long breath. "Waterstone wasn't overreacting, asking for Lord Tarkyn's shield. The danger from these people is real."

Chapter 28

Through the kitchen windows of the inn, the darkness outside seemed to loom with hidden danger. The whole Vine family sat around the kitchen table with Jackson, drinking tea, each of them taking a turn to go through and look after the bar. Initially, they had been dismayed when the situation had been explained to them and were inclined to cast blame on Tarkyn for meddling.

"Maybe he should have left well alone," said Ivan heavily, "but it's done now and I think Vera and I should come and meet these woodfolk of yours, Stefan."

"They're not my woodfolk," said Stefan tightly. Unable to sit still, he carried cups to the sink and began to wash them.

Anton walked over and put his arm around Stefan's shoulder. "Don't worry. I think we're safe enough. It doesn't sound as though the local woodfolk are going to storm in here, especially with other people around. Just as your friend, Waterstone, said…"

"He's not my friend," countered Stefan belligerently.

"Oh, put a sock in it, Stefan," Marjorie retorted.

Stefan scowled but before he could say anything further, Anton continued as though he hadn't interrupted. "…these local woodfolk wouldn't want to provoke a manhunt."

"No, but they will be a continuing threat until this is resolved," said Javier, joining Stefan at the sink to wipe the cleaned cups, "so you're going to have to help High Lord Tarkyn and his woodfolk negotiate with these local woodfolk, Stefan, since the whole issue pivots around you."

Stefan exploded. "No, it doesn't! I didn't ask them to come."

"No, you didn't," replied Marjorie, in a patient tone that conversely indicated she was losing patience with him, "but regardless of that, it does pivot around you. I don't know whether the local woodfolk are just about to discover your existence or whether they have been turning a blind eye all these years." She threw another cup to him. "Here! But when the Eskuzorian woodfolk go home, you'll still be here and so will we… and so will the local woodfolk who, at the moment, apparently want to kill us. You have to be part of the solution."

Just then Marin, the wiriest of the Vine brothers but still far bulkier than Stefan, walked into the kitchen and gestured with his thumb over his shoulder. "Tom the Baker has just accused Jack the Smith of, and I quote, 'blowing his bellows in other people's forges.'"

Jackson chuckled, Marjorie mouthed, "Ooh dear," and Anton glanced at Ivan who said, "You can do it, son. Vera and I are off out with Jackson and Stefan. Marjorie, you can come with us too, if you'd like to."

Anton grinned. "Right. Thanks, Dad. I'd better get out there." He clapped Stefan on the back before heading to the door to the bar. "Good luck. See you whenever you get back," and left before Stefan could reply.

Stefan straightened and swivelled to lean back against the sink. He crossed his arms and glowered at them all. Then suddenly he let out a gusty breath. "I'm being a pain, aren't I?"

"Yep," said Marjorie without a second's hesitation.

"Hmph. Sorry." He gave a lop-sided smile. "Well, we'd better get organized and get going then."

Marjorie, Jackson and Stefan brought in several loads of wood until it was stacked high in the corner of the kitchen and filled the water butt and a couple of extra buckets, while Ivan and Vera gathered supplies for the woodfolk and themselves.

"What about the horses?" asked Javier suddenly. "I need to check on them before bed and feed them first thing in the morning."

"I'll help," said Stefan.

"I'll take you over there now before we go," offered Jackson, "and I'll come back early tomorrow, if we're not back by then anyway." Grimacing inwardly, he asked, "How early?"

Javier gave him a knowing grin. "Before dawn." He laughed. "No. Not really. The travellers we have staying here aren't planning to leave before midmorning. So maybe an hour after cockcrow would do."

"Fine. I'll be here."

"Thanks."

As he forked hay down out of the loft, Stefan's mind began to reflect on his belligerence. He knew he had a tendency to become tetchy if people assumed things about him. All his life, people had sniped at his lack of height and assumed a corresponding lack of fighting ability. Now his family were assuming that just because he looked like these woodfolk, he would feel close to them. Well, he didn't. He wanted nothing to do with them.

He thought about that a bit longer, in light of his sister's unequivocal reaction to his behaviour. *Maybe I'm not being fair to these woodfolk. It's not their fault I look like them and am probably one of them, any more than it is mine. They are deadly fighters, but no one has been aggressive to me or my family. And after all, I too am a fighter to be reckoned with.*

Stefan climbed down the ladder and started forking hay into the stalls that had already been cleaned by Jackson and Javier.

Rainstorm was unnervingly honest about the consequences for breaking their blasted oath of concealment, but not with any malice, he thought. *In fact, the woodman had assumed the consequences were irrelevant because he trusted our honour.*

He felt himself beginning to thaw.

And from the beginning, Waterstone understood my reticence and was sympathetic and gently amused by it... but not at me, with me. And Lapping Water, seeing that I was feeling overwhelmed, orchestrated the immediate disappearance of the woodfolk to give me breathing space.

He gave a grunt of censure at himself.

Jackson looked around from the next stall along. "What's up?"

"Nothing." Jackson didn't press but Stefan saw his shoulder lift in a shrug. After a minute, Stefan asked, "What do you think of these woodfolk?"

Jackson straightened and leaned on his broom. "If I say I like them, you'll bite my head off, thinking I'm trying to talk you into liking them. If I say I don't like them, it will worry you because, let's face it, whether you like it or not, you're definitely a woodman, at least by birth."

Stefan let out a low whistle. "You don't beat around the bush, do you?" He frowned. "Sorry I'm being so difficult. It's a lot to come to terms with. But I've been giving it some thought so I would really like to know your opinion, since you have the least emotional investment of all of us."

"Huh." Jackson did one of his long pauses while he decided whether or not to risk Stefan's reaction. Finally, he said, "Ok, I'll tell you, but just remember you asked for it." He took a breath. "From what I have seen, they are close-knit, just as your family is. They are kind, clever, and seem to have a dry sense of humour, which I like. They are magically talented with their mind talking and their flicking, and very skilled at woodcraft and weaponry. But, saying that, they live very differently from us. In fact, I'm amazed the High Lord can live almost permanently with them." He gave a couple of sweeps with the broom before stopping again. "I'm sorry that their past has taught them to avoid sorcerers. I can understand, but I think they underestimate themselves, and overestimate us." He took a breath, but Stefan made no move to interrupt. "I have a strong sense of identity as a sorcerer and I would not wish to be a woodman and live purely within the woodlands, virtually camping all the time." He waited and when Stefan still did not respond he added, almost defiantly, "There! I have told you what I think. I like them, a great deal actually, but I wouldn't want to be one of them."

Jackson held his breath, waiting for the reaction. When no response came, he picked up his broom and swept out the last of the old straw from the stall he was working on.

"Huh," said Stefan's voice from behind him. He sounded quite cheery, if a little bemused. "Huh." He started forking straw into the newly cleaned stall. "Well, I do like camping. Maybe not all the time but a lot. Interesting. Thank you for being honest. You have given me a lot to think about."

Chapter 29

Twenty minutes later, Jackson, Stefan, Marjorie and his parents made their farewells and headed out into the night beneath Jackson's burgundy shield, all bearing baskets of food and drink, and a bag full of blankets for those who chose to stay the night out there.

They walked beneath high branches, which hung over the track and partly obscured the moon and starlight. A soft wind wafted through the leaves, making the shadows dance on the trail in front of them, obscuring obstacles and forcing them to place their feet carefully. From time to time, Ivan and Vera murmured to each other, but mostly they were silent, listening for any sound of their attackers.

Once or twice, stones clattered against the outside of Jackson' shield but it was a half-hearted attack and Stefan suspected the woodfolk had figured out that stones could not penetrate the shield and so had desisted.

Sure enough, a few minutes later, four arrows struck hard against the shield. Those within its burgundy dome cowered instinctively but the arrows fell, ineffective, to the ground. Gradually those within the shield straightened and Vera moved closer to Ivan, who put his arm around her. She drew in a breath and lifted her head high. "Come on then. Let's keep going."

Marjorie glanced at Jackson, but seeing that he didn't look concerned, folded her arms around herself and kept walking.

They rounded the last bend with no further attacks and saw the translucent bronze dome of Tarkyn's shield, twenty feet in diameter, lit up from within.

As they drew close, Jackson waved his hand, actually more of a wiggle of his fingers since he was carrying a big wicker hamper, and his burgundy shield blinked out. Immediately, Tarkyn expanded his own to include the newcomers.

Ivan looked around the inside of this new dome. "Well, that's interesting," he said. "I've never been inside a sorcerer's shield before and now, look at this! Two in one night. And they're different colours. Amazing!" He grinned, obviously enjoying himself. He quickly surveyed the woodfolk who were looking less tired but still ill at ease, and his grin broadened further. "Well, will you look at that? All of you, just like our Stefan here. That's marvellous." He placed a huge basket on the ground. "Look. We've brought you everything we would have given you, if you'd come to our inn for dinner... and more besides." Feeling a dig in his ribs, he added hastily, "Hello, I'm Ivan, Stefan's dad."

Stefan felt a rush of warmth for his kind, outgoing father who welcomed these kin of his without hesitation.

"Hello," said Vera a little shyly. "We brought more cups for tea, and more tea. We have flagons of wine, and the makings of a beef stew." She gave a shrug. "I've already got a good stew hanging over the fire in the kitchen, but it was too hot and awkward to bring and besides, we really need it for the customers tonight." At the end of all this, she bobbed a curtsy. "Hello, I'm Vera and I'm very pleased to meet you."

"No need for that," said Waterstone, standing up to greet her. "Hello, Stefan's mother and Marjorie. It's a pleasure to meet the people who have brought up one of our own, however extraordinary that may be. I am Waterstone." He caught the beginning of a scowl on Stefan's face. *"Sorry. Didn't mean to be provocative. I know you're not too pleased at having a bunch of primitive forest dwellers as relatives."* He grinned, as Stefan, who had been taking a drink of water from Jackson's waterbag, choked and spluttered a spray of water over those nearby. In the general uproar from the people who had been sprayed, Waterstone added wickedly, *"And you think we're uncivilized!"*

"Sorry," gasped Stefan, adding mentally, *"I don't think that,"* and sending a searing glare at Waterstone, who merely smiled in return.

Ivan frowned at Stefan, not best pleased with his manners and having no inkling of the silent exchange that was going on between Waterstone and him. Stefan sighed as his father turned his attention to everyone else, a tacit demonstration of his displeasure, and took control, just as though they were in the bar room of his inn. "Well now, let's get this food and drink sorted out, then you can tell us what's been happening. Nothing good, I gather."

Waterstone and Rainstorm helped Vera cut up the meat and vegetables for the stew, while Sparrow and Marjorie went for a short walk with Jackson, carefully shielded, to collect wood for a fire. Once a big pot of stew was simmering over a newly lit fire, Ivan passed around wine, bread and cheeses.

Waterstone took a sip of the white wine and raised his eyebrows in surprise. "Oh, lovely. Where did you get this?"

Ivan thought for a moment. "I have a few travellers come through with wines, ales and food that we purchase. Now, this particular wine came through about a year ago." He clicked his fingers. "I know. It was that old bloke, strange name, but always has good wares at reasonable prices. Always saying his wares have the Royal Eskuzorian seal of approval, whatever that's supposed to mean. He's a theatrical sort of chap."

"That strange name wouldn't have been Stormaway Treemaster, would it?" asked Watertone, his eyes twinkling.

"That's him. Do you know him?"

"He's... a friend of ours," said Tarkyn, clearly not wanting to provide too much detail. "And he does indeed provide wares to the Royal House of Eskuzor, both to my sister and to me."

"And the wine we are drinking comes from woodfolk vintners, the Mountainfolk, who live on the northern side of the mountain range that we've just crossed," said Waterstone. He raised his goblet. "And I thank you very much for it because it is of excellent quality and, I suspect, quite expensive."

Ivan went pink with pleasure. "You are welcome, sir. This is, after all, a momentous occasion." His face fell a little. "It is a shame that your visit to our country has been marred by such unpleasantness that you feel the need to be shielded. Even with a bar full of hooligans, I have never felt that need."

"You have never encountered the woodfolk of your forests," said Autumn Leaves bleakly and went on to describe what had happened for those who had not heard the first time. "In their eyes, all of us have transgressed, you as much as us."

"They didn't give us a chance to explain and we didn't want to risk the verdict of a formal trial." The strain had returned to Rainstorm's voice. "If they had taken us into custody, we could never have escaped from so many and you may never have been able to find us." He shook his head. "We don't work like that in Eskuzor. We don't put strangers on trial the second we meet them."

"Of course you don't," said Stefan spuriously. *"You just kill them out of hand, if they mess up."*

Rainstorm promptly rose to the bait and smiled sweetly. *"No. Not woodfolk. Woodfolk, we banish. Only outsiders, we kill.*

Ivan's brows drew together. "What's going on? Young man, why are you smiling like that? I hope it is not at our expense."

The smile was immediately wiped from Rainstorm's face. "Oh, not at all. If you must know, I was just teasing Stefan."

"Well, don't," said Ivan firmly. "The poor man has been teased all his life for looking different. I would hope that people who look like him might have no reason to tease him."

"Thanks Dad, but I think I can look after myself," muttered Stefan, embarrassed.

Rainstorm, distracted for the moment from his fears, gave a jaunty grin. "Plenty of other reasons to tease, I'm afraid. But if it makes you feel any better, Ivan, I only tease people I like."

Tarkyn, who had been overseeing a game between Midnight and Gurgling Brook while listening in, raised his head at that and gave Ivan a reassuring smile. "Don't worry. Rainstorm can be devastatingly straightforward, but he is never cruel. In fact, he is kind, quick-witted and frequently sails into awkward situations to repair them, while everyone else is just sitting around wondering what to do."

Rainstorm rubbed his face with his hands. "Oh, my word," he grumbled. "Tarkyn, you are every bit as embarrassing as Ivan is."

Stefan laughed, happy that the focus had been taken off him.

Once the stew had been cooked and served, Waterstone broached the question on everyone's minds. "So what are we going to do?"

"We will have to find a way to contact them, I suppose," said Autumn Leaves. He took a spoonful of beef and gravy. "Hmm. Very good. Well done, chefs. We don't usually get the chance to eat beef."

"Not easy to contact woodfolk, unless they want you to." Lapping Water ate a spoonful and expressed her appreciation, but the strain was back on her face. "And there is nowhere we can hide except out of the forest and we can't do that." She bent her head over her stew to hide panicked tears that sprang unbidden to her eyes.

Tarkyn saw that she was upset, but also saw that she was trying to hide it in front of people she didn't know, so he did not put down his dinner and go to her, as he wanted to. Instead he said firmly, "You woodfolk can't send a mind message through a sorcerer's shield to see whether they would respond, but I can send images. Failing that, I will find another way to contact them. I can use birds or animals to help, if I need to. Above all, we will protect you with our shields until we have come to some resolution with these local woodfolk."

"It would be our honour to assist you." Jackson gave a courtly nod and a smile from where he was sitting. "We can take it in shifts. Holding a shield is something I do well. I can last for several hours."

Sheldrake nodded his agreement. "And I, too, would be pleased to provide my shield. After all, you are here because of my country's need to protect its borders within the forests, so I feel partly responsible for your predicament."

"And he loves any excuse to use magic," added Maud, in an effort to make the woodfolk feel less beholden. Suddenly, she realised that no one was listening to her.

Chapter 30

A stream of people was emerging from the forest to the left of the path that led to the inn. Their stature, which was all that could be seen in the half-light, suggested they were woodfolk.

Tarkyn's woodfolk ranged themselves around the arc of the dome of his shield, facing the oncoming woodfolk. Tarkyn stood behind them. The other non-woodfolk people seated themselves around the fire in the middle of the dome but Stefan was unsure where he should place himself.

After a moment, he mindmessaged Waterstone. *"Where do you want me?"*

"Back with your parents for now. We'll call you forward when the time is right."

The number of woodfolk outside the dome was already larger than the group that Tarkyn's woodfolk had previously encountered and still more were flowing out of the forest to join them. Upward of forty faces glared in through the bronze-tinted translucent shield.

"Flood and fire!" exclaimed Autumn Leaves in horror. "I have never been on the receiving end of so much animosity."

"They can't hurt you," said Sheldrake, thinking he was reassuring them.

Autumn Leaves glanced at him. "It is the intent, not the danger, that worries me. I'm glad Tarkyn reached us before they did."

Even as he spoke, several arrows flew from different directions to ping against the shield and fall harmlessly to the ground outside.

Waterstone's eyes narrowed as he considered the trajectory of the arrows. He took a breath and let it out. "Well. That's something, I suppose. None of those arrows would have hit any of us, had the shield not been there. They were just testing the shield."

"Those ones may have missed us," said Stefan trenchantly, "but the ones that hit Jackson's shield on the way to and from the inn were aimed directly at us. Most definitely."

Waterstone raised his eyebrows. "Uh-huh. So perhaps their intentions have changed? No. I think not. No doubt those who fired at you earlier reported it to the others. So perhaps they are now trying to work out a way to deal with sorcerers and outsiders so that they can exile or eliminate all of us who have, in their eyes, transgressed."

Maud stood up from where she was seated near the fire, gathered her voluminous green skirts and walked over to join them against the inside of Tarkyn's shield. "Clearly, we need to negotiate with them."

"Can you mindtalk through the shield?" asked Sheldrake.

Waterstone shook his head. "No. We can mindtalk among ourselves, however."

"Let's not do that." said Tarkyn "We don't want to antagonize them further. Besides, we are all in this together. So, I think woodfolk and outsiders alike should be included in our discussions. I can send images through my shield to those woodfolk outside, if any of you wish it. I am at your disposal."

"Send an image of us and them sitting around a fire with cups of tea," suggested Rainstorm promptly. "Please."

The others nodded assent.

Moments later, Tarkyn said, "I have sent that image, and tried to convey feelings of warmth and friendship. I have received no response."

Sheldrake was impressed to notice that Tarkyn seemed to be spending almost none of his attention on maintaining his shield. He determined to ask him about this later but, as he thought about it, he realized that Tarkyn was showing signs of strain

"Would you like me to take over making light?" he offered.

Tarkyn nodded and as soon as Sheldrake put words into action, some of the tension leeched out of him. "Thanks."

"At least they have come forward to confront us," said Lapping Water suddenly. She smiled at their surprised faces. "It may be unnerving, but it is actually a good thing. The alternative is that they gradually pick us off from within the shelter of the trees over the next days and weeks."

"I see," said Maud thoughtfully. "Then we had better make this opportunity count." Before anyone could object, she turned to the woodfolk outside the shield and smiled warmly at them. "Thank you so much for gracing us with your presence. I understand you have never met people from outside your forest before. So, it must have taken great courage for you to venture out to meet us. Oh, I almost forgot. My name is Maud." She waited but when no one responded, she continued. "Perhaps I should explain that all the outsiders you see before you have sworn an oath, on pain of death, never to reveal the existence of woodfolk."

"But someone must have told you about us in the first place," said Red Gum, her voice determined but sharpened by an undercurrent of panic. She folded her arms across her chest, blustering her way through her fear of strangers. Almost huffily, she added, "I am Red Gum."

"That would be me, I'm afraid," said Tarkyn disarmingly. "But I did insist on their oaths before I revealed anything. I am Tarkyn, Prince and High Lord Guardian of Eskuzor, none of which titles will mean anything to you."

Red Gum looked Tarkyn up and down, taking in his bright amber eyes, his long black hair and the long wolfskin cloak hanging from his shoulders. Tarkyn smiled to himself. He suspected she wouldn't be half so bold if she knew that, for him, the shield was one way. He could attack her, if he chose to, but she couldn't attack him.

"But," continued Tarkyn, "I am also a forest guardian, which may mean something to you." He turned around and gestured to Midnight to join him, adding, "And this is Midnight. He too is a forest guardian, perhaps the youngest ever known."

A ripple of amazement flowed through the local woodfolk.

"I beg your pardon," said the white-bearded man the Eskuzorian woodfolk had met before. "Did you just say that you're a forest guardian? Oh. How do you do? I am Sphagnum Moss."

Tarkyn nodded.

"Oh my word! This changes everything. How very interesting. We have not seen a forest guardian for generations. But now, *two* forest guardians." Sphagnum Moss turned to Redgum and his companions and a protracted silence of mindtalking ensued.

"He sounds just like Sheldrake," murmured Maud while they waited.

Eventually, the old woodman turned back and asked, "Now Tarkyn, as a forest guardian, you can communicate with animals, can't you? So, was it you who sent those birds to interfere with our pursuit of these woodfolk?"

Tarkyn smiled and turned to Midnight, translating Sphagnum Moss's words into images. "Did you do that?" When Midnight nodded, his smile broadened. "You're a clever one, aren't you? And you did that in the middle of running away, did you? Well done."

Midnight beamed.

Tarkyn returned his attention to the old woodman. "No. Midnight did it."

Spinifex wound his way through the crowd to the front. "If you're a forest guardian, what made you betray the presence of woodfolk? Surely you understand the importance of keeping our existence secret?"

"I do, although being a forest guardian does not come with built-in omniscience."

"Being a forest guardian means," butted in Rainstorm, Tarkyn's self-appointed champion, "that he can communicate with animals, heal and make things grow. But more than anything, it means that he uses his enormous power to protect the forests and those who dwell in them."

"But," said Autumn Leaves, "we had to teach him woodfolk lore." He shrugged. "Most of it he accepts and lives by. Some of it, he can't or chooses not to. He is a sorcerer, after all," he chuckled, "and a prince."

Tarkyn spread his hands. "And here we are again; people talking about me as though I were not here."

Rainstorm and Autumn Leaves just grinned at him.

Another mind conference ensued. Then Banksia, a dumpy, comfortable woodwoman, spoke on behalf of her companions, "I'm being honest, here. We are in a quandary. We see before us, a flagrant flouting of woodfolk lore. No Carradorian woodfolk has ever spoken to outsiders before. Not to one, let alone... how many of you are there?... eight of you." She turned to Waterstone. "You should know this is forbidden. Yet not only have you revealed yourself to them, you are hiding behind their protection against us, your kindred."

"There are not eight outsiders here," replied Lapping Water, "There are only seven. We have travelled from Eskuzor exactly because of one of *your* Carradorian woodfolk has been permitted by *you* to live among outsiders." She stepped to one side indicating Stefan behind her. "This man, Stefan, is a woodman. He is no kin of ours, so he must be kin of yours. And yet you have allowed him to be brought up by outsiders, right in front of your eyes at the Creeping Vine Inn, within your forests, without lifting a finger to rescue him and bring him back into the woodfolk community." She paused. "We can explain our actions if you are willing to listen, but can you explain yours? I am Lapping Water."

Chapter 31

Come forward, Stefan, requested Waterstone silently.

Spinifex frowned at Stefan. After a moment, he shook his head. "No. You're mistaken. He's not a woodman. This is the son of Ivan the innkeeper. He has lived there all his life. He is just shorter than the rest of his family and happens to have green eyes."

Before anyone could stop him, Ivan surged to his feet and stomped forward. "You're right. He is my son and always will be." He put his arm around Stefan before saying, "But Stefan was not born into our family. He was found near the river after the great flood." He smiled at his son and gave him a squeeze before continuing, "I have worked at the inn for nearly fifty years, ever since I was a lad. In that time, I have seen hundreds, possibly thousands of people pass through our inn but no one…no one other than Stefan, has had green eyes." A little crease appeared between his eyebrows. "Actually, I'd never really realized that before. Hmm. I am Ivan, by the way."

"And take it from me, as a forest guardian," said Tarkyn, pressing home their point, "no one but woodfolk can mindtalk. I can exchange mental images with humans and animals, but not words. No other sorcerer or outsider can even do that." He hesitated. "If I remove my shield, will you undertake not to harm or take captive any of us, at least until we have reached an agreement? Then Stefan can demonstrate his ability."

After a brief mental consultation, Sphagnum Moss nodded. "We agree."

Tarkyn swept away his shield. Suddenly, everything felt more open and people from both sides breathed an unconscious sigh of relief. "Say something, Stefan."

Stefan was looking a little dazed. "What?' he asked out loud.

Rainstorm laughed. "You poor bugger. Tell them what you think of Tarkyn for turning your world upside down."

"Thanks, Rainstorm," said Tarkyn dryly.

Stefan took a deep breath to steady himself and began to mindspeak. *At first, I was resentful that Tarkyn had destroyed my whole view of my life but then, as I came to know Rainstorm and the other Eskuzorian woodfolk, I thought it might be all right to actually be someone other than who I thought I was. And after Lord Tarkyn's displays of power last night, I felt privileged that he had spent the time on me.*

Rainstorm rolled his eyes. *That's not very interesting. Everyone thinks he's great... well, arrogant and great... but basically great. I thought you'd be mad at him.*

Stefan laughed. *I was, at first. Very.*

And how long have you been able to mindtalk? asked Banksia.

"About four days." Stefan replied out loud. He shrugged. "Well, probably all my life, but no one was there to tell me I could, before Tarkyn came along." After hearing Lapping Water's diatribe, he was not feeling very friendly towards these people who had let him grow up unaware of his abilities. He was not going to let them indulge in a private conversation with him in front of his friends.

Banksia, Sphagnum Moss and Spinifex looked stricken, as did those around them. Grevillea had tears in her eyes and Red Gum looked shamefaced. Many of the woodfolk clustered closer to Stefan, studying him.

After a moment, Banksia held up a hand. "Could you give us a few minutes, please?" When she came back into focus, she gave a sad smile. "You have really caused a furore with this information. We are truly shocked. The forests are ringing with contrition, and renewed grief for those lost in the great flood… But a query has arisen." She addressed Vera, who was still seated in the background beside the fire. "We don't actually spend our lives spying on your family. It is more that we notice various aspects of your life over time as we pass by. But… I hope I am not rude in asking this, but weren't you swollen with child before Stefan appeared?"

Vera nodded. "Yes." Even in the dim light, her eyes seemed to be shining over-brightly. "But I lost the babe. It is the only child I lost, from six pregnancies. When we, or rather Anton, found Stefan and brought him home, the loss was so recent that I was still producing milk." She cleared her throat uncertainly. "Hello. I am Vera."

"Oh. That explains it," said Banksia thoughtfully. "You see, while we were in turmoil following the flood, we missed the event of Anton finding the baby. We don't see everything that happens in the woodlands, you know. Far from it. And when we saw a new member of your family, we just assumed it was your child." Her face crumpled. "Oh dear. That poor little boy." She drew a handkerchief out of a pocket and buried her face in it.

Amidst the grief, Sphagnum Moss braved the proximity of outsiders to walk over to Stefan, and take his hand, clasping it between both of his. "I am so sorry that we have neglected you. It is our fault, not yours, that this has happened. We will do everything we can to repair it." He, too, was, holding back tears. "It will take time. We don't know what to do."

Tree Fern threw a defiant glare at the outsiders as she, too, moved forward. But she had no interest in Stefan. Instead she placed a supportive, slightly protective, arm around her grandfather. Sphagnum Moss looked more annoyed by this than grateful.

"Leave me alone, girlie," he said tetchily. "Can't you see they're not planning to hurt us?"

Tree Fern's arm dropped to her side and for a moment she looked a little forlorn. Then she crossed her arms across her chest, attempting to reassert her belligerence to cover her uncertainty.

"It is confusing, isn't it?" said Waterstone into her mind. *"Don't worry. Your grandfather is safe among us."*

Sphagnum Moss half turned and took one of his hands from Stefan's to place it on her arm, but she shrugged it off. He gave a little sigh of resignation and said silently to Stefan, *"She is all flame and no coals. It's nice that she's worried about me, but I can look after myself… I shouldn't have snapped at her. I suppose she's just frightened and upset. We all are."*

In the midst of the maelstrom of emotion, Tarkyn had retreated to the fire and wrapped his arms around himself, his face pinched with suffering.

Lapping Water noticed him go. "What is it?" she asked gently.

Tarkyn looked down at himself, realized what he was doing and with a grimace, let his arms fall. "I can feel their sorrow. The forest is full of regret, and guilt and self-retribution." He shook his head. "It is as though all the trees are wailing."

"Gather yourself, Tarkyn," she said softly, coming to put her arm around him. "Help them."

Tarkyn, forest guardian, took a deep breath and nodded, looking across at Stefan, who stood among his true people with his foster father's arm around his shoulders and his hand held by the old woodman. He studied Stefan's firm mouth and the eyes that lit with humour, the arms and hands that handled weapons so well and thought about Stefan's perceptiveness that made him such a good teacher. He smiled at the way Stefan met everyone eye to eye, a legacy of his woodfolk heritage, he was sure. He remembered the flashes of resentment that showed through when Stefan thought he was being teased, which were allayed by his rock-solid belief in himself, instilled by Vera, Ivan and Stefan's four siblings with their fierce devotion to each other and to Stefan... And Tarkyn sent out emotion-charged images that showed to the grieving woodfolk the reality of Stefan.

Gradually Tarkyn straightened as the emotions flowing through the trees changed slowly from grief and guilt to the realisation that one of their number whom they had thought lost, had survived the flood and, despite his alien upbringing, had flourished. Then wonder and a sense of rejoicing washed like a wave through the hundreds of woodfolk throughout the forest.

All around the clearing, even more woodfolk, young and old, simply appeared between the trees and in the branches above them. Vera and Jackson, still seated at the fire, watched, knowing the something momentous was happening.

"Open your mind, Stefan," said Autumn Leaves quietly. "Come and join him, Vera. And Marjorie."

Slowly, the woodfolk converged on Stefan, now flanked by Vera, Ivan and Marjorie. As they drew closer, they encompassed both Stefan and his family members in their arms from all sides; layers upon layers of arms interlaced over each other. Jackson, who had seen little of woodfolk, looked on, his eyes bright with tears.

Stefan's mind was swamped with messages of welcome, not just from the thirty touching him now, but also from the hundreds of woodfolk elsewhere in the forest.

From somewhere inside the huddle, Banksia spoke out loud, "Vera and Ivan, we have seen over the years – although we didn't realise what we were seeing – and the forest guardian has shown us today, how well you and your children have cared for our kin, who is also your kin. Since Stefan is our kin, then so too are you, and we welcome you and your family."

Luckily Ivan, Vera, Marjorie and Stefan were used to an effusive, demonstrative family, which saved them from feeling completely overwhelmed by the flood of emotion that flowed to them from all sides. Gradually the woodfolk pulled back, many of them smiling shyly.

A small girl grinned up at Marjorie. "You're the first outsider I have ever come near. I am Lorikeet."

Marjorie smiled down at her and tousled her light brown hair. "Then I expect you have just been very brave."

The girl nodded solemnly. "Yes, I have." She waved her hand around to indicate her fellow woodfolk. "We all were." She glanced at Tarkyn and Jackson and took a little breath. "We still are."

At that, Jackson walked over slowly and crouched down in front of her. "Hello. My name's Jackson. I hope you don't stay scared of me. I am just the same as you, but just a bit less clever. I can't flick into hiding or mindtalk… but I can make a magical shield. That's about all the magic I can do. Other than that, I walk, talk, run, climb a bit, not much, and ride horses a lot." He grinned at her. "I have a mum and dad, just like you, although at the moment they are far away… and I have two sisters."

The little girl studied him. "Hmm. I suppose you are the same mostly. Just longer and … leggy. And your eyes are a bit different, but brown eyes are good for hiding, just like green ones are." She looked across at Tarkyn and leaned forward to murmur quietly to Jackson. "His eyes are too bright, though. They're almost orange and you'd see all that black hair a mile away unless he was deep in the shadows."

Tarkyn rolled his eyes. "Have I mentioned how much I love being talked about?"

"That's lucky, isn't it?" said Jackson to the girl. "Because I bet people talk about him all the time."

As Lorikeet giggled, Jackson grinned at her and stood up.

"Hello, young lady." Sheldrake walked over and sketched a small bow that made Lorikeet giggle even harder, a puzzled frown appearing on her face.

Rainstorm laughed. "Don't worry. It is just a gesture that means something like, 'Hello' or 'Happy to be of service.' " His laughter faded away as he and all other woodfolk received a report from the lookouts that an unknown outsider was approaching their firesite. He sent an image of a dusty, travel-weary man to Tarkyn, who indicated that he did not know him.

Instantly, all the woodfolk disappeared.

Part 5

Chapter 32

Jayhan slowly became aware that he was being jostled as he lay in the dark. His first thought was that he was late getting up and someone was shaking him awake. His mind galvanised into action, in his fear that he might get into trouble for sleeping in too long. But as he tried to heave himself upward, he realised he had it all wrong. The jostling was not someone waking him, his limbs were restricted and could not respond to his wish to move … and it was as dark as midnight. He didn't persist in struggling to rise. He dropped back and lay in the dark, trying to make sense of his situation.

He could feel a tight pressure around his hands and ankles and realised they were bound. He could smell a damp, earthy, leaf mouldy odour around him but he could see no light through a cloth covering his face. A surge of panic welled up, but he clamped down on it before it overwhelmed him. Suddenly another surge of panic hit him.

"Sasha?" It came out as a croak and he realised his mouth was dry.

A grunt sounded behind him.

"Sasha?" he whispered again. He swivelled a little and his arm connected with someone else's arm behind him in the darkness. A small someone else. He swung his arm up and down, using his elbow to feel the ropes on the wrists and the softness of the arm muscle. Definitely, probably, almost certainly, Sasha. He pushed his elbow down a little harder on the arm. "Sasha? Is that you? Are you all right?"

"Of course it's me, you idiot," came a hiss. "Who'd you think it would be?"

Jayhan subsided, feeling hurt.

After a minute, he felt a soft jab in his back from Sasha's bound hands. "Sorry," she whispered. "I feel sick and my head is all muzzy and I'm scared."

At that, Jayhan wriggled until he had turned over and was facing her, even if he couldn't see her. Bits of damp leaves and twigs trickled down the neck of his shirt, as he moved. He felt around until he found her hands and clasped them. "At least they haven't killed you… us."

"It's those escaped prisoners, isn't it?" she whispered. "We never did tell anyone about that person I saw on the way to the palace."

"Idiots!" replied Jayhan vehemently. After a pause, he asked, "How long do you think it'll be before they notice we're gone?"

"Dunno. That grumpy old gardener, Kate, will just think we've run off."

"Huh. Probably not 'til teatime then."

"That's *hours* away."

"I know," replied Sasha gloomily. "We could be anywhere by then."

Suddenly the jostling stopped and they could hear the sound of feet on cobblestones close by. Then each of them was grabbed and dragged upward, pulling their hands away from each other, cascades of compost falling from them as they rose. Both of them began to wail, hoping someone would hear but a hand was clamped over each of their mouths. Sasha bit the one holding her mouth and her kidnapper let out a yelp and the hand whipped away.

"Don't you dare!" commanded a harsh voice.

"She bit me! She deserves a thump." The man sounded aggrieved.

"Leave her alone. Use a rag around your hand so she can't bite. Shut her up but don't hit her."

"Blood and thunder! This is the namby-pambiest abduction I've ever been involved in."

"This is the most important abduction you've ever been involved. So get it right!"

If Sasha and Jayhan had harboured any hope that this might be a random abduction, they didn't now. The men began to feed them into sacks, feet first. They wriggled and tried to make it difficult, but their captors were too strong. As soon as the men let go of their mouths to tie the sacks, the children both began to shout but Jayhan received a savage kick and let out a gasp of pain.

"Jayhan," cried out Sasha.

"That's right, young lady. We won't hurt you, but if you cause us trouble, we *will* hurt him. Do you understand?"

Sasha thinned her mouth and refused to answer. Another cry of pain issued from Jayhan and she forced out, "Yes."

They heard the sound of metal scraping on cobblestones and were carried downwards. After a brief descent, they felt themselves bumping on the men's backs as they were carried forward. They could hear the sound of water trickling and the smell that now permeated the air was disgusting. Both of them struggled not to gag.

As time passed, the sound of the water changed from a trickle to lapping and gurgling, then to a distant roar. Just when they feared they might be caught in a torrent, they felt themselves bumping as the men climbed upwards. They heard the scraping of metal above them and after a few more bumps, they breathed in fresh air.

"Right. Carry them into the trees over there. Then we'll let them out."

A few minutes later, they were swung off the shoulders of the two men and deposited on the ground. Jayhan did not feel the thump of landing that he had anticipated. Maybe the men were only unkind when they felt it was necessary. He hoped so. His thigh still hurt where he had been kicked.

The men hauled them out of the sacks and unknotted the ropes binding their legs, the ropes being carefully coiled and put away in a rucksack for later use. They pulled the coarse hessian hood from Sasha's head but left Jayhan's in place. Sasha nearly protested but didn't want to risk them hurting Jayhan again. Besides, she recognised two of the three men as members of the assault party who had tried to capture her and kill other shamans in the woods a few months ago. She would never forget how Jayhan's horror had transmitted itself through great beams of white light from his eyes to freeze his opponents with dread.

Clearly they had not forgotten, either and were taking no chances with him this time. Poor Jayhan. He didn't even know how he'd done it, but she didn't expect they'd believe her or risk it happening again.

She risked a question. "Why have you abducted us?"

"Because you have something our queen wants and only you can give it to her."

Sasha raised her chin. "It is mine by right."

"Don't care." The man shrugged. "I work for Queen Toriana and she wants it."

Sasha glared at him. "I will not say the words of transfer and if I don't, she cannot take it from me."

"You will," said the man calmly. "Because you don't want your friend here to suffer, do you?"

The men tied a loose rope between the bound wrists of the two children, then led them in single file deeper into the woods. One man placed his hand under Jayhan's elbow to steady him, whenever he tripped or became unsteady. Each time Jayhan tripped, the bruise on his thigh hurt where he had been kicked. So he worked at lifting his feet a little higher and landing each foot a little flatter so that he could adjust for bumps and hollows underfoot.

Jayhan didn't like having a hood over his head but he liked the smell of the hessian. Now that he wasn't covered in compost or upside down in a sack in dark tunnels, he found he could see light and shade from within his hessian hood and could make out vague shapes. In fact, as they walked, his vision became clearer and clearer until he seemed to be looking straight through the hessian, as though it were no longer there. *Huh*, thought Jayhan, *that might be useful*, and proceeded to trip artistically every now and then, to maintain the illusion that he couldn't see.

At one point, the men hoisted the children onto their shoulders as they forded a swiftly running creek. The men simply waded through the water, putting up with wearing their wet boots until they dried. Jayhan did not enjoy hanging upside down and completely lost his sense of direction. When he was put down, they were well within the forest again and it crossed his mind that they could be heading back the way they had come, for all he knew. So, for the next little while he watched the shadows, seeing they were mostly facing ahead of him, which meant the west was behind them and they were still travelling east.

Gradually the light dimmed until he felt the patter of rain drops on his hood. He groaned inwardly. Now they were going to get wet and cold, on top of being frightened and tired. He heard the men muttering among themselves, followed by someone flinging a cloak around his shoulders as they walked. He bit back his thanks but couldn't repress a grunt of acknowledgement. He hunched his shoulders in disgust at himself and kept on tramping.

The shower passed and Jayhan felt the sun on his back. A shudder went down his back as its warmth began to thaw him.

The man guiding him noticed his reaction and said, "Count yourself lucky. We just caught the edge of that storm. I bet it's teeming closer to Highkington."

"Good," came a voice from further up the line. "Rain might wash away our tracks and make the going slower if anyone works out where we've gone."

Jayhan's spirits sank further. His legs were so sore and tired that it was all he could do to keep going. He was genuinely tripping more now, as his legs refused to work properly. There seemed to be more roots and small branches in their path now and he often had to dodge branches that swung back into his face as Sasha pushed through. Since her hands were tied, she couldn't do much about it, other than call a warning to him. As another thin branch thwacked him in the face, he decided there were benefits to wearing the hessian hood.

The man guiding him said gruffly, "Shay. Take a rest. The kids need a break. Otherwise we'll have to carry them. This one's nearly done in."

"It's only another half hour, Bart."

"Don't care. We need to rest now."

Shay reluctantly called a halt, but only allowed them ten minutes before they were ordered back onto their feet and on their way again.

The long summer day was drawing in by the time they turned off the track to approach a shabby hut, almost hidden by the overhanging branches of a stand of huge myrtle trees. The walls and roof were made from long thick strips of bark overlaying each other. One upright of the verandah had rotted through, so that its roof sagged alarmingly at one end. Accumulated leaves and twigs threatened to cascade down at any moment. Jayhan could see so well that he spotted a small skink scurrying up a verandah post to disappear into the bark of the roof. Luckily, his natural instinct to blurt out this piece of fascination to Sasha was dulled by his tiredness. Instead, it was all he could do to put one foot in front of the other.

They were ushered inside to a single room that was lined on three sides with built-in wooden benches. A fire burnt cheerily in a fireplace in the fourth wall where the mantelpiece and shelves were dotted with filled jars, bags and various utensils. A big pot hung over the fire, emanating the tantalising smell of stew. Jayhan suddenly realised he hadn't eaten for hours. A large kettle sat on the side of the coals, steam wafting from its spout. The only furniture was a farm table and six wooden chairs. The entire hut seemed to be just a large kitchen.

A tall woman was leaning over the fire stirring the contents of the pot, but she straightened as they entered.

It was the shaman who had been among those who had attacked them at the meeting of the refugees in the forest near the Creeping Vine.

At the time, Sasha's amulet had caused this woman to falter and lose consciousness but unlike Lady Electra, who had immediately switched allegiances, this woman was here working with kidnappers for Queen Toriana against Sasha.

The woman walked over to Sasha, leaned forward and pulled up the chain that hung around the girl's neck until her black amulet came into view. Immediately, a responding pale light from the woman's own amulet beamed though the material of her bodice.

For a long moment, dark eyes stared into Sasha's. Then she said roughly to the men, "Lock the door. Sit them at the table, untie their wrists. Shay, how is that child going to eat with a hood on him?"

"It can't come off, Ruby," growled the man who seemed to be the leader of the three men. "His eyes are too dangerous."

"Then put a blindfold on him," she snapped.

The man who had been leading Jayhan rummaged in his pocket and produced a red and white spotted scarf. He handed it to Shay, who raised his eyebrows in surprise, his lips twitching with the beginnings of a grin. "Lovely, Bart. Where did you get this?"

"Oh, just from a friend of mine." Bart said airily but his heightened colour betrayed him. "She gave it to me for good luck when we left Kimora." He scowled. "So look after it."

Shay smiled. "I will, Bart, I will. Now, turn the boy towards the wall so he can't see us when we take the hood off."

Jayhan, now blindfolded by the polka dot scarf, was guided to a seat beside Sasha at the table where the others were already seated, waiting while Ruby dished out bowls of stew. Sasha patted Jayhan's knee in sympathy a couple of times before withdrawing her hand.

The scarf had been folded so that several layers lay over his eyes. At first he couldn't see anything. But gradually, his eyes adjusted and he could see through it, although shade and dark were interfered with by variations of colour on the scarf. He was so busy dealing with being blindfolded and working out how to act so that he seemed blind that he'd almost forgotten to care for Sasha. As the thought struck him, he turned instinctively to look at her, then hoped his head movement hadn't given away that fact that he could see. Her face was drawn and her eyes were big with fear. He gave her comforting squeeze on the leg in return.

Ruby claimed his attention by saying, "Your stew is in front of you, young man. The spoon's sitting in the bowl."

Jayhan didn't want to answer her but he couldn't overcome his training and muttered a reluctant, "Thank you."

Sasha took his hand and guided it to the spoon. He pretended to grope for the spoon awkwardly until he had his fingers around the handle.

"I'd lean over, if I were you," murmured Sasha. "Otherwise you're going to get it all down your front while you're finding your mouth."

"I know where my mouth is," he grumped. "It's the bowl I'll have trouble with."

"Keep your other hand on it," Sasha suggested.

"Hmph." Jayhan decided he would eat with his eyes shut for a while so he could work out how to act. He soon found that he couldn't quite estimate where the end of the spoon was relative to his hand and he did, in fact, often slightly miss his mouth and spill some of the stew.

"Hold your bowl under your chin," whispered Sasha, "You know, to catch the bits."

"I can't. The bowl's too hot to hold." He threw down the spoon in disgust.

"Then keep trying as you are, I'm sure you'll get better at it."

"Or I can feed you," said Ruby dryly, "or you can go without."

Jayhan heaved a sigh, felt around for the spoon and pulled the bowl closer to the edge of the table so he could lean over it. Suddenly, he could barely repress a grin at the thought that they were all playing along in his game while he was the only one who knew he could actually see if he wanted to. Then the gravity of the situation bore in on him and he remembered the kicks to his leg. Suddenly, his near laughter converted to a rush of fear. His breath hitched on a sob.

"It's all right, Jayhan. Take your time. You'll get the hang of it," crooned Sasha.

"It's not all right." Despite his best efforts, the tears welled up. Between sobs, he mumbled, "They're going to make you hand over your amulet to that bad queen, then hundreds more people will die. So you know you can't do that. But it's going to hurt me and I'm scared."

Sasha put her arm around his shoulders. "Oh Jayhan." She wanted to reassure him, but escape seemed the only thing that could save him and she couldn't mention that possibility, even unlikely as it was, in front of their captors.

"What have you done to this boy?" demanded Ruby, glowering at the three men.

Bart shrugged. "Nothing much. Just gave him a couple of kicks to go on with, to shut the two of them up."

"And threatened to slit his throat," interrupted Sasha indignantly, "until I let them put a handkerchief to my mouth back in the palace garden."

"Bart didn't hurt him too badly," said Shay. "The kid's just scared about what'll happen when we get to… But if the girl cooperates, he won't have anything to fear."

Sasha saw a glance pass between Shay and Bart and knew with absolute certainty that once they had forced her to transfer the amulet to Queen Toriana, they planned to kill them. After all, she and Jayhan would pose an ongoing threat of exposure to the queen. Why would they keep them alive?

Despite their fear, Jayhan and Sasha felt a resurgence of strength rise in them as they ate. Perhaps they had just been too hungry. Once their meal was finished, the two men retied the children's hands and directed them to sleep on adjoining benches, flinging cloaks over them for warmth. Two of the men and the woman also settled down to sleep, just as the first drops of rain fell outside. The third man stayed sitting near the dying fire, keeping watch and listening to the steadily increasing drumming of rain on the roof.

Jayhan manoeuvred himself around so that his head was close to Sasha's.

"Are you awake?" he whispered.

"Yes." She wriggled closer. "That man, Shay, has the door key in his pocket. I can't see how we'd get it without waking him."

"No." Jayhan's voice sounded disheartened, but he perked up almost straight away. "Maybe tomorrow when we're travelling through the forest."

"Hey, You two! Go to sleep!" came a heavy voice out of the darkness. "We all have a long walk ahead of us. No more noise or I'll come over and clout you."

Chapter 33

Jon was seated at his desk in the palace, studying a sheaf of reports about damage to the roads from the previous week's heavy rainfall. He sighed. The bundle of reports foreshadowed extensive discussions with Crabtree, the civil engineer in charge of road maintenance, who would bemoan the costs, the insufficient staff and the unfortunate need to prioritize. His hand was just on the bellpull to have Crabtree sent to him when he heard the unusual sound of running footsteps in the corridor; adult footsteps.

Jon frowned and was already half-risen from his desk when a knock sounded on his door. "Come in."

A liveried page walked in quickly, trying to hide the fact that he was panting from his long run and stood before Jon. Despite his best efforts at maintaining decorum, every muscle was stiff with the urgency of his message.

"Sir, the two children, Lady Natasha and Lord Jayhan, have disappeared," he blurted out. "It looks like they've been abducted."

For a moment, Jon stood stock still, his face pale and rigid. Then an anguished cry broke from him. "Ah no! No, no, no, no, no." He grabbed his coat from the back of his chair thrusting his arms into it as he headed for the door. "They're not just hiding?" he asked without much hope, knowing that abduction would be the last possibility considered.

"Mistress Josie believes not, sir. She is waiting for you at the rear gate, sir."

"Right. Thanks." Jon sped off, his long loping strides soon leaving the young page behind.

He arrived at the back gate to find Josie and Lady Teresa waiting with stoic calm while one guard after another reported back on their search to the Sergeant standing beside them. Once Jon had been apprised of the facts, all he wanted to do was saddle a horse and join the search.

"No, Jon," said Josie firmly. "Many men are already searching. You must remain here to decide on further courses of action. I'll have your horse saddled. Better to be ready for any eventuality, but for now, stay." She beckoned to the page who had fetched Jon and sent him off to the stables.

Jon ran a hand across his forehead and started to pace in agitation. After a few turns he stopped in front of Josie. "How can you be so calm?"

In an unexpected gesture, the fearsome woman reached out and grasped Jon's arm, giving him a slight smile. "It is worse for you; she is your sister. But we all care about her… and

Jayhan." She took a breath. "Jon, what you see before you is controlled panic. And to help her, you must control yours."

"Oh." In response to her kindness, tears sprang to his eyes. He nodded until he could regain control of his voice. "I will." With a supreme effort, he pulled himself together and gave her a crooked smile. "I have. Sorry. Emotional family."

It was then that the news of the abandoned cart arrived. Luckily for Jon's continued sanity, his saddled horse arrived a few minutes later and, with a quick look at Josie for approval, he set out with a squad of soldiers and a tracker to investigate.

The cart was neatly parked on the side of a residential street, looking for all the world like the cart of a tradesman visiting one of the terraced houses. A small group of children had gathered to gawk at the two soldiers who had been left to guard it. Other than them, everyone was keeping behind closed doors.

Jon dismounted and beckoned to the children. These weren't street ruffians, but they weren't rich either. They approached nervously, their eyes wide with interest.

Jon squatted in front of them and gestured to the cart. "Did you see this cart arrive? And where the people went to?"

The children consulted each other with looks, then a little girl piped up, "We were playing ball in the alley down there. Carts come past all the time, but soldiers don't. Jim saw the red and gold of the uniform. So we all came out to watch."

Jon gestured to three houses closest to the cart. "Do you know who lives in these houses? Might they have seen anything?"

A boy shook his head. "No one there, at the moment. They's all gone off to some big market. They's all traders, you see."

"How convenient," muttered Jon. "And the houses on the other side of the road?"

"The middle one's my Aunt Marcie but she's not well. Her bedroom's at the back of the house, so she won't have seen anything. Cassie's mum lives next door. She might have seen something but the parlour's at the front and I reckon she'll be in the kitchen getting dinner ready."

"Old Joe might have seen something. He sits in the front room all day long smoking his pipe," said the little girl, eager to be helpful.

Jon felt in his pocket and pulled out a silver coin that he held up. "Who will I give this to, to buy sweets for all of you?"

Several grubby little hands thrust forward but Jon held the coin up, eyebrows raised, until they all looked to the first girl who had spoken.

"Give it to Cassie. She'll be fair," said a boy with a smudge on one knee and a gap in his smile. "Thanks."

By the time Jon had disengaged himself from the children, a soldier was already returning from questioning the old man in the front room across the road.

"He's a sharp one, sir," the soldier reported. "Saw the cart draw up. Saw the driver pull up and get down from the cart. Two men came out of one of those apparently empty houses to join him. Two of the men stood on the street side of the cart, which blocked the old man's view. Then he reckoned they walked around the kerbside of the cart, bent down and disappeared. He hasn't seen any of them since."

Jon frowned. "They could be shimmerers like me," he said, thinking out loud. When the soldier looked confused, Jon shimmered before his eyes, disappeared then returned into view, a wry smile on his face at the astonished stares. "I doubt it though, even though they are probably Kimorans. We're a pretty rare breed."

"Perhaps we should consider more prosaic solutions," suggested the tracker, who was dressed differently in a dark brown, loose-fitting uniform with discrete insignia on his shoulders and lapels. He was a taciturn, serious man who did not suffer fools gladly and clearly did not appreciate Jon's little display. "There's a scattering of compost around the back and kerbside of the cart, so I think the children were definitely taken from the cart here."

Jon glanced up and down the street then nodded grimly. "I agree and I know where they've gone. I lived on these streets for years. Look under the cart, Trevor." As the tracker ducked his head under the cart, he said, "There's a manhole there, isn't there?"

"Yes sir." His voice held a note of surprise. "And there are recent scrape marks on the cobblestones." Trevor straightened. "There is a huge network of tunnels under the city, sir. They could be anywhere. We'll try to track them but if they walk for a while in the water, it could be tricky."

Jon held up a hand to forestall him. "Just a minute. Let me think." He shut his eyes and let his mind wander through the vast network below them and as he did, memories of being frightened, hungry and alone, running for his life, nearly overwhelmed him. He opened his eyes and shook his head to clear it.

"I know these tunnels," he said quietly and couldn't overcome the need to share just a bit of what he had endured. "They are not warm, but they are a lot warmer than being on the streets during a blizzard. And if you know them, you can escape from gangs and marauders. You just have to know the tunnels better than they do." He gave a whimsical smile at the soldiers' stares. "I wasn't always a lord, you know. Well, I was, but I didn't always live a lord's life."

He took a breath to bring himself firmly back into the present. "Anyway, I think I know where they have gone. They will be taking the children to Kimora. There are three outlets that come out close to the edge of the Great Forest. One outlet to the east on the main road, Park Lane, which I think they will avoid, one outlet in the northeast which opens close to the dense northern part of the forest and one beyond the southeast of the city which opens into the southern part of the forest. The route through the southern part of the forest is narrow and overgrown in places but leads more directly to the capital of Kimora, so I think they will go that way. Trevor, you and I and a squad of soldiers will travel to the south eastern outlet, but I think we should send people to the other two outlets just to check those possibilities." He looked around him. "Agreed? Any suggestions or comments?"

"Send back messengers to report our plans to Josie and to organise for provisions to be sent to us at the south eastern city gate, sir," said Trevor, for the first time a note of genuine respect in his voice.

Chapter 34

An hour later, Jon and Trevor were inspecting the ground around another metal manhole set into a grassy knoll, fifty yards outside the city's wall.

Jon pointed towards the forest. "The tunnel goes for another three hundred yards then opens into the Taramine River. The river is flowing fast after all that rain last week, so I doubt that they will have gone that way, even if they could find a way to open the gating without the key."

Trevor squatted down and ran some earth through his hands. "No. I think you're right. People have definitely come out of the manhole here, quite recently." He looked around himself then his eyes travelled along a line towards the forest edge. He stood up and walked along his line of sight for several yards before reporting, "The footprints are all intermingled and there's a bit of a mess near the manhole, but then the tracks head in a clear line towards the forest. So, it looks like they walked in single file. I've found a few clear prints here and there, enough to say there were three adults and two children."

Jon blew out a breath. "Oh, thank goodness. Sasha and Jayhan must be unharmed enough to walk. That's something."

Trevor frowned and focused on one set of small prints amongst the rest. After a minute, he said, "One of the little ones is limping a bit; not badly, but enough to make the steps uneven." He glanced up, saw the query in Jon's eyes and added, "Can't tell which one. They're both wearing boots, about the same size. Josie might know from the treads, but I don't."

A fresh squad troop of eight men and a sergeant jogged up, barely out of breath after their trip from the palace, packs of provisions on their backs. They too were dressed in the camouflaging dark brown that Trevor was wearing. The sergeant, a neat, well-mannered man in his mid-thirties with a crop of black wavy hair over serious grey eyes, presented himself and saluted. "Afternoon, sir. I'm Sergeant Reece. Seventh squad relieving fourth squad, sir. We have provisions enough for several days if needed, sir."

"Several days?" That flustered look was back on Jon's face.

"Not saying we'll need them, sir, but better to be prepared."

"Seventh squad is one of our elite squads, Jon," said Trevor. "Experienced at... hmm... less straightforward approaches, shall we say, fitter and more used to bivouacking and working in the field."

Jon managed a tight smile. "Indeed? Then welcome."

As they followed the footsteps into the tree line and along a narrow but well-defined path, large raindrops started to spatter on the trees, falling through the canopy to land on their heads.

"Blast!" exclaimed Jon. "Halt, everyone. Get your cloaks out. It looks like this is going to get heavier, but we can't afford to stop."

It only took a couple of minutes for the experienced soldiers to drag their cloaks out of their rucksacks and don them, pulling their hoods up. Then they were on their way again.

The rain gradually gained momentum until the men's cloaks were close to saturated and water dripped from the edge of their hoods into their eyes. Nevertheless, they marched on stoically. Soon bushes began to impinge heavily on the path, and wet branches brushed against them as they passed.

Then they came to Flushing Creek.

Normally it was a trickle, but the recent rains had swollen it, making the water knee-deep in the shallower stretches, opening into deeper pools, its pebbly bottom interspersed with strands of reeds and underwater grasses, waving downstream.

The rain pelted down, making visibility poor. Trevor waited for Jon and Sergeant Reece to join him on the banks. He pointed down to the remains of footprints in the mud along the bank.

"Their prints're nearly gone." He gestured across the stream. "The path continues through the trees just over there and that's probably where they went, but if they've deviated in the water, it's going to be hard to pick up their tracks. The rain is washing them away, even as we speak." He indicated the squad of men who had emerged from the trees behind them and had now gathered along the bank of the fast-flowing creek, hunched against the rain. "Once they get over to the other side, there will be no chance of seeing any last remnants. I propose our men take a rest while I cross over and scout about."

Jon nodded, sending a shower of droplets from the front of his hood.

Reece agreed. "I'll take them back under the cover of that large gumtree we just passed. It wasn't waterproof but I noticed a few dry patches under it. It would be better to take off our boots for the crossing anyway."

The men settled under the tree, taking the opportunity to light a fire, make tea and bring out rations of dried meat and apple, talking quietly among themselves. Jon was given a share, but he could not sit still, and instead paced back and forth just inside the shelter provided by the tree.

After several minutes of this, Sergeant Reece approached him. "Two things, my lord. Firstly, if you use all your energy now, what will you have to draw on, if or when we find the abductors? Secondly, these men are seasoned campaigners, but they respond better to calm authority."

Jon stopped dead and looked at him. After a moment, he heaved a sigh, pushed back his hood and ran his hand through his hair. "Sorry." Immediately, a swirl of wind sent down a flurry of raindrops out of the leaves. He shuddered as cold water found its way down the back of his neck, but he didn't replace his hood.

"No need to apologize, sir. You are not accountable to me. Just an observation, that's all."

"Thank you." Jon gave a wry smile. "Besides, I would spend the time better, getting to know your men… and vice versa."

Reece gave him a strange look.

"What?"

The sergeant frowned. "Not quite what I meant. Not common for nobles to hobnob with the men. Nobles tend to stay aloof, sir."

"I was staying aloof by pacing… not intentionally, I'll admit. And I would rather not. I find my own company has limited attraction… unless you were planning to stay aloof with me?"

Sergeant Reece looked flustered. "I, uh, no, I usually stay with my men when we are out in the field."

Jon raised his eyebrows. "So you expect me to stand here on my own, with nothing to do and no one to talk to?"

"Of course I will join you, if you'd like," said Reece hastily. "I was not meaning to ostracize you, my lord."

Jon grinned. "As much as I'm sure your company is delightful, I would rather hobnob with your men… and you, of course."

Half an hour later, Trevor returned, his boots in one hand, to find Lord Jon sitting at his ease on the ground, chatting amiably with the troopers. Trevor's boots seemed to be the driest thing about him. Jon sprang to his feet as soon as the tracker appeared and Reece handed the tracker something to eat in exchange for his boots and saturated cloak, which he took to the fire to dry out. "Cup of tea coming up."

"Thanks." He turned his attention to Jon. "I can't be certain, I'm afraid, sir." Trevor took a bit of dried beef and chewed it before continuing. "No sign of footsteps left at all, anywhere on the other side. There are a couple of places where the bank has fallen in a bit, as it might when someone climbed out of the creek there, but equally it could be from the current undermining the bank."

Jon glanced at Reece to gauge his reaction, then asked, "So what…? What does that mean? What do we do about it?"

"We can play the odds and assume they have continued to follow the path we're on, sir," said the sergeant, "but it might be wise to send a few men along any other paths that lead away from the creek on the other side." Reece turned to Trevor. "Did you see any?"

The tracker shrugged. "Nothing as clear as this path and even this path is not obvious. The forest is pretty dense around here. If they did push through into the bush further down the creek, I would have expected signs of their passage; torn fern fronds or recently snapped small branches, but I didn't see anything. I waded through the creek water several hundred metres in each direction – in some places the bush was too dense and close to the creek's edge to walk around."

"You've done a thorough job, by the sound of it," said Jon. "My thanks. So, we head straight on?"

"I think so, my lord." Trevor glanced at the sky. "The rain's not as heavy as it was but we're starting to lose the light. We'd better cross and get on our way while we can still see our feet."

The rain was easing, and they traversed the creek without incident. More time was lost while the men redonned their boots on the other side of the creek, but after that, they kept up a steady pace, their eyes adjusting to the gathering gloom until it was fully dark. Then Reece called a halt.

"Two choices, my lord. We either set up camp or light torches. If the moon were out, we could keep going, but the cloud cover is still heavy, and we may miss the path or trip over roots or obstacles if we keep going in the pitch dark. If we light torches, we can keep going but it will warn the abductors of our approach… and make us sitting ducks if they plan an ambush."

Jon repressed an exasperated sigh. He knew Reece was right. "Trevor, your opinion?"

"I'm pretty sure we're on the right track. Since we left the creek, I've seen parts of foot-prints in places where trees have sheltered the path from the bulk of the rain but, if you really want to know, I'm developing a headache from concentrating so hard in such poor light." He gave a grunt. "Even with torches, we might miss a small path running off to the side."

"Sir," another voice piped up.

Jon swung around to find a young trooper tramping through the mud to join them at the front of the line.

"Yes…" Reece peered through the gloom for a moment before adding, "Warren. What is it?" His tone indicated that he knew the trooper would only interrupt if he had useful knowledge.

"I used to come out here hunting with my dad when I was a boy. There's an old disused woodcutter's cottage not so far from here, off to the right."

"How far?"

"Dunno. Maybe ten minutes?"

"Could be where the abductors are holed up," said Jon, unable to keep the excitement out of his voice.

"At the very least," said Reece more prosaically, "it will give us somewhere to camp for the night. We can't camp on this narrow path. We had better not use torches, though, if it is possible the abductors are there."

Without torches, Warren's estimated ten minutes took them nearly half an hour in the pitch dark, with Warren becoming increasingly unpopular as time passed. Finally, they reached the edge of a small clearing, just as the clouds parted to bathe the area in moonlight. Instinctively they drew back into the cover of the trees.

They could see an old stone cottage on the other edge of the clearing, a straight dirt path leading up to the front door between two small stone-edged gardens.

With calm efficiency, Reece deployed his troops to circle through the vegetation so that they could come at it from all sides. Jon found it hard to stand still as Reece signalled for the troopers to approach the cottage. They ran quickly from one patch of shadow to the next, until most of them were pressed against up the stone walls of the cottage. Silently, they drew their daggers.

One trooper peered cautiously through a window. Inside the cottage, all seemed dark and quiet. He carefully tried the doorknob and pushed gently on the door. It wasn't locked, although no one expected it to be, this far into the woods. As the door swung open, a slight breeze eddied in the doorway.

He glanced at his companions and in a coordinated rush, he and three other troopers threw open the door and ran in, daggers drawn. Another coming behind them lit a lantern. As the lantern lit the room, they gaped in astonishment.

Jon stood before them, hands on hips. "No one here, I'm afraid."

One of the men ducked his head out of the door, then back in again. He grunted. "Just checking there aren't two of you."

"Ah. That's right. You weren't there when I demonstrated earlier." Jon shimmered out of sight then reappeared. "It's called shimmering."

The troopers looked at each other but said nothing. One of them walked outside and signalled the 'All clear' to Sergeant Reece and the other men.

Reece, when he arrived, was not pleased. He tersely ordered his men to bring their packs inside and to get settled for the night.

"We can't go further in the dark, Jon," said Trevor, not unkindly, in response to Jon's ill-concealed concern. "As it is, I think they may have turned off the path and I might have missed it. I'll backtrack at first light and see if I can pick something up."

As Jon nodded reluctant acknowledgement, the sergeant caught his attention. "A word with you outside, my lord, if you please."

Jon grimaced in Trevor's direction before following Reece outside, aware that the sergeant was not happy. Once they were out of earshot, Reece swung around to face Jon, his hands on his hips. "We are not playing games here, my lord. In case you hadn't noticed, my men were careful, stealthy and approached that cottage in a manner least likely to attract the attention of anyone inside."

"I did notice. In fact, I was impressed... but so too did I, in case *you* hadn't noticed."

Reece gave a snort of exasperation. "But you acted impulsively, without my knowledge, without my men's knowledge and without a plan."

"And what exactly was your plan?" Jon's usually cheery voice developed an edge. "What would your men have done if they had broken in, to find a Kimoran with his knife to my sister's throat? Or Jayhan and Sasha tied in the corner and several abductors between them and the door? Pretty risky plan, if you ask me."

"But you placed yourself at risk and reduced everyone's effectiveness by acting alone," protested Reece vehemently. "What if the situation had demanded that you stay shimmered, or invisible, or whatever you call it? Not knowing you were there, one of my men could have inadvertently swung his dagger straight through you, had there been a fight."

"I doubt it," said Jon. "I'm fast on my feet and I'm used to street brawling with knives." He gave a wry smile as his anger evaporated as quickly as it had come. "But I concede your point. We would work better in concert. In fact, I was caught out by the suddenness of our coming upon the cottage and the immediate deployment of your men." He gave a laugh that held no trace of bitterness. "And I am pretty sure you consider me an inconvenient, decorative addition to your force. So, I decided that by the time I could persuade you to take me seriously, the moment would well and truly have passed. So, I just acted."

The two of the had been glaring at each other but at these words, Reece looked past Jon and slowly swept his gaze around the trees on the edge of the clearing then down at his feet as he considered. When he met Jon's gaze again, there was the hint of a smile in the corner of his mouth. "Fair point. In fact, now I think about it, your particular talent could come in very handy… if you were willing to work with me."

Jon smiled. "If that means 'work under your command', the answer is no. But I am happy to use my skill in consultation with you."

"Fair enough, as long as we don't argue in front of the men. Discuss, yes; argue, no."

Jon gave a small bow. "I am not argumentative by nature, so unless you are, we should rub along well enough."

Reece chuckled. "You're a funny one, for a noble."

"I've had a funny upbringing." The smile on Jon's face slipped a little. "Well, not funny. Not at all funny. But unusual."

"That's what I meant, unusual. And I'm beginning to like you, which is more than I can say for most noblemen I've met."

"Are you? Well, that's nice. Thank you very much."

Reece laughed and shook his head. "Very unusual. Come on, m'lord. Let's go and get some sleep so we can be on the trail of your sister at the crack of dawn."

But all night long, the rain hammered down and by morning, no trace was left of the abductors' footsteps. Even their own footsteps had washed away.

Chapter 35

Someone thumped loudly on the door, the sound jerking Jayhan awake. He felt he had only just drifted off to sleep. A surge of adrenalin rushed through him, leaving him feeling jarred and dazed.

It was still pitch dark and rain drummed steadily on the roof. He tried to rub his eyes, but his hands encountered the cloth of the polka dot scarf. After a moment of uncertainty, he worked out that it actually *was* still dark, and it wasn't because he was blindfolded.

"What's going on?" whispered Sasha.

"Come on, you two!" bellowed Shay. "Our squad has arrived. Up and out with you."

Before they could react, the children were hauled to their feet and pushed towards the door. Shay pulled the door open and shoved them outside into the cold of the pre-dawn darkness, where they found themselves surrounded by black-clad figures. The rain was easing, but big drops still fell from the eaves of the hut and from the tree branches overhead.

The children huddled close to each other, pushing against each other for warmth and comfort. Sasha tried to remind herself that she was supposed to be these people's queen, but this only served to convince her that queens were just people like everybody else. She was scared and cold and tired, just as Jayhan was. Someone flung dark grey, hooded cloaks over them, but by then their clothes were already damp.

"Right. This is Brinta," said Shay, indicating a short, dark-haired, dark-faced woman who was thin but bursting with contained energy and, Sasha suspected, hidden strength. "She and the other three will be coming with us to Kimora from here. Do what we say, and Jayhan will not be hurt."

Beside her, Sasha felt Jayhan shudder inside his cloak.

For several minutes, Shay and Carl bustled back and forth into the hut, collecting provisions for their journey and stuffing them into their backpacks and handing supplies out to the newcomers. Just as the children were being ushered off into the darkness, Ruby came out of the hut and handed each of them a small satchel to throw over their shoulders and a freshly baked herb and cheese scone to hold. "Here," she said gruffly. "Eat that now. There are cookies in the bag to eat over the next few days." She stared hard into Sasha's eyes "They will give you the strength and stamina that you will need."

Sasha gazed back at her, trying but failing to discern her motives, then nodded her thanks. Beside her, Jayhan mumbled something incomprehensible.

They barely had time to eat their scones before they were pushed roughly in the direction of a narrow easterly track. It was still dark, but when Jayhan and Sasha looked up, they could see a pale grey sky in the gaps between the trees and could discern the shapes of nearby bushes.

Jayhan shrugged off the big fist on his shoulder. A small flame of resentment bloomed inside him, blotting out the fear. *These bastards are not going to take us and hurt us and kill us. We are going to get away. Don't know how, but we are.*

As they walked, he thought about what weapons he could use to free them. He could shape shift but only to the shape of a person, not an animal as his mother could. And he had his eyes. He now knew he could see through hessian and scarves. What else could he see through? And on that one occasion, his own terror at Jon's impending death had ignited his eyes and sent forth streams of white light that had paralysed their enemies with fear. He gave a little grunt of frustration. But he didn't know how to consciously make them do that.

"*I will work on it,*" he decided, his mouth setting in a determined line that might have given his captors pause, if they could have seen it in the darkness.

Behind him, Sasha, too, was walking with new purpose. She was thinking about the time her amulet had thrown Yarrow across the room and then surrounded Sasha in a black, impenetrable cloud while she recovered from an overload of images. If her mother had lived to see her grow up, she would have taught Sasha the secrets of her amulet, but that knowledge had died with her mother. She frowned. Hadn't Sheldrake said that she was gradually gaining knowledge as she grew up, just by wearing the amulet?

"*Hmph,*" she thought, "*Maybe I know more than I realise. I will focus on my amulet as we walk and see what I can learn.*"

After two long, dark hours they stopped for a break. It was full daylight now and the clouds were beginning to clear. Jayhan and Sasha were both dragging their feet and tripping from fatigue.

"It must have still been the middle of the night when we left," whispered Sasha. "Dawn's very early this time of year."

"No wonder I felt like I'd just gone to sleep... I had."

Shay tied them to a tree and wandered off to chat with the other troops and to eat the freshly baked bread provided by Ruby. It smelt wonderful, but it was not offered to the children.

"You've got your own," growled Brinta, as she left to join the others.

Sasha and Jayhan turned their attention to their little satchels and, manoeuvring awkwardly with their tied hands, each pushed a cookie out of the other's satchel so they could eat it.

As their lips touched the cookies, a zing of energy jolted through them. They jerked their heads back, then they looked surreptitiously around before meeting each other's eyes.

"Try that again?" murmured Jayhan.

Sasha nodded.

Steeling themselves, they each took a careful bite of their biscuit and chewed, actually enjoying the initial zing. Strength flooded through them... and something more. A sense of hope.

"Huh." After a moment, Sasha whispered, "Hey, have you been planning what to do instead of just being paralysed with fear? Since we left the cottage, I mean."

"Yep. You?"

Suddenly Sasha's face lit with a smile. "Yep. I think she put something in those scones she gave us and now something even stronger in these cookies."

"What're you grinning at?" demanded Jayhan.

"That means the amulet worked on Ruby after all, just as it did on Lady Electra. I thought, when she was working with the kidnappers, that maybe my amulet hadn't overpowered hers, but she's actually helping us, so it must have."

Jayhan thought about it. "Huh. Maybe this is the best she could do without getting herself killed."

"In which case we'd better hide how much better we're feeling."

"And anyhow, if we still look scared, they won't think we're up to something."

"True."

However, this plan was destined for failure. As soon as Jayhan tried to look doleful, Sasha glanced at him and got the giggles, which set him off too. When Brinta broke away from the others to find out why they were laughing, Sasha improvised wildly and said it was because Jayhan's spotty scarf made him look silly. Brinta frowned furiously but in the end, let it go.

As soon as she was out of earshot, Jayhan murmured dryly, "Hmm. So that could have gone better,'' which nearly set them off again.

With an effort, they pulled themselves together so that they could tell each other what they had been thinking about as they walked.

Sasha said urgently, "I think the key to controlling our powers is imagination. I have to imagine a situation is so bad that my amulet springs to life to defend me. You know, putting me in that black cloud thing and shoving my enemies away, like it did with Yarrow."

"Yeah, but the trouble with your amulet is that it only protects *you*, which," he gave a lop-sided smile, "makes it next to useless if you care about me."

Sasha frowned. "True. That's why they could kidnap me, us. I'll have to think about that."

"And also, remember that somehow, touching me might increase whatever magic you have."

They had no more time for plotting. Brinta called them all to order and the children quickly stuffed down the rest of the cookies they were holding. Begrudgingly, the Kimorans stood up and fell into line in single file; Shay in front, then three more in front of Jayhan and Sasha, with Brinta and Bart bringing up the rear.

"You two looked pretty tired by the time we stopped. We won't go so long without a break this time," Shay reassured them, as they set off once more. "Otherwise we might end up carrying you, which would slow us down even more."

It soon became apparent that while Sasha and Jayhan had gained strength and vitality, Brinta and her troops were feeling grumpy and lethargic. Sasha caught up to Jayhan long enough to jab him in his back with her fist. When he glanced around, frowning at her, she nodded towards their kidnappers and mouthed, "Tired."

"What are you two up to?" growled Brinta from behind them.

"Nothing," they chorused.

Not surprisingly, this did nothing to allay Brinta's suspicions.

Sasha improvised again, trying to sound aggrieved. "Jayhan tried to trip me up as we got back into line, so I just got him back by giving him a jab."

Brinta rolled her eyes. "Just shut up and keep walking."

"Any more of that bread left?" asked Sasha.

"Yes, we've got enough for a few days. But I told you, it's not for you. Now, be quiet."

Sasha hoped that Jayhan would understand the implication; that Ruby's bread was making the captors tired and grumpy, maybe less alert.

He understood all right, although he didn't know what he could do about it. But he would work on it.

All that day and over the next two days, they slogged their way through dense forest, trudged along miles of boring, uneventful straight stretches, stepping from tussock to tussock through sodden ground, and skirting along rocky sections that wound up and over sparsely wooded hills. Occasionally they would jump from rock to rock or be carried across one of the burbling streams that cut through the path.

All the while, as Sasha and Jayhan ate their cookies, they resisted the dragging urge to become disheartened and instead, maintained their energy and sense of hope.

Jayhan worked hard on trying to remember how he had felt, how his eyes had felt, when the Kimoran trooper had grabbed Jon by the neck and threatened to cut his throat. As tiny droplets had appeared in a line across Jon's throat, Jayhan's horror had engulfed him and his eyes had shone forth. But how? Then he remembered that Yarrow had said he couldn't just summon the power. But maybe it would ignite in response to his imagination, as Sasha had suggested.

He tried thinking of himself being threatened. He tried to imagine someone bringing down a knife to slice his arm, but his mind baulked at the image. At first, he couldn't even follow the image through to its conclusion, but after several attempts and a lot of determination, he brought it to the point where the knife touched the skin of his arm. But, try as he might, he couldn't imagine the pain at all. He had no concept of how it would feel. And through all these images, his eyes seemed completely unchanged.

Sometimes he was so busy concentrating that he would trip over a rock or raised root in the path, but it didn't worry him. In fact, as he recovered his balance, he would be glad he had tripped, because he knew that he kept forgetting to act as though he couldn't see.

Then he'd go back to his ruminations.

Chapter 36

Jon slept restlessly, waking often to see whether it was yet dawn. At the first greying of the sky, he was up and out of the cottage. He splashed his face with water from the tank that abutted the cottage and after a slight hesitation, drank from his cupped hands. The water had an earthy taste that was quite pleasant, and he suspected leaves had fallen into the tank over time. He stood up, shaking his hands to dry them, and turned to find the other men emerging from the cottage.

As Sergeant Reece strode over to him, Jon gave him a friendly nod and said, "Good morning. I'm glad to see you're all up. I was just wondering whether I should risk your wrath to wake you all."

Reece gave a grunt of laughter. "We are used to rising with the dawn. Trevor has just headed off to look for tracks but after the night's rain, I don't hold out much hope. I think we will just have to continue on the track we were following yesterday. We just have time to light a fire and make ourselves some tea before he gets back." As Reece saw a wave of impatience cross the young lord's face, he added, "It won't slow our departure, I promise you."

True to Reece's word, half an hour later, everyone was packed and ready to leave. Trevor was handed a cup of tea as soon as he returned and gulped it down as he reported his findings – or rather, lack of them.

Jon reached out and put a hand on his shoulder. "Don't scald your mouth on my account. I can stand another minute or two of inaction." While Trevor gave a quirky smile and took a slower sip, he said, "So we follow the main path from the Flushing Creek again today, do we?"

"Yes. I think it is a reasonably safe bet. I saw no other paths leading off from it and it will only take a few minutes to return to it in daylight."

Once they were back on the main trail, they settled into a fast but relaxed pace and, a little over an hour and a half later, came upon the dilapidated old bark hut, huddled under the trees, where Sasha and Jayhan had slept only a few hours before.

This time Jon glanced at Reece who nodded his agreement. Jon shimmered and approached the hut soundlessly, the only sign of his passing, the appearance of muddy footprints in the wet, scattered leaf mould of the clearing. The soldiers spread out slowly on either side, out of line of sight with the door. As everyone waited with bated breath, the door swung slowly inwards, apparently by itself.

A minute later, Jon's voice sounded cheerily from inside. "No one here. Safe to come in."

Outside, Trevor raised his hand. "Not so fast. Let me go in first and see what I can see before you lot destroy it all."

Reece nodded. "Agreed."

As Trevor entered, Jon pointed to marks on the floor that hadn't been made by him. "Not here now, but they were, I think. So, we're on the right track."

It did not take Trevor long to find the footprints of three adults and two children in the dust and mud on the hut's floor. "You're right. They were here, all right. But they must have met a third person either here or somewhere after Flushing Creek." He looked around. "Here, I'm guessing. Looks like someone used that fireplace for cooking. A new set of prints, only one, near the fireplace." He pottered around the hut and then moved outside to inspect the ground all around the clearing, gradually working his way east, while Jon wandered back out to join Reece and his men.

When he had finished, Trevor reported, "Three more people arrived here from the east. They milled around for a bit, then all six headed eastward, taking the children with them."

"How long ago?" asked Reece. "Any idea?"

"Not sure. Depends when the rain stopped here. My guess is that we're four hours behind them, maybe more. They may have left earlier than us. They have the advantage of knowing where they're going while we had to wait for the light to see tracks." He pointed eastward. "Still on the same path so far."

"Right. Ten-minute break, then we move on." Reece sent a perceptive glance at Jon. "You holding up all right?"

Jon gave a wry smile. "Physically or emotionally, do you mean?"

Reece shrugged. "Either. Both. You haven't had the rigorous training than this lot have had."

"Physically, fine. I do a lot more than you'd imagine. I have projects outside my work at the palace that keep me moving around." Just as Reece was thinking that he had over-stepped the mark and was just going to get a defensive answer, Jon gave a little grin. "But emotionally, I'm a bit up and down. I was on tenterhooks going into that hut, and full of hope. Then, no one there. Grim… But…" he shrugged, "at least we know they've been here and we're still on the right track."

"You're good at pulling yourself together when you need to, aren't you? Even if you get wound up in the first place. Your voice sounded quite cheery coming from that hut." Reece pulled out two hard biscuits and offered one to Jon. "Here. Let's sit down while we eat."

They sat down on a damp log on the side of the clearing, somehow not wanting to go into the hut.

"Thanks," said Jon, accepting the biscuit. He bit into it, having to clench his jaw muscles to get through it. After a few chews, he added, "… for the biscuit and the comment. I think I'm just a naturally cheerful person, so I bounce back to cheery as my default position, even if I sink at times." He glanced sideways at the sergeant. "Sometimes, it has taken quite a bit of effort."

"At least, being a lord, you've never had to worry about where your next meal's coming from," said Reece, with a faint touch of bitterness.

Jon decided to sidestep the possible one-upmanship about who had had the harder past and instead, chose to seek the source of the sergeant's bitterness. "And you have?"

"Often. My father was a lawyer, so to start with, we were comfortably off. But when I was eleven, he was killed by a runaway cart. From then on, my mother had to find work, as a seamstress or a scribe. She was well-educated... her father was a well-to-do merchant... but few people would turn to a woman for their letters." Reece took a rather savage bite of his hard biscuit. "She had trouble getting regular clients and she was proud. She had fallen out with her family and wouldn't turn to them for help. And she never got over the death of my father, either. She took to drinking. Sometimes she spent all the money she earnt on drink... and she lost clients because she didn't deliver on time. Daisy, that's my little sister, and I tried to find odd jobs, but we weren't brought up for it."

"Neither was I," said Jon, then kicked himself for interrupting. "Sorry. Go on."

Reece stared at him for a few seconds then shrugged. "Not much more to tell. As soon as I was sixteen, I enlisted in the army so I could support Daisy and myself, and Mum, if she needed it."

"Huh. I thought you seemed more educated than the average enlisted man."

"I suppose I am. Despite it all, Mum found time, mostly, to teach us our letters, numbers and a bit of history."

"And etiquette, I think."

Reece smiled. "We were just brought up that way. Not strict court etiquette, of course but hmm, I suppose you'd call it genteel manners." He chuckled. "It doesn't always go down well with the men, but they're a great bunch and put up with me."

"You're perceptive and care about the people around you. I'd say you're worth putting up with," said Jon, standing up and holding out his hand to pull Reece up.

"Thanks... for the hand and the comment," Reece said, echoing Jon's previous words. "Sorry I dumped all that on you. I don't usually talk about it. No point really. The past is the past." He called his men to order and they set off down the path that Sasha and Jayhan had been taken down in the pre-dawn.

Once they were settled on their path, Jon continued the conversation. "Sounds like your mum had a hard time of it. But you have a good, interesting job now, don't you? Why are you bitter still?"

Reece hitched his pack more comfortably on his back and blew out a huff of air. "I shouldn't be, I suppose. It's just that... ah, you know. If my father had lived, I'd probably have been a lawyer too, or if I'd joined the army, it would have been as a commissioned officer. Now, I never will be. You're either enlisted or commissioned. You have to buy a commission and pay for the training, all of which costs far more than I'll ever earn." He gave a self-deprecating smile. "I do my men a disservice complaining like this. Enough. I am proud of them and we have a job to do. Let's focus on that."

Jon gazed around at the tall trees above them, the wet leaves shining in the mid-morning sun and the patches of blue sky appearing amongst the clouds. He smiled. "It may not be just what you want, but you seem to have earned yourself a place in a skilful, elite squad who have interesting assignments out in the countryside. Seems pretty good to me. Much better than being a footman."

Reece exploded with laughter. "That's a random comment, if ever I heard one. What made you say that?" He waved his hand. "Never mind. You're right, of course. It is a pretty good job. And I actually love it, most of the time anyway."

Suddenly one of the men came jogging up bedside them. "Sir, someone is travelling parallel to us through the bushes to our left."

Before Sergeant Reece could react, Trevor signalled from up ahead. "Someone off to the right up ahead," he interpreted for Jon.

Then they saw a figure waving frantically from high in a tree further up ahead.

"Weapons ready, men," ordered Reece. "Whoever that is could be trying to catch our attention to distract us, or warn us of an ambush. Be ready for an attack from any side."

Without further instruction, the eight men moved into formation; two facing forward in front of Jon and Reece, two backwards and two facing each side, all with swords and daggers drawn. Then as one, they moved swiftly into the cover of the bushes on the right of the road and kept moving forward along the track. Up ahead, Trevor ran from tree to tree along the side of the track trying to get closer to the gesticulating man. But despite all their precautions, he or any of them would have been sitting ducks if their opponents had archers among them.

Soon, Trevor could hear what the frantic white-haired man was shouting as he waved his scrawny arm. Trevor signalled to the sergeant who turned to Jon. "He wants you, whoever he is. He is specifically calling your name. We'll move up as a group until we're close enough for you to see whether you know him. Then we'll decide what to do next."

As they drew nearer, Jon recognised the scrawny old man. "It's all right. He's safe. He's a Kimoran refugee. He is loyal to me."

Reece gave Jon a strange look, knowing him only as a noblemen in charge of the Transport Ministry. Then he listened to what the man was saying.

"Jonboy. Jon. We have to talk to you. It's urgent."

Jon straightened and moved away from the squad to stand in the middle of the road close enough to shout up at the man. "Beetlebrow. I didn't know you could climb trees. Come down. These men won't hurt you." He glanced at Reece for confirmation before adding, "You have my word."

"Right. Give me a minute. Argus is close by, too. I'll signal to him to join us too. All right?"

Jon looked at Reece. "I can vouch for him too." When Reece nodded, he replied to Beetlebrow, "Yes. Better to have him out in the open with us. No misunderstandings then."

Reece raised his eyebrows. "They're *loyal* to you too? What going on? You're not some bandit lord, I hope."

"What?" Jon frowned in surprise then laughed. "No. Nothing like that."

Beetlebrow had made it down the tree by now. He gave Trevor a friendly nod as he passed him and shambled over to stand before Jon, gasping from the effort. Then he surveyed the armed squad of men arrayed behind Jon and brought himself up short. He gave an awkward little bow before saying stiffly, "Good morning, Your Highness. Sorry for calling you Jonboy."

Jon placed a hand on his shoulder. "Stop it, Beetlebrow. You can call me Jon or Jonboy just as you always have. Save all that stuff for if we ever get back to the Kimoran court. Now, tell me why you need me."

"Oh yes. Right. We saw Sasharia and her little friend with the pale eyes being marched off, further down this track. Their hands were bound and they had Kimoran special forces troops behind and ahead of them. We ran back this way looking for help. We were planning to go all the way into Highkington to report it until we saw you. Lucky we saw you. I'm puffed out already."

"How many?"

"Four in front and two behind," replied Beetlebrow promptly. "Draya and Rhoda are keeping track of them, but we didn't want to attack in case the kids got hurt. We're farmers and tradesmen, not fighters."

Argus stepped out from the bushes on the left-hand side of the path and raised his hands disarmingly when he saw a swathe of swords swing his way.

"This is Argus," said Jon. "Let him through."

"Ah, Jon. Thank goodness you've come. We've been shadowing your group for a little while now, trying to work out whose side they were on. Then we saw you. So Beetlebrow raced up ahead and climbed a tree to get your attention from a safe place." Argus ran a hand through his mane of greying hair. "We've been worried sick. We just find our true queen is alive and now we're losing her. Those bastards will kill her as soon as she hands over the power of that amulet." He gave an apologetic shrug. "We're no heroes. There's only the four of us. We couldn't do it on our own."

"Don't worry," said Reece, entering the conversation. "We'll get her back and the little fellow too. How long since you saw them?"

"We saw them about two hours ago, but we've been walking this way ever since and they'll have been getting further away all this time."

The sergeant turned to his men. "Hear that, men? We're only four hours behind. Let's step up the pace. We'll jog four hundred yards, then walk for four hundred yards on the east stretches. Can you people keep up or should we keep to your pace?"

Angus and Beetlebrow glanced at each other, then shook their heads. "We can't do that, but you go on. We'll bring up the rear."

Jon nodded. "Thanks, you two. I'll go on with the squad," he gave a wry smile, "although it may kill me trying to keep up."

"Keep an eye out for Rhoda and Draya. They might have more news further along the track," said Beetlebrow. Then he grinned. "See you later, Your Highness. You'll have to get used to using your title sooner or later."

Jon rolled his eyes. "I was trying to keep that quiet, but never mind. See you later."

For the first four hundred yards of jogging, no one spoke but when they slowed to a walk, Reece turned to Jon. "Would you care to explain? I understood that two children, one of them related to the king, had been kidnapped, presumably for the ransom. I wasn't sure why you were coming along, even if the girl's your sister. These jobs are better left to professionals." He shrugged. "But noblemen don't usually have to explain themselves to me, so I just accepted it…"

Jon's eye twinkled at him. "With barely concealed ill-grace, I might mention."

Reece gave a grunt of laughter. "Sorry." He waited.

"It's a long story," said Jon finally. "If I tell you the short version, you'll just ask me lots of questions. So, I'll start at the beginning."

So he told Reece and the listening troopers who he was, of the attack on his family by his aunt, and of his flight from Kimora as a twelve-year-old, with baby Sasha in his arms. He glossed over his years of living on the streets of Highkington and finally, gave a light-hearted sketch of his time as a footman in the Kimoran embassy.

Overcoming his laughter, Reece shouted, "Jog!" and the squad set off for another four hundred yards. Once they were walking and breathing evenly again, Reece considered Jon out of the corner of his eye for a few minutes. Finally, he asked, "So how do things stand now?"

"I am in disguise, or was, as Lord Jonathan instead of Prince Jondarian, and I work as Minister of Transport while I try to organise the Kimoran refugees into a force to be reckoned with. We only recently revealed to the refugees that my sister Sasharia, the true queen, had survived my family's slaughter. With their approval, Sasha appointed me as regent until she comes of age."

Reece stopped dead, open-mouthed, nearly causing a pile-up. "So you're telling me that rightfully, you should be the current ruler of Kimora?"

"Only until Sasha turns sixteen."

Reece shook his head and turned to keep walking. "You are far too self-deprecating. You have all the authority of a fluffy kitten."

Hearing murmurs of agreement from the men behind them, Jon smiled his sunny smile and shrugged. "Haven't you noticed how fluffy kittens usually get what they want?" Suddenly he looked worried. "That's not to say that I'm friendly just to get what I want. I just find people are usually happy to cooperate with me and I'm happy to work with them." He glanced sideways at Reece. "You can't live on the streets for years without realising that everyone has worth in their own way; sometimes well-hidden, I must say." He chuckled. "Perhaps I've never pulled rank because, until recently, I didn't have any recognised rank to pull."

"Perhaps." Reece didn't sound convinced. He gave a wry smile. "Maybe your parents, while they had the chance, brought you up well, or maybe they, too, had sunny dispositions."

"They did."

Jon's words sounded strangled and when Reece looked at him, he realised the young man was holding back tears. He wasn't sure what he should do, especially in front of his men, and finally settled on placing his hand on Jon's back as they walked.

After a couple of minutes, Jon drew a deep breath and as he let it out, gave Reece a grateful smile. "The sadness wells up from time to time. I suppose it will never really go away. And I don't want it to. My mother and my father and my brother and my sister deserve me to remember them. That's the price I have to pay for being cheerful most of the time."

Reece gave him a couple of firm pats on the back and withdrew his hand. "I like you even more, the more I get to know you."

And like the sun from behind a cloud, out came Jon's cheery grin. "Thanks."

Reece grinned back. "Jog!" he shouted.

Part 6

Chapter 37

Instantly, all the woodfolk disappeared... except Stefan. He had been aware of the urgent, collective mind message to hide, but he had no idea how to flick into hiding. Besides, his loyalties lay with his parents and his employers. Still, it left him feeling a little bereft. The woodfolk had said they would include him and introduce him to people who might be his kin. Instead, they had left him behind as they disappeared.

Despite himself, Stefan smiled when he saw his parents, Sheldrake and Maud, staring around themselves in shock as hundreds of woodfolk disappeared instantaneously.

"My word," exclaimed his father, wide-eyed and taking a gulp of his wine. "They are most magical, aren't they?"

"And can you do that too, dear?" asked his mother.

Stefan grimaced. "I don't know. I haven't tried and don't know how." Even to his own ears, he sounded petulant.

"Now, dear, I'm sure they're not deliberately leaving you out. They do have a lot on their minds at the minute."

Stefan felt his cheeks growing warm with embarrassment. His mother knew him too well.

Vera leaned forward and whispered, "I can't believe how many people have been living in these forests around us and we never knew."

"It's amazing, sure enough." Ivan looked at Stefan. "Look at all these people who must be your kin." He gave a wry smile. "Pity they don't frequent taverns. We'd make a fortune."

Just then, Stefan became aware of Waterstone sending an image to Tarkyn requesting him to shield himself. Concerned that imminent danger threatened, Stefan whirled around ready for action, only to find Tarkyn clucking his tongue in amused irritation.

"Such a mother hen," mouthed Tarkyn.

Remembering that Tarkyn was, in fact, a visiting dignitary who would normally be given protection, Stefan offered to intercept the new arrival and check their credentials.

Tarkyn gave a wry smile, "You don't have to do that."

"I am a member of the King's guard and as such, it would be my honour." Stefan gave a small bow, and set off down the dark track towards the Creeping Vine.

"Just a minute," called Tarkyn softly. "Sheldrake, are you able to create an enduring orb of light for Stefan to take with him? I could take over the light for our firesite, but I am only able to create light where I am."

Sheldrake beamed, delighted that he had finally found a skill he possessed that the powerful sorcerer did not. "I would be charmed," he said, pushing his glowing orb towards Stefan, as Tarkyn ignited a new one over the firesite.

Stefan caught Sheldrake's orb a little apprehensively but found that it was quite cool to the touch. He nodded his thanks.

"I'll go with him," offered Jackson.

"Good. Then he'll have your shield, if he needs it."

"For goodness' sake," growled Ivan, "it's just a stranger approaching. Happens to me a hundred times a day in the inn. I don't go rushing around taking precautions every time. I wouldn't have time to do my job, if I did."

Tarkyn grinned. "Ah, but you don't have an anxious blood brother badgering you about your safety. In times past, I was outlawed by my sorcerer brothers, with a price on my head. Old fears die hard, I suppose. Besides, as you can see, it's in the nature of woodfolk to be wary of strangers." He surveyed the group sitting around the fire. "Please remember not to mention the woodfolk. The secrecy of their existence underpins their whole way of life."

"We won't," rumbled Ivan. "You'd be surprised how many secrets an innkeeper overhears and keeps to him or herself." He shrugged. "And threats aside, I wouldn't want to betray their trust."

Minutes later, Stefan and Jackson re-entered the firelight, escorting a tired, dusty King's Messenger.

"This is Lerrin. We both know her," said Jackson. "I, because I am, or was, in the equivalent messenger service for the Eskuzorian Embassy and Stefan, because he has seen her around the King's castle."

"I know her too. She has often been to the inn on her way past. I'll get you a drink, Lerrin," announced Ivan. "You look parched."

The messenger ignored them. She was focused solely on her task of delivering her message. The tension of her movements telegraphed that it was urgent. Without a word, she approached Sheldrake, who stood as she approached. Lerrin produced an envelope from her satchel and with a bow, handed it to Sheldrake who nodded his thanks. Tarkyn redirected his sphere of light for the mage to read by.

As Sheldrake read the single sheet from the envelope, his face paled. But with years of experience in subterfuge, he did not exclaim. He glanced quickly around the firesite, evaluating Ivan, Vera, Tarkyn, Jackson and Stefan. Maud watched his reaction but said nothing. Then he considered the possible loyalties of the woodfolk who might be out of sight, but not necessarily out of earshot. Rather abruptly, he asked Tarkyn, "Do your friends read?"

"Not in general, no. They communicate mentally, so do not need messengers." Tarkyn hesitated. "Some of my closer associates have chosen to learn to read, but no one else that I am aware of."

Sheldrake grunted and handed the letter to Maud, indicating that she should pass it on when she had finished reading it. Effusive though she might be, Maud, too, had years of training behind her. She breathed out, "Oh no," and passed the letter to the others without another word.

They sat in stricken silence, not knowing what they could and couldn't say in front of the hidden woodfolk and the messenger, who was unaware of woodfolk.

Having had time to think it through, Jackson let out a breath. "Well, this is awkward." He turned to the messenger. "Lerrin, let me take you back to the inn and get you settled for the night. Is that all right with you, Ivan?"

"Of course. Thank you. We'll be along shortly, I think."

"Thank you indeed, Jackson," said Tarkyn. "You are a prince among aides-de-camp. Don't forget to take Sheldrake's light orb with you."

Sheldrake held up a hand. "Lerrin, just before you go. How soon will you be rested enough to take a return message to Highkington, should I require it?'

"Sir, with a fresh horse, I could leave in half an hour, given the urgency of the situation." Lerrin glanced up at the sky. "The moon is at three quarters, although there are some passing clouds, but generally, visibility will be adequate." She hesitated. "But might I suggest that you wait for further bulletins? When I left, the news was new," she gave a self-deprecating smile at her choice of words and added, "so to speak. I would expect another messenger within the hour with further information."

"You are right, of course. Thank you." He blew out a breath. "Nothing is to be gained from acting precipitously, much as I would like to," he said tightly and nodded to her in dismissal.

As soon as Jackson and Lerrin were out of sight, Autumn Leaves, Rainstorm, Sparrow and Midnight reappeared. Everyone but Tarkyn jumped, still not used to the woodfolk's coming and going. Midnight went straight to Tarkyn and climbed up on his knee.

Rainstorm, who had reappeared next to Stefan, grinned at their reaction but then put an arm around Stefan's shoulder, "Sorry, my friend. We were so preoccupied with all of these new woodfolk, we didn't even send you a message. That was wrong of us. And we must teach you to disappear. I expect you wanted to stay anyway, but in future, we must give you the choice."

Stefan's resentment melted. He gave a wry smile and said, "True on all counts."

While they were speaking, Autumn Leaves was surveying the rest of them seated around the fire. After a moment, he crossed to Maud, squatted down next to her and took her hands in his. "Your hands are shaking. What has happened?"

He glanced at Sparrow, who looked around the whole shocked group and responded promptly with, "Cups of tea, coming up."

In response to his kindness, Maud's professionalism broke down and tears coursed down her cheeks. He took away one of his hands to rummage in his pocket and produce a rather crumpled piece of cloth. "Here," he said, removing his other hand from hers and, instead, putting his arm around her shoulders, leaving her free to wipe her eyes.

Between sobs, she managed to get out, keeping her voice low, "J... J... Jayhan and Sasha have been abducted. It is our worst fear come true."

For several minutes, she couldn't speak as she sobbed into the handkerchief. Sheldrake watched her from the other side of the fire, a frown on his face, but he made no attempt to go to her. Stefan suspected he was working at keeping himself together so he could act.

Autumn Leaves took the opportunity to send a query to Tarkyn, who murmured, "Jayhan is their son and Sasha... hmm... Sasha is their stable boy." He glanced at the darkened trees around them. "Perhaps Stefan can give you more information? Stefan, can you direct your thoughts directly to only one or a selected few people?"

Stefan nodded. "I think so. Let me try it out to check first." After a pause, he asked, "Autumn Leaves, did you get that?" When Autumn Leaves nodded, he glanced at Rainstorm. "Did you?" Rainstorm shook his head.

Ever curious, Rainstorm asked, "What did you say?"

Stefan gave a slight smile. "I said, 'I am sending this to you but not to anyone else.'"

"Oh."

Tarkyn turned to Sheldrake and Maud and said quietly. "I would trust my own group of woodfolk – my home guard, as I call them – with my life and with all my knowledge. As yet, however, I have little knowledge of the woodfolk of these forests."

Sheldrake pre-empted the permission request and nodded. "Go ahead, Stefan. Explain the reasons to Autumn Leaves and he can relay it to the others of Tarkyn's home guard."

A few minutes later, Waterstone appeared at Sheldrake's elbow, shaking his head, as though he had been there all the time. "This couldn't have come at a worse time, could it? With you two, miles from your home and us, in the middle of getting to know the local woodfolk. How can we help? What do you want us to do?"

Stefan saw Sheldrake stand a little straighter in reaction to Waterstone's practical energy. He even managed a smile. "Thank you, Waterstone. Above all, we need to know where they are. We know they will be taking the children to..." He glanced at Stefan who mindspoke the word, *Kimora*. "The only question is, by which route?"

Maud gave a final sniff and said, "Jon is... was, at the palace. He will have heard sooner than us and be hot on their heels, as best he can be."

"I need to study my maps," said Sheldrake, his voice firmer now. "They are in my room at the inn." He spoke more quietly, "We need to be able to discuss the possibilities away from people whose allegiance we are unsure of."

"I understand," said Waterstone.

Sheldrake's eyes widened. "No. I didn't mean you."

Waterstone smiled reassuringly. "No. I realise that. When you go back to the inn, we will keep in touch with you through Stefan, while we get to know the local woodfolk. Is that all right with you, Stefan? You can join us later if you like." He glanced around. "Tarkyn, where are the local woodfolk at the moment?"

Tarkyn let his senses rove. "They have moved further away now. Lapping Water is talking to three of them about two hundred yards that way," he said, pointing to the south. "They have a lookout posted thirty yards closer, presumably to keep an eye on us. The rest have retreated further from the wiles of man." He gave a little grin at his phrasing.

Sheldrake watched Tarkyn's ability to scan the surrounding woodlands enviously. What an asset his skills would be to the King's Spiders. No use dreaming about that. At least Tarkyn was available to them for the time being. He returned his attention to Waterstone, whose firm kindness had given him direction when his feelings had threatened to railroad his thought processes.

"Thanks, Tarkyn," Waterstone was saying. "So, while no one else is currently within earshot, we can speak plainly. I presume you would like us to find out, if we can, whether any of them have had dealings with the current Kimoran monarch. That would be the only basis for mistrust I could think of." He raised his eyebrows in query at Sheldrake and waited for his confirmation before continuing, "I think it unlikely that they have, given our natural reticence, but we will check. Then, when we are clear about their intentions, we will ask for their assistance in finding your kidnapped children."

"Judging by their attitude to us," said Maud dryly, sipping her tea, "I can't imagine that they have had any interaction with outsiders before."

"No. Neither can I." Autumn Leaves smiled at her as he stood up. "You people head back to the inn as soon as you've finished your tea. We will pack up your things and you can collect them in the morning. You have more important concerns on your mind tonight."

Chapter 38

The tables in the private parlour were covered in maps. After some debate between themselves, Maud and Sheldrake had decided to include the Vines in their knowledge of Sasha's heritage and its implications. The Vines' actions and attitudes, reflected in those of Stefan, deemed them to be people of integrity. Besides, several of them had known about Maud's shapeshifting for years and had never breathed a word. Their local knowledge of both the area and the people who passed through the inn was too valuable to exclude.

Sheldrake began by studying a map that showed the whole of Carrador running to its eastern borders and beyond. It was less detailed than some of the more specific maps but gave a better overview. Jackson, as a messenger, and Stefan as a soldier, had a passing knowledge of most areas of Carrador, while Maud brought to bear her knowledge of the people at court, their connections and the location of their holdings. Ivan and Vera had sent Marjorie in to join them, to provide titbits gleaned from the locals. Apparently, customers talked more freely when she was serving them than when Ivan or one of her brothers was nearby.

So, five people clustered around the map as Sheldrake expounded on the possible routes from Highkington into Kimora. Tarkyn took not the slightest interest. He sat at his ease in a chair against the wall, sipping a glass of very fine port. He was a man of many talents, but navigation was not one of them. Leave that to those who had an aptitude for such things.

Stefan glanced over at him and unintentionally caught his eye. Tarkyn smiled and raised his glass, sending a little wave of friendship across the space between them. Stefan couldn't help but grin back. Having seen Tarkyn at work this evening, waving shields and orbs of light in and out of existence, Stefan felt deeply honoured that this powerful sorcerer, the highest power of Eskuzor, had thought it worth his while to delve into his heritage.

Discovering that he was not Ivan and Vera's biological son had hurt Stefan. Deeply. But now a whole new view of his beloved forest had opened up to him. It still amazed him that it was full of people, that their isolated inn was in fact in the middle of a different community.

His distraction must have conveyed itself to Tarkyn, perhaps by the simple medium of his facial expression. Tarkyn rose, holding his glass in one hand and the nearly full bottle in the other.

"Come with me," he said quietly.

Stefan glanced around the people at the table and realised they would barely notice his absence at this stage. After all, Sheldrake was the head of Carrador's intelligence network and knew far more than he about the castle's security and the layout of the kingdom. They would need him more, if the discussion homed into possible paths through the forest. Besides, he thought wryly, his mind was too overwhelmed at the moment to concentrate properly. He nodded and followed the High Lord out of the room.

As they passed the end of the bar, Tarkyn said, "You can bring your own glass or share mine. Up to you."

Stefan gave a little grin, pleased that Tarkyn had thought to include him in the bottle of port and rather liking the idea of casually sharing a glass with someone so exalted. "I'll share yours."

The front bar had only a few patrons left at this time of night and no one paid particular attention to the tall man with the long black hair followed by the familiar sight of Stefan, whose head barely reached the taller man's shoulder. They walked outside into the forecourt of the inn, bathed in a warm light by torches mounted in sconces on either side of the door.

"Let's walk down Park Lane a little, to get away from the light," suggested Tarkyn.

"We're not off to meet up with the woodfolk again, are we?"

Tarkyn looked down at him, his strange amber eyes glinting in the light from the torches. "You don't like them?" He didn't seem to take offence at the possibility, merely holding out his glass of port for Stefan to take.

"Actually, I do. I'm really coming to like your people." He took a sip of the port. "Hmm. That's a good one. Dad doesn't usually let us near that one. No, I like them. It's just that I've had enough woodfolk for the moment. I need time to think."

"Hmm. I thought so. Too much too fast."

Stefan handed the glass back to Tarkyn as they walked away from the glare of the inn's light and into the dimmer light provided by the three-quarter moon. Ahead of them they could see the orange brown of the track spearing off into the darkness between the tall shadows of the trees. Above them, thousands of silver stars shone, their light unhindered by the glow of civilization.

Tarkyn pointed upward. "Beautiful, isn't it? I love being out in the open these days."

Stefan took a deep breath and let it out slowly, letting the tension leech out of him. "Yes, I have always loved it. I spent my childhood disappearing into the forest and watching the stars at night." He cocked his head at Tarkyn. "Do you think that is the woodfolk blood in me?"

"Possibly. Do your siblings feel the same way?"

"Not to the same extent. In some cases, not at all. Anton and Javier would rather be in beside the fire or behind the bar."

Tarkyn sipped the port and walked on for several paces before asking, "Have you forgiven me yet?"

He handed the glass to Stefan again, almost as a gesture of reconciliation.

Stefan didn't hesitate. "Yes. I didn't realize it at first, but you have given me a great gift. Now, when I stand short beside my brothers... and my sister, I will know that I have talents and another heritage that they can never possess."

"Have they been unkind to you?"

Stefan shrugged. "No. No more than to each other. But I have always had a feeling of difference. I look different, I move differently. It is not just my height. It's my whole appearance and demeanour… even my voice, now I come to think of it."

"And I suppose you've had a constant stream of customers coming through your inn commenting on it."

"Yep," said Stefan tightly. He took another sip of port and handed the glass back to Tarkyn. "And all my life I tried so hard to fit in, to be just like my family." He smiled, a flash of white in the darkness. "But now? Now, I don't have to keep trying to be something I'm not. And they all still love me anyway, just as I am. In fact, just as I always was. They don't mind the difference. Only I did."

Tarkyn chuckled. "And how does it feel to be on the cusp of two civilizations? To be the product of two complex cultures? You are unique, as far as I know. The only woodman living among outsiders."

"Hmm, that's something, isn't it?" He walked several paces in silence before saying slowly, "I don't know. I haven't even got to know the local woodfolk yet and I don't even know who my true family is." He glanced at Tarkyn. "I like being able to mindtalk but I can only mindtalk with woodfolk, and exchange images with you. When you and your woodfolk leave, the local woodfolk may just fade back into the forest and I'll have no one to use it with. Not so 'on the cusp of two civilizations' then."

Tarkyn refilled the glass and took a sip before replying. "No. I don't think they'll do that. Woodfolk have a very strong sense of family. All woodfolk must belong to a family. If all of a person's blood relatives die, then that person is officially adopted into a new family. That's how I became a woodman; by being adopted into Waterstone's family." He shook his head. "No. They won't leave you behind, now they know you exist. They'll find your family or adopt you into a new one." He took a sip and handed the glass back to Stefan.

"I don't want to live with them, you know. I don't even know them or their way of life. I have my own life, my own responsibilities." He frowned as he took another sip. "Speaking of which, I suppose we should be getting back shortly. Protecting those two children is partly my responsibility and I want to do everything I can to retrieve them."

Tarkyn smiled rather smugly. "I thought of that. That is why we are on the road to Highkington. When the next messenger arrives, then we will know it is time to go back inside." Stefan raised his eyebrows in surprised appreciation, making Tarkyn chuckle. "It just shows how preoccupied you are at the moment. I'm sure that would normally have occurred to you."

No sooner had he spoken than they heard the distant sound of hoofbeats that drew slowly closer until a figure on horseback rounded a bend and came into sight, head bent down over the horse's neck.

Stefan swivelled on his heels and headed back to the inn at a dead run. Tarkyn, smiling to himself, wandered back at his own pace.

Chapter 39

When Tarkyn arrived back at the inn, Sheldrake rushed outside to meet him, his black coat tails flapping behind him, and blurted out, all protocol forgotten, "They are travelling through the dense, southern part of the forest. Jon worked out they had been taken through the sewers out of the city. He found their tracks near the south eastern outlet leading into the forest and followed their trail with a tracker and a squad of specialist troopers. He sent a message back to Josie, who is coordinating from the palace, and she sent the news on to us." Sheldrake had to draw breath at this stage.

"We will find them," said Tarkyn, with quiet certainty.

He gently but firmly steered Sheldrake back inside. "Let's go and see what the Vines know of that part of the forest."

They passed the two messengers who were seated at a table in the front bar, drinking tankards of ale and eating a late supper. Clearly the first messenger, Lerrin, had been so sure that second messenger was on the way that she had waited for him before eating.

Sheldrake and Tarkyn entered the private parlour to find four heads bent over a map that gave greater detail of the forest. Stefan looked up, his green eyes shining with excitement, as they entered.

"Lord Sheldrake, I can see where they must have taken Sasha and Jayhan. Look, sir." He traced his finger along a faint, dotted, winding line that traversed the southern part of the forest. "This is a narrow track that winds through the forest here from the outskirts of Highkington right through to Charville River. It is ironically referred to as The Way Through, because, for most people, it's not. It is very hard to navigate, and few people know about it or use it beyond the first fifteen or so miles. There are a few woodcutters' shacks and hunters' cottages dotted through the trees, close to Highkington but nothing further in, as far as I know." He shrugged. "Many of these places are deserted now."

"I remember," said Sheldrake, nodding slowly. "There was a period a few years ago when bandits were hiding in the woods in that area, in close striking distance to the capital. They preyed on local inhabitants as well as on the city dwellers. Many people had been killed or driven from their homes by the bandits before we finally tracked them down and cleared them out. A big operation, as I remember it." He looked at Stefan. "You said the forest is too large for anyone to know it well, but you have explored more of it than most people, I gather. Have you been along this 'Way Through', the one they appear to be following?"

"Yes, at least I think I have. It took me five days from end to end. It is very convoluted and almost disappears in places. It winds around a marshland and through some of the tallest timber and thickest brush in the forest. I followed what I thought was the trail, but I may have missed a turning that had become overgrown. It is so obscure and so rarely used that sometimes I wasn't sure that I wasn't just bashing my way through."

"So they won't be making very good time," said Maud, straightening from the table. "That is mildly encouraging."

"They will have covered several miles tonight." Stefan carefully didn't meet her eyes so that she could stay focused, but it wasn't necessary; Maud had herself well in hand, now. "But you couldn't travel that path in the dark. So they will have to stay somewhere, probably in one of the abandoned buildings, and leave early tomorrow morning." He grimaced. "Unfortunately, the same applies to Jon and his company. In fact, even more so, I'm afraid, because they will need enough light to follow the abductors' tracks."

Maud heaved a sigh of frustration. "If we travel back to Highkington tonight, we won't arrive until the early hours of the morning. Even if we set out at dawn, just as they will be doing, we will be tired while they are fresh, and we will be at least five or six hours behind."

"And you can't take horses, ma'am. It is far too overgrown for them to be able to force their way through."

Maud looked down at herself and gave a wry smile, "I may appear unfit; solid is how Sasha describes me, but I could easily keep up with you and Sheldrake or whoever accompanied us, on foot. I travel with much less effort as a four-legged animal, perhaps a wolf or large cat... "

Stefan grinned, unaware that he had already been visited by her in the form of a grey cat. "I would be entranced to see it, ma'am."

Marjorie straightened from where she had been studying the map and stood for a moment, a frown between her straight black brows. Obviously too preoccupied to appreciate the moment of light-heartedness, she announced, "I think we need a different approach. Going back to Highkington is completely counterproductive." Before anyone could object, she raised her hand to stop them. "Think about it. You are already twenty miles east of Highkington. I'm guessing they are only ten miles east at the most. It's just they're further south..."

"And cutting the diagonal. So they'll have less distance to travel to Manissa, the Kimoran capital," Stefan pointed to the path on the map "They'll have a longer distance to reach the border than a direct route, maybe one hundred miles, with the path's twists and turns, but they'll hit it a lot further south."

"True, but I think we are all agreed that we can't allow them to get across the border." They were all a little taken aback by Marjorie's sudden decisiveness. "Now Stefan, how far south is this track, and do you know of any tracks that intercept it along the way?"

Sheldrake was nodding his head in appreciation. "Good thought, Marjorie. Stefan?"

"The path begins in the south east corner of Highkington. So that's about eighteen miles south of the start of Park Lane. But it drifts further south as it goes east. By the time it is due south of here, I would say it is forty-five miles south and by the time it reaches the Charville River, it would be... hmm, about seventy-five miles south of Park Lane. But it's not straight by any means, so these are very rough calculations." He leant over the map and propped his head on his elbow as he considered the possibilities. "Hmm. I know a few paths that go south from here, but most of them stop within a few miles." He grimaced. "Actually, *all* the paths I know of stop within a few miles of here. I suppose we could trail-blaze our way through, but it would be difficult. There's a reason other people haven't done it before."

Jackson tapped Stefan's elbow. "Hoy. Move your arm."

Stefan sent him a frown of irritation but complied.

Once he could see the whole map again, Jackson pointed to the eastern half of the forest. "What about the river?"

Stefan stood up suddenly, clearly about to point out how impossible that idea was. Then he paused. "Huh. Let me think about it. It is way longer than the route they will be taking. We would be doing two sides of a triangle while they cut the corner; thirty miles to Bridgetown then, as the crows flies, about seventy-five miles south along the river." He pulled his mouth down at the corners, "But as the river flows, probably more like one hundred and twenty miles, at least, but it would be an easier trip. Not sure whether we'd get to the other end of The Way Through in time though."

A small frown flitted across Marjorie's brow at this last piece of information. "So Stefan, where along the river did you come out when you reached the end of that path, The Way Through?"

Stefan glanced at his sister, so much taller and darker-haired than he. Then he scrunched his face in embarrassment and confessed. "I don't know."

There was an incredulous silence.

A low chuckle came from the armchair in the corner where Tarkyn was sipping his way through the rest of the bottle of port. "*Stefan!*" he exclaimed in mock severity. "How could you? And you were doing so well." Stefan frowned, but Tarkyn smiled sunnily back at him.

"I'm sorry, but no," Maud interrupted them firmly. "That river is the Kimoran border. It is too risky to let them get so close to Kimora before intercepting them. We must find a way through the forest."

Tarkyn nodded his agreement. "Don't worry. We will. You can fly reconnaissance as can Bird, my eagle. We also have the possible resource of the local woodfolk and we definitely have my home guard. I can contact many creatures of the woodlands if need be… forest guardian, remember?… I am sure between us, we will find a way through to your little ones."

"Are you coming with us?" asked Maud, surprised. "I thought you had other priorities."

Tarkyn raised his eyebrows. "I did, until this one came along. I still do, but there is no way in the world that I will leave your dear little son and your dear little stable hand to the machinations of an immoral monarch." Anyone who knew Tarkyn would realise that he had possibly drunk too much, but his sentiments were genuine. He waved his arm, encompassing everyone in the room. "I presume all of you will be coming on the search for Sasha and Jayhan? How could you not?"

Marjorie looked flustered. "I would love to come, but I…"

"You will come with us," said Tarkyn firmly. "Your parents have plenty of help to manage without you for the next week or two. It was your idea after all to cut them off."

Stefan grinned at her. "Well done, sis. Come on. Here's your chance to get out of the pub and see some of the places you hear people talking about."

And Marjorie, her eyes shining with excitement, nodded her head.

Tarkyn unfolded his long frame from the armchair and stood for a moment, checking his balance. The port was strong and he had perhaps imbibed too much. He gave a little smile as he realized his balance was unaffected. Then he transferred his attention to the others in the room. "I will bid you goodnight. I am, of course, off into the forest, to spend the night with Lapping Water… and Midnight… and Gurgling Brook."

From the other people's point of view, there was no 'of course' about it and they all looked surprised.

Tarkyn grinned at their expressions. "You assumed a prince would prefer to stay in this comfortable inn? No. I love my family and my woodfolk friends and they have walked more than a hundred miles to join me. I can neglect them no longer. Jackson and Stefan, could you walk with me some of the way, please? We have arrangements to make for tomorrow."

As they approached the woodfolk's firesite, Rainstorm suddenly appeared next to them and proceeded to walk beside them. "So, tell us. Have they found the little ones yet? Do they know where they are? Can we help?"

"Hello, Rainstorm. No. Yes. Yes," replied Tarkyn as they walked into the firelight. "They have a rough idea of the children's location. They are being taken along a trail in the forest some forty-five miles south of here. We will cut further to the east to intercept them."

The woodfolk were relaxing around the fire, glasses of wine bedside them. The fire cast huge shadows of them against the surrounding trees. Gurgling Brook was asleep, curled up on Lapping Water's lap, while Midnight and Sparrow were snuggled up on either side of Waterstone.

Waterstone breathed out a long sigh. "South east, eh? Even further from Eskuzor."

"I'm sorry, Waterstone, I know you're all tired but…" Tarkyn paused, searching his friend's eyes, knowing that behind the rigid adherence to woodfolk principles was a kind, strong man who had befriended him when all other woodfolk shunned him, exactly because his woodfolk principles insisted that he treat all people as equal. "These two little children need our help… and their kidnappers intend to torture one of them to force compliance from the other." He shook his head. "We can't let that happen, not while there is something we can do to stop it."

Waterstone snorted. "No, of course we can't."

"Tea or wine?" queried Autumn Leaves of the three newcomers, preparing to rise.

"Stay there. I'll get it." said Stefan, heading over to the cache of leftover wine.

"We've been talking to some of the local woodfolk, you know," said Autumn Leaves. "We don't think they are involved with this unpleasant Kimoran queen, but predictably, they could not understand what business it was of theirs that one set of outsiders was abducting another set."

Stefan poured out three glasses of wine, kept one for himself and handed the other two to Jackson and Tarkyn. "Anyone else?" When he had topped up glasses, he sat himself down and took a sip. Then, as his eyes travelled around the group, a big grin slowly spread across his face, completely out of keeping with the spirit of their discussion about abducted children. He tried, unsuccessfully, to hide it by burying his face in his glass.

Lapping Water smiled back at him from across the fire and in response to her mindmessage, Autumn Leaves, Waterstone and Rainstorm focused on him and smiled, too.

Jackson and Tarkyn, watching them, also smiled but they were the audience while the others were the participants.

"I believe," murmured Tarkyn, "that our arms master is enjoying being surrounded by people who look like him. It has been a lifelong bone of contention for him that he looks so different from his family."

Jackson suddenly realised that he was the only non-woodfolk among them and immediately felt that he was intruding. Some of this must have shown on his face because Autumn Leaves looked across at him to say, "You're fine, Jackson. Consider yourself an honorary member of Tarkyn's home guard. After all, you *are* working with him."

Jackson noticed that he didn't say 'working for' and remembered their views about ranks. He smiled to himself as he realised that in their eyes, he held equal status with his country's ultimate authority. "Thanks," he said, meaning it in more ways than one.

Stefan and he only stayed long enough to finish their drinks, by which time they had sketched out plans for the morrow. They took their leave, knowing they had a lot to do and a short time to do it in before their departure.

Chapter 40

Well before dawn the next morning, Sheldrake and Maud were seated in the public bar, eating a quick breakfast. Anton was waiting on them while Marjorie dashed in and out asking last minute questions about what to take. Ten minutes later, Stefan and Jackson returned from the rear of the inn to join them.

"Everything is packed and ready to go," reported Stefan.

"But where is Lord Tarkyn?' asked Maud impatiently. "We are ready to leave."

Jackson gave an apologetic smile. "His woodfolk are exhausted after yesterday. They walked all morning, had to flee through the forest in the afternoon, followed by stressful confrontations and negotiations with the locals in the evening."

Maud was unimpressed. "Lord Tarkyn didn't walk miles in the morning. He was here with us."

"Oh." Jackson looked startled. "Didn't you realise? Lord Tarkyn's woodfolk are coming with us, to help retrieve your son... and Sasha, of course."

"Good Lord! That's most decent of them," exclaimed Sheldrake. "I thought they were just going to tell us how to get to The Way Through."

Maud's face screwed up with worry. "But we have to leave as soon as possible. Time is of the essence. I can't possibly just sit around, waiting for them to get up. I'll go mad."

Jackson gave a little bow with his head and said, "Lord Tarkyn said to tell you, that is, to *suggest* to you, that Stefan and I guide you for the first part of the morning and meet them further down the track."

Maud's eyes flashed. "There is a certain high-handedness in that young man's approach."

"Yes, ma'am. I believe the woodfolk berate him frequently for being arrogant and he is, after all, used to his word being law in Eskuzor, although obviously it is not, here in Carrador."

"I may perhaps have to remind him that he has no authority over me," said Maud, prepared to battle it out with him when she next saw him.

Jackson's eyes shone with poorly suppressed mirth, "As to that, ma'am, he authorized me to apologize in advance for his presumption and to explain that he, too, has family responsibilities and, perhaps more importantly, that his little daughter would not be an asset if she were too tired." He couldn't help adding with a grin, "And I think he prefers to sleep in, if possible."

The frown disappeared from Maud's face and she grinned back. "The man is incorrigible. Very well. Sheldrake and I will leave in ten minutes."

"By the way, Stefan," said Sheldrake, "I have sent the King's messengers back to Highkington to inform Josie of our plans, and the King, of course, if he has returned. I have also sent a message to Leon to take charge of the network while I am gone. He's my second-in-command." He shot Jackson and Stefan a glance. "No one else knows, of course. It would never occur to anyone that my coachman-henchman would have any real authority."

"He's always struck me as pretty clever," said Stefan. He chuckled. "No wonder you couldn't trick him into fighting me."

Sheldrake gave a slight smile. "His big, bovine, ignorant look is just his disguise. We both do everything we can to perpetuate it." He rose from the table. "Shall we go, my dear?"

They emerged into a cold, grey morning, misty rain drifting through the trees. The light had come up just enough to see by, but it was not yet full daylight.

Rather self-consciously, both Maud and Marjorie were wearing leggings, not their usual billowing skirts. Sheldrake, Stefan and Jackson pretended not to notice.

Maud frowned when she saw only four backpacks waiting for them. She looked around at her companions. "Which of us is not coming?"

Jackson grinned. "We are all coming. It is just another of Lord Tarkyn's suggestions that it would be better if your belongings were distributed amongst our packs."

Maud raised her eyebrows, once again displeased with Tarkyn's high-handedness. "And why is that? I am perfectly capable of carrying my own pack."

The colour heightened in Jackson's cheeks. "I believe it is so that you can shapeshift if need be, without then leaving a pack that someone else would have to carry."

Her eyes narrowed while she thought this over. "I would have preferred him to discuss it with me but…" She let out a breath. "I can see the merit in it. In that case, I will take turns with Marjorie for the time being."

An hour and a half later, the track they were following petered out at a pleasant little picnic spot near a burbling stream. Stefan swung his pack off his shoulders. "This is as far as I can guide you. Now it is up to the woodfolk."

Moments later, Tarkyn's woodfolk melted out of the seeming impenetrable stand of bush and brambles that barred their track. Tarkyn himself walked up from the stream in muddy boots, holding Gurgling Brook's hand.

"Good morning," he said cheerily, holding up an old cup triumphantly. "Look what we have caught. You show them, Gurgling Brook."

Smiling proudly, the little girl brought the cup over to the new arrivals. Inside it was a large spray of gum leaves and some soap. When Maud looked puzzled, Tarkyn said, "Look under the gum leaves."

Maud gingerly pushed the gum leaves aside and found herself looking at a dozen little freshwater crayfish.

"Yabbies," announced Gurgling Brook.

Maud smiled. "Very good. How exciting."

The little girl nodded, beaming.

Seeing Maud's uncertainty, Tarkyn said, "These ones are a bit small for eating but very good for bait. Rainstorm and I may do a bit of fishing later to see if we can catch something for dinner." He intercepted her gathering frown by adding, "… if we have a break near a stream."

"I might join you in that, if I may," said Sheldrake, as he dropped his pack on the ground and unstoppered his water flask.

"Of course."

"And me," chorused Jackson, Marjorie and Stefan, with varying degrees of assertion.

Midnight, seeming to understand what they were saying, looked up at Tarkyn and smiled while Maud became very busy putting her pack down and not looking at anyone. Without even thinking about it, Tarkyn sent her a wave of warm strength. "We'll have to make sure we do some fishing with Jayhan and Sasha on the way back, won't we?"

She raised glistening eyes and nodded.

Rainstorm walked over and put his hand on her back. "We can't promise to bring them back safely, Maud, but we can promise you that we will give you all the help we can. And remember; within the forests, the skills and knowledge of outsiders are no match for ours." There was no hint of bragging in his voice. His calm assurance steadied her more than any empty promise could have. Then he smiled cheekily. "I like your leggings by the way. Yours too, Marjorie. Much more practical."

Maud's returning equanimity was once more overset, but this time by embarrassment.

Rainstorm chortled. "Don't worry, Maud. None of the people at your court need ever know. And here in the forest, you can merely think of it as fitting in with the mode of dress worn by one of the highest-ranking women in Eskuzor."

"Rainstorm! Stop it," snapped Lapping Water, scowling furiously at him. "You know I don't think of myself like that."

Rainstorm turned an unrepentant grin on her. "Of course I know. You and I don't give a fig about rank, but I bet Maud does."

Maud was saved from replying to this by the appearance of Sphagnum Moss, Tree Fern and Spinifex, accompanied by two woodfolk, previously unknown to them. A woodwoman of late middle age, statuesque and graceful with long silver hair shimmering down her back stood next to a ruggedly handsome woodman of similar age. The woodwoman held such an aura about her that everyone stopped what they were doing or saying to stare at her. She showed no sign of nervousness even though she had almost certainly never met outsiders before. The man beside her, however, was taut with wariness.

She bestowed a smile on them. "Good morning. Welcome to our forests. I am Silverwood, healer and keeper of the lore." Her voice flowed over them, rich and deep.

Stefan frowned. "Like a bailiff?"

She gave a slight shake of her head. "No. A storyteller. I tell and listen to the stories and legends of the woodfolk and make sure they are told truly. You, Tarkyn, and you, Midnight, spring from our legends and will become part of our future legends." She turned to Stefan. "As will you. Already the woods are ringing with the story of your loss in the great flood, your extraordinary upbringing among outsiders and your reappearance among us. It is truly a wondrous tale."

Stefan's face reddened and he crossed his arms, looking acutely uncomfortable.

Silverwood smiled and the whole area seemed to light up. "Unlike the forest guardian, you are not used to such attention." She paused for a moment, giving him time. "Stefan, in the days since it became known that you are a woodman, have you not wondered who your actual birth family is?"

Stefan glanced uncomfortably at Marjorie, before looking back at Silverwood and muttering, "Constantly."

"So too have we," she said, rather to the surprise of her listeners. "Many people were lost in that flood. Not just you. Two newborn male babies were among those lost, along with their mothers. Their fathers, who happened to be rostered on to guard duty high in the trees at the time, both survived. An hour earlier and it would have been the mothers safe in the trees and the fathers swept away. Thus are the vagaries of fate." She gestured at the unknown man. "This is Ironbark. Ironbark and Spinifex are my brothers. Spinifex was married to Flowering Gum and Ironbark was married to Wattle Bird. They are the fathers of those two lost babies. Sphagnum Moss is your grandfather and Tree Fern is Spinifex's daughter." She waved an arm that took in all four of the people with her. "We do not know which of them is your father and which your uncle. We could think of no way that we could work it out. But all of us are your family," she moved her gaze to Marjorie, "and yours."

Ironbark hesitated, then walked over to Stefan, even though he stood close to outsiders, and placed his hand self-consciously on his shoulder. "I welcome you back into our family. I am sorry I was not present last night, but I was on lookout duty," he said in a deep, mellow voice. He turned to look up at Marjorie and took a quick breath. "I also welcome you." He gave a lopsided smile. "That wasn't as warm as I meant it to be, but I'm a bit nervous meeting you for the first time. I will thaw over time."

Marjorie smiled and flung her arm around his neck in a hug. He nearly jerked back but stopped himself. "There. That will progress things faster," she said with the cheery warmth of the Vines. "I welcome you to our family, too."

Ironbark gradually returned her embrace and included Stefan in it.

Silverwood approached them more slowly and hovered a little beyond their reach. Suddenly Stefan realised that despite her apparent poise, she was more unsure than Ironbark. He disengaged himself and walked over to her. "So, you are my aunt then and Tree Fern is my cousin…or sister?"

She nodded but made no move. As he stood there wondering what to do next, Marjorie sailed past him and put her arms around both of them. Ignoring Silverwood's lack of effusion, she said, "So look at you, little brother. Two uncle/fathers and an aunty. Plus a grandfather and a cousin-sister."

Stiffly, Silverwood put her arms around them, completing the triangle, while Ironbark stood grinning at them. "Silverwood, they won't bite."

"Be quiet, Ironbark," she threw at him. "I am doing my best. It is not my usual practice to hug complete strangers."

It was now some time since they had reached the end of the track and Maud, although pleased for Stefan, was restraining herself from dancing from one foot to the other in her impatience to be gone.

Seeing this, Jackson spoke up for the first time. "How do you do, Stefan's family? I am Jackson. Do you intend to accompany us because I'm afraid we cannot linger here much longer?"

Spinifex replied, his voice thinner and scratchier than his sister's. "Maud and Sheldrake, I believe your children have been taken. We understand such loss, but we have never involved ourselves in the affairs of outsiders."

"You're bound to take more of an interest now," said Jackson tartly. "Your son or nephew is an outsider as much as he is a woodman." He shrugged. "Besides, your forests are now rife with Kimoran refugees and special forces because of this false Kimoran queen, Toriana. Surely this must be inconvenient for you."

"It is," said Silverwood. "Until Autumn Leaves explained the situation to us last night, we had not realised why so many people were in our forests."

Spinifex looked at Stefan. "What is your connection to these abducted children, Stefan?" he asked.

"I live at the house of Sheldrake and Maud, working as an arms master to train them and their staff to protect these two children. I am also developing the children's fighting skills. Sasha and Jayhan matter a great deal to me. They are almost family."

A brief mental conference concluded with Ironbark saying to Stefan. "Then, if these children matter to you, we will help you find them. Consider it a gesture of..." he shrugged, "friendship, kinship, solidarity... welcome." Then he gave a self-conscious laugh. "I sound silly. I simply mean that woodfolk work together. As a woodman and particularly as a member of our family, you merit our assistance, if it matters to you. That is all."

"Besides," said Spinifex with a flash of humour, "these Eskuzorian woodfolk have no hope of finding their way quickly through our forests."

"He's right, of course," said Waterstone. "We could get you there, but we don't know the fastest routes. I'm glad you're coming with us."

Chapter 41

Once they had woven their way through a mile of dense thickets, the first day of the journey took them south east through light woodlands where the travelling was easy.

Halfway through the morning, Ironbark noticed an eagle circling high above them in the clear morning sky. He pointed up and said. "Unusual for a mountain eagle to be this far from the Darkstone Mountains. They are usually further south on the eastern side of the Charville River."

Autumn Leaves watched to make sure, then smiled at the woodman. "No. She is a long way *south* of her territory, not north. That is Bird, Tarkyn's eagle. Make sure your woodfolk know not to shoot at her when she comes in to land."

"We never shoot raptors," said Ironbark, with a hint of censure. "Do you?"

Autumn Leaves glanced at him. "No, but I wasn't sure how similar our creeds were."

Even as he spoke, they could see that the eagle was gradually losing height and as they crossed a clearing where an old tree had fallen, the huge black and gold eagle glided in at speed to land neatly but with great force on Tarkyn's shoulder. Tarkyn staggered backwards but managed to keep his feet under him. Then, as she turned to face forward, her tail brushed across his face.

"Ah phtewy," grumbled Tarkyn, his face full of feathers. "Can't you turn the other way, you annoying bird?"

Bird just ignored him and ran her beak down a strand of his long black hair as though grooming him. Autumn Leaves laughed while Ironbark boggled.

"She does it and he does it, every time," chuckled Autumn Leaves. "It's almost a ritual for them."

"Great, isn't it?" Stefan was grinning. "I've only seen it a couple of times. It's wonderful, and the funny thing is Tarkyn just thinks it's a pest having to carry her. See? He has pads sewn on his shirt so that her talons don't destroy his shoulder."

Tarkyn, inevitably, heard them. "It's a pest to have to carry her but I don't think *she's* a pest. I love her dearly. But she weighs more each year. She was just a baby when I first got to know her. Well, not a baby exactly, but quite young. She was heavy then but now she must weigh close to ten pounds."

"And is this part of being a forest guardian, having a familiar animal?" asked Ironbark.

"Not that I'm aware of." Tarkyn flexed his shoulder under her weight while she bobbed contentedly up and down as he walked. "Though I suppose it is a consequence of it. I asked her to track some people for me when she was younger, but she flew too close to them and was speared by an arrow. I rescued her and brought her back to health, which was the least I could do, since she had been helping me at the time. But since then, she has never wanted to leave. I hope one day she'll find a mate, an eagle mate, not me, and raise a family." He smiled and raised his hand to stroke her. "But I would not want to lose contact with her."

Tree Fern kept a covert eye on Stefan as they walked. He noticed but didn't say anything, giving her time to get used to being around outsiders. Besides, he was feeling awkward and couldn't think of anything to talk about. He was just about to comment on the lovely sunny morning when she said abruptly, "You're leaving tracks, you know."

He looked at her in mild surprise. "Does it matter? No one is after us, are they?"

"We *never* leave tracks. Never."

"Oh."

From the other side of him, but in a friendlier tone of voice, Ironbark joined the conversation. "If we did, sooner or later, someone would see them and wonder who had been here."

"It is not just luck that no one has learnt of our existence," added Spinifex. "We work hard at it."

"Oh dear," said Stefan, looking flustered. "I'm a failed woodman before I even start."

Tree Fern sidestepped a dusty patch of path, stepping lightly from stone to stone. "Of course you are. You haven't had our years of training."

"Actually, he has," said Rainstorm, coming to his new friend's rescue. "It's just been different from ours. He is a master arms man, you know. He can hold his own against us in archery. He is so good at weaponry that he teaches other people."

"But we haven't had time to teach him any specialist woodcraft skills yet," said Autumn Leaves. "He only met woodfolk for the first time yesterday. So give him a break. And Tarkyn showed him mindtalking only a few days ago, mostly to check out whether he was truly a woodman. He hasn't even had time to learn the full extent of image and memory sharing."

Up ahead, Silverwood stopped and looked back at Stefan. "Don't let Tree Fern wind you up, Stefan. We will teach you. In fact, you will have to learn if you wish to spend any time with us. But it is our fault, not yours, that you have gaps in your training." She turned a stern glare on her niece. "And just you remember that, young lady, and be kind."

Tree Fern's eyes narrowed and she looked anything but repentant.

Gradually, the land began to rise and soon, people were saving their breath for walking. Silverwood and Spinifex led them unerringly between the tumbled boulders that lay along the crest of a line of hills, following a narrow, convoluted trail that led to a viewing point where they could look out across the wooded hills to the south. Below them, white water gushed over cataracts into a river below.

"That's not the Charville River, is it?" asked Maud in some alarm.

"No." Silverwood's voice was soothing. "That is much further east. This is the Wandigo River. A lot smaller than the Charville. It has even been known to dry up completely."

"Not often though," said Sphagnum Moss, who was leaning heavily on his walking stave after the long walk uphill. "It springs from the caves that riddle these hills. So it has to be a bad drought indeed, for it to dry up."

Ironbark pointed to the distant horizon. "The Way Through is still far to the south. From what you have said, we need to keep heading southeast. So, we can follow this river for a while, but eventually it turns due east to flow into the Charville."

Bird, whose grip on Tarkyn's shoulder had been taxed by the constant change of direction among the boulders, chose that moment to launch herself off into the space above the falls. Warned by the tighter grip on his shoulder and the tensing of her leg muscles, Tarkyn thrust his right leg backwards to counteract her push from his left shoulder. Bird spread her wings and soared out to circle over the falls, her black and gold wings shining in the sunlight.

"Oh! She is beautiful," breathed Silverwood.

They watched her in awed silence, taking the opportunity to catch their breaths after the long upward incline. When they could drag themselves away, Spinifex led them back from the lookout for a hundred yards before turning hard left, to take them down a steep, narrow path that paralleled the course of the falls. The trees were denser and greener on the steep slope, kept moist by the spray from the falls. The ground underfoot was muddy and slippery, forcing them to hang on to fern fronds or mossy branches as they passed, to keep from sliding.

Three quarters of the way down, Sphagnum Moss lost his footing. He fell heavily and skittered for several yards before he could grab a passing plant to stop himself. Unfortunately, the plant he grabbed was the leaf of a stinging tree. The old man sat hunched in the middle of the path, cradling his stung hand and resisting the impulse to rub it. His face was drawn with pain.

Maud, who had been preceding him, turned back and bent over him. "Are you all right? Have you broken anything? Can you stand?"

"Stinging tree," he managed to gasp.

"Oh no," breathed Silverwood as she glided down the path to reach him. "Oh dear. We'll need something for the pain and some resin."

Maud looked confused. "What has happened? What stinging plant?"

Silverwood looked up and down the path at the party strung out in either direction. "Oh dear. We should have told you. Please listen, everyone. Within these damper forests, a stinging plant grows. It is much more vicious than a normal stinging nettle." She pointed to an innocuous looking plant with slightly furry, spade-shaped leaves, that was growing beside the path next to Sphagnum Moss. "Look. It produces a severe sting, not just when you touch it but for months afterwards. Every time you wash your hand the pain will return. Sphagnum Moss has just grasped one." Her voice became directive. "Spinifex, Tree Fern, Ironbark, we need some resin. See if you can find a black wattle tree or a gum tree that is exuding some. If we can warm the resin and put it on his hand, the tiny barbs may stick to it and we should be able to pull most of them out."

She reached into a pouch she had strapped around her waist and pulled out a small bundle. "Pa, we have to get you down the hill. Can someone go ahead and boil up some water to steep willow bark for the pain, please?" She leant over and tried to get her hand under his elbow without touching the hand that was stinging.

"Wait!" said Tarkyn firmly, coming up behind the old man. "You go ahead and get things ready, Silverwood. I will take Sphagnum Moss down the hill."

She looked dubiously at him. "Don't touch his hand or that plant," she warned him.

"I won't." Tarkyn leant over Sphagnum Moss. "Take a deep breath. I am going to lift you off the ground and down the path. Are you ready?" When he nodded, Tarkyn intoned, "*Ka liefka,*" and lifted Sphagnum Moss into the air on the end of a shaft of bronze magic.

Sphagnum Moss let out an undignified squawk. "Aah! Oh! That sort of lift!"

Grinning slightly but maintaining his concentration, Tarkyn carefully sidled past those ahead of him on the path, intoned, *"Kaya Reeza Mureva,"* and glided Sphagnum Moss through the air in front of him, to deposit him gently on his feet at the point where the ground levelled out. Autumn Leaves was waiting to hold him steady as he landed, while Waterstone and Sparrow were already gathering wood for a fire.

Silverwood led them to a clearing where they could set up a firesite and solicitously settled Sphagnum Moss against a log.

"It's damp here," he grumbled. "I'm going to get wet trousers."

"Good," she said, obviously used to his grumpiness. "It'll keep your mind off the pain."

"Huh," and, after a moment, "it'll take more than that."

Tarkyn walked into the clearing with a small bundle of sticks that he dropped where Lapping Water was setting the fire. He ruffled the top of her head affectionately and she smiled up at him briefly before he turned to Silverwood. "Tell me about this stinging plant. Can my healing powers help?"

"I don't know. The problem is that the little barbs break off inside the skin and stay there for months until the body gradually expels them. If we can drop liquid resin onto Pa's hand and let it harden, then hopefully the barbs will stick to it and be pulled out." She screwed up her face. "Trouble is, we may burn Pa's hand in the process."

"Oh, don't worry about that," said Tarkyn airily. "I can fix that."

"And," continued Silverwood, "it probably won't get them all out, but it is the best we can do. That and painkillers."

Tarkyn squatted down in front of the old man. "Show me your hand." When the old man's eyes narrowed, he added, "Please. I promise I won't lift you up again."

"Just make sure you tell me what you're doing next time." Sphagnum Moss held out his hand, palm up. It was a little pink but nothing to indicate that apparent degree of pain.

"I did. You just misunderstood."

Sphagnum Moss growled. "Of course I did. We've never seen anything like that before."

Completely unfazed by the old man's irritation, Tarkyn grinned. "I promise I'll be clearer next time." He inspected Sphagnum Moss's hand but couldn't really see anything, then sat back on his haunches. "Let me think about it while you prepare the bark and resin. And I'll be standing by to heal your hand if it gets burnt."

Just then Stefan entered the clearing at a dead run and rushed over. He held out his hand to Silverwood, showing her several knobs of amber coloured, hardened resin. One of them was hard on the outside and still contained liquid resin on the inside. "Look. I found some."

The healer raised her eyebrows. "Well done, nephew. I didn't think you would know what to look for."

Stefan smiled with a hint of pride. "I use wax and resins for my bow strings and I teach the use and care of weaponry. Not quite the same but I know what to look out for."

Silverwood's smile dawned. "A mixture of wax and resin is just what we need, but we need a higher concentration of resin than you would use for your weapons."

"Just a minute. I'll get you some of the stuff I use for my bowstring and you can add this resin to it," Stefan offered.

Ironbark and Spinifex returned, also bearing resin, just as the wax and the resin Stefan had collected were being placed in a small pot on the fire to heat until they liquified. They seemed unconcerned about their efforts being unneeded and gave the resin they had collected into Silverwood's safekeeping.

Once the mixture was ready, Silverwood applied it to Sphagnum Moss's hand. The old man, for all his grumbling, bit down and barely made a noise as the hot liquid made contact with his palm. He endured in silence as the mixture of resin and wax hardened.

When Silverwood peeled the wax and resin away, the skin of his palm was red but not burnt. "Any better?"

Sphagnum Moss frowned as he thought about it. "Hard to tell. My poor hand has been battered by poison and now by heat. I think the stinging has eased but not completely. Can't tell yet if it's the poison that's still stinging, or whether there are barbs left in there. If it's just the poison, it will ease soon, I suppose." He gave a gruff smile. "Thank you, my dear, and thank you, everyone, for trying."

"Would you like me give you *esse*, my healing power?" asked Tarkyn.

The old man waved his hand irritably. "No. Not right now. Don't crowd me. I just need some time to gather my resources."

Sparrow, who was on her way over to him with a carefully prepared cup of steeped willow bark, hesitated, unsure what to do.

Sphagnum Moss waved her over to him. "It's all right, girlie. What's your name?"

"Sparrow."

"It's all right, Sparrow. I need that... and a cup of tea afterwards wouldn't go amiss. Dreadfully bitter is willow bark."

Chapter 42

They made good progress for the next few hours, although Sphagnum Moss struggled to keep up. He had jarred his right hip when he had fallen, and he could only hold his staff in his right hand because his left hand still stung whenever it brushed anything.

By mid-afternoon, Tarkyn could stand it no more. When they stopped for a tea break, he walked over to Sphagnum Moss and sat down beside him. "Sphagnum Moss, I admire stoicism as much as the next man, but your unnecessary suffering is distressing me. I don't know whether I can fix your hand, but I can definitely fix your hip, if you'll allow me to."

"Don't force him," said Tree Fern, coming to sit on the other side of her grandfather as she handed him a cup of tea.

Perversely, that was enough for Sphagnum Moss to agree. "I don't need protecting, Tree Fern. I am perfectly capable of sticking up for myself," he grouched. He cocked his head at Tarkyn. "Your healing power comes from being a forest guardian, doesn't it?"

Tarkyn just waited and after a moment, the old man gave a decisive nod. "I'd be mad to pass up an opportunity like this. When it first happened, I was befuddled by the pain and the care from all directions but I'm all right now." He nodded. "Go ahead, young man. What do I need to do?"

"Tree Fern, could you take your grandfather's cup and put it out of the way for a few minutes, please? Then put your hand on his back to keep him steady. We don't want him falling backwards off this log while he's concentrating on the healing."

Sphagnum Moss narrowed his eyes, suspecting, quite rightly, that Tarkyn was including the young woodwoman simply to sidestep her opposition. But he said nothing.

"In a minute, I will ask you to close your eyes. Then I will place my hand on your shoulder and follow my *esse*, my healing power, down into your body. It will feel like a warm stream. Firstly, I will direct the power to your hip, then your hand. If your hand suddenly hurts, don't worry. The feeling will pass."

Waterstone stood close by, cup of tea in hand, watching. "Why might his hand hurt? Healing is not usually painful."

"I don't really know how to counter any barbs or poison that might be left, but it occurred to me that I might treat them as invaders, as I did the virus that attacked Rushwind a few years ago."

Waterstone nodded. "Worth a try."

"Ready, Sphagnum Moss?"

The old man nodded and closed his eyes. Immediately, Tarkyn placed his hand on his shoulder, felt inside himself to his core then sent his *esse* down his arm into Sphagnum Moss. He let it flow down into the damaged hip, soothing and repairing damaged blood vessels and strengthening the tendons. Then he returned briefly to the site of his own hand on Sphagnum Moss's shoulder, to orient himself before coursing his actual consciousness down to the aggravated left hand. Even from within, he could not see the tiny barbs and he could certainly not see the residual poison. But he knew how to counter invasions. Tarkyn drew on his outrage at the concept of the woodman being assailed by outside forces and sent forth a short, sharp blast of anger that burnt through the area around the damaged palm.

Outside, Sphagnum Moss grunted with pain and a short gasp escaped his lips. Tree Fern went to knock Tarkyn's arm away but was stopped by Waterstone.

"Don't you dare," he growled.

A soft warmth coursed through Sphagnum Moss's hand as the abused flesh was soothed. Then he felt the warmth contract up into his shoulder and dissipate entirely. He opened his eyes and looked down at his hand. He carefully flexed his fingers then, gingerly at first, rubbed his hand against the front of his shirt.

"Huh." He smiled broadly and stood up, giving his injured leg a shake. "Huh. That was amazing, truly amazing. Well done, young man, and thank you for your perseverance in getting me to agree to it."

The party was able to move faster after that and by dusk, they had reached the point where the river curved to flow due east. Close by, a sheltered clearing within tall river gums provided a suitable firesite and once they were unpacked and a fire had been lit, a keen group of anglers headed for the river to use Gurgling Brook's yabbies.

Most of the anglers used hand lines wrapped around short, thick sticks, but Lapping Water rigged up a pole with a long piece of line dangling from its end for Gurgling Brook and Midnight to hold so they didn't get their line tangled.

Stefan was diverted from joining them by Rainstorm, who gestured for him to come into the trees away from the others. As soon as they were alone, Rainstorm pointed up into the trees above them. "Look. Autumn Leaves is on lookout duty on this side. So I... we, thought I could teach you how to flick and merge into your surroundings before you get any more grief from your relatives. There is still a lot more to learn, but at least you would know the basics."

Stefan's eyes gleamed with excitement. "I'd like that. I'm dying to learn how to flick. The older relatives aren't unkind, just a bit incredulous. It's only Tree Fern who's snaky about it. I don't think she likes me being foisted into her family."

"No... Maybe not," admitted Rainstorm cautiously. "She's been Sphagnum Moss's only grandchild until now and she seemed pretty possessive of him even before you came along, let alone now."

Stefan nodded. "I think I'll have to tread carefully."

"And she's either your sister or your cousin, and you don't know which man is your uncle and which is your father. That must feel pretty weird." Rainstorm was busy scouting around the gaps between the trees looking for an easy spot to flick to, but he glanced at Stefan to gauge his reaction.

Stefan shook his head from side to side a few times, filled with confusion. "Very weird. I had envisaged a mum, a dad and one or two siblings. Nothing like this. I'm glad I have Ivan, rock solid in my background, to fall back on. He is my real dad, as far as I'm concerned. Ironbark and Spinifex? Well, they feel like a fiction someone is trying to impose on me."

"Give it time." Rainstorm hesitated then stood to face Stefan. "It must matter hugely to them. Ironbark and Spinifex each lost a son and a nephew. And now here you are, and they don't even know which of them you belong to. They too must be feeling uncertain and confused... and sad, too."

Stefan gave an unhappy shrug. "Hard, isn't it? For all of us."

"Yep. Very. Anyway, I'm here to talk to, if you need me. And Autumn Leaves and Lapping Water and Waterstone. We can help you understand the woodfolk perspective outside the fraught knots of your new family." Without waiting for a response, he clapped Stefan on his back. "Now, come on. Let's do some flicking."

By the time, Stefan was ready to re-join the anglers, Marjorie and Jackson had already headed back with three good-sized fish to begin dinner preparations. Ironbark and Spinifex were still seated on the riverbank, fishing peacefully, when Stefan appeared suddenly between them, his face flushed with pride and a hint of embarrassment. They started, then laughed in pleasure at Stefan's achievement.

"Well done, young one," said Spinifex, with the ease of someone who was already a father.

Ironbark just smiled warmly at him and said nothing.

In the next instant, Stefan appeared beside Midnight, grinning his head off. Even before the little boy had finished reacting, Stefan had disappeared to reappear between Sparrow and Tree Fern.

His antics drew a reluctant smile from Tree Fern, who said, "It's not a game, you know. It's a survival skill."

Stefan just shrugged. "They're not mutually exclusive. A lot of people do archery for relaxation and competition and it's also a survival skill."

Moments later, Rainstorm appeared beside him.

"You must use this so effectively when you're fighting," exclaimed Stefan, full of enthusiasm.

Rainstorm chuckled. "No. We use it to avoid fighting."

"Oh." He gave his head a little shake. "You people have such fearsome fighting skills that I keep forgetting you're not at all warlike."

Sparrow shrugged. "We're not great at hand-to-hand combat, because we never allow ourselves to get up close to people who might be a threat. So, we don't practice it as much." She smiled impishly at Rainstorm, her soft green eyes shining. "But wresting is fun, and I think we could add in a bit of flicking. Could make it interesting."

Waterstone jumped lightly to his feet and wound up his fishing line around a smooth stick before walking over, without flicking, to join them. "I can see having an arms master amongst us is already leading to new fighting tactics. I think we could stage a few wrestling matches at some stage and try it out," his remarks gently reminding them that Stefan had his own special skills that he brought with him into the forest.

By the time the fishing party returned to the firesite, the nervous energy that had been spurring Maud forward, was long gone. In fact, more than that, it had caused her to overtax herself ever since they left the Creeping Vine and she was now struggling to stay awake long enough to eat dinner before retiring. She slumped next to the fire, leaning against Sheldrake, who had returned early from the fishing expedition and was also looking looked drawn and tired. After all, they were the only two who were not used to lives of constant physical activity and, in addition to that, they were bearing the burden of the fear for their own child.

As Maud and Sheldrake watched, several fish, still fresh from their successful fishing, were wrapped in large leaves and buried in the coals to bake.

Tarkyn moved quietly around the fire and sat down beside them. "How are you bearing up?"

"It helps to be doing something; walking," said Maud, with a sad little smile. "But now that we've stopped, it has all come rushing back again, as it always does... and I am so tired and sore."

Tarkyn took one of her hands in both of his. "Lady Maud..."

"Just Maud, if you please."

"Maud. I can't miraculously restore your son to you, although I will do all I can to help. But, will you allow me to use my *esse* to ease your aches and tiredness?"

Sheldrake leaned forward, full of interest, and gave Maud an eager nod.

"If you think it will help." Maud gave a tired smile. "Besides, I couldn't deprive Sheldrake of another opportunity of seeing you at work."

Tarkyn placed a hand on her shoulder. "Close your eyes," he said, then, closing his own, he sent his *esse* into Maud through her shoulder, lacing it with comfort and reassurance. Since she was suffering from overall tiredness and soreness, he did not bother to direct the flow but let her body disseminate it to where it was needed. Maud felt a soft warmth spreading through her, while Sheldrake saw a faint bronze haze hanging in the air around her.

Tarkyn took his hands away, opened his eyes and waited.

A few moments later, Maud opened her eyes and breathed out. "Oh, that's much better. Thank you." She hesitated for a moment, before saying, "I think Sheldrake could do with some of that, if it would not be too much of an imposition and he is willing to accept it. After all, he hasn't done this much walking for a while and must be aching, too."

Tarkyn looked a query at Sheldrake, who said stiffly, "I would be honoured to experience your magic, whether I need it or not."

"Close your eyes then... and allow me in." Tarkyn repeated the process. He became aware that beneath Sheldrake's austere shell, the man was straining to keep himself together as fear for his son threatened to overwhelm him. Amidst the *esse*, Tarkyn sent in waves of compassion and strength, acknowledging Sheldrake's fears while at the same time shoring up his defences. When he felt he had done enough, he withdrew and opened his eyes.

A full minute passed before Sheldrake opened his eyes. A shudder passed down his whole body, leaving him looking more relaxed and more focused than he had been. Suddenly, his face broke into a broad grin, much less restrained than the usual Sheldrake. "You are a true genius. It is not just your power, which is remarkable. It is your understanding, your connection with other people." He shook his head. "And you are so young for such wisdom. No wonder you come across as arrogant sometimes. You must know so much more than you show, and so much more than those around you."

The colour in Tarkyn's cheeks heightened. "Hmm. I'm not that wise. I have a temper that gets me into strife from time to time."

Sheldrake chuckled. "If that's what rocked the inn the other day, I'm sure it does."

Chapter 43

Stefan waited until the next day to try out his new skill on Marjorie. They were walking along a wallaby track that wandered through dense scrub in a south-easterly direction. Unfortunately, wallabies were happy to jump over low bushes, so now and then the track would disappear. Then the local woodfolk would have to lead them around the bushes and either join the original track or find another one for them to follow.

Stefan had been waiting all morning for a chance to get Marjorie on her own. Finally, after passing through a stand of long grass, she sat down on a rock to remove a grass seed that had worked its way into her sock. Stefan took a breath, concentrated and flicked to stand in front of her. She was looking down at the time, so all she saw was a pair of booted feet suddenly appear. She flinched back in surprise, then looked up to see Stefan standing with his hands on his hips, grinning at her.

"Do that again," she demanded.

He obligingly flicked to stand several yards further along the path, then flicked back to stand in front of her.

She grinned in delight. "Oh, well done, Stefan! That's marvellous. So magical. How do you do it?"

"You just have to envisage yourself at that particular place then concentrate on it really hard and then... there you are!" He waved his hand theatrically before giving a grunt of laughter. "Actually, I don't think the woodfolk have to concentrate very hard. Just I do, at the moment."

Marjorie smiled, the supportive older sister. "I'm sure you'll be able to do it with less effort over time." She nodded at him. "Go on. Show me again. Use it to go up the path and I'll join you by foot. We'd better get going and catch up with the others."

As they hurried along the path, a gentle rain began to fall from the low grey clouds overhead. No one thought of stopping and by midday, the clouds had lifted and they were able to dry off in the sun as they walked. By the time they reached a suitable place for their second firesite, they were tired but dry.

After dinner, Ironbark brought over a flagon of wine and poured drinks for Sheldrake, Maud and himself. Then he sat down, just a little further from them than they were from each other, inadvertently reminding them that he was still uncertain in the company of outsiders. He was making an effort, however.

"I thought you would like to know, Maud and Sheldrake, that some of our kin further south have reported sighting a party of black-clad men and women with two children among them, walking from west to east along The Way Through."

Maud, who was sitting closest to him, reached out impulsively and clutched his arm. His eyes dilated briefly but he stopped himself from pulling back. "Oh, Ironbark. What a relief to know they are still alive!" Her eyes glistened and she swallowed before adding, "And that we know where they are. Up 'til now, it has largely been conjecture. Thank you."

Silverwood spoke from the other side of the fire. "It is hard to gauge exactly where they are, relative to us. We have more ground to cover than they do in order to intercept them, but I think we are travelling faster, even though we are not on a designated path. We need to. It would help to be able to see exactly which direction they are in so that we could adjust our path if we need to. Still, we are doing well so far, I think."

Maud glanced at Sheldrake, who gave a little nod. She drew a breath and said, "I have not mentioned this until now…" She gave an embarrassed shrug. "Not many people know of it and I wanted to get to know you woodfolk first." She had the undivided attention of the whole firesite by now. "I am a shapeshifter. I could become a peregrine falcon and fly over the forest tomorrow and reconnoitre for you. If you give me the general direction, I should be able to go from there."

A hubbub of voices filled the firesite, everyone commenting and asking questions at once.

At last, Rainstorm's voice could be heard clearly above the rest. "But why didn't you just change to something that would have found it easier to travel over the last two days? Then you wouldn't be so tired."

She shrugged. "I can't talk when I am in other shapes, although I can share images with Tarkyn. So I would have missed the chance to get to know you, both for your own sakes and for gauging the advisability of telling you my secret." She smiled. "It is useful and fun to change shape, but also isolating. I can't just socialize with the people around me and that is important to me, especially with a new group."

Silverwood's smile dawned. "It has been important for us, too, but your help will be invaluable."

"Excellent idea, Maud, you reconnoitring for us," said Tarkyn, used to working with animals and therefore the quickest to understand the possibilities. "Bird could do it, if she agreed, but a peregrine falcon is much faster. You can fly over the forests, down to The Way Through and be back by mid-morning. Besides, once you are there, you can make decisions about where you need to go to see what you want, whereas Bird would have to be guided from here. You can send images and I can… No, wait. Midnight can sketch out a map with their position and our position marked on it. Pity Sparrow can't do it. She is the best map drawer."

"Midnight and I can do it together. He can share his images with me," suggested Sparrow.

"I think one of us should join you in that," said Ironbark. "We can add our local knowledge, after all. We may be able to help you understand what you are seeing from above, Maud."

The energy levels around the firesite rose and, in working on a joint venture, the gaps between the two groups of woodfolk and the outsiders narrowed appreciably.

Early the next morning, once they had packed up and were ready to leave, Maud prepared to depart.

"By my calculations," said Stefan, "The Way Through should be about thirty miles directly south of here by now. If we are making the progress we need to, in the right direction, they should be on The Way Through but further west than that point. We started out ten miles further east, didn't we?"

"When they were seen yesterday, they had just traversed the Hidden Swamp, which is about thirty-five miles east of the last of the outsider dwellings." said Spinifex. He grinned. "I wonder how they fared with the sand flies? Nasty little things if you don't have the right herbs to deal with them."

Ironbark explained to Maud the route they would be taking until lunchtime, so she would know where to return to. Although she could search for them from overhead, it would be easier if she knew their general location.

She was just about to retire behind a tree to shapeshift when Rainstorm exclaimed in disappointment, "Where are you going? Can't we watch? Or do you have to undress?'

The colour heightened in Maud's face. "No. I don't have to undress. I always leave from and come back to my original form in whatever I was wearing," she rolled her eyes and gave an embarrassed laugh, "…luckily." She hesitated. "I just find it a bit, hmm…awkward. Most people don't know about it, so I keep it private. Only on one occasion have I changed in front of people. Even Sheldrake usually discreetly turns his back."

Rainstorm held up his hand. "Sorry I asked. I didn't mean to embarrass you."

She frowned, letting her gaze travel around the woodfolk; both local and Eskuzorian, the outsiders; Sheldrake, Jackson, and Marjorie and the inbetweeners; Tarkyn and Stefan.

"No. I will show you," she said decisively. "Think of it as a token of thanks for helping me to find Jayhan and Sasha." She gave a wry smile. "It's not very exciting though."

With that, she squinted her eyes as she focused on imagining the form of a peregrine falcon. Then, very quickly, she shrank and coalesced into the shape of a streamlined bird of prey, yellow beak and talons, grey back and wing feathers with a cream chest barred with fine brown stripes. She stood blinking for a minute then stretched her wings experimentally. Her wingspan was surprisingly large, more than a yard across. She drew them into her side momentarily before launching herself up from the forest floor, her beating wings drawing her swiftly up into the air. She flew twice around the onlookers at breakneck speed before spearing off above the trees to the south.

"Wow," breathed Rainstorm, "That was really something."

"Yes, it was," said Sheldrake softly, his eyes shining with pride.

Although they were still some thirty miles north of The Way Through, only thirty minutes passed before she began to send images of the path. She flew straight and true on her mission to find her son, but she also revelled in the joy of speed, her feathers ruffling in the wind of her passage.

Following the information she had received from Ironbark, she soon located the Kimorans. She swooped low over them and could see Jayhan and Sasha walking stolidly, hands tied, in their midst. In a confused surge of rage and relief, she swept up into the air to glide in a circle high above them, ready to plummet down on the person in the lead, to frighten him if nothing else. Then she remembered that if there were a shaman among them, they would be able to tell that she was a shapeshifter. So, reluctantly, she stopped herself. She saw Jayhan squint up at her, then nudge Sasha who followed his gaze, smiled broadly and murmured something to him. Then he too smiled. Maud glided from side to side above the path then, with great resolve, flew upward and away. No animal she could transform into, no matter how powerful, could take down a column of men on its own.

From there, Maud flew along the path towards Highkington until she spotted Jon walking with the squad of Carradorian militia. They were still more than eight miles behind Sasha and Jayhan. She considered shape-changing back to her normal form to talk to Jon, but on balance decided that she didn't want so many Carradorians knowing of her secret. Besides, no plans had yet been devised by Tarkyn, Sheldrake and the others and, at the moment, her own group was significantly further from Sasha and Jayhan than Jon's group was. She was here purely to gather information and relay it back to Midnight and Sparrow, the map makers. She could come back and talk to Jon later when plans were clearer.

Maud had not held the position of first lady in the land for so many years by making hasty, ungoverned decisions and so, she resolutely flew in a broad arc before heading eastward, past Jayhan and Sasha and on further for more than an hour until she could see all the way to where The Way Through met the Charville River. As Stefan has said, The Way Through twisted its way around denser patches of bush, boggy ground and steep hills. At one point, it curved for several miles to the north, before winding back to the south-east, cutting across the last ridge on a long line of hills that were probably the beginnings of the foothills of the Darkstone Mountains. Maud and Sheldrake's party would have far less ground to cover if they intercepted The Way Through at the apex of this northerly curve.

She estimated that it would take Jayhan and Sasha's group another day and half, maybe two days, to reach that point. She thought that Jon's party would be hot on their heels by then, unencumbered as they were with unwilling children, and with less need to follow footprints so closely, now that they were following the same path.

She took herself up higher so that she and the map makers could gain a wide view of the forest. She had now been flying for nearly two hours, mostly at high speed, and she wasn't used to extended periods of exercise like a true peregrine falcon would be. Time for a break. Then, far below her, she spotted a hapless mudlark flitting about in the morning sunshine, catching insects just above the tops of the trees. Without a second thought, she closed off her images to Midnight, folded her wings and dropped into a dive, grabbing the mudlark between her talons with a satisfying crunch. The mudlark never knew what hit it.

Then she settled on high branch and proceeded to devour her mid-morning snack, inwardly smiling at the distaste Sheldrake would feel if she told him. When she was rested and satiated, she flew back in a leisurely manner, enjoying the sunny morning, to rejoin Sheldrake and the others.

Part 7

Chapter 44

It was four days since Jayhan and Sasha had left the hut. The last three days had been a continuous slog of long hours of walking, punctuated by short, dismal rest breaks, and surrounded by unfriendly Kimorans. Today didn't look like it would be much better.

But late in the morning, Jayhan had a breakthrough. They were walking through a long valley of tall mountain ash, interlaced with tree ferns. If he had had any interest in his surroundings, he would have realised that it was quite beautiful, but his mind was intent on working out his powers.

He remembered that his eyes hadn't reacted when he'd been in danger, when he'd fallen from the tree on top of Sasha's attacker. Hmm. His eyes had only reacted when Jon was in danger. Ha! Maybe his eyes reacted to protect other people, not himself. Behind his blindfold, Jayhan squinted his eyes in concentration, envisioning Sasha being held by two roughnecks before the Kimoran Queen, her arms twisted painfully behind her back, a thug aiming a kick at her thigh. He knew how that felt. Immediately, he felt power surging through his eyes, moments before he received another jab in his ribs from Sasha.

"Stop, Jayhan!" came her warning hiss from behind him.

The sensation cut off abruptly. *Oops.*

Brinta's suspicious voice came from behind Sasha. "Stop what? What's he doing?'

"He's driving me crazy," said Sasha, improvising frantically. "He keeps tripping, which makes me nearly run into him all the time."

To Jayhan's surprise, Brinta stood up for him. "Give the kid a break. He's wearing a blindfold. What do you expect?"

Sasha gave an artistically disgruntled sigh and subsided.

After another dreary two hours, they stopped for another break. While the other Kimorans settled themselves beneath an array of tree ferns, Brinta herded the children to a young eucalyptus tree whose trunk was narrow enough to tie a cord around it. This she secured to the bonds around the children's wrists. Once she was sure they were firmly tied, she handed Sasha a canteen of water.

"Here, share this with the lad. Drink up and eat the rest of that food Ruby gave you. We'll have a twenty-minute rest here," she said, before re-joining her comrades.

As soon as she was out of earshot, Jayhan moved so that Sasha was between him and their guards, screening him from their view. "Right," he said decisively. "First, I'm getting out of these ropes."

Before Sasha could say anything, Jayhan shrank before her eyes into a younger version of himself. When he spoke, his voice sounded higher and more childish. "Shape shifting. Now my wrists are smaller. See? The ropes come off easily." He grinned, then reshaped himself to his true size.

"What about the blindfold?" hissed Sasha.

He shrugged nonchalantly. "Doesn't matter. I can see straight through it anyway."

"You little bugger! You could have told me." Sasha was partly cross and partly impressed. "It's slipped, you know. So you might as well pull it down completely."

Jayhan grinned unrepentantly. "Easier to pretend I couldn't see, if you didn't know."

"But can your eyes send out that white light through the blindfold?"

Now Jayhan looked uncertain. "I don't know. I don't even know for sure that I can make them do it. What did you see? You must have seen something to jab me before."

Sasha nodded. "Yes. I did see white light ... but it might just have been seeping out round the edges of the blindfold."

While they were talking, Jayhan was busy loosening off Sasha's bonds. Suddenly a thought struck Sasha. "Why are they leaving us to ourselves, if they're so worried about you that they keep your blindfold on? I mean, even with your hands tied, you could slip the blindfold off."

Jayhan frowned and glanced over at Brinta's squad. "Just a minute. Weren't there six of them? Brinta, Shay, Bart and three others?"

Sasha nodded.

His blood froze. "Well, now there are only five. Where's Bart?"

"Oh, well done, my little mate," came a deep rumble from the other side of their small tree. "You are a sharp little fella, aren't you?"

Bart stepped out from the shadows of the undergrowth, towering above them. "Got our ropes off, have we? Not for long."

Sasha jumped away from him, but he reached out with his big, beefy hand and grabbed her arm. As she cried out in pain, white light poured forth from Jayhan's eyes. The huge man drew back, cowering in terror. Jayhan pulled Sasha out of Bart's now unresisting grasp and drew her towards him.

But in the other direction, the other guards saw what was happening, threw down their water canteens and ran towards the children.

Sasha grabbed Jayhan around the waist and glared at the oncoming guards, concentrating fiercely. Her amulet seemed to burn on her chest. Suddenly, a silent detonation pulsed out from her, throwing the Kimorans backwards to lie sprawled in the dust. Jayhan felt the power thrusting him outward too, but Sasha's grip on him held him against her. Then, he could see nothing but a thick, velvety blackness.

Beside him, he heard Sasha say jubilantly, "I did it! I made the amulet realise that it has to protect you too, to protect me."

"I don't think so," muttered Jayhan. "I just got pushed pretty hard by it. If you weren't holding onto me, I'd be halfway across the clearing by now."

"Hmph." Sasha sounded disappointed. "You might be right. I did have to strain to keep hold of you. But," she regained her enthusiasm, "you're inside the protection with me now. So even if I have to hold you, I can protect you."

"Stars above, I hope so. I don't feel very brave about being hurt, you know, just so that horrible queen can get her hands on your amulet."

Sasha's arm tightened around him. "Neither do I."

It was then they became aware of noises outside their cocoon of darkness. They heard the shuffling of feet on the soft ground, then Brinta said harshly, "They're in that dark oval thing. Two of you, grab it. We'll just pick it up and keep going. One of the shamans can work out how to break into it when we get to Manissa."

A woman's voice spoke from closer to them. "You get that side and I'll lift from this die."

They heard Bart's angry voice close by. "Little swine. I'll teach them for making a fool of me." After a minute of foot shuffling and grunts of effort, Bart's voice came again, sounding aggrieved. "I can't get a grip. It's sort of spongey and tingly… Ow. My hands are burning."

"Ow. Mine too."

"Find some gloves then," said Brinta unsympathetically.

Inside the oval blackness, Sasha and Jayhan waited in tense silence, Sasha's arm firmly around Jayhan's waist.

"Why didn't my mother do this when my family was attacked?" whispered Sasha.

Jayhan thought for a moment. "Because you weren't near her. You were on the other side of the tent, from what Jon told us. So it was either you or her."

There was a delay, presumably while gloves were being fetched. Then another voice said, "Why don't we throw a cloak over them and roll them up in it?"

"Good idea," came Shay's voice. "Try it."

Jayhan and Sasha heard the swishing of a cloak flying through the air followed by the sounds of material being wrapped around the outside of their cocoon. They heard grunts of effort, all coming from one side, but only felt a slight pressure until suddenly, they were toppling over. They braced themselves but their landing was cushioned by the black oval of the amulet's shield. Then they felt themselves being rolled over and over.

"There," gasped a voice close to them. "They're wrapped up. I think I need a drink after that."

"Rubbish," said Brinta. "You can drink as we walk. We need to get back on the road and get this lot into Kimora before they think of anything else."

"Get a grip. You make it sound as though Kimora's just around the corner. We have the rest of today and at least half of tomorrow, slogging through this, to get to the river. If we don't pace ourselves, we'll never make it."

An exasperated sigh came from Brinta. "All right. Five minutes. Then we leave."

Chapter 45

It was dark inside the cocoon of Sasha's shield. Jayhan and Sasha were being carried on their sides within the swathe of cloaks that covered the soft but impenetrable black oval. All around them, they could hear steady, rhythmic breathing punctuated by occasional grunts of exertion as their bearers altered their grips, or had to manoeuvre the cocoon past obstacles in the increasingly narrow path.

"So now what happens, do you think?' murmured Jayhan, then, in a lower whisper, "Do you think they can hear us through all this?"

"Don't know to both, but maybe they can."

"How long's this shield of yours going to last?' whispered Jayhan.

"I don't know. It's only happened once before. It knocked me out while it protected me last time. Remember? Because Yarrow's memories were too much for me. You were watching, so you know as much as me, maybe more."

"Hmm. It lasted about two hours then, but you weren't in danger except at the start. It was just healing you." Jayhan gave a disgruntled sigh. "We don't have a clue, do we? We might be in here for days if this thing still thinks you're in danger. What if I need to go to the toilet?" He groaned. "Oh. I wish I hadn't said that."

Sasha chuckled. "Idiot! You'll just have to hang on." After another few minutes, she asked, "Do you still have some of that food Ruby gave us?"

"Yep. I still have a few of those cookies in my satchel. You might have to move your arm a bit so I can reach them." As he felt her arm slide upward, he said in sudden alarm, "But don't let go! I might get thrown out of here."

"I won't. I promise. Anyway, you'd only end up inside the roll of cloaks at the moment."

"Yeah, but when they unwrapped us, they'd be able to hurt me and make you come out, too."

"True. Good point, except I don't know how to stop it or come out of it."

"But they mightn't believe you and then…" Jayhan's voice trailed off and she could feel his chest heave under her arm.

Sasha gave him a squeeze, and said soothingly, "Come on, Jayhan. We'll find a way through." She gave her head a little shake, wondering where she came up with this nonsense. She had no idea how they were going to get away. But never mind. She was ten and he was only eight, so she had to look after him. "Now, where are those cookies?"

For hours, they were carried within their cloak-wrapped cocoon. From time to time, they could feel jolting as they were passed to a new set of bearers. Now and then, they were dropped onto the ground with a thud as the Kimorans stopped for a rest. Jayhan's bladder became an increasing focus of his attention.

When he whined about it, Sasha said shortly, "I will never speak to you again if you wee on me," which was enough for him to maintain his self-control for a while longer.

On their fourth stop in their cocoon, which must have been sometime in the late afternoon or early evening, they heard new voices outside.

Brinta greeted the newcomers and explained about the cloak-wrapped lump lying on the ground. "We have seen no sign of pursuit, ma'am," she said. "Which doesn't mean there isn't any, just that they are not close enough for us to see. With any luck, they haven't figured out which way Shay brought them out of Highkington. But even if they have, I am hoping that they are still a few hours behind us."

"Good," came an unknown woman's voice, carrying a note of authority. "But we don't want to take chances. You people have your work cut out for you over the next few days making sure you get them to the border. Leave the pursuers to me. I intend to make life very difficult for them."

Even as she spoke, Sasha and Jayhan heard the rattle of leaves, as a light breeze sprang up.

"Ooh," breathed Sasha. "I think she's a shaman. My amulet feels warm on my chest."

Outside, something light skittered past them, driven by an edgy breeze. The breeze gradually became a wind.

"Is she making a storm, do you think?" asked Jayhan. "Can shamans do that?"

"Think so. Yarrow says they, we, can work with natural elements. She'd have to be a strong one, though."

"Well," came Jayhan's voice in the dark, in that familiar tone that meant he was coming up with a hare-brained idea that might actually work, "No matter how strong she is, your amulet's stronger than hers. So, can you stop her? If someone's trying to rescue us, we don't want her making it hard for them, do we?"

Sasha sounded doubtful. "Maybe. I don't know what I'm doing, you realise. And what about the shield? If I focus the amulet's power on this shaman, maybe there won't be enough power to keep the shield up. What d'you think?"

"That would be a blessing in disguise, if you asked my bladder."

"Jayhan! I'm trying to be serious."

Now they could hear the wind beginning to roar through the treetops.

Sasha felt Jayhan's shoulder move as he shrugged. "Just seems to me that while we're in this cocoon, we have no hope of escaping, have we? So maybe we have to take our chances."

"Hmm." There was a long silence within the cocoon. Outside came the first faint rumbling of thunder. Using every ounce of his will power, Jayhan did not press her further and eventually Sasha heaved a sigh. "All right. I'll try."

Sasha focused on her heartbeat and the warmth of the amulet on her chest. She didn't think about overcoming the other shaman or the forces that were being unleashed. She just focused on her own heartbeat, slowly becoming aware of herself as a small part of the forest around her. It was almost as though her heart was beating with, and for, the forest, in concert with the trees' own ponderous rhythm. Gradually the darkness in the cocoon around Jayhan and Sasha began to pulse in time with her heartbeat, gently at first then growing more insistent.

Outside, everyone was intent on watching the shaman as, head thrown back, she held her arms aloft, muttering incantations up into the sky, drawing air from the east to lift and swirl it into the growing storm. No one noticed when the cloak-wrapped bundle lying on the ground began to throb like a huge, dark grey heart. The pulsing grew stronger and stronger until suddenly, the cloaks ripped apart, strips of material flying outward, strands of grey cloaks swirling upwards into the roiling clouds above.

Then a spear of black light streaked from the remnants of the cloaks across the open ground. It slammed into the shaman's chest and engulfed her in a dusky cloud. The haze around her pulsed once as though drawing in a breath, then sent a blast of white light shooting upwards to hit the clouds above and spread out beneath them in a silver sheet, crackling with veins of lightning.

The Kimorans watched transfixed, as silver light flickered across the underside of the cloud mass, irritating the clouds into rumbles of discontent. Now and again they heard a half-hearted clap of thunder, but the light was slowly but surely dissipating the storm clouds. A few minutes later, a gentle rain began to fall, bringing the Kimorans' gazes back to earth.

Which was when they realised that their shaman and their captives were gone.

Chapter 46

At lunchtime on the fourth day out of Highkington, Trevor trotted over to Reece to report that they should have a look at strange marks in a clearing before passing it. He led Jon and the sergeant over to a tree where confused footprints overlay each other. The tracker studied the bark of the trees closely and discovered signs of a rope having been tied around a young eucalyptus tree's trunk. The signs were subtle, just small patches of bark rubbed away. Nearby was a patch of singed grass and close to that, an area where the grass had been flattened by something. Further away they found shallow indentations, almost skid marks, on the ground which spread out from the singed grass.

"Almost like marks from an explosion," mused Reece.

They studied the singeing and the patch of flattened grass but couldn't come up with a plausible explanation for them.

"And another thing," said Trevor. "The children's tracks disappear after this clearing. The six adults' tracks still clearly follow the path but... no kids' footprints."

Jon's eye lit up. "Maybe Sasha and Jayhan escaped?"

Trevor shook his head. "I don't think so. Think about it. If they'd escaped, the adults' footprints would head off in several directions looking for them. But they don't. They just keep walking along the path towards Kimora." A thought struck him. He walked along the path a little, bending down and examining the footprints. Then he straightened. "Hmm. Two sets are deeper than the others. I think they are carrying the children. I don't know why or how, but I'm pretty sure that what's happening."

"Well, with any luck, that should slow their pace a little," said Reece.

A crease of worry appeared between Jon's eyebrows. "Oh dear. I hope they're not injured and having to be carried because they can't walk."

"Let's not paralyse ourselves with grim imaginings." Reece gave Jon a clap on the back. "Come on. The best we can do is to work on closing the distance between us and them." He turned to make sure the squad were watching him. "Right. Fall in. Jog!"

By mid-afternoon, Jon was at the end of his strength. The last stretch of the path had been smooth and relatively wide, so they had alternated jogging and walking for the last four hours with only short rest breaks, but Jon had not had the months of rigorous training that the elite troopers had had. As Reece once more yelled, "Walk!" Jon bent over, gasping for breath.

Eyeing him, Reece waved a hand at his troops, "Right. Fifteen minutes' break. Trevor, when you've recovered, could you go ahead and scout the terrain? Just to the top of that next hill will do. I just want some idea of how much longer the terrain will be suitable for keeping up this pace." He smiled wryly at Jon who was still gasping between swigs from his water canteen. "If the terrain becomes more difficult again soon, we might as well persevere and keep up this pace up while we can. If it continues to be easy traveling, we'd better pace ourselves enough for you to keep up."

As Jon went to protest, Reece raised his hand. "No, I won't leave you behind. There is no way I am leaving a prince assigned to my troop, alone in woods that may be swarming with Kimorans,"

Jon bit his lip. "I'm sorry. You were right to be so longsuffering at my addition to your troop, weren't you? I'm holding you all up, and really, all that matters is that we catch up with the abductors." He ran his hand through his wavy, sweat-darkened blond hair. "But I couldn't have stayed behind, you know. I'd have gone mad." He gave a whimsical little smile. "Perhaps my sanity counts for something."

Reece gave a grunt of laughter. "Perhaps it does. We can't have a madman running Kimora."

Jon looked uncomfortable. "No, not ideally. Although I fear my aunt, the current ruler, must be close to mad, to be so cruel to so many people and so power-hungry. I hope I haven't inherited any of the evil that runs in her veins."

"I don't think for a moment that you have."

"Maybe I have a darker side you just haven't encountered yet?"

"Have you?"

Jon thought for a moment, particularly about his time on the streets, then shrugged. "Maybe. But I wonder how I would react if I had my aunt at my mercy... or Sasha's abductors..."

"Jon, we all have a darker side. It's just a matter of degree and what we do with it. Do we allow it to rule us, or do we rule it?"

"Huh. You are wise for your years, Sergeant Reece. I wish I had met you sooner. I would have liked someone like you – well, you – to talk to, over the last few years." He gave a shy smile, then looked away. "Do you think, when this is all over, that you might like to stay in contact with me?"

Reece gave a shout of laughter, and slapped him on the knee, grinning broadly. "You really are one out of the bag, aren't you? I've never met such an illustrious person who is so diffident. Actually, I don't think I've ever met anyone as illustrious as you; not to talk to, at least. Of course I would love to stay in touch. I think some of the boys would, too, if you asked them."

Jon smiled and looked around at some of the closer men. He cocked his head and raised his eyebrows in query, which prompted cheerful acceptances from everyone.

"Of course we would. You may be slow as a tortoise, but you're good company," said Warren. "And very interesting," he added, with a quick grin.

"Oh, you have no idea how interesting I can be," said Jon dryly. "I can tell you all about new road surfaces they're trying out and which streets have potholes, which roads have been washed out by the recent rains. Absolutely riveting." His smile faded as he saw Trevor returning.

"Sergeant, in half a mile or so, the road seems to disappear into a thicker section of the forest. If it's as dense as it looks, we won't be able to run through it. In fact, we'll be lucky to find where the path goes and push through it."

Reece blew out a sigh of exasperation. "Well, we've done the best we can. On these open stretches, we will have been travelling at one and half times their speed, may be more. So I reckon we've made up at least two, may be three hours, which means we're five or six miles closer to them than we were three days ago." He grimaced. "We're getting closer but they're still an hour or two ahead of us." He looked at Jon. "You ready? We'll do one last run while we have the chance." He checked that all his men were up and packed. "Right. Walk for four hundred, so His Highness here can catch his breath. Then we jog."

As they reached the dense tangle of the thicker forest, having jogged the final five hundred yards, Jon gave a gusty sigh of relief. His head was throbbing from over-exertion, his legs felt wobbly and his knees were threatening to buckle. He had to grab hold of a tree to keep himself upright.

"Look," said Trevor, giving him time to rest by pointing to a discernible line of broken or bent branches and fern fronds. "This dense bush is making it hard for them to carry their load. So, even walking at a normal pace we'll be gaining on them. It can't be long now."

Reece gave Jon an encouraging smile. "In fact, we may be getting so close that I should probably send Trevor and one of the lads up ahead to make sure we don't stumble upon them unawares." He passed his water canteen to Jon. "Here. Have a drink. We'll give it another five minutes then get moving again."

The next two hours were slow going, as they pushed their way through long grass and undergrowth that had a nasty tendency to be prickly. The canopy was high above them and blocked out a lot of the sunlight. Gradually, the ground began to rise as they made their way from the valley floor up to the top of a line of granite-strewn hills. It was a hard slog, warm, damp and steamy. Reece keep them going by promising to stop when they reached the top.

Towards sunset, the last branch was pushed aside, and they finally crested a rise that didn't lead to yet another rise. On the plateau at the top, ragged gumtrees and soft grasses grew between rocky outcrops.

Jon was not the only one this time who was tired. The entire troop threw themselves down on the grass amongst the rocks and broke out their water canteens and rations.

Trevor, who seemed indomitable in all circumstances, walked to the edge of the plateau and looked out across the next valley. The side of the hill they were on was thick with trees, but a grassy section ran along the valley floor before the track once more disappeared into the forest. The tracker squinted into the fading light then turned to Reece. "I think I saw movement over there, just at the bottom of the next incline. We'd better stay away from the edge in case we can be seen against the skyline. Anyone watching the sunset, which I do every chance I get, might see us as silhouettes against the sky."

"Hear that, men?"

Someone gave a tired guffaw. "No chance of me standing up anytime soon."

Trevor studied the wisps of cloud in the eastern sky that seemed to become more substantial as he watched. A cool breeze sprang up and sent him diving into his pack for his cloak. When he looked again, woolly white clouds had formed. As he watched, the clouds expanded, rolling in on themselves as they grew in height and width. They darkened into storm clouds and the wind picked up. Soon it was howling through the treetops up the hillside towards them.

"Storm coming," Trevor said over his shoulder, as the first rumbles of thunder could be heard. A loud crack of thunder and the raging wind nearly drowned him out as he shouted, "I've never seen a storm build up so fast. We need to find shelter or get the tents up. No, wind's too strong. We'll never get tents up in this." Even before anyone started moving, he said, "Just a minute. Something strange is happening. Quick. Get over here and look. But stay low. I felt... I'm not sure what... a detonation of some kind." He pointed. "Look. Over there. Just inside the tree line."

Drawn by the urgency in his voice, the men scrambled to the edge of the plateau and lay on the grass, looking out, just in time to see what appeared to be, from this vantage point, a flash of black light. Then they drew in a collective breath as a pillar of white light streaked upwards and bled across the underside of the clouds. The thunder rumbled a few more times then faded away completely and the wind began to die down. Then, before their eyes, the clouds began to dissipate.

"What on earth was that?" asked Warren.

Trevor shook his head. "I have no idea."

"Whatever it was, it wasn't natural," said Reece, frowning. "That storm came out of nowhere. Then, *poof*! It was gone."

"Poof, eh, sir?" quipped one of the men.

Reece gave an amused smile. "Yes. Definitely, poof!"

Jon was looking thoughtful. "Shamans can raise storms."

"Can they? Hmm."

"Maybe someone tried to raise a storm, probably to cause us some grief, but overcooked it and burnt themselves out," suggested Trevor.

Jon shrugged. "Maybe. It certainly looked something like that." He smiled wryly at them. "Well, at least we know they are up ahead and, at the moment, in sight. We're doing well, aren't we? Now all we have to do is catch up the last couple of miles, approach them unseen and somehow extract the little ones without endangering them."

"So, one last push before dark?" asked Reece.

Jon rolled his eyes. "I asked for that, didn't I? At least it will be downhill."

Chapter 47

By the time Jon and the Carradorian troopers reached the source of the flash of black light, daylight was almost gone. There were two black, seared patches on the ground and the remnants of one, maybe two, shredded dark grey cloaks. Trevor lit one of their lanterns to study the ground in the fading light. He circled the whole clearing, squatting down from time to time to check particular spots. Then he walked a short way to the east examining the footprints, before reporting to Reece.

"Sir," Trevor glanced at Jon then back to Reece, "two things. The abductors were joined from the east by at least five more people. But more importantly, I think the children are no longer with them." He waited for the exclamations to subside before giving the reasons for his conclusions. "I don't know whether someone took them in another direction, or whether they escaped, or what happened, but no footprints head east. Footprints are chaotically superimposed over each other all around the clearing, then they head in all directions, but mainly in several northerly directions." He gave a slight smile. "Just as I said they would, if the children had managed to escape."

"So, can you see the children's footprints?" asked Jon eagerly.

"Maybe," said Trevor uncertainly "It's been raining, you see. Not enough to completely wash away their prints but enough to obscure them. He walked to the rags of the cloaks that lay strewn on the north-west edge of the clearing and squatted down. "Come over here and have a look." He pointed to four small footprints. "See? They look like they might be heading north, but once they get off the track, the grass and undergrowth, especially after rain, has obscured their trail."

"And look, larger feet have followed them," said Jon, his blood chilling at the thought.

Suddenly Reece was all business. "Right, we'll set up camp here tonight. Be aware that the Kimorans are all around us in the surrounding woods, looking for Sasha and Jayhan. At any time, one or several of them may return to this clearing. So, I want two men on guard at all times. Trevor, is there any point in trying to track the children tonight? We will, if you think there's a chance we may find them."

Trevor looked at Jon, but after a moment's hesitation, shook his head. "No, Sergeant, We're more likely to run into a Kimoran and get ourselves killed. I'm sorry, Jon. So near and yet so far."

Suddenly, one of the men spotted a light off the road to the north, back along the track towards Highkington.

Jon, Reece and Trevor exchanged glances.

"There's the remains of a fire here," said Reece. He kicked it with his boot. "Still some glowing coals in the ash."

"They probably lit oil lamps with brands from the fire before they headed off," suggested Trevor.

"If that's the Kimorans, why is the light down that way?" asked Jon. "The children's footprints head straight off the road, due north."

Trevor came back to look at the point where the small footprints had disappeared. He stepped off the road and walked several paces into the scrub before coming up against a barrier of thorny bushes. He shrugged. "Can't get through here. You'd have to go around."

"If they have lights and we don't," said Reece slowly, "we may be able to sneak up on them in the dark and at least eliminate a few Kimorans. It'll give the kids a better chance of getting away, even if we can't track them ourselves in the dark."

Trevor studied the sky. "Not much light left, but the moon's coming up soon. I think we can manage to find our way if we're careful."

There were grunts of assent from the men.

"Good. We'll leave two men here to guard our gear."

"Sir," said Warren, excitedly. "There's another light down there in the trees to the north-east."

"In that case," Reece amended, "we'll split into two groups. Jon with me and three troopers. We'll head towards Highkington. Trevor, you lead the other three towards that light to the north-east. Warren and Davis, stay here and guard the camp. Now men, make as little sound as possible; it's better to be slow and silent. We don't want them to know we're following them."

As they crept along the side of the road, Reece whispered in Jon's ear, "Now Jon. No shenanigans. Please. I can't order you but I'm asking you, let the five of us act as a team, watching each others' backs."

Reece felt a pat on his back. "It would be my honour to be part of your team," whispered Jon back.

Reece smiled in the dark.

It was not long before they drew level with the light in the trees. By this stage, they realized that the light was actually two lamps, two or three hundred yards north of the trail, moving in two zig-zagging paths between the trees as the Kimorans searched for the escaped children.

Reece called a halt while they considered their next move. Keeping his voice low, he said, "Including the five newcomers, there were at least eleven Kimorans, weren't there?

"Sir," murmured one of the troopers, "they might have thought it more likely that the children would head back towards Highkington, in which case they would have sent more people down this way."

"Good point," agreed Reece. "I think, however, they would have sent at least a pair in the other direction. But our group of five may be dealing with seven or more Kimorans."

Jon watched the steady movement of the lights. "Our advantage is they don't know we're following them."

"And," added another trooper, "that they will be night blind from their torches and won't be able to see beyond their ring of light, while our eyes have become accustomed to the dark."

"However," said Reece, "should they turn suddenly and flash their light in your face, you will be dazzled while they will be used to the glare. Keep your eyes down as much as possible so their light doesn't catch a reflection in your eye and give you away, and to stop you from getting dazzled."

Since the men had had extensive training in night combat, this last little speech was actually meant for Jon, without Reece explicitly saying so. Jon listened earnestly and only realized much later that he had been its sole target.

"And also remember," said Jon quietly, "if you want to disappear completely, just ask. You must be touching me or touching someone who is touching me. Then I can shimmer you and myself invisible." He smiled cheerily. Although no one saw the smile in the dark, they heard it in his next words. "As long as Reece thinks that's a good idea."

"Would this shimmering affect our perceptions, or our ability to act or hit the enemy?" asked Reece.

"No."

"All right. Thank you. We'll keep it up our sleeves as a possibility. Each of you men may choose independently to avail yourselves of Jon's offer if the situation calls for it." The sergeant waved a hand forward. "All right. Spread out. Let's catch them before they catch us."

As they crept nearer, they could see that all the Kimorans held long, curved swords at the ready and in the other hand, either a lamp or a foot-long dagger. They were working their way methodically through the trees, sweeping their lamps back and forth in front of them.

Jon, whose survival on the streets had depended on being one step ahead of the opposition, considered their apparent single-minded focus on finding the lost children and decided all was not as it seemed. Surely the Kimorans would know that pursuit was not far behind. Even in their panic to regain their prize, they would not forget to guard their backs. Would they?

Then Jon spotted a man fifty yards ahead and to his left, leaning against a tree, on the side away from the lamps. The man's night vision would be as unimpaired as his own. Jon let his gaze wander to the right and found another man in a similar position near the other lamp. Reece and the three troopers were slinking forward, crouched down, heading more towards the righthand lookout, too far away for Jon to gain their attention in the dark without making enough noise to alert the enemy. He had only moments to intercede before the lookouts saw them and ambushed them or raised the alarm.

He shimmered and ran forward lightly. As he ran, he drew his stiletto, a memento from his years on the street that he carried with him always. He circled around behind the man on the left, then closed in and clamped his left hand across the man's mouth. As soon as Jon touched him, the lookout disappeared within the shimmering. Then Jon brought the stiletto up and slid it silently between the man's ribs, straight into his heart. Jon held the man's weight as he slumped to the ground, keeping the death as silent as possible. He pulled out his blade, wiped it on the man's jacket and let him go. Immediately, the man re-appeared, lying motionless on the ground, still on the far side of the tree from the lamplight.

None of the Kimorans had seen a thing.

But Reece had. His eyes widened in alarm as he caught the movement in the shadows, and he signalled to his men. Now they were within twenty feet of the man on their right, but they had still not seen him. Their focus was on the dead man. Jon caught the flash of steel in the lamplight of a knife raised, ready to throw.

Reece was looking Jon's way and there was no time to warn him. Unless Jon acted, one of the troopers would be killed. Jon reversed his knife in his hand and gripped it firmly by the long, narrow blade. He couldn't see the other lookout in the gloom, but he had seen where the knife glinted. He drew back and threw, aiming for a spot two feet lower and a little towards the road.

He saw Reece and the three troopers flinch back as the knife flashed past them, its flight caught in the lamp. A gasp of pain and the dull sound of a weapon hitting the forest floor made them turn and finally they saw the man on their right, now clutching a slim, wicked blade protruding from his chest.

But the Kimorans had heard it too, this time.

"Go, go, go!" yelled Reece, all efforts at subterfuge abandoned. "Keep your eyes down."

The numbers were even but the Carradorians had the element of surprise and their night vision intact. Reece and his troopers surged forward, catching the Kimorans before they could turn properly and prepare themselves. As the Kimorans squinted into the darkness, the troopers kept their eyes trained on the ground, using their peripheral vision to dodge the flailing swords of their opposition and to stab upwards with their own weapons.

It was over in minutes. There was no chance for finesse in the poor lighting and three of the Kimorans lay dead and the fourth badly wounded, when Reece stayed his hand from a killing blow.

"Hold," he shouted to himself and his men. "I'll let this one live. Then we can find out what happened."

A slight rustle in the leaves on the forest floor, left of the Kimorans, had them whipping round, ready to attack, but Jon's voice said, "Don't worry. It's only me." When he was sure they weren't going to rush him, he shimmered into view, his stiletto once more sheathed and out of view.

He bent down and picked up a fallen lantern that had managed to stay alight during the little melee and was now threatening to light the detritus on the ground. He raised it so that he could study the faces of the fallen Kimorans. When he swung it onto the face of the man Reece had spared, he grunted in disgust. "Shay. He betrayed his fellow refugees and nearly killed Lord Sheldrake... and me, of course. He must be one of those who escaped from prison. And here he is, straight back to work, hurting my family and my friends."

Jon took a breath and spat out, "You're a bastard, Shay." He straightened up and produced a small cloth bag from an inner pocket, opened the draw string, extracted two small packets and handed them to Reece. "Here. I presume you have some sort of bandaging with you. Moisten these with a bit of water and smear them on whatever you bind his shoulder with. They will deaden the pain and prevent infection."

Reece looked puzzled. "Why are you helping him?"

Jon glanced at Shay then back at Reece. "Because he will slow us down if we don't look after him and I presume we will be taking him with us. And because… I don't do unto others what they do to me, just for the sake of it." Reece and his men had seen a new side of Jon, confident and deadly, but suddenly he smiled his sunny smile. "Just part of being a fluffy kitten, I suppose."

Reece's eyes narrowed, not buying Jon's disarming charm so easily this time. "And are both of their look-outs dead?"

"Yes," said Jon quietly, his smile gone. His eyes slid away from the sergeant's face, uncomfortable with people seeing this side of him.

Seeing this, Reece reached out and gripped him by the shoulder. "You, Lord Jon, are an enigma. Your skills with a knife are as breathtaking as they are unexpected… and we have you to thank for at least one of our lives."

Jon gave a self-deprecating shrug. "Years of practice. I'm not too skilled with a sword but I can wield a knife." He met Reece's eyes. "And I learned to fight when, every day, my life depended on getting it right. Self-preservation is a great motivator." And beneath his voice, they could hear a faint trace of well-hidden bitterness.

Chapter 48

Jayhan and Sasha plunged through the long grass and threw themselves into the under-growth.

"Ow," muttered Jayhan, as he pushed his way under straggly, sharp-twigged bushes. Their thin branches caught at his clothes and he kept having to drag away or unhitch parts of his surcoat that were caught.

Sasha was not faring much better. "Blasted bushes! We would have to find the clingiest, sharpest bushes in the whole forest to crawl through."

"Ow," yelped Jayhan again. "Something bit me."

Sasha curbed a sigh of exasperation. "No, it didn't. It's just the thorns. Some of them are razor-sharp. Come on. We're nearly through."

They wriggled and crawled their way through the dense bank of prickly shrubs, Sasha leaving shreds of her dress behind her on the sharp thorns, until finally, they could drag themselves free and stand up. Sasha's gown, not that she cared, was a tattered wreck. They found themselves inside a tall forest, where little light, especially now that it was dusk, penetrated. High above them, they could hear rain pattering on leaves. Now and then, a large drop of water would fall from above to land close by, or, if they were unlucky, down their necks or on their faces.

Few bushes grew beneath the distant canopy. The forest floor was damp and much of it was exposed earth or leaf fall. Knobbly tree roots snaked their way across the ground in places, some of them tall and thin like miniature curved walls. Mosses grew on tree trunks and fallen logs. Although it was beautiful, Sasha and Jayhan could barely see it in the fading light and to them, it seemed dark, lonely and threatening.

Jayahn took a deep breath. "Right. Stay here. Back in a minute," he said quietly and stepped off to the side between the trees until he was out of sight of Sasha. He returned a few minutes later. "Phew! That's better. Now I can concentrate on running away."

"Know what you mean," said Sasha, with a grin.

Jayhan looked surprised. "Did you go too?"

Sasha nodded. "Come on. I don't think they can get through the bushes we crawled through, but they'll find a gap somewhere and we have to be as far away as we can be when they do."

They walked away from the bank of bushes and the path as quickly as they could. Even though their eyes adjusted to the gloom, it was too dark to run. Jayhan's pale eyes saw better in the dark than Sasha's and so, after a short protest, Jayhan took Sasha's hand and led her from one tree trunk to the next, murmuring directions as they went. A few times, one or other of them tripped over raised tree roots or rises in the ground. Only having their hand held by the other saved them from falling heavily.

Then they heard voices off to their left.

"Oh no. They've found a way into the forest," whispered Sasha.

"Well, we knew they would," said Jayhan.

"Yes, but I was hoping they'd take longer."

Jayhan gave a little snort in the darkness. "Yeah. So was I." He increased the pressure on Sasha's hand. "Watch out. There's a big tree root to step over here."

Once the root was safely negotiated, they turned to look in the direction of the voices. As they watched, a pinprick of light came into view. It was still distant, flickering in and out of sight as it passed between trees.

"If they have a light, we can't outrun them," said Sasha. She looked around at the smooth towering trunks. "We have to find somewhere to hide."

"And hide our tracks."

"We can't do that in the dark." Sasha sounded close to panic.

"We can a bit. Wait here. I'll walk on damp patches off to our right for a hundred yards, then come back on leafy bits. Then we'll walk on leaves."

"Go on then. Hurry."

Two minutes later, he was back. "Forget it!" he said. "There's a light in that direction as well."

Giving up all thought of covering their trail, they blundered on through the trees, panic making them clumsy in the dark. It wasn't long before they missed seeing an obscured root and fell heavily in tangled heap, both gasping in fright.

Sasha was the first to recover. She worked hard to slow her breathing and when she felt able to speak, said, "Right. Let's think. What did we trip over? If you didn't see it, maybe it was covered in bushes or leaves or something we could hide under."

"I'm sorry, Sasha. I should have seen it. I should have looked better." The little boy sounded close to tears. He gave a little hiccough of suppressed sobs. "And my leg hurts."

From her wise old age of ten, Sasha ignored this last little gambit and patted his arm. "Don't worry. We're both doing our best. Let's feel around and see if there is anything here to hide under," she gave a forlorn attempt at a giggle, "since we're down on the ground anyway."

Jayhan gave a dutiful grunt of laughter in response, knowing she was trying to cheer them both up, before turning his attention to their surroundings.

Suddenly, a hand clamped over his mouth and an arm grabbed him around the chest. He flailed and writhed, trying to break the grip.

"Shh," came a quiet voice in his ear. "I'm Draya. Remember me? I'm one of the Kimoran refugees. I'm not abducting you. I'm saving you from my countrymen." She paused to let her words sink in. "All right? Can I let go, without you screaming blue murder?"

Jayhan thought about it and realised that if he screamed, the nearby Kimorans hunting them would hear him, which would be counter-productive whoever this person was. He nodded and the hand was removed.

He looked around at Draya and saw an older woman holding Sasha around the shoulder, but not forcibly. He squinted through the gloom. "Rhoda?"

"Hello, Jayhan," she said quietly. "We've been shadowing you for days. Beetlebrow and Argus headed back to Highkington to bring help three days ago when we first saw you, and we two have been following you and your abductors, hoping that something would happen so that we could help you."

"We would have loved to attack them and stage a daring rescue, but we'd just have been captured ourselves. Brave, we are. Silly we are not." Draya stood up and virtually lifted Jayhan to his feet. "Come on. Up you get. We have boltholes all through the forest but there are none nearby. Those bastards are hot on your trail. We have to go."

"If you show me which way to go, I can help guide us in the dark," piped up Jayhan. "My eyes, you know." Despite his best effort, he still sounded embarrassed saying it.

Sasha brushed herself off. "He's really good at it," Jayhan heard the grin in her voice, "except when he's panicking." She took hold of Rhoda's hand. "It's better to hold hands in the dark… to hold each other up if we trip."

Draya took Jayhan's hand and they led the way deeper into the forest. Concentrating as they were on the way forward, no one looked back. So none of them saw the lights swing wildly, or that the lights returned to the road, now in the hands of Jon and his companions.

Part 8

Chapter 49

Once Maud had returned from her flight, Ironbark, Spinifex and Silverwood conferred with the local woodfolk to adjust their path so that they would intercept The Way Through at its most northerly point. Now that Maud had actually seen the children, the whole group felt a renewed sense of urgency.

The revised path began by leading them through a swamp, winding from one piece of dry land to the next. The ground underfoot was spongy peat, which was pleasant to walk on, but the air was full of midges and mosquitoes. It was not long before a halt was called so that Silverwood could dole out an herbal salve to keep the insects at bay. Maud and Sheldrake exchanged dubious glances at the windiness of the path but Ironbark, intercepting one of these, assured them that it was still quicker than detouring around the swamp.

By mid-afternoon, they had left the swamp behind them and were threading their way through scrubby bushland composed mainly of scratchy paperbarks. On the other side of this were a series of low hills, covered in a forest whose dense canopy filtered the light and reduced the amount of undergrowth. Tree ferns filled the gullies, but the ridges were only lightly covered, making them easy to traverse.

The party made such good time that they decided to keep going for a couple of hours after dark, using luminescent orbs provided by Tarkyn and Sheldrake to light their way. They camped in a pretty clearing next to a cold, clear creek that gurgled its way over rounded pebbles, providing a friendly backdrop to their conversation around the firesite. Cold meat and fire-baked damper were prepared and eaten. Tarkyn noticed, but knew not to mention, that Waterstone's and Gurgling Brook's voices blended in with the sound of the creek so much that they had to speak up to be heard.

They set off early the next morning, hoping to reach The Way Through by mid-afternoon. A slight breeze played through the trees and soft white clouds floated in the strong blue sky overhead. A perfect day for travelling.

But as they emerged from the trees on the other side of the hills, Rainstorm stopped dead, his eyes widening in horror. "Oh, my stars! What do we do now?"

Before them stretched a flooded plain, hundreds of yards across.

Stefan turned to Spinifex. "Is this normal? Do you know the way around it?"

"No," replied Spinifex slowly. He scratched his head uncertainly. "The recent rains must have flooded the creek. Usually the path we're on would lead us straight to a series of stepping-stones that would take us across it without a second thought."

Waterstone considered. "If it's not too deep, we could wade through, I suppose."

"How can we tell?" said Ironbark. "It's so wide. Could be anything under there."

"We might have to go around," said Silverwood. "I wonder how far it stretches to the left and right?" She went out of focus for a few minutes but then shook her head. "No woodfolk nearby to tell us."

"Could Bird have a look at it for us from overhead?" asked Rainstorm. "Maybe there's a ford nearby."

Tarkyn shook his head. "Not right now. She's far away, hunting, at the moment. I think she needs to feed before she would be willing to return."

Almost as one, everyone turned to Maud.

She gave a scowl in return that was, fortunately, underpinned with a glimmer of laughter. "You can see why I don't want my gift widely known. I am *far* too useful… and," she added primly, "I don't always want to be useful." She waved her hand and smiled, "Obviously today I do, since I want us to reach my son as soon as possible. Very well. Hmm." She thought carefully for a few minutes, keeping them all waiting. "Right," she said suddenly. "An osprey is what we need. Very good at seeing into the water."

Moments later, a beautiful brown and white bird of prey stood on the ground before them, her head just above the height of their knees. Although her head was white, broad brown streaks ran horizontally through her eyes prompting Rainstorm to say, "Those stripes almost look like heavy eye makeup."

In response, Maud turned her hard eyes on him and, even though she glared up at him from only a bit above knee height, he wished he hadn't spoken. Then she turned towards the water and took off, beating her wings strongly to pull her upward. She circled above them, appearing almost all white from underneath, only dark at the wrists of her wings.

For a time, Maud simply circled a little above tree height over the area in front of her friends, but she soon discovered that, despite her excellent vision, she could not see very far into the muddy water. So she turned her attention to the objects that stuck out from the top of the water at different places, using the tops of trees, bushes and grasses to try to gauge some idea of the water's depth. It looked as though it could be at least five feet deep in places and who knew what potholes, ponds or streams lay beneath it.

She flew slowly off to the east to check the extent of the flood, noticing that her wings felt more powerful but carried her more slowly than her peregrine falcon form had done. The water extended for several miles in this direction, spread out across the plain. It looked like it was a water course that had overflowed its banks. Her heart sank. It would take at least half a day to skirt around it to the east. To cheer herself up, she banked into an unnecessarily tight turn as she headed back to scout out the western extent of the flood.

The land rose in this direction and it did not take long for her to find the stream that fed into the flooded plain. As it flowed down through the hills, the stream was deep, contained by steep rock banks. She flew slowly along its course, looking for somewhere they could cross. With a start of hope, she saw up ahead a huge mountain ash which, at some time in the past, had fallen across the stream. Its trunk was broad and still strong but covered in mosses and possibly slippery. Still, it would do. This time she did not stop to hunt since everyone was waiting on her information to be able to move on.

As she flew back towards the group, she noticed a shadow on the water below her Suddenly, she felt the force of a strong predatory mind challenging her right to approach Tarkyn. She sent out an urgent image to Tarkyn, even as the size of the shadow on the water increased alarmingly.

Maud threw herself sideways and fled into the shelter of the trees, just as the talons of a great mountain eagle raked along the edge of her wing. Bird was huge, so much bigger than she was, and Bird was angry; protective of Tarkyn and of her unique connection with him. Heart pounding, Maud winged her way carefully through the confines of the trees. This was not her osprey form's normal territory. She preferred the open cliffs, plains and water. She heard Bird's shriek of outrage above her, as the mountain eagle shadowed her, gliding over the trees, waiting for her to re-emerge.

Maud landed under a tree fern and, after giving herself time to catch her breath, transformed back into her own shape. She found she was panting in fright and trembling. She inspected the outside of her right arm and could see beads of blood soaking into her shirt. She took some time to recover before edging out from under the tree fern, scanning the sky above the treetops for Bird. Sure enough, the eagle was still there, circling overhead. Squaring her shoulders, Maud stood straight and walked firmly towards the rear of their group.

Jackson spotted her first and ran over to her. "Are you all right? We saw Bird go for you, but she wouldn't respond to Tarkyn."

She nodded, still shaky. "Yes. I avoided her. Just. But I might need a new shirt."

Jackson put his arm around her shoulders and steered her towards the group, forbearing to ask her what she had discovered.

Since they had been due for a break anyway, a fire had been lit and Autumn Leaves approached her bearing a cup of tea. "Looks like you need this. That bloody Bird has no manners at all."

They led her to the firesite where Sheldrake took over from Jackson. "You gave me the fright of my life, my dear, or rather Bird did. You did very well to dodge her."

Silverwood rolled up Maud's bloodstained sleeve and inspected her wound. "Not too bad. Just a long scratch. A bit deep in places." She frowned in thought. "Hmm. It may get infected, depending on what has recently been on Bird's talons."

"No, it won't," said Tarkyn firmly, walking over to place his hand on her shoulder. Without any preamble, he sent a stream of *esse* into her arm, laced with a quick jab of irritation, which he had no trouble in summoning at the thought of Bird's behaviour, to combat any lurking germs.

"Thank you both," said Maud, feeling a little swamped by the care being shown her by so many people at once.

Tarkyn gave her shoulder a final pat before walking to the other side of the fire, looking thoroughly disgruntled. "Least I can do. I will be speaking to Bird at some length about this."

Maud smiled. "Don't be too cross with her. I don't think she understands shapeshifting."

"No. That is what I will try to explain to her. But also, she needs to desist if I demand it." He gave a lopsided smile. "She won't follow commands automatically. She is far too independent for that. But she has to realize that if I am emphatic, I may know something about the situation she doesn't and to at least give me a chance to explain."

"I can see why you said 'speak to her at length'" said Waterstone. "Pretty difficult to explain all that in images."

Waiting for the briefest pause in the conversation, Sheldrake interrupted, "So, Maud. What did you find out? I don't like to press, but I fear we are running out of time."

Maud swallowed her mouthful of tea, then described what she had seen.

"Hmm. Sounds like a doddle for us woodfolk, but possibly a bit trickier for you outsiders," said Rainstorm.

"My thoughts exactly," said Maud. "If the worst comes to the worst, and it is too slippery for us to keep our footing, we can bum across, I suppose. I am not shape-changing again until Tarkyn has spoken to Bird."

Tarkyn shook out his cup and walked over to put it in his backpack. "Don't worry. I will stand close to the end of the log, ready to levitate anyone who slips."

Following his lead, everyone prepared to leave. Lapping Water and Autumn Leaves put out the fire and covered the ashes, while others packed away the kettle and tea leaves.

"Pardon me for asking," said Sheldrake, "but why don't you just levitate everyone over the flood?"

"Too far and too many," replied Tarkyn shortly. "Besides, I don't usually do things for people if it is possible for them to do it themselves." This may have sounded selfish if they hadn't already seen him use his power to help Sphagnum Moss, Maud and Sheldrake at various times. "Firstly, I'd end up at everyone's beck and call, and secondly, it would diminish their own independent skills."

Sheldrake smiled broadly. "I can see you've thought this through."

"Always," said Waterstone, his blood brother. "Well, almost always. Many issues have arisen from Tarkyn living among us as a sorcerer and as our liege, that have required … hmm… guidelines, you might say."

In a very short time, they were on their way again. As they emerged from the trees, a great shriek heralded Bird's arrival. She flew in, landing on poor Tarkyn's shoulder, digging in with her talons before going through the rigmarole of turning herself to the front. As they walked west along the edge of the flooded plain, Tarkyn was clearly preoccupied with trying to explain things to his ferocious, independent pet.

When they reached the huge log, they found a thick rope strung from one side to the other, about five feet above the log.

Spinifex grinned at their surprise. "As we neared this part of the forest, we were able to contact some woodfolk in the area. They offered to help but," he gave an embarrassed grimace, "they don't actually want to meet you."

"Understandable," said Sheldrake. "In that case, thank them for us, would you please?"

Despite the rope, Tarkyn stood by, waiting to catch anyone who slipped, but everyone crossed safely, and they were able to continue on their way. However, skirting the flood had cost them a couple of hours and so, as dusk approached, they were still more than an hour away from The Way Through.

The wind was picking up and dark clouds were beginning to form overhead. It looked as though they were going to get wet if they kept going and didn't find shelter.

Suddenly Tarkyn stopped dead, causing Lapping Water and Rainstorm to canon into him. He raised a hand to silence any protests they may have been going to make and gazed far into the forest. Without a word, he walked to large ghost gum and placed his hand on its trunk.

"Someone or something is connecting with the forest, drawing on its power," he murmured.

The clouds above them were thickening and darkening. A distant clap of thunder heralded the coming of a storm.

Moments later, a concussive force thrummed through the trees, making every person catch their breath. Then silver light streaked across the underside of the clouds. The clouds rumbled and grumbled above, as the silver light seemed to eat into them, breaking them apart.

"What on earth is that?" demanded Rainstorm. "It's not normal lightning. I've never seen anything like it."

Without another word being spoken, the entire company broke into a run, anxious to reach the source of the disturbance. It only took them a couple of hundred yards, however, to realise that a precipitous entry into an uncertain situation was impractical and dangerous. Besides, although everyone was pretty fit, none of them were trained long distance runners and were running out of breath. They slowed and came to a halt, gathering together to confer. Autumn Leaves, who had been carrying Gurgling Brook, breathed a sigh of relief.

By no coincidence at all, Sheldrake ended up next to Tarkyn. "Tell us about this power you sensed."

Catching his breath, Tarkyn glanced at Sheldrake who seemed unperturbed by their run. "You're fitter than I thought you were." Tarkyn, who had run with Bird bobbing unconcernedly on his shoulder, took another breath before answering, "Someone was drawing on the power in the forest, not just from the trees as I do, but from everything around them; trees, rocks, earth, air." He shook his head. "Do you know anything about this?"

"Perhaps," said Sheldrake. "Go on."

"Then another power, similar but far greater and less disciplined, overwhelmed the machinations of the first and…" Tarkyn hesitated, trying to find a way to explain, "and blew it apart."

"Is the wielder of the first lot of power still alive, do you think?"

Tarkyn shook his head. "No idea. I can't imagine that person is very well, after having their power swamped like that, but I have no idea what we're dealing with. Do you?"

Sheldrake nodded briskly. "I think so. From what I have read and from what I have learnt from Yarrow, Sasha's shamanic teacher, and from watching Sasha herself, I would say that Sasha has overwhelmed a lesser shaman."

Tarkyn looked startled. "What? A little girl, using magic aggressively? I thought shamans were all about healing and mysticism, not attack."

"They are, as a general rule. But Sasha is the High Shaman despite her lack of years, and, in the natural course of events, all other shamans are linked in with her. If they have been corrupted by the current Kimoran queen, Sasha can break that compulsion. We, *she*, did it with Lady Electra and, I think, with one of the women who attacked a group of refugees we were with, a few months ago."

"And did it cause that great lightning display?" asked Tarkyn.

Sheldrake shook his head. "No. Something else is at play here that I haven't yet come across. The only pertinent knowledge I can offer is that I believe shamans can affect the weather."

"I hope the Kimorans have not hurt Sasha in retaliation," said Lapping Water, "… or she has not hurt herself. That's a lot of power for a little girl to wield."

"We need more information before we barge into a rescue." Maud held up her hand. "You don't even have to ask this time. I will be our scout and try to find out what is going on."

Sheldrake gave a sigh of relief and smiled gently at her. "Thank you, my dear. But do be careful." He turned to Tarkyn. "I trust your eagle will allow her safe passage?"

"If you transform in front of her, Maud, she will understand that you are one of my friends." Tarkyn, with Bird glaring down from his shoulder, stroked her head. "She doesn't attack my friends."

"No, not quite," put in Rainstorm caustically. "She just intimidates us."

Maud shrugged. "An eagle couldn't catch a peregrine falcon even if it tried." She took a breath to ready herself. "Right. Watching, Bird?"

Without further discussion, Maud transformed herself into her favourite peregrine falcon shape. Bird squawked in surprise and ruffled her feathers. Tarkyn took the opportunity with Bird to pair images of Maud with images of the peregrine falcon to reinforce the point. Maud simply took off and sped through the trees, leaving them all behind, as they turned and kept walking towards The Way Through.

Chapter 50

When Jon, Reece and his men returned to their campsite and their gear, they found two rather bemused troopers making polite conversation with a middle-aged woman, whose upper-class accent and general air of grooming belied her style of dress. Her face lit up when she saw Jon.

"Maud! What are you doing here?" He ran forward and before he had time to think, grabbed her in a bear hug. "It's terrible, isn't it? Your Jayhan and my Sasha. How did you get here? Where's Sheldrake? We've been closing on the abductors for days, but now Sasha and Jayhan have run off into the forest somewhere and it's too dark to look for them. We've just killed a group of Kimorans and taken one prisoner, but there are a few more to the east. With any luck, Trevor and his group will have taken care of them. Then at least, Sasha and Jayhan will be safe from Kimorans and all we'll have to do is find them."

Maud was laughing and crying all at once. Finally, she pulled back and wiped her eyes, but didn't disengage herself from his arms. "Jon. Jon. Calm down. Sheldrake and Lord Tarkyn and Stefan and... a few others are about an hour north of here. Less by now." She straightened herself up and eying the gathering troops, inclined her head. "How do you do? I am Lady Maud Batian. I would like to thank you all, for coming to the aid of my son and his friend."

Reece gave a stiff bow. "How do you do, ma'am? I am Sergeant Reece. It is surprising to come across you so far from Highkington. We are doing the best we can for your children." He caught sight of Trevor and the other half of their squad approaching. "But if you'll excuse me, we are rather busy at the moment."

"I should hope so," she said acerbically, displeased at being dismissed so quickly. Then she turned and saw the men arriving. As they came withing the corona of the lanterns, she could see that one man was limping and another's sleeve was slashed, the edges of the cloth soaked in blood. A third man was holding a piece of cloth to a gash in his forehead, trying to staunch the flow of blood.

Without instruction, the two men who had been left guarding the camp immediately rummaged through packs to produce bandages and salves. They sat the incoming men down and set to dressing their wounds.

Trevor resisted their ministrations until he had limped over to Reece to report, glancing with some curiosity at Maud. "We killed five, I think, but three more got away. As they ran off, one of them yelled over her shoulder, 'You haven't won yet.' " He shook his head tiredly. "Well, we haven't, until we've found those children…"

"No, you haven't," growled Shay, their Kimoran prisoner, to himself. Seeing they were listening, he glared up at them from where they had dumped him on the ground.

Maud looked curiously at him. "You're the man who betrayed your fellow Kimoran refugees and struck Sheldrake with that tree branch, aren't you? Up to your old tricks again. Do you specialize in hunting down children?" she asked scathingly.

Even as she said the words, she exchanged a glance of dawning understanding with Jon.

"Oh, my word!" exclaimed Jon, turning to Shay "You're the expert shaman hunter that Queen Toriana sent two years ago to find Sasha and her amulet. You're the reason she had to leave the orphanage early."

Shay gave a nod of acknowledgement. "I nearly had her then, and I just missed her at Bryson's. By the time I'd tracked Bryson and his family down, she was no longer with them." He shrugged. "Lucky for her. Unlucky for them." He gave an unpleasant smile. "It took a lot to convince me they no longer had her… and that they didn't know where she had gone."

"Huh." Maud expelled a breath in surprise. "So, for all that he beat her as his wagon lad, he didn't betray her. Strange man."

"Brave, determined man, if he knew and didn't tell me," said Shay, giving Bryson a dispassionate evaluation. He held their gazes, a smug smile playing around his lips. "It's not over yet, you know. Three of my team got away and they're already scouring the forest while you stand here exchanging revelations with me. Three of them. That's enough."

Not surprisingly, this galvanised Maud into action. "Right. Nothing for it, I suppose." She looked around at Jon and the troopers before homing in on Reece. "Sergeant Reece, this man is an encumbrance. Would you be so kind as to have him blindfolded and tied up, well away from us?"

When Reece frowned, Jon said, "Lady Maud knows what she is doing. She is the King's personal advisor, based on her merits."

Reece's eyes narrowed. "So, does this mean you are taking over command, ma'am?"

Maud waved her hand airily. "Oh, not at all, young man. I don't have the authority to do that. I merely made a request. If you accede to it, I will take you into my confidence and work with you. If you don't, I will work alone."

Reece glanced at Jon, clearly feeling beleaguered by the presence of two nobles.

Help came from an unexpected quarter. "Come on, Reece," said Trevor, clapping the young sergeant on his back. "Give them the benefit of the doubt. After all, Jon has proved himself to have hidden depths and he vouches for the lady." His eyes twinkled, rather uncharacteristically for the prosaic tracker. "And speaking for myself, I would like to know what secrets Lady Maud may reveal."

Reece's mouth twisted into a reluctant smile and Maud could see he was trying to find a way to save face in front of his men. He gave a little bow. "Since it is in our own best interests to be as informed as possible, I will accede to your request, ma'am."

Maud smiled broadly and murmured, so quietly that only he could hear it, "Well done, young man."

Once Shay had been hauled away to a distant tree and blindfolded, Reece turned to her.

Maud made sure she was close enough to the injured troopers so that they were included, then looked around at the others. "Now, do I have everyone's attention?" Until this point, she had been the confident *grande dame*, but now she looked a little embarrassed. "I have a particular talent that allowed me to arrive in your midst so suddenly and will help us to track down the children. I do not share knowledge of my talent widely, as I use it to assist Sheldrake and his Spiders. So, I would appreciate it if you kept it to yourselves. The more people who know of it, the less use it is." She took a breath. "I am a shapeshifter."

The troopers, who were very well disciplined, did not betray any reaction but Jon grinned broadly. "Marvellous, isn't it? I expect that's how you got here. Is it, Maud?"

Despite themselves, several of the troopers exchanged little grins at Jon's enthusiasm.

"Yes, it is. I arrived as a peregrine falcon, but it is too dark and the canopy of the forest too dense for me to have spotted the children on my way here. I now intend to become a bloodhound to track the children, now that I have a starting point," Maud smiled disarmingly, "unless you have any better ideas, Sergeant Reece? I am happy to consider all options."

Reece blinked. "Uh, no ma'am. To be honest, you have caught me by surprise and my mind is struggling to catch up." He gave a little smile. "I'm glad I chose to listen to you, though." He gave a little bow. "And I am sorry if I was less than helpful. Things were rather fraught when you arrived."

"Quite all right. Things are still rather fraught, Sergeant, and I wish to be on my way immediately. Jon, of course, will wish to accompany me, but who in your squad will come and who will stay? It seems to me that some must stay here to care for the wounded and to guard your belongings."

"Yes, ma'am." Reece sent forth a string of orders which left a disgruntled Trevor and four troopers at the campsite, while Reece and the other four troopers stood ready to accompany Jon and Maud. "I'm sorry, Trevor. You, of all of us, other than Lady Maud apparently, is best qualified to track the children, but you are injured, as are Morris and Symmons. And you three need at least two men to protect you and our gear. You know I would take you otherwise."

Trevor nodded reluctantly and gave a tight smile, little more than a quirk of his mouth, in acknowledgement. "It's just as well the only Kimorans left are focused elsewhere. We would have little hope of repelling an attack."

"If you need it, I may be able to provide extra protection, but how, is one secret I will not share." Maud smiled around the group. "By the way, as a dog, I can receive images from Lord Tarkyn and I can understand you. But I cannot speak orally to you in return. Feel free to treat me as you would any dog, assuming you are kind." Maud took a deep breath, glanced around self-consciously, then transformed before their eyes into a droopy-eyed, long-eared, solid bloodhound.

For a moment, she sat still as she conveyed images to Tarkyn, apprising him of the current state of play. She knew no more about the cause of the surge of power they had witnessed from afar, but she could tell him that the children had escaped and were heading northward. She also sent a suggestive image of woodfolk protecting Trevor and his men. She followed this with an image of herself as a bloodhound and left Tarkyn to reach his own conclusions.

With that done, she dropped her head and began to sniff around the campsite. She quickly picked up Jayhan's scent. She needed none of his clothing or belongings to use as a starting point. She knew her own son's scent. Maud followed it off the path to the point where it disappeared into the dense, straggly bushes. She huffed and padded westward until she found a gap large enough for her and the men following her to crawl through. As soon as they left the path and entered the tree cover, the darkness pressed in.

"Just a moment, ma'am," murmured Reece. "We can't see where we're going. We are going to have to light a lamp. I know it's risky, but it's just as risky trying to keep up in pitch black. Um…" He glanced at Jon beside him for direction, but Jon had no idea what he wanted. "Um, ma'am… if you catch the scent of people other than the children, could you alert us? Then we'll dowse the lamp immediately."

Maud wagged her tail a couple of times, which he took as acquiescence. Once the lamp was lit, she doubled back and snuffled around until she picked up the scent, at the place where Sasha and Jayhan had emerged from the bushes. Then she sat and waited for the men to catch up.

Jon couldn't help himself. He stroked her head and crooned, "Good girl," then grimaced in embarrassment, which was luckily lost in the dark.

Maud nudged her head under his hand, indicating that she wanted more stroking. He chuckled and stroked her again. Reece frowned, giving Jon a quizzical half smile. Jon shrugged in return and kept stroking her head until everyone was bunched up around them.

"Right Maud, onward."

Chapter 51

Sasha and Jayhan stumbled on through the dark with their two companions. Sasha wondered whether meeting up with Draya and Rhoda had been all that helpful. It made them feel safer, she supposed, but it slowed them down. She was sure that just she and Jayhan would have made better progress. For a start, they now had to wait for twice as many people to recover from tripping over tree roots and rocks in the dark. And without Draya and Rhoda, Sasha could have been holding Jayhan's hand and been in direct contact with the person with the best sight, instead of groping along in his wake. Admittedly, Jayhan and she had fallen over a few times too, but… And another thing, Rhoda was wearing a voluminous skirt which kept billowing out in front of Sasha and nearly tripping her up.

Sasha gradually became aware of the sound of wheezing and, looking up, realized that Rhoda was struggling with the pace. Thinking about it, she remembered that Rhoda was a few decades older than Draya. *Oh good. Best of intentions but not really up to the job of running wildly through the night, chased by abductors. And where are we going? Do they really have any idea where we are headed in this darkness?*

Suddenly, a huge shape loomed out of the trees to Sasha's right and grabbed her arm. She let out a shriek of fright then immediately wished she hadn't, knowing it might alert everyone for miles around of their location. She tried to yank herself free, but the big hand held her firmly and dragged her away from Rhoda. Now, the last thing she wanted was to be parted from Rhoda.

"Jayhan!" she yelled desperately, giving up any hope of subterfuge.

But Jayhan was already spinning to face her, his eyes as bright as searchlights, white light streaming from them. He pulled his hand out of Draya's grasp and rushed at the attacker, who stared in horror at the apparition approaching him. The attacker's grasp on Sasha's arm went limp and he stood defenceless as the little boy barrelled into him, sending him a few steps backwards. Then Sasha, too, threw herself at the attacker and got in a hefty kick to his shin, causing him to howl in pain.

Everyone in the forest would have heard that, she thought, *but too late now.*

Her blood was up and she and Jayhan kept flailing at him with their fists, all the pent-up fear and frustration of the last few days powering every blow, while the searing white light from Jayhan's eyes kept the man cowering in fright, unable to react. Then a movement in her peripheral vision caught her attention, as Draya swung a solid branch in an arc to connect with the Kimoran's head. He dropped like a stone.

As they stood there panting, both from fright and effort, Sasha heard a mournful baying somewhere in the trees.

"Listen! That's Maud!" she exclaimed. "Jayhan, your mum's here! Let's go."

Forgetting all about heading further from the road, they ran and stumbled back the way they had come. Minutes later, Maud loped forward to greet them, with Jon and the troopers strung out behind her.

Sasha and Jayhan threw their arms around her neck, sobbing in relief. Then Sasha disentangled herself, threw herself into Jon's arms and cried into his shoulder. Reece and his four troopers looked on in great satisfaction, pleased their chase had had a happy ending.

But they were not out of the woods yet.

Rhoda and Draya caught up and stood uncertainly just outside the ring of people. Alerted by movement in the gloom but unable to see what it was, Reece and the troopers went on the offensive, but relaxed when they saw that the two women weren't clad in black.

Jon peered through the gloom at them, then broke into a smile. "Hello. Reece, men, this is Rhoda and Draya. They are the other half of the little group of Kimoran refugees we intercepted a couple of days ago. So, you kept up with them, did you, Rhoda? And you were there to protect them when they managed to escape? Well done!"

They glanced at each other. "I'm not sure how much help we were," said Rhoda. "I suspect we may have actually slowed them down."

A wave of guilt flowed through Sasha as these words so accurately reflected what she had been thinking, and she hoped that none of her thoughts had conveyed themselves to Rhoda. She slipped down out of Jon's arms and walked to take hold of the older woman's hand. "You helped. You made us feel safer. So thank you." She gave a little smile. "And don't forget, Draya did hit that man with a big branch."

Suddenly, Maud shook her head, her long, soft ears hitting Jayhan in the face and pushing him, laughing, away. As soon as he had let go, she transformed into her true form. The first thing she did was scoop Jayhan into her arms and hug him close. The second was to turn to Jon and Reece, her voice tight with urgency.

"Sheldrake, Tarkyn and the others are another mile or so north of here. Not far. But we have trouble. According to Lord Tarkyn, scores of Kimorans have been spotted moving towards us from the east."

"*Scores?*" Reece's voice came out as a squawk, much to his embarrassment. For a moment, he felt a flicker of panic as he considered his wounded men, his split force and its small size compared to the incoming threat. "Scores of them?" he repeated in a deeper voice. He straightened up, pulling himself together.

Maud was reassuringly calm. "Lord Tarkyn has suggested that we would be safer if we joined forces with them." She omitted to mention that his communication had been considerably stronger than a suggestion, aware that she had to tread carefully with Reece. "Do you agree?"

He nodded firmly. "I agree. We must keep these children safe at all costs. Even four more people will help."

"Oh," said Maud, "there are more than…" She trailed off as she realized that her need to reassure the sergeant had nearly led her into betraying the presence of the woodfolk.

"Uh, what I mean is, they are far more in power than just four. Lord Tarkyn is a fearsome sorcerer and Lord Sheldrake is a mage, more learned than fearsome I'll admit, but still with powers greater than your average man."

"That's my dad," put in Jayhan proudly. "He's pretty good."

Reece noticeably brightened. If he hadn't been in front of his men, Maud suspected he might have let out a sigh of relief. "Right. Let's go."

Chapter 52

"Local woodfolk report that the first Kimoran attackers will arrive within minutes." Silverwood's mellifluous voice held no hint of fear. "They are spread out on a wide front, threading through the trees, searching as they come."

"How many?" asked Tarkyn.

After a brief mental consultation, Silverwood replied, "Not sure, but over eighty and less than two hundred."

Tarkyn felt a wave of consternation emanate from his companions. He quelled his own reaction and sent back a wave of reassurance. "Sheldrake and I have shields. We can keep you safe."

"Not if we want to fight off the invaders," said Waterstone tersely "We can't shoot through your shield and even though you can, you can't attack that many at once on your own, even with your power ray and your *Shturrum* spell, particularly if they are spaced out among trees."

Spinifex looked puzzled. "We don't need your shield. Why would we? We'll just flick into hiding."

"You forget, Spinifex. Sorcerers and outsiders can't do that," said Lapping Water.

Tarkyn's mouth twisted ruefully. "And *I* forget that woodfolk rarely need my protection and have evaded outsiders in their forests for countless generations."

"Let's walk and talk. We must hurry," urged Sheldrake tensely. "We must reach Maud and the children before this new wave of Kimorans does." As they turned and began to stride south, Sheldrake asked Stefan to walk beside him. "Stefan, when the woodfolk flick into hiding, what will you do? Decide now, so that when the time comes, you don't hesitate."

"I'm not leaving my sister in danger," replied Stefan firmly. "I'm staying with Marjorie."

Marjorie, who was walking just ahead of them, turned and waited for them to catch up with her. "No, Stefan. I will be safely inside a sorcerer's shield if they attack us. You are a master arms man. Get up into those trees with the rest of them and use your expertise. We will need every competent arms man or woman to defeat them, if it comes to a confrontation."

Just then Tarkyn received new images from Maud. He turned, smiling broadly. "Maud has found them."

A quiet cheer went up.

"How did they look?" asked Sheldrake, his narrow face alight with excitement. "Are they all right?"

Tarkyn grinned at him. "Fit and healthy and smiles all over their faces."

"They must be very relieved, poor little things," said Lapping Water. She shifted Gurgling Brook from one hip to the other but kept walking. "How many are with them now? How much protection do they have?"

"They have two women with them. I don't know where they came from... and Jon and five Carradorian men in dark brown uniforms, if that tells you anything, Sheldrake. And Maud, of course."

"Men in brown uniforms are elite Carridorian troops, specialists in survival and under-cover work. The women..." Sheldrake shrugged. "I don't know. Maybe some of the Kimoran refugees. Couldn't say without seeing them."

"They're not far away. I have told them of the approaching Kimorans. Maud thinks if they walk towards us, and vice versa, we should meet up in about fifteen minutes."

"Let's go then," urged Sheldrake, as he started walking, half jogging with excitement. A few minutes later, he asked Silverwood, "Can any of your people see them, so we know that we're heading in the right direction?"

Spinifex answered for her. "We're right on track. Keep going. See that hill up ahead? They are coming up the other side of it."

But suddenly, ahead of them, they saw dark figures emerging from the trees on their left and spreading across the narrow path to bar their way.

"Woodfolk, go!" ordered Tarkyn, all thought of handing over control lost in the urgency of the moment. "And you too, Bird." He shrugged his shoulder, getting a squawk for his trouble. But he was determined. "Go Bird. I can't deal with you and all of this at once."

With a disgruntled shriek, she flapped her great wings, giving Tarkyn a thump on the head for good measure as she rose into the air and disappeared above the trees.

"Jackson, Marjorie, mind Gurgling Brook," said Lapping Water, thrusting her child into Jackson's arms. "Please." She gave a brief smile and disappeared.

Tarkyn frowned in surprise at her unilateral decision to allow their woodfolk sorcerer child to be seen by outsiders, but he had no time to worry about it now.

In an instant, only Sheldrake, Marjorie and Jackson stood with Tarkyn on the path, one holding a little woodchild, encased inside the bronze dome of Tarkyn's shield.

"Keep walking," he said. "We have to get to those children. They only have eight adults with them and some of them aren't fighters."

As they neared the first of the Kimorans, Tarkyn received a query from Waterstone that he relayed to Sheldrake. "Arrows or slingshots? Do you want them dead or unconscious?"

Sheldrake looked startled. "Oh, my word. They are good, aren't they?" He would have preferred more time to think through the political ramifications but with the need for a snap decision, he erred on the side of mercy and political caution. "Slingshots."

Even as the word left his mouth, seven of the dark clad figures blocking their path slumped to the ground.

"Keep walking," said Tarkyn grimly.

Six more fell. Those left standing looked frantically around themselves, torn between fear of the unseen attackers and their need to keep Tarkyn's small group from joining up with the children. But they took heart as more of their comrades emerged from the trees to bolster their numbers.

In the distance now, they could hear the sounds of blades clashing. Both sides redoubled their efforts.

Tarkyn's shield came up against the first line of Kimorans. He sent a shaft of power through his shield that tore into the ground at the feet of their attackers. As they stumbled backwards in shock, Tarkyn pressed forward, gaining several yards before they recovered.

Suddenly, the sound of clashing steel stopped. A sense of dread crept over Tarkyn and Sheldrake.

"They've stopped. Why? They can't have beaten the Kimorans so quickly. There are too many of them," said Marjorie, voicing everyone's fears.

Chapter 53

Reece, Jon and the four troopers had deployed themselves around Sasha and Jayhan as they set off on the final leg to join Tarkyn, Sheldrake and the others. At her request, Draya had been given someone's spare sword so that she could take her place among them. Maud and Rhoda stayed beside the children.

"We can help too, you know," protested Jayhan, looking up at his mother, who was firmly holding his hand.

"Especially if there are any shamans among them," added Sasha.

"I'm sure you can," replied Maud, her tone placating rather than convinced, even though she had seen both of them in action in the past, "but you are their target. They won't even bother to fight us if they can just grab you and run."

"True," said Sasha in a small voice, but she clasped her amulet and focused hard on her heartbeat, hoping that she might be able to affect any shamans who came in range, even if she couldn't see them. She could only try.

They trudged on up the hill between shadowy bushes and under dark branches, whose leaves gained colour and lost it as they passed beneath them with their lamp. They were all tired after a long day but were driven by the wish to join up with allies against the incoming Kimorans. It was now full dark, and although the lamp was a risk, they had decided on speed over caution. But every sense was stretched for sight or sound of new interlopers.

"Look!" said Jon, pointing ahead. "I think I can see a glimmer of light reflecting in the trees."

Reece frowned. "Rhoda, could you shield the lantern for a minute, so we can see better, please?" After a few moments, he nodded. "You're right. Jon, I think the source of the light we can see is somewhere over the other side of the hill. Not far now," he said he6eningly. "They must be just over that ridge."

It was just as well they had shrouded their lamp. It meant their adjusted eyes took a split second less time to see the dark shapes swarming towards them out of the shadows.

"We're under attack!" shouted Reece. "Keep the lamp dowsed. Stand firm, men… and women."

Blades came whistling out of the darkness. Jon ducked under a sword and stepped in, driving his dagger into his assailant's chest. A slighter but muscled woman came at him from the side with a roundhouse swing of her blade. As Jon tried desperately to wrench his blade from the first assailant to defend himself, the woman fell to the ground without a word. Jon frowned, unable to see who had saved him.

"Thanks," he muttered, as he turned to face the next assailant.

Beside him, Reece was clashing blades with a tall man whose longer reach was making his defences difficult to breach. His attacker pressed him hard, but Reece refused to step back and let him get any closer to his charges behind him. In a sudden movement, the man dropped the tip of his blade, unbalancing Reece. The Kimoran drew his arm back for a killing blow, and with sickening clarity, Reece knew he wouldn't have time to recover. Then the Kimoran's eyes rolled up in his head and he fell limply to the ground. Reece blinked in surprise. He looked around for his saviour but could see no one in reach.

"D'you see that?" he muttered. "He just dropped where he stood."

"Yep. Happened to me, too," replied Jon, between heavy breaths.

Hearing this, Draya gave her head a slight shake but had to keep her focus, as two assailants rushed her in a pincer movement. She sidestepped one and swung her sword around just in time to block the other, but as soon as she had her eyes on the second, the first one closed in behind her, swinging a backhand cut at her ribs. She braced for the blow, but instead, the sword clattered from the man's nerveless hand. Draya glanced at the falling man without comprehension, but had no time to contemplate the cause, as the second man came at her again.

Dark-clad figures were rushing them on all sides. Reece and his men were hard-pressed. Jon and Draya helped to make the circle stronger, but it was still a pitiful few against scores of well-trained opponents. All around them, Kimoran men and women dropped in their tracks. No one understood why. But heedless of their falling comrades, the black-clad figures came on, stepping over their bodies.

A shout of pain issued from the circle protecting the children, as one of the troopers was sliced across the forearm. Then Jon, stepping sideways, stood on a loose rock and his foot went from under him. As he slid down and sideways, three assailants homed in on him, seeing him as easy prey.

From behind Reece, came an anguished yell as Jayhan twisted his hand out of his mother's and rushed forward, his eyes blazing with white light. Immediately, the three assailants and the attackers on either side of them cowered back, all the fight gone from them. Then, they simply keeled over, and lay unmoving.

Jayhan stopped dead, shocked by the unexpected success of his charge. He had never knocked people out before. But the light from his eyes could not reach all the attackers. Shielded by those in front of them, many kept pushing forward. Jon rolled to his feet and bodily returned Jayhan to his mother, saying, "Thanks, young one, but stay back," before returning to his place beside Reece.

Jayhan frowned in frustration as Maud took a firmer grip on his hand. "Ow, Mum. You're hurting me."

Her grip lessened only slightly.

"Well done, Jayhan," murmured Sasha. "*I* thought that was great… but stay with me. I don't want to lose you," she said. "Your eyes worked really well, but they only affect the first row in a crush like this. Not enough people can see them."

They stood in the darkness, surrounded by larger people, hearing the grunts of effort, yells and screams of pain, and the constant clash of steel. Sasha watched in gathering horror as angry, hate-filled faces loomed out of the darkness, all with the sole purpose of capturing her. She clung close to Rhoda.

At least one Kimoran was on her side... and Draya. *But all these other people... Was Kimora just a land full of vicious killers, now that the refugees had left?*

Unseen in the trees around them, a score of woodfolk took careful aim to send small rocks speeding viciously towards Kimoran attackers, whenever the need was dire or when they could get a clear shot.

Directly above Maud, Stefan lay along a branch with Autumn Leaves on the next branch to his left and Spinifex to his right. He sent a constant barrage of pebbles from the small shanghai wherever he could get a clear shot at a Kimoran's temple. Silverwood, Tree Fern and Iron Bark stood in the next tree along.

Other woodfolk he had not met were strung through the surrounding trees, all firing on the enemy to protect the children in the beleaguered group below.

Suddenly a feeling of kinship, of being part of a powerful, skilful nation of people, welled up inside him. For a few moments, Stefan let his gaze take in the hidden might of the wood-folk around him. He glowed with pride that he was one of them.

"Quick! That one," said Autumn Leaves in his mind, bringing him back to his task. "She's about to chop into Reece. I can't get the angle from here."

Stefan sent a small stone whizzing towards the side of the attacker's head and a moment later the Kimoran fell, knocked out cold.

"Well done," came Autumn Leaves' mindtalk. "Another to your right."

Stefan continued to aim and release, aim and release, with a growing sense of desperation. There were so many of them. He knew that, in the end, the woodfolk would prevail, because the Kimorans couldn't fight off an unseen foe.

But not fast enough.

A constant stream of black figures appeared out of the darkness and despite their best efforts, he and the woodfolk couldn't dispatch them fast enough to save the depleted circle that was fighting with growing desperation to protect the children.

Below him, another trooper cried out and collapsed as a sword was driven into his thigh. Draya moved to stand over him, lashing out savagely at anyone who came within reach until Rhoda and Maud could pull the wounded man back behind the fighting. As Rhoda and Sasha struggled desperately to staunch his bleeding leg, the circle contracted to keep him and them safe within it. Jon, Draya and even Reece and his remaining troopers were breathing in ragged gasps as they blocked and thrust, their arms growing sluggish against men and women who stepped forward, fresh and eager to fight.

Another wave of assailants thrust at them. In answer, the gallant defenders dredged the depths of their strength in what they feared would be a final effort.

Then, at the back of their awareness, they felt a movement within the circle behind them.

Suddenly, Maud bellowed, "Disengage and step back. NOW!"

Her voice was so sure and so vehement that they obeyed without question. Immediately, a dark haze appeared between them and the Kimorans.

In their surprise, several of them stepped back even further, treading on the feet of people behind them. Most managed to stay upright, but Jon fell in a tangled heap. From his position on the ground, he looked up to see the haze extending in a dome over them and a small boy standing close to Maud, looking down at him.

Jon wiped his sweaty forehead and frowned. "Who are you? Where did you come from... ? What's going on?"

Maud calmly re-ignited the lamp, showing them a small boy with dark brown hair and brilliant green eyes, watching them warily. Maud put her arm around his shoulder. "This is Midnight. He is... a sorcerer and, I believe, a guardian of the forest. He is also Lord Tarkyn's ward." She waved her arm at the dome which covered them and which they could now see was dark green. It was holding at bay a bevy of frustrated Kimorans. "This is his shield. He has just saved our lives," her mouth twisted, "... unless you thought you were going to continue to hold out against those hordes out there."

Reece ran a hand through his hair and got out between gasps, "No ma'am. I did not. We would never have given up, but it looked like we were going to die trying." He glanced out at the faces surrounding them in the darkness. "They seem endless. They just keep on coming." He took a deep breath and let it out, releasing some of the tension from the fighting. Then he squatted down in front of Midnight and smiled. "Thank you, young man."

Midnight glanced at Sasha and Jayhan then around at the men and women towering over him in the close confines of his shield. He brought his gaze back to Reece and nodded solemnly.

"He's deaf," explained Maud quietly, "but I think he understood what you said. He is frightened of strangers, so it has taken great courage for him to come amongst us." She gently stroked his head. "Now I think about it, he is the only one who could have. Tarkyn and Sheldrake can raise shields but neither of them could have flicked to stand among us."

"Flick?" asked Jon.

"Flick, uh, move instantly from one place to another, only within sight and not through objects, only around them. So you couldn't escape from jail by flicking, but you could flick into hiding behind a tree."

Jon raised his eyebrows and smiled. "Very interesting." He reached into his pocket, pulled out a bit of dried apricot and held it out to Midnight, with an encouraging nod.

Midnight took the offering, the side of his mouth quirking slightly in acknowledgement. He didn't eat it but put it in his own pocket for later.

After a bemused moment, Jon turned to Maud, "So, can we keep walking up the hill inside this shield or do we have to stay still? I have had no experience of sorcerers' shields."

"We can move, provided, of course, that Midnight does." She frowned out into the darkness. "But I'm not sure how well we will be able to plough through all those people between us and the others." She tapped Midnight on the shoulder and pointed at him, then everyone in the shield, before making a walking motion with her fingers and pointing up the hill. She tilted her head in query.

Midnight turned to look up the hill and came face to face with a montage of angry faces. He jolted backwards and for a moment, his shield flickered. But he took a deep breath, clearly steadying himself and the haze around them became, if anything, denser.

"Sir," said Warrun, "these Kimorans are still dying all around us. I just saw another one keel over."

For a minute, everyone watched the people outside the shield and sure enough, their attackers were slowly but surely succumbing to some unknown phenomena. Despite their comrades falling all around them, a horde of determined men and women still stood across the upward path, pressing in against the outside of the shield.

"I don't know who's doing it, sir. I can't see anyone. Maybe it's some strange malady. Whatever it is, it saved our lives over and over out there."

"I don't know any more than you, Warrun," replied Reece.

He was distracted from saying anything further by the sight of Midnight, who tilted his head as he tuned in to a distant mind. Midnight gave a little grin before thrusting one hand forward, sending a ray of dark green magic spearing though his shield to blast the dirt at the feet of the Kimorans blocking their path.

The Kimorans stumbled backwards in shock.

Midnight immediately pushed his shield forward into the gap. Then he glanced around his companions to check their reaction. Jon and Reece nodded vigorously and smiled. Jayhan and Sasha patted him on the shoulder, their eyes shining with excitement.

So, he turned once more and tried it again. But this time, his shaft of power didn't have the shock value and although the Kimorans shied out of the way, they quickly regrouped. Midnight tried again but the same thing happened. The Kimorans regrouped before he could move the shield forward.

"Jayhan, he needs more power. You can help him," said Sasha urgently.

Jayhan's eyes widened. "Yeah. So I can."

He grabbed Midnight's hand, which made the boy jump with fright and shy away from him. For a moment, the shield flickered.

"Gently, Jayhan," scolded Sasha.

Jayhan grinned sheepishly at Midnight. "Oops, sorry." He pointed at his hand that was still holding Midnight's and gestured to indicate that Midnight should send another shaft of power. Midnight frowned in confusion but after a moment, took a deep breath and sent forth another shaft. This time, the power hit the ground with a sharp retort, sending dirt flying high into the air and gouging a deep rut in the path. Some of the assailants were thrown off their feet by the strength of the blast. Before they could press back in, Midnight pushed his shield forward and glanced at Jayhan

"Onward!" shouted Jayhan, grinning and waving his other arm.

Midnight almost smiled in return. Almost. Then he turned forward once more and thrust his hand out, sending another blast of power scattering the opposition and tearing up the path. As he pushed forward, he began to grin and suddenly, he and Jayhan were just playing a game and having fun with his power. Over and over, he sent forth Jayhan-enhanced shafts of power and slowly they progressed up the hill.

Now they could see that Sheldrake's light orb had crested the hill and they could see that it came from a bronze-coloured dome containing four people. A tall man with unusually long, black hair stood at the front of the shield, employing the same tactic as Midnight and sending forth bronze power rays that forced back the Kimoran attackers. And all the while, the numbers of attackers thinned as they dropped one by one to the ground.

Within minutes, the two hemispheres of light had forged a path to each other. When they were touching, Tarkyn stood with his hands on his hips looking down at Midnight, his strange amber eyes glowing with pride at his ward's achievement. "Well done, Midnight. You are the cleverest, bravest boy in the whole world," he said, matching images to words.

Midnight beamed.

Part 9

Chapter 54

With a flick of his wrist, Tarkyn enlarged his shield and lifted it up over Midnight's so the little boy could drop his. Instantly, the dark green dome disappeared, and Midnight sagged a little at the release of effort, then ran forward to jump into Tarkyn's arms. Tarkyn hugged him tightly and swung himself in a full circle, while Jackson and Marjorie patted his back as it flew past. Jayhan dodged past them into his father's waiting arms.

Tarkyn swung Midnight onto one hip and collected himself enough to welcome the new arrivals. "Hello, Maud. Well done to you, too; finding the little ones in time. Close run thing, I gather." He looked at the others in the little group. "Hello, Lord Jon. I believe we met at that excruciating, formal luncheon at the King's palace. Hello, Sasha. I don't know the rest of you, but I am very glad to see you. I am Prince Tarkyn, High Lord of Eskuzor." He smiled disarmingly. "But if you wish, you may call me Tarkyn for now." He raised his eyebrows. "Now, who are you people?"

Reece gave a neat bow and said, "I am Sergeant Reece and these men are half of my squad, Your Highness. The rest of my men are back on The Way Through."

"So I understand. Don't worry," said Tarkyn. "We're protecting them." He transferred his attention to Reece's men. "And your names?" Long gone was the time when Tarkyn would take anyone for granted.

Warrun and the other three troopers looked faintly surprised but introduced themselves.

"And may I also present Draya and Rhoda, refugee shamans from Kimora," said Jon, "who shadowed the attackers for several days and were ready to intercept the children and look after them when they escaped."

"Pleased to meet you all. The actions of all of you have been heroic in protecting the children." Then Tarkyn frowned and looked closer. "I see two of you, at least, are wounded. What we need is a fire and cups of tea while I repair the injured."

"We can do it," said Rhoda firmly. "We just haven't had the chance 'til now, other than a quick bandage."

"Really? Are you forest guardians, then? Can you communicate with animals?" asked Tarkyn, intrigued. "I thought forest guardians were very rare. They are, in Eskuzor."

Draya gave a short laugh. "No. We're shamans. We can't talk to animals, but we can heal; some of us better than others."

Reece looked puzzled. "But My Lord, we are still surrounded by the enemy."

Tarkyn waved his hand dismissively. "Oh, very few left now. Don't worry about them. The important thing is that you're safe."

"Right." Reece just looked dazed. He felt his command had well and truly been wrested from him but didn't have the energy to resist, or even the wish to, at the moment.

Marjorie glanced at him to see if he was going to say more, before offering, "Jackson and I will make the tea. We didn't have to fight like you did, so we're not tired."

"Thanks. Thank you very much." Reece pulled himself together enough to ask, "And might I ask, Sire, who your companions are?"

"Oh, I beg your pardon," said Tarkyn. "I should have said. This is Lord Sheldrake. He's the one hugging Maud and Jayhan, and this is Stefan's sister, Marjorie."

"You already know Stefan, Reece," put in Jon. "The arms master."

As Reece nodded, Tarkyn continued, "And this is the estimable Jackson, my aide-de-camp, who is holding my daughter, Gurgling Brook. Jackson, could you please take over shielding us? I am growing weary. I would ask Sheldrake, but he is providing us with light which, I must say, he is managing to maintain while reuniting with his wife and child. You never know, Sheldrake, I might be able to teach you to do two spells simultaneously."

Sheldrake held his little family close to him. "Not right now." Maud and Jayhan exchanged a glance of surprise. That Sheldrake so easily dismissed a discussion of magic showed them, even more than his embrace and his beaming smile, how much they meant to him.

Tarkyn gave a grunt of laughter. "No. I didn't mean right now." He stared around into the gloom, completely ignoring the remaining Kimorans. "Any trees nearby? I'm feeling a bit light-headed."

Sasha watched the bemused looks on her companions' faces as Tarkyn bounced from one topic to another. He was so energetic and enthusiastic and... commanding. She wondered whether she would have to be like that to be a queen. She didn't think she had it in her. She wondered whether the people in Eskuzor were nicer than the Kimorans.

"Midnight might find it helpful, too," he was saying. "He used an enormous amount of power for a little one... and doing two spells at once. That takes a lot of concentration."

"Impressive little fellow," said Sheldrake, his arm still around Jayhan.

"Jayhan helped Midnight, you know," said Sasha, loyally giving him credit while at the same time envying him the attention that Sheldrake was giving him. "Jayhan increased Midnight's power so that he could make bigger blasts."

Something in her voice or her stance must have given her away. Sheldrake looked over at her, where she stood holding Jon's hand. He smiled at her and tweaked a finger. "Sasha, my little stable hand. Come and give your employer a hug. I missed you, too, you know."

Sasha took two nonchalant steps towards him, then, giving up all pretence, rushed over to him. Sheldrake disengaged himself from his family to pick her up and hug her to his chest. Maud and Jayhan had never seen Sheldrake so demonstrative.

Tarkyn watched Jayhan stand to one side, quite happy, in fact pleased, for Sasha to share his family. "You're an impressive young man," he said to the little boy, meaning it in more ways than one. "What an interesting skill you have. Well done."

Jayhan gave a little shrug. "Thanks, but Sasha thought of it." He turned and grinned at Midnight, "and it was really fun, wasn't it, Midnight?"

Midnight grinned back and sent Tarkyn images of them blasting their way up the hill, showing him the difference Jayhan's power had made, and at the same time, without consciously meaning to, showing him the friendship they had struck up.

Tarkyn smiled down at his little Midnight and stroked his hair, beginning to slow down. "Thank you, Jayhan. He loved it."

Maud waited a moment before saying, "Tarkyn, there is a good-sized gum tree a few yards to your left. It may involve stepping over a few Kimorans, though."

He peered in the direction she had pointed. "Only a couple. We'll push them out of the way and deal with them later." Once he had sat down with his hand on the tree, he exhaled and let his shoulders drop. He looked around at everyone watching him and gave a slow smile. Then he said, speaking more slowly, "Sorry. I've been babbling, haven't I? I'm a bit wired up. I suppose all of you are too, aren't you? I am so pleased that we have Sasha and Jayhan safe. Congratulations to all of you." He took another deep breath. "Right. Bring forth our wounded, Pieter and Ramon, isn't it? Then I can watch Rhoda and Draya strut their stuff while Sasha and Jayhan can tell us what caused that amazing lightning in the sky and how they got away."

"... and you can tell us how Midnight found us," added Jon.

"Oh, that's easy to answer. He felt Jayhan's strong reaction to something, probably one or all of you under threat, and followed it to its source by flicking several times until he reached you. I didn't ask him to. He was up in the trees at the time and just realized your need was dire." Tarkyn smiled down at Midnight, who was sitting within the crook of his arm, munching the apricot Jon had given him earlier.

Sometime later, when everyone was installed with cups of tea and the wounded troopers had been healed by the two shamans, Tarkyn drew a long breath and said, "Once all the Kimorans are knocked out, we'll have some work to do, disarming them all and trussing them up before they come round again."

"Only knocked out, are they?" Jon gazed around at the bodies strewn around them; large, small, wiry, solid, many dark-skinned like Sasha, many as light-skinned as he was. "I'm glad." He gave a slight, self-conscious smile. "After all, these *are* my people."

That smile spoke volumes. Jon and Tarkyn both came from a royal family and both were, according to birthright, brother to a queen. They were both tall, but Jon was fair and willowy, while Taryn was strongly built and dark-haired. Jon was friendly, gentle and whimsical while Tarkyn was sure and strong, but also kind. Tarkyn had always lived with the sure knowledge that it was an honour for people to meet him, whereas Jon had lived for the last ten years in obscurity, alone and unsupported.

Tarkyn gave him a gentle smile. "So I understand. Sheldrake and Maud have honoured us with your story; yours and Sasha's. So I have some idea how you must feel. When I was trying to prevent my brothers from beginning a civil war, I always tried to avoid killing their soldiers. I wanted to protect Eskuzor, but not by destroying its citizens."

"Huh." Jon looked thoughtful. "I'm pleased to hear that..." A frown gradually gathered on his face. "But how exactly have you managed to disable so many without killing them and without any visible armed force?"

Chapter 55

Jon expected Tarkyn to explain proudly how he or they had managed it but instead, he looked uneasy and embarrassed. After some hesitation, he replied, "I'm afraid I can't tell you that right now."

Jon and the troopers and the shamans looked intrigued and Tarkyn could see they were conjecturing wildly.

"Interesting," said Jon. "So, it's secret sorcerer's business, is it? Some kind of spell that will wear off over time?"

Tarkyn was almost tempted to let him think that it was. It was a good explanation that would cover up the existence of woodfolk. He let out a sigh and gave a wry smile, aware that his integrity often landed him in difficult situations that dissemblance could avoid.

"Not exactly," was all he said. He diverted the conversation by becoming business-like. "Now, time to get to work. Reece, I think we need to look after the wounded men you left at The Way Through. Jackson, would you take Draya and Rhoda down there, please? Can you hold a shield for that long?"

"How far is it?" asked Jackson. "How long will it take us to get there?"

"About an hour, maybe less," said Reece. "Maybe one of my men should accompany them to show them the way."

"No need," said Draya. "We know where we're going. Are all the Kimorans unconscious now?"

Tarkyn looked distracted for a moment before saying, "Yes, I believe so."

Draya nodded briskly. "Then we have no need of a shield. You have a lot of Kimorans to disarm and tie up and a short time to do it in. So, you get cracking and so will we."

Ah, thought Tarkyn, *matriarchal society. Like the independent woodwomen but more so.* He didn't like her tone of voice but didn't argue. "Very well. We'll meet you there as soon as we can."

As they watched the lantern carried by Rhoda bob its way down the hill and into the trees, Jackson said, "Does that mean I can drop my shield now?"

Tarkyn considered the options. "I think so, but until tomorrow morning when we can see what we are doing and are sure the threat has passed, I want Jon, Jayhan and Sasha to remain within a shield. I don't mind whether it is yours or Sheldrake's."

"I would like to stay with Jayhan... and Sasha," said Sheldrake. "Midnight might like to join us, too, if they have become friends. Then I can bed them down and they can get some sleep. We won't need a light. We can just settle down somewhere and wait."

"If you can manage it, Lord Sheldrake, and if you children aren't too tired," said Reece, "I suggest that you walk down to The Way Through before bedding down. The site down there is better for a large group to camp the night and it is close to a stream, whereas here, we are on top of a ridge with no water supply close by. Then, we can work our way down the hill to join you and we can all bed down in the same place."

Jon, who was actually the most tired of this little group, having walked all day like the others and then fought a pitched battle, nodded. "We can do that, can't we, little ones?" He smiled at Midnight. "Are you coming too? Then we can use your shield while Sheldrake provides us with light for the walk. What do you think?"

Tarkyn relayed Jon's words into images, knowing Midnight was much more likely to feel brave enough to go with relative strangers, if he had a role to play. Midnight glanced up at Tarkyn, who assured him that he would join him in a while.

Soon after they had departed, Stefan appeared beside Tarkyn. "Well, that was a close call, despite our best efforts. Midnight came just in time." He swung his rucksack off his shoulders and proceeded to bring out several large rolls of thin leather strips, which he laid on the ground. He grinned. "You might need these if you're going to truss up scores of Kimorans."

Tarkyn's face cleared. "Oh, good. That's one problem solved."

"And I think you'll find that many of them have already had their weapons removed and their hands tied. Some of them still have wounds that need to be bound."

"Hello, Stefan," interrupted Reece. "Haven't seen you since I finished my training. Where did you spring from?"

In answer, Stefan flicked twenty yards to appear right next to Reece, making him rear back in surprise. "I can flick like Midnight does; a recently discovered talent I didn't know I had."

Reece raised his eyebrows. "That's bloody handy. I wish I could do that. So why weren't you with Lord Tarkyn and the others?" he asked, a hint of censure in his voice.

"We decided that I could use my archery skills better by positioning myself in a tree. So I was above you, but not within the shield, helping to stave off the hordes that were attacking you."

"So that why some of those Kimorans just dropped where they stood. Good work. You saved Jon and me more than once." Reece smiled in apology for doubting him. "You should have come down sooner. You missed out on a cup of tea." Then a frown developed on his face as he thought about it. "I know you're good, but you couldn't possibly have felled all of those Kimorans on your own... could you?"

"No, of course not."

Reece was clearly waiting for further clarification, but Stefan dodged the unasked question by addressing himself to Tarkyn. "Sire, do you think someone other than you could direct the operation of securing the Kimorans? I need to speak privately with you."

Tarkyn nodded, glad to have a way to escape, in order to confer with his woodfolk. "Reece? Could you organise your troopers, please? Work your way from here down towards The Way Through. Maud, Marjorie and Jackson, are you happy to work with the troopers? Stefan and I will meet you at the other end, if not before." He reached out to Marjorie, who was now holding Gurgling Brook. "I'll take her off your hands now. Thank you for looking after her."

"It's a pleasure." Marjorie smiled and tapped her on the nose. "She is such a sweetie and she stayed so calm amongst all that noise and turmoil. No trouble at all."

Gurgling Brook smiled sunnily and waved at her over her father's shoulder, as she was borne away. "Bye-bye, Marjee. Bye, Jasson."

Stefan followed Tarkyn off the track into the trees on the right. As soon as they were out of sight and earshot, Stefan's family and Tarkyn's woodfolk appeared around them.

Tarkyn beamed at them. "Well done, my friends. What a marvellous job you've done. And I presume, Silverwood, that your kin also assisted us. So, thank them too, if you would."

Rainstorm bounced up to him. "I liked your power blasts through your shield. Very spectacular. And what about Midnight? One minute, he's next to me in a tall gum down the path a bit; the next minute, I see his shield appear way down the track, right in the thick of the fighting." He shook his head admiringly. "Brave little fella, especially after all he's been through."

"But now," said Waterstone, cutting to the chase, "we are in a right pickle. How are you going to explain all these unconscious bodies strewn about the place?"

Autumn Leaves huffed, "Jon came up with a perfectly good explanation, but did you accept it, Tarkyn? No."

Tarkyn, who knew his extreme integrity sometimes drove Autumn Leaves to distraction, smiled sympathetically. "It did cross my mind that it would be convenient to let him think that it was some sort of magic spell. But," he shrugged, "you know I don't like deceiving people. It's so disrespectful to them. But also... well, you know me. I couldn't have pulled it off. He'd have asked how it was done, or something else that would have had me floundering in prevarication in no time."

Autumn Leaves gave a grunt of laughter. "True."

"I'm afraid none of us thought this far ahead," said Ironbark. "After all, we thought we would only be dealing with the original abductors. It was only at the last minute that we realised the numbers involved. By then, we were committed to assisting you."

"Knocking out a few here and there could have passed unnoticed." Sphagnum Moss sighed. "But now... "

"Now, if we leave it unexplained..." Lapping Water reached out for Gurgling Brook, "I'll take her. Hello. Did you have fun?" Once the little girl had nodded, her mother continued, "If we leave it unexplained, these troopers and Jon and those children will make up all sorts of stories, and rumours will fly all over Highkington. Fairly counterproductive, I would have thought. It would direct too much attention to the forest."

"And by the time those troopers tie up the last of the Kimorans and remove their weapons, they are bound to notice bruises on some of them from the rocks we shot at them, even if they can't identify the ammunition," said Tree Fern.

Lapping Water noticed that Tree Fern sounded more mature and less defensive than usual. Maybe the action had given her a sense of purpose.

A gloomy silence fell.

After a minute, Lapping Water said, "We might as well sit down. I don't know about you people, but I'm tired from all that climbing through the trees looking for good positions to aim from. We haven't stopped since those Kimorans appeared."

"I'll make tea," said Rainstorm brightly.

"Good idea. I'll get a fire going," said Tree Fern, causing some raised eyebrows amongst her family, who were used to her being abrasive.

Sphagnum Moss settled himself against a fallen log and watched as a small fire sprang to life in the midst of a neat pyramid of small twigs. As Tree Fern fed large twigs then small branches onto it, he asked, "How many of these outsiders are there altogether? Not counting the Kimoran intruders, of course."

"Sheldrake, Maud, Marjorie and Jackson, you have already met, "said Tarkyn, ticking them off on his fingers as he brought them to mind. "Then there are Jayhan and Sasha, the two children we rescued, and Jon, who is Sasha's older brother. There are also the two shamans, Draya and Rhoda, and couple of Kimoran refugees, Argus and Beetlebrow, who are likely to join us later, I understand. Besides that, there are ten troopers. That is all."

Spinifex boggled. "That's *all*? That is at least seventeen new outsiders who are probably working out, as we speak, that a hidden force of people has come to their aid."

"Oh well, don't worry," said Stefan, with a touch of acid in his voice. "There are hundreds, possibly thousands of outsiders who have seen me over the years. So it's not as though they haven't seen a woodman before. I've met Jon, Reece and all the troopers before and even trained some of them."

Spinifex spluttered. "Yes, but..."

"Yes but what?" pressed Stefan. "What are you going to do? Kill them off because they might work out the existence of woodfolk? Why don't we just go for wholesale murder of everyone I've ever met?"

Waterstone moved quietly over and put his hand on Stefan's arm.

"Stefan," he said in a low, calming voice, "I think some of your resentment at being abandoned, however unintentionally, by your woodfolk kin, is currently getting in the way of rationale argument. No one has suggested killing them all off..." he gave a cheeky smile, "although it is, of course, an option."

"Not a good one though," said Ironbark repressively, worried that Stefan would fire up again. "After all, what's the point of saving them all, if we just turn around and kill them? Not sensible."

"Stefan, my son-nephew," said Spinifex patiently, "give us a chance to adjust. Four days ago, I had never met an outsider in my life. But more than that, our whole creed forbids it. You think nothing of it, but for us, these last few days have been a constant strain, interacting with outsiders. It's not that I don't like them. I do, actually... and I am becoming easier with them. But..." he waved his hand. "... never mind."

Stefan stared at him. "So does that mean you're uneasy with me?"

Spinifex stared back at him. Then his mouth quirked. "Oh, totally." This rather took the wind out of Stefan's sails. "Be honest. Don't you feel a little awkward with us? You're an unknown quantity to us, just as we are to you. I'm sure we'll get over it in time, but at the moment, we're all unsure and self-conscious."

Suddenly Stefan chuckled. "True. Now at least we can all be self-conscious together." He grinned around at the other members of his woodfolk family and they all laughed or smiled in return, relieved to have it out in the open.

Tree Fern walked over and slipped her arm through his. "So what they're saying, cousin-brother, is that they're nervous about meeting so many outsiders. We can't meet them when the Kimoran invaders are around to see, obviously. Now that *would* be too many. But I think we've decided to let them know who we are." She looked around. "Yes?"

Silverwood glanced at her brothers before saying firmly, "Yes."

"But they have to be sworn to secrecy, of course," said Tarkyn. "Normally, they would make their oath to me, but I'm not their liege lord. Sheldrake or Maud are the King's representatives and since the troopers are the King's men, maybe one of them can take their oaths."

"They can make their oaths to us," said Silverwood firmly, cutting through what was, to her, the irrelevance of hierarchy. "It will, after all, be a pact between them and us; that they keep our existence secret, in return for their lives."

"Right," said Tarkyn, looking a little embarrassed. "Good idea. I should have thought of that." He frowned repressively at Rainstorm who was chortling into his cup of tea, just as an unexpected communication came through from some of the woodfolk stationed further down the path.

Chapter 56

The two shamans strode off down the path, stepping between the unconscious forms of their compatriots. As they reached the spot where they, Jon and the troopers had made their desperate stand, Rhoda heard someone groaning.

She put her hand on Draya's arm. "Wait. Listen." She swung the lantern over the sea of bodies, looking for the source of the sound. "Ah. Here, Draya."

Rhoda held the lantern up while Draya leant over to inspect a young woman who had a shallow sword-cut along the side of her head. Draya squatted down to inspect it carefully. After a few moments, she straightened and said, "I can't see why she was knocked out. That cut wouldn't do it. It looks a bit messy with blood seeping through her hair, but it's not deep. I think we can repair it quickly before we move on."

"But why isn't she staying unconscious like the others? She wasn't knocked out by our friends in the trees. They made sure their victims wouldn't rouse too soon, so we and they could have a chance to immobilise them."

Above them, watching from nearby tree branches, four woodfolk froze in shock. *They know about us.* Frenzied messages shot to the woodfolk stationed above Marjorie and Jackson. They checked with the woodfolk who had been near Maud and then to those with Tarkyn. None of them had told the shamans about woodfolk.

Oblivious to the consternation raging overhead, Draya looked closer then put her hand inside the woman's collar to pull out a moonstone amulet on the end of a silver chain. Without a word, she brought out her own amulet and watched as soft light from the two amulets beat in unison. She looked up at Rhoda. "I think Sasha's proximity must have freed this shaman from Toriana's hold."

Rhoda nodded. "That would explain why she is recovering at a different rate from the others. Her blackout was from a different cause."

"I think we'd better rouse her and take her with us."

Just then, they heard a twig snap under someone's foot, then the crunch of forest floor detritus as someone walked heavily towards them from the south. Rhoda held up the lantern, peering into the darkness, her heart hammering in her chest. "I'm beginning to regret our refusal of a shield. Too independent by half you are, sometimes."

"Rubbish. Whoever it is, isn't a threat. They're making no effort to conceal their approach, are they?" She raised her voice. "Hello? Who are you? Come and join us." As they heard the sound of stumbling, she added, "Are you all right?"

The footsteps righted themselves and a minute later, a disoriented woman in dark clothing came into view. As she came closer, they could see that she was middle-aged with her grey hair dishevelled, fuzzy strands sticking out in all directions. Her uniform was actually dark blue with pale orange trim. Her eyes were unfocused, and she seemed close to collapse.

"Hello?" said Draya again. "Can you hear us?" Then she frowned and looked closer. "Hang on. You're Arquin, Lady Arquin, aren't you?"

"Major."

"Major Arquin?" When the woman nodded, Draya exchanged worried glances with Rhoda and her hand went down to the pommel of the sword she was still wearing. "She's a powerful shaman, this one," she muttered to Rhoda.

The woman gave an out-of-focus smile. "Hello. I'm looking for... I am looking for the true Queen. She's out here somewhere."

Draya narrowed her eyes. "Just a minute. Are you the shaman who instigated that huge storm?"

"Yes. Have you seen her?"

"Who? Queen Toriana? So far from court?" asked Draya, testing.

The woman leant closer and nearly lost her balance in the process. She managed to co-ordinate enough to get her finger up to her mouth. "Shh. No. No, I don't think so. No. It's my amulet, you see. It's changed rhythm. It's beating faster. Not a lot, just a bit. But it's different. I notice these things, you see." She gave a sluggish frown. "And a little while ago, it was beating very fast indeed, several times, in fact."

"Really?" said Draya. Then her voice became hard, "You've come to take Sasharia back to your Queen Toriana, haven't you?"

Arquin reared back at Draya's tone. "No, I came to take an *impostor* into custody, but ..."

Rhoda and Draya looked at each other. Then Rhoda said, more gently than Draya had been speaking, "Could you show us your amulet, please?"

Arquin squinted suspiciously at them. "What for?" she asked drunkenly. In answer, Rhoda held out her own amulet. Arquin peered at it for a time, studying its gentle pulsing. "Hmm... hmm." She pulled out her own and held it beside Draya's. "Hmm. Same. You looking for her too?" She let her amulet fall to the end of its chain then passed the back of her hand across her forehead. "I'm so confused. A huge power swamped me, nearly tore me apart. I don't remember much after that. Might have passed out. I've managed to pull my mind together now... mostly. But now... now..." She gave a gusty sigh. "It's like a huge weight has gone from my mind but I haven't adjusted to the lighter load."

"A huge weight *has* gone from your mind, I think," said Rhoda, "The compulsion placed on it by Toriana. Without that, a shaman would never have set out to hunt down the true High Shaman."

Abruptly, Arquin sat down on the ground. "Oh. That wicked woman. She made us believe that the bandits who had killed her sister were now parading a young girl wearing a false amulet as the true heir. She said she wanted her brought back alive so she could question her about her fellow conspirators and quell any possibility of a rebellion." She smiled mistily up at them. "So I'm right. That young girl really *is* Princess Sasharia." She shook her head in wonder. "Oh my word, she's powerful."

Rhoda and Draya glanced at each other. Then Draya bent down and put a hand under the older woman's arm.

"Come on," she said briskly, helping her up. "We have work to do and if you recover enough, you can help us. Rhoda, see if you can rouse that other shaman enough to get her on her feet. We have to go."

They made their way down to The Way Through, guiding the two dazed shamans. When they emerged onto the track, the two troopers on guard confronted them, challenging their business. When Rhoda and Draya explained their part in the actions over the last few hours, Trevor and the four troopers clustered around them, eager to hear what had happened, and delighted that the children were safe.

The troopers led them over to their fire where Beetlebrow and Argus, dusty and exhausted, were seated. The two refugees had finally caught up with the troopers and were now watching the arrival of the shamans with interest. The second shaman, Berundi, was still looking dazed but Arquin was starting to recover. They sat down quietly amongst the Carradorian troopers without a word. The men offered them cups of tea.

"Hello, you two. Glad you made it," said Draya briefly, before responding to the offer for tea. "Thank you, that would be lovely, but we can repair the wounded while we sip."

"We've already cleaned and bandaged the wounds," said Weston, a trooper whose upturned nose made him look deceptively boyish. He was on the defensive. "I don't think they'll fester."

"Well done. I am casting no aspersions on your first aid. But I'm talking about healing." Draya indicated Rhoda and herself. "We are shamans. We can heal. That's why we came on ahead; to put you boys out of your misery."

The three wounded men glanced at each other, looking anything but convinced.

"Sergeant Reece sent us," said Draya inaccurately, deciding he had tacitly sanctioned it by not objecting.

"Well then," said Trevor, still sounding dubious, "I suppose we had better let you have a look."

Darya began work on Morris, while Rhoda moved over to sit on the ground beside Trevor's bandaged leg. She smiled reassuringly up at him. "Let's take this off and see what we have, shall we?"

She gently unwound the bandage, taking even more care as she reached the point where it was stuck to the seeping wound. She peered closely at it, struggling to see well enough by the light of the fire.

"Would you like more light?" offered a trooper, brandishing a lit stick.

"Thank you," said Rhoda. When she had finished her examination, she looked up at Trevor. "It's deep, isn't it? Sword thrust?"

Trevor nodded, clenching his teeth as she placed a fresh piece of cloth over the wound and placed her hands on it. But she was so gentle that he gradually realised he had no need to brace for more pain and, rather sheepishly, relaxed his jaw.

"And how did you fare, here on your own, Trevor?" asked Rhoda, as much as anything to distract him. "Did any more Kimorans come through here?" She kept her hands carefully in place on Trevor's calf as the wound slowly pulled together under the influence of the healing power seeping into it.

Trevor shook his head. "A few times we thought we heard someone approaching," he jerked a thumb at Shay, "and that one would go on alert. But each time, it went quiet again. After a while, we decided it must have been animals wandering around in the undergrowth that we'd heard."

"Maybe," said Draya noncommittally. She patted Morris's arm. "There. That should be better."

The young man moved his arm gingerly, then through a greater range. Slowly, a relieved smile dawned on his face. "Thank you." He turned to the other wounded trooper, ready to bring him to Draya, but saw that he was already receiving attention from Arquin.

"She is also a shaman," said Draya. "So is Berundi, but she is in no fit state to heal at the moment."

Rhoda gave Trevor's leg a final pat and a couple of troopers helped him to his feet. He tried a couple of experimental, successful steps and his face lit up. "Who'd have thought? It's much better. Thank you."

Arquin was still working on the sword-cut on Symmon's arm, when Jon, Sheldrake and the three children arrived, walking within the green haze of Midnight's shield. It wasn't until they came into the firelight that the green dome could be seen clearly.

Trevor's eyes widened. "Well! Will you look at that? Is that really a magic shield? I've heard of them but never seen one before." He frowned into the green dome. "Now, I know Jon, but who are these little people? Let me see. This must be Sasha, you're the only one in a skirt," he gave a rueful grin, "what's left of it."

At Sasha's name, Arquin's head whipped around and she was torn between rising to greet Sasha and continuing with her healing. After a moment, she resolutely returned her attention and energy to the young trooper's arm, holding to her duty as a shaman.

"And you, with the pale eyes that the king so admires, must be Jayhan," continued Trevor.

The other troopers looked on in surprise as the usually taciturn tracker greeted the children. Unaware or uninterested in the stir he was causing among his comrades, Trevor turned to Midnight. "And you must be Midnight, the hero of the day. Draya and Rhoda told us all about you. Oh yes, that's right. You can't hear, can you?" Trevor gave him an enthusiastic thumbs-up and smiled broadly at him.

Midnight gave a half-hearted wave back and hid behind Sheldrake. Sheldrake raised his eyebrows at being overlooked by Trevor. "And I am Lord Sheldrake, Jayhan's father."

"Don't mind Trevor, my lord," said Morris smoothly. "It's just we've been dying to meet the children we've spent so long chasing down... and I think he must be a bit euphoric because his leg has stopped hurting."

"This is a night of wonders, to be sure," said Symmons, gawking at them. "First, miracle healing and now, a sorcerer's shield."

Arquin had now finished her healing and, motioning for Berundi to join her, walked over to stand before Jon and Sasha. As Berundi and she knelt, their right hands on their hearts, everyone stopped to watch.

"Sasharia," said Arquin, softly but formally. "I acknowledge you as our true queen and High Shaman." She turned her eyes to Jon, "and you as Kimora's regent. And I give you my faith and my duty. All my resources are at your disposal."

Berundi has recovered enough to say, "I too give you my faith and my duty." Her face threatened to crumple but with an effort, she controlled herself. "And I am so sorry we attacked you."

Then they pulled out their moonstone amulets and held them in front of them. Sasha glanced at Jon before pulling out her own obsidian amulet. For a full minute, they knelt before Sasha, watching their amulets pulse in time with hers.

Then Arquin raised her head and smiled mistily at Sasha.

Sasha hitched a breath and whispered, "Thank you."

"Please rise," said Jon, aware, as Sasha was not, that they would not rise without permission.

Arquin rose to her feet. "And, Prince Jondarian, I give you my word of honour, as an officer and a peer of the realm, I will not run and will not try to harm your comrades." Her voice hardened as she glanced over at Shay. "But don't let that snake go. He's the one who sent the carrier pigeon to the Queen requesting a full company to ensure the safe delivery of Sasharia, the true queen, to her, and no doubt giving her all the information he could. Unlike me, he has never been under a misapprehension about the identity of the child we were seeking." Her voice gathered anger. "He has no soul. He is a mercenary who works purely for money, not honour, and he won't stop until he fulfils his contract. A failed contract would damage his reputation and mean less work for him in the future. That's all he cares about."

As she stepped back, she seemed to calm herself. "However, he too has been injured and I think I should put him out of his misery."

This was just ambiguous enough to delay people's reactions. Unopposed, Arquin walked up to Shay, who watched her warily as she approached. Before anyone thought to stop her, she thrust a sharp little dagger deep into his chest. With a grunt, he slumped forward against his ropes. Without a backward glance, she turned and walked away.

She raised her eyebrows at the shocked silence and addressed Lord Sheldrake, who was the most senior Carradorian present. "He is, *was*, a known traitor to the true queen... and he betrayed his fellow Kimorans. Your jail did not hold him. I do not want to chance having him abroad again in Carrador, threatening Sasharia and her brother." Arquin gave a little satisfied smile. "So, as my first act of fealty, I have just made the world a little safer."

After a moment, Trevor said quietly, "Warrun, Symmons, move him out of sight. Not nice for the children."

Sasha crossed her arms and said in a sharp little voice, "I'm glad he's dead. He hurt Jayhan and was going to keep hurting him." But her face was tight with shock and she looked close to tears.

In the trees above them, woodfolk were waiting for Tarkyn, Reece and the rest of them to arrive before introducing themselves but, at the sight of her distress, Rainstorm couldn't contain himself. He flicked down to appear in front of them and smiled at her. "Hello, Sasha. I am Rainstorm."

Autumn Leaves appeared next to him, giving Rainstorm a harassed glance. "Rainstorm. You were supposed to wait. Hello, all. I am Autumn Leaves."

Rainstorm just grinned cheekily at him before turning to the troopers and shamans. "Hello, all. We woodfolk have been your back-up team. Those animals you thought you heard out there in the undergrowth? They were Kimoran soldiers that we knocked off before they got to you."

Lapping Water, deciding it would be better if she, too, came down to keep Rainstorm in check, appeared on the other side of him holding Gurgling Water, who promptly leaned dangerously far out of her arms towards Midnight. "Minnight. Minnight."

Rainstorm grabbed the little girl before she fell and placed her gently on the ground beside him, keeping her hand in his.

"And I am Lapping Water."

The troopers and shamans were still staring speechlessly at them when Tarkyn, Maud, Reece and the others walked up. Not having seen them flick into existence, Reece frowned at the woodfolk in suspicion. "And who exactly are you?" he demanded. He scowled at Rainstorm. "Hang on. You look like Stefan. Are you his brother?"

Silverwood, not liking his tone, decided to shock him into civility. She flicked from a tree further down the road to stand in front of him, her long, silvery hair shining in the light from the fire.

"Good evening," she said formally, "my name is Silverwood. I believe you know my nephew, Stefan, the arms master." Ironbark and Spinifex appeared behind her and she waved vaguely to indicate them. "And these are his...father and uncle. Stefan is not related to Rainstorm."

Sphagnum Moss and Tree Fern appeared and were introduced to an increasingly stunned audience.

Waterstone and Sparrow stayed up in the trees above, watching with unholy mirth. They decided they would stay put, since the troopers and shamans had more than enough to cope with at the moment and besides, father and daughter were having far too much fun watching from the sidelines.

For several minutes, pandemonium reigned as those who had only just met the woodfolk asked question after question of those who already knew of them, or of the woodfolk themselves.

When the noise level subsided enough for him to make himself heard, Tarkyn raised his hand, then his voice. "We still have much to sort out, but, thanks to the concerted efforts of everyone here and of those watching from the surrounding trees, Sasha and Jayhan are now safely among us." He paused briefly, but not long enough to allow the chatter to start up again. "There is, however, a consequence for receiving this help from the woodfolk. Silverwood will explain."

Silverwood came to stand beside Tarkyn. "We woodfolk, as you may have gathered, live deep in the forest, apart from outsiders. Before today, no woodfolk in Carrador have ever interacted with outsiders." Seeing puzzled glances at Stefan, she faltered.

Iron Bark took over. "Stefan was lost to us during the great floods and was brought up by the outsiders who own the Creeping Vine Inn. He is one of us and yet he is also one of you. Because he cares for Jayhan and Sasha, we made his cause our own and fought by your side to rescue them."

Silverwood gave a small smile of thanks, before continuing, "Despite the anomaly of Stefan, keeping our existence secret from outsiders is still central to our whole way of life." She turned to Draya and Rhoda, her green eyes hard. "So we were shocked to hear you two casually revealing your awareness that we were in the trees above you. For how long, and how, have you known about us?"

Rhoda and Draya looked at each other for direction. Then Rhoda shrugged and turned back to Silverwood. "Not sure how long. Maybe always. We knew you didn't want anything to do with us, so we didn't try to make contact." She gave a little smile. "Your business is your own, after all. You allowed us to live as refugees, unmolested, in your forests. So, that was enough."

"We have people like you in Kimora," Draya explained, "but we call them treewrights. They, like you, keep to themselves. People outside the forests know of them but accept that they wish to be left alone."

"I see," said Silverwood slowly, again unsure how to proceed.

Lapping Water came to her rescue. "That is not the case here, or in Eskuzor. In Carrador and in Eskuzor, the secret of woodfolk's existence is sacrosanct."

"Any woodman or woman who betrays our existence is exiled," continued Autumn Leaves, "and only under very special circumstances have we ever allowed outsiders who have seen us to leave the forests."

Sheldrake turned to Stefan. "Perhaps in the years to come, your unique position may bridge the gap between our two peoples, so that woodfolk will feel less need to isolate themselves from us outsiders."

Stefan's gaze wandered from Silverwood and his family to the group of Eskuzorian wood-folk, from whom Rainstorm stood grinning at him, and then onto the more familiar figures of Marjorie, Reece, Sheldrake, Maud, the children and the troopers.

Lastly, he glanced at Tarkyn, who had engineered the whole discovery of his dual heritage and gave him a wry smile. "I hope so. For better or worse, some outsiders in Carrador now know about woodfolk and know what they are looking at, when they see me. It is a beginning."

"Perhaps it is," conceded Silverwood. She took a breath. "But as things stand now, all woodfolk are sworn to keep our existence secret and now we ask, *require*, of you that you also make this oath…" her mouth quirked as she added, knowing this would be unpopular, "… on pain of death."

Reece scowled. "On pain of death? That seems extreme."

"Not as extreme as killing all the outsiders who saw us today," said Spinifex phlegmatically, "which was the other option."

There was a fraught silence…

"In that case," said Jon, smiling cheerily, "this oath sounds like a great idea."

The Dark-Eyed Shaman
The Dark Amulet Book 3

I would like to dedicate this to all of us who have had to come to terms with lockdowns, especially those alone and feeling lonely, those who are trying to juggle working from home with home-schooling their children, and those whose livelihoods have been damaged or even destroyed.

Acknowledgments

I would like to thank Wendy Ealey and Neil Gardner for editing and providing ongoing enthusiasm. I would also like to thank my narrator, William Merryn Hill, for creating such wonderful audiobooks from my manuscripts.

And lastly, I would like to thank William Shakespeare for Cleopatra's words, "Oh, happy horse, to bear the weight of Antony," which always come into my mind when Sheldrake is riding his wife, Maud, when she has shape-changed into horse form.

Characters

Sasharia (Sasha): Shaman, usurped Queen of Kimora, residing at Maud and Sheldrake's
Jondarian (Jon): Sasha's elder brother, will be regent if she regains throne

Lord Sheldrake: Mage, head of the Carradorian King's Secret Service
Lady Maud: Shape-shifter, advisor to the king. Sheldrake's wife
Jayhan: Their pale-eyed son. Apprentice mage.
Prince Tarkyn: High Lord of Eskuzor, forest guardian, sorcerer.
Stormaway Treemaster: Tarkyn's wizard
Lord Stefan: King Gavin's ambassador to Carradorian woodfolk
Marjorie: Stefan's (foster) sister
Jackson: Tarkyn's aide de camp

Woodfolk

Waterstone: Tarkyn's bloodbrother
Sparrow: Waterstone's daughter
Lapping Water: Tarkyn's wife
Midnight: Tarkyn's ten-year-old ward
Gurgling Brook: Lapping Water and Tarkyn's two-year-old daughter.
Autumn Leaves
Rainstorm
Mountain Wind: A treewright (Kimoran name for woodfolk)

Sheldrake & Maud's staff

Beth: head groom.
Clive: butler Beth's husband
Leon: coachman and henchman
Hannah: the cook
Rose: Housemaid
Edgar: Rose's brother
Eloquin: Governess for Jayhan

King Gavin: King of Carrador
The King's Staff

Josie: King's steward.
Stevenson: Butler
Neville: Valet
Captain Bryant: Captain of King's guards.
Cyrus: Pigeon handler
Crabtree: Gifted but cranky civil engineer
Kate: Literate kitchen maid

Lord Argyve: Eskuzorian ambassador
Lady Electra: The Kimoran ambassador.
Lieutenant Reece: friend of Jon's.
Cassie: Jon's informant, street girl.

Toriana: Queen of Kimora, shaman
Corinna: Mother of Sasha and Jon. Toriana's elder sister, killed by Toriana.
Toriana's staff
Major Waldarion: Advisor to Queen Toriana
Pansy: maid
Barton: Dresser
Hardikan: Chief shaman adviser
Gordon: Gardener
Jenkins & Simmins: Coachmen

Argus, Beetlebrow: Kimoran Refugees
Rhoda, Draya, Yarrow: Refugee shamans from Kimora.
Graham: Rhoda's brother

General Kazak: Commander of central Kimoran invasion force.
Captain Marlene: Senior shaman in Kazak's force.
Lieutenant Hagan: non-shaman officer.
Major Arquin: Commanding officer of a 160-strong Kimoran incursion force
Miriam, Rayna, Fortuna: Shamans living in The Rapids township

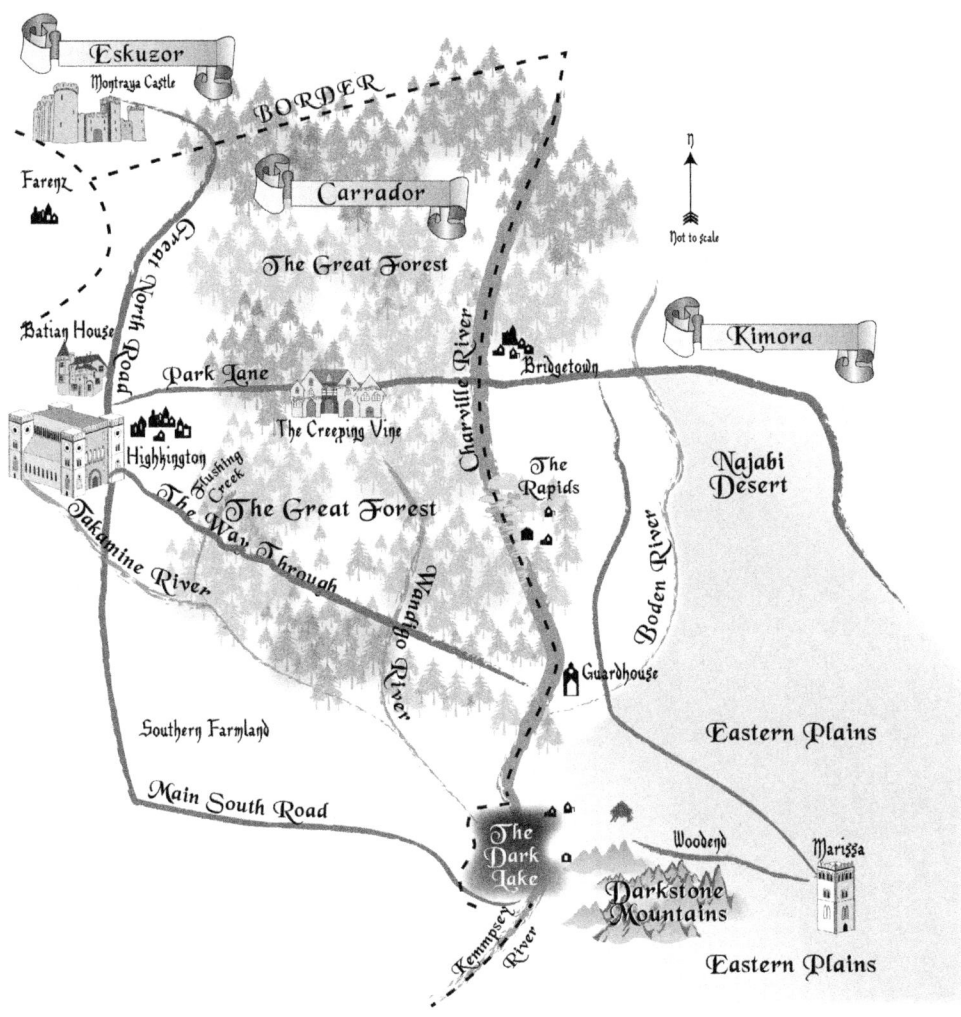

Map of Carrador and Kimora

Part 1

Chapter 1

Gavin, King of Carrador, sat at his desk in his favourite sitting room looking out into his garden, but not seeing the sunlight sparkling on the lake or the reeds swaying gently in the morning breeze that hid the swans' nest.

Instead he was seeing in his mind's eye a small dark-eyed girl, full of life and joy, holding hard to her recently acquired happiness, and trusting in Sheldrake, Maud, Jon and him to guide her and keep her safe as she grew into womanhood and trained for her future role as Queen of Kimora.

He sighed and ran both hands back and forth through his carefully brushed hair, destroying the painstaking work of his dresser. Then he thumped his hands down on his desk and rose, deciding to walk off some of his nervous energy on the path around the lake.

He stepped out into the soft morning light and immediately felt his tension lessen, but not by much.

No news.

On the first day, a messenger had brought back reports that Jon, Sergeant Reece, and a crack team of specialist troopers were on the trail of the abductors along an obscure trail in the southern part of the Great Forest. Trouble was, there were no facilities for keeping carrier pigeons along that trail and the squad was too small to carry pigeons or to keep sending men back with messages. So how was he to get further news? He sighed. He would just have to grit his teeth and wait.

Gavin walked across the lawn and around the lake to the spot in the reeds where he could see through to the black swans' nest. He spent some time watching one swan sitting on the untidy pile of sticks while the other swan emerged from the reeds to clamber up to join its mate. He wondered if they had eggs incubating and then thought that Sasha would love it if they did. He gave another sigh and turned away.

Just as he headed back towards the rear of the palace, he caught sight of a small falcon spearing into view above the palace. As it glided overhead, and landed in a nearby tree, he could see it was a peregrine falcon. He was entranced to see it. Raptors of any size were rare visitors to his garden. He admired its soft cream, finely barred underbelly, its dark grey wings, and its sharp curved yellow beak. The intelligence in its eyes was disturbing. He watched it as it took off again, soaring twice around the garden before plummeting into the long reeds somewhere near the swans' nest. Perhaps it had spotted a mouse.

Gavin watched the reeds, waiting for it to fly out when instead, he heard a muttered oath followed by the appearance of Lady Maud as she pushed aside some reeds and stepped out onto the lawn, not twenty yards from him, dressed in her leggings and a jerkin.

When she saw the king, she sank into a low curtsy while he tried to stop gawking at her. She straightened and approached him, smiling.

Gavin frowned quizzically, the morning light catching a twinkle in his blue eyes. "Good morning, Lady Maud. This is an unexpected pleasure. Last I heard you were heading into the Great Forest south of some inn on Park Lane in search of your son."

"Good morning, Your Majesty. Yes, that is indeed where I have been. But this seems to be a week for revealing secrets." Her smile broadened. "So now you know mine."

Gavin blinked. "I do? I'm not sure what I just saw… or didn't see, actually."

"I am a shape-shifter, Sire. I flew in as that peregrine falcon you saw. And since I have revealed that information to your little squad of troopers and to Jon, it seems only fair that you know too."

"Thank you," he said dryly. Then his mind computed the rest of what she had said, and his eyes widened in hope. "So you people who travelled from the Inn intercepted them, did you? Have you found Sasha and Jayhan?"

"Yes, we have them safe."

Gavin let out a long breath of relief. He stepped forward and grasped both of Maud's forearms. "Truly? That is great news." His eyes glistened in an uncharacteristic show of emotion. He generally worked on being carefully modulated in his response. When he realized he was holding onto Maud, he let go and stepped back, waving his hand. "Sorry. Sorry, I'm just so relieved."

Maud hesitated a moment then stepped forward and engulfed him in one of her warm hugs. "We all are. It has been a hard few days, hasn't it?"

She felt Gavin's head nodding against the side of her head. After a few moments, she let him go and stood back smiling at him. She went to say something more, but he raised his hand and managed to get out, "Just a minute." After a few moments, he cleared his throat to say, "Come inside and sit down while we talk. I'll ring for tea while you tell me everything that has happened."

"Thank you, I would like that very much," she looked down at herself, "although I am not exactly dressed for court." As they turned towards the palace, she tucked her hand into his arm, "I have just flown eighty miles and must, with your permission of course, return as soon as possible."

Gavin raised his eyebrows but said nothing further until he had rung the bell for tea. They settled themselves in comfortable chairs when Josie, Gavin's steward, knocked and entered, giving a slight curtsy.

Then she raised her eyebrows at Maud but managed to ignore her strange mode of dress. All visitors to the king in his living room, even if they were residing within the palace, which she knew Maud was not currently, were ushered in by Josie personally. "Where did you come from?"

Maud smiled at her, quite uncowed by her severe visage, which had most people running for cover. "I came in through the garden."

Josie transferred her gaze to the king, a frown gathering. "Our security is not doing well, Your Majesty. I thought we had just overhauled it after... hmm... recent events."

"Thank you for your concern, Josie. I will take note of it. Now, could you please procure morning tea for us. Something substantial, I think?" Gavin glanced at Maud who nodded confirmation.

Josie hesitated at the door and looked back at Maud, knowing she shouldn't interrupt unless invited, but unable to help herself. "Please. Any news?"

Maud smiled warmly at her. "They are safe. I have come to tell Gavin."

Josie breathed out and turned quickly so they wouldn't see the tears that sprang to her eyes.

As soon as the door closed behind her, Gavin leaned forward. "She has done so well. From what I understand, she instigated the search and made sure the news of the abduction was conveyed to all of us it concerned. So tell me. Who was behind the abduction? Was it Kimorans? Who rescued them and how?"

Maud let out a breath that was almost a whistle. "Oh my goodness. So many questions and so much you need to know before you can even understand the answers. Briefly, yes, it was the Kimorans behind the abductions. As to who found and rescued them..." She smiled, "It was a joint effort between Jon, Reece, Trevor and the troopers, Tarkyn, a little wood sorcerer called Midnight, Stefan, a small group of woodfolk from Eskuzor and the woodfolk of the Great Forest, two Kimoran refugee shamans, Sheldrake and of course, myself in guises as peregrine falcon, osprey, and bloodhound at various times. But above all, the children themselves."

Gavin leaned back, his eyes wide. "Well, as I live and breathe. I would not have expected it to be so complicated."

Josie reappeared at this moment with two servants trailing behind her.

"Ah, Josie, thank you," Gavin watched her directing the servants to lay out savoury and sweet platters, a large coffee pot, a tea pot, and two cups. "This may take some time, Josie. Please cancel any appointments I have this morning."

"Could I suggest for the rest of today at least, and possibly tomorrow?" Maud interposed.

The king frowned and thought for a moment. "Very well. Josie, cancel all of today's meetings, and I'll decide about tomorrow when I have heard more." He saw the restrained curiosity on Josie's face and gave a short laugh. "I will tell you what I can when I can. Maud hasn't finished telling me yet. But you may inform people that the children have been found and are safe and sound."

Josie gave a small curtsy. "Thank you, Sire." She frowned at the servants. "Come on you two. Haven't you finished yet?"

The two footmen placed the last two platters of sandwiches, cakes, small pies, meats, cheeses, and fruit on the table. One of them caught Maud's eye as he straightened and gave her a little smile of fellow feeling before bowing and retiring with his companion.

By the time she had answered Gavin's many questions, Maud took more than two hours and three pots of coffee to relate the events of Jayhan and Sasha's rescue. As she recounted them, she realized that the children had actually escaped by themselves, had then been rescued by the two shamans, been found by herself as a bloodhound, then defended by

Jon and the troopers. After that, they had all been rescued by Midnight and his shield and finally, by the intervention of Tarkyn and the woodfolk.

"But we now have a full company of Kimoran soldiers under guard," concluded Maud, "and we can't do more until we have clear direction from you." She gave a mischievous little smile. "And we thought you might like to meet the woodfolk and survey the situation yourself before reaching a decision." She became more serious. "And I think it would be helpful to confer with Jon, Lady Arquin from Kimora, and High Lord Tarkyn... and the woodfolk about our next steps. Sheldrake and I, your chief advisors, will also be there."

Gavin frowned. "But it will take days to reach this place you've described. My retinue and a squad of Royal Guardsmen could carry some provisions for you people, but meanwhile, these woodfolk would have to feed many mouths. It seems too much of an imposition on them."

"No, Sire. I believe we could get you there in about three hours' time, but without guards or a retinue." She smiled. "And you already have a squad of loyal troopers at the campsite on The Way Through."

Gavin was not convinced. "What about these woodfolk though? Can we trust them?" He tried not to widen his eyes as Maud took yet another little bacon roll.

Maud grinned as she caught his look. "When did you last travel eighty miles in less than two hours under your own steam? It makes me very hungry."

Gavin threw his hands up. "Sorry. I suppose it would. I have no idea how that would feel."

"And whether you agree to join us or not, I must fly back shortly to tell them what you have decided."

Gavin gave a short laugh. "Then be careful. Your stomach dragging along the ground could slow you up somewhat."

Maud managed to swallow her little snack before she spluttered with laughter. "Oh dear. You're probably right. I'd better stop."

"So tell me how you propose to transport me to this meeting. I don't suppose you can turn yourself into a dragon and I could ride you there?" he asked hopefully.

An arrested look came into Maud's eyes. "You know, I've never thought of that. Mind you, I think I can only change into real animals, but it does bear thinking about." She gave her head a little shake and refocused on Gavin. "No. I have enlisted Lord Tarkyn's help to translocate you there, if you are willing."

For a long moment, Gavin just stared at her. Then he held his hand up. "Wait. I need time to think."

Ten long minutes passed as he stared out into his garden. He thought through his current obligations in Highkington and decided he could ask his sister to stand in for him for a few days. Then he thought through whether it was his interest or his duty that was urging him to go, trying to work out which weighed more heavily with him and whether it actually mattered which it was. From there, his mind turned to the matter of his personal safety. He would only have a small squad to guard him among people from two other countries, including a full company of Kimoran soldiers, albeit secured, and an unknown number of these woodfolk whose loyalties and intentions were uncertain... not to mention placing himself in the hands of a foreign head of state, about whom he had limited personal knowledge.

On the other hand, Sheldrake and Maud, to whom he would turn for guidance anyway, were recommending that he go, and they would be there with him. He gave a little mental shrug. *And, let's face it, I would be very disappointed at this point if I didn't grasp this opportunity to see what it was like to translocate and to meet these woodfolk that Lord Tarkyn has told me about. Perhaps interest aligns with duty in this case.*

Gavin brought the focus of his eyes out of the garden and back to Maud's face. He took a deep breath then gave one of his very rare boyish grins. "I'll do it."

Maud's face lit up. "That's wonderful, Sire. Now. You will have to dress in practical clothes for camping and wear a heavy coat ready for the evening. I believe you can take a small satchel strung over your shoulder or perhaps a very small backpack, but not much. It is difficult for Tarkyn to translocate another person, so luggage would be a step too far." Seeing Gavin's startled look, she smiled kindly. "Don't worry. The people there can provide everything you need."

"Hmph." His eyes lit with amusement. "Josie is not going to like this. I almost feel like sneaking away without telling her and just leaving her a note." He gave his head a little shake. "No, I couldn't do that, especially after the children's abduction. She rose to the occasion magnificently, but I could see she was shaken. She tried to hide it beneath that fearsome exterior of hers, but you saw her. Her eyes were damp when she left us." He took a little breath. "Very well. How do we do this?"

"Tarkyn's translocation ability is a resummoning spell. It takes him to the place that something was created. So I will take a piece of foliage from your garden, back to Tarkyn, which he can use to translocate to here. He will bring with him a piece of foliage from near the campsite that he can then use to translocate back. Both times, his spell will take him to the place at which the foliage was created."

"Huh. Ingenious."

Maud looked smug. "Thanks, I dreamed up this scheme. Now, we need to find a secluded part of your garden that no one can overlook from the upper floor windows."

Gavin frowned. "Why?"

"Because when Lord Tarkyn arrives, he will feel sick and vulnerable for a few minutes and, I assume, will not want to recover in the public view." Maud waited for Gavin to nod before she continued, "Then we pick a small piece of foliage from a plant in this secluded spot and either I carry it in my beak, which strikes me as uncomfortable for a long trip, or you can strap it securely to my leg once I have transformed, so that I can carry it back to Tarkyn."

"Hmm. Perhaps James the falconer would do a better job of that than I," said Gavin, looking dubious.

"Perhaps," agreed Maud, "but with two provisos. He can't attach a permanent ring around my leg. It has to be easy for Tarkyn or whoever to remove it when I get to the other end, and secondly, it would be better if he doesn't learn who I am. The more people who know that I shape-shift, the less useful it is for gathering intelligence."

"Hmm. He will wonder where I acquired such a falcon..." Gavin glanced at her, slightly embarrassed by being on unfamiliar territory. "Would you consider becoming a pigeon instead? It would arouse less comment using a pigeon to deliver something. We use pigeons all the time." He crossed to the bookcase and after perusing the shelves for a few moments, withdrew a book on birds. He flicked through it quickly then opened a page to show her. "Peregrine falcons may be the fastest birds in a dive, but I believe pigeons are equally fast, if not faster, on longer journeys."

Maud gave a little sniff. "Not as exotic though, are they?"

Gavin laughed. "You're a bird snob! Pigeons may not be as exotic, but they are strong, loyal, intelligent, and many of them are beautifully coloured if you take the time to study them." He shrugged. "Anyway, I leave it up to you. It is, after all your area of expertise, not mine."

Maud frowned, thinking through everything she knew of pigeons and visualising a lovely grey rock pigeon flying in a flock and winging her solitary way to faithfully deliver a message. She gave a decisive nod. "I'll do it. Good idea. I'd just better let Tarkyn know before I get there in case the woodfolk have pigeon pie on the menu!" Seeing Gavin's look of enquiry, she explained how she could send Tarkyn images when she was in an animal form. "Because he is a forest guardian, you understand."

"Not entirely, but I don't have to know everything straight away," said Gavin. "Let us begin by finding a secluded spot, perhaps in amongst the reeds near the swans' nest."

Together, they found a dry spot deep inside the tall reeds, hidden from view, and a strip of reed from one of the surrounding plants.

"Are you ready?" Maud asked the king. When he nodded, she said, "Say goodbye to Josie for me. I won't see her for a week or two, I'd say."

With that, she turned into a twinkling column of particles which shrank and coalesced into the shape of a rather solid, grey rock pigeon. She cocked her head then flew up onto Gavin's outstretched hand.

The pigeon cote was situated, conveniently for the pigeons, but inconveniently for people, high in the stone east-facing tower. The higher the king rose up the winding stairs of the tower, with Maud perched perkily on his finger, the louder the sounds of cooing and the more tiny bits of fluff and feathers clung to the walls amongst the dust.

Twenty steps before the top, Gavin stopped to get his breath back before accosting the pigeon keeper. When he finally stepped onto the wooden floor that held the pigeon cote, the rustling and cooing of hundreds of pigeons masked his entrance and it was only when Maud cooed that Cyrus swung round, hearing her particular unknown voice among the others.

As it turned out, Cyrus, the keeper of the royal pigeons, was just as curious about Maud, as the James the falconer would have been about a new falcon.

He was a stooped, white-haired man, with a barrel-shaped body ensconced in a grey tunic that blended in well with most of the pigeons he kept. Unfortunately, he knew every pigeon in the king's service: their age, gender, whereabouts, fitness, likes and dislikes.

When he saw the identity of his visitor, he sank into a low bow. "Your Majesty. An honour."

"Thank you, Cyrus," said Gavin, smiling. "Do stand up. It has been too long since I came up here, hasn't it? I used to love sneaking up here when I was a boy. Do you remember?"

Cyrus chuckled. "How could I forget, Sire? You kept wanting to pat the young chicks and I kept stopping you"

He took Maud from where she perched on Gavin's finger and held her up to admire her. "Lovely little bird, this one, Sire. Haven't see her before. A little overweight, perhaps, but she looks pretty healthy. Where has she come from?"

Gavin improvised by saying that the pigeon belonged to Tarkyn, High Lord of Eskuzor, which made Maud cock her head in his direction. When he heard that Maud had just flown eighty miles, Cyrus suggested that another pigeon should return in her stead. Luckily, Gavin was able to say with complete honesty that no other pigeons knew their way to the particular site she had come from. Once he had fielded Cyrus' suggestion that perhaps a pigeon cote should be set up in the middle of the forest, the king managed to persuade his enthusiastic pigeon keeper to attach a little rolled message containing the piece of reed, to Maud's leg.

Then Cyrus walked to the window and threw Maud out into the warming morning air.

Chapter 2

As soon as Maud left, Gavin sprang into action. He bid farewell to old Cyrus, promising to visit again soon, then ran down the stairs of the tower until his knees threatened to give way and he had to slow to a walk. Once down, he walked to his bed chamber and had an extensive and not altogether harmonious discussion with his valet about the attire he required for his upcoming stay in the forest. He was actually unsure himself about how casually he should dress. After all, he would be there in an official capacity, with all those present waiting on his decisions. But, on the other hand, he had to make sure he wore clothes that were comfortable and practical enough for a night or two camping the forest. And from what Maud had said, everyone else would be wearing very casual wear, and he didn't want to appear incongruous by overdressing. Then there was the matter of a crown or even just a thin band to denote his status. No, he decided. Everyone would know who he was.

Gavin drew a breath, eyed his disapproving valet who was waiting with withering patience beside the wardrobe for his decision, and realised he was nervous about this upcoming meeting. He would have to deal with people from three nations, four, if you counted the woodfolk as a nation, all without his usual bevy of advisors and hangers-on. Maud and Sheldrake would be there, but still... Maybe he shouldn't have agreed to go.

But he had.

He took a deep breath, dropped his shoulders, and smiled at his own temerity. "Neville, please don't glower at me. I need your help. I have to leave in about two hours. Let me tell you who will be there, why, and under what conditions." He wasn't going to tell Neville about the woodfolk, but he would sketch the sort of life they led and describe the others.

Little did he know, but his smile had completely disarmed his stiff-necked valet, even before his admission that he needed help. From then on, Neville eschewed his normal strict adherence to Royal Sartorial Expectations and actually listened to what Gavin was saying.

Once he was dressed in a plain tan ensemble with no lace, practical pockets and soft leather boots, Gavin asked for a picnic table to be set up on the lawn close to the reeds, not so close that he would disturb the swans but close enough that he would become aware of Tarkyn's arrival. He ordered a pot of coffee for himself and a jug of iced water, to be replenished periodically with more ice, and various small, tasty snacks that might tempt a someone who was recovering from nausea. He sat down at the table with writing implements and his diary, to make sure he did not leave chaos behind him. He was, after all, a methodical, caring king.

Once he was clear about possible issues as he saw them, he sent a footman to invite Josie to join him and to bring an extra cup.

When she arrived, he began, as promised, by giving her an edited version of the events that Maud had described. Then they spent half an hour going through his schedule for the next two days before Josie left to organise the changes that would be needed. He had not yet explained to her that he would be heading off into the forest, only that he would be otherwise occupied.

It was after midday before anything happened. Gavin had eaten several of the assortment of snacks as lunchtime came and went, and he had worked his way through another pot of coffee. Judging by the way his jaw kept clenching, he was beginning to think the extra pot of coffee, on top of what he had already consumed with Maud, had been a bad idea. Still, it might just be the tension of waiting.

He'd just decided he might stand up and take a turn around the lawn to ease his growing stiffness when he heard a thud and a low groan issuing from the reeds. Restraining himself from rushing in, he granted Tarkyn a few minutes' grace before calling softly, "Lord Tarkyn? Is that you? When you are ready, follow the sound of my voice. I have chilled water waiting for you."

"Of course it's me. Who else did you think it would be?… Sorry." After a lot of rustling, the voice came again. "How do I get out of these bloody reeds?"

Gavin gave a low laugh and stepped forward to hold the nearest pair of bulrushes apart, expecting to find Tarkyn behind them. Instead, he heard splashing and quiet cursing. He manoeuvred his way into the reeds to be confronted by the sight of Tarkyn up to his ankles in water, completely disoriented and headed away from him towards the lake and the nearby swan's nest.

Gavin suppressed a chuckle and called quietly, "This way. Turn around. I'm right behind you."

Tarkyn turned and frowned fiercely at him. "And you can wipe that grin off your face. Navigation is not my best suit, not at any time, let alone when I'm feeling sick and in a strange place." He clambered out of the water and stood with his hands on his hips, green slime, mud, and water trickling down the lower part of his legs. Slowly a grin spread over his face. "You are being most forgiving of my crankiness. You have no idea how much grief I get from the woodfolk for my atrocious sense of direction. Lapping Water is continually amazed and amused by my ineptitude. She will be delighted to hear of my latest effort." He looked down at his sodden boots and trouser legs, then up at the cloudless sky. "Oh well. They will dry soon enough." He gave a sudden shudder. "Ah. Well, at least that's over for now. I'm beginning to feel better. Chilled water, did you say?"

When they exited the reeds onto the lawn, Tarkyn noticed two guards on either end of the terrace and several on the ramparts above, with their arrows trained on him. He looked at Gavin and raised his eyebrows.

Gavin shrugged. "Best I could do, I'm afraid. Their preference was to dog my footsteps and stand just at the edge of the reeds, ready to pounce on you as you emerged." Gavin gave them a hand signal that caused them all to stand down. As soon as the king and the high lord reached the table and took seats, Gavin poured a glass of water for Tarkyn and indicated the food platters that had recently been refreshed. "For you, if or when you are hungry."

Tarkyn nodded his thanks and took a long draught before saying, "I'm not surprised your guards are overprotective, after what happened." He lowered his voice. "Have you told them of your plans to come with me, unguarded, into the forest?"

"I have left a note." Gavin gave a small smile. "I don't like having arguments I may not win, when I am determined for the outcome to go my way."

Tarkyn smiled in return, not for a moment considering it a sign of weakness that the king was avoiding a confrontation with his guards. "After all, it is their duty to protect you, and protocol dictates that you should be guarded at all times, so you don't stand much chance of winning that argument." He took another draught of water. "Aah. That's better. Any chance of a coffee while I'm here. We have a variety of teas in the forest but no coffee."

Gavin raised his hand, and a footman came running, took the order, and left. He was not particularly surprised when he saw the coffee tray being borne by Josie, rather than one of her underlings.

"Good afternoon, Josie," said Gavin, his eyes twinkling at her ill-concealed curiosity. "I believe you have met High Lord Tarkyn. As you know, he and I hold the same rank, more or less, in our respective countries."

Josie dropped a curtsey to Tarkyn, "How do you do, Sire? A very unorthodox mode of arrival, might I say?"

"Lord Tarkyn and I will be spending the next day or two together."

Without allowing her eyes to travel over the men's attire, she said, "I gather this is an informal visit, Sire?" While she was speaking, she emptied the tray of a coffee pot and two fresh cups, a jug of milk, and a small bowl of sugar.

Gavin nodded his thanks. "Yes and no. Matters have arisen from the abduction of Sasha and Jayhan that I need to resolve." He took a deep breath, knowing he was about to outrage his steward. He handed her an envelope. "Here are written instructions. But basically, Lord Tarkyn and I will be absent for a couple of days while I travel into the forest with him, using translocation." He had limited knowledge of magic, so he glanced at Tarkyn to make sure he had used the term correctly. Tarkyn gave a tiny nod. "I will take no guards from here, but a squad of my troopers awaits us at the other end. I plan to return sometime on the day after tomorrow," he turned to Tarkyn, "if that is convenient to you?"

Josie's mouth pinched as she took in his words and both men braced themselves for her next utterance but instead, she smiled. "Sire, I think a short adven… sojourn away would do you the world of good. Your role dictates that you must be so serious, so much of the time, and we wouldn't want your eyes to lose their twinkle." A faint flush rose in Gavin's cheeks, which made Josie's smile broaden. "I can see you've already worked your way around Neville, Sire."

At Tarkyn's look of enquiry, Gavin said shortly. "My valet."

"And what about Captain Bryant?" asked Josie.

"You will find a letter for him in the envelope I have just given you."

"Very wise, Sire."

A small grin of understanding passed between king and steward.

"Have I covered everything, Josie?"

"I don't suppose you could take a carrier pigeon with you, could you, Sire?"

Gavin glanced at Tarkyn who shook his head and replied, "No. It would be convenient for us, but I am pushing my powers to take another person with me. So I don't want to jeopardize the two of us by straining my powers even further. We'll get word to you if we need to."

"And when do you intend to leave?" asked Josie.

"As soon as Tarkyn has recovered, I think."

Tarkyn smiled at her. "In half an hour or so. That should give me time to enjoy your excellent coffee and these lovely little delicacies. And it is a pleasant change to sit in manicured gardens. This is a beautiful area you have here."

"It is, Sire," Josie took a deep breath, and they could see she was finding it hard to depart. "Look after him, Lord Tarkyn," she said in a rush, then bobbed a curtsy and walked briskly away across the lawn before he could reply.

Chapter 3

While Maud was winging her way to Highkington, Sparrow, Tree Fern, Spinifex, Autumn Leaves, and Waterstone had set out to hunt for red deer. When Stefan, Jon and Reece asked if they could join them, Waterstone had noticeably hesitated before agreeing.

"I won't come if I'm going to hinder you," said Stefan, a little stiffly. "After all, the important thing is to find enough meat to feast the king and feed the hordes this evening. I know I don't yet have your woodcraft, but I have spent a lot of time in the woods, growing up."

Waterstone considered him for a minute. "I am not so concerned about you as about your two friends here. Jon, what experience do you have?"

"I've done a lot of sneaking around but in the city not the country. And I can use a knife." Jon's eyes twinkled. "I'm willing to learn and will stay out of your way when I need to."

Spinifex grimaced. "We can't give you a crash course in stealth in the forest. Just try to put your feet where we do and avoid leaves and twigs. It takes concentration, especially at first. Not sure about the knife but…"

"Reece, if you are the equivalent of Eskuzor's elite guard, you should be pretty good." Waterstone grinned. "Not as good as us, perhaps, but pretty good. One of our friends, Danton, who is an elite guard, travelled with us for a while and he was skilled at stealthy movement."

As they threaded their way through the trees, looking for tracks, a thought struck Reece. "Just a minute," he whispered to Sparrow. "Danton. Isn't that the name of the prince consort?"

Sparrow nodded. "Yep. That's him. He's Rainstorm's bloodbrother," she added, clearly considering this far more important than his high rank.

"Huh."

They soon picked up the trail of a small herd of deer and tracked them over the next half an hour, keeping quiet and low. Stefan thought he might have missed the first signs of the deer's passage that they picked up, but once Sparrow had pointed them out, he could follow the trail from there. He found it slightly galling that a thirteen-year-old noticed things he missed, but he reminded himself that she had learnt it all her life from experts, whereas he had had to teach himself.

As they crept forward, Waterstone said quietly to him. "Stay low. The deer are up ahead behind that next line of trees. Hear them?"

Stefan cocked his head and listened. He nodded.

"We are going up into the trees," murmured Waterstone. "To do that quietly, you have to look for a solid branch to flick onto that is on the other side of the tree from the deer, not too close to the outer foliage so that you don't rustle the leaves."

Spinifex frowned at the two outsiders, wondering what to do with them. "Reece and Jon, what weapons do you have?"

Reece patted his sword and knife while Jon indicated his sheathed knife.

Spinifex screwed his face up. "I'm not sure how much good they'll be against deer. Might be better if you just wait here and watch what you can through the trees. We should have armed you better. Just make sure you don't get yourselves trampled if any of them break in this direction."

Stefan experienced a moment of torn loyalties. Should he stay with Reece and Jon or go with the woodfolk? He had met Jon several times at Sheldrake's place, and he had trained Reece over many months and knew him well. He also knew his archery skills might protect them if they got into difficulties. On the other hand, he still had a lot to learn from his woodfolk kin.

Seeing the indecision on his face, Jon patted him on the shoulder. "Go, my friend. You will get a better shot from the trees, and we need all the food we can get."

Stefan's brow cleared. Then he was gone.

Jon and Reece hunkered down behind a large tree and waited.

A few minutes later, they heard deer crashing through the undergrowth, as the small herd broke into panic-stricken flight. To their left, a doe and two fawns jumped through a small screen of saplings and fled past them. Then, further ahead of them, a recently matured buck plunged through long grass into the open and headed straight for them.

Jon stepped out from behind the tree, took aim and threw his long stiletto, all in one fluid movement. The buck kept coming and Jon ducked back behind the tree. But well before it reached them, its forelegs buckled, and it sank to the ground. Jon peered around the trunk of the tree and gave himself a nod of satisfaction before glancing back at Reece, who hadn't moved.

"Got it. But we'd better stay here in case any more come through."

They heard three more crash past on their right and a few seconds later a straggler galloped past on their left. Then quiet returned to the bush.

Reece gave a self-deprecating smile. "I didn't even try. A sword would be no good against a speeding deer. I'd have to get too close and risk injury. And I only use my knife for thrusting and slashing, not throwing. So it would have been worse." He looked cautiously around the tree at the still form on the ground. "Well done."

They emerged tentatively, still listening for any stragglers. Jon walked over to inspect his prey and squatted down to pull out his dagger.

"You did well to get its heart," said Autumn Leaves, appearing beside him. "Luck or skill?"

Jon considered. "Bit of both. I am practised with a knife, but I've never aimed at a deer before. However, I attended many hunting parties as a footman and learnt the anatomy of deer and knew where the heart was. So it was just a matter of aiming well."

Autumn Leaves turned to Reece. "And you too did well. Knowing your limits and staying out of the way."

"Excellent shot, Jon, with the animal coming straight towards you. Made aiming easier but it took nerve to hold your ground and keep your aim true," said Waterstone. He smiled. "And you had to be quick. You rival our skill level."

Jon gave a little grin, knowing that what he was about to say would shock them. "Probably my woodfolk heritage."

It certainly did shock them. The jaws on six green-eyed faces dropped.

Jon chuckled. "Not pure woodfolk heritage. It's mixed with plainsman… and probably a few other strains. When drought-stricken woodfolk first sought sanctuary in Kimora five hundred years ago, some of them interbred with the plainsmen who inhabited the forest edges, while others kept strictly to themselves. It is they we call the treewrights."

The woodfolk were so overwhelmed by this information that they forgot to accommodate the two outsiders and went into a silent flurry of mental exchanges.

A few minutes later, Spinifex leaned in and studied Jon's eyes. "Hmph. Now you mention it, I can see tiny flecks of green in your blue eyes. Not noticeable unless you're looking for it."

"And I think my shimmering may be a variation on your flicking," said Jon.

At their looks of query, Reece explained, "Jon can appear and disappear. I don't think you can flick somewhere else though, can you?"

Jon shook his head. "Although I can walk away while I'm concealed."

"Could you show us?" asked Waterstone.

"Certainly." Jon shimmered and disappeared, then walked away from them and around behind them, speaking as he walked, "So as you can hear, I am moving around so I can reappear somewhere out of view if I choose to."

As Jon reappeared in front of them, Waterstone said thoughtfully, "Hmm. So the effect would then be the same as flicking, but the mechanism would be different."

Jon nodded. "And the shamanism in our women has its root in woodfolk affinity for forest life." He shrugged. "The shimmering ability is very rare. Shamanism less so. But I think both are the product of woodfolk qualities blended with the magic of other cultural groups within Kimora: the plainsmen, the under-dwellers, and the high people." He shrugged. "Most people in Kimora have more than one strain in their blood."

"In Eskuzor," piped up Sparrow, "We only have three people of mixed blood that I know of: Gurgling Brook; Midnight; and Tarkyn's wizard, Stormaway."

"And in Carrador, as far as I know," said Tree Fern, "there is no one except Kimoran refugees. Even Stefan, who bridges our two cultures, is pure woodfolk."

Everyone pondered this in silence for a minute before Spinifex pulled himself together and said, "Well, we'd better get cracking. That was the easy part. Now we have to get three carcasses back to camp and prepare them."

Chapter 4

When they re-entered the firesite in the late morning, Jon's eyes automatically sought out Sasha. He spotted Midnight and Jayhan playing a complicated game in the dirt with sticks and pebbles. Gurgling Brook squatted nearby, contentedly hitting the ground with a stick, gradually gouging a small hole in the middle of a bare patch.

Sasha was nowhere in sight.

Jon wandered over and squatted down next to the boys.

"Jayhan, where's Sasha?" he asked, trying to keep his voice casual.

Jayhan glanced up at him and grimaced. "She's in bed still. I don't know what's wrong with her. She wouldn't get up, not even for breakfast. Maybe she's sick." He focused on his game long enough to move a pebble for a reason Jon couldn't fathom, then added, "Mum took her in a cup of tea, but she still wouldn't get up."

"I see," said Jon slowly. "Perhaps I had better visit her myself."

"Yeah. Good idea. She might listen to you."

Jon made his way out of the clearing to a nearby larger shelter that had been constructed for Sheldrake, Maud, Jayhan, and Sasha. They had arranged their bedding so that Maud and Sheldrake lay across the doorway, thereby guarding the entrance as they slept. In addition, woodfolk lookouts kept a close eye on that particular shelter.

Jon pulled aside the brush that covered the entrance and ducked inside. Sasha was lying with her back to the doorway under a washed horse blanket that Maud had especially brought with her to comfort Sasha when she was found.

"Sasha," called Jon softly. When he received no response, he entered and sat down, cross-legged, beside her. He put his hand on her shoulder and tried again. "Sasha, wake up. It's Jon."

A hand came out from under the blanket and pulled it more firmly over her shoulders.

Jon thought for a moment then started stroking her dark wavy hair. He used long rhythmic strokes as he would to calm a nervous horse. For a long time, nothing seemed to happen but slowly he saw her shoulders unhunch themselves. Listening closely, he heard a quiet sniff and then another.

"Sasha, Sasha, Sasha," he crooned. "It's all right. I'm here. I shouldn't have left you this morning. But I'm here now."

He didn't try to pull her around, just kept up his stroking and finally, when she half turned towards him, he scooped her up, blanket and all, and held her close against him, her head buried in his chest, as she sobbed her heart out.

His heart was wrung as he listened to her and felt her shoulders shaking against his chest. He wished he had the woodfolk's facility for mindtalking so he could get someone to fetch a drink of water for her. Looking around the inside of the shelter, he spotted a stone just within his reach. By stretching one arm, he could just get a hold of it. He picked it up and tossed it behind him out through the brush of the opening, hoping someone would notice.

Moments later, Jayhan's head appeared in the opening. Jon pointed down at Sasha and with one hand, mimed having a drink. Jayhan nodded and disappeared. Two minutes later he snuck into the shelter with a large beaker of water that he placed where Jon could reach it. Then without a word, he backed quietly out.

"You have a very good friend in Jayhan, don't you?" he murmured, as Sasha began to settle.

Rather than cheer her up, this set her off all over again. Jon grimaced, wondering what he'd done wrong. He gave a mental shrug and just kept holding her.

Eventually, she rolled so that she was looking up at him with red-rimmed eyes, still hiccoughing with the aftermath of the sobs. "You don't understand," she managed, "I can never have a friend again." She tried to contain her sobs, but they overwhelmed her again and she buried her head once more in his chest, mumbling almost incoherently, "And I love Jayhan, not like a boyfriend, like a brother. He's the best friend I've ever had. But I can't be his friend anymore."

"Because Toriana might use him against you?" hazarded Jon.

Sasha nodded and let out another little sob. "They hurt him, Jon, and they were going to hurt him more and it's all my fault."

Jon didn't think that disputing with her at this juncture would be productive, so he just urged her to sit up enough to drink and handed her the water. "Here. Take your time. We have all day if we need it."

When she had taken a good long draught, she handed the beaker back to Jon and muttered her thanks.

"And," she continued, "there's a whole field of people, a whole *field* of them, who came here to kill me or capture me and take me back to my horrid aunty. And all she wants to do is hurt Jayhan and kill you." She wailed, "And I love both of you. And I'm so scared of all those people, even if they are tied up. What if they get away? And I'm scared of Arquin and Berundi. And I'm scared of all these green-eyed people who've suddenly appeared out of nowhere. And this Lord Tarkyn. How do we know we can trust him? He might be as power-hungry as my aunty." She buried her head and said in a muffled voice, "It's all too hard."

"Oh, you poor little one. It is far too hard, isn't it? Too many people too fast and the Kimorans, with whom we should feel most closely aligned, are our worst enemies." Jon handed her the beaker for another drink. "At least we have Rhoda and Draya and Beetlebrow and Argus. You trust them, don't you?"

"Maybe. I don't know. Shay was a refugee too…" she replied in a small voice.

Just then, a cheery voice asked, "May I come in?"

Jon frowned and was about to say 'no', when Rainstorm pushed aside the barrier and entered, carrying three cups by their handles, all filled with tea. As he sank down to sit cross-legged beside them, he handed two of the cups to Jon.

"Hello, Sasha, I hope you're impressed. I didn't spill a drop as I sat down." He smiled at her and tousled her hair. "We scary, green-eyed people are a nosy lot, and this shelter isn't very soundproof. Not at all, in fact. And we are sad to hear that we scared you. So I am a delegation of one, sent to try to cheer you up."

Sasha frowned at him as she sipped her tea and tried not to smile.

"So, we green-eyed people live deep in the forests. We've always been here. We haven't appeared out of nowhere. We're just letting you see us now. Perhaps you're worried about the 'be silent or be dead' oath we insisted on." He took a sip of his own tea. "But you're not planning on telling anyone about us, are you? So, you're perfectly safe."

She watched him steadily.

"And," here Rainstorm pulled a sorrowful face, "we've all done our level best to save you from that horde out in the field and instead of thanking us, you're upset with us."

She almost giggled but after a few moments, asked, "But why would you protect me? I don't even know you."

"True. Good point," said Rainstorm. "Well, the Eskuzorian woodfolk, of whom I am one, were present when Sheldrake and Maud found out about your abduction and we all wanted to save them from their distress, by finding you two. Neither Tarkyn nor we could contemplate leaving you to your fate. In the ordinary course of events, the Carradorian woodfolk... you know, Silverwood, Ironbark and Spinifex and the others... would not have concerned themselves with outsiders. But they had just discovered they were related to Stefan and so took up Stefan's cause to support him."

Sasha nodded her head slowly as she thought about what he had said. "Hmm. So you didn't fight for me or Jayhan exactly. You fought, on principle, to protect children you didn't even know, from being abducted and treated badly."

"Yep. Pretty much." Rainstorm squinted in worry. "I hope you're not disappointed that it wasn't your personal charms that brought us to your aid?"

Sasha gave a choke of laughter. "No, not at all. It feels much better that everyone is not just focused on me."

Something rustled in the doorway, and they turned their heads to see Midnight sidling through the brush barrier. As soon as he was through, he thrust out a hand holding a rather scruffy but colourful bunch of wildflowers towards Sasha and smiled hopefully.

Sasha's face lit with a smile, and she accepted his offering. "Oh thank you, Midnight."

She glanced at Rainstorm. "Will you tell him?"

"No need. He can see your reaction." Rainstorm's eyes went out of focus for a minute then said, "Midnight says he didn't mean to scare you with his magic. He thought he was helping."

"Oh, he *was* helping. We were all a bit dazzled by his magic, but we didn't feel threatened by it. I'm sorry. I'm not scared of Midnight at all. I'm just upset by everything that's happened." She gave a little sob. "And hundreds of people out there hate me."

Rainstorm glanced at Midnight before saying, "Midnight wants you to know that when he was a little boy, all the woodfolk he knew reviled him and made him live outside their community. So he understands how you are feeling."

"Why did they do that? He's such a such a kind, helpful person."

"Long story. But he had a very hard start to his life through no fault of his own, until Tarkyn rescued him when he was seven." He gave a little smile, "He has just shown me images of Tarkyn, Lapping Water, and me paired with Jon, Maud, Sheldrake and Jayhan."

Sasha smiled. "Yes. I do have people who care for me."

"And the people who rejected Midnight now accept him. So I hope the same will hold true for you."

Jon smiled at Rainstorm and Midnight. "Thank you. I'm sure it will."

Suddenly sounds of shouting and people running came to them from outside. Midnight grinned and Rainstorm rolled his eyes as they received images from watching woodfolk.

"What is going on?" demanded Jon.

Rainstorm chuckled. "Your little friend Jayhan..."

"He's not my friend, and I'll tell all the Kimorans that so they leave him alone," stated Sasha hotly.

"Too late, I'm afraid. As we speak, your little friend Jayhan is striding up and down in front of the captured Kimoran troops declaring that he is your lifelong friend and that nothing they can threaten him with will change that."

"Oh for heaven's sake! What's he doing that for? He's such an idiot sometimes."

Rainstorm smiled warmly. "He is making sure there is no point in you abandoning your friendship with him. No one's going to believe you now, if you run along behind him saying you're not friends anymore."

"Ugh," Sasha groaned. Tear sprang to her eyes again. "He was so frightened of being hurt, you know." She shrugged her way out of the horse blanket and off Jon's lap. "I'd better go and get him. He might whip those people into a frenzy."

Before anyone could stop her, she grabbed her boots and dodged out of the shelter. She stopped only to drag her boots on before running in the direction of the field. Jon had to untangle himself from the blanket and unfold his large frame, but Midnight and Rainstorm quickly caught up with her.

But before Rainstorm could say anything, Sasha found her way barred by Arquin and Berundi.

"Your Highness, we need your help," said Arquin.

"Not now," replied Sasha, trying to push past them. "I have to stop Jayhan from inciting your troops."

Berundi smiled. "No, you don't. Sheldrake has already taken him in hand and is bringing him back here." She chuckled. "Marching him back here actually. I don't think Sheldrake is at all pleased. And he didn't catch him before Jayhan had declared to every Kimoran in earshot that he is your lifelong friend. I'm not sure why he did that suddenly. It seems a strange thing to do." She shrugged. "Maybe he is trying to ensure a place at your side when you become queen."

Sasha frowned. "Of course he's not. No. But he overheard me saying that I would have to end our friendship to protect him. He just wants us to stay friends. That's all."

"Aha."

Sasha's eyes narrowed, unsure how to take Berundi's ambiguous response. With a flash of acumen, she realised that if she pressed her point, Berundi would just think she was too young and naïve to understand that people would want to court favour with her, as a future queen. On balance, she held her peace.

Arquin glanced from one to the other to see whether they had more to say. Then she spoke slowly and calmly, giving Sasha time to take in what she was saying. "Sasharia, Berundi and I have been trying to convince my troops of Toriana's perfidy. But my other captain, Katya, and two of my sergeants are also shamans who have been corrupted by Toriana. So they contradict everything Berundi and I say. And as they have been confined with the troops, they have developed a greater influence on them."

As Sasha listened, she felt Rainstorm's steadying hand on her shoulder, and she became aware that Jon had joined her and was standing just behind her. She was glad they were there. "So you want me to free these shamans from Toriana's binding? Is that right?" she asked, feeling a wellspring of panic rising inside her again. When Arquin nodded, Sasha looked around at Jon. "What do you think?"

"As your brother, I think you need time to settle down. There is no rush. Chat and play with your naughty little friend, and with Midnight. Have something to eat, gather your resources, then we'll see." Jon gave a little smile, "As your regent, I think we need to think this through carefully, perhaps with the help of others. What are the ramifications of having one hundred and fifty odd Kimorans, who are not shamans, becoming aware of who you are and the fact that you can break shamans' bonds with Toriana? They are not connected to you through the amulet as shamans are. And if any of them went to Toriana with that information…" Arquin went to speak but Jon quelled her with a glance. "Later," he said firmly.

Chapter 5

Gavin felt as though all the breath had been sucked out of him until he had almost ceased to exist. Then, with a suddenness that made his stomach heave, he was reinflated and dumped unceremoniously on the ground with Tarkyn's arms encircling him. Immediately each pushed away from the other as the contents of their stomachs threatened to exit.

As they lay next to each other recovering, Gavin became aware that he was lying on soft moss, looking up through the fronds of a tree fern to huge soaring eucalyptus. Gradually he tuned into the sounds of birdsong and the smell of rich damp earth, eucalyptus, and a myriad of other scents. He took a deep breath and closed his eyes, taking in just the scents and sounds for a few minutes.

He opened his eyes again and looked across to see that Tarkyn was sitting up, looking tactfully away from him into the trees, giving him time to recover.

Gavin sat up gingerly and Tarkyn turned, handing him a water bottle from a large rucksack that was propped against a nearby tree.

"Thanks." After he had taken a drink, he wiped his mouth and said, "And thank you for putting yourself through that unpleasant experience twice to bring me here." He looked around himself. "It is truly beautiful here, isn't it? And we're now eighty miles or so from the palace? Just like that."

Tarkyn smiled. "Just like that. Useful but not much fun."

"Interesting though. I've never done anything like it before." Gavin stood up and brushed himself down, not that he was dirty. It was reflexive as much as anything. He took a deep breath, readying himself to face a crowd of mostly unknown people. "So, now what?"

Tarkyn, who was still seated, looked up at him and smiled. "Unless you are dying to step straight into your official role, I thought we could just talk for a while, you and I, and when you're ready, I could introduce you to my family and friends who came with me from Eskuzor, seven of them altogether. Then we can spend some time together before meeting the Carradorian woodfolk then the others for dinner. How does that sound?"

Gavin let out his long pent-up breath and let himself relax a little. He nodded but then frowned. "Are they in the trees around us, watching us, and waiting for your summons?"

"No. We are quite alone. No one can hear us. There is a wide ring of woodfolk around us standing guard, but the nearest person is over hundred yards away. I will send a mental image to my woodfolk when you wish to meet them. No one is standing by on tenterhooks, awaiting my summons. So we can do things in our own time."

"Huh." He eyed Tarkyn speculatively. "And do you have anything in particular you are wanting to talk about?"

Tarkyn chuckled. "You are too used to court, where everyone had a motive for speaking to you. I just thought we could get to know each other better. I liked what I saw of you the other day, and I know being the highest authority in the land can be... isolating. I don't want to chat about the strength of your armed forces or trade agreements. I just want to hear about your family and tell you about mine, answer any questions you might have about my magic or my woodfolk or whatever else you're interested in." He smiled. "I suppose from a political point of view, increased knowledge of each other should lead to a greater accord between our nations but that is incidental."

"Huh," said Gavin again. "Well, I have one sister and my mother, who both have their own apartments at the palace, as you probably know. My mother is..." And he was off, talking to Tarkyn, as he could to no one else, about his hopes and fears for his family, his projects, his country, and his associates. From time to time, Tarkyn commented or asked questions but generally, he let Gavin have his head.

While Gavin talked, Tarkyn casually sent a small fireball into a preset pyramid of twigs and small branches then fed in larger sticks and small branches as the fire took hold. He interrupted briefly to ask, "Tea?" He peered once more into the rucksack and produced a small bag of tea leaves and then an assortment of bowls that had been carefully stacked inside the bag, containing nuts, cheeses, and dried meat. Finally, he drew out a round loaf of damper that had been baked in the coals of the fire. He spread his hands in invitation. "Lunch?"

Gavin nodded with a quick smile of thanks and kept talking. The tea had been brewed and drunk before he slowed. Suddenly, he gave Tarkyn a sheepish grin and said, "Whoops! I haven't asked a single thing about you yet." He gave a relaxed sigh. "But it is so good to talk to someone who is not involved with any of it." He looked hopefully at the large kettle nestled in the coals of the fire. "Any chance of more tea?"

As they were settling down against a log with their second cup, a raucous cry rent the air and a shadow flitted over them. Tarkyn hastily put down his cup.

"Stay still, Gavin," said Tarkyn. "We are not under attack."

Moments later, Tarkyn's huge mountain eagle swooped down between a gap in the trees to land with great accuracy but too much force on his shoulder. He rocked back, but the log behind him saved him from being thrown onto his back.

Gavin leaned away from him in shock, his eyes wide, but Tarkyn's words kept him from retreating further, as he suddenly found himself within an arm's length of a wild, fearsome bird of prey. Slowly he straightened up and watched with astonishment and some amusement as Tarkyn fruitlessly scolded Bird for turning in the wrong direction and filling his face with feathers and fluff.

Bird's arrival led the conversation naturally onto Tarkyn's powers as a forest guardian, his ability to share images with animals and its usefulness for surveillance and from there, onto his exploits in his battle to save Eskuzor from his brothers' machinations and to his life among the woodfolk.

It was mid-afternoon by the time Gavin asked, "So may I meet this family of yours and your friends? I admit I am dying to meet these woodfolk you speak of."

Almost before he had finished speaking, Midnight appeared suddenly in front of him and gave a shy smile and wave before walking over to sit in Tarkyn's lap and reaching up to stroke the eagle's chest.

"No, little one. Don't get settled," said Tarkyn, giving Midnight a welcoming squeeze. "I think we'll stand up for introductions. Besides, I'm getting numb from sitting too long. Gavin, could you give me a hand up? Bird is a such a heavy lump."

Midnight hopped out of the way while Gavin stood up, held out his hand and heaved as Tarkyn pushed with his legs to rise from the ground to a standing position. Bird, meanwhile, just rode the sudden jolt upward nonchalantly.

"Really, Tarkyn," scolded a voice from the side. "You indulge that bird too much. Just shoo her away."

Tarkyn smiled and waved his hand to indicate the woodman who had just appeared. "And this, Gavin, is my bloodbrother, Waterstone."

"Hello," said Waterstone casually, "Nice to meet you. Must be good to get away from everything for a while."

Gavin had been forewarned. So he showed no reaction to being accorded none of the formal gestures of the respect due to him as Carrador's king, but inwardly he was watching with interest and no small degree of amazement. He smiled. "How do you do? Yes, it is indeed. I can't tell you how much I've enjoyed just sitting and talking with your bloodbrother."

Waterstone grinned and walked over to thump Tarkyn on the shoulder. "Yes. We think he's pretty good too."

In the next moment, a semi-circle of five more light-brown-haired and green-eyed people clustered around Gavin, all smiling, greeting him, and giving him their names.

Gavin could feel himself stiffening up. He was naturally a quiet, self-contained person and he was not used to close proximity with anyone, let alone a cheery, social, informal group of strangers. He wasn't angry or offended. He was just becoming overwhelmed.

Suddenly everyone went quiet and took a few steps backwards.

"I'll make tea, shall I?" offered Autumn Leaves gently. He sent an understanding smile to Gavin. "Sorry about that. Too many of us too fast. We should have taken more care." He nodded at the surrounding bush. "You might need to take a short walk before you can fit in another cup of tea. We'll all settle in around the fire and chat to you in a minute when you're ready." He gave a little grin. "Don't get lost."

Gavin was disconcerted by Autumn Leaves alluding to his bodily needs so casually in public, but the pragmatic side of him was glad he had. He managed a small smile in return. "Don't worry. I'm not Tarkyn."

He walked into the blissful quiet of the towering trees with friendly laughter ringing in his ears.

Chapter 6

When Gavin returned, the mood had completely changed. Sparrow and Rainstorm were bent over a quarrel looking at a piece of fletching that had come loose. Tarkyn was talking to Gurgling Brook and sending images to Midnight as the two children constructed a little hut from twigs and moss, while Autumn Leaves and Waterstone were setting out cups ready for the tea that was brewing by the side of the fire.

Lapping Water, her soft green eyes shining, came to sit next to the king. "The local wood-folk will not be as relaxed as we are. They only spoke to outsiders for the first time just a few days ago. So they are likely to be more formal than us." She caught a hint of confusion in his face and smiled. "Oh no. They don't believe in hierarchies or rank any more than we do. So I doubt they'll bow or anything like that...Perhaps 'formal' is the wrong word. They will be more reserved than us... and a little wary." She put a friendly hand on his knee, making Gavin's eyes widen, "After all, I suppose you could make life difficult for them if you scoured the forest with your troops for them. But I gather from Tarkyn that you are a far more reasonable king than his father was."

Gavin frowned. "Did he just tell you what we've been talking about?"

Lapping Water shook her head, sending ripples of sunlight through her long hair. "No, no, of course he didn't. But he did report back about your first meeting. After all, we had to consider the feasibility of the local woodfolk being able to work with you."

It was about now that Gavin realised how much power and influence this seemingly casual group of woodfolk wielded. Their unique relationship with Tarkyn, both as High Lord and forest guardian, their experience of conferring with both woodfolk and outsiders and their participation in orchestrating the events in Eskuzor had given them an assurance and breadth of knowledge that few rivalled.

Gavin raised a quizzical eyebrow. "So I passed muster, did I?"

"Oh, better than that," piped up Rainstorm from the other side of the fire. "You're far less stiff-necked than Tarkyn was when we first met him, and streets ahead of King Markazon, his father, of course."

"Not wishy-washy, I hope," asked Gavin, with a faint smile.

"No, not at all," said Waterstone, handing him yet another cup of tea. "Maud and Sheldrake both say that you are your own person and make you own decisions but are open to advice." He grinned. "Couldn't be better, if you ask me."

The colour had heightened in Gavin's cheeks. He looked at Tarkyn. "Are they always this complimentary?"

"No." One side of Tarkyn's mouth quirked ruefully. "They constantly tell me that I am too autocratic, arrogant, impulsive and overbearing… and their favourite hobby is teasing me about my navigational skills."

"He has no navigational skills," said Autumn Leaves flatly, pausing in his pouring of another cup of tea. Then he smiled. "But we also tell him that he handles his immense power amazingly well. He cares deeply about people, and uses his power, both magical and political, to help them. He has a special way with animals, he is kind, fun to be around, and well… just Tarkyn. We all think the world of him, even if he does have a few drawbacks."

Now Tarkyn was looking as discomforted as Gavin. Autumn Leaves grinned and handed Waterstone the next cup of tea, to give to Tarkyn.

Gavin let out a long breath. "You are the most amazing group of people I have ever met."

Lapping Water smiled. "Thanks. I think."

"Now, Gavin," said Waterstone, "No doubt Maud has briefed you about the situation. In our opinion, your best course of action would be to have dinner with everyone tonight… We have all put in together to prepare a feast in your honour, you know… Then you'll get a better feel for the nuances. Then tomorrow, you can hold a formal meeting and decide what to do."

"Why in my honour?" asked Gavin. "I thought you didn't believe in rank, pomp and ceremony."

"We don't, but the Carradorian and Kimoran outsiders do. Woodfolk follow the lead of whoever is best qualified in a given situation to make the decisions which, in the current circumstances, is you. From our point of view, we are simply welcoming you with a special dinner, while it probably means more to some of the others." Waterstone took the final cup of tea from Autumn Leaves and sat down. "Anyway, what I wanted to say was this: Feel free to confer with us or seek our advice, especially related to woodfolk issues. It is a hard situation to walk into. So, just know we are right behind you and will give you whatever support we can."

"Thank you. Thank you very much," said Gavin.

From there they went on to talk about woodfolk society and customs and what Gavin could expect or otherwise of the local woodfolk.

The sun's rays were shining in slanting yellow bands through the trees, when Silverwood, Ironbark and Spinifex, Sphagnum Moss, and Tree Fern made an appearance and were introduced to the king. As Lapping Water predicted, they were stiff and reserved, but not unfriendly. The relationship between Gavin and the local woodfolk was quite different because Gavin was, after all, the king of the country in which they resided, whether they acknowledged hierarchies or not, and so held jurisdiction over them, in the eyes of the outsiders' law.

"Welcome to our forests," said Silverwood quietly.

This statement was immediately controversial, as the forest lay within King Gavin's domain. The air almost hummed with anticipation as everyone waited for his response. Years ago, when the Eskuzorian woodfolk had said that to King Markazon, he had stormed at them that they only lived there at his discretion. It had not been a good start.

"Thank you," replied Gavin gravely. "And in return, may I welcome you to the broader community of Carrador? You do not have to participate in it, but you are welcome to, should you choose to do so. And as the liege lord of Carrador, I offer you my support, should you ever need it." He paused for a moment before saying, "As you know, I have already undertaken not to reveal your presence."

Silverwood's eyes went out of focus for a minute as she conferred with her companions.

Then Sphagnum Moss's eyes narrowed, "If you offer us support, what do you demand in return?"

Gavin held himself more erect and his tone became harder. "I find your response disappointingly discourteous. I have not and will not demand anything of you. If I filled the forest with thousands of troops trying to impose my will, it would merely result in suffering and inconvenience on both sides and no sure outcome." He took the edge off his voice. "I had hoped, very much, that I could work with you as the Eskuzorian woodfolk work with outsiders in their country."

"The Eskuzorian woodfolk's cooperation springs from a disgraceful oath that was forced on them years ago by King Markazon," stated Spinifex baldly.

"That was its origin, yes," said Lapping Water quietly, from where she was standing to the left of the king, "but I would argue that Tarkyn has given us far more than we could ever reciprocate. He has worked with us to battle flood, fire, the incursion of civil war into our forest and to eradicate pestilence, and the effects of a dreadful curse."

Gavin gave a little cough. "Hmm. I'm not sure that I'm that heroic or that powerful. In fact, sadly, I have no magical power at all. But I do have mages, soldiers, and alchemists at my disposal. Perhaps, if you people or your forest were ever sick, I could help. I could mobilize troops to fight a fire and send in people to help with cleaning up the forest after storm or flood, if you requested it."

"And how many troops do you have under your command?" asked Ironbark.

Gavin thought for a moment. "At least ten thousand, I would say, and I also have thousands of non-military personnel I could call on in an emergency." He shrugged. "But to be honest, your need may never arise. You have managed without us until now."

Ironbark grinned. "I like you. I beg your pardon for accepting your reciprocal welcome so poorly. One thing you haven't mentioned is the fact that the Kimorans, both refugees and military, are becoming increasingly frequent in our forests, which is both dangerous and inconvenient for you and us."

"So I think we have a common cause we could work on together." Sphagnum Moss gave a grunt. "Once the Kimorans are sorted out one way or another, we'll see."

Silverwood's mellow voice made itself heard. "With the realisation that Stefan, one of our number, has lived among you all of his life and with the advent of the Eskuzorian woodfolk bringing with them their experience of relating to outsiders, the very foundation of our culture is under review. Whether our future will be better or worse remains to be seen. But it will be different." She gave a slow warm smile. "You have shown yourself to be a man of great power but little pretension. We will work with you for now and see where it leads us."

Gavin felt like dropping his shoulders and jumping for joy, but instead he inclined his head and replied, "I feel honoured that you have decided to trust and support me, and I look forward to our future association."

To his right, Tree Fern let out a gusty sigh and grinned. "Well, that's settled then. Now, can I ask you about your swans' nest? Sasha was telling me about it."

Moments later, Gavin found himself in the middle of an animated conversation about swans, and how he had had to retrieve Tarkyn before he blundered into their nest. He looked up and caught Tarkyn's eye as he watched him from the other side of the clearing.

"Well done," mouthed Tarkyn.

The king permitted himself a small private smile before reimmersing himself in the conversation around him.

Chapter 7

As the day wore on, the firesite was made ready to receive the king for the welcoming feast. Sheldrake sent the children off with Draya and Rhoda to find flowers and thin leafy branches that could be entwined into garlands to hang around the clearing. Woodfolk gathered edible plants and the troopers prepared the three carcasses to be spit roasted over the fire. Ideally, they would have been hung for a day or two, but not this time.

Jackson and Marjorie collected enough wood to see them well into the evening and then helped Ironbark and Silverwood prepare a shelter of woven brambles and branches for Gavin to sleep in. As a special concession they gathered armfuls of bracken to make up a bed for him to sleep on, aware that he wouldn't be used to their rough conditions.

In the late afternoon, Tarkyn's woodfolk melted away and at dusk, the local woodfolk also disappeared. Except for Stefan.

Stefan kept working with the troopers, feeding the fire, and helping Reece to organise a roster of people to keep the spits turning. Of course he was aware that all the woodfolk had disappeared and again, left him behind. At first, he was philosophical, reasoning that really, he was more at home with the people he had been raised with, but as time progressed, his resentment at being sidelined grew. How could these woodfolk call themselves his family and not include him?

He had just placed one end of a long stick on a rock and had stomped on it with excessive force to snap it when he heard Waterstone's cheery voice in his head. *"Now, now, don't break your foot. We've just been sorting out a few things with Gavin and now he wants to see you... if you can drag yourself away from destroying the firewood. Just flick into the trees on the north of The Way Through and you'll see us about a hundred yards further to the north-east in a small clearing. Join us as soon as you can. You might like to let everyone know that Gavin will arrive soon after sunset. See you in a minute."*

Stefan beckoned to Maud, who was organising seating arrangements against trees and logs, working out who would sit closest to Gavin and where the guards would station themselves.

"Apparently the king wishes to see me." A certain dryness in his tone betrayed his resentment that he had been sidelined. "Then he will arrive here in," he glanced at the sky, "about an hour for our feast."

Maud smiled warmly and gave him a pat on the shoulder. "I'm sure there was a reason. They didn't just forget you. You're not at all forgettable." She gave him a final pat. "Off you go then. We'll see you soon."

When Stefan appeared in the other clearing, he found the king being regaled with the reasons for Stefan having two father-uncles instead of one father and one uncle. The king turned to him, and Stefan went down on one knee and bowed, flushing slightly as he realized he would be the only woodman who had shown that sign of respect.

"Please rise, Stefan," said Gavin. He noticed Stefan's heightened colour and gave a wry smile. "I am pleased to see you. It must be, and will continue to be, difficult for you to span two such different cultures." He nodded at Ironbark and Spinifex. "If you would excuse us, Stefan and I will take a short walk. I presume someone will keep an eye on us."

Gavin led the way from the clearing, heading northward. "Tarkyn suggested that you could take me up the hill where you all fought against the Kimorans, and we could watch the sunset from the top of the rise."

"Certainly, Your Majesty."

After a loop past some straggly bushes, their path took them beneath towering gums whose leaves shone in the late afternoon sun. Stefan fell into step beside his king. He had never met Gavin personally before, although each knew of the other. He glanced sideways at the quietly self-assured man and wondered what he should say, or whether he should speak at all. He had a notion that he wasn't supposed to talk to a king until he spoke to him first, but the king had already spoken to him. He waited.

Finally Gavin spoke. "So Stefan. I am sorry we have kept you waiting. It was not the choice of your woodfolk family to exclude you, but they understood when I explained. High Lord Tarkyn and his woodfolk wanted me to become acquainted with the woodfolk of these forests as they have lived here for centuries... and we did not want you caught in the crossfire if our negotiations became heated." He smiled. "As it turns out, they didn't... although Silverwood and Sphagnum Moss tested me."

"Did they? How?" asked Stefan and then wondered if he should have asked.

"Silverwood welcomed me to what I have considered until now to be my own forests," Gavin raised his eyebrows, inviting a response.

Stefan chuckled. "I can see that could have led to conflict. Both of you think of the forest as yours."

Gavin nodded. "Indeed. And when I welcomed them into the wider kingdom with an offer of assistance if they ever needed it, Sphagnum Moss demanded to know what I wanted from them in return." The king frowned. "I must admit I found that a little trying." He waved his hand. "Anyway, we have agreed to work together to keep the Kimorans out of the forest and when that threat passes, to reconsider our alliance." He stopped and turned to look at Stefan. "My thought was that during that negotiation, you wouldn't have known where to place yourself. If we had ended up in conflict, you would have been in a very awkward position."

Stefan nodded slowly, clearly taking it in. "You're right. I wouldn't have known where to put myself if you'd argued with them. In fact, I don't know where to put myself a lot of the time when I'm with outsiders and woodfolk. Just this morning when we went hunting, I didn't know whether to go with one or the other."

They turned to continue walking. The ground began to rise, and they were now coming across gouged holes in the ground that led in a line up the hill.

"Look at these, Sire. This is where little Midnight blasted the ground at the feet of the attacking Kimorans to force them back so that he could bring Sasha, Jayhan, Jon, Maud, and the others in his shield up the hill to join Tarkyn at the top." He pointed to where the gouges became deeper and wider. "And this is where Jayhan held his hand to enhance his power. Did you know Jayhan had that special gift? He can magnify another person's power. Clever little fellow."

"My word! It's lucky we had the Eskuzorians fighting for us, isn't it?"

"Yes, yes, it is. Although for a while, I wished I had never met Lord Tarkyn." He glanced at Gavin then took a quick breath, "He destroyed my life, my certainties and my place in the world."

Gavin just nodded and waited.

Stefan let out a breath. "Then he gave me another life and another place in the world but… it is strange and new and not as comfortable." He flashed a smile at Gavin, "But it is also interesting and exciting, and I have discovered talents within myself that I never knew I had." He grinned. "Look, Sire. Watch this."

He flicked to reappear twenty yards further up the hill then flicked back to the king's side. "Pretty good, hey?" He shook his head and frowned at himself. "Whoops, sorry, Sire. Getting a bit too familiar there."

"Not at all. I am pleased you are finding advantages to this upheaval of your life."

They reached the top of the hill where Gavin swung around and sat on a patch of stony ground to watch the sky above the trees as the sun set. He patted the ground to indicate that Stefan should sit beside him. Gavin waited a moment, then continued. "I have not had the chance, since I found out about your origins, to talk to you about your loyalties." He gave a little smile. "I can only imagine that they are in a state of flux but the more you get to know your woodfolk family, the more your loyalty may swing in their direction. They are, after all, a remarkable people."

"I am no less loyal to you or those outside the forests, Sire," said Stefan hurriedly. "After all, the family I grew up with and whom I love are not woodfolk. And I have not yet come to care deeply for my family of origin. In fact," he added with flash of candour, "I can't help feeling a bit peeved that they watched me grow up in front of them and didn't manage to figure out that I was one of them."

Gavin gave short laugh. "You have only just begun the journey of getting to know them. I suspect you will go through many emotions on the way. But Stefan, you have suddenly become a pivotal person in this kingdom. You have always been talented and well-respected, but now, I would like you to become my ambassador to the woodfolk and theirs to me." He gave a wry smile. "I will give you the title of Minister for the Great Forest and officially, you will be in charge of caring for the forest and all who dwell in her or pass through her, including of course, keeping our border with Kimora secure. Unofficially, you will also liaise between the woodfolk and me." He shrugged. "I also think it will make your position clearer for you and the woodfolk, if you have a role that bridges the gap between us."

Stefan gave a slow smile as he thought about it. "You know, this might just help. Thank you for trusting my loyalty enough to offer me that role." Then he trained his green eyes firmly on Gavin's face. "I like you as a man and as a king. I believe you to be fair and well-intentioned, with the strength to back your beliefs. I have always considered myself loyal to you. If I am able to come to you in the future with any doubts I may have, then I can guarantee to remain loyal to you."

"Coming from a man in such a state of flux as you, that is an honest, convincing avowal of faith. Thank you. I will accept that. Besides, if I demanded unquestioning loyalty, the woodfolk would not trust you." Gavin smiled. "So, the next time I negotiate with the wood-folk, you will not be excluded. In fact, you will be the arbiter. I am counting on you to keep the peace between us."

Stefan's eyes widened. "Wow. That is a responsibility."

"It is. But in any liaison between us, you will understand the perspective of both sides more than anyone else, so they will follow your leadership in that situation."

Stefan gave a quick smile. "So they will. They always give the lead to the most expert in any given situation." He heaved a sigh. "Aaah. Maybe some good will come of all this, after all. Thank you, Sire. Instead of being the new uncertain woodman, I can now be a man on a mission. It feels much better."

"And one last thing. When woodfolk are present, seen or unseen, you may dispense with bowing to me in greeting and just give a nod of respect. I think that is a fair compromise that will discomfort you less. In other circumstances, we will follow normal protocols."

Stefan let out a gusty sigh, watching the sky blaze in a display of gold and orange-rimmed dark clouds with sweeping wisps that turned to pink and blue behind them. "I look forward to working with you, Sire. Very much."

Chapter 8

Everything was ready; the fire was blazing, the venison was nearly cooked, and filled the firesite with a tantalizing aroma. There was no table, but plates of nuts and cheeses and small rolls had been set out on logs. Table mats of woven branches had been placed in regular intervals around the edge of the clearing ready to receive the vegetables that were cooking in the ashes of the fire, while garlands of flowers and leaves decorated the surrounding trees.

Lapping Water entered the clearing carrying Gurgling Brook and smiled at the display and a sea of expectant faces. "Oh. This looks beautiful. King Gavin is about to arrive."

"Please stand," said Sheldrake, in a quiet but authoritative voice, "For His Majesty, King Gavin of Carrador."

Everyone stood up nervously, brushed themselves down, then watched the north-east corner of the bush where Lapping Water had emerged. Moments later, the king entered.

He stood just inside the clearing near Lapping Water and waited while Maud, Sheldrake, Reece, his troopers, and the Kimorans bowed.

"Please rise," he said in a low melodic voice. "I am pleased to make your acquaintance and look forward to getting to know you all over dinner."

He was not a tall imposing figure like Tarkyn or even Jon, but he carried himself with quiet confidence. His thigh length frock coat was a soft russet, his favourite colour, and he wore tan knee-length boots over dark brown breeches. His apparel was not at all ostentatious but despite his valet's best efforts, was clearly less casual and of far finer quality than everyone else's. However, he was the king after all, and he did not look jarringly out of place.

Then Sheldrake spoke again. "We are also honoured to welcome His Highness Prince Tarkyn, High Lord of Eskuzor. And as you know, we have among us, the rightful queen of Kimora, Sasharia, and her regent, Prince Jondarian."

Tarkyn, with Bird riding determinedly on his shoulder, followed Gavin into the clearing after a discreet pause, but merely nodded his head in greeting. Sasha and Jon, taking their lead from him, did likewise. After all, this feast was in the king's honour.

Gavin worked his way around the firesite, with Maud presenting each person to be greeted, in descending order of rank. Sasha was unaccountably shy, as she and Jon were presented.

Gavin's eyes twinkled at her, and he held out his hands to grasp hers. "Why so shy, my little cousin? I am so very pleased to see you and your young friend safe and sound. You have given me sleepless nights this last week."

She cocked her head. "Have I?" Sasha leaned in close to him and muttered, "I'm not used to formal events. I don't know how to act properly." She managed a smile, but it lacked her usual insouciance. "But I am very glad to see you too."

"You have been through a hard time, haven't you?" Gavin said softly. "We will talk more later."

She nodded, trying unsuccessfully to keep the tears from her eyes. Beside her, Jon put his arm around her back, giving her support without a blatant hug.

Gavin grinned up at Jon. "And I hear your years on the street have paid off, leading the chase through the sewers, then using your knife skills to kill a deer and more importantly, a few of the abductors. You have hidden depths, my friend."

Jon gave a wry smile in return although he looked a bit uncomfortable. "Not a side of my life I am used to showing others… but useful all the same. I'm pleased you came."

"So too am I." He gave a little chuckle. "It is all most interesting." He gave Sheldrake a brief but warm greeting then bent down to talk to Jayhan. "Hello, young man. We meet again. I am very pleased to see you safe. I have been worried sick about Sasha and you. I hear you have been helping Midnight to blast wads of earth into the air. Fun, was it?"

Jayhan grinned and nodded. "Once we realised Midnight's shield could protect us from those mean people trying to kill us, it was fun… really fun. You should have seen that dirt fly and those mean people jump back."

Gavin smiled, but after a moment said, "But it must have been very frightening to be under attack like that."

Jayhan's face became tight. "It was. Very. I used my eyes on a few but there were thousands of them coming at us from all sides and all trying to kill us. Not just me or Sasha or Jon. All of us." He shuddered. "I've never been in a war before."

Gavin resisted the urge to correct him. Little boys were, after all, prone to exaggeration and even if it had only been a skirmish, it had been a deadly one. He tousled Jayhan's hair as he straightened. "You must tell me more about it later."

Then, as he turned to have Lady Arquin presented to him, his smile faded and he said formally, "How do you do? It is unfortunate that we meet in my country without my authorization for your entry."

Lady Arquin dropped another quick curtsey even though it was not required. "Indeed, Your Majesty. Most unfortunate. And even more so, that my countrymen and I have been deceived by our reigning monarch into hunting down our true queen. You have my humblest apology for our intrusion into your country and for our offence against your cousins."

"Thank you," replied Gavin neutrally.

Arquin hesitated but said in a rush before he moved on, "And, Sire, I must speak to you before you return to Highkington. It is most important. Not now, but before you return. If you please."

Gavin stared at her a moment then nodded curtly before turning to Berundi.

When Berundi had been introduced, she said, "And I too am truly mortified that we took arms against our true queen, Sasharia, and against Prince Jondarian. I can only be thankful that your brave troopers and the woodfolk stopped us."

Gavin nodded. "I agree. We are all in their debt." His quiet courtesy gave no sign whether he really believed their contrition. He moved on to meet Rhoda and Draya. "And I believe you two shadowed the abductors and were there to support the little ones when they escaped. Wise tactics."

"The best we could do, Sire," said Rhoda.

"And I thank you both for healing my troopers. I, and I'm sure they too, are most grateful for that."

Draya smiled. "You are welcome, Sire."

He moved on to speak to Reece and Trevor, who were heading up the king's elite squad of troopers. "Sergeant Reece. I believe you and my old friend, Trevor, here, with the help of your men, made short work of the original group of abductors. A job well done. We do not need their like polluting our fine country."

"We did, Your Majesty, but the children actually freed themselves," replied Reece, not wishing to take undue credit. "I believe Sasha used some sort of magic to counter a building storm and dazed her captors long enough for them to flee into the forest. We merely spotted their pursuers and dispatched them before they could close in again on the children."

Trevor gave a low chuckle. "Then, when we returned to this spot here, we found a court-bred lady had suddenly appeared and then, blow me down, if she doesn't turn into a dirty great bloodhound and lead most of our squad off into the woods to track down the little ones."

"Found them too, Sire," Reece gave a stiff smile that, if he had been speaking to anyone else, would have been a grin. "You should have heard her baying to greet them when we were getting close. Absolutely blood-curdling." He glanced at Maud, who was standing next to the king, looking primly as though this had nothing to do with her.

Gavin turned to her and said, with a twinkle in his eye, "I have always known you were deeper and cleverer than your frivolous reputation. But this, Lady Maud! This is astonishing... and so unbecoming for a Lady of the Court! I am delighted. What else have you become?"

Maud turned pink and her face screwed up in embarrassment.

Seeing this, Gavin raised his hand and said, "No. I did not mean to discomfort you. Don't tell me now. I don't wish to make you a source of entertainment. But I would love to hear about it at some later date."

Maud let out a breath of relief. "Thank you, Sire. Although circumstances dictated that I shared the knowledge of my talent with many here, it is generally a private thing. But of course, I would be happy to talk to you about it... later."

Once Gavin had spoken briefly to each member of Reece's squad, he moved on to Stefan, Marjorie, and Jackson. "Maud has left you three until last because you keep company with Stefan, and I have an announcement to make concerning him. Jackson, I thank you for lending your support to our cause and for acting as my aide-de-camp too while I am here in the forests."

Gavin turned to Marjorie and smiled at the tall woman, her blue-eyed face framed with black hair. "And you must be Marjorie, Stefan's sister." Then, despite the formality of the occasion he chuckled, "You look just like him."

Marjorie grinned back and put her arm around her shorter, green-eyed brother, as a ripple of laughter coursed around the firesite. "I've always thought so."

"And now... Stefan." Gavin promptly turned away from him and instead, addressed the assembled crowd, "As most of you know, Stefan has recently discovered that he was born a woodman but raised as an outsider by the Vine family. Because of his unique connection to both communities and his skills and experience, I am appointing him as Minister for the Great Forest to liaise between us."

Marjorie gave a squeak of delight and threw her arms around Stefan's neck. Stefan grinned and returned her embrace but disentangled himself as quickly as he could, as the king was waiting to continue.

"Sorry about that," they chorused.

Gavin shook his head and smiled, thinking privately that this would never happen in the formidable, formal atmosphere of his court. He continued his address. "Of course, in public, his role will be to oversee the training of elite squads such this one," he indicated Reece and Trevor with their men, "and to check on logging, excessive poaching, any banditry and particularly, to prevent unauthorized entries across our borders within the forest. But his greatest role will be to liaise with the woodfolk." He waved his hand. "I give you, Lord Stefan, Minister for The Great Forest."

As everyone applauded, Stefan's eyes nearly fell out of his head. "*Lord* Stefan? You didn't mention that."

Gavin chuckled. "I wasn't sure how you'd react, being born a woodman."

"... but raised an outsider." Stefan reflected for a moment, "I suppose I don't pay rank as much reverence as some, but still..." He smiled. "Thank you very much, Sire. It doesn't seem quite fair that I should be so elevated because of an accident of birth but I will accept and do my best for you, the woodfolk, and the forests."

The applause had died down enough for everyone to hear the last part of this speech, which incited another round of applause. Under its cover, Gavin said quietly, "Most positions of rank are accidents of birth. It is the way of the world."

With introductions now complete, Maud received a stone goblet of wine from Lapping Water, which she presented to Gavin. "Your Majesty, may we present you with a wine that the mountainfolk, a branch of Eskuzorian woodfolk, produce and store in caves under their mountains. It is of excellent quality," she gave a little smile, "and I suspect you may have tasted it before."

"Thank you," He took a sip, then nearly dropped the goblet in surprise as the woodfolk appeared suddenly around him, watching expectantly. He took another sip, then raised his eyebrows. "It is indeed very good, and you're right, I have had it before. Well, fancy that! I wonder what other woodfolk products I have been unknowingly imbibing?"

"Any goods you have sampled would only have come from the Eskuzorian woodfolk since until now, we have never dealt with any outsiders," Silverwood gave a broad smile. "But I am pleased you appreciate their quality."

"I do. Amazing. There is a whole world within my world that I knew nothing about." He turned to Stefan, "And you, my new Minister for the Great Forest, can lead me through it."

The woodfolk's casual delight in surprising him had broken the air of formality engendered by Gavin's presentation and the firesite gradually filled with the sounds of conversation and laughter, as everyone began to relax in the presence of the king and settled back to enjoy the evening. There were no servants, but a variety of people kept Gavin supplied with food and wine all evening, as they did for each other.

Gavin, for his part, relaxed his stance but not his guard. He had enjoyed the afternoon with the woodfolk with their cavalier disregard for rank but here, he had a role to play, however casually. And he only had a short time to become familiar with a situation that everyone else already understood. However, as the wine flowed, quite slowly in his case, the people around the firesite became less guarded and more candid and he learnt more in that evening than he could have from any number of briefings. He privately applauded Maud and Sheldrake's guidance in asking him to take the time to get to know the players before the match and determined to inspect the captured Kimorans before retiring.

Part 2

Chapter 9

The following morning, Gavin awoke stiff and sore. Tarkyn may have become used to sleeping on a pile of bracken or just on hard ground, but he had not. He suppressed a groan as he stretched the worst of the cramps out of his muscles and pushed back the screen of shrubbery to crawl outside and stand up, stretching his arms above his head, before dropping them and looking around.

No one was in sight, but he had been told that woodfolk lookouts would be up in the surrounding trees, keeping guard. He glanced around and could see none of them, but apparently that was to be expected. He heard the sound of voices and followed it along a short path to its source, to find a fire lit, with several woodfolk and most of the troopers sitting around it, waiting for a large kettle to come to the boil.

They smiled when they heard someone approaching but when they realised who it was, the troopers scrambled to stand up.

Gavin waved them back down. "Stay there. Too early in the day for formality. How close are we to a cup of tea?"

"Five minutes, I'd say," said Autumn Leaves. "You're an early riser. Not like your Eskuzorian counterpart. Tarkyn is a notorious late riser unless there is a particular reason to get up. He's even worse now that he has Gurgling Water to play with in bed."

Just at that moment, Tarkyn appeared, running his hands back and forth through his hair. "I heard that." He grinned. "I'm not disputing it, just saying I heard it." He nodded at Gavin. "Good morning. Looks like being a beautiful day, doesn't it? Listen to those birds." He gave a shiver. "Bit chilly at the moment, but it will warm up."

Over the next hour, the firesite gradually filled up. A second fire was lit so that there was enough room for everyone to sit close to the fires and keep warm in the crisp morning air, while large pots of porridge cooked.

Once breakfast was over, Gavin asked Maud and Sheldrake, Tarkyn, Jon, Stefan, Silverwood and Waterstone to accompany him to the clearing where he had spent the previous afternoon with the woodfolk. He decided that he would perhaps include Lady Arquin later, since he considered her an uncertain quantity.

Sasha watched them go but knew that Jon would be representing her as her regent. She turned to find Jayhan at her elbow, waiting to embroil her in a new game with Midnight, in a deliberate attempt, she suspected, to keep her mind off the decisions being made.

Gavin sat down on the ground against a log, vaguely wondering whether the dewy moss under him would stain his coat. When the others were seated and listening, he said, "So, the question is, what do we do with one hundred and sixty Kimoran soldiers that we have captured? Do we send them home or do we keep them as prisoners of war and put them to work on our roads? I know the issues are complex but firstly, let us consider this one issue from Carrador's point of view."

"Do you want to keep them as prisoners of war?" asked Maud.

Gavin shook his head. "Not particularly. In fact, no. I would not want anyone to mis-interpret my actions and think that I was mustering a rebel army. But on the other hand, will I appear over-conciliatory to Toriana, if I allow an invading force to go home, virtually unscathed?"

"You could hold Lady Arquin and Berundi and perhaps other officers as hostages for ransom," suggested Sheldrake.

"Hmm," Gavin pondered a moment, "And if I send these people back to Kimora, will they face excessively severe retribution at the hands of this unstable monarch?" He shook his head. "But on the other hand, if we keep them, might that retribution be rained down upon their families instead?"

"I think returning them may be to your advantage, Sire," said Maud, "as they can provide good reasons for their failure. They can honestly report that the children had already es-caped, and their abductors had been slain, before they arrived. Furthermore, they can report that they were overcome by a far greater force, which now patrols your borders."

"A force so skilful that they could choose to disable, not kill," added Stefan with a note of pride in his voice.

Waterstone smiled at him but said nothing.

Gavin nodded. "True. And it will help our security, if they report that they were stopped at the border by our troops." He smiled apologetically at Silverwood. "I know you are not our troops, but I can't say it was woodfolk, can I?"

Silverwood did not look perturbed. "No, you can't."

"Very well," said Gavin, coming to a decision. "I will send them home, minus weapons of course. And I will write to Toriana reiterating my displeasure at having shaman hunters within my borders and warning her of our increased border presence. I will demand repa-ration for the incursion of her armed force and will hold Lady Arquin as surety, until it is paid." He rubbed his forehead between his thumb and fingers as he pondered. "I am tempted to say that any further invasion by an armed force will be considered an act of war, but I don't want to risk daring her into it. I don't want a war. I don't want our people hurt, and lands and villages damaged. "

He stood up suddenly, slapping his hands on his thighs. "Good. That's decided then." As Maud, Sheldrake, and Stefan went to rise, he waved his hand to keep them where they were. He smiled. "Stay there. Just stretching."

"Well, that was quick," said Tarkyn, startled. "Maybe you didn't need to come here after all."

Gavin gave a brief smile. "It is because I am here that it could be so quick. But that is only one aspect of the situation. I fear the issues surrounding our little cousin, Sasharia, are far more complex." He paced slowly around the perimeter of the clearing, then stopped and looked around at the people he had gathered together. "Comments?"

"Toriana will now have confirmation that Sasha is alive, since Shay must have sent her a message telling her of the abduction and requesting the troops," Maud replied.

"Hmm. So Sasharia is even more at risk than before," concluded Gavin.

"I'm afraid so, Sire. But at least Shay didn't know of Sasha's ability to dispel Toriana's binding," said Maud. "Ruby, the shaman with the abductors, did not let on to him that she was no longer held in thrall by Toriana."

Sheldrake grimaced. "Toriana may not *know* of Sasha's power, but she fears its existence."

"Unfortunately," said Jon, shifting uncomfortably, "Arquin and Berundi have already told the Kimoran troops that Sasha, as their true queen, has released them from the binding. But three other officers are shamans still under Toriana's sway, and they are undermining Arquin. So, the troops' loyalties are divided, and they will carry that debate back into Kimora."

Sheldrake nodded. "Arquin has requested that Sasha release the other shamans in her troop from Toriana's binding and I must say, I agree with her."

Jon hesitated, before continuing, "Speaking for myself, I would like to see them freed from delusion, even if it is a lot to ask of Sasha. It pains me to see Kimorans' free will compromised. And if we are ever to depose Toriana, Sasha will have to break her aunt's hold on the shamans in Kimora. We could start with these people."

Maud put a finger to her mouth as she considered. "Hmm. I agree. I would think that this is an untenable situation for Arquin. They know she has shifted her loyalty. As things stand, her shaman officers and the troops most influenced by them will almost certainly inform on her when they return."

"Too dangerous," said Gavin firmly. "It would be safer if all the shamans among them regained their independence so that they could provide a consistent message to their troops."

Silverwood frowned. "But can we then rely on these troops not to spread word through Kimora that their shamans have been freed from Toriana's influence?"

"I think so," said Jon. "People follow their local shamans, above all else, and will want to protect them."

"Will they?" Gavin sat down again and reached for a waterbag, giving himself time to decide as he drank. "In that case, we will ask Sasha to release these shamans."

"And I think it would work more effectively if she were to do it in full view of the Kimoran troops," suggested Maud.

"Only when she is ready," said Jon, the light of battle in his eyes.

Gavin smiled gently at him. "I agree. Having had so much hatred directed towards her has shaken her confidence. We will look after her, I promise you. But perhaps if she meets those troops again, once the released shamans have had time to talk to them, they may be kinder to her and restore her faith in Kimorans and herself."

Chapter 10

When Stefan left the meeting with King Gavin, he spotted Midnight, Jayhan, and Sasha playing marbles around a circle they had drawn in the middle of The Way Through. Normally, a thoroughfare would not be an ideal place to play but there was no traffic at all on The Way Through, so they were quite safe. He thought Sasha looked strained.

He wandered over and knelt down next to Midnight who, as the current leader, had the most marbles. Midnight smiled at him and good-naturedly offered him a handful of marbles so he could join in.

"Thanks" he said and proceeded to show a degree of skill only rivalled by Midnight.

As Stefan's marble cracked one of Sasha's last marbles out of the ring, she asked tensely, "So what's happening? What did Gavin decide?"

"He's sending the Kimorans home but keeping Lady Arquin as a hostage for ransom."

"Huh," Sasha became thoughtful. "That means they'll be waiting for us in Kimora if we ever go there, waiting to attack us."

"Possibly," said Stefan, but left it at that.

Before long, first Jayhan and then Sasha lost all their marbles and naturally began to lose interest.

Seeing this, Stefan suggested, "What if we ask Midnight to show us his archery and slingshot skills? Perhaps we could borrow someone's bow and have a go ourselves?" He shrugged. "After all, I am supposed to be teaching you to bear arms effectively."

Sasha turned a woebegone face to him. "Yes, but now you've got a new job, you won't have time to bother with us anymore."

Stefan tousled her hair. "Don't be such a gloomy guts. Of course I will. If I can't do it in work time, I'll do it in my spare time."

"Are you sure?" Jayhan's face lit up.

"Yes, I'm sure."

Sasha and Jayhan immediately perked up, so Stefan enlisted Rainstorm's help to acquire a couple of bows and a quiver of arrows. Needless to say, Rainstorm was keen to join them too.

While Midnight and Rainstorm set up targets, Stefan revised Jayhan and Sasha's knowledge of the basics of holding the bow correctly, how far back to pull back the drawstring and how to release the arrow without jerking and ruining their aim. Rainstorm kept a weather eye on what they were doing but either approved of what Stefan was saying or decided to hold his peace.

As they practised, Stefan said casually, "You know Sasha, you and I have a lot in common."
"We do?"

"Yes. Just think about it. We both span two cultures, which Jon, Tarkyn, and even Midnight do." He walked to the tree that had been marked as their target and pulled out the last flight of arrows to return them to the younger ones for their next attempt. "But you and I, Sasha, we have both just discovered we're not who we thought we were. I thought I was the son of an innkeeper and a Carradorian arms master but discovered that I'm also a woodman. You thought you were a simply an orphaned stable girl but now find you're rightfully the Queen of Kimora. "

"Hey yeah," said Jayhan enthusiastically. "That's true. Amazing."

Sasha scowled. "But your true people want you. Mine don't. They're all trying to kill me off."

"Your truest person is Jon, and he loves you to pieces," retaliated Stefan. "And the others would if they hadn't been corrupted either directly or indirectly by Toriana. Once that's sorted, they'll be right behind you."

"Huh."

As he handed out the arrows for the next try, Stefan glanced at her and said, "Well, I don't know about you, but I've had a very hard time these last few days."

Sasha looked startled. "Oh." After a moment, she sighed, "Sorry, Stefan. It's all been me, me, me, hasn't it? I should have thought." And she did. She stopped fitting her next arrow to the draw string and thought while the others waited. Slowly she said, "And you're so proud of your family that owns the Vine, aren't you? You must have almost felt like you lost them."

Stefan's mouth twisted. "I did lose them for a while. All in my head, not theirs." He looked across at Rainstorm and Midnight, "And then these miscreants came into my life …"

Rainstorm grinned. "And showed you that being a woodman wasn't as bad as you feared it might be."

Stefan chuckled. "Exactly. And you probably don't know this yet, Sasha and Jayhan," he added, "but because I was one of two baby boys who were lost by the woodfolk in a flood long ago, none of my true family knows which man is my father and which is my uncle. So Spinifex and Ironbark are both my uncle-fathers and Tree Fern is my sister-cousin. All I can be sure of is that Sphagnum Moss is my grandfather and Silverwood is my aunty."

"Really?" Jayhan's pale eyes grew round, and he dropped the arrow that he was trying to fit to his drawstring. "Blast!" He bent over and picked it up. "Well," he said to Sasha, as he straightened. "At least *your* family is straightforward. You have one ghastly aunt and one brilliant brother." He grinned "Now all you have to do is help your brilliant brother to have more power than your ghastly aunt."

"Aah. You drive me crazy sometimes, Jayhan," said Sasha, as she let loose her next arrow to land dead on the bull's eye.

He took this to mean, quite accurately, that she agreed with him, even though she didn't want to. He grinned at her. "I know."

Chapter 11

It was mid-afternoon, six hours after Gavin's meeting. As a rising wind swept rolling grey clouds before it, the sun came and went, with the clouds' shadows scudding across the ground.

A storm was brewing.

Sasha stood in the field, fifty yards away from the Kimoran captives, facing three shamans, each one guarded by a Carradorian trooper. Jon, Jayhan who had insisted on coming, Maud, Arquin and Berundi stood to her left, on the far side from the Kimorans so that they didn't block the soldiers' view.

"Lady Arquin," murmured Maud, "All of your shamans are female. Is that just a coincidence? I distinctly remember Lady Electra referring to her countrymen and women as being shamans, but I have yet to meet a male one."

Arquin raised her eyebrows. "Did she? I suspect that was merely a sop to your patriarchal society. Our society is matriarchal, and we have no male shamans and few men in positions of power. But power in the hands of women does not always improve our relationship with other countries. So perhaps ambassadors are instructed to soften the impression they give neighbouring countries."

Maud pondered this. No wonder Yarrow had been so reluctant to include Sheldrake and Jayhan in her training of Sasha. She gave herself a little shake and returned her focus to the scene before her. She noticed Gavin, Tarkyn, and several others watching from a distance and knew that most of the woodfolk had positioned themselves in nearby trees for a grandstand view.

No one had asked Sasha to act so quickly, but she had insisted. In the end, Jayhan's words had decided her. She had formed a resolve to help Jon and by implication, herself, and wanted to get it over and done with and, if at all possible, dissolve the hatred that she knew the Kimoran captives were directing towards her. She had decided that if they remained stalwart in their hatred of her, she would walk away from the whole future rebellion. She had been brought up without the bedrock of even one secure parent, and at times like this, she could feel no inner strength to draw upon, to hold up against the concerted antagonism of a full company of Kimorans, however misguided she knew them to be.

Sasha glanced up at the clouds and then across the field at the ranks of Kimoran soldiers, all disarmed but still aggressive, kept at bay only by the ropes that tied them to the trees and the threat of unseen archers. Then she studied the three shamans standing in front of her, who glared at her, tight-lipped and resentful.

She drew a deep breath and closed her eyes, blanking them all from her mind. She lifted her amulet out of her jerkin into clear view and held it in her hand. Then she focused on her heartbeat, oblivious to the world outside.

The carved obsidian in her hand began to glow.

A single answering pulse of pale light emitted from the three shamans, where their amulets hung inside their tunics against their chests. Then, as the light from their amulets began to pulse arrhythmically, the shamans clutched at them, staggering as Sasha's influence fought against Toriana's hold on them. Each shaman was supported by the trooper guarding them as their knees began to buckle.

Then, the audience watched as a strong steady rhythm superimposed itself over the erratic pulsing of the shamans' amulets. Suddenly a stream of black power speared from Sasha towards them and billowed out to surround them in a dark transparent cloud. Inside the cloud, the shamans' bodies began to glow with a light that intensified until it flashed brilliantly.

An answering strike of lightning streaked down from the clouds and struck Sasha. A gasp rose from the onlookers, but the small girl appeared to be unaffected. Thunder rumbled all around them and another flash of lightning struck a nearby tree, leaving the bark smouldering, as the storm moved slowly to the east. As the thunder growled, the lightning struck a bare patch on the top of the next rise. Then the rain came, sheets of rain, drenching everyone instantly.

While the audience was focused on the storm, the three shamans had been gently lowered to the ground where they lay senseless. Ignoring the angry shouts that erupted from the Kimoran captives, Sasha opened her eyes, wiped water from her face and waved her arm slowly, murmuring, "Birth, Life, Death… Always."

Then she turned and walked away through the deluge, away from the angry Kimorans and back towards the firesite, Jon's arm across her shoulders, Jayhan's hand in hers and Maud beside Jayhan.

At the firesite, Rhoda was waiting for her with a cloak, a cup of tea and encouragement. Sasha just looked at her, dazed.

"Give it time," said Maud gently from within the hood of her cloak. "At the moment they think you've attacked, and possibly killed, their shamans. They will soon learn differently. You were very brave, my little Sasha."

The rain was still pouring down. People ran in to huddle around the fire, some feeding it to keep it alight in the rain. Most gave Sasha a wide berth, giving her time to recover. Ten minutes later, the rain eased, and the sun broke through the last of the dark clouds. The storm continued on its way to Kimora, leaving the earth steaming in its aftermath.

Arquin, Berundi, Rhoda and Draya returned to the firesite half an hour later, in the company of the three shamans.

Sasha glanced at them, then away.

Arquin walked over and stood in her line of vision. "Your Highness, may I present the other shamans of my home county company?"

Jon watched from across the fire as Sasha raised her eyes reluctantly and stood up, turning to face them.

As one, they dropped to one knee, heads bowed.

She took a deep breath and let it out in a rush. "Please rise."

She waited until they were facing her, standing as tall as her young frame would allow, her dark eyes gauging them. Then she spoke. "I am sorry that my aunt tricked you into becoming linked to her in a way that meant she could deceive and control you. You and I now have a link through our amulets, which some or all of you consider sacred. However, I do not want you to be in thrall to me, as you have just been to Toriana. If you wish to walk away, do so. If you wish to work with me, you may only do so as free, independent women. I will not have mystery and magic determining your loyalties. I am, I believe, the true High Shaman and rightful Queen of Kimora. My brother," here she gestured to Jon to join her, "Prince Jondarian, will act as my regent. You do not have to follow us. The choice is yours. I ask only this, that you do not betray your fellow shamans who are unregistered or who have been freed."

The power of her amulet imbued her address with greater gravitas and wisdom than anyone could have expected from a ten-year-old, and unknown to her, Sasha's words reverberated around the firesite.

But despite giving them the freedom to leave, she felt warmth radiating from her amulet and being returned to her from theirs. In a surge that took her totally by surprise, the six shaman women stepped forward and embraced her from all sides, towering over her small frame, surrounding her with kindness, strength, and warmth. When they finally pulled back, Sasha had tears rolling down her cheeks.

She sniffed. "So that's settled then, I suppose," she said, and gave a watery smile.

On the other side of the firesite, Gavin murmured to Tarkyn, "She is magnificent." He gave a quiet chuckle, "She and that brother of hers!" He shook his head, smiling in fond recollection. "I have never met two people so vulnerable and yet so strong. They wear their hearts on their sleeves. Without the corruption of Toriana's binding, every Kimoran they meet, including Arquin's troops, will fall all over themselves to support them."

Chapter 12

A few minutes later, Lady Arquin approached Gavin and Tarkyn. She nodded acknowledgement to the High Lord before curtseying to the king and waiting for him to address her.

"So Lady Arquin, Sasharia has freed your shamans from Toriana's thrall as you wished… at no small personal cost to one so young."

Arquin's eyes glistened with tears. "Your Majesty, I realise that Berundi and I inadvertently forced her into this by trying to convert my troops to her cause. For that, I am sorry. In my enthusiasm, I forgot the power of Toriana's enchantment would stop the other shamans in my company from being able to believe what I was saying to them." She took a deep breath. "But this was not what I wished to speak to you about."

The king raised his eyebrows. "Indeed?" His cool response showed clearly that he had not yet forgiven her for invading his lands.

"Sire, I believe the Queen may be planning a full-scale invasion of Carrador."

"Go on," said Gavin quietly.

"Our orders were not just to escort Sasharia and Jayhan back to the Queen. I was also asked to report back on your border defences and to gauge the viability of sending a large force along The Way Through."

"How large a force?" Gavin's tone was so well modulated that he could have been discussing plans for next week's garden party. Not a hint of tension showed in his demeanour.

"That was for me to determine, but the Queen was considering full battalions of a thousand each, not just companies."

"I see." Gavin thought for a moment then beckoned to Jon, who was watching their interchange with a weather eye from the other side of the clearing and so, responded immediately to the summons. When he arrived, Gavin asked Arquin to repeat what she had just told him. Unlike Gavin, Jon looked horrified at the prospect of an invasion.

Then Gavin asked, "Lady Arquin, was your impression that the intention to invade was a backup plan in the event that the Queen failed to secure Sasharia or was she intending to invade anyway? In other words, if she had Sasharia, would this avert an invasion?"

Jon frowned fiercely, ready to interject, but Gavin held up a finger. "Jon, I asked you to join us to hear the answer to this question, so that the issue was not raised behind your back. Do not make assumptions about my intent."

Jon gave a small stiff bow. "My apologies." He waved his hand to indicate that Arquin should answer.

Arquin sent a worried glance between the king and her new regent. "The Queen has become increasingly… annoyed with Carrador as her shaman hunters have been impeded by your express command. That traitor, Shay, was her chief shaman hunter. His last report, which accompanied his request for troops, explained clearly that you, Sire, were knowingly harbouring Prince Jondarian and Queen Sasharia under the pseudonyms of Lord Jonathan and Lady Natasha. Queen Toriana was apoplectic with rage."

The king took a deep breath and let it out slowly. "Oh dear. I fear our subterfuge has failed dismally. And Jon, that your plans for a subtle resistance are in tatters before they begin."

Jon looked stricken. "This is terrible. We will have to leave. We cannot stay and endanger your kingdom. I am so sorry we have brought this upon you."

Gavin placed a firm hand on Jon's tense shoulder. "Not so fast, my young cousin. Let us hear more." Still with his hand on Jon's shoulder, he turned to Arquin. "What more can you tell us? Did she calm down? The information was, after all, still new to her. What is Kimora's capacity to invade?"

"Kimora is huge. Her population is far larger than Carrador's," Jon butted in, close to panic.

"Jon," said Gavin patiently, "Allow Arquin to answer."

"Sorry."

"She did calm down, of course, but she remains angry." Arquin shrugged. "However, I would have to say she has spoken of invading both Carrador and Eskuzor at various times in the past. Kimora has suffered drought for the last decade and many of her crops are failing. On the other hand, Carrador's southern farmlands are rich and productive, Sire, and Toriana has her eye on them. Her current focus is on Carrador but if she succeeds in annexing your country, I am sure she will broaden her scope to include Farenz and Eskuzor. And she is definitely moving from talk to action. She is actually investigating the feasibility and the logistics of an invasion here." Arquin gave a brief humourless smile. "Your one saving grace is that many of her troops are currently tied up with quelling at least two separate rebellions. She may not have the strength to move against you until she has her own population under control."

Jon's eyes lit up. "We can help with that," he said to Gavin. "My refugees can support those uprisings and incite others. We can stall her until we're ready to make our move."

"She is a dangerous force to have in our region," said Tarkyn, entering the conversation for the first time, "If you wish it, Gavin, my woodfolk and I can spend some time here, developing the woodfolks' lines of communication in preparation for your defence, should it come to that. I think your woodfolk would see the value in preventing large contingents of armed troops stomping through their beloved forests and would be keen to assist. Their communication network could be established more quickly using the experience gained from our own network."

Gavin smiled warmly. "Thank you. I would appreciate that… a great deal, provided Eskuzor can spare you for a month or two."

"My woodfolk are too far away to receive mindmessages from home, but normal messengers could get word to me within a couple of days if something urgent crops up in Eskuzor." He smiled. "And I think my people would like the opportunity to get to know a whole new nation of woodfolk. Besides, it sounds as though Carrador's fight is also Eskuzor's fight, if this woman is as aggressive as she sounds."

Gavin nodded. "I will meet with my military advisors to review our defences, our troop numbers and their level of training, and to plan supply lines." He looked across the clearing at Sasha, who was sitting close to Maud talking quietly to Jayhan. She looked tired but calm. "Let's keep this between ourselves for now. I will, of course, inform Sheldrake and Maud but I think Sasharia has plenty to deal with, at the moment, without this. I will leave it to you, Jon, to tell her, if and when you think she is ready."

Chapter 13

Soon after this, Tarkyn bid his family and friends farewell, explaining he might be gone for a few days, and translocated with Gavin, back to Highkington.

As they lay in the reeds recovering, they could hear the gentle musical honks of the nearby black swans on one side and a couple of coots thrashing around in the reeds. Then they heard boots thudding across the lawns on the other side of them.

"Stand down," croaked Gavin. He cleared his throat and said more firmly. "Stand down. High Lord Tarkyn and I will be out to join you in a minute." He looked at Tarkyn who was now getting to his feet. "Just a moment," Gavin said to him, "let me lead you out of here. I have no wish for wet breeches."

"Hmph." Tarkyn smiled despite his lingering nausea and nodded. "Good idea."

Gavin stood up, brushed himself down and straightened his shoulders. "This way."

When they emerged from the reeds, they found themselves surrounded by alert guardsmen who, true to their liege's command, had sheathed their weapons, but had not relaxed.

"Good afternoon," said Gavin calmly. "I am pleased to see you so alert. Jenkins, could you send word to Josie that I have arrived back and that she may join us for coffee and afternoon tea in my study."

Jenkins, a young man who had only been with the guards for a year, grinned. "It has already been done, Your Majesty."

"Good heavens. Well done." Gavin glanced at Taryn. "My staff know me well, it seems, even in unusual circumstances."

They walked across the manicured lawns, past flowering garden beds and in through the French windows of Gavin's study. The king had enjoyed his foray into the forest, but he was also pleased to be back within the ordered beauty of his palatial surroundings. As he entered his study and headed for his favourite armchair, upholstered in a beautiful tapestry of browns and golds, he suddenly remembered that he had not bathed for two days, and his breeches carried evidence of him having sat on mossy logs and on the detritus of the forest floor. He gave a mental shrug. Upholstery could be cleaned, and he had more important things on his mind.

They had barely had time to sit down when a knock sounded on the door and following Gavin's reply, Josie walked into the room decorously, but with every line of her body betraying that she had had to restrain herself from bursting in. She gave a deep curtsy and waited.

Gavin smiled. "Good afternoon, Josie. I have returned fit and well, as you see. Did Annabelle strike any problems while I was gone?"

"No, Your Majesty. She held court most admirably in your stead."

"Excellent. I will catch up with her over dinner. The High Lord will be staying for several days and for dinner tonight, of course."

Josie nodded and gave a small curtsy in Tarkyn's direction.

"Take a seat, Josie," Gavin was saying, "We have a lot to discuss."

Chapter 14

Three days later and two and fifty hundred miles away, a sweet-faced, middle-aged, unremarkable looking woman was sitting in the sun, throwing out seed for a flock of blue and crimson parrots that were strutting around her on the lawn. She laughed as two of them snatched for the same corn kernel and while they were squawking at each other, a third parrot snatched the seed from under their beaks. She heard footsteps padding across the lawn behind and in the next second, the parrots screeched and took off in a whirl of colour.

She was sitting with the rising sun behind her, so her face was cast in shadow, but as she turned, the newcomer saw a flash of irritation in her large dark eyes, understandable he thought, since he had sent her favourite birds into flight.

Wincing inwardly, he walked around to stand in front of her, bowed and waited. The sun lit his tanned, careworn face, making him squint a little. Metal buttons shone in reflected light against the dark blue of his dress uniform. He had the broad physique of an older man who had trained hard for most of his life. He was one of the few men in the higher echelons of power. As a colonel, he had risen as high as a non-shaman could in Kimora.

The Queen gave a little sigh. "You could have timed your arrival a little better, Colonel Waldarion."

"My apologies, Your Majesty." He hesitated, then held out a letter bearing the seal of the King of Carrador. "But I thought you would wish to receive this as soon as it arrived."

The Queen had not heard from Shay or Lady Arquin since she had sent the company of troops forth to bring back Sasha, so the arrival of a letter from the Carradorian king did not bode well. Colonel Waldarion had drawn the short straw in being nominated to deliver it to her. He remembered all too well the rage with which she had greeted Shay's most recent report.

Toriana gave a tight little smile. "Perhaps he is apologizing for harbouring these impostors," she said, as she slid her thumbnail beneath the red seal to open the letter. "Let us hope so, for his sake."

As she opened it, another letter slipped to the floor. Waldarion bent to retrieve it and saw that it was a smaller letter addressed to the Queen in a different person's handwriting. He handed it to the Queen who took it without a word and held it while she read the king's missive.

Waldarion watched with gathering apprehension as high spots of colour appeared on Toriana's cheeks. When she looked up, her eyes were glittering with anger.

"He is demanding… no, *requesting* reparation for our troops trespassing into his king-dom. Very polite, I'm sure, but he is holding Lady Arquin as surety." She waved her hand. "Well, he can keep her, as far as I'm concerned. I'm not paying for my own troops to be re-turned. Presumably, they have failed ignominiously. So what need would I have for troops of that calibre?"

Waldarion gave a little cough. "Perhaps more information is contained in the other let-ter?"

Toriana's eyes narrowed. "Of *course*, more information is contained in the other letter. Why else would they have sent it? If you have nothing worthwhile to say, keep silent."

Waldarion wisely followed her instruction and merely nodded his acquiescence.

Rather theatrically, she threw Gavin's letter to the side so that it spiralled to the floor. Then she ripped open the second letter and began to read.

> *Your Majesty,*
>
> *I deeply apologize for our failure to bring the impostor to you. She had already escaped from Shay's custody before we arrived.*
>
> *Our intelligence regarding the border regions was quite inaccurate. We were completely overwhelmed by a large, well-trained force that has apparently been recently deployed within the Great Forest close to the Charville River.*
>
> *Obviously, King Gavin has perused this missive, but its contents are accurate, never-theless.*
>
> *We will await your instructions on the Carradorian side of the river. A message delivered to the guardhouse on the river will reach us.*
>
> *I will tell you more when I next see you.*
>
> *Your obedient servant,*
>
> *Arquin,*
>
> *Lady of Morville.*

"Well, she won't be seeing me, that is certain," said Toriana tartly. "I am not going to pay for her return. Send King Gavin a message by carrier pigeon: If those incompetent troops try to return, they will be shot at the border. And he can keep Lady Arquin. I don't need an officer who has failed us so comprehensively." She gave an unpleasant laugh. "Huh. I'd like to see his face. Now he'll either have to kill them all or pay for their food and lodgings in his prisons. He won't like that."

"And what about the families on Lady Arquin's estates?" asked Waldarion.

Her eyes narrowed as she considered. After a moment she huffed. "I would not like to think I was an unreasonable monarch. The families cannot be blamed for the failure of these troops. I shall requisition Lady Arquin's lands for the crown and those people left on the estates can continue to work the lands and provide me with income from them." She nodded in satisfaction with her idea, quite unconcerned that she had just condemned the whole area to losing their most able-bodied, leaving the rest to combine working the fields with child-rearing and caring for the elderly.

527

Waldarion, who knew she could be far more savage than this, gave a slight bow, "You are most merciful, ma'am."

Toriana threw a few more morsels on the grass as three green and yellow parrots flew back down onto the lawn. She sighed and gave a wistful smile. "Yes, I know. It is my great besetting sin.

Chapter 15

Lady Arquin, now supported by her full complement of shaman officers, gathered her troops together. Her troops were no longer bound but were acutely aware that archers monitored their every move from the trees above them.

Hours before, the warriors from Lady Arquin's estates had watched in horrified, helpless anger as the power of Sasha's amulet had overwhelmed their shaman officers sending them senseless to the ground. Now those same shamans were here in front of them looking not only recovered, but more relaxed and confident. It seemed obvious to most of the troops that their officers had fallen under some enchantment. So they waited with deep scepticism to hear what they had to say.

Captain Katya stepped forward to speak first. She was a wiry, cheery woman with bouncy black curls clustered around sparkling, almost black eyes. She was popular with the troops and had their trust. Previously, she had been the most senior officer arguing against Arquin and Berundi when they had tried to tell the troops about the truth of Sasha's claim. "You all witnessed the power of Sasharia's amulet. I understand that you were angry and feared for our safety, for which I thank you. You may think that our will was being overwhelmed and that we are now in deluded service to Sasharia. But in actual fact, the opposite is true. Our free will has been returned to us. Toriana magically bound our service to her. Sasharia freed our amulets from that binding."

"So now you're bound to her instead, then," growled an old campaigner.

Katya shook her head. "No. Our amulets beat in time with her heart, which shows us that she is the true High Shaman. But she said to us, quite forcefully, that she would not demand our fealty and would only accept service freely given." She gave a little smile. "I don't think she knows how to bind a person's will and would not do so, even if she could."

Sergeant Maslin, a no-nonsense middle-aged woman, who was respected but not generally liked, said unexpectedly, her eyes misting with tears, "But she is so fragile and earnest and good-hearted… and we can all feel her heart beating through our amulets." She glanced at the others and gave a wry smile, before saying. "So we have individually and freely given her and her brother our oath of fealty."

"Her brother? That little boy? But she was the youngest," clamoured several voices, and conversations erupted everywhere.

Arquin held up her hand and when they had quietened, she addressed them. "I'm sorry. I… we forgot that you have been kept away from the unfolding events. Prince Jondarian, who is now twenty-two years old, is among those who came searching for Sasharia when they heard she had been abducted. The little boy with the pale eyes, Jayhan, is merely her friend, as I believe he told you." She smiled. "A very loyal friend, willing to remain by her side, even though our Queen Toriana had intended to use him to make Sasharia hand over the One True Amulet."

"Prince Jondarian is also alive?" murmured several voices, answered by others doubting his identity.

"Yes, he is," said Arquin, tears in her eyes, "And he has been protecting our true Queen and High Shaman as well as he could, since he was twelve."

Pandemonium erupted as speculation turned into heated debates. As verbal disagreements threatened to become physical, their Lady raised her hand and projected her voice in a sharp reprimand. "The people of Morville do not behave like hooligans. Control yourselves."

Such was the respect that she commanded, that her troops fell silent almost immediately.

"I am not surprised you are upset and sceptical. After all, it is hard to come to terms with the possibility that the queen we have accepted all these years actually attempted to engineer the deaths of her sister and her sister's family." Her face tightened with sorrow. "And succeeded, with all but Sasharia and Jondarian."

"How do you know they're not impostors?" asked a sassy woman, who was young enough not to weigh up the disadvantages of antagonizing her superior. Her tone was assertive but not aggressive. "How do you know the girl didn't steal the amulet, even if it is the true amulet? After all, we were told robbers attacked Corinna's family."

"I'm glad you asked that question. All shamans know the answer, but lay people do not. Only the true High Shaman can don the amulet and only then if words of transfer have been spoken to them by the previous wearer, in this case, Princess Corinna. Neither shaman nor lay person can put the amulet over their heads. A pain too great to bear envelopes them if they try."

The sassy young woman looked thoughtful. "And you can tell it's the true amulet because your amulets beat in time with it. Is that correct?"

A weather-beaten man with a firm mouth but laughter lines around his eyes, had been studying the shamans before him and said, "Meaning no disrespect, ma'am, but you shamans are definitely looking... hmm... not sure how to describe it... brighter. I don't mean smarter," he added hastily, "although maybe that too. But shining more brightly, less stern and tight, if you know what I mean."

The shamans broke into smiles and looked at each other.

"That's how we feel, too," said one of them.

Lady Arquin changed the subject then and informed them of the king's decision to allow them to return home. They expressed concern when they heard that she was to be held as surety until compensation was paid. She thanked them but assured them that King Gavin was an honourable man who would treat her well. "A letter has been sent to Queen Toriana and you will return home once the king receives a reply. As you are no doubt aware, the distance between the two capitals means that you will be waiting several days for your marching orders. In the meantime, if any of you wish to help with foraging and hunting, you may do so, but be aware that archers will guard your every move wherever you are.

Since you are being sent home, escape attempts seem pointless anyway and would run counter to my wishes."

"So what about this Princess... *Queen* Sasharia?" asked a thin man with a scratchy, almost insolent voice. "Do we get to meet her?"

Arquin drilled him with her stare. After a moment, she replied, "She may honour you with a visit tomorrow, depending on your attitude, which I will gauge before letting her come near you."

Chapter 16

That night, the wind blew restlessly through the trees of the forest. High above them, clouds scudded over a waning moon and the world felt as though it were waiting for momentous events to unfold. Inside her shelter, Sasha shivered as a tiny breeze found its way through the brush door. She pushed herself back into the comfort of Jon's chest and felt his arm tighten around her.

She thought back to the shamans who had gathered around her, flooding her with the warmth of their connection to her. She let out a long sigh. Now that she had experienced the gentle strength of the shamans, she knew she could never walk away and leave shamans to suffer under the blight of Toriana's thrall. Whatever the cost, she now felt committed to the salvation of Kimora, just as her brother did.

Then she thought about the angry hordes of Arquin's troops awaiting her in the morning and her breath caught in her throat. How could she face them? What if they just shouted her down and abused her? How could she save people who didn't want to be saved? Should she even try? Her thoughts broadened from the hundred and sixty men and women to the wider population of Kimora. She was not some evangelist, skilled at preaching her own cause... and she didn't want to be.

She sighed. But she did want to release those people from the terror of unjust arrests and the merciless quelling of dissent. Too many families had been torn apart or interned to guarantee family members' compliance.

She found Jon's hand in the darkness and grasped it with her small fingers. Jon would help her and keep her safe.

"All right, little one?" came his voice quietly in the darkness.

She nodded and pressed back against him.

When she next awoke, the sun was streaming in through gaps in the brush of her shelter. Jon was still holding her, but as soon as he knew she was awake, he propped himself up on one elbow, leaning over to look into her eyes.

"Good morning, Sleepy Head. I'm stiff as a board from waiting for you to wake up."

She frowned up at him. "You could have got up without me."

He smiled at her, his blue eyes twinkling with good humour. "Could have but didn't. Ready for breakfast?"

She looked around the shelter and realised that Maud, Sheldrake and Jayhan had already left. "Oops. I *am* late, aren't I? Will they be mad at me?"

Jon laughed. "Not at all. They knew you were tired. That's why they snuck out."

"Oh dear," she said fretfully. "That's two days in a row that I've been the last out of bed. Usually I'm up at dawn."

"You're not usually having to cope with being abducted or facing a bevy of angry shamans. Cut yourself some slack, young lady."

She gave a grimace that turned into a smile. "True. So, are we off to face some more nasty Kimorans this morning?"

"Not nasty. Misguided," said Jon repressively.

"They're nasty to *me*."

"Only until they get to know you." He shrugged. "Anyway, Arquin and I aren't letting you anywhere near them unless they have mellowed a bit."

Sasha giggled. "You make them sound like bottles of port."

As it turned out, Jon decided to meet the Kimoran troops, accompanied only by Arquin and Reece, to determine for himself how receptive they would be to a visit from Sasha.

Arquin introduced him then she and Reece took a step back. Jon simply stood there, hands held loosely behind his back, waiting for their reaction.

Little did he know, but Jon looked a lot like his maternal grandfather, whom many of the older troops had known as the Prince Consort. Jon was taller and fairer, but his eyes and cheekbones were similar. The older men and women murmured their observations to the younger ones and gradually the whole company sank to one knee, hand on heart.

And as they did, Jon's sunny smile spread across his face. "Thank you very much. Please rise." As they got to their feet, he said, "I know it is hard to change one view with another. If it will help to dispel any lingering doubts, please feel free to ask me questions."

"Aren't we going to see your little sister?"

"I hope so. Consider me the vanguard. Until she is sixteen, I will act as regent protecting her and governing in line with her wishes. Let us get to know one another a little more before I decide."

"Excuse me, Your Highness," said a diminutive young soldier, her eyes sparkling with newly formed hero worship, "but could you tell us how you and Princess Sasharia escaped from the bandits."

"They weren't bandits," said Jon heavily, his smile fading. "They were assassins." He told them how he had seen his father, brothers and sister brutally murdered and then Corinna's desperate effort to save Sasharia and the true line, by throwing the amulet over the baby's head as she intoned the words of transfer. And that, even as the assassins were attacking her, she had charged Jondarian with the duty of saving his baby sister before turning back to stave off the attackers one last time.

Despite his best efforts, his eyes glistened with tears by the time he had finished his tale. But no one doubted him now and if surges of anger rippled through his audience, they were directed at Toriana and the assassins, not at Jon and Sasha.

"And you were twelve?" said an older man, possibly a grandfather, incredulously. "How on earth did you get out of Kimora with a babe in arms?"

Jon's mouth curved up in a half smile. "I stole an assassin's horse and suckled Sasha on nursing goats and sheep I found along the way." He chuckled at the aghast faces that gradually joined him in laughter. "It wasn't easy. Hard to find them, and even harder to catch them."

"And where have you been living in Carrador all this time?" asked one of the shamans sympathetically.

Jon immediately looked apprehensive. "I couldn't look after Sasha on my own. I placed her in an orphanage."

"You what?!" thundered the old grandfather.

Jon winced. "It was the best I could do. Old Tom who runs the orphanage is a kind man, but I didn't know how to look after a baby, and I couldn't stay with her because I was too old. So I visited as often as I could without arousing suspicion."

Disgruntled murmurs ran through the crowd. Then someone asked scathingly, "And what about you? Stayed with some swanky relatives, did you?"

"Not exactly. I didn't know who had sent the assassins, you see. So I couldn't approach anybody."

"And so?" persisted the voice.

"And so I lived on the streets of Highkington until I was eighteen when I finally landed a job as a footman in the Kimoran Embassy." Jon had folded his arms against the barrage. He glanced at Arquin. "I think I've had enough," he said quietly and turned to leave.

Immediately an uproar broke out as people apologised and begged him to stay.

He turned back to them and ran his hand through his hair. "I don't like my past any more than you do. I have lived in fear for the last ten years, fear for myself and fear for Sasharia. And it's not over yet. It will never be over while my aunt sits on the throne of Kimora."

"So, our young Queen was brought up in an orphanage, was she?" said the grandfather ruminatively. "Well, she'll have a feel for the common people, which can't be a bad thing. Where's she living now? Still there?"

"No. Lady Maud told the king of our existence." He gave a self-deprecatory grimace. "I should have gone to him sooner. He is our cousin, you see. His uncle, our father, was killed in the attack on our family. But I didn't know whom to trust." Jon glanced sideways at Reece who gave him an encouraging smile. "The king is supporting us and we are better off than we were, although we have both insisted on working for our living."

For a few moments there was silence while Jon looked down and brushed a twig off his shirt. Then he raised his eyes and surveyed the faces in front of him. "I don't know what you people have experienced, but many Kimoran refugees now inhabit these forests. They have fled from persecution, brutality, and coercion in Kimora to protect themselves or their families. For several years, I have been supporting and organising them. They, too, have only recently found out who I am." He gave a grunt of bitter laughter. "And straight away, we were attacked by Shay and his cronies."

"And by us," said a sturdy middle-aged woman. She glanced around herself then back at Jon, "for which we are sorry."

Jon smiled. "Thanks. It is a big gnarly mess, isn't it? But with your help and Sasha's power, we can start to unravel it." He turned to the shaman. "Lady Arquin, if you and your people could wait a few minutes, I will bring Sasha to meet them."

Arquin's face lit up. "Thank you, Sire," she said quietly.

When Jon returned with Sasha, she was flanked on the other side by her determined champion, Jayhan. She was not holding the hand of either of them but walked, head up and shoulders squared, looking straight ahead. As they turned to face Arquin's troops, Jon and she presented a picture of contrasts. Jon was tall, fair-skinned, blond, and blue-eyed while Sasha barely reached his chest, her black wavy hair framing her dark face and liquid brown eyes. But she too resembled her maternal grandfather and, coming from Kimora where different colourings ran in the same family, no one in the audience doubted that she was Jon's sister.

Jon indicated Sasha. "This is my sister, Sasharia, rightful Queen of Kimora and High Shaman."

Without a murmur, the entire company sank to one knee, hand on heart.

Sasha took a deep breath. "Please rise." She waited until they were standing and said, "I am pleased to meet you. I hope you have forgiven me for putting your shamans through such a difficult experience yesterday and that you understand why it was necessary." She indicated Jayhan at her side and managed a tight smile. "And this is my friend, Jayhan, whom I believe you have already met. He too was abducted, to be used as leverage to make me transfer the power of the amulet to my aunt. But he has chosen to remain my friend despite the risks, for which I thank him."

Jayhan blinked in surprise at the formal tone of her thanks, then grinned at her. She couldn't help herself. She grinned back. Applause and hoots of appreciation both for Sasha and Jayhan broke out in the crowd. In the blink of an eye, formality gave way to friendly questions and people wanting to talk to her.

Through the throng that surrounded her, she managed to catch Jon's eye. He just crossed his arms, raised his eyebrows, and shook his head in amazement, smiling at her, not really grasping that it was his groundwork that had made her reception so enthusiastic.

Chapter 17

Waiting for Toriana's reply forced the whole camp to remain in one place. By the end of the week, members of Toriana's forces were conversing amiably with Beetlebrow, Argus, Darya, and Rhoda, hearing about the plights of their compatriots and asking after lost relatives. The woodfolk insisted on staying out of sight of Arquin's troops which led to some awkward moments as the outsiders tried to explain why they couldn't all just eat, talk, and camp together.

In the end, Arquin had to pull rank and say that she wanted her company to maintain their discipline while they were officially deployed, which meant organising their own campsite, posting guards, and rostering tasks. They were required to seek permission if they wanted to leave their campsite for any reason, ostensibly so that she could ensure that no one was shot inadvertently, but in reality, so that woodfolk would have warning of their approach.

Finally, late on the sixth day, a signal was received from the small guardhouse across the river that a message had arrived. The flotilla of small boats that had brought the company across over a week ago was moored along the bank near the guardhouse, having been returned to the Kimoran side of the river once Arquin's company had debarked. One of these boats, bearing a Kimoran messenger, was being rowed across by a local fisherman. The current was strong so that the boat finally landed several hundred yards downstream.

Arquin, shading her eyes against the setting sun, frowned. Why just a message? Why weren't the other boats being brought over to take her people back home?

The messenger hopped agilely out of the boat, ran along the bank, and bowed, presenting Arquin with a sealed envelope.

Her heart sank. The handwriting was Colonel Waldarion's, not the Queen's. Keeping her feelings to herself, she slit open the letter and read:

> *My dear Lady Arquin (Major),*
>
> *You will not be surprised to learn that your failure angered the Queen, even if it was based on inaccurate intelligence.*
>
> *She has no intention of paying your ransom and has forbidden your company to return home.*
>
> *Your estates have been forfeited to the Crown. However, your tenants will be allowed to continue to work the land so that its revenue is not interrupted.*
>
> *The Queen has sent a reply to King Gavin by carrier pigeon but omitted to inform you. So, I am informing you in her stead.*

Yours Faithfully,
Waldarion.

She looked up blindly, trying to come to terms with the catastrophe that had befallen her and her people. She didn't even see the curious stares of her troops as she gathered her wits enough to walk past them to seek out Maud and Sheldrake.

She found them seated at the firesite, talking to Stefan, Jon, and Reece. Without a word, she thrust the letter into Maud's hand. Maud read it silently before handing it to Sheldrake.

"Come and sit down," said Maud gently. "Can you trust this Waldarion chap?"

Arquin nodded. "He is an old friend. He risks the Queen's ire by writing to me. She wanted us to attempt to enter Kimora then to be shot down without warning. Waldarion has saved the lives of many of my company by writing to me."

"Oh my dear!" Maud was shocked. "She is a terrible woman. Sergeant Reece, we need tea. Sheldrake, we must bring them all back to Highkington. We will leave first thing tomorrow morning. Don't worry, my dear. King Gavin will not leave you or your people destitute. Now, go with Berundi and tell your people. By the time you've done that, a nice hot cup of tea will be waiting for you."

Maud's kind but firm managing style was just what Arquin needed to pull herself together. She rose from where she had sat so briefly and, taking a deep breath, sallied forth to tell her people of their exile.

"That poor woman! What a poor reward for loyal service." Sheldrake stood up and stretched to get the stiffness out of his limbs. "Well, my dear, I hope an invasion isn't imminent, but we shall certainly keep our ears to the ground. Until the prospect becomes more immediate, I think we should carry on as before, training Sasha in history, etiquette and magic for as long as we can." He looked across at Stefan, his arms master who now had the added responsibility of liaising with the woodfolk. "Stefan, now that Toriana knows the true identities of Lord Jonathan and Lady Natasha, do you think the security arrangements and the staff's training are sufficient to keep Sasha safe at Batian House?"

"They will be, sir, if you can place a warning ward around the whole perimeter. The current ward that only stretches across the front is no longer sufficient, I think."

Sheldrake nodded. "I will write to Tarkyn's wizard, Stormaway Treemaster, seeking advice. He is, apparently, a master in the use of wards."

Part 3

Chapter 18

A click sounded in the darkness.

Then the faint protest of a hinge as the heavy wooden front door was swung inward. A pause as the intruder waited, checking for any disturbance, then quiet, almost silent, footsteps slipped along the edge of the wooden floor of the hallway, avoiding the possibility of creaking floorboards.

They passed the corridor on the left, which led to the kitchen. The stairs were in sight now, even in the darkness of the hallway.

BANGGG!

Hannah, the household's head cook, stood over a crumpled figure, a huge cast iron frypan held in her two hands. From further up the corridor, a light appeared held by Rose, the maid.

Rose hurried down to join the cook in looking down at the black clad intruder. She gave a little grunt of satisfaction. "Well done, Hannah. How are your hands?"

The rotund cook grunted. "A bit jarred but they're fine." She gave a chuckle. "More than I can say for his… " She frowned and looked closer, "… or her head." She shook her head. "No, it's a him."

Another light made its way down the stairs to join them, held by Sheldrake, the master of the house. "Excellent work Hannah." He frowned. "I hope you haven't killed him. Your backhand swing with a frypan is becoming quite fearsome."

Rose gave the prone body a little push with her toe, which elicited a groan. She smiled briefly at Sheldrake. "No. He'll live, sir."

The front door pushed wider open, and the slight figure of Stefan entered. "Stables are secure, Sheldrake. Leon and two other guards are combing the grounds, but I think this, like the others, is a lone intruder."

Sheldrake shook his head. "This is the third in a fortnight. Poor Hannah's sleep, all of our sleep, is being constantly interrupted."

Hannah gave a grim smile. "We don't mind, sir. Rather keep the little one safe. And speaking for myself, I enjoy the chance to use that training Stefan's been giving us." She glanced at the patch of grey that could be seen through the front door. "Nearly dawn anyway. Better get on and get the bread in the oven."

"Thank you, Hannah… and Rose," said Sheldrake, heartfelt but also a dismissal. "Stefan, can you organise to have our latest offering," he indicated the body at his feet, who had not regained full consciousness, "taken to the king's prison and a note sent to the king please? I will write it directly."

"Will do." Stefan bent over and deftly secured the man's hands with a strip of thin rope he had produced from his pocket. After a moment's thought, he also secured the man's ankles. "There! Just until I can get someone in here to take him away. Save you having to keep an eye on him if he can't walk anywhere."

"Good. I will be upstairs if anyone needs me." As he reached the foot of the stairs, he had a thought and turned to Stefan. "Join us for breakfast, would you, when you're ready? It won't be for another couple of hours. I think we need to talk about this."

Over in the loft above the stables, Sasha was just beginning to stir as the sky turned from grey to pale yellow in the small skylight above her. Her bedroom was no longer a pallet tucked away amongst the straw. She had a proper bed, dressing table and wardrobe, still tucked in a corner of the straw-filled stable loft, but her court dresses were housed in her official boudoir in the main house.

Officially, she slept in the main house, a widely disseminated piece of information that kept any would-be attackers heading in the wrong direction. It seemed that Shay had never thought to pass on the information that Sasha worked as a stable hand. Perhaps he had assumed that once she had appeared as Lady Natasha, she would have left her working role behind her.

In a very short time, the stable had been extended to provide Stefan with his own quite extensive quarters so that he could combine his role as Minister for the Great Forest with training Sheldrake's staff and overseeing Sasha's protection. Since he had been elevated to the title of Lord, albeit a minor one, he was almost on a par with Sheldrake, certainly close enough to be on first name terms. And he had his own set of rooms at the palace, as did Maud, Sheldrake, and Jon.

Stefan divided his time between these two establishments and visiting the woodfolk. He would be able to see his family at the Creeping Vine more often than he had previously since his liaison with the woodfolk took him more frequently into the forest. However, he had come to think of his cottage behind the stables at Batian House as his true home and Maud had assured him that he would always be welcome to live there, even after Sasha had grown up and moved away.

Stefan entered the stable and walked between two rows of interested but calm horses. Their demeanour told him that no stranger had entered. The horses had been trained to react if a stranger, unaccompanied by a member of the household, came into the stables. Maud had made the training easier by shape-shifting into her guise as Maisy, the solid brown mare, to communicate horse-to-horse with them. And now their solid unperturbed presence reassured him.

Nevertheless, he climbed the loft ladder and gave a soft rap on the wood of the closed hatch that led into the loft above. The hatch door was a relatively new addition, made to be bolted closed, from above.

"Coming," came Sasha's voice. A moment later, her voice asked from right above the hatch, "Who is it?"

"It's me, Stefan. Hannah needs your help in the kitchen before you clean the stalls."

Sasha sat bolt upright, her heart hammering. "Not again," she breathed, knowing his words were code for "Intruder in the grounds."

The sound of a large bolt being drawn was followed by the hatch door swinging upwards to be secured against a roof strut. Sasha peered down to see Stefan looking up at her. "Morning. I'm here. Safe and sound." She pulled a hooded jerkin over her clothes, raising the hood over her head before descending to the stables below.

By the time her feet touched the ground, Beth had walked over from her office which was part of the living quarters that she and Clive the butler shared. "Good morning, Sasha. Off you go!" she said, giving her 'stableboy' a little pat on the backside to send her to the door at the rear, which led into Stefan's quarters. From Stefan's front door, it took only a few steps in the open to reach the kitchen.

As soon as Sasha arrived in the kitchen, Hannah murmured quietly, "Morning, young one. All is safe, we think. He's trussed up in the corridor." She crossed to the far wall and opened a hatch that led to a large dumbwaiter. The cook nodded at her. "In you go."

It might have been large for a dumbwaiter, but it was still meant for crockery and food items, not people. It was a tight squeeze for a person, even an eleven-year-old, to fit into. Nevertheless, Sasha did not protest and manoeuvred herself into it. Hannah shut the door and Rose pulled the ropes until the dumbwaiter had risen to the first-floor level.

As soon as the dumbwaiter stopped moving, the doors were opened by Sheldrake, who was waiting for her in the corridor outside the dining room upstairs. Sasha gave him a brief smile of thanks as he helped her out before running quietly down the corridor to her indoors bedroom. There, she quickly donned a nightgown, dressing gown, and a pair of fine silk slippers. Then she took a deep breath and breezed out into the corridor and down the stairs. When she reached the bottom, she saw the intruder had regained consciousness, so she held her hands over her mouth in a gesture of shock she had seen court ladies use and gave a squeak of fright.

Hannah rushed out of the kitchen. "Oh, miss. Don't worry. He can't hurt you."

She put an arm around the apparently shocked girl and guided her towards the kitchen. "Come on. Come and have a cup of tea. Breakfast won't be ready for a while."

Sasha gave an artistic sniff and replied querulously. "Thanks. Milk will do. I was just coming down for a glass of milk when I saw him." She looked back over her shoulder into his hate-filled eyes and gave a genuine shudder. "Do you think he's misguided or a mercenary?" she asked softly.

Hannah glanced back at him and grimaced. "I'd say misguided. He has passion in his eyes, not the calculating stare of a blade-for-money."

Sasha sighed. "I wonder whose orders he's under? Has he been misguided by a shaman spellbound by Queen Toriana, or does Toriana influence non-shamans directly?"

"No good asking me, poppet," said Hannah as she led Sasha to a chair, while Rose poured her a glass of milk. "Not my field." She chuckled. "I just cook and fight." She grinned proudly. "It was me as laid him out, you know."

"Was it? Well done. You're getting good. Frypan, was it?" When Hannah nodded, she managed a smile she did not feel, but said with real gratitude. "I am so lucky to be surrounded by kind people who want to protect me. I thank you both very much."

Hannah smiled while Rose bobbed her a curtsey. Once Rose had understood that Sasha was actually the legitimate ruler of Kimora and was not just a stableboy, she had fallen all over herself to be helpful and, to Sasha's intense discomfort, to demonstrate her respect for her rank. No amount of persuasion could budge her from her determination to give Sasha her due as a queen, albeit unacknowledged by the Kimoran state. Only when Sasha was in her role as stableboy did Rose desist and then, having to treat her as an outside servant seemed to make her more determined than ever to make up for it the next time Sasha appeared as a court-bred lady. Sasha suspected Rose was still trying to make up for having been unkind to her when she had first arrived as a stableboy. For Sasha, it was water under the bridge, but clearly not for Rose.

Sasha was halfway through her glass of milk when she heard a piping voice issuing from the entrance hallway where the intruder had been left. She walked quietly down the short corridor from the kitchen and peeped around the corner.

There, squatted on his haunches next to the bound intruder was Jayhan. The intruder had managed to work himself upright so that he was now sitting awkwardly against the wall with his tied hands behind him. Jayhan was gazing earnestly into his eyes, having completely forgotten the unnerving effect his pale eyes had on strangers.

The little boy had obviously already introduced himself and was now saying, "You know Sasha?... Sasharia?" He assumed that the man knew that Lady Natasha was really Sasha. Otherwise, why would he want to harm her? "Well, she is my friend and she's never done anything to hurt anyone."

The man just stared at him in horror.

Jayhan frowned. "What's wrong? I'm not going to hurt you."

"Your eyes. What's wrong with your eyes?" he breathed.

Jayhan waved a hand impatiently. "Nothing is wrong with them. In fact, they're good for seeing in the dark,"

Sasha was pleased to hear Jayhan advocating for his eyes instead of being embarrassed about them.

"Anyway," Jayhan continued, "did you know your Queen Toriana killed her family?" When the man's mouth tightened in disbelief, Jayhan nodded. "I know. Shocking, isn't it? Toriana killed her own sister and her family... on purpose."

"Who fed you this nonsense?" demanded the intruder who was clearly recovering from his bang on the head and from the sight of Jayhan's eyes. "That girl is an impostor. Bandits stole a black amulet and now they are setting this girl up to pretend that she is the legitimate heir. And if she is agreeing to it, she is dangerous. She's just a fake who could cause a civil war. She has to be stopped."

Having heard this story many times before, Jayhan remained unperturbed. After a minute he asked. "Do you know anything about the High Shamanic amulet?"

The intruder gave a derisive snort. "Do you?"

Jayhan grinned. "Yep. Quite a lot, actually." His grin broadened. "Comes from living with it. Sasha wears it all the time."

"Oh yeah? And how can you prove it's the true amulet? I don't believe you for a second."

The boy grimaced. "I don't know. It's easy to convince shamans but I don't know how to prove it to non-shamans."

An arrested look came into the man's eyes. After a few moments, he said, "And I'm hardly likely to tell you. Then you'd know what you had to fake, to trick people into thinking this impostor had the real amulet."

Jayhan laughed and stood up. "Now you're trying to trick me. There is no way to show non-shamans that the amulet is true unless they are with a shaman when they see it." He carefully didn't mention that watching the amulet break a shaman's bond to Toriana was very convincing, because Jon and Sasha did not yet want that specific detail known.

"You certainly know what you're talking about. I'll give you that," conceded the man.

"Yep. But my father is a mage and I'm his apprentice. So maybe I just learnt it." Jayhan shrugged, dismissing the argument. "Do you want a drink of water?"

The man's eyes narrowed. "You're very phlegmatic for one so young."

"I'm what?"

"Phlegmatic. Not easily unnerved."

Jayhan's brow cleared. "Oh. No, I'm not always. But we have intruders like you pretty often, so I'm just getting used to it, that's all... Water?" When the man nodded, he grinned and added, "In fact, it makes the start of the day more interesting, and it shows that our security is working." His face darkened. "But I wish you people would stop trying to hurt Sasha."

Chapter 19

A knock sounded on the dining room door and at a word from Sheldrake, Stefan entered. Maud, Eloquin the governess, Sasha, and Jayhan were already seated.

"Good morning, all," he said cheerily as he sat down at the table and unfolded his napkin.

"Good morning, Stefan," replied Maud. "Once more, your notion of training our entire staff, rather than introducing men-at-arms, has proved its worth. Well done."

Stefan chuckled. "The congratulations should go to Hannah. She is becoming a dab hand with a frying pan... as a weapon, I mean." Everyone around the table smiled but he noticed that Sasha's smile was forced, and that she was looking down at her plate, which was currently empty. "Are you still not feeling safe, little one?" he asked.

She gave her head a tiny shake then dragged her dark liquid brown eyes up to meet his green ones. "No. Not really. They get so close before they are caught."

"We know of them long before they are caught, Sasha," said Sheldrake reassuringly. "My magical wards alert the staff as soon as someone crosses the boundary. That's how Hannah came to be waiting with her frying pan at the ready."

She gave a wan smile. "I know, but still... And now I'll have to miss the morning chores in the stable and work with Eloquin instead. No offence to you, Eloquin. I love learning with you, but I worry that Beth will get worn out, covering my work all the time. "

"We do have Edward now, dear," said Maud gently. "He can help Beth. We won't let her wear herself out, I promise you."

Tears sprang to Sasha's eyes. "And then I won't be needed anymore."

"Oh dear. You are upset, aren't you?" Maud raised her voice. "Clive? Where is our tea?"

The door opened and Clive entered, bearing a steaming silver teapot on a silver tray. "Just coming, my lady. Things are a little behind in the kitchen, but breakfast is on its way."

"Thank you. Serve Sasha first, if you would. She is a little upset."

"I'm not surprised," said Clive dryly, as he padded around the table to her and poured tea into her cup. "There you are, young one. Chin up. You're amongst those who love you." Balancing the tray skilfully on one hand, he gave her a couple of circular rubs on her back with the other, before moving on to fill everyone else's cups.

No one commented or sent him odd looks. They knew Clive lived in the stables as Sasha did and that he, as much as Sheldrake, was a surrogate father to her. Sasha wandered between being a stableboy and a young lady of the house, which led to some unusual crossovers of others' roles, as well as her own.

Maud leant forward and said earnestly. "Clive is right. You are among people who love you and will still love you, long after you stop being our stableboy and even if, *when* you move away from us."

Jayhan, who was sitting next to her, put an arm around her shoulders. "Yeah, but it's still horrible having all these people coming after her, one after another. And they definitely don't love her at all. In fact, …"

Sheldrake waved him to silence. "Yes that will do, Jayhan. I don't think Sasha needs to hear more about their feelings on the subject. Clearly, they are all being driven by Toriana's propaganda that Sasha is an impostor. Either that or they're just in it for a reward. None of them is driven by their knowledge of Sasha as a person since they have never met her."

Jayhan's face brightened. "True. That's true, Dad." He turned to Sasha. "See? It's not you."

"No." She let out a long breath. "No, I know that with my head, but my heart still gets bruised when someone stares at me with hate-filled eyes."

"Hmmm." Maud sipped her tea then put down her cup and tapped its rim with her fingernail while she thought about it. "I think you and I, and perhaps Yarrow, need to work with you on separating yourself as a person, from your role as a queen in exile. Public and political figures, my dear, whether they are in power or not, attract a great deal of criticism, no matter how popular they are. We must find a way to help you to deal with that."

Sheldrake nodded. "Even King Gavin, much as we admire him, is criticized constantly by people who are on the losing end of his decisions, or who think he is too young or too autocratic or too soft. Whatever he does, someone will not like it."

The discussion ceased as Clive and Rose entered with trays bearing bowls of porridge soon to be followed by plates of eggs, bacon, tomato, and mushrooms. Maud believed a solid breakfast was the foundation of a productive day and the conversation became desultory as those around the table applied themselves to their breakfasts.

Just as Eloquin and the two children were leaving to go to the library for morning lessons, Sasha turned back in the doorway and said, "I know you're going to talk about these people who are trying to attack me. The attacks are coming more often, aren't they? I am now eleven years old, you know, and although I get upset by their hatred, I don't want to just sit here, avoiding being the victim while I wait to grow up. I want to stop it. I want to take the fight back into Kimora and overset my ghastly aunt and support my brilliant brother." She gave the ghost of a smile as she used Jayhan's nicknames for Toriana and Jon, "It won't be easy or safe and I know that sometimes I'll get upset. But that's what I want to do."

Jayhan ducked his head under Sasha's arm to look at his parents, "Me too."

Sheldrake, who had been taking Sasha seriously, rolled his eyes. "Jayhan, this is not a game."

Jayhan looked crushed. "I know. I didn't think it was a game when we were abducted. I was scared stiff. But if Sasha goes, I want to go with her. I'm her protector."

No one knew quite what to say to this. It was true that he had saved her life on at least one occasion, but a nine-year-old was not a strong contender for the role of protector when many strong adults could fill the role so much more convincingly.

"No one is going anywhere but to the library for lessons at the moment," said Maud firmly, wisely choosing to avoid debating the issue with him. "We will take your views into account."

"Thank you," said Sasha. "Just thought you should know, that's all."

"Much better than running away behind our backs," said Maud approvingly.

Sasha gave a little chortle and disappeared from the doorway, taking Jayhan with her.

Maud leaned back in her chair and let out a huff of breath. "Well! Look what a small avowal of love does to bolster that child's courage. We must remember that."

"Yes, we must," said Sheldrake, "although we may have unleashed a tiger. We don't want her rushing off on some wild, poorly-prepared crusade."

Stefan looked up from buttering a piece of toast. "It would be less wild and poorly pre-pared than even a few months ago. Jon has been working hard to organize and train his groups of refugees. With the help of the woodfolk, the border is more secure within the forest and those of Toriana's agents who do make it through along the roads or across the fields, are now solely focused on finding Sasha. So the other refugees, even the shamans, can move around more freely."

Sheldrake tapped his forefinger on the table while he thought. "That is good as far as it goes, but how are these assassins still getting through?"

"You would know better than I, Sheldrake," replied Stefan. "They're not coming through the Great Forest. So I can only assume they are arriving disguised as merchants or other non-military travellers, either straight from Kimora or via Eskuzor."

"Or hidden in merchandise," added Sheldrake. He sighed. "We've curtailed the entry of their elite squads, but these individual specialists are very hard to spot. They differ in age, gender, size, racial group... there is no description we can circulate to catch the next one."

"The only additional action we could take to reduce their numbers, is to close our borders completely with Kimora and Eskuzor," Maud smiled at their looks of shock, "which would, of course, create political and economic mayhem, and is therefore unconscionable."

Sheldrake gave a perfunctory smile, but the look of concern did not leave his eyes, He began to drum his fingers rhythmically on the table. Maud was just about to ask him to desist when he did so of his own accord. "You know, I think Sasha may be right. I don't think we can expect to field these assassins successfully forever. So far, we have done well. Your staff training has paid off a hundred times over, Stefan, but sooner or later, someone will slip through. It doesn't matter how many we foil. It will only take one assassin, cannier, quieter, more deadly than his predecessors, and Sasha will be dead." He sat up. "We have to do more than just protect the victim. Sasha's right. We will have to move against Toriana sooner rather than later."

Maud put her hand on his arm. "Sheldrake, dear. Aren't you forgetting just one thing? The king is not going to sanction a war against Kimora."

Sheldrake waved his hand dismissively. "No, of course he's not, and rightly so. We, Car-rador, may well lose a direct conflict. Their forces are greater in number and because of the compulsion Toriana has placed on the shamans, more fanatical."

"No, Sheldrake, I don't think we'd do as badly as you think," countered Maud. "But certainly our lands and people would suffer, which is what Gavin wishes to avoid. This fight must be seen to be only between Kimorans. Sasha, the true heir, and Toriana, the usurper."

"This fight must not be seen at all," Sheldrake retorted. "Toriana is ruthless. She will trample any sign of insurrection and use her binding power mercilessly to force her shamans into fighting their friends, neighbours, and relatives. We can't allow that, because when her hold breaks, those shamans will be devastated by what they had been forced to do."

"Just as Lady Arquin and Berundi were," agreed Stefan. "We need to talk to Jon … and Electra. As the Kimoran ambassador, she can give us information that Queen Toriana is sending her while Jon can give us a picture of the Kimoran refugees' readiness within Carrador." He gave a little grin. "I expect Colonel Argyve will want to come too, more because Electra is coming than because he needs to, as the Eskuzorian ambassador."

"Stefan, we do not have to pander to Argyve's wishes," said Maud primly. "This is a serious business. If we don't need Eskuzor represented, he can stay away."

Stefan grinned. "You don't mean that for a minute. Besides, if some of these assassins are coming via Eskuzor, he probably should join us anyway."

"As you know perfectly well, Maud," said Sheldrake dryly.

Maud grinned. She dabbed her mouth with her napkin and prepared to stand up. "I will inform Gavin of this meeting and its intentions. I don't want him thinking we're working behind his back. I will invite him to attend but I don't expect he will." She paused for a moment. "What is the status of Lord Argyle and Lady Electra with the woodfolk? Do they know of them?"

"Lord Argyle has known of woodfolk for a long time," replied Stefan rising, as Maud did. "That's why he looked at me so strangely when he first saw me…. And because he has become so closely associated with Electra, we… the woodfolk that is, agreed to let Electra know of their presence. She is, after all, one of the key players in the Kimoran issue." He shrugged. "Besides, Kimorans seem to know about the Kimoran treewrights who are, according to Jon, woodfolk by another name."

Maud nodded decisively. "Good. Then let us arrange to meet at your family's inn. Electra and Argyve can join us there under the pretext of having a social outing in the woods. A couple of Sheldrake's agents can check that they are not followed beyond the city limits and if they are, find a way to hinder them. I don't want Kimoran spies noting Electra meeting with us or coming to our house too often, since they know Sasha resides here, even more so, if Jon will also be there. Electra must be kept above suspicion, or her life will be in danger."

Chapter 20

Two hours later, Stefan walked around the corner of the stables to be ambushed by two small children.

His eyebrows shot up. "I thought you two were supposed to be in lessons."

Two pairs of eyes looked earnestly up at him: Sasha's liquid brown eyes in a dark face, and Jayhan's pale lavender eyes in a pale face. What a contrast.

"We were," said Sasha, "but we rushed through our work and Eloquin let us out early." She leaned closer and murmured, "Where is that man, the intruder? Is he still here somewhere?"

Stefan frowned. "Are you still worried?"

Sasha straightened up. "Um... no. Not really. Not about him, at least."

"He's gone. We sent a message to the palace and two Royal Guards came by an hour ago and took him away."

"Oh. Never mind then. I was just thinking maybe I should have talked to him."

Stefan considered Sasha. She was dressed in a neat, dark blue pinafore over a white blouse, suitable for young ladies to wear at home. Although she still preferred her jerkin and leggings, she had gradually become comfortable in skirts and dresses and no longer raised such fierce objections when she was required to wear them to court or at home when she had to play the part of Lady Natasha. After a moment he asked, "What would you have gained from talking to him?"

Sasha shrugged and looked away. "I don't know. I thought maybe I could change his mind, or I could..." she grimaced, "start getting used to people hating me."

Beside her, Jayhan rolled his eyes. "I told her that was a bad idea. I'm glad the man's gone. Then she can't go and hurt herself by talking to him."

Stefan put his hand on Sasha's shoulder and waited until she looked at him. "I'd have to agree with Jayhan. No point shoving your face in it if you don't have to. And if you tried to convince him you were the true queen, and failed, which you almost certainly would, you might start thinking you just weren't good enough to convince him, when the truth is he can't see past Toriana's enchantment."

"But *he's* not enchanted," objected Sasha.

"No. Not that we know of. But the people he has known and trusted all his life are, and they are telling him that you are a fraud."

"Humph." Sasha still didn't look satisfied.

"Sasha, you're a complete stranger to him. Would you trust the words of a complete stranger who walked in through the front gates, in preference to everything Sheldrake and Maud and Jayhan and I had always told you?"

Sasha cocked her head and frowned while she thought about it. After a few moments, she said, "No. But I would think about it, and I would wonder why that person had said it and whether there might be some truth in it."

Jayhan snorted. "Well, this man today would think he knows why you said it, because you're trying to usurp his queen."

"Yes, all right, smartie. But if some other piece of information came up in the future to back up what I was saying, it might make him think about it a bit more. That's all."

"She's right, you know," said Stefan slowly. "It's worth a thought. Not," he added hastily, "that I'm advocating you upsetting yourself, Sasha, by trying to talk to these people. But a continual drip feeding of facts might change some people's minds. I'll mention it at the meeting."

"What meeting?" chorused the two children.

Stefan rolled his eyes at his mistake but gave in to the inevitable. "I might as well tell you, as I'm sure you'll find out one way or another."

When he had explained, Jayhan said. "Oh good. So if the woodfolk are involved as well, it means we get to go on a trip into the forest."

"Not necessarily. I represent the woodfolk and liaise with them. Though, as it happens, we do intend to meet at my parents' inn." The arms master frowned at him. "But when I said we, I didn't mean we here. I meant Sheldrake, Maud, and I."

"But you couldn't leave Sasha here without any of you to guard her," protested Jayhan, in what Stefan knew to be a spurious argument. "I mean, Hannah is good and so are Rose and the others, but it's not the same."

"What you actually mean is that you want to come."

Sasha beamed at him. "Exactly."

"Not my decision," said Stefan firmly. "Let's see what Sheldrake, Maud, and Jon think."

With this, they had to be content. But Stefan, watching them walk off towards the top paddock with their heads bent together in earnest conversation, suspected that they would come whether permitted to or not. The pair of them were generally well-behaved but they shared a wilful streak that knew no bounds when they thought it mattered enough. On balance, he thought Maud and Sheldrake would be wiser to sanction the children coming, rather than risk them trying to find their own way there.

After a minute, Stefan sighed, and followed after them. He had a lot to do but he didn't feel right about letting them get too far from the house after an attempted attack. His concern wasn't particularly logical. He knew another attack was no more or less likely to occur after one had already taken place since he was fairly sure the operatives worked independently of each other. Certainly, those they had questioned seemed to have no knowledge of the movements of other Kimoran intruders, although they admitted their existence.

A magical ward informed the staff members of Batian House and the woodfolk in the bushland whenever an intruder breached the perimeter. Sheldrake had corresponded with Tarkyn's wizard, Stormaway Treemaster, and between them, they had devised a huge ward that ran along the street front, along the perimeter boundaries on either side of their paddocks and bushland, then through the bushland at the rear of the property, one hundred metres beyond the creek. Because the distance it covered was so vast, the ward was actually comprised of several smaller wards strung together. It didn't keep people out, just gave warning of their arrival. So the nearer Sasha and Jayhan came to this invisible boundary, the less time members of the Batian household would have to react and come between them and any intruders.

Stefan grabbed three staffs and ran after them.

By the time he caught up with them, they had left the dirt road and were walking across the rough dry grass of the paddock towards a small dam that lay close to the border of the bushland at the rear of the property. The magical ward was still several hundred yards further into the bushland.

At the sound of his footsteps, Sasha looked around. Lines of apprehension on her face smoothed into a welcoming smile. "Hello Stefan. Have you come to look at the tadpoles too?"

"They are starting to get little rear legs now, you know," chimed in Jayhan. "We were thinking of catching some and putting them in a jar to watch them grow."

"But then we decided that we could just come and watch them here because they'd have more fun in their pond than in a jar, wouldn't they?"

Stefan smiled in return. "Yes. I think they would." He held out the staffs. "Here. One each. I thought we could spar after we've looked at tadpoles. We could practise on this uneven ground. Meanwhile, you can use them as walking staffs."

Sasha gave him an intense, considering look before accepting the staff with thanks and saying to Jayhan, "Look. I think they're around the other side among those rocks. It's too shallow on this side now. No cover from birds."

The three of them made their way around the dried, cracked mud that ringed the dam and squatted down where they could peer into a deeper puddle of the murky water.

Jayhan pointed. "Look. There they are. So many of them. More than last time, don't you think?"

"Definitely." Sasha screwed up her face. "They're hard to see properly though, aren't they? They keep wriggling into the shadows. Maybe we should bring a jar and catch some so we can get a good look at them. Then we could put them back as soon as we've looked at them."

"Good idea." Jayhan grinned. "And then we can have all the fun of catching them every time we come. I've got a little butterfly net somewhere. That should do." He lay down on his stomach and dabbled his hand in the water near them, making them wriggle off in panic into the deeper shadows among the fuzzy greenery that clung to the rocks.

"Jayhan! Now you're scared them off."

"Have not," he replied indignantly. "You watch. They'll come back. I thought they might swim against my hand and that would tickle."

However, the time it took the tadpoles to overcome their fright was far longer than the time it took for Jayhan's patience to run out. So, after a few minutes, he gave up and withdrew his hand. As soon as the huge alien shape had left their environment, the tadpoles cautiously began to re-emerge.

Jayhan huffed. "Huh. Unfriendly little things."

Stefan laughed. "How friendly would *you* be to an object hundreds of times larger than your house that appeared suddenly in your backyard?"

The little boy glowered for another few seconds then broke into a grin. "Not friendly at all."

Sasha reached her hand out over the water, trying to keep the sun's reflection off the water so they could see the tadpoles better. A shiver of tiny ripples spread concentrically across the water.

Stefan frowned. "That's odd."

Sasha shrugged. "Maybe one of the tadpoles broke the surface."

"Maybe." Stefan did not sound convinced.

"So, do it again," said Jayhan. "Take you hand away from the water then put it back over and see what happens."

Sasha looked at him for a second then took her hand away, waited for the water to settle and did it again.

Wherever her hand moved over the water, little ripples formed as though the water was lifting, trying to reach her hand.

She moved her hand around and back and forth, watching the effect it had on the water. Leaving her hand over the water, she looked up at Jayhan and Stefan and gave a little smile. "Some shamans can affect weather, Yarrow said. Maybe I..."

"Of course you can," cut in Jayhan. "You got rid of that storm Arquin was making. Remember?"

Sasha gave a little frown. "I didn't think that was because I could affect the weather. I thought that was because I wrecked her spell."

"And what about the lightning that struck you when you were freeing Arquin's shamans?"

She shook her head, straightening up, and moving her hand away from the pond. "No. That wasn't me affecting the storm. That was the storm affecting me. I didn't call down the lightning. It just came. I was concentrating on freeing all those shamans."

Stefan eyed Sasha. "It looked to me as though the storm responded to the light that blazed forth from the shamans when you and your amulet shattered Toriana's link with them. It was almost as though the storm were joining in or giving its stamp of approval." He gave her a quizzical look. "You do realize that if anyone else had been struck by that lightning, they would probably have died?"

"I was scared to death when I saw it come down," Jayhan burst out, finally admitting something he'd been keeping to himself for a long time. "I thought you'd be burnt to a crisp." He took a deep breath to rein in his remembered fear and gave her a gentle smile. "I'm glad you weren't."

Sasha responded by giving him an embarrassed punch in the arm.

"Ow. What was that for?" he demanded, rubbing his arm.

"Sorry. I care about you too. Not," she added hastily, "in a boyfriend way, of course."

Jayhan rolled his eyes. "Don't be silly. I'm only nine." He grinned. "Anyway, you'll probably have to marry some fat old lord or prince," he put his hand on his chest, raised his eyes skyward and said melodramatically, "for the sake of your kingdom."

Sasha scowled. "I don't think so. Anyway, Kimora is not a kingdom. It's a queendom...Hmm. Is there such a thing? There should be if there isn't. Anyway, it's a country or a realm but not a kingdom. Matriarchy. Remember?"

"Still has to make alliances. That's why your mum married King Gavin's brother, I'll bet."

"Oh." Sasha's face dropped. "I hadn't thought of that. I just thought they'd married for love." After a few moments she said wistfully, "I hope they at least liked each other."

"If your father was anything like his brother, Gavin's father, he would have been a very nice man," said Stefan. "I'm sure your mother would have liked him, at the very least. You could talk to Jon or King Gavin about it. They'll probably have some idea." He stood up, shaking one leg then the other to take the stiffness out of them. "Now, do you want to experiment more with your hand over the water or spar with the staffs for a while? Up to you."

Sasha glanced at Jayhan who gave a slight nod in return. "Let's spar. That'll be fun. Then we'll have to get back for lunch and magic tutoring with Sheldrake... and I think Yarrow might be coming this afternoon."

Chapter 21

As it turned out, Yarrow, the unregistered shaman who had been helping Sasha to develop her shamanic powers, did come for lunch and for the afternoon's magic workshop. She was dressed in her mirrored, embroidered black dress, set off by gold loop earrings, inside each of which dangled an emerald droplet. Her thick black hair was caught up in a brightly coloured bandana that allowed her hair to fall in thick waves down her back but kept it off her face.

She brought news of Jon and a report about the progress that the refugees were making in organizing themselves into a potential resistance force. It had only been two months since Sasha and Jayhan's abduction, but it seemed that outrage at the abduction coupled with the recognition of Sasha as their future queen, and Jon as their regent, had galvanised the resistance effort. Now the various groups were training hard and had already developed hierarchies, roles, and communication lines within and between the groups.

For Sasha, it felt as though the future was rushing shockingly fast towards her. She didn't say anything, but she became unusually solemn during lunch.

Even now, as they stood in Sheldrake's hallowed shed, while Yarrow and Sheldrake decided what they might work on, Sasha was quiet and withdrawn. The adults didn't notice but Jayhan did.

"What's wrong?" he muttered, making sure his father didn't overhear him.

Sasha crossed her arms. "Nothing."

"Yes, there is. Go on. Tell me," he urged.

She huffed and sent a speaking glance at the adults. "Later."

"Oh. All right. Later. But don't forget."

Sheldrake tuned into the last few words and swung around. "Don't forget what?"

Luckily for Sasha's equanimity, Stefan chose this moment to knock and poke his head around the corner of the door. "Hello all. Just thought I'd mention that Sasha had an interesting experience at the pond this morning. I'll leave you to tell them, Sasha. See you later on."

With that, he was off, leaving four people staring at the door.

Sheldrake blinked and turned to Sasha. " Aah. So that's what you don't want to forget." He raised his eyebrows. "Well?"

Happy with this diversion, Jayhan and Sasha related what had happened at the pond and the discussion that had followed.

When they had finished, Sheldrake turned to Yarrow and said, "I believe Sasha's aunt can manipulate either water or weather or both, and obviously Lady Arquin can. So, since we know Sasha is powerful, does it naturally follow that she, too, can manipulate the weather? And if so, how?"

Yarrow had the good sense to look at Sasha to make sure she was included in the conversation. "Only powerful shamans can manipulate the weather, but power alone is not enough. Weather-working is a particular talent that only a very few are born with. Unless it is nurtured and trained, it will lie dormant within the individual." She grimaced. "I'm afraid I know little about it."

"But if Sasha is the High Shaman, shouldn't she have all the talents that shamans have?" asked Jayhan, championing his friend.

Yarrow nodded. "I would think so, but all I can do is help her to access her power through her amulet."

Sheldrake considered Sasha. "Well, you have already gained considerable knowledge just from wearing the amulet. Perhaps knowledge about weather-working will come too." He smiled at her. "Let's go and see what you can already do."

"Just a minute, Dad," said Jayhan. "I'll just nip up and get my butterfly net. Sasha, can you get a jar from the kitchen?"

Before Sheldrake could object, his son had shot off out the door.

"Tadpoles," explained Sasha, not feeling as free as Jayhan to leave without permission.

Sheldrake sighed. "Off you go then. While you procure a jar, Yarrow and I will stroll up to the back paddock and meet you at the dam, if not sooner."

Sasha grinned. "Thanks. I'll be right back."

Yarrow frowned in her wake. "That young lady is still too self-effacing. She will be... well, she already *is*, a queen, just unrecognised by her country." She shook her head. "She doesn't act like it at all. How will she cope at court with everyone hanging on her every word and gesture?"

Sheldrake held the door open for her. "Come on. We'll talk while we walk." As they passed along the side of the cottage and the redbrick of the kitchen garden wall, he said, "You didn't see her when she freed Arquin's shamans. ... " He gave a little smile, with a hint of pride in it. "Gavin, our king, thought she was magnificent."

Yarrow looked surprised but pleased. "Was she?"

Sheldrake nodded. "She wasn't grandiose or regal or theatrical. She was just her straightforward, vulnerable little self. She told them she was their rightful queen and that they shared a link with her through their amulets. But she made it clear that she would hold them under no compulsion and would not demand, only ask, that they follow Jon and herself. Every last one of them came forward and wrapped their arms around her in an overwhelming gesture of support."

Yarrow's eyes widened. "That is encouraging. Sasharia doesn't exude any obvious power at all, here."

"No. That is not her role here. Here, she can just be a young girl earning her living, learning her heritage and developing her magical skills." As they passed the kitchen garden and the paddocks came into view, Sheldrake looked up at the hard, blue sky then across the brown fields and sighed. "Our fields are dry. The dam we are heading towards is a third of its usual size. I must say I would love it if Sasha could make it rain."

As they cut across the fields towards the dam, the brittle grass crunched beneath their feet. Sheldrake looked down and grimaced. "Even sheep can't get much sustenance out of what's left of our grass. I've already had to buy in fodder."

He stopped and squatted down to run his hand over the brown withered grass blades.

"How long since it rained?"

Sheldrake looked up at her, squinting against the sun in his face. "We haven't had decent rain for nearly a decade, but this year we've had no rain at all."

"It's not Sasha, is it?"

Sheldrake frowned. "Why do you say that? She wasn't even here in the previous years when the rain has been scarce." He rubbed his hands together to get the residual dirt off them and stood up again, turning once more towards the dam.

"She was in the vicinity, living at Stonehaven. How widespread is this drought?"

Sheldrake thought for a moment. "It hasn't affected the forested areas and the fields are far greener in the south of the kingdom." He stopped walking and turned to face Yarrow. "Now I think about it, the drought-stricken area is all north of Highkington, and the rains began to fail about the time Sasha came to Carrador." He snorted and turned to keep walking. "Perhaps we are reading too much into this. It may just be a coincidence."

"I doubt it. That amulet and its wearer are at the heart of shamanic power and shamanic power is at the heart of the whole natural environment."

"But it rained all over them in the forest," objected Sheldrake.

"The forests are in their natural state and so have an intrinsic strength that the fields, shaped by man, lack." Yarrow shrugged. "Besides, how long was Sasha in the forest? It would take time for the imbalance caused by the disrupted power of the amulet to have an effect... and in the forests, much longer, if ever." She glanced at him. "You are aware, I suppose, that Kimora is in the throes of its worst drought for centuries? Crops have failed for the last three years, and yet starving farmers are still being taxed at the same rate. Their whole agriculture is at breaking point. That's the main reason Toriana is setting her sights on Carrador."

Sheldrake grunted and lapsed into silence as he thought about it. He was just about to make another remark when Jayhan and Sasha caught up with them, laughing and puffing because, as usual, they had been racing each other. Sheldrake looked into Sasha's grinning face and marvelled that so much untapped power, both magical and potentially political, could reside in such a cheery, unaffected little girl.

He took a small breath and smiled. "Come on then. Show me your tadpoles. Then we'll have a look at the effect you have on the water."

Chapter 22

For the next half hour, Sasha and Jayhan had a lovely time leaning precariously out over the rocks, shrieking in mock terror as they nearly fell in, and splashing each other, intentionally and unintentionally, as they took turns in swooshing the little butterfly net through the water. Eventually, due more to luck than skill, they proudly presented a jar with eight little tadpoles swimming around in it for Sheldrake and Yarrow's admiration.

The two adults duly exclaimed and inspected the tadpoles while the children beamed at their achievement. But their eyes, which initially shone with excitement, gradually lost their sparkle as Sheldrake gave them a comprehensive discourse on the life cycle of frogs.

Seeing this, Yarrow cut in just as Sheldrake was about to expound on the difference between lung and gills. "I'm so sorry to interrupt, but I will have to leave in an hour or so. Do you think we could have a look at what effect Sasha has on the water before we run out of time?"

Sheldrake was instantly contrite. "Oh my word! You should have stopped me earlier. I can always tell them more about frogs later."

Although from the children's point of view this was not ideal, at least it was better than standing around and continuing to listen now. Sasha might be ambivalent about being a future queen, but she had no such qualms about being a shaman and she was keen to learn all she could about her power.

She smiled. "Ready?"

Sheldrake's lecture had given the surface of the little dam time to settle, and it was now so still that they could see the reflections of themselves and the nearby trees in it. Sasha clambered out over the rocks, knelt down, and reached out with her hand, holding it palm down, a foot above the water. She swept her hand slowly in an arc sending a series of small waves speeding to the further shore of the dam.

Sheldrake and Yarrow both watched with brows drawn, concentrating on what she was doing.

"Very interesting," said Sheldrake. "What happens if you hold your hand over one spot but move it up and down instead?"

Sasha followed his suggestion, and her audience could clearly see the water rise and fall in time with her hand, as though a piece of string joined the surface of the water to her palm.

"Huh," said Sheldrake. "Fascinating. You are actually drawing the water up with your hand."

"And repelling it," added Yarrow. "See that? The centre dips below the rest of the surface as her hand comes down."

"Are you concentrating on doing it at all?" asked Sheldrake.

Sasha thought for a moment before shaking her head. "Not really. I'm concentrating on moving my hand. That's all."

Following Sheldrake's next instruction, Sasha focused on bringing the water to her as she slowly stood up with her hand over the water. The water rose into a muddy shimmering column to three feet high before collapsing back into the dam.

Jayhan's eyes were round. "Wow, Sasha. That was amazing."

Sasha grinned. "Pretty good, hey?"

Sheldrake stood in thought, tapping his teeth with his long bony forefinger. Eventually he turned to Yarrow. "What do you think? Could we try asking Sasha to draw water towards her from the atmosphere… in an effort to break the drought, you understand?"

Yarrow shook her head. "Moving water three feet, even if it is straight upwards is nothing like the scale needed to change the weather." She shrugged. "Besides, she needs to learn what she is doing and how to control her ability to move water in the atmosphere first. Otherwise, you risk a deluge." She smiled at Sasha, who was looking a little crestfallen. "Well done. You have made a very good start. You can keep playing around with the water in the dam. Practise holding that column of water and walking around, perhaps seeing if you can hold it up from further away and maybe making it taller."

"Yes, very impressive," chimed in Sheldrake, realising he had been remiss. "I think Yarrow is right though. We need to tread carefully with such potential." He grimaced. "I wish I knew more about weather-working. I think we need an expert to guide you, Sasha."

"Lady Arquin knows how to work weather," piped up Jayhan.

"True. She does," Sheldrake replied, "And so too does Tarkyn's wizard friend, Stormaway Treemaster, to whom I wrote for advice about warding the property. He is a master of weather-working, I believe. I remember Tarkyn telling me about a storm that he and Stormaway diverted or dissipated, I'm not sure which, under Stormaway's direction. Well, the wizard's name says it all really, doesn't it?" He turned, full of purpose. "Come on. Back to the house. I will write to him forthwith and invite him to come and stay again, the next time he travels through Carrador selling his wares."

They were just turning to leave when they heard a thud. They looked around to see a large goanna standing under a tree, staring at them. In an unusual gesture for a lizard, it shook its head as though trying to clear it, turning its long neck from side to side. It was close enough for them to see the cream stripes on its legs and tail as it turned and crashed away through the undergrowth.

"Wow," breathed Jayhan. "That was a big one. Must have been five feet long if you count the tail as well."

Sheldrake smiled at his son's reaction. "Yes. It was a beauty, wasn't it? They don't usually come so close to the paddocks."

Neither of them noticed the look that passed between Sasha and Yarrow who could discern shape-shifters.

"What is Maud doing?" murmured Sasha.

Chapter 23

As soon as Yarrow had departed and they had endured the last of the information on frogs, Sasha and Jayhan finally had half an hour on their own before dinner.

Jayhan came straight to the point. "So, come on. What were you worried about before? You were happy again this afternoon, but something was wrong at lunchtime."

Sasha sighed. She glanced at him then looked away. "I'm… I suppose I'm frightened. I've always thought about going into Kimora, rescuing shamans, and becoming queen as a sort of horror fantasy. Far in the future and not really going to happen."

"But you told Mum you wanted to fight them."

Sasha scrunched up her face. "I do but… I don't. At least, not yet. I just want those intruders to stop coming and to stay here with you and Beth and Clive and Sheldrake and Maud."

"Well, that's not going to happen," said Jayhan prosaically. Then he saw tears forming in Sasha's eyes and rushed on. "I would love it too. I want you to stay here always too. But, well, lots of things don't happen that we want. I want to be a shap\

shifter like Mum who can become types of animals." He made a disgusted face. "But can I? No. I can only become different people."

Despite herself, Sasha smiled. "Most people would love to be able to transform as you can. It's only because Maud is around that you feel bad about it."

"Most people would love to be a queen," retorted Jayhan. He chortled. "Well, most women, anyway."

"Maybe some men…" Since they had a traditional view of men, they spent some time giggling at the vision of a hairy legged man in a long fluffy white dress. Eventually Sasha drew a breath and continued, "Yep. Maybe some people would want to be a queen. But maybe they haven't thought about sitting around in a big chair all day and listening to arguments, then having to decide what to do, knowing one side will be unhappy. And maybe they haven't thought about having to wear huge gowns that make it hard to climb trees."

"I think lots of women like big gowns."

Sasha frowned furiously at him for interrupting, "Not Beth… and not me." She took a breath and continued. "And think about it. King Gavin, who is a really nice person, is lonely in a way. People know he can change their futures. So they can't relax around him. Even Maud and Sheldrake, who know him pretty well, are careful."

"True," said Jayhan thoughtfully. "Maybe we should try harder to be his friend when we're at the palace." He brightened. "Anyway, you'll always have me around. I'll be your friend. You know I will."

"I know." Sasha hesitated. "But you're a Carradorian lord. I don't see how you can leave that behind and move to Kimora."

He screwed up his face. "I suppose we could get married, if we're desperate."

Sasha snorted. "I don't think we'll ever be that desperate."

Jayhan grinned. "No. We'll have to think of something else." He smiled warmly at her. "But we will. And you have Jon as well. It's not all bad. And now I think about it, isn't Jon the one who'll settle all those arguments until you're older. That's what a regent does, isn't it?"

"True. Good point. So all I'll have to worry about is thousands of unfriendly Kimorans trying to kill me. Excellent. Nothing to worry about at all."

Jayhan laughed. "I'm glad you're feeling cheerier. Not much I can say about that. Jon and Stefan and Mum and Dad will have to come up with something for that problem. I'm sure they will, though." He broke into a run, heading for the trees, "Come on. Race you to the top paddock."

"Cheat!" shouted Sasha as she sprinted after him.

Part 4

Chapter 24

Lord Jonathan, Jon to his friends and in reality, Prince Jondarian of Kimora, had a problem.

His name was Crabtree, the civil engineer in charge of road maintenance.

Jon, as Minister for Transport, dealt almost daily with Crabtree. Crabtree was a fussy, neatly dressed man who attempted to hide his balding pate with long strands of black hair, combed from the side and greased into place by an oil that left a faint aroma of cloves behind him when he left the room.

In his favour, he was passionately devoted to his work, the maintenance of Carrador's road system. He was clever, and when he put his mind to it, inventive in the ways he resolved problems.

On the downside, he often did not put his mind to these problems because he felt he should be given more resources to provide an easier solution. But worse than this, he constantly bemoaned the costs, the insufficient staff, and the unfortunate need to prioritize. Every new issue began from the position of 'Can't possibly do it,' from which Jon would have to cajole and placate him then discuss the matter with him until he would eventually sigh and agree to see what he could do.

After months of this, Jon's patience, which was extensive, was wearing very thin. Crabtree, for his part, had taken advantage of Jon's good nature and had learnt, perhaps unconsciously, that no matter how much he complained, Jon did not lose his temper. So over the months, it was taking longer and longer to convince him to act.

With a mounting sense of dread, Jon sat at his desk in his big well-appointed office in the king's palace, riffling through a pile of reports that all pointed to the need to resurface the road from Highkington to the Eskuzorian border, a distance of over one hundred and twenty miles. It was an extensive project, but piecemeal repairs were becoming too frequent and, in the end, more expensive than doing a complete overhaul. Some stretches were still in good repair but too many were not. But although it was large, it was not the project itself that worried Jon. It was Crabtree.

With a sigh, he rang the small bell on his desk. Immediately the door opened and one of the palace footmen, a slight young man with auburn hair and twinkling eyes, stepped neatly into the room.

Jon dragged himself out of his trepidation to smile. "Good morning, Franz. How are you this morning? Any news from around the palace?" Having been a footman himself, Jon never took the staff for granted and, unless he was in a tearing hurry, took time to have a chat with them. An unlooked-for advantage in this was that he picked up interesting snippets of gossip from time to time.

"Good morning, my lord. I sprained my ankle last week playing streetball with my little sister but it's feeling better now. Cook's had a bit of a row with Stevenson and she's gone off in a huff to stay at her sister's for a week. So you'll be getting your meals cooked by Diedre, Cook's second." He grinned. "Diedre's a pretty good but Cook never gives her a chance. So, you never know, the food might be better."

Jon raised his eyebrows. "I look forward to trying it. Now, will you please let me know if your ankle starts to get sore. Standing on it all day will not help it to heal. I can send you on a message or let you sit in here for a time with your leg up, as long as no one else is around. But please, do tell me."

"Thank you, sir." His mouth quirked. "You never know. I might take you up on it. It's fine now but it mightn't be later. Uh, was there something you wanted, my lord?"

"Ah yes. Could you ask Cra…" At the last moment, Jon quailed. "Uh no. Not Crabtree. Ask Lieutenant Reece to join me please?"

Franz smothered a smile, bowed, and left the room.

Half an hour later, a knock on the door preceded the entry of Reece, smartly dressed in his new Lieutenant's uniform, his serious grey eyes guarded as he waited to find out why he had been summoned.

After Jon and Reece's report of the squad's role in the rescue of Jayhan and Sasha, augmented by a quiet word from Jon to King Gavin, it had been agreed to give Reece a commission in the king's guard. Because of his expertise as sergeant of a specialist squad, he had been appointed to command one of the specialist divisions, which was made up of four of these squads.

Jon beamed at him. "Impressive. Are you enjoying your new role? Do you have half an hour to spare now, or are you in the middle of training?"

Reece smiled. "I was in the middle of training, but an important lord summoned me, so here I am."

"Oh." Jon's cheeks flushed. "Sorry. I should have phrased my request differently."

"Not at all," said Reece, grinning as he realised that Jon hadn't changed. "I was saved from doing a fourth circuit of jogging around the perimeter of the castle. I was delighted."

Jon's face cleared. "Oh good. Glad to be of service then. Take a seat." He rang the bell on his desk and when Franz's head appeared around the door, ordered iced water and a pot of tea. A little crease appeared between his eyes. "Do you always train in dress uniform?"

Reece spluttered with mirth. "Very funny. Of course not."

Jon nodded. "Hmm. It's a bit pestilential, having to see me, isn't it?"

"Extremely," said Reece cheerily. "But I'm glad to see you. The boys and I were wondering whether you were ever going to come down to the Ox and Cart Tavern or whether you'd forgotten us."

Jon was taken aback. "Of course I haven't forgotten you. I just… well, I wasn't sure you'd still feel as friendly towards me now that you don't have to be in company with me, if you know what I mean. We were thrown together in our search for the children, and everyone was kind to me then but now… now I haven't seen hide nor hair of any of them and I've only seen you at your promotion ceremony or in passing." He fiddled with his letter opener, turning the long gold blade with its onyx handle over and over in his fingers. Suddenly he looked up and smiled. "I didn't ask you here to beg your friendship, but I would like it. When are you next at that tavern?"

"Tomorrow night. Six o'clock. Dinner and ale. I think a bard from out of town will be singing." He gave his head a slight shake and smiled warmly. "I'd forgotten how self - deprecating you can be. Of course we'd like to see you. We just felt the same way as you did, that perhaps our friendship was transient and dependant on the circumstance. After all, you tend to move in different circles from us and we'd have to get through a barrage of protective servants to contact you."

"Hmm. I'll let Stevenson, the butler, and Josie, the steward, know to give you easy access. Then any of the others can send a message to me through you, if that's all right with you."

Reece's face lit up. "Great. I'll tell the lads."

Franz appeared and delivered the cold water and a pot of tea, giving a small, un-footman-like smile before departing. Reece's eyes followed him out of the room. He turned back to Jon and said, "Am I right in thinking you have a friendlier relationship with the staff than most of the lords and ladies?"

Jon gave his sunny smile. "Probably. Once a footman, always a footman. It would be the height of hypocrisy for me to turn around and pretend they were different from me. We all have our jobs to do, and I know from experience that theirs can be very tedious and tiresome. The least I can do is be friendly."

Jon came around from behind his desk and sat at the other side of the coffee table, pouring tea and cold water for both of them. Then he sat back and said, "Actually, I asked you here for some advice, or at least as someone who might listen while I try to work out what to do."

Reece put down his cup and sat up. "Did you now? I'm honoured." It crossed his mind that Jon must be feeling a little isolated if he needed to turn to him for advice, but he didn't say so. "So what's the problem?"

"Crabtree, the chief civil engineer. You may have seen him around. Nattily dressed, balding with black hair combed across..."

Reece nodded. "Yes, I think so. Poncy sort of a fellow. Fusses along the corridor as though he is the only one who is busy."

Jon gave a little smile at the accuracy of Reece's description. "That's him. Well, I have to work with him on a daily basis. And every new project is a new battle." He went on to explain the difficulties he was having. He pointed to the pile of papers neatly stacked on one corner of his desk. "And now I have to present him with that sheaf of reports, all of which point to the need for a major overhaul of the North Road." He let out a gusty sigh. "And I've just had enough. I went to summon him and found myself sending for you instead." He smiled wryly. "Much better outcome in the short run, but I can't shirk my responsibilities indefinitely."

"Can he read?" asked Reece.

Jon snorted. "Of course he can read. He studied engineering."

"Easy then." Reece waved his hand. "Just give him the reports to read himself and reach his own conclusions. Better still, *send* him the reports and ask for a written response. Then you don't even have to see him for the time being. Give yourself a break."

Jon frowned quizzically. "But it's my job to oversee the maintenance of the transport system."

Reece shrugged. "You are. You've read the reports and know what's needed. Now leave it to him and set him a deadline."

"But he'll complain about the budget. He always does and says he can't do it."

Reece took a sip of his rapidly cooling tea and said, "Pre-empt him in your cover letter, instruction note, whatever it is. Tell him you know the budget is always insufficient, but that miraculously he always finds a way, and you're depending on his genius to find a way this time. Tell him to come back to you only when he has come up with a workable proposition."

"Worth a try." Jon took a slow sip of tea while he thought about it. "Definitely worth a try.... I wonder how Sheldrake managed Crabtree when he was temporarily Minister for Transport?"

Reece chuckled. "Didn't put up with any shit, I expect, and wasn't so worried about the man's feelings."

Jon coloured. "I'm not very good at this, am I?"

"No. No. I didn't mean that," said Reece hastily. "You're very good at it. I've been out and about. No one's complaining about the state of the roads or the docks. Obviously, there is the odd comment about a pothole that's just opened up here and there, but nothing much. You're getting the job done. You just need to protect yourself a bit."

"Maybe you were right when you said I had all the authority of a fluffy kitten."

Reece smiled warmly. "Perhaps, but you have managed to get him to do what you wanted. Maybe that fluffy kitten just needs to keep its distance and show its claws from time to time, even if it doesn't use them."

"But I don't want to ride roughshod over Crabtree."

"By sending him the reports to reach his own conclusions, you will be giving him more authority, not less." Reece shrugged. "Besides, at the moment, he is riding roughshod over you." When Jon frowned, he added, "Think about it. He knows the outcome before the conversation starts. He's just putting you through your paces and following his own time-honoured pattern of behaviour."

Jon sat back suddenly. "So he is. That cranky bastard." He grinned. "I'm so glad I asked for you to come up here rather than head straight into battle with Crabtree again. Thanks." He reached behind himself to reach the bell on his desk. When the footman appeared, he said, "Franz, could you take these papers to Crabtree please?" Then he realized he had been too precipitous in his wish to try the new ploy with Crabtree. "No. Wait just a minute." He stood up and went to the desk, drew a piece of paper from the drawer and penned a quick note. He handed the note and the reports to Franz. "There. Take all of these to Crabtree. If he's not in his office, just leave them on his desk. Thanks."

Jon couldn't help noticing Franz's slightly raised eyebrows. "Franz, I hope you're more discreet with your reactions when you're with other people."

Franz grinned. "Of course I am."

Jon grinned back. "That's all right then. Now, go away. Let me know how you get on."

Reece watched this interchange with some amusement. Once Franz had left, he said, "You could have asked Franz what to do. I suspect he could be quite helpful."

Jon folded his long frame back into the comfortable chair at his coffee table. "No. That wouldn't be right. Franz is too young and has his own role to play. I like him but I do not consider him my friend. You, on the other hand, I do consider to be my friend, or at least I was hoping you were, and you are, as it turns out, which is good." He raised his eyebrows and shook his head at his own drivel. He drew a breath and gave a rueful smile. "Anyway, you are uninvolved in the situation... and older and wiser."

"I'm only thirty-three," Reece protested. "You make me sound like I should have a long white beard. But you're right, I am uninvolved and have had no interactions with Crabtree at all."

From here, they went on to talk about their respective training regimes and the doings of their mutual acquaintances, which included squad members, Tarkyn, the members of Sheldrake's household and the woodfolk. As they talked, they both realised that they shared many areas of discussion that they could not talk to many others about: woodfolk, the progress the Kimoran refugees were making in organising themselves, Jon's aspirations as Kimora's regent, and Reece's feelings about his new role.

An hour later, the ice that had threatened to form on their new friendship had been well and truly thawed.

Jon had just reiterated his intention of joining Reece and seventh squad at the Ox and Cart when the door burst open and Crabtree, stiff with indignation, stood on the threshold of Jon's office.

Jon stared in shock at him before slowly rising from his chair to stand looking at him from his superior height. Aware of Reece watching him, Jon debated how outraged he should appear in view of Crabtree's uninvited entry. In the end, he decided to react minimally, even though Crabtree had actually succeeded, this time, in angering him.

"Good morning, Crabtree. Obviously, you were unaware that I was in the middle of a private conversation. But I believe knocking before you entered would have precluded you from interrupting, which I am sure you would not have wished to do."

Crabtree, who had expected Jon to be defensive and ready to be badgered yet again, stopped short. He shot a glance at Reece who, in his full dress uniform, looked impressive and clearly relaxed in Jon's presence, in a way he had never been.

"I beg your pardon," he said stiffly. For a moment, he stood nonplussed. Then, his sense of ill-usage reasserted itself and he drew a sheaf of papers from behind his back with a flourish "But my lord, I must speak to you."

Jon held up his hand. "No, you must not. You are interrupting. Even had you already finalised your plans for this project, which I very much doubt even you could have done in an hour, you would have to wait." Before Crabtree could stop goggling enough to reply, Jon added, "Now, when you do have a proposition to put to me, perhaps you could tell Franz and he will let you know when I am next available." Jon reached past him, opened the door wide and stood beside it, clearly expecting his stunned engineer to leave.

For a long moment, Crabtree just glared at him. Then he transferred his gaze to Reece, who simply kept his visage bland. Seeing no help or challenge from that quarter, Crabtree gave a derisive sniff, put his nose in the air, and stalked out.

As the door closed behind him, Reece raised his eyebrows "Well, he is a piece of work, isn't he? Well done. Would you have done that, had I not been here?"

Jon's blue eyes twinkled. "I have no idea. It certainly helped having you here to bring me up to the mark." His mouth quirked. "Yes. I think I would still have reacted that way. He finally pushed me too far. Rude bastard. And he didn't even leave when he realized he'd intruded. The nerve of him."

"Hoo! If this is you at your most angry, watch out world!"

Jon laughed. After a moment's hesitation, he said with unwonted seriousness, "My anger is as deep as the ocean, as wide as the world. I saw my family slaughtered. The rage inside me is… well, it is too dangerous to ever allow out. It would poison my friendships, my intentions and my whole view of life." He shrugged. "I let it fuel my thirst for justice for my people, the people of Kimora. But other than that, I mostly keep it at bay."

Reece blew out a long breath. "Whew! You're amazing, you know. You hide it so well."

Jon shrugged aside his intensity and relaxed into his sunny smile. "It's only a small part of who I am, and I prefer the other parts."

Reece smiled. "I like all the parts."

"Thanks."

"I'd better go. I have to run squad training this afternoon. See you tomorrow night?"

Jon nodded. "You will."

Chapter 25

After Reece had left, Jon returned to his desk and spent some time considering a petition that had been presented by the Merchant Guild and the Seaman's Guild to extend the docks at Waterhaven. He knew that, at best, they would have to wait until next year as the kingdom could not afford two major projects at the same time. He hoped Crabtree would come up with a reasonable timeline for the reconstruction of the North Road.

This naturally led his thoughts back to his confrontation with the man. Jon had not missed the flash of what... jealousy? resentment? in Crabtree's eyes when he had seen Reece sitting in a comfortable chair sharing a pot of tea with him. He realized that he had never taken the time to get to know Crabtree as he had other people in the palace, because the man was always so belligerent towards him. He determined to find out more about him.

He penned a short note to Sheldrake, master of the intelligence network fondly known as the King's Spiders, which he asked Franz to have delivered. He toyed with the idea of going on the journey down the stairs, along the long southern corridor and then down another flight of stairs to visit the Road Maintenance Department. But he knew it would give Crabtree an opportunity to harangue him before the engineer had had time to come up with a proposal. Jon did not want to weaken his stance before they had established a new way of working together. No. He would have to wait.

The hours ticked by. Jon had lunch delivered to him in his office and as the afternoon wore on, he became more and more apprehensive about Crabtree's reappearance or worse, possible non-reappearance because he had resigned. For all his faults, Crabtree was a gifted engineer, and his departure would leave a hole in the Ministry for Transport that would be hard to fill.

Finally, as the last light was fading and Jon was watching the lamplighter working her way around the inner courtyard and the gardens, a knock sounded on his door. Jon's heart leapt to his throat. He gave his head a small shake of self-reproach and, after clearing his throat to make sure he sounded calm, answered, "Enter."

Franz came in and handed him a letter. "From Crabtree, sir."

"Thank you. You must be nearly due to go off duty. How did your ankle hold up?"

"Not too bad, sir. I lifted my foot and wriggled it when no one was in sight."

Jon nodded. "Well, look after it."

"I will, sir. I'll just light the lamps before I go." Franz set about lighting the candles on the wall sconces and in the lamps on his desk.

The lamps in Jon's room all contained candles, rather than the smellier oil that filled the lanterns lining the pathways outside. Candles were more expensive but preferred by those who could afford them, because they burnt more cleanly. Needless to say, the palace provided candles.

"Thank you. The night draws in and I shall need to read this before I leave."

When Franz exited, Jon was left looking down at a well-stuffed envelope.

With any luck, that meant it was not merely a note of resignation. Jon extracted several pages of neat writing and began to read. When he had finished, he sat back and huffed in exasperation. It was simply another harangue. In essence, the pages contained a written version of the objections that Crabtree usually raised face-to-face.

Jon threw the pages down on his desk. "Blast the man!"

Pages of objections without a single suggestion for solutions.

After some thought, Jon opened his drawer and drew out a pair of scissors and a small pot of glue. He was just about to start cutting the missive into sections when he realized his plan wouldn't work because Crabtree had written on both sides.

He stared out the window and saw people walking across the courtyard as they headed home for the night. No. He would not let Crabtree ruin his evening. He would come back to this in the morning. He had other things, more important, to worry about. He had arranged to meet with Beetlebrow at the Crowing Cock. Time to go.

He lifted his sky-blue cloak off its hook and swinging it around his shoulders, walked out the door. A new footman, Arnold, was standing in the corridor.

Jon paused briefly. "Good evening Arnold. Could you arrange for a scribe to come to my office first thing tomorrow morning? Thank you."

With that, he strode down the corridor towards the front stairs of the palace. Once outside, he headed across the main square before diverging into a small alley that would take him the two blocks to the Crowing Cock. Halfway down the alley, he turned into a side alley that ended in a dead-end and waited behind a pile of rubbish for ten long minutes. Good. No one seemed to be following him.

He let out a low whistle and waited. Three minutes later, a small thin girl skulked into the side alley and walked around the pile of rubbish, straight to Jon's side. She gave a tight smile of relief once she was sure it was him.

"Hello, Cassie. How are you keeping?" Jon murmured quietly.

Her hazel eyes regarded him for a minute, as though checking that he was really interested before replying, "I'm all right. Me mam's pretty crook though. Her stomach hurts her. It's getting worse." The little girl's voice was sharp with worry.

"We'd better get a doctor to her, hadn't we then?" Jon reached into his pocket and produced a silver coin. "Now this is for the doctor and whatever medicine she needs." He prodded Cassie gently in the chest. "Now, what I need in return is a note from the doctor, telling me what is wrong. Got that?"

Cassie flounced her head, her curly auburn hair bouncing with the movement and pouted. "You don't trust me, do you? You think I'm making it up."

"Mostly I trust you, but I want to know what's wrong with your mam. Besides, if I just took everything you said as true, you'd think I was a fool ripe for the picking, wouldn't you?"

Cassie stared up at him for a minute, then grinned. "Maybe."

"Definitely," said Jon, still keeping his voice low. "Now. What's happening on the streets? Anyone watching for me? Any shamans being targeted?"

"No one's watching you at the moment. Some bloke came by asking questions a few days ago but he's moved on."

"Did anyone tell him anything?"

Cassie shook her head. "Well, I didn't. Don't know about anyone else but probably not. He was a stranger, and we all look out for you. You know that. Even though you've moved away, you're still one of us."

Jon gave a quick smile. "Thanks. Anything else?"

"Word on the street is there's big money being offered for a hit."

"Who's the target?"

"Not you," Cassie reassured him. "Just some girl. Dunno why."

"What girl?"

"She's not from round here. She's from up north a bit. Big house, magical ward, I hear. Think there's a mage lives there as well. Pretty tricky hit, I reckon. So I guess that's why the big money."

Jon's blood ran cold, but he didn't let it show in his voice. "Who's putting up the money?"

"They say a cloaked woman approached the Assassin's Guild. She posted a promissory note under their door and left."

"Did anyone follow her?"

"O' course. She went into a tavern, the Bent Bow, I think, but never came out. She must be pretty smart to evade the Assassins like that."

"What do you know about the Bent Bow?" asked Jon.

Cassie shrugged. "Not much."

Jon handed her another silver coin. "This is for you now. Do a bit of snooping around the Bent Bow and I'll give you another."

Cassie's eyes widened. "Wow. Thanks. That's more than usual."

"You're doing a good job… and if your mam's sick, you might need a bit more to tide you over." Jon put up his forefinger, "And don't forget the doctor's letter."

Cassie scowled. "I won't."

"One last thing. I really appreciate you being loyal to me. It means a lot to me. But if anyone should ever offer you so much money that you are tempted to betray me, please come and tell me. To start with, I need to know who and why but also, I need the chance to match it." As he saw a frown appear on the young girl's face, he smiled. "Cassie, I know you're loyal to me, as I am to you, but sometimes the stakes become very high. What if they threatened your mam? Or offered you fifty crowns? If anything like that happens, just get word to me. All right?"

Cassie shuffled her feet and looked down. "I will. I promise. I want to be on your side, but I see what you mean."

Jon ruffled his hair. "Good girl. You and I, Cassie, know the streets can be a tough place. If we stick together, we have a better chance of finding our way through safely. Now, just check that all's clear and I'll be on my way."

Chapter 26

The girl crept to the end of the side alley and peered in the direction from which Jon had come. Suddenly she heard a noise behind her. Even as she whirled, a knife slashed down at her. She managed to dodge a lethal blow, but the blade intended for her throat struck her shoulder instead. She howled in pain. As she staggered, she glimpsed a flash of light on steel, as another blade spun out of the darkness and caught her assailant in the chest. The cloaked figure dropped to the ground.

Cassie clutched her shoulder, sobbing, blood pouring out between her fingers as she too, sank to the cobblestones. "Jon. Help me. Oh, it hurts. I'm going to die."

Jon's figure loomed out of the dark. He quickly glanced up and down the laneway before crouching down beside her. "It's all right. I'm here." After a cursory inspection, he said soothingly, "No. You're not going to die. I promise I would tell you if you were. But you're going to be very sore for quite a while. Now, I'm going to rip a bit of material off your skirt. All right? Don't worry. I'll buy you another one." He tore a strip off the bottom and folded it up, pressing it against her shoulder to stem the bleeding. As the blood soaked through the makeshift bandage, he said, "You're going to need a doctor." Jon scrunched his face in thought. "What to do? What doctor would you have called upon for your mother? Could he help?"

"No." Cassie's words came out as though they were being squeezed. "He's very proper… or scared. He wouldn't touch a knife wound. The Assassin's Guild would know someone, but I don't really know them. Owww. It's hurting."

Jon had thought through all the options and found most of them wanting. "Right. Nothing for it, I think. I'll have to take you back to my rooms and call for help from there." He put his hand under Cassie's armpits and lifted. "Come on. Be brave. I think you can stand if you try. Use your other hand to hold your bandage in place." Jon encouraged her as the small girl struggled to her feet. Then he put his arm around her and led her back the way he had come. As they neared the palace, Jon deviated to the left and entered through a side door that led into the kitchen.

"Where's Stevenson?" he demanded, as they entered to the astonished stares of the kitchen staff who were in the throes of last-minute preparations of a dinner party for the king.

"I believe he is receiving guests, my lord," said a footman.

"Then can *you* help me get this child up to my rooms, Keith, then fetch a doctor?" The urgency in Jon's voice had the footman jumping to assist, leaving the others to cover for him. "Someone else, bring cleans towels and warm water please."

Luckily, Jon's ongoing friendliness and genuine care for the kitchen staff meant that when he needed them, they fell all over themselves to help him. Keith took the other side of Cassie as they headed for the stairs while the little scullery maid, Emily, brought up the rear carrying a quickly filled bucket and an armful of towels.

As they emerged at the top of the stairs and headed down the south corridor to his rooms, footmen converged on them. No one was po-faced with disapproval. All of them were eager to help in any way they could. In their midst, the woebegone little girl sobbed and hobbled along between the two men towering either side of her. If she hadn't been hurting so badly, she might have been overwhelmed by her surroundings but as it was, she was oblivious to everything but Jon close to her, taking her to somewhere safe.

Once they had her inside Jon's sitting room, Emily placed a towel on the sofa before they lay Cassie down on it, in the faint hope that the sofa would be saved from the blood that still seeped from the wound in Cassie's shoulder.

Keith headed off to find the king's doctor while Jon remembered to send Arnold with a message to postpone his liaison with Beetlebrow. "Make sure you only say 'Jon,' Not Lord Jon, just Jon. Clear? We don't want any flapping ears overhearing."

"Yes sir." Arnold kept his curiosity to himself, nodded and left at a near run.

Jon knelt beside the little girl, holding a warm damp towel to her shoulder to staunch the bleeding with one hand and stroking her hair with the other. In the light of the candles, he could see just how dirty the piece of skirt was that he'd pressed against her wound on the way to the palace and wished he'd thought to use something of his own. He gave his head a little shake. Too late now. He'd just have to make sure she didn't get an infection.

While they were waiting for the doctor, Stanley, an off-duty Royal Guardsmen, took a look at the wound. He was an older, avuncular man with grown children of his own and a couple of grandchildren.

"There, there, dearie" he said comfortably. "Someone's taken a good swipe at you, haven't they, but your collarbone's caught most of it. Lucky, really. No damage to ligaments and such. Hurts though doesn't it when it hits a bone?"

Cassie nodded and sniffed pitiably. "Hurts lots."

The room was crowded with staff, anxious to help. Jon was too busy focusing on Cassie to worry about it, but a stir at the door heralded the arrival of Stevenson, the butler, not a hair out of place.

The hubbub quietened instantly

"Lord Jon," said Stevenson dryly. "Do you have need of this many people? I suspect other members of the king's household would appreciate some of their attention, if you could spare them."

Jon brought his strained face around to meet Stevenson's eyes and only then did he realise the extent of the crowd. He gave the faintest smile. "Thank you everyone. I'll let you know how she gets on with the doctor."

"Tea, I think," said Stevenson, taking charge. "Emily, more towels and more hot water. You two, go with her to help carry things and bring back a pot of tea as well." He scrutinised Jon for a moment. "And bring up a bottle of brandy. The '84 from the second shelf in the cellar. I think his lordship needs sustenance." He brought his gaze to bear on the small girl and added, "I think we may also need cake and lemonade... and whatever spare morsels that may be from His Majesty's dinner party for Lord Jon. No rush on those. We'll wait until Lord Jeffrey has seen her."

"Thank you, Stevenson," said Jon, relieved that someone else had taken over. "Poor little girl. She was just walking in the laneway when, out of the blue, a hooded figure attacked her. She dodged sideways or it would have been a lot worse."

"And where is this assailant now?" asked Stevenson, taking the story at face value. "Not lying in wait for another unfortunate, I hope?"

Jon concentrated on looking at Cassie's face. "Uh no. I managed to... um... dispose of him."

Stevenson raised his eyebrows just the tiniest bit. "Indeed my lord? Well done."

Happily for Jon's equanimity, the doctor arrived at this moment and the next forty minutes was spent in watching him examine the wound, listening to his diagnosis, which tallied with Stanley's, and in assisting him while he cleansed and stitched the wound then bandaged it and put her arm in a sling. When he had given Jon some medicine for the pain and packed his bag, he stood up to leave.

Jon also rose. "Thank you so much for coming," he said. "I am sorry we dragged you away from your evening. Were you at the king's dinner party?"

Lord Jeffrey's lined face broke into a smile. "No. I rarely attend them. I find they are generally less interesting than the smaller dinner parties I go to, either in my own rooms or in those of my close friends. But you did drag me away from one of those." He gave a warm smile and patted Cassie on the hand, "But it was well worth it, for your sake and mine. I have just avoided losing at Bridge. I loathe the game, but my wife loves it. So I endure it from time to time." He tapped Cassie on the nose. "So you see, young lady, you have done me a service."

Cassie actually giggled, which was as much a credit to his bedside manner as it was to his medical skill.

"Goodbye, sleep tight tonight. I'll drop by and see you tomorrow." And with that, he was gone.

Chapter 27

Soon afterwards, several laden trays were brought up and placed on the dining table in the next room. Jon's suites included a sitting room, which was where Cassie reposed on the sofa, a dining room with sufficient seating for eight people off to the left, while the bedroom and a private privy and bathing room could be accessed off to the right of the sitting room. Doors opened from the corridor into both the dining room and the sitting room.

Cassie, who was beginning to feel better, watched with round eyes as the trays, carried by uniformed footmen and maids, were placed on the dining room table which, although in the next room, was within her line of sight. Jon, who hadn't left her side, smiled at her expression.

"Hungry?" he asked.

"Yeah. Starving." She dragged her eyes away from the table in the next-door room to say, "But I'm worried about me mam. She won't know where I am, and I'd usually be home long ago... Plus she's sick."

"Good girl. That's why I like working with you. You're very responsible." He caught the eye of a young footman who was heading towards the door with an empty tray. "Just a minute. Tomkins, isn't it? You're new, aren't you? Could you arrange to deliver a couple of notes please?"

Tomkins smiled. "Certainly, sir." While he waited for Jon to cross to his small writing desk in the corner and pen the notes, the footman turned to the little girl. "And how are you getting on, little lady? Ready for some supper?" When Cassie nodded, he said, "Just as well. There's a lot there to choose from." He glanced at Jon and decided that if he had wanted Cassie served, he would have said so. His efforts at conversation, a skill not required by footmen, faltered to a stop.

After a moment, Cassie said, "I like your clothes. They're very smart."

"Thank you." Tomkins smiled. "I'm very proud of them."

Jon glanced up at that. "They look good on you. Liking the new job?"

"Yes. Mostly." He grinned. "Food's good... People are friendly."

"Here we are," said Jon, rising from his escritoire. He handed Tomkins the notes and two silver coins. "One for Cassie's mother and one for the doctor. Hmm. It would be better if whoever delivers the notes does not wear a palace uniform. It would be very conspicuous in that part of town."

Tomkins gave a bow as he accepted the notes and coins.

"Understood, sir," he said as he left.

Once they were alone, Jon surveyed Cassie, noting her dirty clothes and shoddy little boots. She wasn't destitute but he guessed her mother had bought her shoes second-hand and struggled to make ends meet. Cassie's clothes were not ingrained with dirt, but she had fallen into the detritus of the alley and blood smeared the parts of her clothes that hadn't been totally soaked.

"Hmm. I think you need to get cleaned up sooner, rather than later. Just a minute." He was halfway to the door when a knock preceded the entry of a maid carrying clean nightclothes with Josie, Gavin's fearsome steward, right behind her.

Despite himself, Jon quailed at the sight of her. Josie walked into the middle of the room and stood frowning down at Cassie. "Young lady, what is your name?"

"Cassie, ma'am," said Cassie in a small voice.

"Well Cassie, my name is Josie. I have come to see that you are well looked after." Josie threw Jon an amused glance, knowing she could be intimidating and that he would be waiting to see which way she pounced. She turned back to the girl and said firmly but kindly, "I expect you are hungry after all you have been through, but you will enjoy your food and your sleep much better after a bath."

Two more maids carrying buckets of warm water entered the room and, bobbing curtseys to Jon on the way past, went through his bedroom into the bathroom beyond and emptied their loads into his bathtub. Cassie looked on in mute astonishment.

Josie indicated a dark-haired maid with a creamy complexion and dark blue eyes, holding the night clothes. "This is Kate. She will help you bathe and get dressed."

A look of fear crossed Cassie's face, making Josie frowned more severely. "I hope you are not afraid of bathing?"

Cassie shook her head. "I'm scared of hurting."

Kate's dark eyes twinkled kindly at her. "Don't worry, I'll be gentle with your shoulder."

"By the way, Jon, I hear you asked for a scribe for tomorrow morning. Kate may be able to help you between looking after Cassie." Josie took her leave, a gaggle of maids and footmen trailing after her, leaving Jon blinking in surprise in her wake.

Before Jon could say anything to Kate, she had borne Cassie off into the bathing room. Half an hour later, Cassie re-emerged, dressed in a long flannelette nightgown, and shaking back her damp, auburn hair. Her hazel eyes glowed with pleasure. "Jon, Jon. They have beautiful smelling soap. Just like lilacs." She pranced over and beamed up at him. "And Kate was really careful, so it only hurt a bit."

Suddenly she started tilting backwards. Jon reached out and grabbed her around the waist to steady her. He smiled. "Not quite up to prancing, little one. Take it easy. You lost a lot of blood, you know. Now, do you want to sit at the table or on the sofa?"

"I think I'd better lie down." Tears sprang to her eyes, and her face scrunched in disappointment. "But I'm really hungry."

"Don't worry. Kate and I will bring all the dishes to you, one by one, so that you can choose what you want."

Cassie brightened. "Really?" As she was led to the bed, she gazed around the sitting room then back at Jon, eyes wide, as she finally had time to take in the grandeur of their surroundings. She looked as though she were about to say something but then just gave her head a little shake, a dazed look in her eyes, and sank down onto the sofa.

She only had time to work her way through three small platefuls, before her eyes started to droop, and the plate threatened to slide onto the floor. Kate scooped the plate deftly out of harm's way and settled the blankets around her.

She looked at Jon. "Poor thing is exhausted." She hesitated. "Josie says I'm to set up a truckle bed in here with her. For tonight. Just to keep an eye on her."

Jon's blue eyes twinkled. "Just to keep an eye on the proprieties, you mean. I would have thought Cassie was too young to worry about. She's only eight or nine, I think."

"Yes sir, but she's not family, is she? Sorry. I'll try not to get in your way."

Jon laughed. "No trouble at all. And we wouldn't want to cross Josie, now would we?"

Kate let out a breath of relief. "No sir. We wouldn't."

Privately, Jon thought that any impropriety was far more likely to occur with Kate than with Cassie, and that Cassie would be far too deeply asleep to act as chaperone, but he had no intention of taking advantage of the situation.

Chapter 28

As soon as he was sure Cassie was asleep, Jon walked quietly to his escritoire and wrote another note to Sheldrake, this time telling him about the price on Sasha's head. Jon was alarmed that she had become such a high-profile target. It was becoming too dangerous to keep her at Sheldrake's. And Jon didn't feel sure she would be any safer here at the palace, even with the increased security that had been put in place at the palace since the abduction. He wondered if perhaps Sheldrake, Maud, Stefan, and the others should meet, unaware that they had had the same thought.

He wrote his thoughts to Sheldrake and crossed to the door, handing the note to the footman outside for delivery. It was still early but he wouldn't go out and risk having Cassie waking up and finding him gone.

He stopped beside her as he walked back to his desk. She moaned in pain as she moved in her sleep. Poor little girl. She had taken a blow meant for him. He, too, was not safe.

He wished he'd been able to see Beetlebrow tonight. He needed to gauge the readiness of the Kimoran refugees to move against Toriana. Could he ask Beetlebrow here? No. Here, he was Lord Jonathan. The fewer people who knew his true identity, the better. But someone out there had known who he was. He didn't think for a minute that the attacker had been some random mugger. And another attempt had been made on Sasha, only two days ago… and that was before the reward letter had been delivered to the Assassin's Guild. It was getting worse. He sighed. The risks were becoming untenable.

"Are you all right?" came a soft mellow voice.

Jon had forgotten about Kate, sitting quietly in the corner, waiting for him to retire before she could set herself up in the truckle bed.

Jon rubbed his forehead and gave a wan smile. "No. Not really, I suppose. That knife was meant for me, you know. That alone is upsetting enough, but then to have an innocent girl hurt in my place…" He shook his head. "Poor Cassie…"

"You know her, don't you? She's not just some chance victim you rescued from a mugging?"

"Yes. She is someone I go to for information. I have become quite fond of her." Jon knew that many members of the nobility had a variety of information sources, so it was not giving too much away to tell Kate this.

"Would you like a brandy, sir? Stevenson ordered up a very good one for you, I think."

"Thank you. That's a good idea." Jon smiled. "Would you like one too? And have you had anything to eat yet, yourself?"

"I had a bit to eat before I came up here." She glanced longingly through the door into the dining room, but then turned back to Jon. "And I'm not sure I should. I mean, what if Miss Josie came in and found me eating and drinking with you, sir?"

"Good point. But although she makes me quiver in my boots, I think I can hold my own if I need to." He walked to the table, took a plate, and handed it to her before taking one for himself. "Now come on. You'll be no help to Cassie if you faint halfway through the night from hunger." He looked at her quizzically. "Do you like brandy?"

She smiled. "I have no idea. But I don't know how much help I'll be to Cassie if I'm drunk as a lord. Whoops. Sorry, sir. No offence intended."

Jon laughed. "I will give you one little glassful, then strictly tea. How's that?"

Kate's eyes shone as she enjoyed the novelty of the situation. "Sounds just right."

As they ate, they talked about various members of the serving staff around the palace, the upcoming Spring Carnival and about good eateries and pubs each of them had been to. Jon enjoyed chatting as he had done when he had been a footman, but he was careful not to speak slightingly of any of the nobility and certainly not of the king himself. He would have loved to tell her about Crabtree, but he felt it might set the unpleasant man up as a butt of ridicule and he did not want to risk that, much as he struggled with him.

As they rose from the table, Kate said, "You might want to get some warm water up here and have a wash yourself before retiring, sir. You cleaned your hands after the doctor came but you've still got a smear of it on your face and some on your cuffs."

Jon rolled his eyes. "You could have mentioned that sooner."

Kate merely chuckled and went to the door to order up some water for him.

"You can read and write, I gather," Jon said, as she turned back into the room. "Josie said you could help me with some scribing."

"Yes. I can, as a matter of fact. My father had great ambitions for me and wanted me to become a governess." She shrugged and looked down. "Never got anywhere. People want genteel women to be governesses, not some working-class daughter of a wood carter. I suppose it's my accent as much as anything. Tried for scores of jobs. Never got one of them."

He smiled. "Well, I need a scribe tomorrow morning. So, if you're here anyway, perhaps you could copy a letter for me. I would give you a little extra for the extra work. What do you think?"

Kate beamed. "Love to. Thank you."

He showed her the letter he wanted copied and where he kept the ink and pens. "One copy, but only write on one side of the paper. Don't do it until tomorrow morning when the light is better."

Once the water arrived, he bid her good night and retired to his chamber to wash and go to bed.

The next morning he awoke to the sound of female voices murmuring on the other side of the door. A young giggle was quickly suppressed, which led to more giggles and a splutter of laughter. After a low "Shh," and a brief silence, the murmuring recommenced. Jon smiled. It sounded as though his little informant was recovering well.

He swung out of bed, pulled his bathrobe around himself, and went out into the sitting room. He was not a later riser like Lord Tarkyn, but he definitely rose later than the servants.

When he entered the room. Kate looked up from where she sat chatting to Cassie. Cassie was now dressed in a simple, but good quality skirt and jerkin. Jon marvelled at Josie's resources. He had no doubt she was the source of Cassie's new outfit.

Kate smiled. "Good morning. I hope we didn't wake you."

Jon raised his eyebrows. "Hard to say, but it was time to get up anyway. Quite a cheery sound to wake up to." He grinned, then looked at Cassie. "And how is your shoulder, young lady?"

"Not too bad, except when I move it. Then it hurts… a lot." She grinned. "But it's almost worth it to come here and see your amazing room and eat your amazing food. When's breakfast? I'm starving."

Jon crossed to the door, poked his head out into the corridor and spoke to a footman. "On its way," he reported.

Minutes later, a knock sounded on his door.

"Yes?"

It was not breakfast. Instead, a footman walked in and said, "Lord Jonathan, His Majesty has decided to breakfast with you. He expressed a desire to meet both Kate and the young lady. He will arrive in half an hour."

Carefully po-faced, he withdrew, leaving three shocked countenances behind him. Jon imagined the unexpressed hilarity the footman was feeling at the moment.

He was the first to recover. "Right. I'd better get dressed." He surveyed the other two. "Don't worry. You two look fine. You've obviously have been up for a while." He realised Kate was looking nervous and Cassie had actually gone pale with fear. He smiled reassuringly at them. "It is all right. The king will not be coming to punish or reprimand you, I'm sure. I expect Josie has been telling him all about you and he just wants to meet you."

"But I don't know how to talk to a king," exclaimed Cassie.

"Don't worry," said Jon. "As soon as I'm dressed, I'll give you a few lessons. Once introductions are over, it is pretty straightforward."

Half an hour later, a knock preceded the entry of a footman who announced the king.

Gavin walked in and paused on the threshold. He was wearing a dove-grey thigh length coat over cream breeches and a silver-embroidered waistcoat. Cassie blinked and wondered whether the waistcoat contained real silver. Kate and Cassie, who had stood up for the occasion, curtseyed deeply, Cassie suppressing a grunt as her shoulder hurt her. Jon gave a bow commensurate with his role as Lord Jonathan, which was deeper than he would have as Prince Jondarian.

"Please rise. Good morning, Lord Jon."

"Good morning Your Majesty, an unexpected pleasure to see you."

Gavin gave a faint smile. "Since my trip to the woodlands, I have realised that my life has lacked… hmm… spontaneity. Josie told me of the occurrences here last night and I thought I would come to see for myself, instead of relying on reports as I usually do." He nodded at the other two. "You may introduce yourselves."

"I am Kate, daughter of Royce the wood carter, Your Majesty. I work here as a maid."

"And Josie tells me you are literate. I'm pleased to hear it. I have a great interest in providing education to those who wish to have it." He looked at Cassie, slightly raising his eyebrows in query.

"Hello, Your Majesty. My name is Cassie and I live in Charters Street."

"Ah, do you indeed?" Gavin's eyes twinkled. "Unless I'm much mistaken, that is where the cart carrying Sasha and Jayhan was taken when they were abducted. Is that where you met Lord Jon?"

"Ooh. You're pretty sharp, Sire." Cassie watched him, waiting to see whether she had used the right title for the time of speaking. Jon had given her a quick lesson on protocol, but she was by no means sure of herself.

Gavin smiled, apparently finding her form of address unremarkable. "I like to think so."

He led the way into Jon's dining room, where the table had already been laid. At first, conversation was stilted, but not only was Gavin an expert at small talk, but he also had a genuine interest in hearing about the lives of the two young ladies.

As the meal drew to a close, the king said to Kate, "As I mentioned before, I would like to provide education to a broader range of my subjects. Would you be interested in helping me to establish a school in the poorer part of town? You are uniquely placed because you are educated, but do not sound... hmm... but your roots are still discernible."

Kate gave a little laugh. "I still have a working-class accent, you mean?"

Gavin grimaced. "I was trying to avoid saying that."

"Yes, I would like that very much, but you'd have to think about what you'd do with all of these educated people who can't get jobs with your noble families anyway."

"If that were a person's ambition, I believe an elocution coach would take of that," said Gavin, "But I think many people are proud of their particular accents and have no wish to change them. Being a governess to a noble family is not the only use of education. Employment can be found in the trades, bookkeeping, and negotiating for merchants, reading plans for builders, and in teaching, if I can increase the number of schools."

"There is also the possibility of apprenticeships with mages if the students have any magical abilities or with scribes or lawyers. But for all of these, they need to be literate," added Jon. At that moment, a footman entered bearing a note for Jon. "Excuse me," he said, giving it a quick perusal. When he had finished, he glanced at Cassie before handing the note to the king.

The contents were terse:

Nothing wrong with her that a little food won't cure. She is suffering from malnutrition. She has been giving her daughter what little food she has and neglecting herself entirely.
Yours
Grimsby. MD

"What is it?" asked Cassie, alarmed.

Jon took a breath and forced a smile. "It is from the doctor I sent to your mother. You will be pleased to know she is well and should make a full recovery. A tummy bug that is almost past."

Cassie frowned at him but when he returned her gaze blandly, she let out a sigh of relief. "Oh good. Thank you for helping her."

The king looked up from the note and asked her, "Can your mother read and write?"

"No, Sire. She used to work as housekeeper to a chandler down near the docks, but he died suddenly a month ago and she's had trouble finding more work, because she didn't have a reference from him." She gave a tight smile. "We'll get by though, Sire. We always have."

"Would she be willing to learn and to help Kate establish my new school?"

Cassie's eyes grew wide with excitement. "Oh, Sire, I think she'd love that. I could help too."

Gavin smiled at her. "You, young lady, will humour me by getting well first then learning your letters from Kate. If you do that, I may consider taking you on to assist Kate and to run various errands and discover information for me."

Cassie was about to gush her thanks until the last phrase when her face clouded over. She looked at Jon, trying to put a question into her gaze. When he did not return her gaze, she turned resolutely to the king. "Sire, I would be happy to learn my letters and help Kate but I'm not sure I can run errands for you." She grimaced unhappily. "It is just that I already work for Jon."

"But I am your king. My wishes override all others."

Cassie was almost in tears, but she held fast. "I am a loyal subject, Your Majesty. I really am. But I promised I would be loyal to Jon." She scrunched her napkin in her hand. "Now I don't know what to do. I can't betray Jon." She turned beseeching eyes to Jon. "Jon, help."

Jon glanced at Gavin, unable to take much more of Cassie's distress. To his relief, Gavin broke into a warm smile. "Young lady, your loyalty does you proud. It takes great courage to stand up to a king." He placed his hand on Jon's back. "You have my assurance that I would never work against Lord Jon. I might like to know what he is doing sometimes but I won't ask you to break his confidence."

Cassie let out a long sigh of relief. "Then I would love to work for you, Sire."

Chapter 29

Not long afterwards, Gavin took his leave but requested that Jon attend him in his own quarters later in the morning. In the interim, Jon entertained Cassie while Kate copied the contents of Crabtree's letter, writing each objection at the start of new page. Only in the palace, could one consider being so generous with paper.

When she had finished, Jon perused her work then looked up and gave a nod. "Excellent. Now I will write a short letter asking him to write the solutions below each of his objections before consulting with me again. At the very least, he must provide options to discuss with me." Jon frowned as he realized he had just gone against his intention of not discussing Crabtree with Kate. "Hmm. This is strictly between us. I don't want Crabtree's performance discussed in the kitchen."

"No sir. His dress and style have been the butt of the occasional joke, you know, but I promise I won't add to it."

Jon smiled. "Thank you." He turned to Cassie. "And now, young lady, I will escort you home. We are going via the kitchens to put together a hamper for you and your mother. I will also give you two silver crowns to tide you over until you and your mother start work with Kate."

Cassie's eye grew wide. "Oh thank you." She chuckled. "I must get myself hurt again. It is very profitable."

"Cheeky brat. You must be feeling better."

In full daylight, they walked through the streets with far less trepidation. Cassie's house was a mile from the palace in the middle of a row of terraced houses, south of the commercial area. The street was neat and well kept. Jon remembered from the last time he had been here that a few merchants lived here and some retired people. Not wealthy merchants, he suspected.

Cassie's house had no front garden. The bright blue front door opened straight onto the footpath and was flanked on either side with rather neglected pot plants. As Cassie put her hand on the doorknob to open it and stride in, Jon stopped her.

"Just a moment. I would prefer to knock to give your mother some warning that she has visitors."

Cassie considered him for a moment before nodding and giving the door a hearty rap. A few minutes later, the door was opened by a tall, thin woman, whose hair showed signs of having been quickly dragged back from her face and pinned up. Wisps of hair hung limply on either side of her hollow cheeks and dark eyes, dulled by hardship, stared up at him.

Jon produced a pleasant smile. "Good morning. My name is Jon and I have come to return your daughter to you. As I mentioned in my note, she was set upon in an alley and was wounded. She has been seen to by the finest doctor in the land and is now on the road to recovery."

The woman considered him for a moment before saying with quiet dignity, "Thank you." She transferred her gaze to Cassie. "All right, love?" and held out her arm. Cassie walked straight into the shelter offered by it and burst into tears. Her mother held her close and for a while, stood with her head bent over her daughter. As Cassie settled, she looked up and said, "The doctor read the note to me. Thank you for telling me, sir. I was worried sick by the time it arrived."

A sniff emitting from the level of her chest heralded Cassie's recovery. The girl looked up and gave her mother a watery smile, her eyes glistening with both tears and excitement. "But guess what, Mum? I went to the palace and all the walls were bright cream and all the trim was gold. GOLD!!! They had men in uniform standing around waiting to help, and beautiful carpets and paintings and ... "

The rest was smothered by her mother who pulled her close, effectively gagging her. "I'm glad you're all right, my little Cassie." She looked sternly over her daughter at Jon. "I thank you for looking after her, but now you'll have put a whole lot more wild ideas into that head of hers."

Before Jon could reply, Cassie dragged herself away from her mother enough to be able to speak again. "And mum, I met the king."

"Go on with you!"

"No really, I did. And I had *breakfast* with him."

Her mother frowned a query over Cassie's head at Jon, who smiled his sunny smile. "She did. She and I and a kitchen maid called Kate. The king heard about Cassie being injured and visited us this morning."

The woman's eyes grew round. "Well! What an honour."

Jon remembered he was holding the big basket of food from the kitchen and proffered it. "This is from His Majesty's kitchen."

Cassie's mother frowned. "I don't hold with taking charity, young man."

"Consider it compensation for Cassie's hardship, ma'am."

Her eyes narrowed. She was clearly torn between taking the basket and standing on her dignity.

"I read the doctor's report, ma'am," said Jon gently. "And I think it is in your daughter's best interests if you are well. *She* has been worried sick about *you*." He waited a moment. "Of course, your business is your own and Cassie is just pleased that you are recovering from your tummy bug."

The woman took a deep breath. "You'd best come in, I suppose. That is, if you want to. Where's my manners? My name's Gwen and of course you're welcome to come in." She looked back over her shoulder at the dingy brown walls. "Not up to your usual standards, I expect, if you live at the palace."

"Thank you. I would be delighted," said Jon, stepping over the threshold before she could change her mind.

A packet of tea and bag of freshly baked biscuits were produced from the basket to provide the basis of a lovely morning tea. Cassie's mother struggled to hide tears of relief, which turned to excitement, as she unpacked meats, cheeses, vegetables, and bread from the big basket. They drank tea and ate biscuits as Jon explained the king's scheme for a local school to Cassie's mother.

An hour later, Jon took his leave, pleased that at least one little family was facing a brighter future.

Chapter 30

Jon returned to the palace only just in time for his appointment with Gavin. He walked down the long corridor past paintings of Gavin's ancestors, aristocratic gatherings, and bucolic vistas. He turned left into the northern wing of the palace, walked down a flight of stairs to the ground floor then walked still further until he reached the door of King Gavin's private office. He knocked and waited.

A minute later the door opened to reveal Josie who gave him a considering stare before saying, "Good morning young man. You may go in. I was just leaving."

Jon gave a courtly nod of his head. "Thank you, ma'am."

Josie chuckled. "Don't you ma'am me, you young rapscallion. Josie will do for you."

Jon grinned. "Yes, ma... Josie."

"Cheeky boy," she said as she swept past him, a smile lingering on her usually stern visage.

Jon walked through the doorway to find Gavin seated at his desk, watching their interchange with interest. To Gavin's right, French doors gave onto the vista of the palace gardens and lake. Jon gave the king a shallow bow.

Gavin smiled ruefully. "You have Josie wrapped around your little finger."

"So, too, do you," replied Jon.

"Ah yes, but that is because she is in my employ, whereas you just charm her into working with you. Not many can do that, except perhaps Maud."

Jon laughed. "Don't worry. I am still nervous of her. She's a force to be reckoned with, that one."

Gavin sighed. "She is. As is Neville, my valet and Bryant, the captain of my Guard. They all apparently have my best interests at heart, but that does not seem to include automatically following my orders."

"Of course not. They all have their areas of expertise, and you allow them to bring their specific knowledge to bear on a given situation. You are served far better that way, even if you don't get instant obedience." Jon smiled. "It takes more strength to give power to other people than to completely squash them."

"*I* know that, but some of my nobles haven't figured it out and try to take advantage of me." Gavin waved his hand in invitation. "Do take a seat."

"Thanks. " Jon settled himself in a well-padded armchair. "Of course they do. Being tyrannical with your staff wouldn't stop that though. Your nobles would just look for more roundabout ways to get what they wanted if they thought you were sterner."

Gavin grunted. "I suppose there are advantages to people confronting me directly, although I won't tolerate belligerence or blatant disrespect." A silence descended and something in the way the king fiddled with the paperweight on his desk stopped Jon from saying anything further. Then, with a sigh, Gavin looked Jon directly in the eyes. "Jon, I don't think we can maintain our current arrangements. I fear too much for your safety and for that of Sasha. Sasha, in particular, is the target of constant attempts on her life. And now, that little girl, Cassie, has taken a knife blow meant for you." He shook his head. "It will not do. Things must change."

Jon's face went rigid with shock.

"No Jon, I'm not throwing you out on your ear. Of course I'm not. But I think you should take Sasha and move to somewhere safer until you're ready to make your move. Do you have any suggestions?"

Jon's mind was having trouble working. All the fears of the twelve-year-old he once was, alone in a hostile world with a baby sister to save, rose within him. "Um, no." He rubbed his hand across his face. "Just give me a minute. I'll think of something."

"No. You don't have to do this alone," Gavin smiled sympathetically. "Maud has already proposed a meeting to discuss the current situation and what to do about it. She suggested the Creeping Vine Inn as a venue, but I have asked them all here instead. Lady Electra will rouse no suspicion coming to an audience with me, while she would if she visited Batian House too often."

Jon looked like a rabbit caught in the headlights. "Are you all working behind my back?"

"No. Maud only contacted me this morning and I am extending her invitation to you now." Gavin's voice was even, but the faintest edge to it showed that his patience would not last much longer.

"Sorry." Jon drew in a deep shuddering breath and managed a wan smile. "Sorry. I don't know how I can ever be a regent if I get upset so easily."

Gavin shook his head at his cousin. "Tea, coffee, or brandy?"

Jon pulled himself together enough to reply, "Brandy please, followed by a tea. But only if you have time."

"I have time. This is important. You are important. I have made time."

"Have you? Thank you. I know you are always busy with a hundred demands, so thank you."

Gavin gave a warm smile. "You are welcome, cousin." He rang a bell prompting the arrival of a footman. Once he had given the order for tea, he stood up and poured the brandy himself from a crystal decanter which stood on a sideboard in the corner of the room. "Here," he said, handing a glass to Jon and reseating himself, this time in an armchair. "I was thinking about what you said. When you are acting as regent, if you are so upset by some news that you stop being able to think, just clear the court and give yourself time to think. Even if it is only for ten minutes, but longer is better. Otherwise, you may buckle to unwise pressure."

Jon sipped his brandy and gave a sigh as he began to relax. "Have you ever done that?"

"Oh yes. Often. But for longer than ten minutes, usually for at least several hours, quite often for several days. Besides, if a piece of news oversets your thinking, you almost certainly need more information, different perspectives, and the counsel of your advisors before reacting to it."

"Oh. I see." Jon's brow cleared and a glimmer of his sunny smile appeared. "So I just have to teach myself to think 'Clear the court' or 'Give yourself time,' when I am stunned or confused."

Gavin nodded. "Just remember, they are at your beck and call, not the other way around."

Jon chuckled and took another sip while he thought about it. After a while he said, "Probably a bit easier for you to remember that, than it is for me. You have always had authority and a clear place at court."

"True, and even harder for Sasha who has no memory of the Kimoran court at all."

"Maud, Yarrow, and Eloquin have been teaching her etiquette and Kimoran customs, but no one has been teaching her statecraft. Has she even been to the audience chamber?" asked Jon.

Gavin nodded. "She has. Twice. But I think her focus was on the expected behaviours, not on the strategies of being a ruler."

"Such a lot to learn." Jon sighed, raised his hand, and let it drop. "And now…"

"And now, you are both in constant danger." Gavin finished for him. He leaned forward and said gently, "Jon, all the statecraft in the world will be useless to her if she is dead."

Jon sipped his brandy, looking somewhere far past the confines of the room. After a moment, he roused himself from his reverie, glanced at Gavin and gave a rueful smile. "True. And I have just discovered that a contract has been put out on Sasha through the Assassins' Guild." He sat up straighter in his chair and said briskly, "I, too, was thinking we needed to meet and work out what to do. Well, I had better get an update from my refugee compatriots beforehand." He paused as he was about to leave. "Is Prince Tarkyn still around? Could we ask him too?"

"Currently he is with his family, deep in the Great Forest somewhere. But he is due back here tomorrow. I will ask him, but he may not see it as his priority."

Jon nodded. "Understandable. Thanks."

Chapter 31

In the drawing room of the Manissan palace, Toriana glanced up from her desk where she was working her way through a pile of documents. She watched the heavy carved wooden doors open to reveal Colonel Waldarion, who entered, and bowed. Once she had allowed him to straighten, she returned her attention to the reports from her generals for a full ten minutes before deigning to acknowledge him. "So Waldarion. Your demeanour tells me that you are not the bearer of the news I am waiting to hear. How can a whole nation fail to kill two people?"

Colonel Waldarion repressed his irritation and managed a faint smile of unfelt apology. "Good morning, Your Majesty. How indeed? Unfortunately, you are correct. No success so far. I believe one specialist came close to this man whom King Gavin thinks is Jondarian, but he made the mistake of attacking the impostor's lookout instead of waiting for the man himself to emerge."

"And we know this how?"

"We found our man dead in the alley and asked witnesses what had happened. Few people were around but eventually we tracked down a street cleaner who had been further up the alley and had seen most of it, although he did not see the blow that killed our 'specialist.' Apparently, a girl was injured and taken to the palace for treatment."

Toriana drew in a sharp breath. "Most unfortunate. The specialist must have been an imbecile. Now they will increase security around the impostor and make our work even more difficult."

She narrowed her eyes, staring at a row of tiny black ants that were trekking along the edge of her desk towards a half-eaten cupcake. She had not enjoyed the cloying sweetness of it, so she had decided the ants could have it. She pinched part of her skirt and began working the cloth back and forth between her fingers. The major noted this sign of frustration with trepidation.

Suddenly she lifted her head to glare at him. "And what of the girl? She is even more of a danger to us. If she has found herself a black amulet, some will give credence to her claim that she is the true queen..." She gave an angry titter, underpinned with anxiety. "Only until the shamans realize she is fake, of course." She sniffed. "But I do not want false pretenders to my throne causing unrest among the people."

"Of course not. It would be most upsetting," said Waldarion soothingly. "We are doing everything we can to prevent that possibility."

"Troops are being readied, are they not, just in case?"

"Yes ma'am."

Toriana gave a little huff. "I was led to understand that this girl lives in a normal residence. Is that not so? Surely, that should present no problem."

"That is true, ma'am. But again, we have had no success. Several have been killed or, worse still, captured." He winced at the thought of his queen's possible reaction. "I believe the property is magically warded."

Toriana's finger rubbed the material of her skirt back and forth between her fingers more tightly to the point where Waldarion wondered whether she might actually wear it through in that spot.

He continued quickly. "We have now issued a reward through the Assassin's Guild. It is only a matter of time, I think, ma'am. She cannot elude us forever."

"Well, she will have nowhere to run when we invade Carrador. But I want her out of the way before then."

Chapter 32

They gathered three days later in one of the king's smaller dining rooms. The sun was just setting over the lake, sending deep orange rays of light through the floor length windows onto the tapestried carpets.

They took their seats around the highly polished, round mahogany table. Gavin, of course, was seated at the head of the table, which was denoted by a larger, more ornate chair. Sheldrake, Maud, and Stefan sat to his right, squinting against the last rays of the sun, while Jon, Lady Electra, and Colonel Argyve sat to his left. Tarkyn had decided to join them, as much as anything to give himself the chance to see Argyve and the others he had come to know since arriving in Carrador.

Opposite Gavin, two seats remained empty. These were for Jayhan and Sasha, who would be allowed to join them later, perhaps for dessert, depending on where they were in their discussions by then.

Servants circled them, unfolding starched white napkins, and placing them on the diners' knees. Drinks were poured and the first course choices of smoked salmon, pork terrine, prawns fried in lemon and spices, and a duck pate were presented.

During the first course, the soup and the main meal, conversation remained desultory, while the servants still hovered. But once the main course plates had been cleared away, Gavin made sure there was sufficient wine and water on the table then dismissed the servants, saying he would ring for them.

Once they were alone, Gavin turned to his spymaster. "Now Sheldrake, how secure is this room? Could a servant be listening at the door? Are there any peepholes that you know of?"

Sheldrake glanced across at a darker corner of the room where the flock wallpaper was cast into shadow by the edge of the dresser. Then he waved his hand and murmured a few words under his breath. "No one is at the peephole, Sire, and I have just shielded the room against listeners."

Gavin raised his eyebrows then smiled. "The things I don't know about my own palace." He turned to the table at large and said, "And now, we must talk. Lady Electra, Lord Argyve, are you aware of what is happening?"

"Not entirely, Sire," said Electra. "I received your invitation which contained the words, 'if you can spare the time.' This is the innocuous inclusion devised by Sheldrake to alert me to the fact that either Sasha or Jon or both needed me." She smiled apologetically. "That's the sum total of my current knowledge, I'm afraid. I was just glad to see that Prince Jondarian was looking well and was safe when I arrived. I presume, from your demeanours that Sasha too is safe and well."

"Yes, she is," Maud assured her. "But it is difficult to keep her so. That was what we wanted to talk to you about."

"Maud and Sheldrake's staff are intercepting would-be assassins nearly every week. So far, their interceptions have been successful, but for how much longer?" Gavin's quiet voice held everyone's attention with no conscious effort. "And an attempt was made on Jon's life only two days ago." He leant back and sighed. "Clearly, the Kimoran assassins are all working on information provided by Shay, regarding the true identities of 'Lord Jondarian,' and 'Lady Natasha,' although they don't seem to know about Sasha, the stableboy. However, they do know she lives at Batian House."

"I agree," said Sheldrake. "We stopped the abduction, but we lost the subterfuge, with Shay's intelligence reaching the Kimoran Queen."

"So our present arrangements are no longer adequate to keep Jon and Sasha safe," concluded Maud.

Lady Electra looked at Jon, "How do you feel about this?"

Gavin was intrigued that she had said 'feel' rather than 'think'.

Jon grimaced. "I feel desolated. Confused, sad that I will have to move on, worried about Sasha, fearful about Kimora's future and worried about the fate of the refugees, if they choose to help us." He took a deep breath, raising his shoulders and letting them drop. "But… I agree. We cannot continue as we are."

"Why desolated?" asked Stefan. "That's a pretty strong word. You have friends, us, who are here to help you."

"Ah. Because we had the semblance of a normal life for a while, maybe not the one we were born to, but productive, comfortable." He shook his head. "But now the illusion has slipped, and we are once more as we were, on the run and hunted by our homicidal, *regicidal* aunty." Suddenly he gave a quirky smile. "On the other hand, I won't have to deal with Crabtree, if I leave."

Sheldrake, Maud, and Gavin, who knew the man he was talking about, gave grunts of laughter.

"A very awkward engineer who reports to the Minister for Transport," Sheldrake explained to the others.

"A few more details, if you wouldn't mind," said Argyve. "Not of Crabtree, obviously. Of these assassination attempts and the measures you have put in place and why you think they are insufficient. Then we can consider our options."

Gavin nodded approvingly. "Trust a military man to get down to the essentials."

Once Electra and Argyve had been filled in, Colonel Argyve concluded, "There's no point in maintaining Jon and Sasha's aliases if they stay here. Sasha is learning fast but still needs more training. How close are you to being able to attempt an incursion into Kimora?" he asked Jon abruptly.

"There are six main refugee camps, holding in total nearly five thousand. Two of these camps are predominantly people who are too old, sick, or infirm in some way or with young children. So we can discount their numbers in any calculation we may make of the people ready to travel into Kimora. The other four camps contain men, women and older children, twelve years old and above."

Argyve raised his eyebrows. "This does not sound like an army ready to march."

"No. It's not, but..." started Jon.

"I'll answer that, since I have been overseeing their training," Stefan interrupted. "Each of the small incursion groups numbers forty, but many will work in pairs or small groups. In consultation with the local woodfolk, who remain hidden, I have been teaching them wood-folk skills: hunting, tracking, hiding themselves and their tracks, archery, and knife throw-ing." He gave a self-conscious grin. "Obviously some woodfolk abilities, such as mindtalking, flicking into hiding and melding into the background cannot be taught."

"We have also developed a signalling system so that we can leave marks on trees with a time and basic information," added Jon. "And the refugees themselves have developed a hierarchy of command and a system of reporting between the groups."

"I have also taught them hand-to-hand fighting techniques and the rudiments of sword-play. Few of them have swords but they enjoy learning to use them." Stefan took a long draught of water. "They have trained hard and, in my opinion, are more ready for action than your average green recruit. Obviously, time will improve their skills, but they will do now."

Gavin's eyes narrowed. "I hope you have not been neglecting your work in liaising be-tween Carrador and the woodfolk and in training Sheldrake's household."

"Not at all, Sire," said Stefan, who had been clearly prepared for the king to raise this. "Generally, I merely oversee the training. I do not do it myself. I train the instructors for each group, and they do the rest. Once in a while, I watch a training session to make sure they are developing their skills correctly but being in the forest gives me the opportunity to visit my woodfolk contacts and family anyway."

"So you would have over three thousand trained soldiers? An impressive force," said Argyve, "but not, I think, sufficient to meet Toriana head on."

"No," said Jon firmly. "We would never want to do that, even if we could. These peo-ple would end up fighting their friends, neighbours, and family if we did that. Worse still, shamans under Toriana's compulsion, who are the people who hold the positions of com-mand, would direct their troops and use their powers against the refugees and regret it bitterly later once they were freed from her influence."

Argyve leaned back in his chair and took a sip of wine. "I see."

For a few moments, a thoughtful silence filled the room.

"As you know, Kimoran society is a matriarchy built on the power of the shamans," said Electra. "In some areas, people are rebelling against their local shamans who, driven by Toriana's compulsion, have become overbearing and, in some cases, brutal. But it is rare. On the other hand, if you can turn the shamans, you can turn the whole population to your side."

"But Sasha is the only person who can break the queen's compulsion on her shamans," objected Maud. She shook her head in distress. "And she is so young to become embroiled in such danger."

An uncomfortable silence followed.

Then Jon spoke. His words, heavy with regret, thudded like a door closing on Sasha's childhood. "I'm afraid she must."

Chapter 33

"So if Sasha moves through Kimora, freeing shamans, " said Tarkyn, entering the conversation for the first time, "more and more people will be on your side. But what will you do with them? Use them as an increasingly large army to march on the capital?"

"That would be a logistical nightmare," objected Argyve, "trying to organize an army over and over on the march, as more soldiers join it."

"No," said Jon firmly. "Toriana would get wind of it, long before we were strong enough to outface her. No. We must send small squads into areas of unrest to keep Toriana's focus away from Sasha and to frustrate her wish to invade Carrador."

"And what will Sasha be doing?" asked Maud.

"She will release as many shamans as she can along the way, but ultimately," Jon took a deep breath, "ultimately, she will have to face the strongest shamans of Toriana's court, who are based in the capital, Manissa. And the greatest challenge of all, of course, will be Toriana herself."

"Ooh dear," breathed Maud. "I suppose you're right. But it is a terrifying prospect for a small girl just coming into her powers."

"It would be a terrifying prospect for anyone," said Sheldrake drily. He hesitated, before addressing the king. "Sire, is Carrador... are you, planning to lend support to Sasha's quest? Practical support, I mean."

Gavin looked from Sheldrake to Maud and back again. "Are you asking whether you may go with her? And whether I might construe your concern for her as divided loyalty?"

Sheldrake glanced at Maud before answering, "We could build a case by saying that to help Sasha is to help prevent an invasion by Kimora." He shrugged and gave a self-deprecating smile, "But to be honest, I think we just want to look after Sasha and so are unable to be objective about other justifications. We will, of course, abide by your decision."

Gavin drummed his fingers on the table as he thought. Finally, he said, "Thank you for being honest with me. I am pleased that you are so fond of my cousin. So too am I. Both cousins," he added, his eyes twinkling at Jon. "Toriana killed three of my blood relatives; my uncle and two cousins. So, for me also, the issue is personal as well as political."

No one spoke, understanding that the king was still thinking through his position.

"Jon's refugees will provide sufficient armed support, I think, and I do not wish to be construed as going to war by providing more troops." He said, more or less thinking aloud. "In the end, the outcome will hinge on Sasha's ability to stay safe and to hold up under pressure." Then he smiled, having reached his decision. "For this, your support, Maud and Sheldrake, both as quasi-parents and as magic users is justified. So you may accompany her. Stefan, your friendship with Sasha and your knowledge of arms and woodfolk would also be invaluable. You may also take the opportunity to liaise with the Kimoran treewrights, if you can contact them."

Jon's face had lit up. "Oh this is marvellous. Gavin didn't mention it, or perhaps didn't think of it, but I too would greatly appreciate your support, friendship, and wisdom."

Tarkyn smiled at Jon's enthusiasm. He took a sip from his wine glass before saying, "I too would like to accompany you. I think you will need all the help you can get. But I am, after all the Guardian of Eskuzor. For how long may I neglect my duty to my country?"

"If this ruthless Kimoran queen has designs on Eskuzor, however far down the track, I think that justifies your involvement," said Argyve. "Your decision, of course, but that's my opinion."

"Thanks." Tarkyn had always found Argyve to be a rock of certainty in a changing world. "I won't leave my family again, though. So I must discuss it with my home guard who have already walked so far to get here from Eskuzor." He gave a wry smile. "The outcome is by no means certain."

Gavin raised his eyebrows, having experienced the understated strength of Tarkyn's family and friends. "I imagine not. However, please tell them that we would all appreciate their skills being added to Sasha's protection."

"I will." Tarkyn smiled at Argyve. "And I will continue my requisition of Jackson from your messenger service if you don't mind. He is an invaluable aide de camp."

Gavin turned to Maud with a rueful smile. "I am also assuming your determined, young son will be accompanying you, despite the dangers. I cannot imagine anyone being able keep him from following you, short of imprisoning him, which would be a little drastic for one so young."

Maud glanced at Sheldrake and sighed. "Yes. It would certainly be the course of least resistance."

"And he does have useful powers," added Sheldrake, " and more importantly, provides companionship for Sasha."

With that settled, Gavin let his gaze travel around the people at the table. "Are we ready for dessert and to invite the little ones in?" The king pulled an embroidered, tassled cord that hung against the wall within reach of his chair.

In response, Josie entered and curtseyed.

"We're ready," said Gavin.

"Thank goodness, Your Majesty. They are becoming quite restless." She withdrew and returned minutes later, opening the door to admit Sasha, dressed beautifully in a teal blue gown with cream trim, and Jayhan, looking neat in jacket, waistcoat, and knee-length breeches.

Sasha curtseyed and Jayhan bowed. When they straightened, their little faces were alive with apprehension but, rigidly minding their manners, they waited for the king to speak first.

Gavin smiled warmly at them. "Good evening, you two. You both look very smart this evening. I'm glad you managed to keep your clothes clean for so long."

Jayhan frowned. "It was definitely an effort, Your Majesty."

Gavin chuckled. "I thought it might be. Now, you are just in time for chocolate pudding, lemon pie and ice cream. We will continue our discussion shortly." He nodded at the footmen to show them to their seats and waited while the servants served dessert to each person and then withdrew.

As the door closed behind the last one, Sasha let out an impatient sigh, making Gavin laugh.

"I know, Sasha. It's torture, isn't it? But we must not let anyone know of our plans. Your safety is worth a little patience."

Sasha gave a little grin. "Sorry."

With no further ado, Gavin told them what had been decided. He did not let them react or interrupt until he had finished. When he stopped speaking, Sasha just sat there in stunned silence.

Jayhan jabbed her in the ribs. "Well, go on. Say something. Come on. It's exciting, isn't it? A bit tricky in spots, I expect, but exciting."

"When? When are we going?" She wiped shaking fingers across her brow. "Sorry. I thought you were going to come up with new ways of staying safe here. I knew this was coming sometime. But not yet. I'm a bit shocked. Sorry. Thank you, everyone, for wanting to come with me. Well, not everyone, but lots of you." She went to take a sip from her glass of juice and found her hands were shaking. She quickly hid them under the table. This was not lost on the adults watching her.

"Oh dear," said Maud fretfully, "do you think she needs a cup of tea?"

This was so typically Maud's reaction to distress, that Sasha burst into laughter. "No. No, I don't, thank you. " She took a deep, deep breath and put her hand over her amulet. A faint dark glow emanated from her bodice. She looked at her brother. "It must be done, mustn't it? So we will do it. When do we leave?"

Part 5

Chapter 34

Although every day that Jon and Sasha remained in Highkington posed a risk to their safety, the travellers decided that two weeks was a minimum for putting their affairs in order in preparation for a lengthy absence. So they agreed to gather at the Creeping Vine in two weeks' time and leave from there, arriving separately to delay watchers' realisation that Jon and Sasha had left the city.

Maud and Sheldrake were important, high-profile members of the Carradorian court, and they had many matters that had to be either postponed, deputized, or finalized before they left. Jon, as Minister for Transport, could not just walk away, much as he would have liked to, especially from Crabtree, and he needed time to make arrangements with the most trusted of his refugees. At Gavin's request, Argyve, who had known of, and worked with, woodfolk for years in Eskuzor, agreed to step into Stefan's role while he was gone. So Stefan needed to spend time with him, introduce him to the local woodfolk, and give them time to learn to trust him. Tarkyn needed time to consult with his woodfolk.

Until they left, life had to appear as normal to give no hint of their intentions.

Attempts on Sasha's life escalated to two per week. Three would-be assassins who were after the big reward were less skilful that those who had come before, but a kindly-looking old woman selling herbs, spices and mushrooms almost succeeded. The magical ward had not alerted anyone since she came openly through the front gate and made no attempt to seek out Sasha. Instead, she had conversed pleasantly with Hannah while selling her fresh herbs and mushrooms. It was only because Sheldrake had walked into the kitchen looking for sage to burn to give himself some clarity of thought, that he had spotted the pile of mushrooms next to the stove.

"Just a minute," he'd said. "Let me squeeze their stems."

When he did, the stalks turned purple, giving off a musty unpleasant smell. He'd sniffed them and asked Hannah where they came from.

Hannah had wrung her hands and said they'd looked and smelled like normal mushrooms when she'd bought them, then confessed that she'd bought them from the kindly old lady.

"A new supplier?" Sheldrake asked, and without waiting to be told, Hannah realised what a fool she had been and burst into tears of remorse.

Meanwhile, as though nothing beyond the castle walls was happening, Jon had returned to his battle with Crabtree.

On the following morning, with Kate's assistance, he had presented Crabtree with a sheaf of papers, each headed with one of Crabtree's objections and beneath each objection, another heading: Solution? Jon sat back and waited, occupying himself with other matters and wondering who he could put forward as his successor or whether the king already had someone in mind.

Then he remembered that he had never made any overtures of friendship towards Crabtree. So he sent him a note inviting him to have a drink with him in three days' time, at which time he could give Jon his proposals.

At the appointed time, Crabtree knocked and was given entry by the footman outside. He kept sliding his hand nervously over his slicked back hair.

"Good afternoon, my lord."

Jon beamed at him and strode forward to meet him, ushering him to a chair. "Crabtree. Delighted to see you. I realise I have been very remiss and have not taken the time to get to know you. New role, you see, and I was preoccupied with learning the ropes. I do beg your pardon."

Crabtree raised his eyebrows, looking thoroughly overwhelmed. "Not at all, sir."

"Now, what would you like? White wine from Eskuzor or red wine from Kimora?"

"The red, if I may," replied Crabtree querulously.

"Of course."

Once Jon had poured drinks and seated himself, he asked Crabtree about himself and discovered that he lived in a street close to Cassie's, with his ailing mother and a cat called Lucy. Much to his surprise, he discovered that Crabtree indulged in learning swordplay and then using his skills to replay historical battles in a society called the Past Revisited.

Jon leaned back, "Well, that's just marvellous. What a wonderful hobby. I wish I could use a sword. I'm a rank amateur. Not bad with a knife, though. Not very classy, a knife though, is it? More wine?"

Crabtree actually chuckled. "No, sir. Not very classy and no call for knife work in historical battles, unless you have a sword in the other hand."

"Ha! Well, there you have it! I can use my dominant right hand for my knife and my left hand for the sword."

"That will trick them. You may have invented a whole new form of swordplay, well, knife play, disguised as swordplay, if you see what I mean."

The wine was beginning to affect them both at this stage.

Jon grinned. "Indeed. I always said you were a genius."

Crabtree goggled at him. "You did?"

"Oh absolutely. Smartest man I've ever met. Bloody cranky, but bloody smart."

"Well, what do you know?" Crabtree gave a smile, which turned into a grin, which turned into a full-throated laugh. "And there I thought you just had a vested interest in making things difficult for me."

Jon looked astonished. "Me? No. Why would I? I just want the job done as well as it can be within the budget and needs of the nation. Not an easy task, as you well know."

"And you think I'm smart, do you?"

"Of course. Don't you?"

"Well, yes."

Jon wagged a slightly uncoordinated finger at him. "But you think I'm an absolute idiot, don't you?"

"Well... I... Well, to be honest I did, but now I'm not so sure."

"Cheerful does not necessarily mean idiotic. Remember that." Jon crossed his arms but was still smiling. "You, sir, have led me on a merry dance: questioning every requisition, every order, every proposal. And I admit, I was silly. Because I let you do it." He gave a lopsided smile, "But I would so much rather that you put that trained and powerful mind of yours to working out how to make the transport system run within the parameters we have, rather than spending your brain power on intimidating me."

Crabtree frowned, taken aback. "You? Intimidated? Not a chance."

"Of course I am. You have more experience, training, and knowledge... and you obviously find everything I say tedious and objectionable."

Crabtree leaned back and blew out a breath, "Ooh. That bad, eh? I'm surprised you haven't sacked me, in that case."

"So am I," said Jon bluntly. "But you're too damned smart and would be too great a loss."

The engineer stared at him for a time then said quietly, "Thank you."

Jon gave a grunt of laughter. "You're welcome. What I would really like is for you to respect me even half as much as I respect you. Take it for granted when I come to you with a problem, that I already know the budget is insufficient for a straightforward solution and that I am turning to you to come up with your stroke of genius to find a way around it."

"Oh my word. I really have underestimated you, haven't I?"

Jon grinned. "Closed your mind to me would be closer. I expect you resent people less clever and less trained than you, being in charge. That's certainly how you act."

Crabtree peered into his empty glass then looked up, unaware that he looked hopeful. Jon responded by smiling and refilling his glass.

"You know," said Crabtree thoughtfully, "I don't think I'm as clever about people as you are." He smiled, "And you have a great generosity of spirit that I am just coming to realise."

Jon held up his glass and toasted him, hiding his regret that he would be leaving this man behind just when they had come to an understanding and hoping that the next Minister for Transport could build on this foundation.

Chapter 35

Jon, Stefan, Maud, and Sheldrake held ongoing discussions about possible routes into and through Kimora. Tarkyn was not interested in navigation and generally left it to them to tell him the route when they were ready. But this time, Jon had asked him to attend.

They met in the parlour at Batian House on a cool, sunny autumn afternoon three days before their scheduled departure. Clive had laid out afternoon tea on a coffee table in the middle of the room and retired to leave them to their discussions.

Jon was wired up and anxious to speak. As soon as they were all seated, he said, "I have been speaking to Beetlebrow, Argus, Draya, and Rhoda, and they have just reminded me of the Midwinter Festival. People celebrate it right across the country. It gives them something to look forward to in the cold days of winter and to celebrate the coming return of longer days and warmth." His blue eyes shone with excitement. "But what I didn't realise is that shamans gather together to celebrate Midwinter. They meet at their gathering place high in the Darkstone Mountains. They share remedies, discuss problems, and offer each other support. They come both as shaman practitioners and as representatives of the communities they lead and serve."

"*All* shamans?" asked Sheldrake sharply.

Jon nodded. "Not quite all, but as many as are well enough to make the journey. Some must travel over one hundred miles. But they come. It is their duty and, generally, their pleasure to see each other again, to swap ideas and to represent their people's interests. They meet twice a year: midwinter and midsummer."

Sheldrake's eyes lit up. "That would be perfect, far easier than infiltrating the capital. If we can get to this meet, Sasha can release them all at once."

Jon grimaced. "Or fail to release them all at once. After all, she will be up against all of these shamans and Toriana. It would be a huge risk. And if Queen Toriana is in attendance, which I assume she would be, she will have an escort of guards."

"True," conceded Sheldrake. "Not easy, but perhaps more possible than Sasha attempting to traverse the length and breadth of Kimora, converting shamans as she goes, all the while concealing her presence."

"And she may be able to release a few at a time, depending on the layout," suggested Tarkyn, standing up and pacing back and forth a few times before turning to them. "I think it is our... *your* best chance. Risky, yes, but so is every alternative."

"But midwinter is only two weeks away" objected Maud. "And we're not even leaving for another three days. Can we make it in time? I can't leave any sooner."

"We won't, if we have to walk through the Great Forest," said Stefan firmly. "We're going to need a quicker way to go."

An hour of energetic debate led to the decision to travel by coach along Park Lane to the Charville River then by boat down to the forests in the foothills of the Darkstone Mountains, where the treewrights apparently dwelt. From there, they could walk up into the mountains to the festival site. Despite the obstacles, knowledge of the Midwinter Festival had buoyed their spirits. They began to feel that the impossible might just be possible.

Tarkyn was not quite so enthusiastic. "Ooh. My woodfolk will love this," he said with heavy irony, heaving a sigh. "The mountain not so bad. The carriage and the boat ride....?" He raised his eyebrows. "Oh my word..."

Chapter 36

"You're joking, aren't you?" fumed Waterstone. "You can't ask us to travel in a coach or a riverboat. It's too much."

"Wow!" Rainstorm's eyes were round with excitement "That's an amazing idea. Don't say 'can't,' Waterstone," he pleaded. "Just ask instead, 'How can we?'.... Please?"

Waterstone glared at him.

It was late, close to midnight. The small group of woodfolk sat with Tarkyn around their fire, the coals glowing deep orange beneath the flames. They had stayed up to see him, knowing he would return to them that night. Lapping Water sat near him. Midnight was on his knee, as usual. On the other side of the fire, Autumn Leaves was checking that their voices hadn't roused Gurgling Brook who lay asleep, wrapped in blankets, beside him.

Sparrow, who was on guard duty in the tree above them, was in full agreement with Rainstorm, but was clever enough to know that besetting her father on all sides was not the way to win an argument. So, she just watched and waited.

"I presume you have thought this through," said Autumn Leaves mildly.

"As well as I can, with the knowledge I have." Tarkyn gave a tired smile and put his arm around Lapping Water's shoulder, giving her back a stroke. "I have missed you, all of you while I have been back and forth to Highkington. I want to help Sasha and Jon, but I won't, if it means leaving all of you again. And you have already walked such a long way. You can't walk to the Darkstone Mountains. It's too far, so soon after your last journey."

"Then don't go," snapped Waterstone.

Autumn Leaves gave an understanding smile. "But I think we have agreed that we want to help Sasha and Jon, both for their sakes and for future peace among our lands."

Waterstone stood up, reaching for another long branch to feed onto the fire. He looked around the group and rolled his eyes. "Why do I get the feeling that I'm a one-man band fighting for our woodfolk values? Lapping Water, your silence is deafening."

Lapping Water smiled at him disarmingly. "You should know that we are all firm on woodfolk values, Waterstone. Tarkyn is not suggesting that we go among outsiders we don't know. The people we would travel with have been sworn to secrecy. There is nothing in our code about coaches or riverboats."

Waterstone spluttered. "No, of course there's not. Woodfolk lore doesn't envisage us leaving the forest at all." He turned to Autumn Leaves, hands on hips. "Isn't anyone else worried at the prospect of being confined to a wooden box on wheels? We've never even been inside anything with straight lines."

"It is a little mind-boggling, I grant you." Autumn Leaves tucked the blanket up a little higher where Gurgling Brook's hand had worked its way out into the cold night air. "I suppose my greatest concern, Tarkyn, is the possibility that people we don't know might look into the coach or stop it and demand that the occupants get out for some reason." He shrugged. "I don't know, bandits or troopers maybe."

Tarkyn nodded. "Unlikely, but definitely a possibility we need to cover. Stefan, Jackson, and I will be with you, either mounted or driving the coach." He grimaced. "I don't think there will be room for me inside the coach with all of you, unless Lapping Water sits on my knee and Midnight sits on someone else's. The coach's interior seating is designed to accommodate four large people. It will fit the six of you with someone holding Gurgling Brook, but that's about it, I'm afraid."

"I could sit on the floor for a while if you wanted to join us," offered Rainstorm. "I'm used to sitting on the ground. In fact, we all are."

"We are getting off the point here," objected Autumn Leaves. "What do we do if someone stops the coach?"

Sparrow unexpectedly entering the conversation from above them, "If we have enough time, you could drive the coach close to the side of the road. Then we could open a door and flick into the nearby woods."

Waterstone eyed his daughter, torn between displeasure at the whole concept and his wish to acknowledge the usefulness of her idea "Humph. True. Good idea. But what if we don't have enough time?"

"If bandits threaten us, Jackson, Stefan, and my shield will keep them away." Tarkyn grinned. "In fact, as a concession to your concern about being seen, I will even guarantee to kill every last one of them, if there is even a chance they have seen you."

"That's a little bloodthirsty, Tarkyn," said Autumn Leaves, raising his eyebrows. "But the concept is reassuring."

Tarkyn shrugged. "Up to Waterstone. I don't expect to meet bandits, at least, not along the road. Troopers are a distinct possibility, but I have requested a letter of passage from Lord Sheldrake which should get us past any challenge."

Waterstone tried one last-ditch stand. "I can't see this endearing us to the local woodfolk. I thought we were here to develop a relationship with them and show them how to develop a communication network."

"They are well on their way. We have been teaching them for over two months now. And true, this may not endear them to us, but Waterstone," Tarkyn tried not to sound too forceful, "little Sasharia is going into Kimora, a country run by the aunt who wants to kill her. And only she, an eleven-year-old girl, has the power to overturn her aunt's binding on her shaman subjects. If Sasha fails, sooner or later, Toriana will turn her power-hungry focus on Carrador and Eskuzor. Kimora is a large country. They may overrun us."

"Besides," said Lapping Water, "We may get the chance to meet these treewrights the shamans told us about. Imagine what stories we could take back to our own woodfolk. Two separate communities of woodfolk we had never known of, before we came here. Once we leave the river, the path takes us through a vast tract of forest in the foothills of the Darkstone Mountains. We are bound to encounter them."

Waterstone gave a wry smile. "I hope they are friendlier than the local Carradorian wood-folk were, at our first meeting." He grunted. "I can see that our skills could help to keep Sasha… and Jon safe. And apparently, she and Jon have woodfolk blood in them. Anyway, above all, we do not want to part from you so soon after reuniting with you or obstruct something you feel strongly about." He busied himself with adjusting the branch he had fed into the fire so that his voice was muffled, as he added, "But I don't much like confined spaces, and I really *hate* horses."

Tarkyn was immediately sympathetic. "Oh Waterstone! Of course you do. I'd forgotten that. I'm glad you reminded me so I can make sure we keep those on horseback away from you when you're getting into the carriage." Aware that, although it had been Waterstone's resistance that was the strongest, it was still a group decision, he looked around the others. "So, will you come?"

"Yes," said Lapping Water, speaking for all of them. "We will come."

Chapter 37

Two weeks after the dinner with the king, Maud, Sheldrake, Stefan, Marjorie, Jon, Tarkyn, and Jackson gathered in the private parlour in the Creeping Vine, to go over their plans one more time. Sasha and Jayhan had already gone to bed upstairs, ready for an early start in the morning. Maud had insisted that Marjorie be invited to accompany them, both to give Marjorie another chance to get away from the Creeping Vine and to provide Maud with companionship and assistance in the absence of her maid and servants.

"Rhoda and Draya, who have knowledge of this Midwinter Festival, will meet us at the end of our river journey and travel with us from there," said Jon.

"Which is where?" asked Stefan.

"The Dark Lake. The Charville River begins in Eskuzor and flows along the border between Carrador and Kimora down to the Dark Lake. "

Stefan peered again at the map before straightening up to stretch his back. They had been poring over maps for the better part of an hour. "So, this Dark Lake looks to be about a hundred miles away but, as the river flows, it's probably more like one hundred and fifty miles, maybe more. Hmm… but," he held up a finger, "the river flows to the south and even on the slow stretches, it flows faster than walking pace. Not much faster, maybe a very brisk walk, but still faster. And on other stretches of the river, it flows very fast indeed, faster than a run."

"Even if it's slower than cutting through the forest, it will be easier than struggling through the undergrowth," concluded Marjorie. "We only have eleven days to the festival site."

"True," said Maud, "Plus it is an easy trip along Park Lane to reach the river."

"What about rapids? Waterfalls? Hidden sandbars?" asked Sheldrake.

Stefan thought for a minute, running his mind over what he knew of the river. "Rapids, yes. Hidden sandbars, probably. They tend to come and go, as the river changes course and brings silt down. Waterfalls, no… and as far as I know, the rapids are negotiable."

"They are," confirmed Marjorie. "We had a group of merchants in here last week who had travelled downriver with goods for Kimora but made the return journey by road."

Jackson frowned. "But people must be able to travel back up the river. Otherwise there would be a stockpile of boats downstream."

Marjorie laughed. "There would be, wouldn't there? Yes, they can travel upstream, using oars and sail, and I believe there is also a towpath. Some even employ a mage to propel them upstream, especially through the rapids. I think the riverboats either need barge horses or mages to get them up through the rapids. In some cases the boats are ported around the rapids. In fact, many boats stay either below or above the rapids and people transfer from one to the other for the second half of the journey. The merchants I was talking to last week came back by road because they met up with friends of theirs and travelled back in a convoy."

"Oh, I see," said Jackson, grinning at her "I didn't realise the Charville was such a commercial thoroughfare I thought it was a dark brooding river that wanders through the thickest parts of the forest."

Sheldrake walked over to the map and studied it with new eyes. "I think it has plenty of scope to be dark, brooding, and isolated in between settlements. See?" He pointed to the map as he spoke, "There's a settlement here, Bridgetown, which sprawls across on either side of the Park Lane bridge but is basically a Carradorian town, one here at the rapids on the Kimoran side. After that, the river sweeps out to the east onto the plains before turning south-westerly to run back into the Great Forest at the foothills of the Dark Mountains then on into the Dark Lake, which has a settlement on its easterly shore. But nothing in between that I know of, except the occasional river pirate, I believe."

"I have already deployed refugees in the towns along our route to call upon if we need them," said Jon. "They will be keeping a close eye on the shamans in particular."

"Isn't there also a guardhouse on the Kimoran side of the river opposite The Way Through where many boats left from, to transport Arquin's troops across into Carrador?" asked Tarkyn. "Just a thought, since my woodfolk are anxious not be seen when they are on the riverboat or in the coach, for that matter."

"They have agreed to travel by coach? And boat?" exclaimed Sheldrake. "I thought they would cross through the forest and meet us further along."

Tarkyn shook his head. "No. They have walked hundreds of miles in the last few months. They have agreed to come, but I wanted them to have a break from walking. "He chuckled. "Waterstone was not impressed."

"Our inn owns a large coach," explained Stefan, "that we hire out to patrons or use ourselves if need be. Tarkyn has hired it, to follow your own coach, which will contain Jon, Sasha and Jayhan, to keep them out of sight for as long as possible." He smiled. "As you can imagine, the woodfolk are extremely apprehensive about the prospect of leaving the forest, but have agreed to do so, provided they are not seen by anyone but those of us sworn to their secrecy."

"Oh, the poor dears" said Maud effusively. "I'm sure they're apprehensive. What a handsome concession they are making."

"Some more than others," said Stefan dryly. "I think Rainstorm's green eyes haven't stopped shining with excitement."

Jackson remembered something. "Ah yes. I am commissioned to remind you, Tarkyn, to tell everyone that Waterstone is very nervous of horses." Since everyone was present, he delivered the message to them himself. "So, if you could keep clear of him when you're mounted," he gave an embarrassed little cough, "or being a horse, that would be helpful."

The frown disappeared from Maud's face, and she grinned. "I will remember that."

"I have already sent a messenger ahead of us to find a boat and an inn," said Sheldrake. "I had better tell them to find a larger vessel. Maud and I will set out first thing in the morning and meet you at the inn in Bridgetown. That way, we won't have to wait for everyone else to get organised…"

Tarkyn grinned. "You mean, you won't have to wait for me to get up."

"Something like that," Sheldrake conceded with a wry smile, "… and we can go at our own pace."

Chapter 38

Very early the next morning, as soon as they had breakfasted, Sheldrake, mounted on Maud, left in company with their family's coach containing Jon, Sasha, and Jayhan.

An hour and a half later the Vine family coach, with Marjorie at the reins and Stefan by her side, trundled to a stop five hundred yards to the west of the Vine Inn. Stefan surveyed the road carefully in both directions before sending a mindmessage through to the woodfolk that the coast was clear for them to come out onto the road and board the coach. Jackson dismounted from Bosco and tied him to the rear of the coach with the other three horses, before opening the nearside door in preparation.

Rainstorm was the first to break cover, but even he looked a little strained. His head appeared between two sheafs of long grass and he glanced both ways, despite Stefan's re-assurance, before stepping gingerly onto the road and sidling up to the old, black-lacquered coach. He peered in through the doorway then pulled his head back out to give the actual door a close examination. He frowned at the brass handle and latch, then rubbed his hand on the green felt lining of the door. He studied the window that was built into the door and then at the other windows of the coach, one on either side of the doors on both sides of the coach. Then he stood back to see how much he could see through one of the windows if he were someone passing the coach.

He frowned at Jackson who was standing beside him and up at Stefan who was looking around from the driver's seat. "You'd have to warn us if someone was coming past."

"Of course," said Jackson. "We will be on the lookout for people, both ahead and behind us."

"Hmph."

Jackson waited quietly.

Next, Rainstorm peered under the carriage, looking up from underneath it at the axles, struts, and undercarriage. He straightened and looked at Stefan, "May I come up there?"

"Of course. Put your foot…"

But Rainstorm was up beside him before he could explain about the step. The woodman gave Marjorie and Stefan a nervous smile. "I'm the vanguard, you know." He stood up on the seat beside Stefan and swivelled round to study the roof of the carriage, then sat down beside him on the driver's bench. He let his eyes travel along the horses' reins to their harnesses and finally to the four horses themselves. He nodded a few times slowly to himself before turning to Stefan. "Hmm. You know, I have no idea what I'm looking at. Not really. I've never been near a carriage before. So, I'll have to rely on you to tell me whether this is a good, safe carriage and whether this hare-brained idea of Tarkyn's is safe for us." His mouth tightened at the corners in an effort at a smile. "Please. As a fellow woodman… I know you don't know us very well, but as one who shares our blood… can you be honest with me?"

Impulsively, Stefan put his arm around Rainstorm's shoulder, understanding what courage it had taken him to come out of the forest into the open of the roadway. "This carriage is old, but well looked after. She is sturdy and reliable, although not particularly fast. The horses are our own and we know how they react and how long they can go without a break. You will find little curtains," he paused at a certain blankness in Rainstorm's expression, "… little pieces of cloth, hanging inside each window that you can pull over if someone is coming. If the curtains are drawn over the windows, you can't be seen from the outside. Of course, you can't look out either, but you don't have to leave the curtains drawn when no one is around. We will be here to warn you if anyone is approaching and when it is clear to open the curtains again."

Rainstorm looked into his eyes. Stefan felt as though his soul were being searched. Finally, the young woodman gave a decisive nod and smiled, almost relaxed. Without another word, he hopped down and asked Jackson "Can you show me these curtains, please?"

Once Jackson had complied, Rainstorm took a deep breath and climbed inside. He sent his gaze around the whole interior, studying the lacquered black wood of the floor and ceiling and the stained wood panelling of the walls. Then he pushed experimentally on the green, padded, leather seats with his hand, before sitting carefully on the edge of one, gradually working his way back until he was leaning against the back cushion. He leaned forward and looked out a window then pulled the curtain over it to block it.

Then he shut his eyes, opened them again, and grinned.

Moments later, the tall figure of Tarkyn emerged from the roadside bushes holding Gurgling Brook in the crook of his arm, with Sparrow and Midnight on either side. Lapping Water, Waterstone, and Autumn Leaves followed. They all looked carefully up and down the road but then moved straight to the carriage door and climbed inside. Stefan couldn't help himself from climbing down to watch their reactions.

Autumn Leaves caught Jackson looking puzzled at their decisive entry into the carriage, compared to Rainstorm's thorough investigation. He gave an amused smile. "Rainstorm transmitted to us the images of everything he saw over the last few minutes. We already knew what to expect." He climbed in and looked around himself. "Hmm. Quite alien, really, isn't it? No leaves, no branches, moss, or soil. No birds or insects or little animals scurrying through the undergrowth. It's completely lifeless." He gave an involuntary shudder.

"But you have to give it to them," said Rainstorm, "The craftsmanship is excellent." He saw Stefan's quizzical smile and added, "My family come from a long line of craftsmen. Remember the bow I made?"

"It's just I've never looked at it like that. I've always just taken the woodwork and upholstery for granted."

Rainstorm nodded understanding. "We probably appreciate things more than you, since we have to make most things from raw materials and go through all the processes to reach the finished product."

Lapping Water and Rainstorm sat with Midnight between them on one seat, while Sparrow, Autumn Leaves and Waterstone with Gurgling Brook on his knee, sat opposite them. They looked around themselves with lively curiosity but no fear, just excitement at the prospect of a new experience.

"You can put your packs up there on those racks," said Tarkyn, pointing upwards. "Do you want me to travel inside with you?"

Waterstone laughed. "Much as I would enjoy berating you all the way to Bridgetown with the idiocy of this idea, I'd rather be able to breathe, and I think it would be very squashed with you in here."

"What about Stefan? He's smaller."

"Tarkyn," said Lapping Water patiently. "We are not fearful of this coach or the movement. I doubt anything would be as hard to manage as standing guard duty, high in a tree on a windy night."

"Exactly," agreed Autumn Leaves. "And I'm afraid, Stefan, that you and Tarkyn have scored guard duty for the whole journey. We will be relying on you two to tell us what is happening along the road in each direction. Our only concern is that we might be seen by people we don't know. That is all. We don't want to be exiled from our kin for exposing our existence and equally, we don't want to have to kill innocent people to prevent that."

That was when Stefan became aware that the woodfolk were all armed to the teeth. This was their usual practice, he knew, but he just hadn't taken in its significance in this situation. Each of them wore a hunting knife and kept their bow and quiver propped against the seat on the floor space next to them.

And yet none of them looked threatening. In fact, six pairs of excited green eyes shone out of six friendly faces. Autumn Leaves had spoken matter-of-factly, with no heat or threat at all in his words… but that made it all the more spine-chilling.

Stefan found himself revising his preconceived ideas. Here he had been thinking of the woodfolk as a naïve, uneducated group, fearful of things they didn't know. Instead, he had found them cautious until they had investigated, but then supremely confident, casually deadly, and clear about the perceived threats. Suddenly he felt a wellspring of pride surging up within him that he was one of them.

He grinned at them. "*I will be honoured to be on guard duty for you today,*" he mindspoke to them.

Chapter 39

The morning was cool and sunny, a day to make the spirit soar. Leaves high in the eucalypts twinkled in the sunlight, the sky above them a strong blue.

Marjorie wheeled the carriage carefully so that jolting to the occupants was minimal, then set off eastward at a trot for the first leg. Half an hour later, Jackson alerted them to a horse and rider, approaching fast. Stefan sent a mindmessage for the woodfolk to draw the curtains. As he drew closer, Stefan and Marjorie recognized the rider as a messenger who stopped regularly at the Creeping Vine for ale, food, and a change of horses. Breathing a sigh of relief, they gave him a cheery wave as he passed and let the woodfolk know they could relax.

After another half hour, Marjorie slowed the horses to a walk for a mile or two, knowing she would have to take them carefully if they were to travel thirty miles by nightfall. Once they were rested, she raised them to a trot again.

For some time, they did not pass any other travellers. Anyone travelling towards the river from the Creeping Vine had left earlier and would be somewhere up ahead. The messenger would have left very early and ridden hard but, by Stefan's calculations, others who had stayed at The Forest Rest, the tavern halfway between the Creeping Vine and the river, would come into sight within the next hour, heading for Highkington. With a certain sense of smugness, he again used his new-found ability to mindmessage this information to the woodfolk in the coach, adding that no one was yet in view.

Marjorie glanced at him and smiled. "You're talking to them, aren't you?"

Stefan was surprised. "How do you know?'

"You go still while you're concentrating, and your eyes go a bit out of focus."

"Huh. I didn't realise."

Tarkyn, who was riding behind them, cantered Flurry up beside them and then eased her up, to fall in beside the driver's seat. "Problem?"

"No," said Stefan. "I was just saying that we should see the first of the regular travellers coming the other way soon." He frowned, noticing that Tarkyn was showing signs of strain. "Are you all right?"

Tarkyn gave tight smile. "Just a bit tired. Waterstone may think I take this lightly, but I don't. I have constantly had my mind scanning the surrounding woodlands, checking for possible marauders or even just local huntsmen or woodcutters who may inadvertently come out onto the road unexpectedly." He stared off into the forest on their right for a minute before returning his gaze to Marjorie and Stefan. "You won't realise this, but the local woodfolk are watching our every move. Word is travelling down the length of the road through the forest on either side. The danger of exile is very real for our woodfolk… and when woodfolk are exiled, they are expected to live in isolation from each other, as well as from the main group. It is harsh. We don't want that to happen, under any circumstances."

Stefan blew out a breath. "No, we don't."

Jackson moved to the side of the road up ahead and reined in, waiting until the carriage came abreast of him. He smiled at Marjorie, "How are you going? Would you like to ride for a while and one of us drive?"

Stefan noticed a slight flush on Marjorie's cheeks as he said casually, "I'd like a turn at the reins, if you don't mind, sis. You can ride Slinky. He's a friendly enough horse. Let's wait 'til we crest that rise. Then we'll be able to see almost a mile ahead. If no one's coming, our friends could get out and stretch their legs, while you hop down and mount Slinky."

"Or you can ride Flurry," suggested Tarkyn, "and I'll sit up next to Stefan for a while, since he can now stand the sight of me."

Marjorie's pale blue eyes shone. "Oh, I'd love to ride Flurry. She's such a big softie."

Tarkyn chuckled. "She is, but she's a bit naughty sometimes, and a bit skittish."

"She's only young. I'd expect nothing less," said Marjorie, completely undaunted by the prospect of riding the huge draught horse.

When they reached the top of the hill, she reined in the four carriage horses as close to the side of the road as she could, right next to a patch of dense scrub, and climbed nimbly down to open the door of the carriage.

She smiled in at the woodfolk. "No one's in sight. So hop out and stretch your legs. You can stay on the roadway or go into the bush. Up to you."

As Autumn Leaves emerged, he stretched his arms above his head. When he dropped them, he enquired, "Time for a cup of tea?"

Marjorie looked a query up at Tarkyn, who was still seated on Flurry on the far side of the carriage, making sure that he kept away from where Waterstone would be.

"Of course. The horses could do with a break, and you can light a fire, away from the road. Half an hour at most, though. We still have a long way to go, and we don't want to annoy Maud and Sheldrake by arriving too late in the evening."

Tarkyn and Jackson dismounted and hitched their mounts to the rear of the carriage. Tarkyn walked around to stand in front of the carriage horses and sent them images asking them to let him know if anyone came into sight down the road. Then it occurred to him that he could contact Maud while she was being Maisy. He sent her an image of where they were currently and received an image of her, with Sheldrake on her back, approaching the Forest Rest tavern. He relayed an image of the spare horses they had brought with them in case Maud tired, but she indicated that she would keep carrying Sheldrake.

"All is well with Maud and Sheldrake, although the children are getting a little restless cooped up in the coach all day. Jon has his hands full keeping them entertained, I gather," he reported. "Let's go."

As they entered the cover of the forest, it was as though the sun had come out on the faces of the woodfolk. They looked at each other and grinned.

"I didn't realise how tense we were, until we got back to the trees," said Lapping Water.

"Not to say we aren't enjoying it," said Waterstone, not wishing to be cast as the chronic complainer. "We are. It is an interesting experience, in fact, for woodfolk, unique."

Sparrow and Rainstorm ran on ahead, quickly gathering enough firewood for a small fire, while Stefan and Marjorie brought up the rear, carrying between them a large wicker hamper which had been strapped to the back of the coach. As they set it down, Stefan performed a flourishing bow and announced, "Compliments of the Creeping Vine... Morning tea, lunch, and afternoon tea. That should get us to Bridgetown in one piece."

Jackson and the woodfolk quietly applauded. Tarkyn, who always assumed his meals would be provided, belatedly joined in. In no time at all, everyone had found a comfortable place to sit around the fire and were sipping tea and eating their way through slices of a large tea cake; freshly baked and smothered in butter.

"Hmm. I really like butter," said Autumn Leaves, licking a dob off his finger. "We don't have it usually. No cows, you see. Tarkyn has occasionally brought us foods from outside the forest, which have contained, or are spread with, butter. Lovely stuff."

Marjorie stared at him for a moment. "Huh. I hadn't thought of that; that you wouldn't have it usually."

It was early evening as the carriage carrying the woodfolk neared the outskirts of Bridgetown. The sun was still above the horizon, but road was striped with shadows. The number of travellers on the road had increased, more locals than long-distance travellers now.

Stefan drew the coach over to the right-hand side of Park Lane. *I think this is the closest we can safely bring you. Once we crest the next rise, we will be in sight of houses on the outskirts of Bridgetown. I hope you've stuffed your backpacks with provisions.*

We have, replied Rainstorm cheerily. *Remind us to thank your family when we get back to the Creeping Vine.*

Then Stefan heard Lapping Water's voice in his mind. *We'll head through the forest to the south-east until we come to the river. Then we'll look for a good place for you to pull a boat up to the bank and let you know where we are.*

Yes. There was a note of worry in Stefan's voice. *But how far can your... our mindtalking reach?*

There was a confused jumble of thoughts before Waterstone replied. *We're not sure of the range but it is several miles. I don't think you'll lose contact with us, but if you do, just make sure you're standing at the front of this boat you're planning to acquire so that, as you near our position, we'll see you and can send you our location in time for you to draw in to the bank.*

Tarkyn, who was seated beside Stefan on the driver's bench swung down and opened the coach door nearest the edge of the road. Autumn Leaves handed Gurgling Brook into his arms, before alighting himself.

"Daddeeee!" The little girl beamed at him, her green eyes catching the light of the sun, and swivelled her head to look around. "Look Daddy. Big hoss," she said, pointing at Jackson and Marjorie who were riding up to join them "Look. Jasson and Marjie"

Tarkyn smiled at her. "Yes, Jackson and Marjorie. You remembered their names. Clever girl. Do you want to pat the horse?" Gurgling Brook frowned, not sure what he meant. So, he carried her to the carriage horse and demonstrated. "See? Pat. Pat the horse."

She nodded vigorously and reached out a small hand, Tarkyn manoeuvred so that she could reach the glossy black neck of the closest horse. She made a few uncoordinated pats, which became rapidly harder. "Gently." Tarkyn took her hand in his and said, "Look. Now we'll stroke the horse." As he ran her hand along the horse's neck, he repeated, "Silky, isn't he?"

She nodded. "S-choke hoss."

"Did you have fun riding in the carriage?" asked Tarkyn as he carried her back to join the others.

She thrust out her am and pointed to it. "Cadge."

"That's right. Fun?"

She nodded many times and smiled broadly.

By now the rest of the woodfolk had alighted and were standing in a cluster at the edge of the road. He carried her back to them and handed her to Lapping Water. "Daddy has to go now but will see you later on."

The little girl's mouth turned down in disappointment and it looked as though she might start to cry in protest, but Lapping Water touched her on her nose and said cheerily, "And he may even bring you a little something, you never know."

For a moment, the issue hung in the balance. Then Gurgling Brook waved her hand. "Bye Daddy."

"Goodbye little one. See you soon."

Waterstone had moved to the edge of the trees with Autumn Leaves and was anxiously scanning the road in each direction. Closer to the carriage, Midnight was standing beside Rainstorm trying not to look wistful at the attention Gurgling Brook was getting. Tarkyn smiled at him, then walked over and knelt down in front of him, sending him images of riding in the carriage with a query. The boy smiled and flung his arms around Tarkyn's neck.

"Anything coming?" asked Tarkyn.

"No," said Waterstone tightly "Not yet."

"You can all wait within the trees if you like. I'll just give Midnight a turn at patting a horse, then bring him in to you."

After giving him a big hug, Tarkyn disentangled the little boy's arms and took him by the hand to Marjorie who had brought Flurry up as close as she could to the rear of the coach. Then he hoisted Midnight up onto his hip so he could reach the huge horse's neck. Midnight had been watching Tarkyn with Gurgling Brooks so needed no instruction. With firm gentle movements, he stroked Flurry's soft coat, smiling with pleasure. He glanced up at Tarkyn, inviting him to stroke her too. Tarkyn and he, both forest guardians, shared a feeling of friendship with Flurry.

"Rider and horse approaching from Bridgetown," reported Stefan tersely.

Tarkyn, facing Flurry at the back of the coach, had his back to the approaching rider, which shielded Midnight from view. Matching images to words, he said quietly. "Off you go then. Flick to Waterstone."

A moment later, Midnight was gone.

The rider rode up and reined in his horse. He was dressed in a well-tailored coat and breeches that suggested landed gentry or well-to-do merchant. He doffed his hat, wished them a good evening, and enquired if all was well, before continuing on his way.

Stefan breathed a sigh of relief. He looked at the spot where the woodfolk had entered the forest and could see no sign of them. *Are you still there?*

In response, Autumn Leaves became visible at the edge of the road, chuckling. "Of course we are."

Stefan frowned. "How did you do that? That's not flicking."

"No, it's not," answered Tarkyn for him. "They have an uncanny knack of blending into their surroundings when they choose to and revealing themselves when they choose not to. Another woodfolk talent that I do not possess."

"Huh."

Autumn Leaves smiled at Stefan. "We will teach you as soon as we can."

Stefan smiled back shyly. "Thanks. I hadn't noticed that skill before."

"We have to go," said Tarkyn. "I want to check how Maud is, after carrying Sheldrake all day and to make sure Sasha, Jon and Jayhan have arrived safely. Stefan, you drive, I will sit in the carriage," Tarkyn sent a cheeky grin to the woodfolk, "as befits my rank. After all, an empty carriage arriving in Bridgetown would look a little odd."

"So it would," said Waterstone, not rising to the bait. "We will see you later this evening?"

"Yes. After dinner."

Chapter 40

"Ah. I'm exhausted, Sheldrake." Maud leant back in her chair and pushed her legs out straight under the table in the private dining parlour of the Riverside Inn. She would never have been so informal in the public bar. "And my legs are still aching, even though I've had a lie down."

Sheldrake poured some more red wine into her glass. "You are quite remarkable, my dear, but thirty miles is a long way even for a horse that is used to being a horse, if you know what I mean."

"If that dratted man doesn't arrive soon, I will have dinner without him and go to bed." She reached for another oaten cookie from a dish on the table and began to munch on it. "These are just what I need," she gave a mischievous little smile, "for the equine side of me. But I could do with a good steak or a hearty stew."

"So too could I," agreed Jon.

Just then, the door opened and Tarkyn walked in. He gave a courtly bow of greeting, waving his hand to indicate they should stay seated, before seating himself. "Good evening. I'm sorry we are so late. You must be famished. I took the liberty of asking the innkeeper to attend to us straight away... unless you have eaten already?"

Maud, who had had every intention of scolding him, frowned in irritation at having the wind taken out of her sails before giving a reluctant smile. "No, we have not... Thank you."

Sheldrake raised his eyebrows in surprise. "You must be tired," he observed. "I was expecting a small tirade."

Tarkyn smiled at her. "Of course she is. Lady Maud, you have achieved an amazing feat today. No one else amongst us could do it, to walk thirty miles, carrying Sheldrake." His smile broadened. "And in that highhanded way I have, I have sent Marjorie and Jackson off with Sasha and Jayhan to look over the boat and make sure that everything is in readiness to leave at first light tomorrow." He saw Maud sag a little in relief. "I thought you might prefer to dine with just Jon, Stefan, and me when you are so tired and have so much on your mind."

Maud glanced at Sheldrake. "You know, this young man may not be so bad, after all."

"And," continued Tarkyn, "it gives the other two a chance to relax away from people of rank. Woodfolk couldn't care less but other people tend to feel constrained around the nobility." He chuckled. "Besides, it will give Jackson and Marjorie more time to get to know each other."

Before they could react to this little tidbit, a discreet knock on the door heralded the arrival of the innkeeper, a scrawny taciturn man, who took their orders and left again with a promise to return shortly.

Just as Tarkyn had finished filling them in on his journey with the woodfolk on their first carriage ride, two servants brought in beef pie for Maud, a salmon in butter sauce for Tarkyn, and lamb stew for Sheldrake. Jon and Stefan both had steaks smothered in mushroom sauce.

Once they had eaten enough to take it at a more leisurely pace, Tarkyn explained his decision to bring his woodfolk with them and the very real threat of exile that his woodfolk were risking both on the road and on the river.

He glanced at each of them as they ate. "I hope you realise how big a step it is for woodfolk to leave the forest. Except under cover of darkness, none of them has ever left the shelter of the trees, except Rainstorm once, for twenty minutes. Ever."

Maud frowned as she dabbed her mouth with her napkin. "I can't begin to imagine how that must feel. They must be very loyal to you to do it."

Tarkyn rolled his eyes. "Don't bring this back to me. They are not an appendage of mine, and I didn't command them to come. They agreed to come to support Jon and Sasha, to meet the treewrights in Kimora, if possible, and, with a longer view, to prevent Toriana threatening their own woodlands in Eskuzor. It shows their courage and caring, more than loyalty."

"I beg your pardon."

Sheldrake smiled. "Take care, Maud," he said lightly. "Tarkyn thinks the world of his woodfolk."

Tarkyn chuckled. "I do. And with them on our side, we have a much better chance of keeping Sasha and Jon safe."

"I must thank them," said Jon, dabbing away a morsel of mushroom sauce. "Even though they have their own reasons for coming besides our safety." A worried frown creased his brow. "So you think Sasha is safe enough out there? Perhaps I should go and find her?"

Sheldrake leaned across and put a hand on his arm. "I have agents everywhere in Carrador. Two of them were stationed outside this inn, waiting to follow and protect her if she went outside." He sat back. "Besides, I think we covered your own departure well enough, and we kept Sasha carefully hidden until our coach was well away from Highkington. Any assassins will still be looking for her at Batian House at the moment."

Jon gave a small sigh of relief, and the twinkle came back into his eyes. "Oh good. I am not the most assiduous of protectors, try as I might."

Not long afterwards, Tarkyn took his leave, promising to meet them somewhere along the right-hand riverbank in the morning. Stefan debated whether to join him and the woodfolk but couldn't resist the pull of a last night in a comfortable bed. Besides, the woodfolk would need him to be on the boat in the morning to make contact.

Part 6

Chapter 41

The riverboat they had hired was really a bit large for only the six of them to manage, particularly since they had belatedly discovered that none of them had any experience of handling large boats. Maud and Sheldrake had travelled on ships and the occasional boat but always with someone else at the helm. Jackson had rowed small boats as a lad on holidays with his father, but never on his own.

Luckily, the river just below Bridgetown flowed sluggishly and they were able to drift down with the current, using the rudders to keep her to the right-hand side of the river, without the need for oars.

The Woodland Rover was a sturdy wooden boat, thirty feet long, with a small cabin towards the rear, inside which a companionway led down to space belowdecks, where there was a small galley, oarlocks, and benches enough for eight people to row, and spaces that could be used either for passengers or cargo. Her deck curved upward at the bow and stern so that those navigating could see over the cabin from where they held the tiller. One tall mast stood in the middle of the foredeck, rigged with a single square sail that was currently furled along its single horizontal spar. A heavy wooden railing ran all the way around the deck, making it safe for passengers to stroll around.

The river had wound through Bridgetown, past warehouses whose wooden landings thrust into the water, past private boat ramps where stairs wound up to expensive houses and past several public jetties. Finally, the houses had thinned out and they were now drifting past dry brown fields on the Kimoran side and the greenery of the forest in Carrador on their right. Up ahead, they could see the end of the farmland, marking the boundary of the forest that surrounded Bridgetown on all sides.

Stefan stood at the bow railing, peering anxiously ahead at the Carradorian forest. Although it was daylight, the sun had not yet cleared the height of the trees and soft mist hung over the river. He heard a reed warbler chirruping somewhere in the bulrushes and saw moorhens and wood ducks bobbing on the ripples that a light morning breeze had whipped up. He took in a long breath and let it out, surrendering himself to the beauty of his surroundings. He would locate the woodfolk just as well, if not better, if he were calmer.

Then, clear as a bell in his head, he heard Autumn Leaves' voice. *Good morning. Wave if that's you."*

Stefan waved with long arm movements, without being able to see what he was waving at. *Good morning. Can you see me?*

Yes. We are waiting in the trees at the next right-hand curve of the river. There is a small grassy patch crossed by a narrow track that seems to run along the riverbank in both directions. The water looks pretty deep here right up to the edge. Plus, there is a fallen tree you can tie up to.

Stefan grinned. *It sounds perfect. I'll tell the others.*

Jon was watching Stefan's face. "You've made contact then?" he asked.

Stefan nodded and relayed the information from Autumn Leaves.

Marjorie and Jackson, who were manning the tiller, pulled the long wooden handles enthusiastically to the left and almost sent the boat careening headfirst into the right-hand bank at least a hundred yards too early.

"Oops," chortled Jackson as they corrected their pressure on the tiller. "More sensitive than I would have expected."

In the hands of inexperienced sailors, the boat wove a drunken path towards the appointed bend in the river. Sasha and Jayhan leant on the railings, giggling at every change in direction. Luckily, no other boats were out so early in the morning so the novice sailors could get the hang of the steering without colliding into anyone.

"How are we going to stop?" asked Marjorie, as they neared the rendezvous point.

"No idea," said Jackson blithely. "Just hit the bank? I don't know how to slow her down. The current is pulling us along."

Stefan peered over the bow of the boat. "Her planks look pretty strong. Should be all right if we hit at a bit of an angle and the bank is soft." *Is the bank soft? We don't know how to stop so we're just going to hit the bank.*

After a hurried discussion, Rainstorm replied. *Tarkyn says to throw the end of fore painter into the air.*

Painter?

Another hurried consultation. *Rope.*

Stefan relayed this to Sheldrake who looked puzzled but shrugged.

"Go ahead. I'll make sure the other end is firmly connected to our boat," he suggested.

Stefan checked that one end of the rope was tied to a ring secured to the foredeck then threw the loose end of the coiled rope into the air.

As soon as it was airborne, a ray of bronze light streaked out and the rope was pulled through the air towards Tarkyn, who was now visible standing on the edge of the bank just before the bend in the river. As soon as he had it in his grasp, he handed it to Waterstone who ran with it to the fallen tree, tying it securely. Then the woodfolk began hauling the rope in and looping it around the log.

"Good plan," said Sheldrake approvingly. "Jackson, get that other rope ready, the one at the rear and we'll send that over to them as we get nearer."

See what we're doing? asked Stefan. *Ask Tarkyn to be ready.*

A short period of highly stressed activity ensued: Marjorie and Jackson at the tiller, Tarkyn summoning the next rope through the air from much further away than anyone could have thrown them, woodfolk pulling on each of the ropes, and Stefan issuing updates on the riverboat's position from his position at the bow. Then, to everyone's amazement, the old riverboat glided neatly in alongside the bank and came to a gentle halt.

There was a collective sigh of relief.

Rainstorm surveyed The Woodland Rover with a rapt expression. "Wow," he breathed, "I can't believe we are going to ride on this beautiful boat. Look at the bevelling on the railings, the beautiful, smooth finish on decking. Look at the craftmanship in curving and fitting those long planks together, so exactly that the water is kept out. Amazing."

"Come aboard," invited Sheldrake. "No other boats are in sight, but you never know when one will round the bend. There is room below the deck for hiding and sleeping."

"And rowing," added Jackson, "If we need extra speed or extra steering through rough sections of the river."

Waterstone jumped up nimbly, grabbed the railing and swung himself up and over onto the fore deck to stand beside Stefan. "Let's have a look around then." He turned back to the rest of the woodfolk who were standing uncertainly on the bank. "Come on. Up you come. This is much better than the carriage. No horses for a start, and you can walk around."

In one of those instantaneous decisions, the woodfolk suddenly appeared on the foredeck, clustered around Stefan. Tarkyn, left standing alone on the shore, put his hands on his hips, and said sarcastically, "Don't worry. I'll be fine. I'll untie the ropes, shall I, before I hop on, as the boat drifts away?"

Lapping Water chuckled, "Sorry, Tarkyn. Yes, that would be good, if you could." She grinned. "I'll keep hold of Gurgling Brook for you, will I?"

Faced with this tacit reminder that she had been solely parenting their child over a large part of the last few weeks, he accepted the inevitable and began to untie the fore painter while the woodfolk explored the boat. As soon as both ropes were free, The Woodland Rover began to drift away from the bank, quickly caught by a current leading her into the middle of the river.

Tarkyn was left standing with the end of the rope in his hand, knowing that he would soon be pulled into the water if he kept hold of it. As the gap of water between the boat and the bank widened, he took a running jump, muttered *"Ma Liefka"* and rose gracefully into the air. He levitated himself until he was over the deck of the Woodland Rover, then lowered himself neatly onto the aft deck to stand beside Marjorie and Jackson, who were manning the tiller.

Jackson grinned at him. "Good trick."

"Thanks. Just as well I had it up my sleeve or I would be swimming to catch up by now."

Sasha and Jayhan rushed up to him, their eyes shining.

"That was great," enthused Sasha. "You're very lucky, aren't you, to have so many good tricks?"

Tarkyn raised his eyebrows then smiled. "Yes, I suppose I am."

"Oh yes," said Jayhan. "Very lucky."

"Lord Tarkyn, you never cease to amaze me," exclaimed Sheldrake walking down the boat to join them. "I considered myself a mage of some skill until I met you."

"You probably are," said Tarkyn. "My powers are nearly all innate. Little skill or study involved. Stormaway, my wizard, has taught me a few things, but mostly I just use instinct, not training. You, on the other hand, are very learned in the use of concoctions and spells, especially spells you can set and leave, like your border barrier or your light orb. Different field altogether… and one in which I have little knowledge."

Maud joined them and smiled warmly at him. "I'm glad you said that. Sheldrake has become quite despondent in the face of your extensive powers, powers that you use adeptly, frequently, and quite casually."

"I wouldn't worry," said Rainstorm, strolling up in time to hear the end of the conversation. "You get used to him after a while and he never misuses them."

"What do you think of the..." Suddenly Maud was talking to thin air.

Sasha and Jayhan nodded at each other. "They have good tricks too," said Sasha.

Tarkyn grinned and pointed ahead to where the nose of another boat had just appeared around the next bend. "They're all hiding below deck, I expect."

Maud shook her head. "My goodness, they're quick. I hope we don't pass too many boats, or they'll be spending a lot of time below decks." She looked out at the surface of water rippling away from the boat's passage. "How fast do you think we are travelling?"

"I don't know," replied Tarkyn. "Jackson?"

"A river's pace varies from about one to seven miles per hour." Jackson smiled at the bemused look on Tarkyn's face. "My mother's a librarian, remember? We picked up lots of random facts from her." He looked back at their wake. "Hmm. I'd say we are travelling at two, maybe three, miles an hour at the moment. We've picked up speed a bit now that we're out in the middle of the river."

"How far do we have to go? And how long do we have to get there?" asked Maud.

"Stefan estimated about a hundred and twenty miles to reach the point where The Way Through meets the river," said Jon, "which is where the Kimoran guardhouse is situated, complete with boats to cross and possibly troops to intercept us."

Jackson and Marjorie pulled the tiller a little to starboard as the river began a left-hand curve.

Maud stared out across the water as she thought about it, watching the trees drift by. A pair of ducks bobbed past on the port side. Then she turned to Jackson with an air of decision. "We will have to be careful. Is it even worth the risk? Should we abandon this boat before we pass the guardhouse?" She turned to Tarkyn. "What do you think? The greatest danger is to your woodfolk and, of course, Sasha and Jon. "

Tarkyn gave a faint smile. "Either you or Bird or local wildlife can reconnoitre before we commit ourselves to passing the guardhouse. As long as the Kimorans are not in the middle of staging an invasion, which is unlikely, there probably won't be more than one or two guards stationed there. Wait and see."

Maud looked across the river at the dark knot of dried, tangled foliage that skirted the edge of the forest. "It would certainly be easier than walking through those forests where there are no trails and much safer than travelling cross-country in Kimora." She nodded decisively. "We'll stick with the boat if we can."

As they finished speaking, the boat that had poked its nose around the corner now drew near. It was a heavily laden, green and white barge, pulled by a large chestnut mare that trudged along the narrow towpath. The bargeman, sturdy and middle-aged with a cheery kerchief tied around his neck, stood at the tiller.

He touched his fingers to his broad-brimmed hat as he neared them. "Lovely morning, in't it?" he called.

Maud rushed to the fore deck with Sasha and Jayhan trailing behind her. While they waved at the man, she asked, "Good morning. How far is it to the rapids? We are new to this river, you know."

The man took off his hat and scratched his head, as his barge came up parallel with The Woodland Rover. "Ooh, not yet awhile. Maybe three days' travel, I'd say."

Maud began to walk slowly aft to keep level with him. "Does that include travelling at night?"

"Ooh no. I never travels at night. Only myself, y'know. Have to sleep sometime." He nodded at the horse. "So does Daffodil."

"So, if we keep going all night, we might get there tomorrow evening?"

"Hmm. Hard to say. Sounds about right but never done it that fast m'self. As I say, I sleeps at night."

"Thank you," called Maud, waving as the barge began to draw away. The bargeman waved back and turned his face towards Bridgetown.

Chapter 42

For a while they drifted down the river peacefully. When they rounded the bend, a long straight section of river, devoid of boats, came into view and the woodfolk reappeared on deck.

Sometime later, Tarkyn was leaning against the starboard railing, watching in vain for any sign of the local woodfolk in the forest they were drifting past, when he felt a slight pressure on his leg. He looked down to see Midnight's vivid green eyes gazing up at him from under his mop of dark brown hair. His small fingers gripped the material of Tarkyn's leggings, transmitting his tension.

Tarkyn's face broke into a smile as he reached down and picked the boy up. "Hello, rascal," he said, matching images to words, "All a bit new and exciting, isn't it?" He saw Jackson and Marjorie watching him and turned so that Midnight could see them. "Look. Here are Marjorie and Jackson. Remember them? They were at the battle to save Sasha and Jayhan."

Midnight wrapped his two hands around each other and smiled a little tentatively at them. Tarkyn nodded encouragingly until they both copied the gesture, smiling. Midnight's smile broadened and he glanced up at Tarkyn as if to say, "You're right. They are friends."

Jackson gestured at the tiller and then at Midnight, with a query on his face. Midnight considered him for a moment but then, in a convulsive movement, threw himself out of Tarkyn's arms towards the tiller. Tarkyn kept hold of him long enough to land him safely upright.

"Menace," he said mildly. He smiled at Jackson. "That should keep him busy for a while. Thanks."

Marjorie watched him for a while, noting his dark hair and brilliant green eyes. She frowned. "Why is Midnight's colouring so much darker than the other woodfolk? Is he from a different region?"

"No," said Tarkyn, wandering over and stroking the little boys' hair as he stood stalwartly at the tiller. Midnight glanced up at him and gave him a quick smile before returning his gaze to the river. "His father was a powerful wizard, and his mother is a woodwoman."

"Goodness. So why is she not looking after him?" asked Marjorie then reddened slightly, "If you don't mind telling me, that is."

"She is a wandering trapper and did not choose to have a child." Tarkyn let the implications of that sink in, before he continued, "It took some time for the mountainfolk to accept him."

"Seven years, in fact," said Rainstorm. "He had a very tough early life. Woodfolk are not usually so unkind but there was sorcery involved, which Tarkyn had to dismantle."

"Fascinating," said Sheldrake, before realising that Tarkyn's colour had heightened, and he was directing a fulminating glare at Rainstorm. "I would love to hear the technical aspects of it, but perhaps at some other time."

Tarkyn gave a slight nod before steering the talk away from his achievements. "Anyway, I have loved Midnight and looked after him almost from the moment I met him." Suddenly he grinned. "He leads me on a merry dance, I can tell you. One does not usually become a model of virtue from a background like that. He has tested my trustworthiness over and over again… And of course, he is naturally mischievous, aren't you, rascal?"

Midnight beamed up at him, clearly receiving some fond images.

"And he saved your life," said Lapping Water, joining them with Gurgling Brook.

"And he's a forest guardian, like Tarkyn." Realising that Midnight was tensing up under the glare of so much attention, Rainstorm squatted in front of him and smiled reassuringly. "It's all right, my little friend. We are all your friends here."

As Tarkyn put a steadying hand on Midnight's back, everyone but Jackson and Marjorie, who were manning the tiller, subtly moved back from him to keep from crowding him.

"What would he have done?" asked Jackson quietly.

"Run away," chorused Rainstorm and Tarkyn.

"He has very rarely hurt anyone, but he runs or flicks away and then can be hard to find." Lapping Water gestured to the shoreline. "If he flicked into the forest, he would hold us up, while we looked for him." She smiled. "Besides, we don't want to upset him. His old fear of people can overwhelm him sometimes and we don't want that."

Stefan, standing to one side, for the moment forgotten, watched the interplay around Midnight and noted the woodfolk's depth of understanding and experience, far greater than he had assumed when he first met them. Once more, he berated himself for underestimating them on the basis of their apparently simpler way of life.

The day passed peacefully. They made sure someone was always in the bows keeping an eye out for submerged logs or sand bars and so far, their trip had been uneventful.

As dusk approached, Stefan and Jon stood with Lapping Water on the starboard railing, watching the sun setting behind the Carradorian forest. The woodwoman held Gurgling Brook in front of her, letting her feet swing over the railing. Next to them, Jayhan and Sasha were trailing thin branches in the water, watching the patterns they made.

Gazing out at the passing river, a thought struck Stefan. "If Midnight and, for that matter, Gurgling Brook, are half sorcerer and half woodfolk, do they still have to hide from outsiders?"

"They do at the moment. But Stormaway Treemaster is also half woodman, half wizard while Tarkyn and his friend Danton are both sorcerers and honorary woodfolk. All three of them live among both outsiders and woodfolk at different times."

Jon interrupted. "Is that Danton, Prince Consort of Eskuzor?"

"Yes," replied Lapping Water casually, reinforcing Stefan's view that woodfolk were more sophisticated that he had thought. She smiled at his expression and added, "What's more, while Danton and Navira do not yet have children, Gurgling Brook is actually first in line to the throne, since Tarkyn wishes to remain aloof from Eskuzor's line of succession." She placed her chin on the little girl's head. "And here she is, being brought up as a woodwoman, hidden from the world."

"Goodness!" exclaimed Jon. "She's actually a princess."

Lapping Water's eyes narrowed. "Don't you dare give her a title in my hearing. It is not our way."

"No ma'am," said Jon, grinning at her.

Stefan's reappraisal of the woodfolk continued, "I am beginning to think that a child could have no better grounding in understanding the world around them and their fellow man." He saw Marjorie scowling at him and added hastily, "Although my childhood was also filled with joy, love and hmm… learning how to clear tables, pour ale, and serve dinners." Then he grinned and she grinned back.

"Just got out of that one," Jon murmured to him.

Lapping Water did not miss this interchange and was just smiling to herself when Jayhan's voice piped up from her other side, "No. I don't think clearing tables and serving meals would be as much fun as learning to shoot arrows and climb trees. What do you reckon, Sasha?"

"Definitely not," said Sasha firmly, suppressing a grin. She distracted herself from bursting into laughter by pointing out a white-faced grey heron that had just taken off from a dead tree on the edge of the river. "Look, Gurgling Brook."

"Bird," pronounced Gurgling Brook. "Heron bird. Flying."

The grey bird flapped its wings with stately grace to soar over their boat, almost buzzing Tarkyn where he stood in the bow, before gliding to a new perch on the other side of the river.

Lapping Water gave a wry smile. "Huh. Just curious. Wanted to meet the forest guardian."

Gurgling Brook turned to Stefan and said seriously, "Bird is gone," and turned both her hands outwards to demonstrate.

Stefan smiled. "Yes. It's flown over to the other side of the river."

"Bird gone," repeated Gurgling Brook.

"Yes, the heron has gone," said Jon in a serious tone of voice but laughing with his eyes at Stefan whose faintly creased brow betrayed his fear of an ongoing repetition.

Luckily, Lapping Water was aware that other people could not endure the same circular interchange that she could as the little girl's mother. She lifted Gurgling Brook off the railing and put her down on the deck. Giving her a gentle shove in the back, she said. "Now, off you go and chat to your father. I'm sure he's dying to talk to you about herons."

Completely missing the irony in this remark, Gurgling Brook toddled off enthusiastically, to regale Tarkyn with the wonders of a disappearing heron.

Chapter 43

All that first day on the river and all through the night, The Woodland Rover floated gently down river, the current taking her past snags and sandbars with little intervention from the rudders. Considering the level of expertise on board, this was just as well.

During the long peaceful night down the river, Autumn Leave and Waterstone alternated with Rainstorm and Lapping Water at the tiller. From time to time they passed moored river-boats, huddled shapes nestled against the banks or almost concealed beneath trailing foliage, sometimes lit by a dim lantern, but no one was stirring so they could remain undiscovered in full view of the boats they passed.

The sky was greying, and the stars were beginning to dim when Stefan trod softly up the companionway onto the deck. A moment later, Sparrow appeared behind him.

He stretched, lifting his hands above his head, then walked aft to join Autumn Leaves and Waterstone. "Good morning," he said softly. He gazed at the starlight reflected in the inky waters and further afield to the dark shape of the forest against the sky. The moon was just setting behind the trees to their right. Patches of mist were hanging low over the river. He breathed out slowly. "Oh, this is beautiful, isn't it?"

Sparrow walked over the Waterstone who put his arm around her. "Morning, Dad." She pulled back a bit to look him in the face. "You're freezing."

He gave a shudder. "Now you mention it, I am. It was quite balmy when we first came out here, but I think the temperature has gradually dropped as the dawn approached and I've turned into an icicle."

"Just a minute," she said and went below to reappear with cloaks for all four of them. "Here."

"Thanks, Sparrow," Waterstone regarded her quizzically. "So you two aren't here to take your turn at the tiller?"

"Oh, happy to do that. In fact, love to." Sparrow's eyes twinkled up at him. "But I just assumed you two wouldn't want to miss watching the sun come up over the river, since you're already awake."

"Absolutely true." Autumn Leaves chuckled. "A joy Tarkyn rarely experiences."

"Just a minute," said Stefan suddenly and disappeared down the companionway.

"Oh, yes. Back in a minute," said Sparrow, following him.

Autumn Leaves and Waterstone frowned, gave puzzled smiles, then shrugged and re-turned their attention to the river.

A few minutes later, Stefan and Sparrow returned more slowly, each carrying two cups of tea. Sasha followed them, bringing a cup of tea and a cloak for herself.

"Sasha's idea," said Sparrow. "She's been watching the kettle boil and brewing the tea."

Stefan beamed at them as he handed them their tea. "Here. Interesting little metal stove they have down there. Mounted on sand and bricks so none of the wooden planking catches alight. We only made a small fire and Lapping Water is stirring with Gurgling Brook now, so she can keep an eye on it."

"What a brilliant start to the day," exclaimed Autumn Leaves. As he took the tea, he nodded to the port side. "And look! The sky is just starting to turn gold."

Sasha gazed at the breaking dawn. "I love to be up for the sunrise," she said quietly. She glanced uncertainly at Waterstone. "I hope you don't mind me joining you. I don't really belong." When Waterstone frowned at her in concern, she gave a lop-sided smile, "I don't really belong anywhere, not with Jayhan's family that I have to leave, not with woodfolk, not with Kimorans whose way of life I have only heard about. Not anywhere." She heaved a sigh and leant on the railings, holding her hands around the mug to warm them, and returning her gaze to the lightening sky above Kimora.

A minute later, she felt an arm across her shoulder and Waterstone's face came into view beside her. "You are welcome to be with us."

He let silence fall as they watched the rims of clouds darken to orange and the tops of the trees light up with the first rays of the sun. Then he said, "I could say you have Jon, but you are both adrift at the moment, aren't you? Besides, I suspect that when you have been brought up in an orphanage, your feeling of not belonging anywhere will never really leave you, deep down inside." He gave her shoulder a squeeze. "All I can say is that you belong to yourself, as we all do. Be true to yourself and find your place of belonging within yourself. Then wherever you are, you will be where you belong."

Sasha let out a long, calm breath and leant her head against his arm. "Thank you."

Chapter 44

Life on the river moved at a leisurely pace, and the moored riverboats were still shuttered, showing no sign of moving until the sun was well established in the morning sky. So, the woodfolk were able to spend long periods of the morning undisturbed on deck. However, as they neared the township, named unimaginatively The Rapids in the late afternoon, river traffic became more common and the woodfolk spent more of their time below decks.

Even so, Stefan found that he was spending more of his time with the woodfolk than with the outsiders, amongst whom he had been raised. He was also drawn to Tarkyn who, like himself, belonged to both worlds. In the late afternoon, he joined him at the foredeck railing where the forest guardian was frowning at the increased speed of the river.

Tarkyn glanced at him as he arrived. "I hope we can get through these rapids unscathed. Look down there. You can see, *feel,* the pull of the water."

He pointed to the water closer to the banks, where twigs and leaves were being swept along with the increasing current. A pair of ducks were playing by letting themselves be dragged downstream then turning and swimming hard upstream for a few minutes before letting themselves be swept downstream again.

"It's all right for them," he said caustically. "They can take off and fly any time it gets too worrying for them. But once that current drags us into the rapids, we have no way out but down the river." Tarkyn shook his head distractedly. "I don't like this. I don't like not being in control. I doubt that we could pull over to the bank even now if we wanted to."

"Where's your eagle?" asked Stefan, realising a practical response would be more useful than reassurances. "Could you ask her to circle over the rapids and at least show you what we are facing?"

"Huh. Good idea. I've been too busy quietly panicking to think. She's off hunting somewhere to our left. Just a minute. I'll ask her."

For a few minutes they stood in silence. Then Tarkyn said, "Look. There she is." The big eagle flew in above the trees and circled over him. After a minute, she flapped her great wings and headed downstream. "Right. She is heading towards the rapids. I'll share the images with you." He gave a tight smile. "You'd better hang onto the railing."

Stefan noticed that Tarkyn was too preoccupied to ask his permission as he normally would but saw no point in commenting on it. He grasped the railing firmly and closed his eyes.

Immediately he saw, far below him, The Woodland Rover with Tarkyn and himself standing at the railing. Then his vision swept around to the water gathering force further down the river. In the distance, he could see a point where the river narrowed between rocky outcrops on either side and then disappeared over the horizon. His stomach clenched in fear. Their information was right, wasn't it? There were only rapids on the river, weren't there? Not a waterfall?

Beside him, he felt the railing move slightly and realised that Tarkyn had gripped it more tightly. At the forest guardian's urging, Bird swept higher into the air and downstream until she could view the river beyond the rocks. The water was white with turbulence, churning in on itself as it thrust through the narrowed opening. Although clouds of spray partly obscured the eagle's view, they caught sight of patches of water rushing chaotically, sweeping from side to side, over and around inconsistencies in the slope of the river for more than three hundred yards.

But it was not a waterfall.

Tarkyn and Stefan blew out simultaneous breaths of relief, opened their eyes and laughed at each other.

"Still rough though," said Stefan, once the moment had passed.

"Yes. I hope this old tub is up to the job. I wonder if boats without competent crew manage to get through. I wonder if they asked that question when they hired her." Tarkyn straightened. "Let's find out. Where's Jackson.?"

Before they could even start walking down the deck, Jackson appeared from behind the cabin, smiling cheerfully. "Did I hear my name? What can I do for you, Sire?"

"When you hired this boat, were they aware that none of us were sailors and that we intended to go through the rapids?"

Their worried expressions brought Jackson up short. "Uh. Getting close, are we? Is it bad?"

Stefan and Tarkyn glanced at each other.

"Pretty bad," said Stefan shortly.

"I think it would tax the skills of an experienced riverman, one of whom we do not have on board," said Tarkyn drily.

"Hmm. Do I detect a note of censure in your tone, Sire?" Jackson waved his hand dismissively. "Don't worry. I thought of that... But then I thought, we have two sorcerers and a mage on board. Well, I'm not too strong a sorcerer, except for shields, but you more than make up for it, and Sheldrake is highly acclaimed, I gather." He shrugged. "And given we couldn't have a stranger on board with the woodfolk, I figured we'd find a way to manage somehow."

Tarkyn glared at him. "And exactly what were you thinking I might be able to do to get us through a chute of churning water between boulders? Lift the boat?" When Jackson looked as though he were about to nod, Tarkyn gave a derisive grunt of laughter. "I appreciate your faith in me, but in this case, it is sadly misguided. I can lift one, maybe two, people or lift a small object like a rope, but a large boat full of people? Not a hope in the world. I couldn't even nudge it sideways."

"Oh." Jackson looked non plussed, but recovered enough to say, "Maybe Sheldrake...?"

"Maybe Sheldrake what?" asked the mage in question, walking over to join them at the fore railing.

"… will have a trick or two up his sleeve to guide us through the quickly approaching rapids," said Tarkyn drily.

Sheldrake peered across at the bank and frowned. "Hmm. We've picked up speed, haven't we?" He brought his eyes up to face Tarkyn. "In my travels, I have had some experience of boats and rivers, but little of rapids. I have read widely, however. What were you thinking I could do?"

Tarkyn gestured towards Jackson. "Oh, not me. Our friend here thought that our magic could somehow bring us unscathed through the rapids. He was a little shocked when I told him I couldn't lift boats."

Sheldrake chuckled. He looked up ahead, saw the line where the river disappeared from sight and then noted Tarkyn's eagle circling about a mile ahead. "Could you describe what we are about to face, please?" Tarkyn did so then Sheldrake studied their speed and the distance ahead to the start of the rapids. "I'd say we have about twenty minutes before we reach it. So, let's plan."

"Can you do anything?" asked Tarkyn. "I can save myself. But what about my family and my friends whom I have dragged into danger?"

Sheldrake smiled reassuringly at the younger man. He was tempted to pat him on the shoulder but on balance decided he had better not. "Your woodfolk can flick away, can't they, if they need to? But the rest of us will have more trouble, I think. However, I can assure you that we will find a way. Now, what is the worst that could happen?"

"The boat capsizes. We all fall out, hit our heads on the rocks and drown," replied Jackson promptly.

Maud, in her inimitable fashion joined in the conversation as though she had heard it all, which she possibly had. Lacking Sheldrake's sense of nicety, she walked up and put her arm around Tarkyn's shoulders. "Now young man. You are not responsible for everyone. We are all adults together, with equal responsibility for ourselves and the children." When Tarkyn made to protest, she overrode him. "Now, it seems to me that this sturdy old boat will have been through these rapids countless times, but," she held up a hand to forestall interruptions, "presumably in more experienced hands."

"We'd better make sure the fire in the galley is out," said Stefan suddenly. "We'll have to tie down everything that could move and make sure everyone has something to hold onto. I'll tell the woodfolk, who can relay to Marjorie."

Maud nodded her approval. "Good thought, Stefan."

Tarkyn frowned, trying to work out a way through. "I wish we could see the course we must travel better. Bird could only show us patches through the spray."

"I can help you with that," said Maud decisively. She nodded at the painter coiled on the deck nearby. "Stefan, bring the end of that rope over here and I'll tie it around my waist. Then make sure you keep the other end secure. I think it's attached to that ring, but just make sure."

"Maaauud?" The way Sheldrake drew her name out said that he knew she was about to do something rash.

Maud smiled. "Yes, dear?" She pulled the knot tight that held the rope around her waist, then swung her legs over the railing and jumped before anyone could react. Before she touched the water, she had transformed herself into a sleek, grey, well-fed seal.

Moments later she shot up out of the water. Even on her furry seal's face, they could see the shock.

Sheldrake chuckled. "Cold is it. my dear?" he managed to say, before gravity pulled her back into the water.

Two minutes later, she surfaced again further off the starboard bow, her liquid brown eyes twinkling with mischief.

"She's heading down river to the rapids," reported Tarkyn. "Oh dear. I didn't mean her to put herself in danger just to chart our course."

Sheldrake gave an amused grimace. "You didn't make her. She loves a bit of adventure. No one at court would even know she is anything but a lady of fashion, but she is a fearless tearaway. She gives me sleepless nights sometimes."

Beneath the surface of the water, Maud was revelling in feeling the water play around her new body, diving and twisting in the water, thrusting herself forward at great speed with her flippers. All the time, she worked her way downstream past waving forests of river grass and soft multi-coloured small-leaved plants. Now and then she would catch sight of a fish darting among the shadows and once or twice let herself become distracted by chasing them. With great glee, she caught a good-sized bream and surfaced briefly to chomp it down before heading on her way.

She could feel herself being swept along by the current, more and more strongly as she neared the rapids. From time to time, she corkscrewed and headed back upstream just to check she could, before relinquishing herself once more to the current. Bubbles appeared in the water around her and then she saw the first rocks. Instead of sand and mud, big boulders and rock walls lined the river on either side of her. Soon the bubbles made it harder for her to see, so she surfaced and turned her head from side to side, calculating distances, studying and trying to memorize the deepest channel between the rocks. Then she dived again to come up a little further down.

Once the water began to calm, she turned upstream and began to swim against the current. It was hard. The current through the rapids was strong. She was able to make headway, but the going was slow, and she began to tire. She spotted a rocky ledge jutting out on the Carradorian side of the river and dragged herself onto it, gasping for breath. She watched the frothing water gush over hidden rocks and was nearly deafened by its roar. She loved it though.

Well, she thought to herself, *if salmon can swim upstream up rapids and waterfalls, so can I.*

With another deep breath, she launched herself into the water and forged her way up the last hundred yards of the rapids. The swim upstream in the broader river was no hardship at all after the ferocious drag of the rapids. She cavorted, diving and twisting, coming up for air from time to time. As she came closer, she shot herself up into the air as far as she could before twisting to swim alongside the boat, looking up at them expectantly.

"Ah," said Sheldrake, used to his wife's forays into other shapes. "No rope. Hmm. As a human, she has a waistline, but as a seal, it slipped off her as soon as she dived."

Sheldrake, Jackson, and Stefan all turned to Tarkyn, who grinned. "I don't know what you lot would do without me." He leant over the railing and pointed at Maud. *"Ka Liefka."*

A streak of bronze magic lifted her into the air and over the railing, plopping her onto the foredeck.

Tarkyn look down at her. "I hope that is what you wanted, Maud. If you were thinking of swimming the rapids again beside the boat, I can always send you back into the water."

This was not, however, her intention. Tarkyn relayed a message from her, which prompted Midnight to appear up the companionway, waving a towel. Maud transformed back into her human form, which was clothed in dry clothes. However, her hair and what they could see of her skin was wet.

She shuddered as she sat down on a coil of rope "No thanks. That was colder than I expected, even as a seal."

"Had a lot of experience as a seal, have you?" asked Jackson.

"No, as it turns out. That was my first time. I did become used to the cold, but now that I'm out, the cold has hit me."

Tarkyn gave a puzzled frown. "How come you wear clothes as a woman, but they disappear when you're in other forms?"

Maud ruffled Midnight's hair in thanks as she answered, "Because the other forms are constructions, but I return to myself as I was." She smiled ruefully. "Actually, I don't know why, but I'm glad that's how it works except this time I am wet under my gown, which is not pleasant. I can also change size. The horse and panther I can become, are bigger than me…" she gave Tarkyn a cheeky grin, "while a cat is much smaller. The smallest creature I've transformed into is a flea. That was to escape someone. *Very* uncomfortable for a few moments. Like trying to cram yourself into a dress that is three sizes too small."

"Maud is a very strong shape-shifter," said Sheldrake with a hint of pride. "Our son also has the ability, but not to the same extent. He can only become other people, much to his disappointment."

Waterstone emerged from the companionway, bearing a steaming cup of tea. "Here. This might help. So, what did you find out?" he asked, bringing them back to the task at hand. "Just asking, because we are definitely picking up speed."

"Thank you," said Maud. "Just what I need." Without pause, she continued, "The rapids are deep all the way through, deep enough for this vessel if you keep her to the centre of the channel. The force of the water may try to push you into boulders, but I think you can use your rudders to steer clear." She blew on her tea and took a cautious sip. "I put some time into memorising the passage, so I should be able to talk you through it. It will be rushed in spots."

"It's a shame you can't transmit images as we can," said Waterstone. "Then those steering the boat could visualize what is coming up."

Tarkyn glanced appraisingly at Waterstone as he made this seemingly casual remark, then transferred his gaze to Maud.

Maud pretended not to notice for a minute, burying her head in her cup of tea, enjoying its warmth. Then she raised her head and smiled at them. "Yes. I can see you two have worked together for a long time. To save you the bother of cajoling me, I will agree to change back into a seal until we get through the rapids. Then, as an animal, I can transmit images to

Tarkyn who can send them through to all the woodfolk. You can throw the towel around my seal form to keep me warm while I do it. I will sit up here on the foredeck and match images of what lies below the water with what we see on the surface as we go through."

Waterstone grinned. "Maud, you're a gem!" From then on, he took over. "We'll have two woodfolk on each tiller in case they need extra strength against the current: Autumn Leaves and Sparrow on the starboard tiller, Lapping Water and Rainstorm on the port side. Marjorie and Jackson, could you mind the kids please? Keep them and Jon below. We don't want to risk any of them getting washed overboard. Maud, can you understand what we say while you're a seal, or does Tarkyn have to translate that too?"

"I can understand. I just can't speak."

"Good to know." Waterstone nodded. "So I'll stand up next to Maud in case we need to ask questions. Tarkyn, all you need to do is transmit Maud's images and we'll do the rest… if that's all right with everyone."

Leaning on the railing watching all the efficiently organised bustle going on around him, Sheldrake frowned. "Tarkyn, why is Waterstone, rather than you, asking the questions? You're the one with the direct line to Maud's thoughts."

Tarkyn smiled. "Because the woodfolk can talk to each other in words while I can only receive images. So if the people on the tiller have a question, they can use words to ask instead of trying to find a way to tell me using images. Besides, they know I have a terrible sense of direction. So, I could get confused when matching underwater with surface images. If time is of the essence, it is better to use someone who is good and quick with directions." In answer to an unspoken question, he added, "And it is the woodfolk way for the most competent in a situation to direct it and I don't override woodfolk custom without a good reason."

"Is everyone ready?" asked Waterstone.

With a sigh, Maud drank the last of her tea, handed the cup to Midnight, and changed back between one breath and the next into her grey, sleek seal form, still damp despite the towel. Waterstone, Stefan and Tarkyn sat down beside her so that they didn't block the view of those on the tiller. Midnight wrapped the towel around Maud and had a quick exchange of images with her, which decided that one towel was enough for now.

Minutes later, they passed the first of the boulders and felt the boat surge forward into the gap.

The next few minutes were uncanny for Sheldrake, Jackson, and Marjorie. No one spoke out loud and yet the people on the tiller responded instantly and in concert with each other, steering the boat away from oncoming rocks before they came in range of them and riding the racing current in a controlled zigzag between the rock walls. The boat plunged and bucked, swinging over onto one side then the other. But no part of her hit a rock.

Then, in a final rush, they were through.

The river widened into calm water and in the distance, they could see the houses and jetties of The Rapids township.

Amid the released tension, Tarkyn turned to Jackson and said drily, "So, in the end, you were right, Jackson. We did use magic to get us through."

Jackson blew out a long breath. "Yes, we did, but nothing like I expected."

Chapter 45

Well before they drifted too close to The Rapids, they brought The Woodland Rover up to the Kimoran bank of the river where the woodfolk could flick off the boat into the cover of the trees. They could have stayed onboard while the others disembarked in the town, but they were worried that some official might want to come on board. Besides which, they were pleased to have the chance to stretch their legs and meet the boat downstream of The Rapids later in the evening.

After listening to their reasoning. Jon belatedly decided to join them. After all, Jon and Sasha were not yet ready to make themselves known to Kimorans and both children were going stir-crazy with the need for exercise. Maud and Sheldrake felt confident that the woodfolk could protect them and were willing to let Jayhan go with them.

Tarkyn and Stefan who planned to stay on board with the other four, sent mindmessages to the woodfolk that Jon, Jayhan, and Sasha were on their way to them.

Tarkyn gave a grunt of laughter. "This will annoy them, not that they'll be rude enough to show it. Woodfolk can travel more quickly and silently on their own. Still, they did agree to help."

Rainstorm, Sparrow, and Midnight were waiting just inside the tree line as Jon and the two children scrambled up the bank. They did not look at all irritated. In fact, Midnight looked excited to be helping the children.

"I thought it was a bit dangerous for you two to go anywhere near a Kimoran town," said Rainstorm cheerily. "Much better for you to avoid towns for now."

"But try to be as quiet as you can. Better silence than speed." Sparrow watched a few pebbles roll off down the bank. "And we'll have to disguise your tracks as much as possible. Midnight will help." Suddenly she realised that Sasha had stopped dead and was looking around herself in wonder. Sparrow waited a moment then said to her. "This is your first time in Kimora, isn't it, since you were a tiny baby. Are you excited?"

Sasha let out a long breath. "Oh. Much more than that. I feel like I've come home." Now they had all stopped and were watching her. "I can feel the forests stretching along the river and out to the plains beyond." She bent down and ran her hand over the dry, dusty earth beneath the trees' canopy. "But I can also feel the wrongness in it. The land is shrivelling up, dying." When she looked up, she had tears in her eyes.

"Refugees have spoken of a drought," said Jon gently, studying the forest around them. "The forests here are similar to those in Carrador, but you're right, they are much drier."

"It doesn't feel anything like Carrador," said Sasha firmly, as she straightened up.

Jon looked askance at her but merely said, "You'll find an even greater difference when you get out onto the plains and into the cities. ... and up into the Darkstone mountains." He added as an afterthought, "You don't get mountains like them in Carrador." A note of pride had entered his voice.

"Have you missed it?" asked Rainstorm quietly as they started forward again, threading their way through the trees. He heard a sniff behind him and turned to see Jon's eyes shiny with tears.

"More than you could ever imagine."

Sasha smiled at him and took his hand as they walked.

Jayhan noticed but decided it was not his business, so he skirted around them to catch up with Sparrow. "It'll be getting dark soon. Did you know I can see in the dark with my eyes?"

Sparrow glanced at him. "That's pretty handy."

He skipped a few steps, smiling proudly. "I know. So I can help to guide everyone if we are walking in the dark."

She grinned at him, not letting on that woodfolk could also see in the dark. "I'll let the others know. I'm sure they'll be pleased."

They made their way up a long, wooded hill, halting every few minutes as Rainstorm and Sparrow listened to advice from the other woodfolk, who were mostly travelling through the treetops, on the best route forward. As they crested the rise, they could see the township of The Rapids in the distance, scattered down the slopes towards the river, lantern light glowing from streetlamps and houses.

Sasha drew in a breath. "Oh, it's pretty, isn't it?"

"It is from here," said Rainstorm dryly. "Who knows what it's like up close. Come on. We have to get past it before we stop for dinner."

Sasha did not move. After a moment she said, "Couldn't we just get up a little closer first? It's the first Kimoran town I've ever seen. I suppose Bridgetown had a few Kimoran boatmen and travellers but it's really Carradorian, is it?"

"Oh, definitely," agreed Jayhan. He turned to Rainstorm and Sparrow. "Come on. Could we? Pleeease?"

"I, too, would like to see it up closer," said Jon quietly. "I haven't been back to Kimora since I was twelve."

Rainstorm and Sparrow looked at each other for a couple of minutes, clearly engaged in a mental debate.

Aloud Sparrow said, "The others agree but you're making them nervous. We'll just go a couple of hundred yards down this trail on our right to that crag that overlooks the town." She pointed. "See? You can just see it outlined against the lights."

"Then no further, and no more arguments," added Rainstorm firmly. "Agreed?"

"We weren't arguing," chorused Jayhan and Sasha.

Jon chuckled. "I promise."

They made their way down the twisting dirt trail until they reached a sheer drop of about fifty feet. In the near dark, they couldn't see the bottom of it. Then the path turned left and skirted along the top until they reached an outcrop of rocks. The six of them clambered up to the top of them and lay down on their stomachs on a flat section, the three children shoulder to shoulder. A light drizzle began to fall which they ignored as they found themselves looking down on the town, so close that they could see a pot plant in the window of the nearest house and a man moving about inside, pouring himself a drink.

Jayhan felt Midnight's jolt of alarm, and Sasha's.

Sasha drew in a sharp breath, unconsciously clasping her amulet to quell a rising surge of panic. "Definitely close enough."

"Don't worry," Jon's voice was calm and unconcerned. "We can see them in the light, but they can't see us." He glanced back to check. "We are not outlined against the skyline. So they would have no hope of seeing us." He smiled at Sasha, which was mostly lost in the dark. "What do you think? See the pretty way they paint their houses different colours? I particularly remember that."

Sasha had quieted her breathing and was able to take in the scene. "Hard to see the colours in the dark, but I can make out colours where the walls are close to lamps. It must be pretty in daylight too."

Jayhan pointed. "And look! You can see the dark line of the river... and a bit of the wharves. Can't see The Woodland Rover from here though. I wonder where Mum and Dad are? And the others?"

"Probably in one of those inns, having their dinner," said Jon. "They should be finished soon. So we had better get moving. We have yet to have ours." He glanced up as dark clouds rumbled overhead. "Looks like a storm's coming and it's already drizzling. I hope you people have a good suggestion for sheltering from the rain."

Rainstorm shrugged. "Don't know the area, so can't promise anything." He too glanced up. "You never know. It might just pass over." As they stood to leave, light flared in three different parts of the town. Rainstorm frowned. "I wonder what that was. I hope it's not a signalling system to tell them they have intruders on the bluff. We'd better get back into the cover of the dense forest and the protection of the others... Fast!"

Chapter 46

The Rapids was a collection of small wooden houses, trading stores, and inns that were dotted across the face of a wooded hill. Most buildings were painted in shades of light blue or green, yellow or pink. It was not a style Tarkyn had seen before, and he assumed it must be particularly Kimoran. The dirt streets were mostly steep and rutted, a smattering of gravel saving them from being swept away by rain. Several wooden jetties, crowded with river craft, lined the banks of the river. As they drew near, lantern lights began to appear as the night closed in.

Sheldrake was interested to see that a boat ramp with damp wheel tracks led out of the water between the jetties and up onto a wide dirt road that veered left and headed upstream, disappearing into woods outside the town. As they drew in towards the wharf, a short, wiry man wearing a deep-brimmed hat gestured at them to throw the fore painter. Stefan grabbed a few coils in his hand and threw the end of it accurately to him. The man ran it around a bollard and used it to slow the boat and draw her into the side of the jetty. Then he gestured for Stefan to throw down the aft painter and secured the stern before it could drift out from the jetty.

Marjorie smiled at Jackson, who was manning the other tiller. "We're definitely getting better at this. Excellent steering, I thought."

Jackson raised his eyebrows. "I think we're in the hands of an expert. That chap definitely knows what he's doing." He grinned. "Takes the worry out of it, I must say."

The six of them were about to disembark when the small man held up a hand in a clear gesture to stop. Two officials wearing black uniforms emerged from a hut and walked briskly down onto the jetty.

"Whew!" breathed Tarkyn. "I'm glad the woodfolk aren't here."

The two officials, a man and a woman, asked to come on board, although it was clear that it was not really a request. They spoke Kimoran but everyone on board understood them to some degree. Marjorie and Stefan had learnt Kimoran from the constant visitors to the Vine while Jackson had picked up quite a bit working as a messenger. Prince Tarkyn, Lady Maud, and Lord Sheldrake had all learnt Kimoran as part of their education, in the expectation that they would be required to interact competently with foreign dignitaries.

Maud produced her best diplomatic smile. "Certainly."

"I have been to Kimora once or twice before," said Sheldrake quietly to those around him. Actually, he had visited Kimora many times over the years, but he was used to downplaying his knowledge. "Let me handle this."

The two conducted a brief search of the boat, including the area belowdecks. They queried the lack of cargo, enquired about the purpose of their travel down the river, whether the company intended to stay in Kimora, and how they intended to return to Bridgetown.

Sheldrake replied, glad that they had thought up a cover story earlier in the day. "We are visiting friends on an estate in Carrador, south of the Great Forest. Perhaps you have heard of them? Lord Cartwright and Lady Carew Simmons." He almost simpered when he said this, at which Tarkyn's eyes widened, and Maud had to suppress a smile.

Feeling he was overplaying it, Maud stepped in. "We have not yet decided whether we will continue overland from there, back to Highkington, or retrace our route up the river. I understand we could get our boat portaged past the rapids or hire a mage if we return this way. Is that correct?"

"For a fee, of course," said the female official. She had a hard voice and a face to match. "How long are you staying here?"

"An hour. Perhaps two at the most," said Sheldrake. "Just dinner and then we'll keep going."

"No cargo. So, no tariff, but," the official planted her feet a little further apart as she said this, "you have to pay to tie up at the wharf, you know?"

"Really?" Sheldrake raised his eyebrows. "I hadn't heard there were new charges being levied at Kimoran borders."

The male official frowned. "Do you want to get off or not?"

"Happy to pay, as long as it's not too steep." Sheldrake smiled disarmingly. "By the way, is old Miriam around tonight? Wouldn't mind dropping in to see her while we're here."

The officials exchanged an uncertain glance.

"Miriam? The mayor, you mean?" asked the male guard.

"Oh. Is Miriam a common name?"

"Of course he means the mayor, you idiot," hissed the female under her breath.

"Harrumph." The male official look artistically across the river at the setting sun and cleared his throat. "You know, I've just realised the time. No charge for tying up once the sun has gone down."

The female waved her hand and gave a spurious smile. "Welcome to The Rapids. Have to be gone before sunup if you want to avoid charges, though."

Maud beamed at them. "Lovely. Thank you." She sent a twinkling glance at Sheldrake before asking them, "Do you know where we could get a good fish dinner?"

Sheldrake rolled his eyes at Stefan and murmured, "Seal's appetite."

Stefan suppressed a splutter of laughter as he leapt over the boat's railing onto the wharf.

They did not intend to linger for long in The Rapids. Maud and Sheldrake booked into one of the better inns, The Queen's Jewel, just so they could have a good hot bath before dinner. Maud, in particular, wanted to warm up after her swim. The pair offered to pay for dinner so that all six of them could dine together, since the establishment they had chosen was beyond the means of Jackson, Stefan, and Marjorie.

As a result, they managed to avoid the seamier side of the town and were not aware that news of their arrival had spread like wildfire through the poorer quarters. If asked, however, Sheldrake would have assumed this was happening.

The Queen's Jewel boasted an excellent menu, and Maud neatly ate her way through a large baked trout, intended to be shared by two. The other five looked on in covert awe.

As the po-faced waiter cleared away their plates, Sheldrake murmured, "Shape-shifting seems to justify an overindulgence. Perhaps it's the expenditure of energy needed."

"Especially swimming back through those rapids, I would think," said Marjorie, rising to her defence.

Maud was completely unmoved by Sheldrake's remark. "Hard but fun. Down through the rapids was marvellous, although it would have been even better had I not been carefully charting our course as I went." She rose from the table. "If you don't mind, I would rather eschew dessert and get going." She gave a little grin. "Perhaps there is a cake shop open on the way back to the jetty."

There was not, but they found a trading post open late, from which they procured cakes, fresh bread, milk, and a large pat of butter.

"Especially for Autumn Leaves," said Marjorie, waving the butter around.

Stefan got chatting with the storekeeper and managed to find a way to bring up the fact that he had traversed The Way Through a few years ago. "Any idea where it comes out along the river? I've never come at it from this side before."

Sadly, the storekeeper was tired and had no interest in prolonging the chat. All he had on his mind was getting home to his tea and his bed. He shrugged and waved his hand in a vague southerly direction. "Dunno. Somewhere down south. Other than that, no idea and don't care. No one comes through there anyway." He thumped their purchase down on the serving counter. "Will that be all?"

Taking the hint, they took their goods and headed out to find the streetlights shining through a haze of light rain. The dirt of the streets was wet and already becoming slippery. They were just turning towards the wharves when several people ran past, looking alarmed.

Chapter 47

Sheldrake grabbed the arm of a man as he ran past, which swung him around in an arc to face the mage.

"I beg your pardon," said Sheldrake, seeing the man's shocked face, "but what is happening?"

"The mayor has collapsed," replied the man tersely, pulling his arm out of Sheldrake's grasp

"Oh dear, I hope she is all right."

Just as they were speaking, a young woman ran up, her eyes wide with fear. "My mother's sick. She's not moving. I need Miriam's help or Rayna's"

"Miriam's unwell too," said the man tersely. "We'll have to get Rayna."

"Perhaps I could help" offered Sheldrake with a small bow. "I am a healer of sorts."

The young woman looked him up and down. "We'll get Rayna," she said firmly and dashed off up the hill.

Six minutes later, she was back, bending over to catch her breath. Between gasps, she got out, "Rayna's collapsed too." She straightened and eyed Sheldrake. "You'd better come. Better than nothing."

"Charming," muttered Stefan from the side.

"Oh well done, Sheldrake! Now you've dumped yourself in it," hissed Maud.

Sheldrake gave a small bow, ignoring his wife's and Stefan's jibes. "Of course. I would be honoured. Who first?"

"We have a healer here," yelled the young woman, ignoring him. "Bring Ma and Rayna down to the mayor's house. There's more room there. Then he can tend to them all at once. Hurry." She signalled to Sheldrake. "Come this way."

"I, too, am a healer," murmured Tarkyn in Sheldrake's ear, as the mage fell in behind the young woman, "in case you'd forgotten."

"No. I hadn't forgotten," said Sheldrake quietly, "but it's up to you, not me, to offer your services. I would be delighted to work with you."

As they hurried along the street towards the mayor's house, people walked out of connecting streets to join them. Not a deluge but a steady trickle, so that more than a score were now hurrying with them along the waterfront street.

As it became clear that their destination was a larger wooden house painted a cheery yellow with blue window frames, Maud said quietly, "What's the betting that the third stricken woman, that young lady's mother, is also a shaman?"

Sheldrake met her gaze and raised his eyes heavenward as realization dawned. "Oh no. What has Sasha done?"

"Let's not jump to conclusions just yet," said Maud. "Examine these women first. Then see where we are. We had better not have any witnesses when they wake up though, just in case."

Sheldrake gave his head a little shake and turned to Tarkyn who strode on his other side. "Did you hear that?"

Tarkyn nodded. "Do you have agents in this town? And I wonder where Jon's agents are. We may need them." He turned to Stefan. "Has Jon mentioned anything to you?"

"Yes. I was with him when he deployed some of his people," Stefan said. "I think a man and woman selling herbs were assigned to this town... Not sure if there were others." He shook his head. "And I have no idea where we could find them."

"Perhaps they'll find us," suggested Jackson.

"Perhaps," said Tarkyn, "But I would like you, Marjorie, and Stefan to try to find them, if you will. Begin in the taverns. There are too many of us to barge into a sickroom anyway."

"We'll do what we can," said Jackson briskly. "Come on, you two."

Jackson, Marjorie, and Stefan turned off at the next rutted street to their right that ran uphill back into the township and were soon lost to sight.

As Sheldrake, Tarkyn, and Maud reached the yellow house, the young woman yelled at people to move aside so that they could enter unhindered. They walked into sudden quietness inside of the house after the noise of the crowd outside.

Sheldrake turned to their guide. "Your name?" he asked as the front door shut on the mob outside.

"Sorry. Wirra. My name's Wirra. I'm just frantic with worry. Thanks for offering to help. With my mother and the other two shamans out of action, we have no one left to turn to."

Maud sent Sheldrake a speaking glance. "See?" she breathed.

Wirra gestured down a wood-lined corridor. "This way."

An older man with a mane of white and a face creased with worry, walked forward to meet them. "Good of you to come. I am Grayson, Miriam's partner. She is in through here, in the sunroom. I have placed her on a couch near the window.

Sheldrake was wracking his brains trying to see a way through, without the whole town witnessing the shamans' reactions as they recovered... if indeed their collapse was due to Sasha's proximity. Suddenly, inspiration struck. He gave a tiny, satisfied smile to himself. He was, after all, supposed to be a master of subterfuge.

He spoke authoritatively. "Wirra, Grayson, as soon as the other two shamans arrive, I want them both brought to this sunroom and then everyone else must be cleared out, in case of contagion. My companions can stay because we all work regularly with infectious people and have built up an immunity. But we don't want the people of your town struck down."

Wirra nodded. "Whatever you say. What about the townsfolk who are carrying the other two down here?"

"Perhaps you and they should keep your distance from the other townsfolk until we know what we're dealing with," said Maud, getting into the spirit of the deception.

Grayson nodded. "Very well. I'll ask the servants to bring you truckle beds and bedding to the corridor outside the sunroom. I'm afraid you'll have to set them up yourselves if we are guarding against contagion."

"Thank you."

Maud, Tarkyn and Sheldrake had barely had time to set up the beds before the other two shamans were borne in on stretchers by four of the stronger townsmen.

Grayson hovered outside the sunroom door. "Do you have everything you need?"

"Yes thank you," said Maud soothingly. "We'll let you know when they recover."

"*If* they recover," said Wirra darkly.

Maud smiled reassuringly. "I'm sure they will. Sheldrake is very experienced, you know, especially at this type of sudden onset malady."

"But not a shaman," she muttered under her breath.

Maud pretended she hadn't heard.

Chapter 48

Maud straightened, noticing the long, glazed windows sending back reflections of three lamps, one beside each of the stricken women. The water on the outside of the windows blurred and distorted the images. She moved over to join Sheldrake and Tarkyn who had already had time to inspect the women. "Well?"

Sheldrake grimaced. "Hard to say until they come round. Their hearts are beating strongly. Nothing obvious is wrong with them and it seems extremely unlikely that they would all fall ill simultaneously, especially when no one else the town is affected, as far as we know. Tarkyn?"

The forest guardian placed his hand on the shoulder of each in turn and sent his senses through their bodies. When he had finished, he shook his head, "I, too, can find nothing wrong. I would notice an infection."

"Look at their amulets," suggested Maud.

One by one, Sheldrake carefully extracted their amulets from within their clothing and placed them in view on their chests. He grimaced, looking unsure. "They are beating in unison, but they would be, under the pull of Toriana's amulet anyway." He shrugged. "I don't know. I don't think they're ill, though."

Maud sat down in a wicker armchair and put her hands in her lap. "So we wait."

Sheldrake also sat down, happy to wait, but Tarkyn glanced at their calm demeanour in irritation and began pacing around the room, peering out into the night before inspecting each of the women in turn, then again returning to the window.

"Oh, sit down, Tarkyn," Maud admonished. "You'll drive us all to distraction."

Tarkyn frowned forbiddingly at her before letting out a long sigh. He gave a rueful smile. "Sorry. Patience was never my strong suit."

"Only sometimes," said Maud. "You are very patient with Midnight and Gurgling Brook."

"Huh. So I am. Well, I'm not patient at waiting."

Luckily for Tarkyn's ongoing sanity, the unconscious women began to stir. Miriam was the first to recover. As her eyes came into focus, she frowned. "Who are you? What am I doing in the sunroom?"

Sheldrake hurried forward. "Hello. How do you feel? I am a healing mage who just happened to be visiting your town. I am attending you because all three of you shamans took ill at once."

She swung her legs to the floor but didn't try to rise. She gave her head a little shake. "Um... My thoughts keep going in circles. Just give me a moment."

Maud offered her a glass of water which she accepted and drank down in one draught, nodding her thanks. The smaller woman to her right began to stir, closely followed by Rayna, further down the room.

Once they had all recovered, Miriam considered Tarkyn, Sheldrake, and Maud. "You're not from Kimora, are you?"

"No," replied Sheldrake, "And whatever you say within these walls, stays between us."

"Hmph." After a moment she turned to Rayna and the young woman's mother. "Rayna, Fortuna, are you having strange thoughts or is it just me?"

Fortuna, short and dark with tight curls pulled back by a blue scarf, shook her head then nodded, obviously confused. "I keep thinking about what we three have to do this week, then thinking, 'No we don't.' Strange, isn't it?"

Rayna let out a gasp. "That's the same as me." She blinked. She looked at Maud, ignoring the two men and explained. "Every year at this time, ... before the mid-winter gathering, Fortuna, Miriam, and I prepare herbal... hmm... relaxants for the young boys who are about to turn sixteen..."

Shamefaced looks passed between the three of them.

Miriam continued, "... so that they will be compliant when the soldiers come and cart them off, some to the mines, some to the Queen's army, and some to her household. A very few are left here to live and work in the town."

"We haven't questioned it before," said Rayna, a dazed expression on her face. "But it's wrong, isn't it?" She frowned. "I feel different... as though I'm less constrained, or adrift. Am I sick?"

Maud gave them a warm smile. "No. I think you are better than you have been for a very long time."

Just then a knock sounded on the door and a rosy-cheeked woman sporting a scrappy straw hat, popped her head around the corner. "Needing herbs, did you say?"

Maud rose quickly and crossed to the door, pushing the women into the corridor before her and closing the door behind herself. "Are you an unregistered shaman, by any chance?" she asked.

The woman pulled back so she could see Maud's face. She squinted in quick suspicion. "Are you Maud?"

"Yes."

"Then, yes, I am."

"Excellent," said Maud. "Come on in."

On re-entering the room, they found the three shamans watching expectantly while Tarkyn and Sheldrake stood off to the left, keeping a weather eye on proceedings. Maud waved the herb seller in. "I'm sorry. I don't know your name."

"Laurel."

Maud addressed the three shamans. "Laurel here is an herb seller but also a shaman. So you should feel more comfortable with her." She turned to Laurel. "Do you know what you're looking for?"

Laurel nodded so that her straw hat shook back and forth. "I think so."

She withdrew her own moonstone amulet and watched it for a few moments, beating steadily in her hand. Then she moved to each shaman in turn, checking whether their amulets, which were still hanging in sight, beat in time with hers. When she had finished, she nodded at Maud. "Our amulets share the same rhythm. Will you tell them, or shall I?"

Miriam frowned. "Tell us what?"

Maud took a deep breath. "I will. Your forced binding to Queen Toriana has been broken. You and your amulets now beat in time to Sasharia, the true High Shaman, and true Queen of Kimora."

Miriam made a convulsive movement forward, her eyes widening in shock. "What!!?" Her exclamation was almost a shout. The shamans' faces had tightened, and they exchanged horrified glances.

Someone hammered on the door. "What's going on in there?"

Miriam gave an exasperated sigh. "Fortuna, tell them to go away."

Fortuna gave herself a little shake, crossed to the door, and spent a few minutes fending off the concern from outside. Then she closed the door and turned to face the others, nodding that all was well.

"How can this be?" asked Rayna faintly. "Corinna's family were killed by bandits. Everyone knows that."

"All but Prince Jondarian and Princess Sasharia," said Maud. "They escaped to Carrador."

Laurel smiled proudly. "I have met them. And my amulet beats in time with Sasha's heart... as does yours now."

The three shamans noted Laurel's use of the diminutive version of Sasharia's name and were secretly impressed.

Rayna took a deep breath and released her shoulders, a smile gradually dawning on her face. "No wonder I feel less constrained. I am. And no wonder we were suddenly questioning our required actions. The compulsion is gone."

Miriam shook her head, frowning. "It should never have been there. Shamans should be bound by common purpose and support for each other, not by compulsion. Toriana has betrayed our code."

"And her family," added Sheldrake dryly. "And every moral standard you would care to name."

Miriam swung round to regard him, considering his words. "Are you saying...? Surely not."

Sheldrake nodded. "She was behind the attack on her sister and her family. That's why Jon and Sasha have been in hiding in Carrador all these years."

"Oh no." Tears welled in Fortuna's dark eyes. "Oh. This is terrible."

"Fortuna, pull yourself together," Miriam admonished. "Now is not the time for tears. We have to work out what has happened, why, and what we are going to do about it."

The smaller woman sniffed, drew out a large handkerchief, and blew her nose. "Sorry," she mumbled. Then, despite her best efforts, she broke into sobs.

Miriam rolled her eyes and decided to ignore her. She crossed her arms and sent her glare around Maud, Sheldrake, and Tarkyn. "So, first of all, how did this happen? What broke the compulsion?"

"No," said Tarkyn in his most imperious tone, looking down his nose at them from his superior height, his amber eyes glinting. "Firstly, you will tell us your intentions towards Sasharia, should you ever come across her."

"And just who are you?" demanded Miriam, used to a female-dominated society.

"Among other things," said Tarkyn in a hard voice, disliking her attitude, "I am a mighty sorcerer who could wink out your life with a wave of my hand. I am here to protect Sasharia, and you will answer my question before we answer yours."

Maud and Sheldrake were just as shaken as Miriam was. Miriam swallowed and looked at the other two shamans for support.

Tarkyn relented and said more reasonably, "I could wink out your life, but I never would. Just answer our question… please."

Miriam let out a gusty breath of relief. "If Sasharia lives, I would give my life to protect her." She frowned at him, her equanimity restored. "Although the fact that she has employed a fearsome, possibly evil, sorcerer does give me pause."

The other two nodded in agreement. Tarkyn's words had shocked the tears out of Fortuna, who was watching him warily.

"What? Me? Evil?" Tarkyn spluttered with laughter. "Sorry. I suppose I did come on a bit strongly, didn't I? I am used to more respect." He shrugged. "Besides, you do realise that Sasha is only eleven years old. She isn't employing anyone, least of all me."

Sheldrake decided to cut in. "Sasha's amulet can override Toriana's hold on shamans' amulets. Previously she has only done it when she is within a few yards of the shaman and is concentrating on her heartbeat. This time?" He shrugged. "I'm not sure. She is supposed to be skirting around town to meet us further downriver. Perhaps her power is stronger, now she is in Kimora. I don't really know."

Rayna's eyes widened. "She is here? Can we meet her?"

Maud looked harassed. "Uh no. Not really. No one is supposed to know she is here. That's why we've kept everyone out of this sickroom, to give you time to get over the bind being broken. She is not ready to make her move yet. We don't want Toriana getting wind of her presence and using your fellow shamans to quell their compatriots."

"I see," said Miriam thoughtfully. After a moment she asked very courteously, "And may I ask who you are, who have taken it upon yourselves to help her and Kimora?"

The three of them looked at each other then Tarkyn spoke. "I am Prince Tarkyn, High Lord of Eskuzor, sorcerer and forest guardian." He gave a slight bow, his eyes twinkling at Miriam's aghast face.

"Oh, I beg your pardon. I should never have spoken to you in that tone of voice. But," said Miriam, rallying, "in fairness, I didn't know who you were."

"True." Tarkyn nodded at Maud.

"I am Lady Maud Batian, and this is my husband Sheldrake, mage. We are close advisors to the King of Carrador." She glanced at the other two, before adding, "We all support Sasharia, partly because we know her and partly to curtail Toriana's plans for invasion."

"What can we do to help?" asked Miriam.

"Two things," said Maud at her organising best. "Keep our identities and the presence of Sasharia secret and carry on as before, until midwinter. Secondly, at the Midwinter Festival, be ready to look after shamans, as Laurel has done for you, when their bond to Toriana is severed."

"We need to concoct a story to cover your sudden, concurrent collapses," said Sheldrake. "Perhaps you can say that you have all partaken of a particular mushroom or herb that laid you low. Have you prepared something together recently that would fit that story?"

Fortuna nodded. "We're always at each other's houses preparing herbal remedies."

"We'll think of something," said Rayna. Her eyes were shining with excitement. She rubbed her hands together. "Oh. How exciting. This is going to be fun."

"Hardly," muttered Sheldrake dryly.

Chapter 49

A knot of grateful townsfolk waited outside the mayor's house to press cloth bags filled with offerings of meat, vegetables and bread upon Maud, Sheldrake, and Tarkyn as they emerged from the mayor's house. But then, with the courtesies complete, the townsfolk turned their attention to their shamans, clustering around them to hear the full story of their malady. Sheldrake hoped the shamans could maintain their cover story in the face of so much interest.

Maud, Sheldrake, and Tarkyn bid farewell, almost unnoticed, and headed through the misty rain for the docks.

The moon had just risen, and a track of silver flowed across the river. By its light, they had no trouble finding their way along the rutted waterfront street, dodging the rivulets that had formed while they were inside healing the shamans. The sound of the crowd faded into the distance. Jackson, Stefan, and Marjorie were waiting for them where the main street ran down onto the jetty. Without a word, they took the heavy bags of food and fell into step beside them.

The quay appeared deserted, and their footsteps echoed loudly on the wooden planks of the jetty.

Maud shuddered as they reached the Woodland Rover. "I don't like the feel of this place," she muttered as she raised her skirts to step up the little gangplank onto the deck.

"The sooner we're gone, the better," agreed Jackson, stepping nimbly aboard, placing his bundle of food neatly against the railing before pulling the gangplank up after him. He moved aft to receive the painter once Stefan, still on the jetty, had untied it from the bollard.

Then Stefan walked to the fore painter and untied it, before flicking himself up onto the deck as the boat began to drift out on the current.

"Very neat," said Tarkyn as Stefan arrived, grinning, beside him,

Stefan nodded. "By the end of this journey, we will all be expert sailors, but no longer need the skills."

"You never know, we might one day." While he was speaking, Tarkyn sent forth a message to the woodfolk that they had left the township.

Once the boat had turned a bend in the river taking them out of sight of the town, they pulled in to pick up those who had travelled by foot. The woodfolk flicked onto the boat's deck while Jon, Sasha and Jayhan followed more slowly.

Jayhan walked up the gangway and went straight to his mother to tell her all about the lights they had seen through the trees and their journey through the gathering darkness. Waterstone joined him and put an arm around his shoulder. Smiling, he said, "And he used his eyes to help us find our way in the dark. Good little chap, he is."

A little frown flitted over Maud's face. "But can't you people...."

Waterstone frowned over Jayhan's head to indicate that she should keep that thought to herself.

So instead Maud smiled at Jayhan. "Well done. You were very helpful, weren't you?"

Jayhan beamed.

Sasha bounced up beside him, grinning shyly. "And I saw my first Kimoran town. It was twinkling with the light of all its lamps. And the houses are painted different colours, although we couldn't see them very well, even up close."

"What do you mean, up close?" Sheldrake's voice loomed out of the darkness behind her.

Hearing a note of censure in his voice, she spun around, looking apprehensive.

"Not very close," Jon reassured him, putting a protective arm across his sister's shoulder. "We merely climbed down to a rocky outcrop close to the village edge. No one saw us."

"Perhaps not," said Sheldrake dryly, "but they felt you, Sasha. What did you think you were doing, giving away your presence like that?"

Sasha looked stricken and bewildered. "I didn't. I didn't do anything."

"The town's three shamans all had their bond to Toriana broken," said Maud.

"Oh."

Jayhan sprang to her defence. "But she didn't do anything. We just lay on the rocks looking down into the town."

"And you saw or did nothing unusual?' asked Sheldrake, thinking hard.

Jon thought back and shrugged. "Bit of a storm brewing that never eventuated. Oh yes, and those three brilliant flashes in different parts of town. Remember them, Rainstorm?"

As Rainstorm nodded, Midnight wandered up and leaned against Tarkyn's leg, chewing on a piece of dried meat. He glanced up at Tarkyn who tried to explain, in images, what the issue was. Midnight stared up at him, clearly communicating.

"Midnight says Jayhan was right next to Sasha, in physical contact with her," said Tarkyn, "Just as he was when Midnight's power was enhanced during the rescue."

All eyes turned to Jayhan, who scowled defensively. "What? How was I to know that would happen?"

Maud took a deep breath, let it out, then ruffled her son's hair. "It's all right Jayhan... and Sasha. None of us foresaw this, although we adults possibly could have. But now, we have learnt that Sasha can release a shaman from right across a township, at least a mile away, if Jayhan is boosting her power." She smiled at the two worried faces. "That is very useful information, just unexpected."

"And I wasn't even trying," said Sasha. She thought for a moment. "I remember now. I did grab my amulet and take a deep breath when I got a shock that we were so close to the nearest house. Maybe that's when it happened. Sorry."

"Not your fault," said Jayhan, springing to her defence. "You didn't mean to."

"No, true. But maybe I could do it from even further away if I focused."

"Maybe you could," said Jon soothingly.

As the Woodland Rover drifted down the river, those on board caught up on the evening's events from the different points of view. The rain had dried up and it was now such a beautiful night that no one went below for several hours. The moon sent a silvery light across the river, so bright that trees and bushes along the banks cast shadows.

Maud positioned herself in the stern, watching the river drift away behind them. Although it was peaceful, she was also keeping an eye out for any followers. She had been seriously disturbed by the atmosphere of the area around The Rapids' docks. She sometimes wondered whether her shape-shifting ability gave her a heightened sense like those of the animals she became. No one else had seemed to have been as disquieted as she was.

Eventually everyone, even Maud, drifted off belowdecks to sleep. Only Autumn Leaves and Waterstone, who had first watch, manning the tiller, remained.

Part 7

Chapter 50

They struck just after dawn.

A sleek, streamlined boat slid out from beneath an overhanging willow tree as they passed and, with six people pulling on oars, quickly gained on them. In the bows and along the starboard side of the boat, a dozen heavily armed men stood, swords in hand, ready to jump aboard the Woodland Rover, as soon as they were close enough.

Rainstorm saw them first. He reached over and touched Lapping Water to alert her, at the same time sending a mental alarm to Tarkyn and the woodfolk. They reached for their bows, which they always kept close by, slinging their quivers on their backs, ready for action.

"How many?" asked Waterstone.

Rainstorm simply sent an image that saved answering a lot of questions.

"Have they seen you?" asked Autumn Leaves.

"If they haven't yet, they will," replied Lapping Water acerbically. *"There are too many, too intent on attacking us. We must defend our boat. Stop hesitating and get up here before we're boarded."*

Even as she mindspoke, the pirates' boat nosed up beside them.

As he emerged from the companionway, Tarkyn sent an image of a shield around the boat, but Lapping Water, who was becoming stressed by the slow response time, snapped back, *"Too late. They've definitely seen us now."*

An instant later, Autumn Leaves, Sparrow, Waterstone and Stefan stood beside them at the tiller, drawn bows in hand.

As soon as Maud, Stefan, and Jon were above deck, Tarkyn placed a shield over the top of the companionway to keep Jayhan, Sasha, Midnight and Gurgling Brook safe below with Marjorie and Jackson, who had limited fighting skills. Then he hurried to join the defenders.

"Fire. Now," ordered Lapping Water.

With a thrum of bowstrings, six arrows, one knife and one spear of bronze magic streaked into the oncoming pirates. Eight pirates dropped where they stood. The shafts were so accurate that not one pirate screamed in pain as he died.

For a moment, the remaining pirates were confused, unable to fathom what had just happened. Then, far from being discouraged, the death of their companions fuelled their determination. They roared in anger. The rowers abandoned their oars and threw grappling hooks over the railing of The Woodland Rover, pulling her fast to the pirate vessel.

The pirates closed ranks, yelling, and brandishing their weapons as they reached out to board. Hands grabbed The Woodland Rover's railing. Rough men and women poured up over the railing onto The Woodland Rover's deck. Suddenly the woodfolk were face to face with snarling pirates and flashing blades. They were so close that Lapping Water could see the stubble on the men's cheeks and the red veins in their eyes.

She sent a silent order and as one, the woodfolk and Tarkyn took two quick steps back. Jon, watching his companions, did the same. Faces impassive, they aimed and fired.

Six more arrows, another knife and another streak of bronze magic found their targets and seven more pirates fell. Suddenly only five pirates were left standing, facing a small but deadly squad of bowmen. The battle rage died on their faces, and they exchanged fear-filled glances. They were used to defenceless victims, not trained defenders. They started to back away.

Beckoning for Jon to follow him, Tarkyn turned and walked back, grim-faced, to join Sheldrake and Maud, who had been waiting to assist, if the pirates boarded. Standing beside the remaining woodfolk, Stefan glanced back at him, puzzled. Then he heard the thrum of bow strings and turned back swiftly, just in time to see the last five pirates collapse onto the deck.

His stomach clenched in shock. Those last five pirates had been retreating. He looked at Lapping Water and saw her face tight and expressionless, her mouth set in a hard line. So too were the faces of the others.

Then, as he watched, the woodfolk lowered their bows and glances passed between them. They were not jubilant or even pleased. If anything, they were shamefaced. He stood among them but not as one of them; not aligned to their way of seeing the world, at least not yet.

Waterstone took a deep breath and spoke to him. "We are as shocked as you are." The others around him nodded. "I doubt that any of us has killed before. Knocked out, yes. Killed, no. We always choose to hide and avoid conflict if we can. This time, because we were out in the open, we couldn't."

"It is a high price for these last five pirates to pay, to protect the secret of our existence," said Lapping Water sadly, her face softer now, but pale with strain. In fact, she looked a little queasy. She raised her head in defiance of the censure she presumed the non-woodfolk were directing at them. "But had we let them live, we would have been exiled by our people, to live separately for the rest of our lives. Perhaps one day, woodfolk attitudes will change but that day is in the future. Today we did what we had to, to stay true to our people."

Maud bustled over to them, smiling warmly. "I think you are forgetting that you have saved our lives. So, I thank you. I don't condemn you. We knew the conditions of you coming with us to aid Sasha and Jon. Although, for justifiable reasons, your actions were more extreme than those of the king's soldiers might have been, don't forget those pirates were the aggressors. Not you." She patted Autumn Leaves and Lapping Water, the two nearest woodfolk, on the back. "Now I think we all need a good cup of tea. And Autumn Leaves, we specially bought plenty of butter for your breakfast."

"Thank you for saying that, Maud," murmured Sparrow who, at thirteen, had played her part without hesitation but was now looking sick and close to tears.

Waterstone put his arm around his daughter. "I am proud of you, Sparrow. I am proud that you acted so calmly and accurately, and proud that you feel bad about it. We all do, but Maud is right. Our skill saved lives today."

Maud called down the gangway. "Stay below a bit longer with the children please, Marjorie. Jackson, could you come up here please?" She turned to Sheldrake. "Now could you and Jackson steer our boat up to the bank somewhere."

"We need..." began Waterstone.

Maud overrode him. "Jon and Stefan, will you retrieve the woodfolk's and your arrows and your knives, Jon, before tipping these pirates back into their boat. When we reach the bank, tie the pirate's boat to a log or use its anchor to secure it somehow, then release our boat from theirs. Once that is done, we will continue on our journey and leave whoever comes down the river next to take the credit, if they want it, for killing the pirates." She shrugged. "Who knows? There may even be a reward for them." She turned and smiled at Waterstone. "Sorry for interrupting. Have I missed anything?"

For the first time since the attack, Waterstone smiled, although the smile was tight. "No. You are an organisational genius."

Maud beamed at him. "I know."

Chapter 51

Waterstone stood leaning on the bow railing, watching the water ripple past the hull of their boat, his back to everyone. He had been there for nearly two hours, his mind closed to the others. As time passed and he remained isolated, debate raged among the other woodfolk about who should approach him.

Finally Tarkyn had said quietly, "I will go."

As he walked with unhurried steps along the deck, he saw Waterstone's shoulders hunch up and gave a wry smile to himself. Clearly, he wasn't welcome.

"Please don't flick away," Tarkyn said as he came nearer.

"Is that an order?" asked Waterstone bitterly.

"Ooh dear, you are upset, aren't you? No, of course it's not. It's a request from your friend and brother."

Waterstone gave a grunt and continued to stare forward but he didn't flick away.

Tarkyn joined him and leaned his elbows on the railing next to the woodman. Since he was considerably taller, this meant that he was leaning at a greater angle, but it had the advantage of bringing their faces to the same level.

Tarkyn wondered how to begin the conversation without stating the obvious, that Waterstone was upset. Perhaps he should just stand beside his bloodbrother and give him time to think. Ten minutes later, this strategy was beginning to wear thin, mainly due to Tarkyn's inability to stay still for long.

As Tarkyn went to speak, Waterstone's mouth quirked and he said, "Good effort Tarkyn. I'm amazed you lasted that long."

Disconcerted, Tarkyn shut mouth with a snap. But then he smiled and said, "Thanks. I try." After a moment, he broached the conversation. "What can I do to help?"

Waterstone brought troubled eyes around to regard him. "Just being here is a good start. I thought you might condemn us for our actions. I do."

Tarkyn looked shocked. "Of course I don't. If I condemn anyone, it is myself for placing you in this situation."

"No." Waterstone returned his gaze to the river ahead. "You gave us the choice. It is our responsibility. I argued against it but... I didn't stand firmly enough to what I thought was right. I allowed the others, and my care for you... and possibly my care for Eskuzor, to talk me into taking chances woodfolk have never taken before." He heaved a sigh. "And now five men are dead who might otherwise still be alive. In fact, if not for the need to protect our existence, all of the pirates could simply have been knocked out and sent off to face their own people's justice."

"… which would have been hanging and a lot more misery than they endured."

Waterstone grunted. "Not the point. What if it had been a little rowboat emerging from the overhanging willows with a harmless young courting couple in it? No other justification then."

"Waterstone," came an unexpected voice on his other side.

The woodman swivelled to see Sasha's big brown eyes staring gravely up at him. "Waterstone, you told me that you belong to yourself where you are. So that means your decision to be here, or not to argue too hard to stay away, is part of you." She put her head on her side and her eyebrows came together in an uncertain frown. "… Doesn't it?"

Waterstone gave his head little shake. "I'm not sure about that logic but I see what you mean. I'm here because that's who I am, the person who chose to be here."

Sasha smiled warmly up at him. "Something like that. Anyway, I am really glad that you are here because, well, we'd be dead by now, which wouldn't be good," She gave a tiny laugh before continuing seriously, "But besides that," she took a little breath, "It's a hard, lonely thing I'm doing. In the end, when I come of age, it will only be me upon that throne, if I ever get there, and only I can release all these magic-bound shamans to save the Kimoran people from persecution." She tucked her hand under his arm. "And I may not belong with you, but I feel that, at least for now, I am among kind, strong, caring people. So thank you for coming. I wouldn't have dared to ask you myself, but I am so grateful you are here."

Waterstone smiled down at her and remembered that he was indeed a strong, kind, caring person. It had not been his weakness that had led him to agree to come. It was his deep-felt convictions that had battled and won against convention.

Tarkyn, watching from the other side of the woodman, decided that Sasha was an interesting little character, whose innate warmth and honesty might yet carry her through the trials ahead.

Chapter 52

Just after midday on the fifth day since leaving Bridgetown, The Woodland Rover slid quietly past the guardhouse opposite the end of The Way Through in mid-afternoon, without any particular notice from the two guards on duty. Although it had been used as staging platform for Arquin's troops to cross the river into Carrador, usually it was a small outpost just keeping an eye on travellers crossing into Kimora from The Way Through. It was not the border guards' job to police rivercraft, although Sheldrake was sure they would report on anything they considered out of the ordinary.

To that end, only Maud and Sheldrake were on deck with Marjorie and Jackson manning the tiller as they glided past. Even Jayhan, with his memorable pale eyes, was banished below with Tarkyn, Jon, Sasha and the woodfolk for the transit.

Autumn Leaves and Rainstorm had been in contact with the local woodfolk, who had sent images of the guardhouse and had invited them to stop in and visit once they were safely past and out of sight of it. Only woodfolk were invited though.

The local woodfolk did offer to provide the outsiders with protection, but only while stationed in the surrounding trees. They did not want to meet them face to face.

Lapping Water grimaced and gave a wry smile. "We still have a long way to go before the people of our nation are ready to interact with outsiders."

"Never mind," said Maud. "At least they are willing to let us know they are there. Even that is large concession in the face of thousands of years of secrecy."

Just before the forest reasserted its dominance with thick trees growing right to the edge on both banks of the river, The Woodland Rover drifted past a tributary on their left.

"That's the Boden River we're passing," reported Sheldrake, studying a map he had laid out on the deck, held down by a coiled rope, a shoe, and the anchor. He pointed out at the river water over the bow. "Look. Its waters are a light brown, almost yellow, compared to the dark brown green of the Charville. You can see where they meet and flow together."

A few hundred yards further downstream, they nestled their boat under overhanging branches hard against the Carradorian bank of the river under mental direction from the local woodfolk. As the woodfolk were about to disembark, Tarkyn pulled Lapping Water aside.

"I know I am officially woodfolk and I feel right at home with all of you here, but perhaps you might have a more relaxed evening with these new woodfolk if you don't have to worry about me and could all just mindtalk?"

Lapping Water holding Gurgling Brook on her hip, stopped to consider his words. "Possibly, although we are very used to talking out loud to include you in our discussions. But saying that, I think the local woodfolk would be far more relaxed without someone they view as an outsider among them. On the other hand, they would be pleased to meet a forest guardian." She tilted her head. "Perhaps come for some but not all of the time?" She nodded over at Midnight who was playing hide and seek with Sasha and Jayhan. "And he might like to play with those two on hard ground for a change. Perhaps you people could have a picnic lunch on the riverbank while we go further into the forest. Then Midnight and you could join us in an hour or so. What do you think?"

She watched him anxiously in case she had offended him but Tarkyn merely smiled and nodded agreement. "You're taking Stefan though, aren't you?

"Oh, definitely. He's their ambassador after all," she said, chuckling at the concept that had been dreamed up by the king but formed no part of woodfolk culture.

"And he's their kin," Tarkyn said repressively, worried that her mirth would draw Stefan's attention.

"Very true." Lapping Water's green eyes twinkled at him, not at all abashed. "So if you're staying here for a while, you might as well mind Gurgling Brook and bring her along later."

As she swung the little girl over to him, Tarkyn grinned. "Good idea. Then you can really relax while I have fun with Miss Madam."

One of the most unexpected aspects of Tarkyn, coming as he did from a male-dominated culture and having been raised himself by nannies, was his unequivocal acceptance of all people, male and female, on their merits and his love of children. Lapping Water gave him a quick hug and disappeared over the side in the wake of the other woodfolk.

As soon as they were gone, Tarkyn turned to see Jackson and Marjorie appear from below decks, laden with heavy bowls of meats, cheeses, breads, and vegetables. Gurgling Brook waved at them and wriggled to get down. As he lowered her to the deck, he asked, "Do I detect the organisational mastery of Lady Maud in this?"

Marjorie laughed. "Yes. She overheard Lapping Water's suggestion."

Tarkyn ran out the gangway and herded the children over the side to a grassy patch under a huge river gum, whose twisted branches provided mottled shade, while the others carried down the food to set out the picnic.

The children ate quickly so that they could head off and play amongst the trees. They discovered that the old gum tree provided excellent handholds and footholds for climbing and before long, the three of them were perched high in its branches surveying the river and the treetops of Kimora. They found a dilapidated bird's nest and an old knot hole in the trunk which, when inspected, was found to contain a grey ring-tailed possum, sound asleep, curled up inside.

They were just about to descend when Jayhan frowned. "What was that?"

"What was what?" asked Sasha, pardonably annoyed by his vagueness.

"I just saw a flash of light over in Kimora, past the trees." He pointed. "Look! There it is again." He peered up into the branches above them. "Do you think it's safe to climb a bit higher?"

Sasha consulted Midnight using gestures. In answer, Midnight climbed up nimbly until he was another ten feet above them. He looked up at the thinner branches further up, gestured at them and shook his head, but propped where he was, waiting for them to join him. Sasha and Jayhan clambered up and settled themselves in forks where they could sit without holding on.

Jayhan grinned. "Just as well you're not wearing one of those gowns, Sasha."

Sasha sent him a poisonous look but other than that, refused to rise to the bait. "So, come on. Where did you see those flashes?"

Jayhan gestured almost due east, where the forest gave way to the farmland near the guard house. "Look! Over there." He screwed up his face in concentration and said slowly, "There seems to be a lot of dust in that field…"

Just then a gust of wind blew a patch of the dust away and he gasped. "It's… I think it's a big column of marching soldiers," he exclaimed, before the dust obscured them again.

"We'd better get down and tell the grown-ups," said Sasha. She turned to see Midnight looking self-satisfied and when she peered down to the ground below, Tarkyn, Maud, Jon, and Sheldrake had already been galvanised into action and were gesturing for them to come down.

When the children dropped the last six feet to the ground, they found themselves surrounded by grim-faced adults. They were not met with a barrage of questions, however, because Tarkyn had already reported the images Midnight had sent him.

"We need more information," said Sheldrake. He glanced sideways at Maud then looked away. After a moment, he looked at her more firmly. "Maud?"

"Yes, dear. I am quite happy to reconnoitre."

Sheldrake gave a relieved smile. "I just don't want you to think I'm exploiting you."

She smiled warmly at him. "You're not. You don't ask too often, and I am perfectly capable of saying no. I will enjoy a bit of flight on this lovely, sunny afternoon."

"As a peregrine falcon?" confirmed Tarkyn. When she nodded, he said, "I could ask Bird, if you'd prefer, although she's off somewhere hunting at the moment. But a huge eagle circling overhead is quite conspicuous. Last time she flew too low and was hit by an arrow when reconnoitring troops for me. She nearly died. So please don't put yourself at risk. Might I suggest that you don't fly too low over the troops, especially if there are shamans among them who can spot shape-shifters?"

"A good warning. I will stay high." With that she walked between the towering river gums until she was out of sight. Moments later, a peregrine falcon sped out from between the trees and hovered briefly over their heads before swooping in a curve out over the river and climbing rapidly above tree height.

For a while they lost sight of her as she flew low over the tree line on the opposite shore to the south but then they spotted her streaking higher towards the clouds as she turned more towards the east and north to where Jayhan had seen the flashes.

Sheldrake tore his eyes away and turned back to the others, a quirky smile on his face. He shook his head affectionately. "I know it's serious, but I also know she will be having such fun. I envy her sometimes."

"I do too," said Jayhan, turning his mouth down at the corners. "I find out I have the ability to shape-shift but then discover it's only to other human forms. How boring is that?"

Jon ruffled his hair. "Very frustrating. So near and yet so far."

"Exactly."

Chapter 53

Maud had been gone for a half an hour when Stefan came into sight, striding energetically towards them.

"I thought I'd better come back when I saw those images," he said. "The others will return shortly. If those troops are planning to cross into Carrador, the king will have to be warned, and I will have to return to help prepare the troops."

Sheldrake held up his hand. "Not so fast. Let us wait for more information. Those troops may simply be marching to quell an uprising somewhere in Kimora."

Stefan cocked his head. "You really think so?"

Sheldrake hesitated before shaking his head. "Their proximity to The Way Through makes me suspect that they intend an invasion. In which case we will need you with us more than ever, Stefan. The only sure way to stop an invasion by Kimoran troops is to cut if off at its source. Toriana must be stopped. Otherwise we will be facing widespread bloodshed."

The arms master scratched his head in indecision. "I don't know what to do."

"Wait until we know more," came a deep elderly voice from behind him. An old man dressed in long, flowing, green wizard's robes stepped out from behind the trees, Tarkyn's woodfolk following in his wake. Although his beard was white and long, it was tidy and well kept, and his hair hung neatly only to his shoulders. His deep green eyes surveyed them. As soon as he had Tarkyn's attention, he produced a low bow. "Good afternoon, Your Highness."

Prince Tarkyn stared in surprise then broke into a welcoming smile. "Stormaway! Please rise. What are you doing here?" He turned to the others in the clearing. "This is my wizard, Stormaway Treemaster. We have had our differences in the past but despite it all, I count him as one of my staunchest allies. He is also the agent who sells woodfolk goods to outsiders and sold that excellent wine to your father, Stefan." Tarkyn then introduced Sasha and Jon.

As soon as Sasha and Jon were introduced to him, Stormaway bowed low again, "A pleasure to meet you, Your Majesty, Your Highness."

Sasha's eyes widened. She almost made to curtsy but was prevented by Jon's hand under her arm, holding her straight. "No, Sasha," he whispered. "Never again."

"Oh." She took a quick breath. "Please rise. A pleasure to meet you too, Stormaway. We have heard that you are a great wizard."

Stormaway straightened and smiled at her. "Indeed? How delightful that one's reputation precedes one in such a way."

Tarkyn then introduced Sheldrake, Stefan, Jayhan, Marjorie, and Jackson, in strict order of precedence, Sasha noticed. With that done, he asked again why Stormaway had come.

Stormaway gestured to Sheldrake. "In response to Lord Sheldrake's letter... among other things."

"Letter?" Tarkyn frowned. "What letter?"

"I requested Wizard Stormaway's assistance in teaching Sasha how to work with the elements, storms and weather in particular."

Stormaway inclined his head to Sasha. "I hear you can attract water towards you. A very promising start. We must speak more." He smiled, his eyes twinkling kindly at her. "Would you like that?"

Sasha smiled and nodded in return. "The more I can learn, the better chance I have of staying alive and defeating my aunt." Her smile turned to a grin. "Besides, magic is fun."

Stormaway gave a deep chuckle. "That's the spirit, young lady. Don't let your predicament get you down."

Sasha was a little taken aback by the familiarity of this interchange after the formality of his initial greeting.

Watching her, Tarkyn explained, "Stormaway has been wizard to the King Markazon, to me and to the royal family of Eskuzor for over five decades. He may be a stickler for protocol, but royalty does not intimidate him." He grinned. "In fact, he considers it his duty to teach and improve any royal personage within his aegis."

"Huh." Sasha pondered the fact that he, in concert with Jon, had already given her the opportunity to learn how to respond correctly to being formally introduced. For the first time, she had a glimmering of what it felt like to be a queen. "Huh," she said again. "Thank you for my first lesson."

Tarkyn frowned. "But Stormaway, surely you didn't come all this way for magic lessons?"

"Sire, as you know, Lord Sheldrake and I both head extensive intelligence networks. I have been receiving consistent indications of the growing threat from Kimora. I believe they have their eyes on the fertile farmlands of southern Carrador and the rich eastern plains of Eskuzor. So I seized the opportunity to meet the possible solution, young Sasharia here." He smiled at Sasha to take any possible sting out of his words. "And of course, I had my usual transactions as a merchant to settle along the way, both for my cover and as a true occupation. I have been delighted to meet the woodfolk of the Great Forest and believe I shall be able to extend my trading services to them." His eyes shone with enthusiasm. "And I have heard that woodfolk also inhabit Kimora. I wonder, would they also wish to have an agent to trade with outsiders?"

Tarkyn laughed. "Stormaway, you will spread yourself too thin. How can you possibly manage such a large area?"

"Oh, I can't, of course, but I can set up agents in several places. Marjorie and Stefan, for instance, could trade woodfolk goods. I believe their brother, Karl, already sells herbs and plants from the forest, so that would be a perfect outlet... and the Creeping Vine, of course."

Sheldrake raised his eyebrows. "You do have a good intelligence system, don't you?"

Stormaway shrugged. "It helps to be half woodman, half sorcerer. A foot in both camps, so to speak."

They were distracted at this point by a black dot appearing in the clouds above them that quickly resolved into a diving peregrine falcon. At the last minute, Maud flattened out and swerved off among the trees. Minutes later, she reappeared as herself, using her hands to brush her hair neatly back into place as she walked.

"I'm sorry I took so long." She stopped when she saw Stormaway. "How do you do?" she said in a reserved voice.

"Ah, Maud," said Sheldrake hurriedly, knowing she would not say more in front of a stranger. "May I present Lord Stormaway Treemaster, wizard to Prince Tarkyn? Completely trustworthy."

Maud gave a minimal curtsy of acknowledgement which Stormaway returned in kind.

"A pleasure, Lady Maud. We are agog to hear what you have seen."

"Well, where to start?" Maud smiled mischievously, "Perhaps with a drink..."

"Sorry," said Sheldrake, not rising to her teasing. "Of course you need a drink. Wine, water or tea, my dear?"

"Water will quench my thirst so that I can begin talking to you while you brew a pot of tea."

Marjorie and Jackson set to getting a fire started, ready to boil a kettle.

Sheldrake frowned. "Shouldn't we be careful to conceal our presence? I hardly think a fire is wise."

Tarkyn waved his hand airily. "Don't worry. Stormaway can disguise the presence of smoke."

Sheldrake sighed. "Oh dear. Yet another magic user who throws me into shadow."

He felt a small hand on his arm and looked down to see Sasha beaming up at him. "But just think, it was your knowledge and research that discovered what my amulet meant, which then led to Jon finding me again. And your magical ward has given us warning of intruders for months now, which has almost certainly saved my life over and over again."

Sheldrake placed his hand over hers and slowly a warm smile spread over his face. "Thank you, Sasha. That is very kind of you."

"No. She's not being kind," said Jayhan prosaically. "Just honest."

"I think it is the timing of the honesty that makes it a kindness," said Stormaway gently.

Jayhan raised his eyebrows, decided this was too deep for him and wandered off to collect some firewood.

"So," said Maud loudly, regaining the attention of those gathered beside the river. "I saw a long column of soldiers, four wide, marching from the south-east. I estimate there were over two thousand of them. They were followed by the usual paraphernalia of an army on the march: supply wagons, civilian hangers-on, mounted officers at the fore and rear... The road they are following crosses over a stone bridge about two miles inland from the Charville and will lead them up the northern side of the Boden River. I am pretty sure they are heading towards a landing stage I saw about four hundred yards upstream from where the Boden flows into the Charville. More than twenty vessels: barges, fishing boats, and other river craft are standing ready, tied to a long wooden platform that juts out from the tall bank of the river. I presume these vessels are intended to ferry the army across into Carrador. Even with that many, it will take several trips to carry all the soldiers and their equipment and supplies, especially if they are transporting the horses."

"And can you estimate their arrival time at these boats?" asked Stormaway.

Maud narrowed her eyes as she thought about it. "I would say that the head of the column will arrive in less than an hour. I think it will take the rest of the day for the full complement to arrive. So they may not begin to ferry troops across until tomorrow morning." She shrugged unhappily. "But they might send the first load across today."

"It is unthinkable that they be allowed to land in Carrador," said Sheldrake, agitated. "We must stop them."

"I agree," said Stormaway. "And clearly, time is of the essence." He rubbed his hands together, his eyes gleaming with enthusiasm. "What a delightful challenge."

"Perhaps so, but the stakes are very high," added Sheldrake drily. Suddenly, despite the imminent threat, he smiled in fellow feeling. "Still, we have averted disaster for Jon and Sasha so far. Let's put our heads and our talents together and work out a way to avert disaster for Carrador."

Chapter 54

General Kazak rode at the head of the column on her strong, pure white charger. Her dark brown hair was pulled back into a neat bun at the nape of her neck, mostly hidden by her peaked hat, but unruly strands kept escaping and dangling down either side of her face. Her tanned, lined face framed slate grey eyes that constantly scanned their surroundings for threats or obstacles. She had been a career soldier for forty years and had risen through the ranks based on her dedication, intelligence, skill, and initiative. She had been a loyal subject of Queen Suriana and had mourned with the rest of the nation when Suriana's eldest daughter, Corinna, and her family had been killed by bandits only months before the old Queen's death.

Kazak had already been a general by then and she had stood, sad but proud, at the head of Carrador's military to take her oath to the new queen, Toriana, soon after her ascension to the throne. She remembered that day with an internal shudder. The sun had shone brightly, lifting the intensity of the colours all around her: the green of the grass, the purples and pale orange of the Kimoran flags, and the turquoise of the Queen's long gown. Then Kazak had sworn the oath and it was as if the light had dimmed. She had experienced an odd sensation as the amulet lying against her chest had hiccoughed and changed rhythm.

And in that moment, she had known that it was all a farce and that somewhere out there was the true amulet, but not at the end of the chain encircling her new queen's neck. It crossed her mind to wonder whose rhythm her own amulet had been beating to before the Queen imposed her own but somehow, she couldn't keep her thoughts trained on that doubt.

She sympathised with Toriana that she must have had to create a substitute, knowing that the Queen had lost a precious, irretrievable part of her heritage. And Kazak grieved for all shamans, knowing that they too had lost the wellspring of their sisterhood.

Caught up in the pageantry of the moment, most shamans had not noticed their amulets change rhythm. But when Kazak tried to talk to her fellow shamans about it, she found she couldn't form the words to voice her suspicion and her thoughts kept slipping sideways. It was then she realised that Toriana had bound her will during the oath-taking. At first she had fought it, trying to find a way to regain her independence but over time, under the influence of the bond, she forgot her doubts and gradually became resigned to the new regime, realising that as long as she performed her duties unquestioningly, not too much had changed. But bowing to her fate had dimmed the fierceness of her spirit and the sharpness of her inventive mind.

Sometimes she wondered whether Toriana realised how much she had lost by dampening the spirits of her most respected, talented citizens. Bitterly, Kazak suspected that Toriana was happy to reduce any challenge to her own authority and ideas, whatever the cost.

And now they were marching to the mouth of the Boden River, in the first phase of sending an invasion force into Carrador. For years now, the rains had dwindled, and large tracts of Kimora had produced less and less of their expected harvests. Kimora needed food and the southern plains of Carrador could provide it.

In what Kazak suspected was merely a pretext for the invasion, the Queen had taken it as a personal insult that King Gavin had been 'parading' at his court, as the Queen put it, a certain Lady Natasha, with secret and presumably false claims to being the true Kimoran Queen with her brother, a certain Lord Jonathon. Despite her doubts about Toriana, General Kazak could understand the Queen's outrage. After all, no one had ever heard that any of Princess Corinna's family had survived. So, much as she might wish it otherwise, Kazak believed these people must be trouble-making impostors. And if King Gavin wouldn't nip this possible insurrection in the bud, then the Queen had every right to take matters into her own hands.

She reined in her steed to the side of the road and let several ranks of soldiers march past her, watching for signs of fatigue or disorder. Then she trotted her horse back to the front of the column and addressed her second-in-command, Colonel Famira. "We will stop for a short break in twenty minutes. After that we should be able to make the river mouth well before sunset with plenty of time to set up camp." She glanced up at the sky, seeing a falcon soaring far above her and then swivelled her head until she had observed the horizon in every direction. She noted a thin dark line on the horizon behind them and nodded at it. "Might be a storm coming."

"Maybe. If so, it would help if we could set up camp before it hits," suggested Famira, whose straight auburn hair always looked immaculate, almost slicked to her scalp, when it was tied back in the regulation bun at the nape of her neck. Kazak often wondered how she managed to keep her hair so disciplined. Famira turned her bay mare to walk it back along the ranks. "I'll pass the word back. It will motivate the troops to keep up the pace."

Kazak turned to her aide-de camp who rode on her left. Lieutenant Hagan was a thin, earnest young man, blond-haired and blue-eyed, a plainsman and one of the few officers who was not a shaman. He smiled nervously at her when her eyes met his. His demeanour often made her wonder whether she was more fearsome than she realised.

"Hagan, we will shortly be arriving at the bridge across the Boden River. Once the troops have rested, ensure that they form into lines only two abreast until we are over the bridge. The bridge is stone and sturdy enough, but not very wide. The wagons will have to cross in single file. Then, as the troops reach the other side, they can reform into their current formation."

Chapter 55

In view of the close proximity of these Kimoran forces, Sasha and her companions revisited their efforts to disguise The Woodland Rover, cutting branches and draping them over any section of the boat that might be visible through gaps in the overhanging branches under which they had hidden it. Then the whole group retired further into the forest to consider their options. Although it was still mid-afternoon, more supplies had been carried ashore in preparation for having dinner and spending the evening within the forest while they worked out what they would do about the column of troops.

"Woodfolk are willing to do all they can, short of being seen," reported Waterstone, as he pushed a long branch further onto the newly lit fire. "Our attacks from the trees overcame the incursion force that tried to take Sasha. But that was less than two hundred people. We couldn't possibly stop thousands from entering the forests."

"I think a direct attack on these troops is out of the question," said Jon. "We need subterfuge, not force. Besides, once Toriana is neutralized, these people will no longer be our enemies."

Tarkyn smiled sympathetically, including Sasha in his gaze. "And they are *your* people, after all."

Sasha smiled shyly back but said nothing.

"The river is wide here and the current is strong. Heavily equipped troops could not possibly swim across it," said Maud. "Get rid of the boats and you remove the threat."

Sheldrake nodded in agreement. "At least until they can assemble another flotilla."

"Which would take at least a week, if not more. There are no settlements nearby from which to procure more boats." Maud pointed out. "It would buy us enough time to travel to this festival and hopefully destroy Toriana's hold on the shamans."

Suddenly Jayhan catapulted into the middle of them, panting with exertion. Everyone jolted forward in alarm.

"What's wrong?" demanded Sheldrake.

Jayhan grinned. "Nothing. I just beat Midnight back, that's all," he said, just as the little wood sorcerer careened into the back of him and sent them both flying.

They picked themselves up and stood, grinning and puffing, in the middle of the discussion, irritating some and amusing others. Sasha watched them enviously, wishing she could just forget all of this and join them to play.

"Jayhan," said Sheldrake reprovingly. "We are in the middle of a serious discussion that you are interrupting."

"Oops. Sorry." He took a couple of deep heaving breaths to make his breathing more even. "But about that… There'll be shamans among those soldiers, won't there? In fact most of the officers will be shamans from what I can work out. So maybe Sasha could break their bond with Toriana? That would confuse everyone, wouldn't it?" He grinned at Sasha. "What do you reckon?"

Sheldrake smiled proudly at him. "Young man, you are a genius. Very good idea. We will consider it."

A little colour came to Jayhan's cheeks. "Thanks."

Jon gave Jayhan a perfunctory smile of acknowledge before saying, "Hard to say what effect that would have on two thousand troops. Judging by the composition of Arquin's company, about one in thirty or forty will be shamans. That will leave well over nineteen hundred troops wondering what to do with fifty shamans who have suddenly become disoriented. The shamans may become disenchanted with their mission to invade Carrador and call a halt to the invasion, but not necessarily."

"No, we can't bank on that. It will depend on the rationale provided by Toriana for the invasion and other stakes they may have, such as the safety of their families, promotion, financial gain, etc," said Sheldrake.

"And most importantly, on their ingrained discipline," added Maud. "Officers often doubt the wisdom of their superiors' orders but in most cases, follow them anyway."

"So even if the compulsion is lifted, if they don't know of Sasharia's existence, little may change."

"Does that mean that maybe nothing may change even if we release all the shamans in Kimora?" asked Sasha in a small voice.

Jon changed positions to fold his long frame into a cross-legged position beside her and put his arm around her shoulders. "That's why I have sent refugees all through Kimora; to help shamans like those at The Rapids. Once you release them from Toriana's binding, their perceptions will change, but they won't know why unless someone tells them and proves it to them. But I doubt that many of our refugees will be among these troops."

Maud smiled at the small girl with so much power and so little confidence. "They won't need further proof at the Midwinter Festival, of course, if you are standing before them with your heart beating in time with their amulets."

Autumn Leaves and Sparrow had been rummaging around in the bags of supplies and now brought out an array of vegetables. Sparrow gestured to Jayhan and Midnight to help them prepare a stew. As an afterthought, she included Sasha in the invitation, but Sasha reluctantly shook her head, with a quick smile of thanks.

"But at the moment, releasing the shaman officers from Toriana's bond will lead to confusion, won't it?" asked Sasha, glancing around the group to make sure she wasn't being too forward. "And the troops couldn't invade while they are leaderless and in turmoil, could they?" At every step she looked around anxiously for confirmation but at least she was putting forward her ideas. "They would have to wait for their officers to recover." She gave a hopeful little smile. "Maybe that would give us a time to destroy the boats."

Sheldrake smiled his approval, "It should give us at least an extra hour, probably more. I hope you can affect them from this far away though. I wouldn't want to risk you on the other side of the river."

"I am prepared to take risks to save Carrador," she said with a quiet dignity that inadvertently gave Sheldrake pause, reminding him that he no longer outranked her. Completely unaware of the effect of her response, Sasha glanced uncertainly at Tarkyn. "Jayhan can increase my power. Do you think you could too? Or Midnight? With the strength you draw from trees? Then I may be able to do it from here."

"I am willing to try," said Tarkyn, careful not to reject her suggestion outright. "But our powers are different. I can give Stormaway power but I'm not sure about you. I think I can only shore up your strength, not add to your power. Still, even that may be helpful. Let's give it a try. Jayhan, over here, please."

Suddenly talk turned to action as Tarkyn called Jayhan over to sit beside Sasha, close to a towering gum tree, while he placed his hand on her shoulder, connecting his other hand to the trunk of the tree.

"Right. Off you go, Sasha," instructed Tarkyn, leaving no room for further debate.

She glanced at the tall sorcerer, whose long black hair seemed so out of keeping with his role as High Lord. As she hesitated, he turned his glowing amber eyes on her and to her surprise, gave her a warm, encouraging smile. Her uncertainty melted and she felt herself, once more, being swept along into her future.

She smiled in return, took a couple of deep breaths, and closed her eyes. She could feel a gentle wave of warmth entering her body through her shoulder from beneath Tarkyn's hand. On her other side, she could feel Jayhan's hand on her knee. She pulled her amulet from beneath her shirt and held it firmly in her right hand, feeling the cold smooth stone beneath her fingers. With her left hand, she traced the lines etched into its surface. Life, birth, death.

She focused on her heartbeat and let herself forget everything else around her. Slowly she lost herself in the steady pulsing until all she knew was her heart thumping strongly within her chest, a sensation that grew until she felt as though that was all she was.

Gradually she became aware that someone was shaking her shoulder. Then she heard a child's voice, tinged with fear, calling insistently to her.

"Sasha, Sasha. Come back."

Her eyelids fluttered and she opened her eyes to see Jayhan's worried face right in front of her, staring at her. She blinked then grinned. "Get out my face, you idiot. I'm all right. I was just concentrating, that's all."

Jayhan shuddered "Ugh. You went all quiet and your heart rate slowed right down. A dark mist has been coming out of you and drifting up into the trees."

Sheldrake appeared behind him, pulling him gently back by his shoulders. "How are you, Sasha? That grey mist became very dense. For a while we almost lost sight of you."

"I'm fine." She smiled at Tarkyn, looking relaxed and sure of herself. "I feel better than I have for days. Thank you." She turned back to Sheldrake. "Do we know if it worked?"

"Not yet, my dear," said Sheldrake. "We may have to send Jayhan up a tree or Maud up into the air to find out."

"I'll go," said Maud hastily. "I don't want Jayhan climbing up too high, craning his neck to see. Besides, I can get closer to see details." She gave a little grin. "I think I'll become a swallow this time. They are speedy enough for such a short distance, very manoeuvrable and even less conspicuous than a falcon."

"Just as long as you can dodge Bird if she returns," said Tarkyn. "I will send her an image of you changing but I can't promise her good behaviour."

Maud nodded acknowledgement even as she retired into the bushes. A minute later, a little welcome swallow flitted out, swooped joyously just above Sheldrake's head, making him duck. Then she wove a figure of eight over the clearing before swinging her way through the trees and out over the river. She dived swiftly down to the river's surface, snatching up a tasty insect then rose quickly and disappeared into the forest on the Kimoran side of the river.

Chapter 56

The last of the long column and its attendant wagons and hangers-on had finally made it over the bridge. General Kazak had sat mounted on her white stallion, watching every last one of them as they crossed. She wanted to inspect her soldiers as they passed, and she wanted them to see and remember her too. As the last cart rumbled onto the dirt of the roadway that ran along the northern side of the Boden, she nodded at them then pressed her heels into her stallion's sides, urging him into a canter, riding forward to regain her position at the head of the column.

She caught up with Hagan and Famira and reined in to join them.

"Ah. I enjoyed that. So did Albin. He needed to stretch his legs." She smiled at them, more relaxed than usual after her canter. "All safely over the bridge. Another hour and we should be at the landing site, ready to make camp." She glanced at the sky. "That line of clouds is still some distance off. We should make it in time, with any luck."

A few minutes later, she pointed ahead and frowned. "What is that? Some sort of mist wafting out of the trees? Smoke?" She considered before answering her own question. "No. It is not moving in the same way. Whatever it is, it is drifting over the trees towards us. I hope it is benign."

The dark mist swirled and thickened as it floated towards the column of soldiers. Strands of it seemed to home in on the shamans among them. Suddenly, within the clothing of every shaman, their amulets lit up, their clear light shining forth to be swallowed up by the encroaching thick dark fog. Then the light of the amulets began to beat wildly.

Panic seized Kazak. She threw up her hands and yelled, "Guard yourselves. We are under attack. "

The next moment, the roiling shadow intensified, and her amulet began to pulse with a strong irresistible beat. Her whole body began to glow. She looked down at herself in terror. Then light exploded around her and with a gasp, she tumbled unconscious from the saddle.

All along the line, light flashed as shamans collapsed, either slumping to the ground where they stood or sliding senseless from their mounts. Around the soldiers, the dark fog swirled and throbbed with that distant beat, flowing between them as it snaked and coiled its way down the full length of their column.

Soldiers had drawn their swords, staring wildly around but unable to find anything to slash at. Soldiers were shouting out in alarm, trying in vain to stave off an invisible foe as many of their officers succumbed to the grey mist.

Lieutenant Hagan rose brilliantly to the occasion, calmly summoning soldiers to tend to Kazak and Famira, before riding down the column, making sure every shaman was tended to by the soldiers of their company, and every perimeter of the column guarded. He was not the most senior officer left standing, but he did have the general's ear. So once he was away from the head of the column, no one knew he wasn't acting under her orders.

But despite his best efforts, there was no way the column could continue to move forward with so many stricken shamans in their midst and an unknown threat attacking them.

And then the mist cleared. It simply dissipated, leaving chaos and unconscious shamans in its wake.

Hagan looked around and scratched his head, wondering what to do. He decided that the first priority was to make sure the fallen shamans were placed together so that they could be safeguarded against conventional attack. Then he wanted each shaman inspected for damage, particularly those who had fallen from their horses. This was made more difficult by the fact that all their healers were shamans and therefore currently unconscious. Consequently he had to rely on a few battle-hardened soldiers who were experienced in dealing with injuries.

From what they could see, there were few outward signs of injury. One shaman had dislocated her shoulder as she fell and a few others had superficial cuts or grazes but generally they looked well, just unconscious.

After some thought, he decided to send the majority of the troops on ahead to set up camp, draw water, and light fires with whatever officers were left while he and a contingent of soldiers remained to guard the unconscious shamans. That, at least, was his intention.

However the lack of leadership led to heated discussions about who should stay and who should go. A couple of more senior officers pulled rank and took over the debate but then proceeded to disagree with each other. Long before the issues had been resolved, the shamans began to come round and the whole discussion was abandoned.

Slowly, the shamans sat up and looked around themselves, frowning in confusion at finding themselves on the ground. Panic flared in Kazak, and she surged to her feet. As she did so, Hagan ran to her side and was at her elbow in time to steady her as she swayed.

"What…" She found her throat was dry and she had to swallow before starting again. She stared around her. Everything seemed brighter, more in focus. But she thrust the strangeness from her mind. Her troops were in disarray, and she had to act to restore order. "What happened here, Hagan?"

A nearby soldier handed her a cup of water and she drank gratefully as Hagan described the mist and the light from their amulets.

"Where's Marlene?" asked Kazak. "I may be the most senior officer, but she is the most venerable, knowledgeable shaman."

"I'm here, ma'am." An old woman in a captain's uniform hobbled over, assisted by a young female soldier. Her wiry white hair had escaped its ties and now stuck out in all directions around her dark brown face. "I've turned my ankle. Must have landed on it badly when I fell off my horse. It's nothing serious though."

"I'm glad to hear it. We're going to need you. Did you hear what Hagan said? What do you make of it?"

All around them, shamans were getting to their feet, running their hands across their faces or through their hair and staring around at the chaos. Despite their confusion at what had just happened to them, many of them were gazing around in dawning wonder.

"I don't know." Marlene pulled out her moonstone amulet and stared down at it, feeling its strong sure beat in her hand. "But something has changed." She frowned as she directed her attention inward. The general waited. Finally, Marlene raised her liquid brown eyes, so much like Sasha's, to meet Kazak's. "I can tell you this. I don't feel under threat. In fact, I feel... lighter, stronger, more alive." She frowned in thought, even as a small smile played around her lips. "Give me time to think about it." She waved her hand in a shooing motion to indicate that Kazak should get on with her other concerns.

Knowing she would have to be satisfied with that for the time being, Kazak nodded and turned away to direct the officers to return to their troops and to get the column underway again. As long as people were uninjured and able to perform their duties, that would do for now.

Chapter 57

Maud did not take long to return. When she emerged in her human form she was smiling broadly. "Chaos reigns. Prostrate officers all the way along the line with frantic soldiers surrounding them trying to revive them." She chuckled. "The last thing on their minds is boarding those boats. Well done, Sasha. We have our respite."

Autumn Leaves promptly handed Maud a cup of freshly brewed tea. "And well done to you too."

Stormaway, who had found himself a comfortable position seated on a log with his back to a tree, addressed the company. "And now we must plan. Quickly. How do we propose to sink those boats?"

"I could become a narwhal and swim under the boats, puncturing them with my long tusk," suggested Maud, only half-joking. She was still buoyed from the thrill of her flight.

"I don't think so," replied Sheldrake sternly, recognising that, despite her light-hearted tone, Maud was looking for a genuine response to her idea. "You are just as likely to get your tusk stuck in the planking of a boat and trap yourself."

Stormaway looked at the forest guardian "What about you, Tarkyn? Could you ask water rats to gnaw through the mooring ropes?"

"They would have to be enormous rats," Maud butted in. "From what I saw from above, the ropes are half a handspan in width."

Sasha looked over from where she had rejoined the dinner preparation and was now struggling to get a knife through a large pumpkin. "What about a storm, Stormaway? Aren't you famous for creating storms?"

The old wizard smiled at her in some amusement. "If I am, a few deeds must have gained in number and size over the years." He nodded. "But I admit that I have a facility with weather."

"Don't let him fool you, Sasha," said Tarkyn. "He's brilliant."

"He is," agreed Autumn Leaves. "We've seen him dissipate a huge storm that had been create by another wizard and we've seen him create a rainstorm to put out a fire."

"But, if you remember," said Stormaway, "on both occasions, I had help."

Rainstorm threw down a bundle of firewood. "So? You can have help today. Tarkyn can give you power and may be even Jayhan can." He grinned before adding, "And of course, you have Sasha, the greatest shaman in existence."

Sasha's eyes widened at this description, and she buried herself in her task of cutting pumpkin, her cheeks flaming with embarrassment.

Jayhan nudged her in the ribs. "Trust Rainstorm to say something like that."

"I'm not great at all," muttered Sasha. "I hardly know anything about being a shaman compared to women who have been practising for years. Some of them have been practising their arts for over fifty years. I've been doing it for what? Less than a year." She snorted. "And here I am, planning to outface a shaman so powerful that she has bound a whole country of shamans to her." A sob of panic welled up, but she pushed it down. "Forget it. Just help me with this blasted pumpkin."

"Sasha," came Stormaway's voice, deliberately deep and soothing. "Leave the blasted pumpkin to your friends. Come and sit beside me." He waited until she had sat herself beside him but just out of reach. "Do not be afraid of your greatness, Sasharia. Embrace it." He waved his hand around the company. "All of us here are great. Maud, a shape-shifter and trusted advisor to the king, Sheldrake, a mage of great learning and head of the King's Spiders, Tarkyn and Midnight, forest guardians and powerful sorcerers, Jayhan, a boy of unique talents, Jackson, who impressed Tarkyn in less than twenty minutes and has been invaluable ever since, Marjorie who is trailblazing her way out of the life that had been designed for her to support her brother and of course, all the woodfolk, including Stefan, who are gifted with telepathy, uncanny stealth, and almost magical marksmanship."

"What about Jon?"

Stormaway smiled, "And Jon, who can shimmer, has those woodfolk marksmanship skills with his knife and above all, has an endearing cheerfulness that infects all of those around him."

Sasha cocked her head at him while she thought about it then nodded decisively. "You're right. They are all great. Really wonderful, in fact." She smiled. "That takes the pressure off me a bit, doesn't it?"

"I hope so. After all, we're all here to help... not just help you, but all the people who have suffered in Kimora under Toriana's reign."

She reached out bravely and put her hand on his arm. "So will we make a storm and sink these boats? You, me, Tarkyn and Jayhan?"

Stormaway chuckled. "You make it sound so simple. We'll give it a go, shall we?"

"And Midnight," said Jayhan. "If he's a forest guardian, can't he draw on the power of trees, just like Tarkyn?"

Tarkyn frowned, "I don't like him forced into adult business." Then he looked at the other two children and shrugged. "Perhaps I'm being a bit precious."

"Oh, definitely," said Rainstorm cheekily. "After all, if he hadn't interfered in adult's business a few years ago, you would not be here, and if he hadn't interfered a few months ago, Jayhan, Sasha, Maud, and Jon would not have made it either, would they?"

Tarkyn threw up his hands. "Very well. Point taken."

Rainstorm grinned. "Besides, he'd love to be included."

"We need to get as close as we can to where the boats are tied up," said Stormaway, seeing this issue had been settled. "Weather-making in the immediate vicinity is hard enough. Long distance is impossible."

So they walked north through the trees until they reached the point opposite the mouth of the Boden River. Then Tarkyn and Midnight took their shirts off and each sat against a large river red gum's mottled bark so that their skin made contact with the bark. Once they were settled, Tarkyn placed his hand on Stormaway's shoulder, leaving the wizard's hands free while Midnight placed his hand on Sasha's shoulder. Jayhan sat between Sasha and Stormaway forming a circle, with a fistful of Stormaway's green robe on his left and his hand in Sasha's on the right.

Sasha's eyes widened. "Ooh. I can feel a warm stream coming into me."

Tarkyn must have sent him an image of Sasha's words because, after a moment, Midnight smiled at her.

Jayhan looked at each of them around the circle. "Right. So what now?"

The wizard frowned forbiddingly at him. "Now, you will need a great deal of patience, which I suspect will be almost as much of a trial for you as it always is for Tarkyn. I must concentrate and look through the surroundings skies for the beginnings of a storm; something to build on, you see."

Jayhan's face brightened. "Oh. I can help with that. When we were up in the trees when I first caught sight of the soldiers, there was a thin line of dark clouds behind them on the horizon." He grinned. "Might even be a natural storm building up and coming this way."

"He's right," said Maud from a short distance away. "I saw a thick bank of clouds advancing across the plains. More than halfway here now, I'd say. " She paused and frowned. "They had a brownish tinge, though. Not grey like storm clouds."

Stormaway frowned. "Hmm. That sounds like a dust storm out on the plains. If the land is dry, a windstorm or thunderstorm can pick up dust particles as it travels. It may still contain moisture though. That should suit our purpose. I will send my senses in that direction first."

"Do I have to do anything?" asked Sasha, anxious to help, but with no idea what to do.

"The last time I did this," explained Stormaway, "I was creating rain to put out a fire over a wide area, not directing wind to destroy a very specific target. This is far more demanding and this time, I do not have Caroman, the strong, weather-wise wizard who helped me on that occasion. The time before, Tarkyn and I didn't create a storm, we dispelled it, using our magic to redirect it. Perhaps we can use a similar technique to redirect the wind within this storm but this time, to intensify it. If we can send the wind back on itself, we can either create more turbulence or, even better, a small tornado, if we can direct the storm in a circular motion." The wizard considered her for a moment before saying, "Unfortunately, I am not conversant with shaman powers… Hmm."

"Sasha," came Sheldrake's voice from the sidelines. Sheldrake, as neat as usual in his black coat and breeches, not a black hair out of place, looked just as he did when he was teaching them back in his shed. "Might I suggest just focusing on your heartbeat and your amulet? Hold your amulet in your hand and think about what you five are trying to achieve and how. Let your amulet and your heartbeat guide you. Remember you have untapped knowledge inside you."

Stormaway raised his eyebrows. "Does she?"

Sheldrake nodded "Yes. As Sasha grows older, her shamanic knowledge has increased more quickly than we are teaching her, and her amulet gives her adult perspectives so that she sometimes comes out with wisdom far beyond her years."

"How very interesting. We must talk further, you and I," said Stormaway. Sasha recognised the same glint in his eye that Sheldrake had when exploring new magical knowledge. Unaware of her scrutiny, the wizard looked around the small circle. "Right. Everybody ready?"

"I can't create wind," explained Stormaway. "All we can do is use what is there and intensify it. If you can focus through my mind, you will start to see the huge cloudbanks that rise hundreds of feet above the line we see from the ground."

Sasha eyed him, wondering how she was going to focus through his mind. With a little grimace, she decided she'd just try to imagine what he was seeing from what he said.

As he spoke, he began to move his hands rhythmically towards himself, muttering incantations under his breath. After a few minutes, he stopped muttering and said clearly, "Now, Sasha, I want to start dragging the approaching mass of clouds anti-clockwise. If you can focus on drawing the northerly clouds towards you, Tarkyn can form a shield to make the cloud front veer to the south while I will work on pushing the more southerly clouds back towards the east. We don't have long. The whole cloud formation will move along the Boden and then cross the Charville River in the next twenty to forty minutes, depending on its size and windspeed."

Stormaway concentrated, his eyes focused far away in the roiling clouds. Sweat dripped from his eyebrows with the effort. A few minutes later, Stormaway shouted, "Now!"

A huge column of green light shot upward curving from south to east while a bronze curved shield rose high above them to block the storm clouds and turn them back on themselves.

"This is only going to work when the stormfront is actually overhead," muttered Tarkyn.

"I realise that. It is nearly here." Stormaway's reply was terse and underpinned with strain. "By the time it reaches us, the rear of the storm still won't have reached those boats four hundred yards upriver. What we do here should affect the whole storm mass."

Beside him, Sasha had her eyes closed, frowning furiously, trying to do what he wanted. As hard as she could, she envisaged drawing the northerly clouds with their moisture towards her. She remembered the water in the pond then focused on her amulet and her heartbeat and pulled with all her might.

For several long minutes, nothing happened. Then the wind began to pick up and Stormaway said, "The front of the storm is crossing the Charville. It will be overhead within the next minute. Tarkyn, Sasha, hold your focus."

The wind grew stronger, whipping their hair around their faces. Now they could hear it roaring through the treetops.

Suddenly, Sasha heard shouting all around her. Not instructions, panic.

"Grab hold of a tree," yelled someone.

She snapped her eyes open to find everyone scattering, grabbing hold of strong branches, logs, or tree trunks; anything that would anchor them against a huge wall of water that was surging out of the Boden River. She stared around wildly as Jayhan grabbed her arm and dragged her with him to a strong sapling that she could get her arms around and cling to. Then she felt Jon's strong arms encircle both of them, holding them to the trunk.

She watched in horror as the enormous wave drew more water into itself as it drove straight across the river towards them. It reared up into the air above her, blotting out the sky. She closed her eyes, took a deep breath, and hung on for dear life as it came crashing down around her, and swept off through the forest.

Water dragged at her, trying to pull her away, but she clung on, tangled within Jon and Jayhan's limbs. Branches were ripped loose and were swept between trees, swirling and snagging on anyone or anything in their way. Sasha felt a sharp stick rip past her shoulder, but she stopped herself from crying out, knowing her mouth would fill with water if she did. In a few fraught seconds, the worst of the wave had passed, and the water level subsided enough for her to draw a breath. Soon it was only swirling past at waist height, then knee height.

Even as she began to loosen her grip, Jon shouted above the noise of the water and the debris rushing past. "Don't let go! That water will be back in a minute. It will lose momentum on the slope behind us and come flowing back down into the river."

"Oh."

When Jayhan made no reply, she bent towards him. "Are you all right?"

He nodded, his pale eyes wide with fear in the gathering gloom of evening. His knuckles were white from holding on so hard, even though Jon had his arm around him and Sasha.

"We're nearly through it," gasped Jon. "Hold on for a bit longer."

Even as he spoke, the water level began to rise and the water pushed against their ankles from the other direction, threatening to topple them. Then it rose to their waist level then to the height of the children's chests but no higher. Only gravity, not Sasha's power, pulled the water back towards the river, but the danger of being swept off by the current into the river was all too real.

Chapter 58

Across the Charville, the Kimoran troops experienced a wind that picked up in strength as the billowing cumulus clouds moved from the east towards their campsite.

"If their tents aren't yet erected, leave them packed up until this storm passes," yelled Kazak over the wind. "For tents that are up, hammer in extra stakes and weight them down as much as possible. I don't like the feel of this."

She turned to find Marlene at her elbow, who leaned over to shout in her ear. "You don't like the feel because it's not natural. There is a powerful shaman at work somewhere nearby. A shaman and... something else." She straightened up and cocked her head as she let the wind flow over and around her. Then she leant back in and shouted. "I think... Yes. I think I detect the workings of a sorcerer. The sorcerer's power is strong and true. Probably an experienced wizard. But the shamanic power is wild and untamed. But why? Why would they want to create a storm?"

"Where's the power coming from? Can you tell?'

Unhesitatingly, Marlene pointed towards the Charville River. "From the west. From Carrador."

Kazak's eyes widened. "Someone's seen us. The boats. They're trying to sink the boats. Quickly," she said to Hagan. "Gather the shamans. We need to resist. We have to divert that wind."

But already it was too late. Even as she spoke, they became aware of a distant roaring that increased in volume with frightening speed.

"That's not wind," exclaimed Marlene. "That's water. Clear everyone away from the river side. Now!"

Shouts of warning rang out and soldiers scrambled back from the river's edge., gathering water canteens and loose equipment as they ran.

"Leave everything. Just run!"

From the safety of the higher ground, Kazak and Marlene watched in stunned silence as a wall of water twenty feet high swept down the Boden River, spilling over onto the campsite on its way past and dragging with it everything it encountered: tents, firewood, cooking vessels, backpacks. One man was caught on the edge of the flow and only a chain of soldiers pulling hard saved him from being dragged away.

When the water had passed, Kazak looked around her. The side of the campsite closest to the river was a mess or completely missing in places. She shook her head. And what about the boats that were meant to ferry her army across into Carrador? She took a deep breath and walked over to the riverbank to inspect the damage.

Chapter 59

Finally the waters were gone, leaving in their wake torn branches, uprooted bushes, scatterings of twigs, leaves, and bark and a swathe of mud covering everything. The makings of their dinner had completely disappeared. As Jon, Jayhan, and Sasha detached themselves carefully from their sturdy sapling, they saw Maud and Sheldrake disentangling themselves from a tree twenty yards further south of them. Sheldrake's neat black coat was sodden, and his breeches clung to his wet legs. With hands that were not quite steady, he pushed his hair back from his face and back into some semblance of order.

Sasha realised Jayhan was shaking. She put her arm around him, and it was an indication of his distress that he didn't even seem to notice, let alone object. Marjorie and Jackson appeared, hair and clothes wet and bedraggled, picking their way among the branches and twigs that were strewn on the ground.

The rain was still falling but it had eased. Sasha glanced up and saw grey clouds billowing overhead as they moved westward.

She drew in a long shuddering breath, surveying the devastation. She didn't meet anyone's eyes as she asked in a voice of quiet dread. "Where are the others?"

Rainstorm appeared before her. "Up in trees, of course," he replied for everyone.

Sasha let out a sigh of relief.

Tarkyn floated down from the branches above, holding Midnight in one arm and Gurgling Brook in the other. "I am sorry, Sasharia, that I couldn't help you more. It happened so quickly we had no time to plan. Everyone just scrambled for safety." He gave a lop-sided smile, "My shield doesn't work against water."

Gradually people reappeared and took stock of each other and their lack of provisions. Several people were sporting cuts and bruises. Generally, those left on the ground had escaped any major injury.

Sasha was dazed, so horrified at the devastation she had wrought that she wasn't aware of any pain until Maud noticed blood soaking through the back of her shirt.

"Sasha, come over here and let Sheldrake look at you. You're injured."

The girl looked vaguely at her. "What?"

When Sheldrake inspected her, he found that Sasha had a deep gash across her back where the branch had slashed her on its way past. "This needs some salves and bandaging." He huffed. "I don't know where my herbs and ointments have gone."

"On the boat?" suggested Jackson.

Sheldrake let out a breath. "Of course they are. Silly of me. I'm feeling a bit disoriented." He looked around at everyone, dripping wet and dishevelled, and gave a wry smile. "I guess we all are. Could you fetch them please Jackson?... assuming the boat's still there." He was just about to return his attention to Sasha's back when he frowned. "Where's Stormaway?... And Lapping Water?"

Tarkyn gave a knowing smile. "I think Stormaway is upset with himself for creating such a disaster and Lapping Water is trying to persuade him to show his face."

"It wasn't Stormaway's fault," said Sasha in a small voice. "I'm the one who called the water towards us. He was pushing clouds away. We were trying to create a spiralling wind, you see."

"No, young lady. It was not your fault," said Sheldrake firmly. "Stormaway, with my acquiescence, allowed you, an inexperienced, partly-trained shaman to be part of a complex, dangerous piece of magic. Stormaway and I knew the risks and must shoulder the responsibility."

An embarrassed, green-robed wizard descended from the trees to lend his voice to Sheldrake's. "No, no, my dear. I asked too much of you with too little preparation and no training. Most reprehensible of me." He raised his eyebrows at Sheldrake. "Generous of you to share the responsibility but not justified, I fear." Then he leaned forward and whispered, but loudly enough for all to hear, "But my word, little one! What power you have. Most impressive. A little ungoverned perhaps, but no doubt, control will come over time."

He looked around at everyone standing sodden and miserable in the rain that had eased still further to a light drizzle. "I can see you all need cheering up. Come on. If you gather a great mound of sticks and branches, I will light you all a fire, regardless of how wet the wood is. The least I can do." He raised his hand and waved vaguely, giving a little cough. "Apologies to everyone, by the way."

By the time the fire was lit, Marjorie and Jackson had returned with Sheldrake's bag of medicaments and much more besides and were able to report that The Woodland Rover had weathered the deluge.

"From what we can see, the wall of water developed in the Boden River and was not very wide. The damage to the undergrowth extends less than two hundred yards south. Luckily, The Woodland Rover was far enough downstream to be out of its direct path."

The two of them dumped bags on the ground. "We also brought more provisions," said Marjorie, her light blue eyes stark in her pale face amidst black hair hanging in rats' tails down either side, "but we've lost our plates and cups. All the food we unloaded earlier is gone, as far as we can see,"

"So we are running lower than we had planned," finished Jackson, handing Sheldrake his bag.

"Not wishing to distract you all from creature comforts but, as you recall, we are in the middle of trying to stop an invasion," said Maud, a little acerbically. "Have we succeeded?"

Sheldrake gave a little cough. "I think, dear, that you would be best placed to answer that question yourself."

Maud crossed her arms and almost looked like she was going to stamp her foot. "Sheldrake, I can't. I'm tired, I'm wet, I'm cold, I'm hungry, and I've already done it twice today. Can't someone else find out if those bloody boats are still there?"

Tarkyn smiled sympathetically. "It would be my honour, Lady Maud," he said with a slight bow. "I don't know where Bird is, but I doubt that she'll be aloft in these conditions. He frowned. "Hmm. I may have trouble getting any bird to come out into the open at the moment, but I'll try. If I have to wait for the wind to die down completely, it will be getting dark, and I may have to look for an owl or bat instead."

"A bat," said Maud, looking thoughtful. "That's an idea I hadn't thought of."

"Don't worry, Tarkyn," said Stormaway, staring up at the clouds passing overhead. "This storm has nearly passed."

Tarkyn nodded. "Thanks. I'll see if Bird will do it then. Lapping Water, could you mind the little ones please? Rainstorm, could you come with me to direct me? You know I'll lose track of the right direction as soon as I'm out of sight of the river."

Ignoring Rainstorm's chortle, Tarkyn turned and wandered off into the forest where he could concentrate away from everyone else.

As the quietness away from the fire settled around him, Tarkyn became aware of the sound of small feet, running to catch up with him. He stopped and swung around to find Sasha's dark eyes staring resolutely up at him. He raised his eyebrows. "Do you want to watch me summon Bird? I don't think there's much to see unless you can join minds as Rainstorm can."

Sasha shook her head and suddenly looked unsure of herself. "No, no. I just wanted to catch you before you started. I was wondering whether you could help *me* to cross the river and look for myself, to make sure the shamans are all right. Please."

Tarkyn eyebrows snapped together. "What? Right into the middle of all those soldiers?" He restrained himself from saying she must be mad, but only just. She was, after all, trying to figure out how to be a queen, and up until now, had behaved quite sensibly.

Sasha gave a little smile. "No. At least not to begin with. I thought I, *we*, could have a look from the southern side of the Boden River. Then decide what to do from there." While he stared at her in bemusement, she cocked her head. "Can you do that, do you think? And more importantly, will you?"

"Sheldrake would have my guts for garters."

"Sheldrake is not my guardian. Jon is."

"Sheldrake would still have my guts for garters, and so would Jon. And Maud come to think of it."

Sasha gave a naughty little smile. "You do not strike me as a fearful man." She heard a low chuckle behind her and swung round to see Rainstorm, hands on hips, his eyes gleaming with amusement. "Stop it! Who are you laughing at?"

"Neither. I'm admiring your tactics and Tarkyn's predicament."

Tarkyn ignored him. "I am not fearful, at least not in this instance, young lady, but I am honourable, and I would not betray these people's trust."

Sasha's shoulders sagged. "So you won't help me?"

"I will help you, but only with the knowledge of the people who care about you. If you can convince me of the wisdom of your idea, I will support you to convince the others." He smiled at her knowingly. "Besides, you would break Jayhan's heart if you went off on a hare-brained adventure without him."

Out of all the arguments, this last held the most weight. Sasha looked most struck. "True. What was I thinking?" She grinned up at him. "Right. So let's organise our argument."

Tarkyn frowned quizzically over her head to Rainstorm's grinning face, feeling that he had suddenly committed himself to something he didn't necessarily agree with.

Ten minutes later, they walked back into the firesite.

"That was quick," said Maud. "What bird did you use?"

"No bird yet, I'm afraid. I was distracted," said Tarkyn. He gestured at Sasha. "Sasharia has a proposition she would like to put to you. After some consideration, I can tell you it has my support, and I am willing to assist with it."

Sasha took a breath so deep that it lifted and dropped her shoulders. "I want to go and see these people myself, see what has happened to the boats, and see how the shamans are faring." She quailed at the shock on Maud and Sheldrake's face but took heart when she noticed that Jon was nodding in fellow feeling. "These are Kimorans. They are supposed to be my people, whether they know it or not. I won't put myself at risk, but I have to start acting like the person I intend to become."

The effect of this mature announcement was rather spoilt by Jayhan gaping at her then breathing, "Wow Sasha. That was great." He stood up quickly. "I'm coming too, of course... And Jon."

Sasha glanced at Tarkyn, before grinning at her little friend. "Of course."

"No 'of course' about it." snapped Maud. "You're not going, and neither is Jayhan. What are you thinking, throwing yourself into danger like that? ... and you, Tarkyn, condoning it?"

The High Lord's eyes glittered dangerously. He allowed no one to speak to him like that. A fraught silence hung in the air while he quelled his first instinct to reprimand her and then debated how to react. He caught sight of Waterstone standing behind Maud, nodding his approval at his restraint.

His dilemma was solved by the lady herself who was, after all, usually an expert at diplomacy. "I beg your pardon, Your Highness. I am tired and damp from the floodwaters and I am frightened for Carrador and for Sasha and Jayhan... and Jon." She gave an endearingly woebegone smile. "I don't want to lose Sasha and Jon any sooner than I have to, and I don't want to lose Jayhan at all."

Tarkyn's face softened. "Of course you don't, and from a purely pragmatic point of view, it would benefit none of us if we lost Sasha. The plan was never for her to go alone. Stormaway, Midnight, and I, who are among the strongest sorcerers in the known lands, will accompany her and, I presume, Jon, as will two woodfolk... if they are willing." He added as he realized he hadn't asked them yet. "You have my word that we will keep them safe... and Jayhan too, if you will allow him to join us."

Sheldrake expelled a breath and glanced at Maud. "And so it begins," he murmured, "She is already becoming her own woman."

Maud met his eyes for a moment longer as she made her decision. Then she took a deep breath and said briskly. "From my earlier reconnaissance, I saw no sign of any troops on the southern side of the Boden. So it seems to me that the safest course of action is to move The Woodland Rover to the Kimoran side of the river, downstream of the Boden. Then, if you have to make a quick exit, you can be on board and floating downstream far more quickly than having to cross back across the Charville. You people go ahead, while the rest of us pack up and prepare to leave."

Tarkyn blinked, realizing he had just locked horns with someone as controlling as himself. "Excellent plan. And which woodfolk? Rainstorm and ...?" He looked at the woodfolk. "Who else?"

"Me," said Lapping Water firmly.

Without any request being made, Autumn Leaves drew Gurgling Brook to his side and nodded.

"We won't be long, I hope," continued Tarkyn, "I will take a mooring rope across the river with me when I go and tie it to a tree over the other side. Then you'll be able to haul the boat across without going too far downstream. And if the rest of you could also put together dinner while we are gone, I will be eternally grateful." He gave a cheeky grin and turned to leave.

Behind him, he heard Sparrow say in a long-suffering tone, "Tarkyn *never* cooks."

They both knew his acceptance of equality had definite limits and his refusal to cook was one of them. He smiled quite unrepentantly as he imagined Sparrow rolling her eyes.

Chapter 60

Under Tarkyn's direction, Sasha's reconnaissance group made their way downriver through the mess left by the flood until they reached The Woodland Rover. They ducked in under the branches that were disguising it and walked to the portside, peering out through the foliage at the river and the far bank.

"You know," said Tarkyn, looking around at the mass of branches artfully strewn over the sides and superstructure of the boat, "I think it will be easier to launch ourselves from the bank rather than from here. We might snag ourselves on these branches. But we need a long rope, maybe two knotted together, for me to take across to the other side when we go."

"I'll sort that out," said Rainstorm, "and make sure the other end is secured to the boat. You go on ahead and I'll join you in a minute."

Once they had regrouped on the riverbank, Lapping Water considered the width of the river and shook her head regretfully. "Too far for us to flick across, I'm afraid. If you want us to come with you, you'll have to transport us over." She gave a little smile. "If you secure that rope high in a tree on the other side, we could climb across but I'd rather not."

Tarkyn shook his head. "No. The river is only fifty yards across. Stormaway and I will provide a ferry service for you all. Midnight can levitate but he is not strong enough to take someone on his back." Tarkyn grinned at Jon. "Let's get you over first while I still have strength. Stormaway, you bring Sasha, and Midnight will come with us and stay with them so that they have the protection of a sorcerer's shield if needed, while we collect the others."

Rather embarrassed, Jon jumped onto Tarkyn's back. The sorcerer grabbed his legs to hold him steady, then murmuring "*Maya Reeza Mureva,*" rose gently into the air and sailed out across the river.

Jon looked down at the water flowing only feet below him and chortled. "This is fun. Why don't you do it for yourself more often?"

"Hmm. I don't know. I use it to keep up with the woodfolk by getting myself in and out of trees, but other than that," Tarkyn shrugged, "I suppose I don't flaunt my magical talents more than I have to. They can be a bit unnerving, you see."

"Huh," As they alighted on the other side, Jon hopped off. "Thank you for the ride. Thank you very much."

"My pleasure." Tarkyn smiled and rose again to return for his next load.

Stormaway landed beside them and Sasha, who was grinning broadly, slid from his back to join Jon. Midnight floated in and let himself down beside them with a little grin.

"Wow. Thanks Stormaway. That was wonderful," said Sasha.

The old wizard smiled at her delight, entranced that she could be so joyful during such a serious undertaking.

"You're welcome," he said.

As Stormaway lifted off to float back across the river, Sasha let her gaze sweep the woods around her then turned her face, filled with wonder, towards Jon. "Oh. Can you feel it? This place, this land, these forests are calling to me. They need me."

Although he loved Kimora, Jon could not feel it as she did. But he put his arm across her shoulder and said quietly. "Yes, they do."

Ten minutes later, all eight of them were gathered on the riverbank. They moved into the cover of the trees and headed north towards the Boden River.

The Boden River was much smaller than the Charville, only twenty yards wide and as they approached, the sounds of voices floated across the water: snatches of conversation, the occasional shout. They could hear axes and hammers. Not the sounds of battle, merely the sounds you would expect from a campsite being set up: stakes being driven into the ground and wood chopped up for fires.

Sasha pulled a face. "They sound pretty organised to me."

"They couldn't sustain chaos for long. Everything and everyone eventually self-organises," said Stormaway. "Let's see how their boats have fared."

Jayhan frowned at him, trying to decide if what he had said was true.

Not being exactly sure where the boats should be, they began near the intersection with the Charville and walked upstream along the Boden, always keeping well within the tree line. If a stand of bushes barred their way, they would deviate away from the river so that, at no time, were they visible from the other bank.

Five minutes later Jayhan, out of the blue, said, "Even if everything does organise itself, it can get disorganised again, can't it.?" He stared seriously up at the old wizard. "Take my bedroom, for instance. It seems to resist being organised."

Stormaway stopped dead in his tracks and blinked. Then a slow smile dawned on his face. "Thank you for considering my words so carefully. Perhaps I overgeneralised or perhaps everything and everyone does self-organise but eventually falls back into chaos or at least, gradually changes its way of being organised."

This was too much for Jayhan to think about all at once. He gave his head a little shake and returned his attention to the far bank.

For the most part, the opposite bank was sheer, rising eight feet above the water. At one point, a small creek had created a valley where it entered the river. Here they could see men and women walking down the slope to the water's edge. This appeared to be where the soldiers drew water for their campsite.

On closer inspection Sasha could see signs of the flood, branches, flattened tents, and scraps of material, strewn across the area close to the river. As she watched, soldiers were picking up pieces of debris and throwing them into to a pile, dragging on sheets of canvas and inspecting them for damage, while others hammered large wooden stakes into the ground, ready to re-erect those tents that could be salvaged. But there was no sign of boats or a wooden landing stage.

They walked on for another hundred yards, carefully studying the far bank.

Suddenly Lapping Water exclaimed and pointed. "Look! That section of the bank has broken away. The top is jagged while the rest of the way along, it is smooth and weatherworn."

"And there are holes and grooves in that section of the bank," added Rainstorm excitedly. He nodded. "I think we're looking at the site of their little wharf. Look! There are some broken pieces of wood sticking out. Look, there and there," he said, pointing. "I think the whole landing stage has been torn away."

"We will walk another three hundred yards upstream, just to be sure," said Stormaway firmly. He, too, was excited, although he was determined to repress it until they were more certain.

Finally, when he had satisfied himself that there was no other sign of the boats or the landing stage, and they had returned to the point opposite the damaged portion of the far bank, the old wizard turned to Sasha and smiled broadly. "Well done, my little shaman. You may have wreaked unexpected havoc, but I think your deluge has completely destroyed their landing fleet."

Sasha smiled back but a little frown appeared between her eyes. "But shouldn't there be some sign of the boats?"

Stormaway shrugged. "If the landing stage tore away with all the boats attached to it, their ropes probably tangled and the whole lot would have been dragged away or smashed. If any of the boats survived, they are probably bobbing along somewhere down the Charville River."

"Or shredded among the trees where we all were," suggested Rainstorm. "Maybe there are some remnants along the shoreline near our firesite."

"Quite likely, I should think," said Stormaway.

"Lucky we weren't hit by a flying boat," piped up Jayhan with relish. He looked at Tarkyn, pleased with his joke that could actually have been a reality. "Could you tell Midnight that one?"

Tarkyn nodded, used to interpreting for his little charge. Midnight grinned.

Chapter 61

"So, now what?" asked Tarkyn, turning to Sasha.

"Um. I don't know," Sasha was looking steadfastly at the ground. "I just wanted to see if they were all right and, I don't know, help if they weren't." She shrugged. "I don't know how we could have helped but..." She raised her eyes and looked forlornly across the river at the Kimoran camp. "Anyway, it looks like they're fine. I suppose the shamans have had time to recover by now and they're just getting on with their Queen's wishes."

As they watched from within the cover of the trees, a gaggle of officers walked along the top of the far bank, from time to time leaning over to inspect the remnants of their landing stage and talking animatedly among themselves.

Jayhan came over and put an arm around her shoulders. "Don't worry, Sasha. It's good they're all right, as long as they stay in Kimora."

Suddenly, Sasha's amulet pulsed with dark light. Sasha looked down in horror. "Oh no. I didn't tuck it away after the flood. Let go, Jayhan. You're enhancing its power again."

But it was too late. A black beam of light shot across the river calling to the amulets of the Kimoran officers. Even inside their uniforms, the clear light of their amulets could be seen shining in response.

As one, the six officers turned to face the source of the black light.

"Who's there?" shouted an older female voice, harsh with authority.

Hearing the shout, soldiers swarmed to surround their officers, staring out across the river, trying to see any potential threat.

"Do they have archers?" murmured Rainstorm.

"Don't know," replied Tarkyn quickly. "Stormaway, you shield Jon and I'll shield Sasha and Jayhan." He looked at Sasha. "I presume you want to show yourself. It seems pointless not to, at this stage."

Sasha gazed up at him, her liquid brown eyes wide with trepidation. "I suppose so."

The four of them walked forward to the edge of the riverbank, only twenty yards from the Kimorans.

Jon nodded at Sasha. "Go on. Tell them who we are."

Sasha lifted her head high, took a breath and held her amulet before her. "I am Sasharia, youngest daughter of Princess Corinna, wearer of the one true amulet, High Shaman and true Queen of Kimora." In her hand, her amulet glowed with an inner black fire. Into the stunned silence, she continued, indicating her brother, who stood within Stormaway's green shield. "And this is my elder brother, Prince Jondarian, youngest son of Corinna."

Pandemonium broke out on the other side of the river as soldiers began to shout that here was the usurper they had been sent to destroy.

But then a strange thing happened.

Of its own accord, their fury faltered and died out while others exchanged glances. A sense of excitement and dawning hope welled up as rumours ran like wildfire through the troops.

"My aunt always said someone was still alive, wearing the true amulet," murmured a young female soldier.

Some soldiers began to wade into the fast-running current, intending to cross over the river, but whether to attack or ask questions wasn't clear. Others hauled them back and fighting broke out in the shallows until the Kimoran general in their midst raised her hand and, using a shamanic spell to raise her voice, called them to order. All around her, the shouting subsided as soldiers stopped where they were, and all eyes turned to her.

"Women and men of Kimora. Comport yourselves with dignity and discipline, while your shamans and officers confer with these people. Only then, will we decide when or if we attack."

This immediately led to a ripple of outrage and shouts of protest.

General Kazak's eyes glittered with anger. "This is not a democracy. It is an army. Keep your comments to yourself or you will find yourselves severely disciplined. Lieutenant Hagan, find Captain Marlene and round up the other shamans and officers. I want all troops to collect their weapons and fall into formation. Officers will line up with them when they arrive."

The discipline of having clear orders overcame the unrest and dampened the heightened emotions.

When Marlene arrived, she was slightly out of breath but no longer limping, courtesy of shamanic healing. Her white hair was more awry than ever. As soon as all officers and shamans had arrived, Kazak quietly described what had happened.

Marlene frowned. "But my amulet did not glow as I approached."

"No," murmured Kazak. "But she is inside that shield now. Perhaps that is stopping it." At last the general projected her voice, using her magic, to address Sasha. "I am General Kazak, the commanding officer of these forces. You are aware, I presume, that I have two thousand soldiers at my command. You must have a large force if you hope to defeat us."

Jon replied for his sister. "We do not wish to defeat you, merely to stop you crossing into Carrador."

Kazak glanced a question at Marlene, who nodded. Then Kazak asked, "So were you responsible for that surge of water that passed through here an hour ago?"

Jon smiled and shook his head. "Not I. My wizard friend," here he indicated Stormaway but did not introduce him, figuring it was up to Tarkyn and Stormaway to decide whether they wanted their identities known, "and Sasharia created that."

Marlene studied the small girl who stood within the bronze shield, her head only just level with Tarkyn's chest. "No wonder the shamanic magic was wild. She is only a child."

With a growing sense of excitement, Kazak asked her quietly, "Do you think she might be *that* child? Could she be who she claims she is?"

Marlene raised her voice and called across the river, "Will you let down your shields? I wish to sense the quality of your power, but I cannot do so through a sorcerer's shield."

Sasha looked up at Tarkyn who in turn checked with Lapping Water and Rainstorm that there were no archers before waving away his hazy bronze dome, leaving Jayhan and her unprotected. Stormaway followed suit.

Immediately Sasha's amulet sent a black shaft of light streaking across the water to make Marlene's and over forty other shamans' amulets shine in response. For a few moments, the whole group was encased in a shining corona of soft, multi-coloured light. Sasha couldn't help herself. She grinned, feeling the warmth of the answering connection and the sense of the magical camaraderie that existed among shamans.

Across the river, Marlene and Kazak exchanged glances, suppressing smiles.

"What are you going to do?" whispered Marlene.

Kazak looked over her shoulder at her troops, who now stood at attention, weapons by their sides. All of them had their eyes on the proceedings.

Hagan, standing by her side, hesitated before asking quietly. "Could you... would you mind telling me what those streaks of light mean? Or is it private shaman business? It's just that if I understand what is happening, I can be of more assistance."

Kazak considered him. His open, honest face wore a wary expression and she realised that it had taken courage to step over the bounds into shaman business. She nodded at the figures across the river. "That girl's amulet is connecting with ours. It is just possible that she is not an impostor."

Lieutenant Hagan's eyes widened. "But... "

"Exactly. I believed, as did all of us, that all of Corinna's offspring were dead. But the behaviour of that girl's amulet and the strength of her shamanic power suggest otherwise."

Panic flickered behind Hagan's eyes. "Then Queen Toriana..."

Kazak frowned. "Don't say it. Not yet." She turned back to Sasha. "What do you know of a malaise that struck down all of my shamans earlier this afternoon?"

"Just a minute," said Stormaway. He muttered a few words under his breath then nodded to Sasha, "Off you go."

"WE NEEDED..." Sasha's eyes widened. "Ooh. Did you make my voice louder?" When Stormaway gave a slight smile and nod, she whispered, "Thanks." By the time she started again she had had time to realise that saying she had released them from Toriana's binding just to stall for time would not be politic. So instead she said, "I concentrated on my amulet and heartbeat, hoping that I could override the binding that was placed on you by Toriana during your oathtaking. The change overloads your senses, but only for a while." She tilted her head and asked anxiously. "Are you all right now?"

A hubbub of noise rose around Kazak. Her shamans' discipline dissolved as they realised their heightened senses and released tension had signalled their freedom from a bond that was against all tenets of shaman philosophy. Their faces suffused with anger and freed from Toriana's constraint, they voiced their long-subdued outrage at their oppressor.

Suddenly from behind them, the lines of regular troopers joined in, all thoughts of discipline swamped by the release of years of pent-up resentment.

"My aunty always knew Toriana's amulet was false. She wouldn't swear the oath and now she's in some prison in Manissa," yelled a female voice from deep within the crowd that was forming.

"My sister was killed because she told everyone that Toriana's heartbeat didn't beat in time with her own amulet," yelled a man. "We always knew a true heir existed."

His neighbour turned to him. "So what were you doing, signing up to hunt her down then?"

"I didn't know that's what we'd be doing when I signed up. Anyway," the man shoved the questioner in the chest, "who had the choice?"

Then individual voices were lost in shouts of recrimination as fighting broke out and feelings ran high.

Once more Kazak's voice rose above them. Gradually they quietened and all eyes turned once more to Kazak, Marlene, and the small dark girl on the other side of the river.

"I don't know who has been training you or how much you know," said Marlene, "but if you are the wearer of the true amulet, our amulets should be beating in time with your heart, if the link has been broken with Toriana."

Sasha nodded, indicating she knew this. She focused on her heartbeat and on the obsidian amulet in her hand. Slowly the black amulet began to pulse more and more brightly, until its beat showed clearly across the width of the river. Then she looked up and tilted her head in query.

Marlene, holding her own amulet, nodded, a smile of excitement dawning on her face.

"But even if your heart is beating with their amulets, how do we know that you haven't just imposed a stronger sorcery on our shamans than the Queen did?" yelled one of the soldiers.

Sasha looked up at Stormaway, who gave a slight shrug.

"I don't know," Sasha replied honestly.

Marlene answered for her. "The link we had with Toriana felt taut and full of compulsion. This link feels warm and soft and full of compassion."

Tara, a younger blonde-haired shaman, spoke up. "Under Toriana's compulsion, we literally, physically, could never say anything against Toriana. Now I bet we can say what we like about that little girl over there." She gave a wry smile and tried, speaking loudly enough for Sasha to hear. "Sasharia has used an excess of shamanic magic to destroy our boats, which we would have returned to their owners when we had finished with them. So she has done a disservice to the local people of this river."

From across the river, they couldn't see Sasha's expression clearly, but they did see her little friend put his arm around her again.

Then, to their surprise, the boy called out. "Don't blame her. You are trying to invade the country that has looked after her all her life. She is just trying to protect us, those she loves. When she comes to love you, she will protect you instead."

Was it their imagination or did his voice hitch on those last words?

Forgetting that her voice was being projected by Stormaway's spell, Sasha put her arm around his waist and murmured, "Not instead, Jayhan, as well as. I would never forget you and Maud and Sheldrake and everyone who has helped me."

In the midst of the Kimoran shamans, Tara smiled.

Then all around her, the full company of shamans sank to one knee and bowed their heads to their High Shaman. But the soldiers, giddy with delight at the prospect of a better future, did not bow. Instead, they sent up a roar of approbation, threw their caps in the air and jumped up and down in excitement, grabbing their neighbours and hugging them.

Part 8

Chapter 62

The afternoon sun streamed into the large, high-ceilinged, stone room on the third floor of the western tower, illuminating ancient tapestries, even as it faded them. A huge, ornately carved four poster bed was the central piece of furniture. A chaise longue under the window was currently occupied by an enormous iron trunk. The Queen sat in one of two padded armchairs watching as her dresser, a stern middle-aged woman, and a young blue-eyed maid, with bouncy black curls held under a white cap, presented possible gowns from the wardrobe for packing. Both were dressed in deep blue shifts with white collar and cuffs,

It had been a long, tedious process. Toriana kept changing her mind.

Finally, as the maid placed the last finely embroidered woollen gown carefully into the trunk and closed the lid, the dresser said, "All packed ma'am." Before the Queen could change her mind again, Barton said to the maid, "Pansy, send footmen to take the trunk down to the carriage. Quickly now."

Pansy hesitated as Toriana let out a long breath. The two servants waited on tenterhooks until the Queen nodded. "And send up Waldarion, and Hardikan. I need to speak to them before I go."

Just as the maid curtseyed again and turned to leave, the Queen's eyes glazed, and she sat down suddenly on the edge of her bed. Hearing the sudden movement behind her, Pansy whipped back around in alarm but was stopped from going to Toriana by a raised hand. The dresser, still standing by the trunk, was also forestalled by the raised hand and made no move but muttered, "Get Hardikan."

The maid turned and fled.

The castle was large, and it took nearly twenty minutes for Pansy to find the senior shaman. Hardikan was strolling through the gardens, inspecting the progress of the herbs that she had ordered to be grown among the other more decorative plants along the garden's borders. As luck would have it, when Pansy finally tracked her down, she had reached the far end of the garden where she was discussing with Gordon the gardener which herbs could be harvested to take to the Midwinter Festival.

Pansy curtseyed and waited until Hardikan finished what she was saying and turned to her. "Ma'am, the Queen requires your presence. She seems a bit...odd." Pansy, who was not a shaman and so was not subject to the Queen's binding, was able to say phrases that might be construed as reflecting poorly on the monarch.

Hardikan raised her eyebrows. "Indeed? I will come at once."

Despite their haste though, a good half hour passed before Hardikan was admitted to the Queen's bedchamber by Barton. Hardikan raised her eyebrows, a favourite expression of hers, in silent query.

"She has recovered, Ma'am. I've sent for a tisane," murmured the dresser.

"Thank you, Barton."

A harsh voice sounded from within the room. "What's all that muttering in the doorway? Stop gossiping and come in here, Hardikan."

Hardikan entered to find the Queen now seated in one of the padded armchairs, apparently fully recovered.

She dropped a deep curtsey and waited for permission before rising.

"You took you time getting here," snapped Toriana.

"Good afternoon, Your Majesty. Yes, I did inadvertently, but I was at the other end of the gardens. I apologize, but you may be pleased to know that I have finalised which herbs we are to take."

"Hmph," grunted the Queen in grumpy acknowledgement. She waved a hand. "Now sit down and listen." Even before Hardikan had time to seat herself, she began, "Someone has been interfering with the weather over Kimora. It was slow but sure, at first. Then a wild, uncontrolled surge of power took over. I wouldn't be surprised to discover there has been local damage." Her eyes glittered. "It wasn't a natural storm. Someone is interfering in my realm."

"But who, ma'am? And can you tell where in Kimora it was?"

"It felt alien at first but then the power was clearly shamanic." She hit her hand down on the chair arm. "A blasted rogue shaman! How many years will it take to register every shaman? And what are they hoping to achieve?" She glared at Hardikan. "As to where, it was somewhere in the west, near the border."

Hardikan's eyes widened in alarm. "Not near the Darkstone Mountains where we will be gathering, was it?"

"No. Further north and further west than that."

Hardikan thought for a few moments, envisaging a map of Kimora in her mind. Then she drew in a breath. "How far north? Our troops should be arriving at the point opposite The Way Through any time now. Could it be there?"

Despite herself, Hardikan drew back in her chair at the look of fury on Toriana's face.

"A renegade shaman working for our enemy. Outrageous!" barked the Queen. She gave a nasty laugh. "Huh. If so, they picked the wrong shaman to help them. Whoever it is has poor control and is just as likely to hurt her allies as her enemies. Her power went completely haywire. Like a child, trying to ride a wild stallion." A fraught silence descended as the implications of this last remark sank in. Suddenly the Queen became decisive, successfully hiding the sense of panic that was welling inside her. "Send a messenger to General Kazak. She must be warned. If that child impostor is in the vicinity, it may be our best chance of apprehending her."

Once Hardikan and her dresser had left, Toriana stared out the window at the western horizon. With growing conviction, she knew that somewhere out there was her young niece. Worse still, somehow Corinna had transferred the true amulet to her. As soon as Toriana had mentioned a child, she had known who she was facing. She had felt the strength of that erratic surge. Ungoverned it may be, but only the wearer of the true amulet could elicit such power.

Her hands curled into fists as a surge of panic welled up. How could this be happening? How could those idiot assassins have let any of her sister's family escape? Such a simple task. And now her whole lifestyle, her very life, could be at risk.

She gave a bitter laugh. She had thought that life would be so good, so glorious, if she could only get rid of her smarter, more popular elder sister. She had wanted the power that beckoned at the end of their mother's life, and she had wanted the friendships that came so easily to Corinna. Well, by removing Corinna, she had certainly gained the power. But only when she had ascended the throne did Toriana realise that the one thing she could not command was friendship.

Sadly, she was discerning enough to know that all the overtures made towards her were either out of fear, duty, or the hope of gaining some advantage. And because she felt spurned, she took refuge in revenge: delighting in making people feel powerless, keeping them on tenterhooks, and punishing them.

She gave herself a little shake. She might be isolated, but she did have power, status, palaces, wealth beyond imagining, and thousands of people under her command. She smiled grimly. She would not give that away for a hundred friendships and she would do everything in her power to destroy anyone who threatened it.

Chapter 63

By the time a stew of wildfowl, root vegetables and forest greenery was simmering over the fire at their new firesite on the Kimoran side of the Charville, Maud had recovered and was becoming restless.

"I think," she said to Sheldrake, "I might just head off and check on how they are getting on. Then I can let you know when they will be back for dinner." She gave a little smile. "I liked Tarkyn's idea of a bat. I think I'll try it."

Sheldrake frowned at her, not sure why she was smiling. "Why?"

"The wings," she answered quietly "They're like the pictures I've seen of dragons."

Something clicked in Sheldrake's brain, and he remembered a large goanna falling out of a tree near their pond at home and a look passing between Yarrow and Sasha that he hadn't really paid attention to at the time.

"Did you try to sail out of a tree as a goanna?" he asked.

Maud looked embarrassed. "Yes. Silly idea, but at least I got the feel of being a large lizard."

"You want to try to be a dragon, don't you?" Sheldrake's eyes were twinkling with mirth.

Maud looked around her, hoping no one else was listening. "Shh. Yes. Just an idea. Something Gavin said about riding on a dragon got me thinking."

Sheldrake whooped with laughter. "Maud. You are incorrigible."

Just then a great roar erupted from the site of the Kimoran camp. All thoughts of dinner abandoned, everyone ran for the Boden River to protect Sasha and the others.

When they arrived breathlessly at the riverbank, an amazing sight met their eyes. Sasha and Jon stood, proud and tall, in full view of the Kimoran troops. The shamans were still kneeling while the troops were still prancing around with joy.

Maud was just in time to hear Sasha say, her voice enhanced by Stormaway's magic, "Thank you very much. Please rise. The future is not yet ours. While my aunt holds sway over the other shamans throughout Kimora, we are still in danger. But I thank you very much for your faith in me."

Maud sought out Tarkyn. "What's going on? How have Sasha and Jon wrought such a change in so short a time? It took far longer for Arquin's troops to soften and there were only a few of them."

Sasha heard the question and looked around, saying with new confidence, "It is because I am in Kimora where I belong. Everything is just falling into place around me." She nodded to indicate the people on the far shore. "They can feel it too. I belong to them and this land, and they belong to me." She smiled mistily up at her brother, "...and to Jondarian."

"I see," said Maud slowly. After a moment she asked, "So what now? Is it safe to meet up with them," she gave a little quirk of her mouth, "bearing in mind that Sheldrake and I are Carradorian, and Tarkyn and Stormaway are from Eskuzor? Not to mention your own status as a pretender to the crown."

"Not so fast," murmured Sheldrake.

Beside her, Sheldrake scoured the far shore, frowning fiercely and muttering incomprehensible words under his breath. Then he swept his hand in an arc and sent a shower of light blue droplets flying across the river to spread among the troops and officers of the Kimoran force. Gradually the droplets sank through the crowd and dissipated as they touched individuals. But the droplets on one hundred scattered individuals didn't dissipate. Instead, they intensified to a dark royal blue and stuck to them.

"Quickly, Sasha. Tell whoever is in charge that she has informers in her ranks. Tell her to apprehend them before the blue fades."

As Sasha conveyed the message to General Kazak, Stormaway murmured to Sheldrake, "Excellent trick. You must show me that one."

Sheldrake smiled, pleased that at last he had been able to exhibit a skill not possessed by the other magic users. "I would be delighted." Then he realised that Sasha was standing beside him, her newfound confidence fast evaporating.

"Do all those people who showed dark blue still hate me?" she asked in a small voice.

Jon was standing beside Sasha with his arm around her shoulders, but he squatted down at this, to be at her eye level. "Remember we said even King Gavin has people who don't like him? You and I will never have everyone on our side. No matter how harsh Toriana's regime, some people will have thrived under it. Some of these people will be mercenaries loyal only to money, as Shay was, completely disinterested in the royal line. Some will have families who have benefitted from Toriana's patronage. Some will have families who will be endangered if they are found to be disloyal." He shrugged. "Some may just like Toriana's style."

"The world isn't perfect, Sasha," said Marjorie. "Appreciate your achievement. You have the vast majority in your favour now when, an hour ago, they were all crying out for your blood."

"No, not *her* blood," said Jayhan quickly, thinking this phrasing would upset her. "The blood of a mythical impostor."

Marjorie suppressed a smile at Jayhan's stoic loyalty, and she replied seriously, "True."

Chapter 64

The rain drifted gently down around them, forcing them to find shelter under tarpaulins, cloaks or under thickly foliaged tree branches so that they could eat their stew without it turning mushy.

"We'd be better off in the boat," muttered Jackson.

"Perhaps," said Autumn Leaves who was more used to outdoor conditions in any weather. "But let's finish Sparrow's excellent stew first." He glanced at Sasha and Jon. "Besides, we can protect you better from the surrounding trees when these Kimorans arrive."

Maud ate a mouthful of stew then frowned, "Well, I don't know what we're going to say to them. Our plans have gone completely belly up. We are supposed to be sneaking down the river to the Dark Lake and from there, up to the shamans' Midwinter Festival."

Rainstorm gave a quiet chortle. "And we can hardly invite two thousand troops to accompany us."

"Exactly. Even the forty shamans would be out of the question." Maud frowned. "Hmm. I presume they were not going to the Midwinter Festival anyway, if they were intent on invading Carrador... which means caches of shamans all over the country won't be able to leave their duties to go. So our plan of catching all shamans together at once was flawed anyway."

Sasha was watching the trees to the east for the first sign of the approaching Kimoran delegation, but she glanced sideways at that and gave Maud a reassuring smile. "It may not matter if I can best Toriana and break the bond from her end."

"Right," said Maud faintly, feeling daunted by the change in her erstwhile stableboy's manner.

"That is certainly the plan," said Sheldrake carefully, "but I wouldn't underestimate its difficulty."

Sasha looked from one to the other before dropping her eyes, her cheeks reddening. After a minute she said quietly, "I didn't say it would be easy. I'm sorry if you thought I was bragging." She raised her head and looked up at the rain falling gently through the trees. "But I am affecting at least this part of Kimora already. When do you think they last had rain?"

"Oh," breathed Lapping Water from under a leafy branch on the other side of the fire. "Is that you? Oh, of course it is. When you look around, the earth is parched, the trees are straggly and most of the undergrowth has shrivelled and died. It's too much of a coincidence, isn't it, that the first good rain arrives as you do…" she sent a grin to Stormaway, "without any conscious weather-working?"

Already puddles were forming, and the ground was becoming muddy as the hard earth resisted the water it needed so badly.

"Bloody inconvenient, if you ask me," grumbled the wizard.

Sasha grinned. "Sorry."

Then she realised that Lapping Water had disappeared, and she swung around just as General Kazak, Lieutenant Hagan, and Senior Shaman Marlene entered the firesite, water dripping from their hair and the ends of their noses. Sasha scrambled to her feet and stood facing them, her breath coming in anxious little spurts. Then she felt Jon's steadying hand on her back as the three Kimoran officers bowed.

She took a deep breath to steady herself. "Please rise," she said and received a nod of approval from Tarkyn on the other side of the fire. "Welcome to our… campsite."

As the three Kimorans introduced themselves, she sent a frown of query at him, wondering whether she should introduce her companions and if so, by their full titles or only by name.

Happily, Jon took over. "Good evening. Let me make known to you the Lords Tarkyn, Sheldrake, Stormaway, and Stefan, and the Lady Maud. Also Lord Jayhan, Marjorie, Stefan's sister, and Jackson, Lord Tarkyn's aide de camp."

General Kazan was no fool and she had moved in the highest political circles for years. She frowned, thinking through what she knew of these casually delivered names. Then she gave another low bow. "Prince Tarkyn, High Lord of Eskuzor, it is an honour to meet you… and you, Lord Sheldrake and Lady Maud. You are, I believe, the Carradorian King's closest advisors. I am not acquainted with the exploits of you others, but I have no doubt you hold positions of power and influence in your home countries."

"Hmm. No flies on this one," murmured Rainstorm in the tree above her.

Kazak turned to Sasha and asked with a hint of dryness, "Have you had any training at all in the shamanic arts, ma'am?"

Sasha took a moment to realise she was addressing her. Then she blushed, partly in embarrassment at her lack of skill and partly in anger at the general's tone. When she spoke, her voice was cool, "Some, but I have only known that I am a shaman for a year. I would assume that in the years that Marlene and you have practised as shamans, you have learnt more." She looked down and drew out her obsidian amulet. Once she had it in her hand, she looked up again and met the General's eye. "And I doubt that any of you, no matter how experienced, can replace the knowledge my mother and grandmother would have given me."

In the tree above, Rainstorm grinned at Sparrow who was beside him, bow at the ready in case of threat "Hoo. That's telling her."

From the side, Sheldrake gave a little cough. "Fortunately, since her mother is not here, Sasharia learns directly from her amulet. I, three unregistered shamans, and surprisingly, my son Jayhan, have been supporting her to uncover her heritage." He smiled gently, "But as she says, she has only just begun. I think she has made tremendous progress, don't you?"

Marlene smiled warmly and gestured at the black amulet. "Her innate and inherited power are breathtakingly strong," she replied diplomatically. She waved her hand around her, "And her connection with our land is indisputable. Already she is healing it."

Lieutenant Hagan frowned. "The rain, you mean?" When Marlene nodded, he smiled broadly. "Oh, well, that's quite marvellous then. I wonder how widespread this rain is." He looked at Sasha and addressed her directly. "Some parts of Kimora are desert plains and have never had much rainfall. Did you know that?"

His tone was friendly and there was only curiosity, not censure, underlying his question. Sasha decided she liked this man and nodded in reply.

"You've been learning about your home country, have you?" he continued. "That's good. So I wonder if the deserts will stay that way with your arrival. I suspect the plants and animals of the deserts would be very put out by too much rainfall, don't you?"

Sasha grinned. "Probably. But I don't think I'm just causing rain. I think the land is coming back into balance around me. So I think the deserts will return to being as dry as they are happy with."

Beside him, Kazak and Marlene exchanged a glance, clearly impressed by her level of understanding. Hagan, completely involved in his conversation with Sasha, didn't notice. "My family comes from those dry plains, you know. The area is called the Najabi Desert, but you probably know that already, don't you?"

Sasha nodded again, pleased that she did. "And it stretches down to the foothills on the north-eastern side of the Darkstone Mountains."

"I know that too," piped up Jayhan.

Hagan grinned. "Good for you. You've been helping Sasha learn her Kimoran geography, have you?"

Incurably honest, Jayhan screwed up his face and said, "Sometimes. Sometimes I get bored and go off to do something else."

"Very wise," said the Lieutenant. "Otherwise you'd end up distracting Sasharia, wouldn't you?"

Jayhan grinned. "Exactly."

Chapter 65

"I wondered if you were a plainsman, Lieutenant Hagan," said Jon, "Some of our ancestors also hail from there. We share the same colouring, you and I."

"Yes, Sire, we do." Suddenly, speaking to an adult, the Lieutenant became far more reserved. In fact, he seemed to be struggling to know what to say.

General Kazak rescued him by asking, "Do you think we could get out of this rain? Perhaps retire to the overhang of those trees over there?"

"Of course. Jackson and Marjorie have rigged up a tarpaulin for us," said Maud. "I'll organise some tea. Stefan, perhaps you could do the honours there?"

Tarkyn grinned at her from the other side of the clearing, admiring her delegation skills.

A few minutes later they sat in relative dryness under a cover patched together from a large and a small tarpaulin and two cloaks, with Tarkyn and Sheldrake providing magical orbs of light. Just as cups of tea arrived, the rain stopped. Stefan shook his wet hair out of his face and sat down among them.

Marlene cocked her head, listening to the occasional big drops falling from wet leaves and asked Sasha, "Did you do that? Stop it, I mean."

Sasha shook her head. "I didn't consciously start it or stop it. But too much rain all at once would cause flooding, especially after all this dryness, don't you think?" She gave a little smile. "Maybe the change will be gradual and less damaging."

Again Marlene and Kazak exchanged glances.

"Toriana will have sensed the flood you created, Sasharia. She is aware of weather patterns across the country," said Marlene quietly.

Then Kazak leaned forward. "And I should tell you that although we apprehended those amongst us who showed up as informers, we discovered that several people had already gone missing from our ranks and, we suspect, are on the way to inform Queen Toriana of the events that occurred here. We have sent soldiers after them in the hope that we may catch up with them, but it is by no means certain that word won't get through to the Queen."

"Aah," breathed Sheldrake. "That is most unfortunate. Toriana has not known that Sasha can break her binding. I don't know what she can do to safeguard against it, but until now, she has not realised the need to."

"I wonder whether she really thinks you're merely an impostor or is actually aware of your true identity?" mused Kazak. "I can't see that it will affect our orders, but it may affect what she, as a powerful shaman, does."

"She has always known that Sasha may have survived, since I'm sure she must have known that her body and that of Prince Jondarian were never found," said Sheldrake.

"A fact unknown by the general public," cut in Marlene acidly. "We were led to believe that the whole family had been killed. Hence Toriana's apparently legitimate claim to the throne."

Kazak nodded in agreement. "Once I inform her of the loss of our river transport, she will redirect us to searching for you, I think, until more rivercraft have been procured." She grimaced "But it will only be a temporary setback in our plans to invade Carrador. Even now, the northern army, four thousand strong, is marching up to the bridge at Bridgetown and a similar army has already left Manissa and will skirt the Dark Lake to march along the southern route into Carrador. Toriana will not abandon her plans of invasion even if she discovers Sasharia is within Kimora. The prolonged drought has led to chronic food shortages that she plans to repair by taking over the fertile farmlands south of Highkington."

Maud's face went white. "Oh no." For once her composure deserted her. "Oh, of course she would have sent more than your small force. Oh dear, what can we do? I must warn Gavin. We could destroy the bridge before the northern army gets there, but it will not be so easy to hinder the army in the south. How are we going to do that? When will these armies cross into Carrador?"

Sheldrake placed a hand on her arm. "Maud, calm down. All is not yet lost... and we will gain nothing by panicking."

Kazak's eyes narrowed. "I'm not sure that I will give you any more information. In fact, I may have given you too much already. I work for Kimora's future, not yours nor Carrador's and our need is dire."

"And does your future Kimora now include me?" asked Sasha acerbically, "... and Jon?" "

"Or were your demonstrations of fealty just hollow gestures?" asked Jon stiffly.

Kazak glanced at Marlene then Hagan before saying slowly, "I believe you are who you say you are. But I am wary of the company you keep and am concerned that your loyalties are, at best, divided or, at worse, completely corrupted, placing Carrador's interests before our own."

Jon jumped up, his sudden movement sending the cobbled-together covering away to one side with a trail of water droplets in its wake. He towered over them, glaring down into their shocked faces. His brilliant blue eyes glittered with a rage no one had ever seen before.

"How dare you!"

Kazak rose hastily to her feet to face him, Marlene and Hagan right behind her. Although impressed by the strength of his reaction, the general squared her shoulders and thrust her chest out in a gesture of defiance and said evenly, "I dare because I command two thousand soldiers and I say what I think to everyone I meet... except Queen Toriana. And I would be derelict in my duty to Kimora if I just accepted the presence of international leaders, unannounced, on my home soil without challenge."

A quiet chuckle came from Tarkyn who stood up at a more leisurely pace as he said, "She's right, you know, Jon. None of us has yet explained our reasons for being here and she must assume, quite correctly, that all of us would put our own country first." He turned his attention to the General and began to speak, "We have come to know Sasha and Jon and have a personal interest in their welfare. But that alone would not be enough. We have heard of atrocities committed under the reign of your Queen Toriana and recently, our agents have reported preparations for war. By all accounts, she is a merciless, ambitious woman who has already killed her sister to ascend the throne and has now set her sights on her neighbouring countries. But neither Carrador nor Eskuzor wants to wage a war with her... with you."

"So it suits our purpose to support Sasha to usurp Toriana and take her rightful place on the throne," continued Sheldrake. "We can offer alternatives to war. If you need food, we will give you supplies to tide you over. Then you can trade for it. You have plenty of minerals and gems that are valuable to us, but in recent years, trade has been strangled by corrupt border officials and Toriana has ignored all communications from King Gavin to remedy this and to withdraw her shaman hunters. He offered to repatriate a whole company of Kimorans who had invaded Carrador, but she refused to have them back."

Kazak's eyebrows shot together. "She *what*?? We were told that Arquin and her troops were slaughtered wholesale, even those who had yielded."

"No," said Jon, his equanimity restored. "As we speak, they are about to start work on repairing Carrador's main northern road. As paid workers I might add, not as prisoners of war. When Toriana said she wouldn't have them back, we devised gainful employment for them."

"How many survived?"

"Nearly the full company. Less than twenty were killed."

"And you may be interested to know, Kazak," put in Sheldrake, carefully avoiding Jon's gaze, "that Prince Jondarian rescued Sasharia from the assassins who killed the rest of their family when he was only twelve years old. He has since worked tirelessly to rescue, support and organise Kimoran refugees, saving unregistered shamans and their families from slaughter and imprisonment."

"Jon is going to be regent until I'm older," said Sasha, her eyes shining with pride.

General Kazak produced a shallow bow and said to Jon, "I beg your pardon, Your Highness, for doubting you."

"No. The fault is mine. I should have been clearer in my introductions." Jon smiled ruefully. "I admit I was concerned what your reaction would be if I were more forthcoming." He shrugged, grinning. "Besides, these people are effectively Sasha's secret army, and I did not want to give too much away before I had your measure."

Chapter 66

Suddenly the ground shifted beneath them. Not a lot, but it was noticeable. Enough to rock them on their feet and to send scatterings of leaves from the trees.

Automatically, people clung to each other, and Sasha found herself grabbing hold of Hagan while Kazak and Jon grasped each other's clothing. Tarkyn found himself with one arm around Marlene and the other around Maud, who was being clung to by Jayhan. Sheldrake and Stefan grabbed Stormaway as the older man threatened to lose his balance and topple over.

Slowly, as nothing further happened, they released each other. But the physical contact, however brief, had reduced the barriers between them.

Sasha and Jayhan's eyes were round with wonder.

"What was that?" breathed Jayhan, half excited, half frightened.

"An earth tremor, I think," said Sheldrake, "…or a distant explosion."

Marlene shook her head. "Not an explosion. Definitely an earth tremor. I can feel it shifting beneath my feet." She looked at the two children and forced a reassuring smile. "Be careful. There may be some aftershocks, but they will be less powerful."

Balanced in the boughs of the trees, the woodfolk had grabbed hold of nearby trunks and branches as the tremor had struck. Their hearts were still thumping with fright when Marlene glanced up into the trees. "Are you people all right?"

Lapping Water and Autumn Leaves exchanged glances just as they received a message from Waterstone, "*Shamans know about treewrights, which is, I suppose, their name for woodfolk. Shall we join them?*" Waterstone sent the query in an image to Tarkyn, who shrugged and nodded.

"*I'm not sure whether the general Kimoran population know about treewrights,*" replied Autumn Leaves doubtfully. "*What about Lieutenant Hagan?*"

Lapping Water grinned. "*After all the outsiders we've already met, I wouldn't worry about him. If he doesn't know about us, we'll just swear him to secrecy too.*"

Waterstone huffed. "*We can't just go breaking our woodfolk oath every time we feel like having a chat with a new outsider.*"

"*She spoke to us in front of Hagan,*" Lapping Water pointed out. "*He must now be aware that people are in the trees around them, even if he doesn't know they are treewrights… woodfolk.*"

"True." With no further discussion, Waterstone flicked down to appear before Marlene. "Thank you for asking. We are quite shaken, actually. Some of us nearly fell. I am Waterstone."

Moments later, the others appeared in a ring behind him.

"Oh, of course you are, you poor dears," said Maud, in a rush of sympathy. "It was scary enough for us on the ground. Jackson, could you put the kettle back on the fire please? I think we need more tea."

Meanwhile, General Kazak was observing the newcomers, noting the small boy with the more brilliant green eyes, the teenaged girl, and the babe in Lapping Water's arms in company with the three men, all armed.

"How do you do? I am Kazak," she said briefly, before turning to Jon and Sasha, her eyebrows raised. "If you have treewrights on your side, as well as a mage, a wizard, and a sorcerer... oh, and a shape-shifter... regardless of their political connections, you have a very powerful force supporting you. Far greater than my army of two thousand. I can see why you felt confident to reveal yourselves to us."

"Oh well, actually, that was..." began Sasha.

"... a good opportunity to get to know a few Kimoran people to gauge how we would be received," cut in Jon.

Tarkyn frowned at the dissemblance while Sheldrake smiled his approval. Sasha noticed both reactions and gave a little sigh. Life under the scrutiny of many people, especially powerful ones with different agendas, was going to be an ongoing struggle.

Lieutenant Hagan, ignoring this interchange, was smiling at the woodfolk. "How do you do? What a pleasure it is to meet you. I have heard of you, of course, but have never met any of you. I do like your green eyes. Quite lovely."

Lapping Water chuckled. "Thank you. I like your blue eyes. Pleased to meet you too. I am Lapping Water." She glanced at Autumn Leaves, knowing he would be pleased that they weren't revealing themselves to someone who didn't know of them.

"Hello. And I'm Sparrow and this is Midnight," piped up Sparrow.

Midnight gave a little wave of greeting before sidling over to put an arm around Tarkyn's leg so firmly that Tarkyn had to take a step to keep his balance. The sorcerer frowned down at his little charge then realised that Midnight was trembling. He bent down and scooped the boy up into his arms.

"Oh Midnight, you've had a bad fright, haven't you?" As Midnight burrowed his head into Tarkyn's chest, he crooned, matching words to images, knowing that the vibration of his chest as he spoke soothed Midnight. "It's all right. You were a clever one and held on up in the tree. Good boy." He glanced at Sparrow. "And how are you?"

Sparrow smiled, pleased that he had asked her. He was her uncle by virtue of Waterstone being his bloodbrother and they had spent a lot of time together when she was younger at a time when Tarkyn was new to the forest, before the advent of Midnight. "I'm all right. It wasn't much worse than a sudden gust of wind."

Just then, another little shudder went through the ground beneath them.

Sparrow grinned at Tarkyn, "Ooh!'

Sheldrake eyed Marlene. "Are these tremors common in Kimora?"

"No." She looked puzzled and a little worried, but she said nothing further.

General Kazak looked around the group. "You are a strange mixture, I must say, half family, half fighting force. You, in particular, Lord Tarkyn, behave so disarmingly and yet I know that you hold the ultimate political power in your country and are a strong sorcerer and forest guardian."

"You appear strongly in command right now, Kazak, but I'm sure you, too, have your softer side. We all do." He chuckled and looked down at Midnight in his arms, "Just as this little worry pot has his fearsome side. He has nearly as much power as I, you know." His smile faded and he brought up serious eyes to meet hers. "I am sure you cannot stay much longer with two thousand troops waiting for you. So let's get down to business. How long will it take the northern army to reach Bridgetown and when will your southern army reach the Dark Lake and cross into Carrador? We can find out ourselves if you decide not to tell us, but it would save us effort. That is all."

Kazak thought for a moment then glanced at Maud. "Shape-shifter. She could fly and find out, couldn't she?"

Tarkyn nodded. "So you see? Having told us as much as you have, you have nothing to lose by telling us more."

"They should arrive at Bridgetown in five days' time, cross the bridge on the sixth day from now. Both armies are scheduled to cross into Carrador three days after midwinter, moving on Highkington simultaneously from north and south. My army was supposed to already be in place in the forest to infiltrate and lend support where needed." The General glared at Sheldrake. "You had better keep your word about providing us with aid."

"I will," replied Sheldrake, unfazed by her challenge. "And in return I will tell you that Sasha is heading to the Midwinter Festival in the Darkstone Mountains. We are meeting two refugee shamans at the Dark Lake."

Marlene's eyes widened. "If you return to Dark Lake after the Festival, you will be there when the southern army arrives." She turned her gaze from Sheldrake to Sasha to find herself being watched by wary, dark eyes. "Do you have any idea what you are taking on?" she demanded. "There will be hundreds of shamans at the Festival and Queen Toriana, the most powerful shaman of all of them."

Sasha reddened and looked down. "I do know. I must trust to my amulet and myself…" Then she raised her eyes and gave a quirky self-conscious smile, "and to my connection with Kimora, which I am only now discovering."

"But on the shores of the Dark Lake, scores of shamans will be preparing to make the trek up the mountain path," exclaimed. Marlene. "We can't have them dropping like flies and causing pandemonium. Your presence would then be detected before you even came close to the festival site. The Queen will have many non-shaman guards who could take you into custody without being affected by your amulet."

"Can she shield her amulet's power until she is ready to use it?" asked Sheldrake.

Marlene frowned at him, clearly not pleased to have a man involved in a shamanic debate.

Sasha's voice, quiet but firm, made itself heard. "If it were not for Lord Sheldrake, I would not even know I was a shaman. He has helped me to uncover what powers I have." She smiled disarmingly. "He has earned the right to be part of your discussions and it will help me if you can answer his question."

This was so clearly a thinly veiled command that Marlene stiffened. Then she gave a respectful nod of her head. "Yes, ma'am."

Sasha was mildly horrified at her own temerity, but she held Marlene's gaze. She knew the old shaman would probably think that she didn't understand shaman custom enough and perhaps she didn't. But she wasn't going to blindly kowtow to their expectations. They would have to justify their prejudicial customs to her before she accepted them. The future started now.

Marlene addressed Sheldrake. "If we consider what she did to transmit her amulet's power to us across such a distance, perhaps she can do the opposite to conceal it."

Sheldrake nodded while he thought about it, "Good suggestion." He turned to Sasha. "Describe exactly what you did to free the shamans from their bond to Toriana."

Sasha pulled out her amulet and looked down at it nestled in her palm. "I just focused on my amulet and my heartbeat. That's all. Then it just takes over."

"Then you must simply block your heartbeat and your amulet from your mind," said Stormaway, walking over to join the discussion. Sasha saw an expression of irritation cross Marlene's face, but the old shaman restrained herself from objecting. The wizard continued, "Place the whole concept of your amulet in a little mental box and put it at the back of your mind." Seeing her frown, Stormaway laughed. "It can be a pretty little box. We are not imprisoning it. Just putting it aside until you need it."

As Stormaway spoke, Sasha saw Marlene nod in reluctant agreement. "I think that will work. You must practise so that you can take the image of your amulet in and out of its box in your mind at will."

"And I think that, for the time being, Jayhan should refrain from touching Sasha, since he amplifies the amulet's power," said Sheldrake dryly.

Jayhan, listening in from behind his father, scowled at having his actions decided for him, but he wasn't silly enough to argue with so many adults at once.

Kazak raised her eyebrows. "Does he? How strange. He is neither female nor a shaman."

"He amplifies all types of magic, not just that of shamans."

"Ah. That explains it."

Marlene turned to Kazak, her white hair wisping around her face. "We must send one of our shamans with her."

"Will you go?" As the old shaman hesitated, Kazak said, "Farima can act in your stead. Supporting Sasharia is far more important." She frowned. "What is your concern?"

Marlene looked embarrassed. "The climb up the Darkstone Mountain to the Festival site is long and hard. I am not sure that I can keep up. The timeline is too short. The full moon is in three days' time."

"We can help," chorused Jon, Tarkyn, Stormaway, and Sheldrake.

Marlene actually laughed. "Thank you, but no, you can't. Men cannot go near the shamans' festival."

"Oh," said Tarkyn, non-plussed, in a reflection of the other men's reactions. Unnoticed by the adult males, Jayhan's face went white with shock. He glanced at the men, waiting for an uproar but none came. He took in a breath and balled his fists. No one was going to keep him from his self-appointed role as Sasha's protector. Wisely, he kept his reaction to himself.

Then Maud spoke. "But perhaps I can help? Although I am not a shaman."

Marlene pursed her lips as she thought about it. She glanced at Kazak before pronouncing, "Since you are a magic user, I think you could be included." Then she smiled. Her eyes crinkled at the corners and her whole face transformed. "So, what do you have to offer?"

Maud grinned back. "I can carry you up, at least part of the way, as a shaggy mountain pony, perhaps."

"Won't you get tired?"

Maud shrugged. "Probably less tired than I would, climbing up in my own shape. Four legs are so much more efficient for uphill climbs."

Sheldrake was not looking pleased. "And just who will protect you and Sasha if we can't go?"

"I will," said Lapping Water, "And so will Sparrow. We, too, are magic users. Admittedly, we don't consider our abilities as magical, but others do. We will go with them."

Judging by the glances that passed between the men, this wouldn't be the last said on this subject but for now, they let it go.

Chapter 67

Two hours later, by the light of an almost full moon, The Woodland Rover was once more drifting down the Charville River. Aware that they had only three days until the solstice, they knew that they needed to travel during the coming night if they were to make their rendezvous at the Dark Lake.

The land had trembled beneath their feet twice more before they left, but they had seen no sign of tremors since they had been out on the water. Whether this was because the earth had subsided or because the tremors couldn't be felt through the water was uncertain. Marlene was inclined to think that they would have noticed ripples or small waves if there had been further tremors, but she was not basing her opinion on experience.

Having been in the saddle all day, Marlene was tired and retired early. Waterstone and Tarkyn took first shift at the tiller, watching the dark waters glide beneath the boat. The night was bitterly cold making Tarkyn draw his wolfskin cloak more tightly around his shoulders.

A small splash made Tarkyn peer over the side.

He watched for few minutes before reporting to Waterstone, "We're travelling more quickly. I hope there are no rapids up ahead."

"So do I."

"Marlene would have mentioned it, surely."

"Maybe. But perhaps she hasn't travelled by river herself," objected Waterstone.

"Hmm." Tarkyn left the woodman to hold the tiller while he wandered forward and stared out over the bow. He turned his head to one side to listen before shaking his head doubtfully. "I can't hear anything up ahead."

"Ask a bat?" suggested Waterstone. "Or an owl?"

Tarkyn nodded. Leaning against the forward railing, he let his mind scan the trees on either side until he located a large tawny owl perched in a wattle tree a couple of hundred yards ahead of them on their right. He sent an image of the river ahead with a query attached to an image of rapids.

In answer the owl took off and glided along the river's path, seeking for prey as she flew. Ten minutes later, she dropped suddenly to the western bank and Tarkyn felt her talons crunch through the body of a small rodent. Feeling that Waterstone should share in this distasteful event, he connected his mind to the woodman's just as the owl's hooked beak tore through the furry body and ripped at the flesh within.

Tarkyn heard a sardonic, "Thank you very much," issue through the gloom from the stern of the boat and grinned.

The two of them endured the discomfort of sharing the owl's meal, as they waited for her to continue her journey downstream. In a remarkably short amount of time, the owl finished her snack and took off over the river again. In another twenty minutes, she was well ahead of them and out of sight, with no sign of approaching rapids being transmitted back to them. Tarkyn sent a wave of thanks and broke the connection.

Tarkyn wandered back to the stern to join Waterstone at the tiller. "Looks like the river is just picking up speed as it gains in volume. There have been a few little creeks joining her as well as the Boden River."

Waterstone nodded. "Means we should make it in good time."

"Hmm. But we'll have to work out what to do about this ban on men at their Shaman Festival before we meet the other two shamans, won't we?" mused Tarkyn. "We haven't come all this way to be sidelined while Sasha is engaged in the most dangerous, critical stage of the whole enterprise."

Waterstone glanced at Tarkyn. "True, but what are the dangers of men being present? Is it purely preference on their part or would our presence interfere with their shamanic magic and put the participants in danger? And politically, it could be a real hot potato if you, a foreign ruler, are discovered violating their nation's laws... and Sheldrake for that matter, as a representative of Carrador's government."

"And even worse, Jon. If he wishes to gain their respect enough to be accepted as their regent..." Tarkyn grimaced. "I know Lapping Water and Sparrow are quite capable of defending themselves and others, but I just wish they could wield magical shields."

"Sasha has her own shamanic shield that appears at times of extremis, I gather." Waterstone shrugged. "I don't know how much use your shield would be, anyway. She and her amulet can't connect with others through your shield and that is what she needs to do."

Tarkyn huffed unhappily. "Maybe I am just prejudiced. After all, in my culture, women don't fight at all."

Waterstone smiled and slapped him on the back. "No. I don't think so. You have spent a long time among woodwomen now. You're probably worried about Lapping Water, just as I am about Sparrow. Besides, Stormaway, Sheldrake, and you have strong magical powers that those particular women do not possess."

"Sasharia has strong magical powers," conceded Tarkyn, "but neither we nor she have the measure of them," he gave a worried little grimace, "and she's so little and young."

Waterstone smiled sympathetically. "Yes, she is. But perhaps the best thing we can do is give her our faith. If she thinks we believe in her, she has a better chance of believing in herself and succeeding."

Tarkyn stared at Waterstone as the woodman's words ignited an idea. A strange, satisfied smile appeared on his face. "Brilliant! I may not be able to go with her physically, but I can support her mentally. I can send her encouragement and warmth and friendship and belief in herself, long after she and I have parted."

Waterstone grinned. "Of course. The wonders of being a forest guardian." He hesitated. "But we might not mention it to the shamans though."

He glanced uncertainly at Tarkyn, worried that his liege's excessive integrity might preclude deception by omission, but for once, Tarkyn was prepared to bend the rules.

"If," Tarkyn said carefully, "the future of three nations can be supported by us without blatantly flouting their restrictions, then we will do it. I think this is a reasonable compromise, so I will not be asking for their permission." He stared out into the darkness ahead of them. "And I will not be guaranteeing that we stay away if Sasha gets into trouble"

Chapter 68

Sometime during the night, the solid mass of the Great Carradorian forest gave way to broad farmlands, so that The Woodland Rover now drifted between open fields on both sides, only thin borders of trees and shrubs here and there along creeks, roads, and some fence lines.

As the sun rose, a mist hung over the river and streaks of soft grey wafted over the fields. The Woodland Rover drifted on a strong current down the final stages of the river. Jackson and Marjorie were now at the tiller, Waterstone and Tarkyn having retired many hours previously.

Well before anyone else had risen, Maud and Sheldrake emerged from below and with a nod at Marjorie and Jackson, moved to the bow of the boat. They embraced briefly, then Maud was gone, and in her place, a peregrine falcon rose swiftly into the sky and speared away from the rising sun towards Highkington.

By midmorning she was back. Her arms and chest muscles shaking from the excessive exertion. But she recovered quickly, sitting in the sun on the foredeck and imbibing tea and freshly baked scones brought to her by a solicitous Sheldrake. Everyone knew that she had flown to warn King Gavin of the impending invasion, but no one said much about it, feeling awkward with Marlene in their midst, and wishing to keep their focus on the upcoming events.

The peaceful holiday atmosphere that had characterized the earlier days on the boat was gone. Everyone was on edge, aware that one way or another, events would reach their climax in the next few days. Jayhan and Midnight squabbled twice over minor incidents and Gurgling Brook became whiney, picking up on the adults' tension. Sasha stood a little apart leaning on the foredeck railing and watching for the first signs of their destination. After a while, Jon walked up to join her but after glancing at her face, forbore to say anything and simply leaned on the railing beside her.

An hour later, The Woodland Rover rounded a curve in the river and there it was. The Dark Lake spread out before them.

The smooth waters were a deep slate grey. A perfect reflection of the tall snow-capped mountain range behind it and the township that ran along its left bank shone on its surface. Behind the lake, in the south-east, the Darkstone Mountains loomed, their wooded foothills running right down to the southern edge of the lake and around into Carrador. On the eastern end of the range an imposing peak, conical in shape, rose above the rest.

Marlene pointed. "That peak is the actual Darkstone Mountain. The range is named for it. See its shape? It is an extinct volcano and its lava flowed down to form the whole range. That is where the obsidian for the one amulet comes from. The Shaman Festival takes place on a small plateau on its northern slope, close to the summit. Above that, there are too many boulders in the way to be able to pitch tents."

"I begin to see why the festival is held here," said Stormaway quietly.

Pretty, brightly painted, wooden houses clustered along the eastern shore and up into the foothills. In keeping with the custom of naming the river towns descriptively, the township was simply called Dark Lake.

As soon as they entered the deep waters of the lake, the boat lost speed and The Woodland Rover only just had enough momentum to carry them to the second, larger jetty that jutted out from the eastern shore of the lake. Debate had raged among the woodfolk down the last part of the river about whether they could appear among Kimorans if the general population knew of treewrights. The issue was resolved when they saw a pair of treewrights walking along the edge of the lake close to the houses of the settlement.

Lapping Water let out a long breath. "Ooh. If we go ashore with you people, it will be the first time we have moved among outsiders in their own territory. I'm not sure I'm ready for this."

Tarkyn walked over and put an arm around her shoulders as the boat glided gently towards the jetty. "You don't have to. You can always skulk in the shadows until you get on the road up into the mountains."

She frowned and pulled back so that she could look up at him. "I'm not sure that I like the word, 'skulk.' It implies nefarious intentions."

Her husband just chuckled. "In terms of Queen Toriana's future, you do have nefarious intentions."

"Huh."

"Don't worry," said Stefan, as he grabbed the rope coiled on the deck near their feet. "We can keep you amongst us, the people you know, until you get used to it."

He hopped up on the railing and balanced there agilely until the boat came within a yard of the jetty. Then he jumped lightly onto the jetty and secured the painter around a bollard. At the stern, Jackson, with a little less grace but equal competence, vaulted the railing and secured the aft painter.

Shortly afterwards the others walked down the gangway and milled on the jetty, waiting until everyone had hitched their packs and were ready to go. Midwinter was in two days' time.

Jon stood with his hands on his hips looking up at the dark, snow-capped cone of Darkstone Mountain. He drew in a deep breath, both nervous and excited. Strictly speaking, he wasn't a fugitive since Prince Jondarian was not even acknowledged as existing. But the fictional charlatan that Toriana declared him to be, was being hunted.

He surveyed the pretty colourful houses, watching thickly clad residents going about their business in the streets. The air was cold and crisp, even though the sun was shining. The streets were slushy with melted ice. It must have frozen here overnight. He scanned the people he could see, sailors working on their boats, couples promenading along the side of the lake, people making deliveries, trading, or shopping. All were dressed in heavy coats or furs. But he could see no sign of Draya or Rhoda.

He left his blond hair uncovered for several minutes in the hope that they were watching the jetties. He wasn't the only blond person in Kimora but the colouring was more common on the plains so he knew it would stand out. But then his fear of discovery by hostile Kimorans impelled him to lift his hood.

He looked down at Sasha and smiled. "You ready? Your future and Kimora await."

Sasha drew her eyes away from the township to return his gaze and he could see that her eyes were shining with excitement as she nodded. For the moment, her fears were overshadowed by the knowledge that she was actually returning to the home of her birth. She had made two quick forays into Kimora in her trip down the river but now, for better or for worse, she was here to stay.

"We will need supplies," Jackson was saying.

Maud nodded as they walked along the jetty. "We will find an inn and hire some rooms where we can leave our packs. Marlene can guide us in what we will need for the trip up into the mountains. Perhaps you could go on ahead and find somewhere suitable."

Sasha walked behind them and, with a quick inward breath of acknowledgement, stepped onto the soil of Kimora.

Chapter 69

Immediately, she felt a tremor beneath her feet. Far from being scared, she looked up at Jon, smiling. "Feel that? Kimora is welcoming me, us, home."

Jon did not seem so convinced. Neither did most of the adults around them, although Tarkyn, who had a strong connection with the forest, looked thoughtful.

Jayhan, however, bounded up without a second thought and grinned. "So it is. That's impressive, isn't it?"

Midnight was standing nearby, clearly wondering what they were saying. So Tarkyn did his best to explain to him in images and using the sign language Stormaway had devised a few years ago. Once he understood, Midnight grinned and nodded.

The people around them were so swathed in warm long coats or cloaks that it was hard to tell their genders. The group of foreigners elicited curious stares, especially at Stormaway in his wizard's robes, which he wore without any warm covering. A few people glanced at the woodfolk but quickly glanced away, as though knowing to leave them alone.

Sasha and her companions were halfway up the street when the next tremor struck. This time it was stronger and everyone on the street stopped what they were doing, staring at each other in fright. Some began running for the shelter of the buildings. Tarkyn's eagle shrieked and took off from his shoulder, leaving him to his fate. Her powerful wings drew her upwards as she soared off over the lake, well away from the turmoil.

"Keep away from the buildings," shouted Sheldrake in Kimoran. "Move to an open space."

Then the shaking subsided.

People looked at each other and around themselves. After a few minutes, when nothing else happened, they tentatively returned to whatever they had been doing before the tremor struck.

"This is more than a welcome for you, Sasha," said Sheldrake dryly.

The little girl looked completely self-possessed. "True. But it is still a reaction to me being here."

"Is it?" asked Jayhan, more willing to engage in the concept than the adults. "Don't tell me you're going to spend your whole life wobbling your way across the country from one shake to the next."

Sasha hit him playfully on the arm and chuckled. "Idiot. Of course not."

"Then what?"

Although Jayhan was asking the question, the adults listened with interest for her explanation.

Sasha frowned, trying to work it out and to explain. "Hmm. It's as though... hmm, it's as though the land is angry... as though it realises it has been deceived."

As one, Sheldrake and Stormaway both swivelled their heads to stare at the great dark peak in the distance.

"Marlene," asked Stormaway carefully, "Did you say there was a connection between Darkstone Mountain and Sasha's amulet?"

"The true amulet was carved from obsidian obtained at its summit."

"And Toriana's black amulet?"

Marlene's eyes narrowed in anger. "We believed that she wore the true amulet, the one Sasha is wearing. She said that it had been returned to her after the bandits attacked Sasha's family, and she had had to devise a new ceremony to receive it into her keeping, since the previous wearer was no longer alive to transfer it." She ground her teeth. Then she heaved a breath and spat out, "So I have no idea where her black amulet comes from and even whether it is obsidian. We all just assumed it was."

Stormaway shook his head. "We don't know enough about all of this."

Aware that the woodfolk were become increasingly tense standing in a shaking street surrounded by outsiders, he turned and resumed walking, his long green robes billowing around him. He wondered whether they would feel better or worse inside an inn.

Seeing Jackson up ahead beckoning, they approached a large, double-storey tavern with log walls and a heavy dark wood door, bound in iron. Faint tremors followed them up the street. They could see light streaming through the lead light windows. The sounds of people laughing and talking increased in volume as Stormaway opened the door.

"Plenty of room in here," said Jackson as he stood aside to let them in. He addressed the woodfolk. "As you enter, turn to your left and you will find a dimly lit, quiet corner close to the fireplace, away from the rowdier elements of the crowd. You can all array yourselves along the wall so that you can keep an eye on proceedings, while we sit at the same long table but closer to other people." He gave a hopeful smile. "Will that be all right?"

"Nothing in the middle of a town of outsiders will be all right, but it sounds as though you've done the best you could," grumped Autumn Leaves. "I don't see why we can't just slip around the town and camp in the pine forests."

"Because we need your help to plan, and we need to protect each other until we know the lay of the land," replied Tarkyn, "And after your initial encounter with the Carradorian woodfolk, it seems judicious to take it carefully with the local treewrights. None of us is here with the blessing of the reigning monarch."

Autumn Leaves subsided into a grumpy silence as he and the other woodfolk followed Jackson's suggestion.

Once they were seated, Rainstorm surveyed the room, noting the row of pegs along the wall near the door for people's cloaks and coats. He realised that people they had seen on the streets were actually much smaller than they first appeared, now that they had shed their outer garments. All the men and many of the women wore jerkins and leggings, although the women's jerkins tended to fit more loosely. Other women wore jerkins above long skirts, heavy woollen tights, and thick boots.

It was late in the day and many of the patrons were fisherfolk and woodcutters who had come in for a drink or a meal after their day's work. Several men and women smoked pipes and the smoke curled up to hang between dark wooden rafters.

Rainstorm looked at Tarkyn, his eyes twinkling. "Not the sort of crowd you're used to hobnobbing with, outside the forest, Tarkyn," he ventured.

Tarkyn swivelled in his seat so that he could see them. Then he turned back with a wry smile, "No. I wouldn't move in the same circles as them, but I like to think I would value what they have to say as much as anyone I would meet at court."

Lapping Water managed a tight smile, "I think you would, these days."

A burly barman crossed to their table. His eyes widened when he saw the woodfolk. He gave a slight bow and said, "I know you don't give trust easily. So it is an honour to have treewrights visit our establishment. Let me know if any of this lot get too rowdy," He jerked a thumb behind him, "and I'll kick them straight out. I am Barney. Barney the Barman," He smiled broadly at what he considered to be a joke. "Now, what can I get you?"

"A good white wine please," said Rainstorm, with a show of confidence.

The barman's face fell. "Oh. A good one, hey? I'm afraid I've only got a few bottles of very rough wine left. We mostly sell ale, you understand."

He looked so crestfallen that all the woodfolk agreed to try ale, as did the other members of the party except the children, for whom fruit juice was ordered. When Barney returned with a large tray full of pint pots of ale, he waited expectantly while they had their first taste. He was proud of his home brewed ale. But the woodfolk had never tried it before and despite themselves, their faces screwed up at the bitter, fulsome flavour.

Rainstorm saw that the innkeeper was disappointed and made an effort to cheer him up. "This foam on top is nice. I'm sure we'll get used to it, develop a taste for it. It's just very different from wine, really. We have to adjust our thinking. That's all." He looked at Jackson. "You'll have drunk ale before. How does this shape up?"

Jackson wiped away a moustache of white foam and smiled. "It's great, Barney. Really. Very good." When Barney looked mollified, he asked, "What's on offer for dinner?"

"Lamb stew, beef pie and roast duck."

All of the woodfolk went for the pie because oven-baked pastry was not part of their normal diet whereas stews and roast fowl were.

Stefan grinned at them. "You're being very adventurous, ordering food you've never had before."

Waterstone shrugged. "We may never do this again. We might as well take the opportunity." He took a deep breath and let it out. "Well. I never thought I'd find myself inside one of these buildings with the straight lines and corners." He looked up. "I like their wooden beams." He chuckled. "Reminds me of home." He nodded at the crowd. "It's noisy though. I suppose none of them can mindtalk. So their only option is speaking out loud."

Just then the door opened. Four rough-looking soldiers pushed inside and stood near the doorway, glaring around the bar room. Sasha's heart constricted in her chest. Immediately, the bar room quietened.

The sergeant raised her voice. "We're looking for a blond man on the run with a small dark-skinned girl. Anyone seen 'em?"

Since the people in the bar ranged in colour from nearly black to pale and blonde, this description was not as telling as it might have been in Carrador where most people were pale skinned. Murmurs ran through the crowd. But with a start, Sasha realised that the people in the bar were looking anywhere but at her and her friends. Perhaps it was because Jon still had his hood up and she was seated up the other end of the table from him between Jayhan and Midnight. But she didn't think so.

The soldiers' eyes ran casually over their group, but the sight of the woodfolk, their bows and quivers leaning casually against the wall behind them, unnerved them. The sergeant even ducked her head.

"Beg pardon, sirs and madams," she said, addressing the woodfolk. "Didn't mean to disturb you."

The woodfolk, frozen with shock, just stared back at her. Ducking her head again, the sergeant sidled back outside, taking her men with her.

For several seconds, there was a stunned silence. Then, as conversations began to resume around the room, a stocky woodcutter, sporting a bushy beard and a clay pipe, disengaged himself from the crowd and walked over to their table. He had a slightly bulbous nose, and his dark skin and eyes were much the same shade as Sasha's. Something about him seemed familiar.

"Good evening, ladies and gentlemen," he spoke quietly in a deep voice, giving a slight bow. "We are deeply honoured that the lords and ladies of the forest have deigned to come among us. Long we have known of you but until now, we have only seen you from afar."

Rainstorm mentally rolled his eyes. *Oh my stars. What have we done? We've changed all these people's expectations of treewrights.*

But despite Rainstorm's consternation, Waterstone was rising to the occasion. "A pleasure to meet you. It is our custom to introduce ourselves the first time we address someone new. I am Waterstone. And you are?"

"Pardon, sir," the stout man replied gruffly. "I am Graham."

"I admire your courage in addressing us," Waterstone hesitated then took the bull by the horns and said, "And I thank you for not pointing out my companions to those soldiers. Whether or not they are who those soldiers seek, you may have saved us a lot of unnecessary inconvenience."

Graham lowered his voice still further. "The Queen's soldiers will get no help from us. Besides, a friend of yours is a friend of ours. We would not dream of betraying the trust you have given us by showing yourselves here tonight."

"And does that apply to everyone here?" asked Waterstone.

"Everyone." He gave a deep chuckle. "Even the soldiers were overawed by your presence and won't breathe a word of your business to anyone else." He gave a little cough. "You wouldn't by any chance be hoping to meet up with a couple of shamans who have been living in Carrador, would you?"

"We might," interrupted Stormaway. "But I would like to know first what connection you have with them. I am Stormaway Treemaster."

Stormaway's back had been towards him until now, but Graham's eyes widened as he noticed him for the first time. "A wizard and a treewright. How marvellous!" He took a long drag on his pipe, deliberately keeping them waiting before he proved his provenance. "My sister told me all sorts of fanciful tales about recent events, many of which now appear to be true. She is a strong woman and her independent spirit forced her to leave us to venture forth into Carrador. Her name is Rhoda."

There was a perceptible release of tension around the table.

"Is she here?" asked Sasha excitedly.

Graham stared at her intently for a moment before answering, "Yes she is... Sasharia." He gave the slightest bow of his head, showing his respect without attracting attention. "It is my honour to meet you." When Sasha jerked her head sideways towards Jon, the wood cutter transferred his gaze and said quietly, "And you, Sire." Then he straightened up and said more loudly, "I will bring my sister and her friend up to meet you first thing in the morning, ready to leave, if that would suit you."

"Oh thank you," gushed Sasha, "I can't wait."

Graham blinked, then smiled, his body relaxing. "You're welcome."

Then with a nod at the whole table, he was gone.

Chapter 70

The ebony carriage emblazoned with the Queen's arms bowled along the road west from Manissa. Four of the Queen's guard rode ahead of it and four behind. From inside, Toriana watched the fields of wheat pass by. The plants were young and green but smaller than at this time in years past. Once more, the crop had been depressingly meagre. She sighed and leaned back against the cushions so she wouldn't have to keep looking at it. In the back of her mind, the faintest dread niggled at her that the land and the climate were out of harmony because of her disruption of the true line. But if ever this thought threatened to surface, she quelled it mercilessly.

Well, she was doing all she could to rectify the situation. She was about to annex the rich farming lands of southern Carrador. That would provide enough grain to cover the shortfall.

She glanced at Hardikan, propped up asleep in the far corner. Hardikan was a dedicated shaman. She might know how to right the climate, but to ask her was to admit that all was not well. She couldn't do that.

Toriana was just dozing off herself when the carriage jolted suddenly, then again, then several times more. She heard the horses whinnying in fear and the voices of the coachmen trying to calm them. They managed to bring the coach to a halt with the horses bucking and sidling within the traces. She stuck her head out the window but could not see enough, so tapped sharply on the ceiling of the carriage.

Another jolt went through the carriage, even though it was stationary, and the descending coachman fell the last part of the way as he was thrown off his foothold. He picked himself up, wincing as he discovered he had turned his ankle in the fall. Nevertheless, he quickly brushed himself down before opening the door for his queen and bowing.

Toriana surged out of the carriage, stepping down just as another tremor hit. The coachman grabbed her under the elbow to stop her from losing her balance. She glanced acidly at him but did not take her arm away.

Then she waved her other hand around. "What is going on here?"

Hardikan, who had descended under her own steam, stood looking bewildered, still recovering from being jolted awake.

The coachman's face was white with shock, and he needed to take a breath before answering the Queen. He swallowed then said, "I don't know, ma'am. The horses are terrified. Simmons is holding them, but only just."

Both Queen and coachman wobbled as another tremor struck. Toriana looked around the fields stretching in either direction, and at the guards ahead and behind her struggling to control their mounts. Somewhere behind them on the road was her luggage coach and Barton, but it was lumbering along at a slower pace and was no longer in sight.

"We cannot travel on until this quake subsides. We shall have afternoon tea here. Simmons, you stay where you are, quieting the horses. Jenkins, you prepare the refreshments." She watched as he hobbled towards the baskets and trunks strapped onto the rear of the carriage. "And do try to stay upright. You will be no good to me if you injure yourself further."

By the time the Queen had finished her afternoon tea, Sasha had stepped onto The Woodland Rover and the tremors had stopped.

For the rest of the day, the land was quiet, and the Queen's carriage made good time.

However, the following afternoon, the tremors struck just as the Queen's carriage was entering Woodend, a town near the base of Darkstone Mountain, on the border between the farming lands and the forests.

Hers were not the only horses frightened by the tremor. The street became a tangled mass of overturned carts, strewn loads of wool and grain, wild-eyed horses straining to get away from their riders or handlers while both men and horses screamed in fright or pain. One of her white carriage horses reared up and when he came down, his leg snarled in the traces. The carriage started pulling sideways and with a remarkable feat of horsemanship, Simmins managed to pull the carriage to a halt, slewed across the thoroughfare. Jenkins ran to the front of the horses, trying desperately to calm them and untangle the traces from their legs before they injured themselves.

The Queen was not pleased. As soon as the tremors subsided, she had herself escorted to the best inn, stalking between small scenes of disaster, and resigned herself to staying the night here.

As they entered the inn, flustered staff ran to prepare for such illustrious company. Toriana turned to Hardikan, "Do you think this is the last of these quakes? Is it safe to proceed up into the mountains?"

"I will ask the locals. I will also find a quiet place to attune myself to the land and see what I can discover." She did not say, as she was thinking, that Toriana, as High Shaman, should be better able to attune to the land than she could.

Chapter 71

Draya and Rhoda met them upstairs in the private parlour. Their eyes widened when they saw the woodfolk clustered in one corner, looking distinctly on edge in a room of straight lines and right angles.

Sasha saw that Marlene was watching the two refugee shamans' relaxed interaction with the woodfolk and thought she looked impressed. The young girl had been worrying about Marlene's reaction to two unregistered shamans.

But her fears were allayed when Marlene introduced herself and said warmly, "I admire the independent spirits that made you avoid the shackles of Queen Toriana's binding. I wish I had known before I took the oath and became bound." She shook her head, looking shamefaced. "So many things I would not have done and many shamans I would not have forced into Toriana's service, had I realised how I was being duped."

"Thank you," replied Rhoda, "I am sorry you have had to endure what you did by staying in Kimora." She smiled at Sasha. "Let us just hope our little one here can bring change to our country."

Waterstone was watching them, his arms crossed in disapproval. "You are placing a lot of pressure on a small girl's shoulders. I remember protecting Tarkyn from pressure like this and he was nineteen, not eleven. Be careful with your little liege."

Surprisingly, it was the feisty Draya who put an arm around Sasha's shoulders. "We will be. We will do everything we can to support her." She gave Sasha's shoulder a squeeze. "But we cannot do it for her, much as we would like to. She, alone, is the wielder of the dark amulet."

Sasha glanced across the room at Jon and shared a little smile. She knew the task and the danger were great but somehow, she did not feel daunted. She would do her best and it would either work or it wouldn't. Perhaps it was because she was so young, she thought, that she couldn't fully comprehend what lay ahead. She chuckled inwardly at herself, knowing her perspective was all wrong. At the moment, she was far more fearful about picking up the wrong fork at a formal dinner.

She turned dark solemn eyes on Waterstone. "Thank you for worrying about me. Your concern adds to the strength I feel radiating from all of you to support me." She gave a warm smile. "I thank you all."

She smiled when she saw tears of pride start in Jon's eyes. Then the tiniest twinge of fear made her stomach clench when she realised that sometime tomorrow, she would have to leave him and the other men behind, to travel with only a few people up into the precinct of the Midwinter Shaman Festival.

That time came all too quickly.

After an early start, the entire company had travelled up a gently undulating road that gradually took them higher and across the northern face of the mountains towards the looming peak of the Darkstone Mountain on the eastern end of the range. The gravel road snaked through dense pine forests. Few birds called or flew overhead. The whole mountain seemed to be waiting.

The earth tremors had started as soon as Sasha had stepped out the door in the morning. They were intermittent, but so frequent that everyone had begun to compensate for the shaking by bracing themselves as they walked just as they would on a ship in high seas.

By mid-afternoon, the company had reached a gateway formed by two large boulders that stood on either side of the road. The boulders were at least seven feet high and carved in intricate runes that had been filled with ochre to make them stand out.

Marlene pointed. "Someone refurbishes these runes every year just before the Midwinter Festival." She turned to the company. "This is where we part company with you men."

"Just so that we are clear," said Sheldrake, "what would happen if any of us went further?"

Marlene's eyes narrowed. "Shamans are not martial as a group, even though some of us serve in the army. We would not attack you. But it would be a gross invasion of our private business and a reflection on your decency and honour."

Tarkyn raised his eyebrows. "Hmm. Possibly more powerful than a physical defence," he gave a wry smile at the men around him, "since we are all honourable."

So Sasha, Maud, Marjorie, Lapping Water, Sparrow, and the three shamans said their goodbyes to Jon, Sheldrake, Tarkyn, Stefan, Stormaway, Jackson, Waterstone, Autumn Leaves who held Gurgling Brook, on his hip and Rainstorm.

"Don't forget to keep your mind closed until the time is right," said Stormaway.

Jon gave Sasha a long hug and it took a huge effort for him to let her go. "We will camp close to here," he said, with a lump in his throat. "So come back this way."

He tried not to show her his glistening eyes, but she smiled up at him, tears in her own eyes. "Goodbye, big brother, See you soon."

Finally, Jayhan and Midnight both gave Sasha a big hug before letting her go with the others through the stone gateway.

As the men turned away, Sheldrake shook his head. "I wonder at the wisdom of all this. I know we can't wait, with Kimora's troops on Carrador's doorstep, but those quakes worry me. Darkstone Mountain has been dormant since living memory but earth tremors such as we have been experiencing are often felt before a volcano erupts."

Tarkyn's stomach turned over. His wife was climbing a rumbling volcano. He turned to Waterstone and said tightly, "Perhaps you could mind-message that information to Lapping Water. Then, at least they will be forewarned."

"Sasha said it is just the earth expressing its outrage," said Jon, looking worried.

Sheldrake stumbled sideways as another small tremor struck. "I hope so."

Chapter 72

A few shamans had been travelling before and behind Sasha's group along the road they had taken from Dark Lake, but as they climbed higher, paths converged from other directions until they were amongst a throng of women all heading up to the festival site.

Everyone, without exception, was rugged up in heavy cloaks or thick fur-lined coats. Now and again Sasha would catch glimpses of dark skirts decorated with beads and mirrors similar to Yarrow's, but most wore heavy skirts or leggings that did not differentiate them from any of the women that Sasha had seen in the township. As was common throughout the rest of the Kimoran population, there was a wide spectrum of skin, eye, and hair colour. Sasha even saw one woman with green hair sticking out from under her fur-lined head covering, but Marlene assured her it was dyed.

When Tarkyn's message came through, Lapping Water stopped the group to transmit his warning but after a hurried debate, they decided to continue. Maud didn't force her opinion, since risk to the others was involved but she blew a quiet sigh of relief at their decision, in view of the impending invasion of her homeland.

After an hour of climbing, both Marlene and Rhoda were finding the steep climb hard going, so Maud offered her services as mountain pony to Rhoda too.

The women stopped beside the road to drink, eat, and rest. No one among the other shamans travelling past them particularly noticed Sasha, although Lapping Water and Sparrow's green eyes drew some curious stares.

Once they were rested, Maud withdrew through a gap in the trees along the edge of the pine forest and emerged shortly afterwards as a brown, solid, scruffy mountain pony. She wore no saddle or bridle which presented a problem for mounting, but she obligingly lined herself up next to a large log, so that Marlene could throw her leg over easily.

At first Marlene, used to riding with saddle and bridle, was a little nervous placing so much trust in her mount. But Maud was sure-footed and steady, even when the slope fell steeply away on one side, or the ground trembled beneath her hooves. So after a while, Marlene just sat back and enjoyed the gentle swaying of the pony's gait beneath her.

Rhoda and Marlene swapped places after forty minutes. Then an hour later, the sun set behind the lower peaks of the mountain range, drawing in the chill of the evening, and it was time to make camp.

Although the people around them seemed friendly enough, the travellers all agreed that they would find it difficult to navigate the usual introductions and conversations while they had Sasha, two unregistered shamans and two woodwomen among them. In case the refugee shamans were recognized, Marlene had agreed to verify that Rhoda and Draya had finally given their oath to Toriana. But neither she nor they wanted to use the story if they could avoid it, knowing it might lead to difficult questions. So they headed off into the pine forest to make their own camp away from other people.

Just as they turned off towards the gloom of the pines, Sasha gave one last look at the sky and thought she saw a plume of white smoke high above the peak against the darkening sky. Perhaps it was just a cloud, she pondered. But she gave her head a little shake She didn't really think so. She didn't say anything to the others because she knew it would worry them. But she was not scared by it, even though she understood its implications.

As they sat around the firesite after they had eaten, the three shamans talked to the others about what to expect on the following day, the day of the winter solstice.

"The best part is the feast, which begins at sunset tomorrow night," enthused Rhoda, her dark eyes glowing in the firelight. "Each shaman contributes an offering of some sort. It can be vegetables, herbs, pork, beef, lamb, breads, or sauces and homemade ale, wine, or fruit juice. Each person just provides one item of food and drink but somehow, there is always a surplus, which is eaten during the following day along with individual provisions people have brought."

"Every year," said Marlene, "a large pine tree is felled on the last day of the festival so that it can dry out ready to fuel the fire for the next year. So a huge fire will be lit by the Queen on her arrival and burn for two nights and the day in between right on the summit."

Sasha looked puzzled. "How can a small point hold so many people?"

Draya laughed. "It only looks pointy from a distance. The summit is actually a flat area a couple of hundred yards in diameter. It's too uneven to camp on, which is why we set up out tents on the plateau, but it is just right for gathering around the bonfire.'

Lapping Water poked at their fire with a long stick, pushing a few glowing embers back into its centre. The night was bitterly cold, and they needed all the warmth they could get from their small fire. "We'll need to keep this stoked during the night."

"And tomorrow night," enthused Draya, "there is dancing. Several shamans are selected to dance to the audience to depict an event that has occurred in their area during the year. Then, just before midnight, we all dance to celebrate the winter solstice, the return of the sun and the longer days of spring and summer. Most of us have had a great deal to drink by then, so it is tremendous fun."

Sasha was surprised. She had never seen Draya so animated. She had always seemed cynical and often abrasive before. She would not forget Draya's sceptical reception of Sasha as a potential leader, scoffing at her lack of martial experience. She had been right, but she hadn't been kind to a young girl who had only just been introduced to them. But now, she was risking everything to support her.

"And when does the Queen arrive?" asked Sasha.

"Tomorrow afternoon, a couple of hours before sunset."

Sasha felt a shudder go down her spine. Less than a full day. "And are we planning to be at the festival site when she arrives?"

"I think so," said Marlene, sending a glance at Rhoda and Draya for confirmation. "She will ascend the mountain from the east, the other side of the mountain. So we will be closest to her at the festival site."

Sasha stood up, looking for all the world like a fluffy ball on sticks in all her heavy clothing, and crossed to the woodpile. She picked out a good-sized branch and fed it onto the fire before replying. Suddenly it was all too real, and too soon. She tried to make her voice sound casual but gave herself a mental kick when it quavered. "And when will I try to overcome the binding on the gathered shamans and Toriana herself?" she asked as she sat down again.

Without a word, Lapping Water walked around the fire, sat down next to her, and put an arm around her shoulder. "I am glad you are showing fear. Were you not, we would all be worried that you didn't really understand the gravity of the situation."

"Oh."

"Don't be brave on our account. We are here to have courage with you," said Marlene. She smiled. "We don't want you to fall into a quivering heap, of course, but just acknowledge the fear and accept our strength to manage it."

"Oh," Sasha gave a wan little grin. "I didn't realise I was worried until just now."

"And we also have the fear of an uneasy volcano beneath our feet," added Maud, now back in human guise, none the worse for wear.

Again Sasha considered telling them about the white smoke she had seen but instead she said, "I have no fear of the land. I am only anxious about Toriana."

"If you can do it, I think you should try to break the shamans' bond to Toriana soon after she arrives," replied Marlene. "She will have non-shaman spies among us, and her guards will precede her up the mountain. If she gets wind of anything amiss, she will retreat. Then you would lose your chance to get close to her."

Unable to speak, Sasha nodded, her dark eyes shining with unshed tears. When Lapping Water hugged her close, she let go and sobbed into the woodwoman's chest. The older women exchanged glances behind her, partly sympathetic, partly fearful. A lot was riding on one small girl.

Soon afterwards, they settled themselves to sleep, wearing every piece of clothing they had, wrapped in their cloaks, and huddled close to each other near the fire. Rhoda had the first watch.

Sasha quietly pulled her amulet out of her clothing and held it in her gloved hand, being careful to keep her mind disciplined. She felt less strung up now that she had cried. Her mind and body felt clearer. She placed her other hand on the ground and let her mind connect with the world around her and the earth below.

At first, she could hear the wind soughing through the trees high above her. Then she tuned in to tiny animals scurrying through the pine needles nearby and felt the might of the tall pines and their roots driving deep below the surface. Slowly she let her mind drift down through the layers below her until she came to the molten heart of the mountain. The magma was churning and pushing upwards, driven by a deep, smouldering anger at the duplicity that had caused such damage to the land.

Sasha did not have the power or the authority to quell its outrage. All she could do was connect with it and make sure that her presence was known to it, knowing in her heart that its outrage was in harmony with her own. She felt it ease beneath her hand and slowly she drifted off to sleep, aware that tomorrow might be the last day of her life.

Chapter 73

She was woken several hours later, but long before dawn, by an insistent tapping on her shoulder. She opened her eyes and by the light of the banked fire, saw a pair of pale eyes peering down at her. They really could be quite spooky at times, she thought.

"*Jayhan*! What on earth are you doing here?" she demanded in a harsh whisper. "No men. Remember?"

Jayhan grinned. "I'm not a man. I'm a boy." He shrugged. "Anyway, my honour would be more betrayed if I weren't here to help you. That's what I always promised you. You need me to make your amulet stronger. Remember?"

"How did you get past our lookout?"

"Sparrow saw me and let me through. She knew she couldn't send me away to go back down the mountainside on my own in the dark."

"Jayhan. You're incorrigible."

"Really? Is that good?"

Despite herself, Sasha gave a snort of laughter. "Idiot. No, of course it's not." She glanced around in consternation as Rhoda stirred but the older shaman just snuffled, turned over and went back to sleep. "Stars above, Jayhan.! We're going to be in such trouble when they wake up in the morning and find you here."

Jayhan nodded sagely. "I know. Mum will be furious. Dad will be aploppic, but luckily he's not here."

"What? Oh, you mean apoplectic. You're right. He will be."

"See how brave I'm being?" He swung himself off his knees to lie down beside her. "I know I'll get into awful trouble, but I also know it's the right thing to do, to be with you when you fight your aunt."

In the darkness she smiled. He couldn't see it, but he could hear it in her voice when she said, "Thank you, Jayhan. I think you're right. Out of everyone, I need your help the most. Let's go to sleep and face the music in the morning."

It didn't occur to her for a moment that she outranked everyone around her.

Sure enough, when Maud discovered Jayhan lying asleep beside Sasha, she was furious. After berating her son, she turned on Sparrow. "Why didn't you wake me or just send him back?"

Sparrow, a lethally trained but generally polite thirteen-year-old woodwoman, folded her arms and refused to speak until Maud took a deep breath and said, "I apologize for my tone of voice, but my questions still stands."

"My role on guard duty was to make sure you were all safe, not to pass judgement on Jayhan's actions." She unfolded her arms and glanced at Lapping Water before adding, "If you must know, I don't like them having different roles for men and women. I will put up with it to help Sasha, but I will not actively support it."

Maud felt harassed, acutely aware of being scrutinized by Marlene, Rhoda, and Draya. "Jayhan, you got yourself up here. We can't have a male among these shamans. So you'll have to find your own way down. It should be safe enough in daylight."

"No."

It wasn't her fiercely independent son objecting. Shocked, Maud swung round to find Sasha's gaze on her, steady and determined.

"No," said Sasha again. "I am the High Shaman, and I say he can stay. You know that his power amplifies mine. I need him."

"Protocol demands that he leave," said Marlene, with an edge to her voice.

"Protocol will bend to me, not me to protocol," said Sasha firmly.

Rhoda gave a sympathetic smile. "It doesn't work that way,"

Sasha looked at her, and Rhoda found herself staring into deep pools of power. "It will work that way," said Sasha quietly.

For a moment Rhoda felt as though the world stood still. Then she looked away. In that moment, the whole dynamic of the little group shifted as they really understood that they had a queen standing in their midst. Perhaps in time, the protocols of court would confine her, but Rhoda was inclined to think that a time of change might be upon them.

A wry glance passed between Lapping Water and Sparrow, who did not share the outsiders' views on rank.

Then Sasha smiled. "So, instead of objecting, let's see how we can make this work."

"I already know," piped up Jayhan. "I can shape-shift to look like a girl."

Marlene studied him. "Most shamans will know that you're a shape-shifter."

"But will they be able to see his original form? Or know he's a boy?" asked Maud, finally accepting the ongoing presence of her son. "I think not."

"No," said Draya, "But it may arouse suspicion. Why would someone be disguising their true form?"

"To cover a scar or because they are recovering from an illness?" suggested Maud.

"That will do as a backup," said Lapping Water. "But as first response, just tell them you would rather not say."

Sparrow smiled at her, knowing Tarkyn's distaste for lying had rubbed off on his wife and, thought Sparrow wryly, on all of us.

Jayhan nodded. "All right. I can do that. Maybe I will make myself look like Sasha. I did it before. Remember?"

"You did it very well, Jayhan," said his mother, "But it might confuse an already complicated situation if you did that here. What about modelling yourself on Sparrow? Not exactly the same. Twins would elicit too much scrutiny, which is something we are hoping to avoid for the time being."

"Right. Back in a minute. I have to concentrate, you know." Jayhan wandered off to a spot a few trees away.

When he returned, he was taller, but not quite as tall as Sparrow. He was slenderer than he had been, with wider hips and small but definite breasts. His hair was past his shoulders, wavy and light brown. His face was shaped like Sparrow's but closer in hue to Sasha's. His eyes were brighter, the same brilliant green as Midnight's.

He grinned. "How's this?"

"Brilliant!" chorused Sparrow and Sasha, laughing.

Maud walked over to him and ruffled his hair. "Well done, my young son. I am proud of you, even though I am cross with you."

It was only another hour's walk to the plateau on the northern side of the mountain where the majority of shamans had made camp. The Queen's tent loomed large and magnificent on the other side of the plateau, awaiting its owner's arrival. Other larger, more ornate tents clustered around it, but the size and luxury appointments of the tents tapered off as their distance from the Queen's tent increased.

Again, Sasha's company chose a firesite a few hundred yards away within the trees. Lapping Water and Sparrow let the others go off into the crowds while they lingered in the peace of the forest, saying they would join them later.

Women were wandering around, talking to friends and acquaintances from across the nation. Others sat outside their tents and waited for others to come to them. Many had displays of herbs and bottles of medicine to swap or sell. Some had books of chants and ceremonies that they had collected and written down. Others had books on philosophy and the human spirit.

Shamans were always healers, but many of them were also celebrants for birth, marriage, and death. They provided counsel and were the holders of their community's history and culture. As with all groups of people, there was a spectrum of expertise and interest varying from considering shamanism as a hobby on the side to those who had dedicated their whole life and passion to it.

As Sasha walked through the mass of tents and people, she began to realise the breadth and depth of the expertise around her. It both excited and humbled her. Her stomach turned over at the thought of standing up and leading these people. How could she? Nearly all of them were older, more knowledgeable, and more experienced than her.

Something in her demeanour must have given away her thoughts. Rhoda crossed over to her and put her arm around her shoulders. "Don't worry," she whispered. "No single person here knows all there is to know. We are all unique. That is why we share our individual knowledge and skills. And you have what none of these people has: the dark amulet. It gives you power and knowledge like no other."

Sasha glanced up at her and smiled. "Thanks."

Chapter 74

Toriana awoke to the sounds of a farmer's market being set up in the street outside the inn she was staying in. The local farmers had developed a custom of holding a three-day market to capitalize on the constant stream of shamans passing through on the way up to the festival, all of whom needed supplies for their time on the mountain.

She had not been troubled by any tremors during the night and this morning the earth was still. When Pansy entered and set her breakfast up for her, Toriana instructed her to pull back the curtains so she could see the sky, blue above, but dark clouds just peeking over the roofs across the road.

"Do you think it will snow, Pansy?" she asked her maid.

Pansy glanced out the window at the barely visible cloud bank. "Good morning, Your Majesty. It snowed during the night, and I think more may be on the way. But there is only a light smattering on the ground this morning and we should be able to continue on our way."

"And our horses?"

"They were restless but uninjured, ma'am. We only have another ten miles to cover in the carriage to reach the standing stones."

"Good. We will leave in two hours. Send Hardikan to me."

For a few minutes, the Queen ate her toast and sipped her tea while she watched people setting up trestle tables and unpacking vegetables, jars of condiments, and slabs of meat. The bustle outside made an interesting change from the quiet atmosphere of her palace grounds.

Then a knock sounded on the door. Once Hardikan had been given leave to enter and rise from her curtsey, and greetings had been exchanged, Toriana asked her, "What did you discover about these quakes? Can you tell whether they will continue? Should we continue our journey onto The Darkstone Mountain?"

Hardikan stood at the foot of the bed as she addressed the Queen. She folded her hands across her stomach and took a small breath, giving herself time to gather her thoughts. "The Darkstone Mountain has been dormant for centuries, ma'am. So it should be safe to continue. But the earth feels disquieted, ma'am, almost angry. I have never felt it like this before. Perhaps it is angry that an impostor is challenging the High Shaman."

"Why would you think that?" snapped Toriana, her stomach clenching in sudden fear. Was the opposite true? Was the land reacting against her duplicity now that the true High Shaman was apparently on Kimoran soil?

A surge of rage welled up so strongly that her cup shook in her hand. This was so unfair. She was sure she had removed all of her sister's family. But if she hadn't, she would.

"Are you all right, ma'am?" asked Hardikan.

Toriana waved her hand dismissively at the question. She heaved a couple of breaths to get herself under control. "I will not have my rule flouted like this," she replied ambiguously. "This child must be stopped before she causes more damage. So is this unrest in the earth just a transient expression of displeasure or might it increase?"

"I have no idea, ma'am. We can only hope that we can locate and remove the threat of the impostor and thus avoid the question." Hardikan glanced out the window. "All has been quiet this morning, but there is a sense of waiting." She hazarded a smile. "Perhaps when you light the Midwinter Log and assert your authority as High Shaman, it will be reassured and settle."

"Perhaps so."

The Queen's carriage reached the standing stones at midday without any further tremors marring their progress. A small pavilion had been set up and she entered with Hardikan to partake of a delicate luncheon since she was looking forward to the evening's feast and did not wish to spoil her appetite.

When she had finished, she exited the tent to find it had begun to snow. A beautiful white mare was brought forward, and the Queen mounted without assistance, her long voluminous skirts allowing her to ride astride. Her bright green, woollen cloak flowed back over her shoulders. Her hands, encased in gold embroidered woollen gloves, held the reins firmly but with care. Her antipathy towards people did not extend to animals and for all her faults, Toriana was an excellent horsewoman.

Snowflakes fell gently around them, but the road ahead had not yet been covered. Once Hardikan was mounted, they rode up towards the summit, in the midst of eight female guards.

Part 9

Chapter 75

Sasha and Jayhan had just bought two sticks each of freshly grilled lamb pieces from one of the little food stalls when they heard trumpets. They turned to face the sound and realized that people on the eastern side of the plateau were moving aside to provide egress for the arrival of the Queen.

Sasha's stomach turned over and she lost her hold on her meat sticks. Beneath her, the ground shuddered. Jayhan grabbed the sticks before they fell and handed them back to her without comment, careful not to touch her and amplify her power before they were ready.

Around them, everyone was straining to catch a glimpse of the Queen. Once she reached the plateau, Toriana rode slowly, controlling her horse in a high-stepping walk. She waved to the crowds on either side of her as she and her horse made their way across the plateau until they were lost from sight behind her pavilion.

The stall holder nodded in the direction of the pavilion. "And now she'll take a break after her ride up here, have some tea and cakes, I shouldn't wonder, and in about an hour, hour and a half, she'll walk up to the summit, just as the sun is setting, and put a taper to the kindling around that whopping great log that's waiting to be our bonfire for the next two nights." The woman methodically turned skewers on her little grill before looking up and smiling. "Have you seen it before?" When they both shook their heads, she said. "They put something in the kindling to make hundreds of sparks fly up into the air against the setting sun. It's a marvellous sight. You wait and see."

Jayhan pointed up at the grey sky and the gentle descent of snowflakes. "Not sure we're going to see the setting sun today."

The stallholder looked up and grimaced. "No, you're right. But it will be spectacular even against grey clouds."

The children nodded and walked off into the woods a hundred yards beyond the edge of the campsite.

"Sparrow? Lapping Water?" called Jayhan quietly.

When the woodwomen appeared, Jayhan and Sasha both held out one of their skewers of meat.

"Here," said Sasha, forcing a smile. "We thought you might like one of these."

"Thanks," said Lapping Water accepting one and tasting it. "Hmm. Good rich meat. What is it?"

"Lamb," said Jayhan. "I suppose you don't get lamb in the forests, do you?"

"No," Sparrow pulled a piece of meat off the skewer with her fingers. "That was Toriana arriving, wasn't it? We could see her well from up in the trees. Beautiful horse. Did you see her, Sasha? What did you think?" She blew on the hot meat and popped it in her mouth.

Sasha was chewing, so Jayhan butted in, "She got such a fright when the trumpets blared that she nearly dropped her skewers."

Sasha sent him a poisonous look. "It wasn't just the trumpets." She huffed. "She looks so grand and so powerful. And she has that beautiful horse that does just exactly what she wants."

"You and Jon are both fantastic with horses, too," said Jayhan, loyal to the last, "Talent with horses must run in your family." Anything else he might have been going to say was curtailed as he used his teeth to pull another piece of meat off his skewer.

"Are you frightened, Sasha?" asked Lapping Water quietly.

Sasha heaved a huge breath and nodded. "I don't know if I can do it," she said in a small voice.

Lapping Water sent a mindmessage down the mountain to Waterstone, who relayed it to Tarkyn.

In the next minute, a warm wave of strength rolled into Sasha. She became aware of the presence of the forest around her, the patterns of deep green branches above her and the roots below the surface. She felt the mass of the mountain holding her and the forests high above the valleys below. It was a strange feeling, the sense of being held aloft, just as she would be by a horse or her loft in the stable. Then she felt the churning deep below the surface, and she quailed at its power. She almost panicked and shouted that everyone should get down off the mountain, but she took a breath to hold herself together, focusing on her belief that her fate was inextricably linked with the mountain's.

Watching her, Lapping Water nodded. "All right now?"

Before Sasha could answer, a Queen's guard crashed through the trees behind her and grabbed her by the arm. "I was watching you. You're coming with me. We have orders to bring in any girls with dark colouring about your age."

Suddenly the guard felt something cold at her neck and glanced down to see a hand holding a thin blade, its point touching her skin. She looked up into a pair of deadly green eyes.

"I don't think so," said Sparrow. "You're not going anywhere and certainly not with my friend."

"You can't do this. I'm a Queen's guard. I'll be missed."

Maud, Marlene, and the other two shamans burst through the forest perimeter into the shelter of the trees. "Oh, there you are. Oh thank goodness. Well done, Sparrow."

"She says she'll be missed if we keep her here," said Lapping Water, "And I'm afraid she may be right. What will we do?"

Maud looked the guard up and down, noting her height, build, finely chiselled features and dark brown hair. "Jayhan couldn't pull it off, not if he had to talk to other guards or report to the Queen. Besides, Sasha needs him by her side. I'll do it. You make sure the guard is hidden and immobilised for the time being - it will only be for a couple of hours at the most – and I will take her place."

"No. They'll know you're a shape-shifter," objected Marlene. "I'll go... as myself." When she received strange looks from the others she explained, "I'm already in army uniform. If they notice this guard is missing, I'll report that Sasha has been seen running off down the mountain in an easterly direction. I'll say this one..." She frowned. "What's your name?" As the guard clenched her jaw, Marlene rolled her eyes. "Never mind. Silly question. Check her identification."

It was not hard. Sasha realised the woman was wearing a small name tag. Using her newly acquired Kimoran, she read carefully, "Corporal Tamson."

"Right. I'll say Corporal Tamson is in hot pursuit." She smiled sweetly at the corporal. "And you will stay here."

Suddenly the guard slumped to the ground, and they whipped around to see Lapping Water standing close by with a slingshot in her hand, "Don't worry," she said cheerfully. "We'll keep her safely unconscious." She glanced at Sparrow. "But let's tie her up as well. We don't want to take the chance that she wakes up and sneaks off while we are otherwise occupied."

The next hour passed slowly. Following Maud's inevitable suggestion, they kept themselves busy by lighting a small fire and preparing cups of tea, a safe distance in from the forest's edge.

Marlene returned from the forest's edge to join them. "No sounds of alarm yet. I'll go out there in a minute when we've finished planning." She looked at Sasha "Now, theoretically, you should have a greater chance of breaking Toriana's bond if you are closer to the crowd than she is. So, wait until she is at the summit, away from the crowd."

Sasha nodded.

Maud accepted a cup of tea from Jayhan who was helping Sparrow. She smiled her thanks at him, before saying, "And you cannot concentrate in the middle of the crowd among distractions and the constant fear of discovery."

Sasha gave a slight shake of her head.

"Don't worry," said Lapping Water, "Sparrow and I have found the perfect place for you."

"Thanks," said Sasha.

"Marlene, Rhoda, Draya, and I will spread out among the crowd so that we can explain to the shamans what has happened to them, if, *when* you succeed." said Maud, "And with any luck, the shamans from The Rapids, Miriam, Fortuna, and Rayna, will be somewhere in the crowd too."

Sasha nodded.

Maud sent her a piercing glance but decided her little stable girl was often quiet unless she had something particular to say. "Right." Maud tossed away the cold remains of her tea and stood up. "Time to go. We want to get you into position before Toriana begins her trek up to the summit."

The three shamans and Maud stepped out into the crowd, checking the whereabouts of the Queen's guards. None were nearby and no anxious questions were being asked. So they walked off in different directions, Marlene towards the Queen's pavilion in case she had to field awkward questions about Corporal Tamson.

Just inside the forest edge on the eastern side of the festival campsite, Lapping Water, Sparrow, Jayhan, and Sasha walked up the slope until they were level with the upper boundary of the crowd.

"Here. This tree," ordered Lapping Water. She helped the two children to climb twenty feet up into a huge pine tree and settled them securely on neighbouring stout branches, with their legs dangling down either side and their backs against the main trunk. Then she tied both of them to the trunk. "Sparrow and I will be here to release you as soon as you ask and to make sure you get down safely when the time comes."

From their position in the pine, they could see the campsite stretched before them and to their left, the sparsely wooded slope that led to the summit two hundred yards away. They could see the huge log, nestled among kindling and smaller dry branches. A few shamans were busy around it brushing off the falling snow before it had a chance to settle and dampen their wood. As they watched, the last snowflakes fell, but the clouds remained low and heavy.

Then the trumpets sounded and Toriana emerged, carrying a large flaming torch and began her walk up the last stage of Darkstone Mountain. She walked slowly, eking out the moment but even so, it only took her a couple of minutes to reach the pyre on the summit.

As Toriana turned to face the crowd of shamans and raised the flaming torch above her head, Jayhan muttered, "Now."

Sasha drew out her amulet and held it in her left hand. Immediately she felt a jolt in the earth below her. She could feel the thick rope around her waist, reassuring her that she wouldn't fall.

She stared down at the obsidian amulet, studying the lines etched into its surface. She barely noticed as Jayhan took hold of her right hand, but the earth below her noticed, and responded with another shudder that coursed up through the trunk of the tree.

For a moment she feared that the tree might not withstand the mountain's unease. But then she felt the strength of the trunk behind her and remembered the deep roots that would be holding the old pine in place, and she gave it her faith.

She took a deep breath, focused on her heartbeat, and lost herself to the outside world.

Chapter 76

No one noticed the two children perched in the branches of the tall pine.

All eyes were on Toriana, dressed in a long, dark-silver gown with her bright green cloak flowing over her shoulders. The contrast in colours was stunning. She stood at the summit of the mountain, her left hand holding out her black amulet on its long gold chain. Her right hand held the torch high, as she pronounced the time-honoured words that would welcome the return of the sun as the world passed through the depths of winter towards the warmth and longer days of spring and summer.

Up in the pine tree, Sasha opened her eyes and stared down at the black amulet in her hand, allowing it time to gather its strength. It began to glow, dully at first, then brighter and brighter. The crowd below seemed to twinkle as the pale moonstone amulets glowed in response. Still Sasha hesitated, worried by the size of the crowd whose bindings she had to overcome. Before her amulet could begin to challenge the shamans' bindings, she withdrew its power and sent a wry smile to Jayhan.

"No. I won't try to overcome the resistance of thousands. I only have to overcome one. Then the rest will follow."

"Yep," Jayhan agreed briefly, careful not to break her concentration.

So Sasha turned her attention from the nearby crowd to the figure two hundred yards away. She frowned fiercely down at her amulet for a full minute. Then, with a thought, she released the full extent of its pent-up power.

Immediately, a brilliant shaft of black light shot forth, burning though the branches in its path, sending them crashing to the ground, before streaking, unchecked, towards Toriana. The black light hit the amulet in the Queen's hand and shattered it with a crack that resounded across the mountains. No gentle responding light as there had been with other amulets. No battle of wills. Just unquestioning annihilation.

Toriana was left holding an empty chain. She turned shocked eyes towards Sasha., who stared back, equally shocked.

Then, where the pieces of the Queen's false amulet had fallen, thin cracks appeared in the ground. A geyser of steam shot upwards and Toriana screamed.

A huge column of black smoke billowed skyward and molten lava burst up through the earth. For a moment, Toriana could be seen as a translucent figure against the brilliant yellow and orange. Then she was gone, vapourized by the extreme heat.

A shock wave swept down the flanks of the mountain as great gouts of molten rock erupted right under the Midwinter Log, sending it flying end over end into the air.

Instead of their midwinter bonfire, a beautiful but deadly, fiery fountain sprayed up from the summit, sending up showers of molten lava and ash. The Midwinter log landed with a thud that could be felt throughout the campsite, then cartwheeled into the forest on their left, smashing through pine trees and completely uprooting two of them on its way past. A rain of fiery rock and ash fell over the eastern edge of the campsite and over the adjacent forest.

The deadly rain fell on scores of shamans and the air filled with shrieks of pain and terror. Behind the nearer cacophony, Sasha heard the scream of a horse and distant cries of distress from beyond the campsite, from the swathe gouged through the forest by the falling log.

A river of lava began to flow slowly, but inexorably, down the north-eastern face of the mountain, the outer edge of it heading straight towards the Queen's pavilion and the tents of officials and nobles. It looked like the lava flow would miss the rest of the shaman campsite, but people weren't taking any chances.

Without stopping to consider the political or personal significance of what they had seen, blind panic took the shamans as they jostled and fell over each other in their rush to escape down the mountain. Some grabbed their belongings and others just ran.

People yelled and shoved, pushing to get away. Sasha saw one little girl huddled against a deserted tent, crying out for her mother. An older woman fell down and was trampled by several behind her who couldn't avoid her as they were pushed from behind.

That's enough! thought Sasha, watching from up in the pine tree. *I can't just let this happen.*

She focused on her amulet, ignoring the fiery spectacle on her right. She had no idea what she was doing but she could feel the mountain settling beneath her and knew that more people would be injured by running riotously down the mountain than by staying.

She thought about the waves of strength that Tarkyn had sent her and decided to focus on sending out reassurance through her amulet. She thought about the unity and sisterhood that was supposed to exist among shamans and sent images of the people who were being hurt by the lack of care in the shamans' stampede. Then she imposed an image of them all slowing down and stopping.

She no longer had the resistance of the Queen's binding to overcome, and she felt the gentle, unrestricted flow from her amulet to all of theirs.

Over and over she repeated in her head, *Stop. Stop. Stop.*

And slowly, they did.

"Time to go," she said to Lapping Water, who instantly untied the ropes holding her to the tree trunk. Relaxed and remarkably confident, now that the threat of Toriana was no longer hanging over her head, Sasha smiled at the two woodwomen, "Thanks for your help." She turned to Jayhan, "And yours. I couldn't have done it without you. But stay here now. I must do this part alone."

She climbed down out of the tree and walked to stand in the middle of the upper edge of the campsite so that she had her back to the fiery fountain on the summit. She held out her dark obsidian amulet so that it was in full view, and waited, still sending forth the message to stop and to calm. Picking up on what she was doing, Marlene, Draya, Rhoda and even Maud and Marjorie, in different areas of the crowd, verbally reinforced her message.

Suddenly, on the periphery, two of the Queen's guard saw her and started rushing towards her. One spoke to the other and they hesitated, but then kept coming. A knot of four shamans grabbed them and Sasha heard one of them say, "Don't be stupid." The guardswomen, who were clearly not shamans, subsided, looking bewildered and deflated.

Gradually the whole crowd returned, picking up the injured on the way through, some staying to look after them while the rest gathered around an unremarkable girl, whose heavy woollen cloak was pushed back by her hand holding the amulet, revealing a plain brown woollen jerkin and leggings. No furs or shining silks or velvet. No beautiful gown. Just workaday travelling clothes.

But she had a glowing dark amulet in her hand and her dark eyes shone with power.

And although she had commanded their attention, her power was laced with the shamans' care for each other, not with force.

Sasharia saw confusion on the faces of many but waited until at least most of them would be able to hear her against the roaring of the lava fountain in the background.

Then she took a deep breath and raised her voice, "Do not fear the mountain's wrath." She glanced back at it for a moment before turning to them once more and holding up her amulet. "This, the one true amulet, was created from the side of this mountain after its last eruption centuries ago. When I, wearing this amulet, set foot on Kimoran soil, the mountain reacted to the dissonance between Toriana's false and my true amulet. But that dissonance no longer exists, so the Darkstone Mountain will return to quiescence." She smiled and half turned to look at the summit again where already the fountain had decreased in size and force. "You can think of this fiery fountain as a celebration of the return to power of the one true amulet and the true High Shaman. Just keep clear of it and avoid the lava flow and you'll be quite safe." She turned back to the crowd, "For those of you who don't know me," suddenly she grinned, "which is nearly everybody, I am Sasharia, youngest daughter of Corinna."

A stunned silence erupted into a deluge of questions, not hostile but overwhelming.

Marlene, Draya and Rhoda managed to push their way through the crowds to the front and came to stand next to Sasha.

Sasha held up her hand. "Now is not the time. We are safe from the mountain's wrath, but we have injured comrades and ruined tents and belongings. Let us all look after one another first. When the crisis has passed, I will answer your questions."

Suddenly, a commotion occurred at the rear of the crowd. Shouts of outrage rippled through the crowd as shamans were jostled aside by four very determined male sorcerers striding towards her within a translucent bronze shield.

When they reached Sasharia, they were breathing hard after their rush up the mountain side. Stormaway, who was considerably older than the other three, was looking close to collapse. Relieved, they observed the contained fiery fountain on the summit and the slowing flow of lava to their left. Then they turned to the people gathered before Sasharia. Tarkyn dropped his shield as the four sorcerers stepped to one side.

"Our apologies," said Tarkyn to the crowd. "We feared for Sasharia when the volcano erupted and couldn't force ourselves to stay away."

Marlene, who was acknowledged as a senior shaman, gave a wry smile. "These are exceptional circumstances and I'm sure we are all grateful for your concern for our High Shaman." She turned to the crowd. "These people and others have supported Sasharia's journey here and her return to our sisterhood. Accept their presence among us for now. We need to look after the wounded and re-establish our campsite."

As the crowd began to disperse, Sasha looked at the four men, her stomach tightening in fear. "Where's Jon?"

Tarkyn nodded towards the east and gave a wry smile. "We were supposed to be protecting him, but before we could raise our shield around him, he shimmered and disappeared from us. We heard him say he would meet us up here."

Sasha turned to see Jon leading Toriana's beautiful white mare towards them. His blond hair was tousled, and he was a little out of breath. He had wrapped a cloth around the horse's eyes to keep her from panicking and she was limping badly. He gave Sasha a brief grin, "Am I ever glad to see you, little sis." Then he turned to the forest guardian. "Tarkyn, a wooden splinter has driven into her thigh, and she has small scratches all over her from her wild charge through the bush. She took some catching, I can tell you. Can you heal her? Please? I didn't ask the shamans because I would have had to field too many questions first and the mare's need is dire."

Despite his words, three shamans converged on him, willing to assist. A middle-aged woman pushed her salt and pepper hair back from her face and said, "I hope, young man, that you don't think we would stand by and argue while a creature is suffering. Let me have a look."

That was, in fact, exactly what he had thought but he wasn't about to say so. "I beg your pardon, ma'am," said Jon with a slight bow, stepping to one side while maintaining his hold on the halter. The shamans let Jon hold the horse's head and soothe her while they examined the wound. One of them gently removed the stake and then pressed a cloth onto it to staunch the bleeding. The mare stamped her hoof in protest at the pain but did not try to pull out of Jon's grip. Once she had settled again, the other two focused their power into the mare to speed her healing, while the first one applied an antiseptic salve. Through it all, Jon crooned to the mare, keeping her still even though it must have been hurting her.

Once the mare was calm and on the road to recovery, Jon smiled at the shamans who had helped him. "Thank you," he said. "And now we had better see what we can do for the people who have been hurt or no longer have tents to return to.

Chapter 77

Watching from up in the pine tree on the eastern perimeter, Lapping Water was startled when an unfamiliar voice said in her ear. "I believe you know a forest guardian. I am Mountain Wind."

She swung around to come face-to-face with a woodman, similar to her but with darker hair, and eyes the colour of pines needles. She blinked before collecting herself. She gave a slight smile. "You could say that. I'm married to him. Pleased to meet you. I am Lapping Water."

The woodman's eyebrows rose so high they were nearly lost in his hairline. "You have married an outsider? Extraordinary."

His voice held astonishment but not censure. "Unlike you, we do not usually associate with others, but our need is great." Lapping Water curbed her urge to explain that they, too, did not usually associate with outsiders. But the explanation was complicated and now was not the time. "That huge log," he was saying, "destroyed two trees and damaged several others on the other side of this campsite. We have three treewrights dead and at least twenty wounded. Could he come?"

"Of course." She turned to Jayhan. "Can you go down and explain to him? Tell him we'll meet him in the area that's been gouged by the log. I'll send him images too "

She sent mindmessages to the other Eskuzorian woodfolk as she set off with Mountain Wind and Sparrow through the trees on the boundary of the campsite around to the site of the devastation. But concealment was fast becoming a pointless exercise.

When Jayhan delivered his message in his high piping voice, several shamans overheard him and offered Tarkyn their services. Tarkyn hesitated, the cultural violation of taking outsiders uninvited among treewrights warring with his wish to make use of these shamans' skills. Finally he sent an image to Stefan requesting his attendance before saying, "I will assess the situation. As you know, treewrights traditionally keep to themselves. I have already violated one tradition by coming into your shaman gathering. I don't want to make a habit of it. I will speak to the treewrights and send Stefan back here to let you know if they would welcome your assistance."

Stefan flicked into view beside Taryn, startling the shamans closest to him. He gave them a little grin, still pleased with his new skill of flicking.

"We'll be ready," said a familiar voice. It was Rhoda. "And tell them that helping them now does not mean we will insist on continued contact in the future, if that is not their wish."

Tarkyn nodded. "Well said. We cannot assume that interaction with those you have previously met in Carrador," he said, avoiding using the word woodfolk, "means that treewrights here will accept you. I'll let you know how I go. Come on, Stefan."

They had to deviate some distance downhill to get around the lava that had already stopped flowing but was still far too hot to touch. As they approached the damaged area of forest, Tarkyn murmured, "*Lumaya*," and raised a glowing orb to provide light in the gathering darkness. What he saw appalled him. So many treewrights lying on the ground or propped up against trees, moaning in pain while others swarmed around them, tending to their wounds.

Without hesitation, he turned to Stefan, "Today is not a day for convention. Get as many shamans here as they can spare from their own needs. Ask them to bring bandages and whatever salves and medicaments they may have. This job is too big for one person."

Stefan turned on his heel and flicked out of sight.

Deep into the night, Stormaway, Sheldrake, Sasha, and even Jayhan worked with the shamans to tend to the wounded and dying treewrights and shamans, bandaging wounds and burns, preparing salves while those who had the power, such as Tarkyn, Midnight, Rhoda and Draya and many of the shamans, provided deep healing. Jon worked hard himself, but also organised Marjorie, Jackson, the Queen's guard, and others who had little medical knowledge, into lighting fires to keep people warm, preparing food, running errands, and repairing tents and equipment. Tarkyn provided an orb of light for the treewrights while Sheldrake and Stormaway provided lighting for the shamans' campsite.

Maud knew her greatest skill in this situation and turned herself into her lugubrious bloodhound shape, then wandered among the wounded treewrights and shamans, distracting them, letting them fondle her long soft ears and giving them something to hug.

As the evening progressed, word of Jon's identity spread through the camp, even though he had not been formally introduced. Although no one commented, the shamans noted both Sasha and Jon mucking in and taking on any task that would further the welfare of either shamans or treewrights. It was not what Kimorans expected from their royalty, but they were impressed.

Parts of the Queen's pavilion had been saved but Sasha and Jon had no wish to assume their new roles and distance themselves from their friends in the middle of the crisis. So when exhaustion overtook them, they crawled in to sleep beside Maud, Sheldrake, and Jayhan.

Chapter 78

Most people slept through the cold light of dawn. But by midmorning, the winter sun was shining in a brilliant blue sky, providing a surprising amount of warmth for the people who began to stir, gathering around the fires that had been kept burning during the night.

They woke to a new day, a new regime, and new friendships between treewrights and outsiders, shamans, and men.

When Sasha and Jon emerged, scruffy and smeared with ash, in search of a cup of tea, they were confronted by several hundred people gathered quietly on the other side of the nearest campfire, just waiting to set eyes on them. A smattering of applause ran through the crowd as they appeared. Sasha's cheeks reddened and she glanced up at Jon, who merely smiled at her. Knowing this was her future, she took a breath and waved her hand in acknowledgement as she walked to the campfire and sat down cross-legged on the ground. Someone rushed off and returned with a chair for her, but she waved it away.

"No thank you. It would feel very awkward, sitting higher than everyone else." It crossed Sasha's mind that this might be something she would have to get used to in the throne room, but not now.

Jon and she had just been handed cups of tea by people eager to please, when an older woman wearing very fine but bedraggled clothes worked her way to the front of the crowd and curtseyed to them.

"Good morning?" said Sasha, with a query in her greeting since the woman clearly wanted to speak to her.

"Good morning, Your Majesty." The woman drew herself up and spoke in a calm, authoritative voice. "My name is Hardikan. I am one of the more senior shamans and I have worked closely with Queen Toriana for many years."

"I see," said Sasha, keeping her voice carefully neutral. "I am glad you were not in the Queen's pavilion when it was damaged."

"So too am I, ma'am. Luckily, we were all out in the open, watching the ceremony, although Barton's arm was broken and burnt by falling rock." Hardikan held out a small laminated wooden box. "I do not presume that my previous service with the Queen will translate into working in your service. In fact, probably quite the reverse. However, I know our plans for the invasion of Carrador are at a critical point and I must not delay in giving you this, the royal seal, so that you can make your own decisions."

As Sasha accepted the box, Hardikan sank into a low curtsey and this time, stayed down. "You may or may not believe me, ma'am, but I wish to thank you for releasing me and all shamans from Queen Toriana's binding, and to pledge you my loyalty."

Sasha produced a reserved smile. "Thank you. Please rise. And thank you for acting so promptly in the interests of the realm." She handed the box to Jon. "My brother, Prince Jondarian, will act as my regent until I come of age and so to him, I give the royal seal for safekeeping."

On the previous evening, this pronouncement would have given rise to heated opposition. After all, appointing a male to such a high position was unprecedented. But this morning, in the light of their work together, Jon was accepted with unreserved approval, murmurs of pleased surprise running through the crowd.

Jon smiled as Sasha handed him the box. "Thank you, Sasharia," he said formally. "Hardikan, do you have writing implements anywhere or were they all destroyed?"

"I will check, Your Highness. If necessary, I will send a messenger down to the village of Woodend to procure some for you."

"Thank you. As you surmised, Hardikan, the need is urgent. Besides, we must send forth news of Sasharia's ascension to the throne and my appointment as regent."

"Indeed, Sire." Without another word, Hardikan curtseyed and withdrew.

As he watched her walk away, Jon became aware of a movement on his left and much to his surprise, turned to find Waterstone and Mountain Wind sitting down in the ash beside him.

Waterstone grinned at him and asked, "Any more tea in that pot?"

Jon merely had to raise an eyebrow to have someone bring over cups of tea for his friends.

"Thanks," said Waterstone, taking the tea and wrapping his hands around the cup as he blew on it to cool it.

"I'm surprised to see you out and about among outsiders like this."

Waterstone shrugged. "Something shifted in all of us last night. I think the era of woodfolk and treewrights living separately from outsiders may be coming to an end. Of course, we will always live within the forests but perhaps Stormaway, Tarkyn, and Stefan will not be the only people moving between the two societies in the future. Even though treewrights don't mix with outsiders, everyone in Kimora has always known of their existence. So several treewrights have agreed to return with us to Eskuzor to discuss how this works with our fellow woodfolk. In return, we will explain how we have come to have outsiders living among us and introduce them to some sorcerers."

"Lapping Water will be pleased," said Sasha.

Waterstone nodded. "Yes, she is. We all are." He frowned. "You haven't seen Midnight and Gurgling Brook, have you? They wandered off together earlier and I've lost track of them."

"Aren't they Tarkyn's responsibility?" asked Sasha quizzically.

"He dotes on them, but we all care for them. That is our way." He gave an indulgent laugh. "Besides, it's a bit early for Tarkyn."

Just as he spoke, Jayhan, Midnight, and Gurgling Brook trotted over from the direction of the Queen's Pavilion. Jayhan grinned when he saw Sasha.

"Hello. Guess what? We've been exploring and you know that beautiful white mare that Jon fixed last night?" he asked, blithely leaving out the shamans' role in healing the mare. "Well, it's *yours.*"

Sasha's eyes widened. "*Mine?* My own horse? But it's the Qu… Oh. It *is* my horse, isn't it?" She turned to Jon, her eyes shining, and whispered rapturously, "My very own horse, Jon. Imagine that." Then she laughed at herself, realising that this was only the beginning of it.

A woman in the crowd shouted, "Get her something her own size. I've seen Queen Toriana riding that mare. She's too big and temperamental for a small girl."

Jon grinned. "Not for this small girl, she isn't. Sasharia will have no trouble with her."

Chapter 79

As soon as writing materials arrived, Jon penned letters to the commanders of the three invading forces informing them of Sasha's ascension to the throne and ordering them to return to the capital.

Seeing what he was doing, Tarkyn, Stormaway, and Sheldrake wandered over.

"Allow us to assist you," said Stormaway. "Time is short. I know we are not Kimoran, but I hope you know by now that we can be trusted."

Sheldrake peered over Jon's shoulder at what he was writing. "Besides, you can ask for a reply from each of the generals. After all, you will want to be sure they have understood and will follow your directives."

Without hesitation, Jon nodded. "Thank you. What do you have in mind?"

Once he had explained, Stormaway used a spell to reduce the size of the rolled-up messages so that they could be attached to birds' legs. Sheldrake was intrigued by the technique, which included an automatic reversal so that the message would return to full size when a hand unrolled the little scroll at the other end of the journey.

"I used to have to say words over the scroll to resize it but after a few experiments, I found a way for the scroll to automatically resize itself when it is unrolled," said Stormaway with a hint of pride in his voice.

"Well done," said Sheldrake. "A most useful improvement. Then the receiver does not have to know magic."

"Exactly."

Tarkyn enlisted a local rock dove, placating him while the first message was attached to his leg. Once that was done, he used his forest guardian powers to guide him, assisted by local treewrights' navigational skills, to deliver Jon's message to the northern army that was approaching Bridgetown.

Through the dove's eyes, Tarkyn watched the consternation on the general's face and her close scrutiny of the royal seal. Then, as she read further, he could see the dawning understanding on her face as she read of the destruction of Toriana's binding spell and realized why she felt different. She sent for several of her senior officers and after explanations and some debate, wrote a reply which she attached to the dove's leg. She also wrote another letter which she sent off by homing pigeon, presumably to the capital.

Nearly three hours after she had left, the dove returned and only after the reply had been carefully removed from his leg, could Tarkyn give his mind a break.

The reply indicated that the northern army would hold its position, pending confirmation of these orders from Manissa.

Tarkyn, who held a ruling position in his own country, shrugged. "I think that response is fair enough. You can't expect blind obedience when she hasn't even set eyes on either of you and, as yet, has no other source of information about the change of leadership. You'd better get messengers on the road to Manissa though and make sure proclamations go out far and wide."

Jon smiled, happy to take advice even if he had already thought of it himself. "Thanks. I have already started, while you were concentrating." He waved his arm around to indicate the people in the campsite. "If we can organise it in time, each of these shamans can take a proclamation back to their communities. We have set people to work writing them and I'll affix the seal to each of them."

Tarkyn's eyes widened. "That's a lot of work in a short time. Aren't there nearly two thousand shamans here?"

"A lot of work," Jon shrugged, "but a big country to cover and the shamans' gathering presents us with an opportunity to disseminate the information quickly. Most of them will be back in their communities within a week."

Waterstone's eyes twinkled. "I think you'll find word of mouth will travel far faster than that."

Jon grinned at him. "I'm sure you're right. But people will be expecting an official communication, even if it reaches them more slowly."

"Good afternoon, Your Majesty, Your Highness " said Marlene, who had just arrived from overseeing repairs to the Queen's Pavilion. She gave a neat little bow, although her frizzy white hair was even more out of control than usual after the exertions of the night before. "I believe what is left of the Queen's Pavilion is ready for your inspection."

Sasha wanted to protest at the formal greeting but knew she couldn't, in front of so many people.

"Thank you, Marlene," replied Jon with unabated good cheer. "Have a cup of tea while Tarkyn guides a different rock dove to deliver an update and an official command to General Kazak. We have already sent new orders to the northern army, but I understand we will intercept the southern army as we travel to Manissa, so we should be able to deliver our wishes personally to them. The southern road passes to the north of the Darkstone mountains and then around the south of the Dark Lake into Carrador. Is that correct?"

Tarkyn, who was waiting for Stormaway to minimize the next message and attach it to the dove, raised his eyebrows. "You're a better navigator than I am," he said, receiving dry looks from everyone who knew him. He laughed. "I know that's not saying much, but it was meant as a compliment."

At this juncture, Sasha cut in. She had been studying the people on the other side of the campfire and had noticed that many of them were listless and tired. She was not surprised after the previous evening of healing and repairs. "Tarkyn," she said quietly so that only Jon, Marlene and the two woodmen could hear her, "before you do that, would you consider giving some of your *esse* to these people? Many shamans have used up nearly all their healing ability and tomorrow they face long journeys home." She put her head on one side as she considered. "I think it has used up their energy too, looking at them. I know you can replenish yours straightaway from the forest's power, but they will take many days to recover." She turned her liquid brown eyes on him, quite unaware of their effect. "So could you, please?"

Tarkyn smiled warmly at her. "I applaud your care for your people. You will make a fine queen, Sasharia. I would be honoured to assist you... and them."

Two hours later, the Queen's guard were lined up outside what was left of the Queen's pavilion. Only six of the eight of them had survived, since two had been guarding the eastern side of the pavilion when it was overwhelmed by flying rocks and ash.

Inside, Sasha and Jayhan were exploring what was left. Jon was standing in the doorway watching them, with his arms crossed, flanked by Marlene and Hardikan.

The two children were stunned by the luxury of this tent that had been carried into the relative wilderness of the Darkstone Mountain while all across the campsite, other people made do with basic accommodation. It had contained four separate rooms, but only two were still intact. The bedroom had been completely obliterated and so had most of the bathing area. Only the dressing room and the reception room remained but they were still impressive.

When they moved from the reception room to the dressing room, they found Barton standing beside Toriana's travelling trunk, waiting to display its contents to Sasha while Pansy hovered uncertainly in the background in case she was called for.

Sasha glanced at Jayhan and grimaced before approaching the trunk.

She nodded at the dresser who had worked for Toriana. "Good afternoon. Barton, isn't it? How is your arm. I understand you broke it and that it was burnt."

Barton curtseyed. "Good afternoon, Your Majesty." She held out her arm and pulled back the sleeve to reveal a foot-long pink scar running down her forearm. "I have a scar but other than that, it is healed, thanks to the shamans who looked after me."

Sasha smiled. "I'm glad you're all right." She peered into the trunk and pulled back a few layers as she looked at the fine textures, colours, and embroidery of the neatly packed clothes. "It's a pity Maud is not here. She would love these." She frowned a query at Jayhan. "Where *is* Maud? I haven't seen her all day."

"She has flown off to report to King Gavin." Jayhan's mouth quirked up on one side in an embarrassed half smile. "As a peregrine falcon, you understand."

"Oh, that's good.," Sasha replied, not at all fazed by Maud's shape-shifting as her son was. "We don't want Gavin worrying about Sheldrake and Maud having divided loyalties."

She returned her attention to the clothes before straightening and taking a breath for courage. "These clothes are very beautiful, but..." Sasha looked down at what she herself was wearing: a practical jerkin with many useful pockets and leggings beneath a warm cloak. She waved her hand down her front. "But this is what I like to wear. I hope you can accept that. I will only agree to wearing gowns on formal occasions, and for that I would welcome your advice." She smiled disarmingly but her smile was underpinned with determination. "I would value your continued service, but only on my terms. I don't want to argue with you every morning about what I should wear. You are free to leave any time if you cannot stomach that, and I will not think less of you."

Barton pursed her lips and let her eyes travel up and down Sasha's small frame, which even Sasha felt was impertinent. Then the dresser nodded briskly. "I can do that, ma'am, provided you allow me to develop your sense of colour with your leggings, shirts, and jerkins. We could also add a little embroidery to decorate them while maintaining their practicality. Would that be acceptable?"

Sasha grinned. "Yes, it would. Thank you."

She turned to find Jayhan nodding his approval. She glanced over at Pansy, who immediately curtseyed.

"Good afternoon, Your Highness, I mean, Your Majesty." she said nervously. She wrung her hands. "Sorry ma'am. You're just so young to be a queen. Even I'm older than you. Oh sorry." She shut her mouth with a snap, looking as though she feared she might be struck.

Sasha crossed to stand in front of her. Then, as slowly and gently as she would with a frightened horse, she placed her hand on the maid's shoulder. "You're Pansy, I believe. Such a lovely name. I am pleased to meet you. I will be depending on you, Barton, and Hardikan, among others, to teach me about the palace and the staff and what I have to do, and when. I hope you are all willing to make changes because I don't think I will behave as Toriana did and I may wish to change some... hmm... expectations."

Pansy's wide blue eyes gradually relaxed. She drew in a little breath and gave a tremulous smile. "Yes ma'am."

"And Pansy, I hope you can come to trust me. I believe I will be kinder than my aunt was."

Chapter 80

The rest of the day passed all too quickly. Maud flew back in time for the Festival Feast, an event no one had even thought of in the chaos of the previous evening. But as things had settled down, the feast had been rescheduled for tonight, the final night of the Midwinter Festival. The proclamations of Toriana's death, Sasharia's ascension to the throne, and Jondarian's appointment as her regent had all been written, affixed with the royal seal, and stowed in shamans' bags ready for their journeys home on the morrow.

Jon and Sasha determinedly maintained their informality, knowing that this was their last chance before assuming the reins of office. But in truth, many people already felt self-conscious around them.

Now that most of the serious business of ministering to the wounded was past, the shamans could unrestrainedly enjoy the newfound freedom of mind and spirit given to them by their release from Toriana's binding. They laughed and smiled, told stories they could not have told before and took great delight in disparaging Toriana. The tales of her perfidy and wrongdoing grew as the evening progressed and, in the end, it was hard to tell what was true and what were joyous flights of fancy fuelled by the shamans' pleasure in being able to deride their late queen.

The woodfolk and treewrights did not venture into such a large, boisterous gathering but they remained in sight, just within the tree line. Stefan, Jayhan, Jackson, and Marjorie brought them a supply of food and drink and spent large parts of the evening with them. Jayhan spent most of his time eating or playing with Midnight.

As the evening progressed, the fellowship that had sprung up on The Woodland Rover gathered together as Tarkyn and Stormaway, Maud and Sheldrake took their leave of the Kimorans and wandered over. Sasha disengaged herself to join them, watched by many eyes following her departure from the main throng.

"Hello, Sasha," said Rainstorm, greeting her cheerfully. "How are you coping with being the constant centre of attention?"

Sasha glanced back at the crowd and saw several people casually watching her as they talked to their friends.

She gave a wry smile. "At least it's friendly attention, though I suppose it may not always be, if disputes arise." She shrugged. "Mostly, I just try to block it out of my mind and concentrate on the person I'm talking to, or on what I'm doing. It feels a bit like holding a deluge at bay."

"Hard work," said Waterstone.

"It is," agreed Tarkyn, who had had to cope with it all his life. "And you can't block it out completely. It wouldn't be safe to do so."

"I suppose not. It's not relaxing," her dark eyes shone suddenly, "but it is fun in a way." She waved at the crowd. "All those shamans are connected to me through my amulet, and I can feel their warmth and kindness and the guilt for what some of them did under Toriana. But more than anything, I can feel their soaring joy at being free and at having me at their centre." She gave a beaming smile. "How could one possibly dislike that?"

Rainstorm handed her a cup of orange juice. "I was going to give you a wine, but I think you are cheery enough. I'm glad that you have found your place in the world and that you like it."

Sasha nodded. "I do. It's as though I have come fully into focus." Her face tightened, as she spotted Jayhan assiduously avoiding her eyes and concentrating on drawing an animal in the dirt for Gurgling Brook. "Jayhan," She called quietly and waited until he looked up at her. "I couldn't have done any of this without you. I don't mean just your power. Without your friendship, I would never have had the courage to even try."

Jayhan tried to smile but he had tears in his eyes. After a couple of swallows, he regained control of his voice and said, "You were the first person who talked and laughed about my eyes as though they were the most natural thing in the world. And you were my first, and still are, my best friend. I will miss you."

"What a brave speech," murmured Sheldrake to Maud under his breath.

Sasha put down her cup of fruit juice on a nearby log. It landed crookedly on a small knot and Rainstorm grabbed it deftly before it tipped off.

She walked over to Jayhan, and as he stood up to meet her, put her arms around him. "I know you don't like huggy much, but I can't help it. From the first day we met, we knew that we'd be friends our whole lives. We will see each other again. You and Sheldrake and Maud will come to my coronation. In fact, all of you must come, if you can. And you can come and stay with me sometimes, even regularly, I hope. But I will miss you too, Jayhan, more than I can say."

Jayhan returned her hug without reservation. After a while, Sasha heard his muffled voice and pulled away enough to ask, "What was that?"

Jayhan sniffed and said, "Well, this is embarrassing. Everyone watching us, I mean."

Sasha laughed and let go. "Idiot." After a moment she said, "You know, I've been thinking. Now that you've got to know Edgar, he might introduce you to those children in the village. Once they get to know you, they'll forget all about your eyes. They're probably quite nice too, once you get to know them."

"Huh. We'll see." Jayhan sounded derisive but she could see he was actually considering the idea.

"And I officially give my half of the cubby house to Edgar, though I expect to be invited in for afternoon tea, if I ever come to visit."

Jayhan gave a watery chuckle. "Deal."

Just then Jon walked over to join them. He took one look at the two of them and said, "Sheldrake and I have been putting our heads together and we have a plan to further your education." He laughed as they both groaned but continued. "Sheldrake will set up a dove-cote at Batian House. You will help him, of course, Jayhan, since you did such a great job with your cubby. And then you and Sasha can write letters to each other as often as you like, and the pigeons will deliver them between Manissa and your place."

"And in addition to that," said Maud, standing beside Sheldrake with her arm around his back, "You can visit Sasha for a month a year to improve your Kimoran and your understanding of Kimoran life and culture. Then one day, you never know, you might become Carrador's ambassador to Kimora or at the very least, feel comfortable when you visit Sasha as an adult."

Jayhan gave a reluctant smile. "It won't be the same, but it will still be good." He frowned. "But what about you, Sasha? Who will you play with? You can't just stand around being queen all the time. You have to have fun."

When Sasha just shrugged, Jon answered for her. "She will find friends if she wants them. The great thing about children is that once they get playing, they forget all about roles and responsibilities. I will bring Argus, Beetlebrow, and Yarrow to join Darya and Rhoda so she has people she knows and trusts around her. And there are displaced children among the Kimoran refugees. It will take time, but she will find friends."

"Oh, good," said Jayhan unconvincingly.

Sasha punched him bracingly in the arm. "Be nice. No one will ever replace you, Jayhan. You and I may make other friends, but those friendships will be as well, as not instead of, our friendship." She put her head on one side. "Don't you think?"

Jayhan thought about it. "Yeah. Like Midnight." Suddenly he grinned. "Do you want to come and see this cave we found? I reckon it's a fox hole, but Midnight thought it might belong to a big cat. A mountain lion maybe. How good would that be? Coming?"

Sasha chortled. "If it's a mountain lion, I hope Midnight's quick with his shield." She glanced back at the gathering of shamans, then grinned at her brother. "All right. Let's go."

And leaving tomorrow to take care of itself, Jayhan, Sasha, and Midnight ran off into the trees

About the Author

Jennifer Jane Ealey was born in outback Western Australia where her father was studying kangaroos on a research station, one hundred miles from the nearest town. Her arrival into the world was watched, unexpectedly, by their pet kangaroo who had hopped into the hospital. Having survived the excitement of her birth, she moved firstly to Perth and then Melbourne where she spent most of her formative years. She took a year off to ride a motorbike around Australia before working as a mathematics teacher and school psychologist in England and Australia, a bicycle courier in London and a publican in outback New South Wales.

She now lives in a country town just outside Melbourne with her two spoodles, working by day as a psychologist and beavering away by night as a novelist. Her first fantasy series, *The Sorcerer's Oath*, has been published by Next Chapter and comprises four novels; *Bronze Magic*, *Wizard's Curse*, *The Lost Forest* and *The Wizardess*. *The Green-Eyed Man* is second in the Dark Amulet Series, which is set in the same world as *The Sorcerer's Oath*, but in a different country.

* * *

To learn more about Jennifer Ealey and discover more Next Chapter authors, visit our website at http://www.nextchapter.pub.

Printed in Great Britain
by Amazon

43336064R00421